Jane Porter
Thaddeus of Warsaw:
A Novel

Edinburgh Critical Editions of Nineteenth-Century Texts

Published titles
Richard Jefferies, After London; or Wild England
Mark Frost

Marie Corelli, A Romance of Two Worlds: A Novel
Andrew Radford

Sensation Drama, 1860–1880: An Anthology
Joanna Hofer-Robinson and Beth Palmer

Agriculture and the Land: Richard Jefferies' Essays and Letters
Rebecca Welshman

Maxwell Gray, The Silence of Dean Maitland: A Novel
Julian Wolfreys

Jane Porter, Thaddeus of Warsaw: A Novel
Thomas McLean and Ruth Knezevich

Forthcoming titles
William Barnes, Dialect Poems in The Dorset County Chronicle
Thomas Burton and Emma Mason

Geraldine Jewsbury, Critical Essays and Reviews (1849–1870)
Anne-Marie Beller

Hartley Coleridge, The Complete Poems
Nicola Healey

George Gissing, The Private Papers of Henry Ryecroft
Thomas Ue

Philip James Bailey, Festus: A Novel
Mischa Willett

William Morris on Socialism: Uncollected Essays
Florence Boos

Hubert Crackanthorpe, Wreckage: Seven Studies
David Malcolm

Visit the Edinburgh Critical Editions of Nineteenth-Century Texts website at: edinburghuniversitypress.com/series/ecenct

Jane Porter

Thaddeus of Warsaw: A Novel

Edited by Thomas McLean and Ruth Knezevich

EDINBURGH
University Press

Edinburgh University Press is one of the leading university presses in the UK. We publish academic books and journals in our selected subject areas across the humanities and social sciences, combining cutting-edge scholarship with high editorial and production values to produce academic works of lasting importance. For more information visit our website: edinburghuniversitypress.com

Edinburgh University Press Ltd
The Tun – Holyrood Road, 12(2f) Jackson's Entry, Edinburgh EH8 8PJ

Typeset in 11/12.5 Baskerville and Times New Roman by
Servis Filmsetting Ltd, Stockport, Cheshire,
and printed and bound in Great Britain.

A CIP record for this book is available from the British Library

ISBN 978 1 4744 4347 0 (hardback)
ISBN 978 1 4744 4348 7 (webready PDF)
ISBN 978 1 4744 4349 4 (epub)

Contents

Acknowledgements

The editors would like to thank the Royal New Zealand Marsden Fund for its support for this edition. We also thank the many librarians and archivists who have assisted our research into Jane Porter and her family, especially Gayle Richardson at the Huntington Library, San Marino, California; Karen Cook and Elspeth Healey at the Kenneth Spencer Research Library at the University of Kansas; and Charles Carter and Elizabeth Denlinger at the Carl H. Pforzheimer Collection of Shelley and His Circle, New York Public Library. It has been a pleasure working with Edinburgh University Press, and we thank Ersev Ersoy, Michelle Houston, Adela Rauchova, series editor Julian Wolfreys and our two anonymous readers for their support and suggestions.

We are grateful to other scholars who have shared their knowledge of and enthusiasm for Jane Porter and *Thaddeus of Warsaw*, including Peta Beasley, Vincent Gallagher, Devoney Looser and Fiona Price. Katarzyna Gmerek generously answered questions regarding Polish names and historical events. Grace Moore and Megan Kitching read through the whole manuscript and provided expert feedback. Many friends, colleagues and scholars offered useful advice; we especially thank Emily Bernhard Jackson, Miriam Burstein, Lydia Craig, Nora Crook, Nicola Cummins, Richard De Ritter, Jocelyn Harris, Wilhelmina Hotchkiss, Maura Ives, Peter Merchant, Melanie Remy and Charles Rzepka.

Thomas McLean would like to thank Grace Moore and Felix Robinson for their patience, love and good humour. He also thanks all the friends, family, colleagues and random strangers who have endured his interest in *Thaddeus of Warsaw* for more than two decades.

Ruth Knezevich would like to thank Sarah Sharp and Leila Crawford for their friendship, wisdom and encouragement.

Series Editor's Preface

The nineteenth century saw an unprecedented, prodigious production of literary texts. Many of these, often best-sellers or offering vital commentaries on cultural, political and philosophical issues of the period engendering debate, did not survive in print long into the twentieth century, regardless of putative quality, however measured. Edinburgh Critical Editions of Nineteenth-Century Texts seeks to bring back to the reading public and the scholarly eye works of undeniable importance during the time of their first publication and reception, which have, often unjustly, disappeared from print and readers' consciousness. Covering fiction, long and short, non-fiction prose and essays, and poetry, with comprehensive critical introductions and carefully chosen supporting appendices, germane to the text and the context of the volume, Edinburgh Critical Editions of Nineteenth-Century Texts provides definitive, annotated scholarly reprints.

Introduction

Thomas McLean

On 3 February 1801 Jane Porter recorded in her diary having 'finished my Introduction to my "Thaddeus of Warsaw." It pleases me more than anything I have written, because it is the most simple.'[1] At twenty-five years old, Porter was an experienced if little-known writer from a remarkable literary family. But when *Thaddeus of Warsaw* appeared in 1803, its success quickly exceeded any of her family's previous achievements.

Thaddeus of Warsaw concerns Thaddeus Sobieski, the fictional descendant of one of Poland's most famous kings, who fights for his country against Russian invaders and then escapes to England, where he encounters British society in all its varieties and solves the mystery of his birth. A mix of historical romance, social comedy and critical commentary on Britain's treatment of foreign exiles, it was one of the most popular British novels of the nineteenth century. Remembering his adolescent taste for Jane Porter's works, William Makepeace Thackeray wrote to a friend in 1848, 'Why, we used to admire the Scottish chiefs once and cry over Thaddeus of Warsaw. – Fond follies of youth!'[2] Children and towns were named after Porter's hero, who became a byword for honourable behaviour. Yet this remarkable cultural phenomenon is all but forgotten now. Why did *Thaddeus of Warsaw* experience such sustained popularity? And why is it worth remembering? This introduction provides a brief overview of Porter's life, some historical context for understanding the novel, an explanation of the novel's key elements, and a consideration of why it deserves to be read today.

Jane Porter: a biographical sketch

Jane Porter was the fourth of six children born to William and Jane Porter. Her father (1735–79) came from County Donegal, Ireland, and served as surgeon to the 6th (Inniskilling) Dragoons, a cavalry regiment in the British army. While stationed in Durham, he met

[1] Diary of Jane Porter, Folger Shakespeare Library M.b. 15.
[2] Thackeray, William Makepeace, *The Letters and Private Papers of William Makepeace Thackeray*, ed. Gordon N. Ray, 4 vols (New York: Octagon Books, 1980), 2. 429.

Jane Blenkinsopp (1745–1831), the daughter of Peter Blenkinsopp (d. 1778), an innkeeper, and Mary Adamson (d. 1761). William and Jane married in July 1770. Their first child, William, was baptised in 1771 but died in infancy. Their surviving children included John (?1772–1811), a soldier and merchant in the West Indies; William Ogilvie (?1774–1850), a naval surgeon and Bristol doctor; Jane (?1775–1850); Robert Ker (1777–1842), an artist and writer; and Anna Maria (1778–1832), a novelist. There is some uncertainty surrounding the place and date of birth for the three eldest surviving Porter children. Though Jane was baptised on 17 January 1776 at St Mary-le-Bow church in Durham, England, several letters and diaries note that she celebrated her birthday on 3 December, making 1775 her probable birth year. But Porter herself claimed that there was a 'secret' regarding her birthday, and some evidence suggests that she was born in Ireland.[3]

The Porters' seemingly comfortable existence in Durham was disrupted by the deaths of Peter Blenkinsopp (4 December 1778) and William Porter (8 September 1779). By November 1779, the newly widowed Jane Blenkinsopp Porter had moved her three youngest children to Edinburgh (John and William apparently stayed with relations in Durham), where she offered accommodation on Buccleugh Street for 'Students of Physic, and other Gentlemen'.[4] In later years, Jane Porter wrote of these Edinburgh days with great affection. The children attended George Fulton's school in Niddry's Wynd, and among their youthful acquaintances was none other than Walter Scott.[5] Stories and images of Scottish history fired their imaginations.

> I may truly say [she wrote years later] that I was hardly six years of age when I first heard the names of William Wallace and Robert Bruce: – not from gentlemen and ladies, readers of history; but from the maids in the nursery, and the serving-man in the kitchen.[6]

But the family struggled financially in Edinburgh, and by 1785 they had returned to Durham. In September 1785 Jane Blenkinsopp

---

[3] Jane Porter to her mother, 3 December 1816, Huntington Library Jane Porter Papers (hereafter Huntington) POR 1972. Regarding Ireland, see Hall, Mrs S. C., 'Memories of Miss Jane Porter', *Harper's New Monthly Magazine* 1.4 (September 1850), pp. 433–8 (435–6).

[4] *Caledonian Mercury*, 10 November 1779, p. 1.

[5] McLean, Thomas, 'Nobody's Argument: Jane Porter and the Historical Novel', *Journal for Early Modern Cultural Studies* 7.2 (2007), pp. 88–103 (89).

[6] Porter, Jane, 'Retrospective Introduction', *The Scottish Chiefs* (London: Colburn and Bentley, 1831), p. i.

Porter wrote to Dr John Sharp, requesting aid from Lord Crewe's Charity:

> I have no one to speak in my favor, but my situation; being left for these six years past, to struggle with the world, & its inconveniencys [*sic*], upon the poor pittance of Ten Pound a year from Government, which (though a blessing) [is] scarce able to afford me the means of supporting myself & children, & my own endeavours not proving successful.[7]

Few documents survive from this period but the family's situation evidently improved, for Mrs Porter was able to move her brood to London, so that her youngest son, Robert, could enrol in the Royal Academy in February 1791.

Over the next decade, the Porters lived at various addresses in central London: 38 Bedford Street, Covent Garden (1792–4); 66 St Martin's Lane (1794–6); 16 Great Newport Street, Leicester Square (1796–9); and 6 Gerrard Street, Soho (1799–1804).[8] Not surprisingly, these are the same streets and neighbourhoods that Thaddeus Sobieski wanders during his travails in the capital city. In 1804, Mrs Porter and her two daughters (who never married) moved south of the city to Soame House, Thames Ditton, and they remained in Surrey for the better part of three decades. After the deaths of her mother and sister, Jane Porter lived a peripatetic life, relying on the generosity of wealthier friends, including Samuel and Mary Skinner of Shirley Park and the Throckmortons of Coughton Court. In the 1840s, she shared her brother, William Ogilvie's, home in Portland Square, Bristol, until her death in 1850.

By the time of Porter's death, *Thaddeus of Warsaw* had gone through thirteen British editions (and numerous pirated American printings), and it remained her most popular work for the rest of the nineteenth century. Porter seems to have been genuinely surprised when *Thaddeus of Warsaw* became a success. As she wrote to her sister in 1804, 'I should have enjoyed living under the shelter of your Laurels, and those of Robert's – but to have planted a tree myself, was beyond my hopes, though not without my wishes.'[9]

---

[7] Jane Blenkinsopp Porter to Dr John Sharp, 5 September 1785, Northumberland NRO 452/C/2/2/5/127. Sharp (1723–93) was a clergyman and senior trustee of the charity, which was then based at Bamburgh Castle.

[8] Dates drawn from surviving letters and the entry on Robert Ker Porter in Graves, Algernon, *The Royal Academy of Arts: A Complete Dictionary of Contributors and their Work from its Foundation in 1769 to 1904*, vol. 6 (1906), pp. 185–6.

[9] Jane Porter to Anna Maria Porter, 17 October 1804, Huntington POR 1523.

As Porter's comment suggests, her younger sister and brother had already made a mark on London's cultural scene. Anna Maria, although the youngest child, was the first to see her work in print: she published two volumes of stories entitled *Artless Tales* (1793, 1795) and two sentimental novels, *Walsh Colville* (1797) and *Octavia* (1798). In early 1801, while Jane Porter was sketching her plans for *Thaddeus*, Anna Maria was preparing a play for Covent Garden.[10] She would go on to publish a dozen more novels before her death in 1832. Their brother, Robert Ker Porter, had studied under Benjamin West at the Royal Academy, and he had gained widespread acclaim for *The Storming of Seringapatam*, a semi-circular panorama exhibited at the London Lyceum from April 1800 to January 1801. Panoramas – large-scale paintings in the round, depicting landscapes or cityscapes – were a favourite attraction at the turn of the century, and Robert became known for his depictions of military battles: he produced at least seven panoramic works in the first decade of the nineteenth century. He regularly exhibited paintings at the Royal Academy and also contributed four images to the Boydell Shakespeare Gallery. In 1805 he accepted an opportunity to paint historical murals in St Petersburg, Russia, and in later years he travelled widely in Europe and the Middle East, producing several travelogues along the way. In 1826 he took up a diplomatic position in Venezuela and remained there for most of the rest of his life.

Jane developed more slowly as a writer. She had contributed with her younger brother and sister to Thomas Frognall Dibdin's short-lived periodical *The Quiz* (1796–7) and co-authored with Anna Maria the pamphlet *A Defence of the Profession of an Actor* (1800).[11] Her first novel, the three-volume *Spirit of the Elbe* (1799), was a Gothic tale set in Germany. It was published anonymously and received little notice, though the younger Charles Dibdin reimagined the work for a May 1800 Sadler's Wells stage production, *Blackenberg, or The Spirit of the Elbe*. At the same time that she was beginning work on *Thaddeus of Warsaw* in February 1801, she was awaiting proof sheets for her second fictional effort, a single-volume work for young people entitled

---

[10] Diary of Jane Porter (27 January 1801), Folger Shakespeare Library M.b. 15. The play, *The Fair Fugitives*, was eventually performed on 16 May 1803 but closed after only one night.

[11] For evidence that the Porter sisters cowrote *A Defence*, see Jane's 22 November 1799 letter to Anna Maria ('But we must not forget that we have our Treatise to present to Longman–I hope he will publish it,' Huntington POR 1445) and her 9 December 1799 letter to the same where, after a discussion of the theatre, Jane writes, 'Alas! I doubt, however enthusiastically and well-intended, our Pamphlet is written, it will be deemed more utopian than real' (Huntington POR 1447).

Two Princes of Persia (1801). 'I. Porter' appears on its title page, leaving the author's gender a mystery.[12] Like its predecessor, it received limited attention.

Thaddeus of Warsaw appeared in the early months of 1803, and response to it among her acquaintances led Porter to believe that she had a success on her hands. On 19 July 1803 she told her sister that their friend 'Dr Maclaurin has read it twice thro' – and concluded that all the <u>military Scenes</u>, & <u>Speeches</u> were copied from some other work. If I have but fair play, I trust I shall "put money in my pocket".'[13] Reviews were uniformly positive, and during a visit to Bath in early 1804 she found herself a celebrated author.[14] Her publishers, Longman and Rees, requested a second edition in March 1804 (see Appendix D) and a third edition in 1805. The work sold steadily over the next two decades, with an eleventh edition appearing in 1826. In 1831 it was the fourth volume in Henry Colburn and Richard Bentley's Standard Novels series (as a measure of changing tastes, Mary Shelley's *Frankenstein* was ninth in the series; Jane Austen's *Sense and Sensibility* was twenty-third); and it appeared in a newly revised and illustrated edition for George Virtue in 1845. The novel's protagonist, Thaddeus Sobieski, quickly became a model for male behaviour. In Scottish author Mary Brunton's 1810 novel *Self-Control*, Laura describes her favourite literary figure:

> I prefer the hero of Miss Porter's new publication – Thaddeus of Warsaw. Truly generous, and inflexibly upright, his very tenderness has in it something manly and respectable; and the whole combination has an air of nature that interests one as for a real friend.[15]

Percy Shelley was said to have chosen to live on London's Poland Street in 1811 because 'it reminded him of Thaddeus of Warsaw and of freedom'.[16] A young woman in Henry Wadsworth Longfellow's 1849 novel *Kavanagh* declares approvingly of the title character, 'he

---

[12] J was still occasionally treated as a variant of I, so perhaps this was intentional. Interestingly, reviews of the novel in the *Anti-Jacobin Review* and *British Critic* list its author as J. Porter.

[13] Jane Porter to Anna Maria Porter, 19 July 1803, Huntington POR 1480.

[14] Looser, Devoney, 'Another Jane: Jane Porter, Austen's Contemporary', in *New Windows on a Woman's World: Essays for Jocelyn Harris*, eds Colin Gibson and Lisa Marr, 2 vols (Dunedin: Department of English, University of Otago, 2005), 2. 235–48.

[15] Brunton, Mary, *Self-Control* [1810] (New York: Pandora Press, 1986), p. 136.

[16] Hogg, Thomas Jefferson, *The Life of Percy Bysshe Shelley*, 4 vols (London: Moxon, 1858), 1. 297.

is not a man; he is a Thaddeus of Warsaw!'[17] At least three towns in the United States, Warsaw and Pembroke, both in Kentucky, and Warsaw, North Carolina, adopted their names in tribute to Porter's novel. Thaddeus even became a popular boy's name: his most famous namesake is probably the American scientist and Civil War veteran Thaddeus Sobieski Constantine Lowe (1832–1913), though his earliest is certainly the son of Jane's brother William, Thaddeus Porter (1803–25).

Porter's literary career would continue for at least four decades. After *Thaddeus*, she produced a volume of commentary on Sir Philip Sidney's writings (1807), and she regularly wrote on historical events and personages for the periodical press.[18] But her fame rested on *Thaddeus* and the several novels that followed it, most notably *The Scottish Chiefs* (1810) and *The Pastor's Fire-side* (1817), both of which also appeared in the Standard Novels series and in Virtue's illustrated editions.[19] All three works were notable contributions to the development of the British historical novel. However, while the subject matter of the latter two – the campaigns of William Wallace and Robert the Bruce, and the political machinations surrounding the Stuart cause in the 1720s – fits into most narratives of the historical novel's genealogy, the historical setting of *Thaddeus of Warsaw* – the 1790s partition of Poland – seems, to the modern reader, a less likely topic of interest. In fact, it was a widely discussed political and military event, though, like the novel it inspired, it is perhaps less familiar today than it ought to be.

Poland in the 1790s

In the aftermath of the American and French Revolutions, Poland – or, more precisely, the Polish–Lithuanian Commonwealth[20] – was a key

---

[17] Longfellow, Henry Wadsworth, *Kavanagh* (Boston: Ticknor, Reed, and Fields, 1849), p. 55.

[18] McLean, Thomas, 'Jane Porter's Later Works, 1825–1846', *Harvard Library Bulletin* 20.2 (2009), pp. 45–62.

[19] Many nineteenth-century readers would have added a fourth work to that list: *Sir Edward Seaward's Narrative*, which appeared in 1831 as 'edited by Miss Jane Porter'. It was widely assumed that she authored the work but it was actually written by her brother, William Ogilvie Porter. See Price, Fiona, 'Jane Porter and the Authorship of Sir Edward Seaward's Narrative: Previously Unpublished Correspondence', *Notes and Queries* 49.1 (March 2002), pp. 55–7.

[20] For brevity, I have used Poland throughout this introduction, though it would be more correct to speak of the Kingdom of Poland and the Grand Duchy of Lithuania, or the Polish–Lithuanian Commonwealth. Most contemporary British accounts simply use Poland.

setting in the 1790s battle between revolutionary reform and reactionary opposition. Its ruler, Stanisław Poniatowski, was a former lover
of Russia's ruler, Catherine the Great. He had been elected in 1764
– thanks in part to Russian influence – to rule the Commonwealth as
King Stanisław II.[21] But if Stanisław expected support from his former
lover, he was mistaken. When civil war broke out in Poland in the
late 1760s – an event alluded to early in *Thaddeus of Warsaw*, when
General Butzou recounts the abduction of King Stanisław – Catherine
and Frederick II of Prussia took advantage of the unrest to orchestrate
the first partition of Poland in 1772, reducing the size and population
of the Commonwealth by about one-third.

Despite this national catastrophe, Stanisław sought to reform the
governmental practices of his kingdom. His greatest achievement was
the 3 May 1791 Constitution. This reforming constitution made the
crown hereditary (though not through the Poniatowski family) and
curtailed parliamentary powers, in the hopes of also limiting the like-
lihood of foreign influence. The constitution received strong praise
in Britain from Horace Walpole, Edmund Burke and even Thomas
Paine,[22] but some Polish nobles saw the reforms as a threat to their
privileges and formed the Targowica Confederation to oppose the
changes. Fearful of how her Russian subjects might react to the
empowerment of their Polish neighbours, Catherine ordered 100,000
soldiers into Poland in support of the confederates. It is at this moment
– on the eve of the Polish–Russian War of 1792, as the King's reforms
teeter in the balance – that the action of *Thaddeus of Warsaw* begins.

The novel's fictional hero Thaddeus Sobieski fights beside actual
supporters of the 1791 constitution, including Prince Józef Poniatowski,
the King's nephew, and Tadeusz Kościuszko, a decorated veteran of
the American Revolutionary War. The Poles won several victories
against the Russians in 1792, but Stanisław ultimately supported a
ceasefire and joined the Targowica Confederation, which led to the
second partition of Poland in 1793. Disgusted with the King's behaviour, the remaining supporters of reform rallied around Kościuszko,
who declared the uprising that bears his name in March 1794. As in
1792, the Polish forces won several early victories, but on 10 October
1794, at the battle of Maciejowice, Kościuszko was seriously wounded
and taken prisoner. Less than a month later, after the slaughter of

[21] The Polish–Lithuanian Commonwealth had a long history of elective rather than
hereditary monarchy. While in theory a more democratic system, in practice it allowed
foreign interests to manipulate the results of the election.

[22] McLean, Thomas, *The Other East and Nineteenth-Century British Literature: Imagining Poland
and the Russian Empire* (Basingstoke: Palgrave, 2012), pp. 23–4.

soldiers and civilians in the Warsaw suburb of Praga by Russian forces under General Alexander Suvorov, Stanisław surrendered his nation. Russia, Prussia and Austria shared in the third and final partition, and in late 1795, in what Lord Acton later declared 'the most revolutionary act of the old absolutism',[23] Poland disappeared from the map of Europe. It would not reappear until 1918, after the First World War.

Poland's 1791 constitutional reforms and the battles that led to the final two partitions were widely reported in the British press, and the heroism of the Poles became a favourite subject. In his 1796 poem 'Religious Musings', Samuel Taylor Coleridge attacked Catherine the Great, 'that foul Woman of the North', and in his 1794 sonnet 'To Kosciusko' he memorialised the defeated Polish hero: 'O what a loud and fearful shriek was there, / As tho' a thousand souls one death-grown pour'd! / Ah me! they view'd beneath an hireling's sword / Fall'n KOSKIUSKO!' The Scottish poet Thomas Campbell adapted some of Coleridge's imagery for his long poem in rhyming couplets, *The Pleasures of Hope* (1799). Campbell's work contains an extended passage on the defeat of the Kościuszko Uprising, which includes the memorable couplet, 'Hope, for a season, bade the world farewell, / And Freedom shriek'd – as KOSCIUSKO fell!'

The image of the fallen Polish hero as synecdoche for the fallen nation was reinforced by a popular visual image of Kościuszko. After the death of Catherine the Great, her son and successor Tsar Paul released Kościuszko from prison, and the Polish hero visited England in 1797 on his way to the United States. He was still suffering from the injuries he received at Maciejowice, and this limited his mobility and his social visits. In London, Robert Ker Porter's mentor Benjamin West painted a small portrait of Kościuszko reclining on a sofa, his sword at his side and papers scattered about him. West's biographer described the striking image as 'a precocious anticipation of Byronic melancholy and mood laden *Weltschmerz*'.[24] Several engravings of Kościuszko, based on similar images, soon appeared, and the image of the honourable, melancholy Pole was confirmed.

Many, if not all, of these works had an impact on Jane Porter. She quotes from Coleridge's 'Religious Musings' and Campbell's *Pleasures of Hope* in *Thaddeus*; and, though she makes no mention of Benjamin West's portrait in her writings or letters, the family was well known

---

[23] Acton, John Emerich Edward Dalberg, First Baron Acton, 'Nationality', in *Mapping the Nation*, ed. Gopal Balakrishnan (London and New York: Verso, 1996), pp. 17–38 (21).
[24] Alberts, Robert C., *Benjamin West: A Biography* (Boston: Houghton Mifflin, 1978), p. 222.

to West through Robert's attendance at the Royal Academy, and she could have seen the image at the 1798 Academy exhibition. Though Jane never met Kościuszko, her brother did so, visiting the fallen hero during his stay in London, and drawing a (now lost) sketch of his head. Furthermore, Anna Maria Porter contributed a quatrain that accompanies Antoine Cardon's engraving of Kościuszko after a sketch by Richard Cosway. It reads, 'O! Freedom! Valour! Resignation! Here / Pay to your godlike son the sacred tear; / Weave the proud laurel for his suffering brow, / And in a world's wide pity steep the bough'. If British newspapers had presented Kościuszko as an honourable and courageous defender of his homeland, British writers and artists (including Jane's own brother and sister) were adding a layer of tearful melancholy to the representation. Both of these representations come together in Porter's creation, Thaddeus Sobieski.

History and romance in *Thaddeus of Warsaw*

Most of the first volume of *Thaddeus of Warsaw* is set in Poland, during the period between the onset of the Polish–Russian War in early 1792 and the fall of Warsaw in November 1794. Though historical figures, most notably Kościuszko, play a significant role in this first volume, the narrative's central figures are all fictional: Thaddeus, his mother, his grandfather, and his British acquaintance, Pembroke Somerset. There was, of course, a long and recognised history in British literature of mixing history with fiction, going back at least to Shakespeare's history plays and including recent works like Sophia Lee's popular novel *The Recess* (1783), whose twin heroines are the secret daughters of Mary Queen of Scots. But the historical romance did not have the familiarity or critical respect it would gain a decade later, when the friend of Porter's youth, Sir Walter Scott, produced his series of Waverley novels. Thus in the Preface to the first edition of *Thaddeus*, Porter felt it necessary to defend her use of a historical setting to explore the magnanimous character of her fictional protagonist. She writes that Poland's

> struggles for independence, and her misfortunes, afforded me situations exactly fitted to my plan; and preferring a series of incidents which are true and interesting, before a legend of war fabricated entirely by my own hand, I have made no ceremony of making Truth the help-mate of Fiction.

Recognising that 'war and politics are not promising subjects of amusement', she assures her readers that the battle scenes 'are neither frequent, nor do they last long'. She furthermore requests that readers do not 'pass over any scene as extraneous, which, though it begins like a political paper, or a sermon, always terminates by casting some new light on the portrait of the hero'. Like Shakespeare and Scott, Porter hoped to use the rigour of historical events to challenge or clarify the personalities of her fictional characters.

This opening volume of *Thaddeus* has received a significant amount of scholarly attention because it seems to anticipate several key aspects of the historical novel as employed by Sir Walter Scott and elaborated by Scott's twentieth-century champion, the critic Georg Lukács. Porter introduces a degree of historical detail that suggests a strong familiarity with the actual events. Her story is set at a critical historical moment, the final partitioning of Poland, when a seemingly feudal society (Pembroke tells his mother that at Villanow he is 'carried back into the fifteenth century') is overrun by its militarily advanced neighbours. As in Scott's novels, historical figures appear mostly on the periphery; the major characters are fictional. Pembroke, an outsider in this world, is not so different from Edward Waverley in Scott's first novel, who journeys to Scotland and falls under the spell of its manners and customs. For all of these elements, *Thaddeus* deserves a place in any account of the British historical novel.

But *Thaddeus of Warsaw* is arguably most successful when its gallant hero leaves Poland and the action shifts to an English setting. By doing so, Porter is able to investigate an important figure of British history that Walter Scott and most of their contemporaries neglected: the foreign exile who makes Britain his adopted home. Porter is not shy in depicting the challenges that Thaddeus faces, and his introduction to London is far from welcoming. After his exhausting journey from Poland, coachmen and hotel workers take advantage of his inexperience; a cloth vendor and picture dealer treat him ungenerously. But Thaddeus also comes to the attention of honourable Britons, mainly through his own virtuous actions. His kindness to the impoverished Mrs Robson results in his finding a residence in St Martin's Lane; his bravery in coming to the defence of Lady Tinemouth leads to his encounters with all of the most important (and well-connected) figures in the second half of the novel.

Part of the pleasure of the novel's London chapters is their presentation of city life through the eyes and actions of an outsider. Readers experience the mix of high and low society in St James's, the bustle and danger of Charing Cross, the entertainments of Covent Garden and Drury Lane, and the sombreness of the City. Porter's narrative encourages readers to sympathise with her Polish protagonist as he navigates these neighbourhoods of London. We cheer for him as he uses his skills to support himself and to assist those less fortunate; we feel sorrow and even guilt when he recognises the inequalities of this modern society, into which he is necessarily inculcated. As Mary Brunton's character Laura suggests, we feel for Thaddeus as we would 'for a real friend'. There are cameos from historical figures, including the theatre manager George Colman, the opera sensation John Braham and the actor Charles Kemble, so that the mix of fact and fiction continues in the novel's later chapters. Interestingly, many of these cultural markers are slightly anachronistic. Though the main action of the later volumes clearly runs from November 1794 to October 1795, Euphemia Dundas reads Frances Burney's 1796 novel *Camilla*, Braham sings an aria from a 1796 opera, and Thaddeus attends a Haymarket performance of August von Kotzebue's *Sighs*, a work first performed there in 1799. Porter must have known this, suggesting that she was more interested in giving a playful and up-to-date sense of the cultural life of 1790s London rather than a precise historical record.

Like the battle scenes in Poland, these moments of cultural encounter in London provide insights into Thaddeus's personality. In her Preface, Porter explains that she wished 'to pourtray a character which Prosperity could not intoxicate, nor Adversity depress'. The defeat of Poland and the challenges of London cause enormous personal suffering to Thaddeus Sobieski, but he responds to all of these trials with sensitivity and generosity. And tears. Twenty-first-century readers may find the overflow of emotion at times difficult to embrace. Some of Porter's contemporary readers felt the same. In *Self-Control*, Laura's father agrees with his daughter's estimation of Thaddeus Sobieski, but he adds,

> your favourite has the same resemblance to a human character which the Belvidere Apollo has to a human form. It is so like man that one cannot absolutely call it divine, yet so perfect, that it is difficult to believe it human.[25]

An anonymous author in 1818 was less subtle, complaining that 'Thaddeus, that elegant Pole, is a monster, being *unnaturally perfect*.'[26] Most readers, however, were only too ready to weep alongside Porter's hero. In transferring the man of feeling from the novels of

---

[25] Brunton, *Self-Control*, p. 137.
[26] Anonymous, *Prodigious!!! Or Childe Paddie in London*, 3 vols (London: W. Lindsell, 1818), 1. 127.

Oliver Goldsmith and Henry Mackenzie to revolutionary Poland and reactionary England of the 1790s, Porter updates the sentimental hero for contemporary times and reminds her readers that a virtuous individual need not be British.

Porter's sources

Jane Porter's surviving letters from 1801 and 1802 say little about the composition of *Thaddeus of Warsaw*. In her retrospective introduction for the 1831 edition, however, she reflected on some of the early inspirations for her novel. She recalled seeing 'hapless refugees' from Poland and France 'wandering about St. James's Park' in the middle 1790s: 'memory can never forget the variety of wretched, yet noble-looking, visages I then contemplated'. To this she adds her brother's personal encounter with Kościuszko, whose 'whole figure bore marks of long suffering'. No wonder, then, that her novel 'should be founded on the actual scenes of Kosciuszko's sufferings, and moulded out of his virtues'.[27] Robert's experiences were an important inspiration in another way. While she was mixing literary fiction with historical events, her brother was using his own imaginative skills to create panoramic paintings of recent battles: he had followed *Seringapatam* with the *Siege of Acre* (1801) and the *Battle of Alexandria* (1802). '[S]eated in my brother's little study', surrounded by relics of these battles, 'I put my last strokes to the first campaigns of Thaddeus Sobieski.'[28] One of the heroes of Acre, Sir William Sidney Smith, was a family friend and a very strong influence on Porter; she dedicated the first edition to him.[29] There is strong epistolary evidence that Jane and Anna Maria Porter contributed to the descriptive pamphlets that accompanied their brother's panoramic paintings, and thus further familiarised themselves with the strategies of contemporary military campaigns.

Porter also turned to published histories of Poland. As our annotations in this edition make clear, her account of the abduction of King Stanisław in 1771 draws heavily on William Coxe's 1784 *Travels into Poland, Russia, Sweden and Denmark*, and her descriptions of the military campaigns and political events of 1790s Poland closely follow the narrative established in Stephen Jones's 1795 *History of Poland*. There

---

[27] Porter, Jane, 'The Author to her Friendly Readers', *Thaddeus of Warsaw* (London: Colburn and Bentley, 1831), pp. viii, x.

[28] Porter, 'The Author to her Friendly Readers', p. xi.

[29] For more on Porter's relationship with Smith, see Looser, Devoney, 'The Great Man and Women's Historical Fiction: Jane Porter and Sir Sidney Smith', *Women's Writing* 19.3 (2012), pp. 294–314.

are no doubt other historical sources that have yet to come to light. Readers comparing passages of *Thaddeus* to Coxe and Jones will agree with Dr Maclaurin that many scenes and speeches 'were copied from some other work', though it is significant that Porter made limited changes to these passages over the many editions that she revised, suggesting that such borrowing might have been interpreted as a sign of careful research rather than thoughtless theft.

Other kinds of personal experience also shaped Porter's storytelling. Besides London, the novel's other key British setting is the landscape around Grantham, Lincolnshire. In 1799, Porter spent several months in Grantham, visiting family friends. While there she visited Belvoir Castle, and it surely provided a model for the novel's Somerset Castle. Belvoir is the historic seat of the Dukes of Rutland; the fifth Duke of Rutland, John Henry Manners (also known as Lord Roos, 1778–1857), was the son of Lady Mary Isabella Somerset (1756–1831), the daughter of Charles Somerset, fourth Duke of Beaufort. Of course, Roos, Somerset and Beaufort are all surnames of key characters in *Thaddeus of Warsaw*. Interestingly, though, this visit to Belvoir also informed Porter's image of Villanow Palace in Warsaw. In a September 1799 journal fragment, she records her impressions of the landscape near Belvoir:

> Autumn seemed to be unfolding all her beauties to delight us – in one part, we beheld the haymakers mowing the hay, or heaping it into stacks – in another, the reapers gathering the wheat, with a troop of little gleaners behind them, each of whom might have tempted some benevolent palemon, to transplant them to a more generous soil.[30]

Readers of *Thaddeus of Warsaw* will notice its striking similarity to Pembroke Somerset's description of the countryside near Villanow in his letter to his mother (Volume I, Chapter IV).

Less surprisingly, Porter's life in London also informs Thaddeus's experiences. Most, if not all, of the historical figures who make an appearance – Colman, Braham, Kemble – were personally known to the Porters. It must have been an amusing pleasure for the author to imagine her fictional hero encountering her real-life friends, and perhaps also for them to discover themselves within the pages of the novel. Thaddeus's experiences as a starving artist surely reflect those of Robert Ker Porter and his associates at the Royal Academy;

---

[30] Special Collections, Spencer Research Library, University of Kansas MS 28, Box 38, f. 29. For Palemon, see note on page 45.

one nineteenth-century source suggested that Thaddeus's visits to the print shops of Great Newport Street were inspired by the similar experiences of Robert's contemporary, the Norwich artist John Sell Cotman.[31] Thaddeus's awkward encounters with the upper classes of British society were perhaps also familiar to the Porter sisters, who had to adapt to a very different lifestyle in London from what they knew in Edinburgh and Durham.

Equally striking are the many and varied literary echoes and quotations that fill *Thaddeus*. While there are numerous biblical and classical allusions, as well as quotations from Milton, Dryden and Thomson, Shakespeare's plays have the strongest presence. Though *Hamlet* is perhaps the single work most often referenced – not inappropriately, for a story about a son haunted by father figures – the narrative's blend of tragedy and comedy and its almost magical conclusion bring to mind *The Winter's Tale* or *The Tempest*. Porter, however, was not averse to quoting her contemporaries, including Samuel Taylor Coleridge, Thomas Campbell (another family acquaintance) and even her sister, Anna Maria Porter. Thus, even in her literary allusions, she presents her readers with a fusion of the personal and historical.

The legacy of *Thaddeus*

To our critical eyes nowadays [wrote Margaret Oliphant in 1882], the all-accomplished Thaddeus looks a little like a waxwork hero; but it will be hard to find in all our over-abundant romances of the nineteenth century so fine a gentleman, so disinterested a lover, an individual so certain to do what was right and best in every possible combination of circumstances.[32]

There may be some truth in Oliphant's suggestion that Thaddeus Sobieski lacks the psychological complexity that later Victorian readers expected in their heroes, and this may well explain the novel's disappearance from print some time in the early twentieth century. And yet, given its long life, one might argue that its influence was everywhere, that every dashing hero of page, stage and (later) screen owed something to the imagination of Jane Porter. In bringing *Thaddeus of Warsaw* back into print, we hope that scholars begin to identify the wider impact of the novel.

---

[31] Roget, John Lewis, *A History of the 'Old Water-Colour' Society*, 2 vols (London: Longmans, Green, and Co., 1891), 1. 101–3.

[32] Oliphant, Margaret, *The Literary History of England in the End of the Eighteenth and Beginning of the Nineteenth Century*, 3 vols (London: Macmillan and Co., 1882), 2. 273.

Its narrower influence can already be traced.[33] Throughout the nineteenth century, there was a steady flow of honourable Polish protagonists in British literature, and many of these clearly owe a debt to Thaddeus Sobieski. In 'The Pole', an 1832 short story written by Claire Clairmont and Mary Shelley, the Polish military spy Ladislas has a countenance that combines 'deep thoughtfulness' and 'calm intrepid bravery'. He eventually marries Idalie, 'a daughter of one of Kosciusko's unfortunate followers'.[34] Mary Shelley's novel *Lodore* (1835) has a tragic subplot involving Casimir, the child of a relationship between the British Lord Lodore and the Polish Countess Lyzinski. One of the great musical successes of the Victorian era, Michael Balfe's 1843 opera *The Bohemian Girl* features a dashing Polish military exile named Thaddeus who rescues, loses and then is reunited with Arline, a Count's daughter. Perhaps the most famous member of this genealogy is Will Ladislaw from George Eliot's *Middlemarch* (1871–2). Will's passion and idealism are no doubt part of his inheritance from his grandfather, 'a Polish refugee', who, as Will states, 'was a patriot – a bright fellow – could speak many languages – musical – got his bread by teaching all sorts of things'.[35]

The novel's impact was felt in another way: throughout the nineteenth and early twentieth centuries, *Thaddeus of Warsaw* reminded its readers that an independent Polish nation had once existed in Europe. Jane Porter developed a sense of the significance of her novel in 1832, when she received a visit from Prince Adam Jerzy Czartoryski (1770–1861) and the writer Julian Ursyn Niemcewicz (1758–1841). Czartoryski had fought in the Polish–Russian War of 1792; Niemcewicz had been taken prisoner with Kościuszko at Maciejowice. Both were leaders of the Polish government in exile. Jane wrote to her brother Robert that the discussion 'often drew tears from my eyes; for they both told me, that they owed to my pen, that Europe in our own times, knew anything of the history of Poland; as my work had excited the general interest among the young readers, to know more about the country'.[36]

But *Thaddeus of Warsaw* is also a parable of our own times. Since the European Union's enlargement in 2004, hundreds of thousands

---

[33] See McLean, *Other East*, for further discussion of the works mentioned in this paragraph.

[34] Clairmont, Claire, and Mary Shelley, 'The Pole', *Mary Shelley: Collected Tales and Stories*, ed. Charles E. Robinson (Baltimore: Johns Hopkins Press, 1976), pp. 347–72 (347, 354).

[35] Eliot, George, *Middlemarch* (New York: Penguin, 1994), p. 365.

[36] Jane Porter to Robert Ker Porter, 31 January to 1 February 1832, Special Collections, Spencer Research Library, University of Kansas MS 28, Box 4, f. 4.

of Poles have moved to the United Kingdom in search of a better life. Many have returned to Poland; many will stay and shape the future of their adopted homeland. For this growing population and their children, *Thaddeus* is a historical touchstone that points to the longer history of European emigration. It is also a reminder that xenophobia is not a new phenomenon. Shortly after Thaddeus arrives in London, one British character tells another, 'it is our duty to befriend the unfortunate but charity begins at home ... and, you know, the people of Poland have no claims upon us'. Another character declares, 'Would any man be mad enough to take the meat from his children's mouths, and throw it to a swarm of wolves just landed on the coast?' Porter's novel is not perfect; indeed, several passages suggest the author's own blind spots when it comes to cultural difference. But for all its history and romance, its challenge to our attitudes toward emigration and humanity remains sadly relevant.

A Note on the Text

Thaddeus of Warsaw first appeared in 1803. There were twelve subsequent editions published in Jane Porter's lifetime, and she revised the novel for most, if not all, of these; she even revised the first edition's Preface. From the third edition, she added new passages to the concluding chapter, some of which appear in Appendix A. For the final two editions, published in 1831 and 1845, Porter added copious notes, which are often informative but tend to weigh down the text with historical and biographical information. Readers interested in Porter's commentary should certainly locate copies of these later editions. Our goal, however, is to present an edition of the text closer to the version that captured the imagination of so many readers at the start of the nineteenth century.

We have therefore returned to the first edition. An 'Errata' page appears in some copies of the first edition, and we have incorporated these changes into the text. Unfortunately, there are many more errors than are listed on the single page. We have corrected obvious typographical errors, standardised capitalisation for titles (Count, Prince), and used single quotation marks for quotes within quotes. Generally, however, we have left Porter's spelling as it appears in the first edition, even when there are multiple spellings of the same word (for example, 'surprise' and 'surprize'). We have been more intrusive regarding punctuation, but we have mostly left the original punctuation in place, revising it only when the first edition punctuation obscures the meaning of a sentence. In these instances, we have followed punctuation as corrected in the second or third edition. If the punctuation survived through three editions, we left it as is.

Our footnotes are not comprehensive; they are mostly intended to identify historical places and figures, suggest likely sources, and provide clarification on the broad outline of historical events. Just as Porter asked her readers in the Preface to bear with the amount of unfamiliar historical material in the first volume, we hope our readers will do the same. The footnotes are most plentiful at the start, for historical context; they lessen as the story proceeds. We hope, too, that readers will bear with Porter's punctuation, which may seem excessive to twenty-first-century readers but was perhaps helpful to her contemporaries, who often read novels out loud.

Our copy text has been the Corvey Collection copy, available through *Nineteenth Century Collections Online*. We have checked this against a first edition held at the Huntington Library, San Marino, California.

We have made use of *Cary's New and Accurate Plan of London and Westminster, the Borough of Southwark and Parts Adjacent* (1795), available on the mapco.net site, for the identification of London streets. Footnotes refer to the King James Version of the Bible; the *Riverside Shakespeare* (1997); the *Riverside Milton* (1998); and the Clarendon Press edition of James Thomson's *The Seasons* (1981). All word definitions come from the online edition of the *Oxford English Dictionary* (hereafter *OED*).

THADDEUS
OF
WARSAW.

IN FOUR VOLUMES.

The time of life is short;
To spend that shortness basely, were too long,
If life did ride upon a dial's point,
Still ending at the arrival of an hour.
                                    SHAKESPEARE.*

BY
MISS PORTER.

LONDON:

PRINTED BY A. STRAHAN, PRINTERS-STREET,
FOR T. N. LONGMAN AND O. REES, PATERNOSTER-ROW.
1803.

* *Henry IV, Part 1*, V, ii, 81–4.

THADDEUS OF WARSAW
is
inscribed
to
SIR SIDNEY SMITH;*
under the Hope, that as
Sir Philip Sidney†
Did not disdain to write a Romance,
Sir Sidney Smith
will not refuse to read one.
Sir Philip Sidney, consigned his excellent Work to the Affection
of
a Sister.
I confide my aspiring Attempt to the Urbanity
of
the Brave:
to the Man of Taste, of Feeling, and of Candour;
to him,
whose Clemency will bestow that Indulgence on the Author,
which his Judgment might have denied to the Book;
to him,
of whom future Ages will speak with Honour,
and the present Times, boast as their Glory!

To
Sir Sidney Smith
I submit this humble Tribute of the highest Respect
which can be offered by a Briton,
or animate the Heart
of his most obedient
and
obliged Servant

THE AUTHOR.

---

* Sir William Sidney Smith (1764–1840) was an officer in the British Royal Navy during the Napoleonic wars. His service at the siege of Acre in 1799 helped halt Bonaparte's advances and secured Smith a heroic reputation. He was also a Porter family acquaintance: Robert Ker Porter painted a portrait of Smith, as well as a celebratory 1801 panorama, *The Siege of Acre*.

† Sir Philip Sidney (1554–86), author and courtier. Porter refers to his most ambitious literary work, the *Arcadia*, which was dedicated to his sister. Sidney died from an injury sustained at the Battle of Zutphen.

PREFACE.

Having attempted a work of four volumes, it is natural that the consideration of so much time and labour as must have been spent in its execution, should occasion to the author some anxiety respecting its fate; therefore, before the reader favours the tale itself with his attention, I beg leave to offer him an account of its plan.

Agreeably to the constant verdict of good taste, I have ever believed the novels of Richardson to be unequalled.* Their pure morality, and their unity of design, which might well entitle them to be called epic poems in prose, have equally been the objects of my respect and admiration. I see the trials and triumph of *Chastity* manifested in the person of *Pamela*: with the same trials and triumphs, *Piety*, in her brightest garb, is exhibited in the character of *Clarissa*; and in the character of *Sir Charles Grandison*, we have a most attractive and charming example of every Christian virtue.

The contemplation of such a model, tempted me to imitation. The pleasure that I found in the employment; the leisure that I possessed to pursue my pleasure; and the eagerness with which the mind prosecutes, and endeavours to accomplish a favourite scheme, gradually, yet with a lively mental activity, conducted me to the end.

Wishing to pourtray a character which Prosperity could not intoxicate, nor Adversity depress, I chose *Magnanimity* as the subject of my story. There is a powerful ray of the Almighty, in truly great minds: it burns with equal splendour in prosperity and adversity; its purity as well as its ardour, declares its divine origin. This is the talisman of those atchievements, which amaze every one but their author. When the eye is fixed on Heaven, "*Ossa seems a wart.*"†

What flattered Alexander into a madman, and degraded the high-souled Cæsar into a tyrant, I have selected as the first ordeal of Thaddeus

---

* Samuel Richardson (bap. 1689–1761), printer and author. Porter mentions his epistolary novels *Pamela* (1740), *Clarissa* (1747–8) and *Sir Charles Grandison* (1753–4).
† A paraphrase of *Hamlet*, V, i, 268. Ossa is a mountain in northern Greece.

Sobieski.* Placed at the summit of mortal ambition, surrounded with greatness and glory, he neither shews pride nor vanity. And when, in the progress of his second trial, he is plunged into the depth of sorrow; the weakness of passion never sinks the dignity of his fortitude; neither does the firmness of that virtue blunt the amiable sensibility of his heart.

This being the aim to which every incident in the book ought to tend, it became necessary to station my hero amidst scenes where events might probably arise that were proper to excite his bravery, his generosity, and to put his moderation to the test. Poland seemed the country best calculated to promote my intention. Her struggles for independence, and her misfortunes, afforded me situations exactly fitted to my plan; and preferring a series of incidents which are true and interesting, before a legend of war fabricated entirely by my own hand, I have made no ceremony of making Truth the help-mate of Fiction.

I have now described my plan, and if it be not approved, let the work be neglected; but if the reader be so candid and generous, as to proceed, I must beg him to peruse the *whole first* volume. He needs not be alarmed at the battles; they are neither frequent, nor do they last long; and, I request him, not to pass over any scene as extraneous, which, though it begins like a political paper, or a sermon, always terminates by casting some new light on the portrait of the hero. As the three remaining volumes are totally confined to domestic events, they have none of the afore-mentioned prejudices to encounter; but if the reader do not approach them regularly, through all the development of character opened in the first volume, what they exhibit, will seem a mere wilderness of incidents, without aim or interest. Indeed, I have attempted nothing in the personages of this story, beyond the sphere of living evidence. I have sketched no virtue that I have not seen, nor painted any folly from imagination. I have endeavoured to be as faithful to reality in my pictures of morals and heroic life, as a just painter is (when he draws a landscape) to the existing and engaging objects of rural nature.

---

* Alexander III of Macedon ('the Great', 356–323 BC) and Gaius Julius Caesar (100–44 BC) were often represented as figures whose greatness was tarnished by their unrestrained ambition.

THADDEUS OF WARSAW.
VOLUME I.

CHAP. I.

The large and magnificent palace of Villanow, which stands on the northern bank of the Vistula, was the favourite residence of John Sobieski King of Poland. That monarch, after having delivered his country from innumerable enemies, rescued Vienna, and subdued the Turks, used to retire to this place at certain seasons, and dispense those effects of his luminous and benevolent mind, which rendered his name great, and his people happy.*

When Charles the twelfth of Sweden visited the tomb of Sobieski, at Cracow, he exclaimed, "What a pity, that so great a man should ever die!"† Ninety years after his death, the spirit of this *great man* appeared to revive in the person of his descendant, Constantine Count Sobieski; who, in a comparatively private station, as Palatine of Masovia,‡ and the friend, rather than the lord, of his vassals, evinced by his actions, that he was the inheritor of his forefather's virtue, as well as of his blood.

He was the first Polish nobleman, who granted freedom to his peasants.§ He threw down their mud hovels, and built comfortable villages.

---

* John III Sobieski (1629–96), from 1674 King of Poland and Grand Duke of Lithuania, defeated the Ottoman army at Vienna in 1683. Villanow (Wilanów) Palace is a baroque residence built for Sobieski between 1677 and 1696. It stands about 3 kilometres west (not north) of the Vistula river. The historical palace did not remain in the Sobieski family; in the 1790s, it belonged to Princess Izabela Lubomirska (1736–1816).

† Charles XII of Sweden (1682–1718), a celebrated military leader to whom Napoleon was often compared in the Romantic era. This anecdote appears in William Coxe's two-volume *Travels into Poland, Russia, Sweden and Denmark* (London: T. Cadell, 1784), 1. 159; and in Stephen Jones's *History of Poland* (London: Vernor and Hood, 1795), p. 207.

‡ A palatine (or voivode) was an official in charge of one of the provinces of the Polish–Lithuanian Commonwealth. Masovia, which includes Warsaw, is a region in north central Poland. Constantine Sobieski and the rest of his family are fictional, but the Palatine of Masovia was an actual office.

§ Many Polish peasants were legally and financially tied to the lands of nobility. Sobieski's liberal policies associate him with the historical practices of Count Andrzej Zamoyski and Tadeusz Kościuszko, and the progressive ideals of Poland's 3 May 1791 Constitution (see below).

He furnished them with seed, cattle, and implements of husbandry; then calling them all together, he laid before them the deed of their enfranchisement. Before he signed it, he expressed his fears to some of their old men, of the probability that they might abuse this new liberty, and become licentious.

"No," returned a grey-headed peasant, "when we held a firm grasp of no other property than the staffs which we have in our hands, we were destitute of all motive for a consistent conduct; and not having any thing to lose, acted on all occasions in an intemperate manner; but now that our houses and lands, and our cattle, are absolutely our own, the fear of forfeiting them, will be a constant restraint upon our actions."

The good sense and truth of this answer were manifested in the event. On their emancipation, they became so cheerful in their circumstances, and so correct in behaviour, that the example of the Palatine was shortly followed by Zamoiski the great-chancellor; Prince Stanislaus, the king's nephew; and several of the principal nobility.*

Thus, within the bosom of his family, did this illustrious man educate Thaddeus, the only male heir of his name, to the exercise of every peaceful virtue, until the beginning of the year 1792, when war began to threaten the tranquillity of a country, which smiled with content and gratitude.†

On the evening of an anniversary of the birth-day of his grandson, the Palatine rode abroad with Zamoiski, and several others of a party, which had been celebrating the festival with its presence. The Countess and Thaddeus were left alone in the saloon. She sighed as she gazed on her son, who stood at some distance, fitting to his youthful thigh a variety of sabres, which his servant a little time before had laid upon the table. She observed with anxiety, the eagerness of his motion, his flushed cheek, and the ardour that was flashing from his eyes.

"Thaddeus," said she, "lay down that sword; I wish to speak with you." Thaddeus looked gaily up. "My dear Thaddeus," cried his mother, and the tears started to her eyes. The blush of enthusiasm

---

* Count Andrzej Zamoyski (1716–92); Prince Stanisław Poniatowski (1754–1833). William Coxe identified Zamoyski as the first Polish nobleman to eliminate serfdom on his estates. Indeed, the narrator's eulogy of Constantine Sobieski closely follows Coxe's description of Zamoyski; see *Travels*, 1. 132–4. See also Jones, *History*, pp. 54–6.

† The Constitution of 3 May 1791, supported by King Stanisław, introduced reforms in Poland that threatened to weaken the influence of Poland's neighbours. Conservative Polish nobles (the so-called Targowica Confederation) and Russia opposed these reforms. The novel opens on the eve of the resulting Polish–Russian War, which occurred from May to July 1792.

faded from his face; he threw the sabre from him, and drew near the Countess.

"Why, my dear mother, do you distress yourself? When I am in battle, shall I not experience my grandfather's care; and be as much under the protection of God, as at this moment?"

"Yes, my child," answered she, wiping her wet cheek, "God will protect you. He is the protector of the orphan, and you are fatherless." The Countess paused, and the heart of Thaddeus drooped. "Here, my son," said she, giving him a sealed packet, "take this: it will reveal to you who was your father. It is necessary that you should know the truth, and all the goodness of your grandfather." Thaddeus received it, and stood silent with surprise. "Read it, my love;" continued she, "but go to your own apartments; there you will be more retired."

Bewildered by the manner of the Countess, Thaddeus instantly obeyed. Shutting himself within his study, he impatiently opened the papers; and soon found his whole attention absorbed in the following recital.

"You are now, my Thaddeus! at the early age of eighteen, going to engage against the enemies of your country. Ere I resign my greatest comfort to the casualties of war; ere I part with you, perhaps for ever, I would inform you who your father really was; that father, whose exist-ence you have hardly known, and whose name you have never heard. You consider yourself an orphan; your mother a widow: but, alas! I have now to tell you, that you are fatherless by the cruelty of man, not by the dispensation of heaven.

"Twenty years ago, I accompanied my father in a tour through Germany into Italy. Grief for the death of my mother, had impaired his health, and the physicians ordered him to reside in a warmer climate: accordingly we fixed ourselves near the Arno.* During several visits to Florence, my father met, in that city, with a young Englishman of the name of Sackville. These frequent meetings opened into intimacy, and he was invited to our house.

"Mr. Sackville was not only the handsomest man I had ever beheld, but he seemed the most elegant in manners, the most noble in principle, and the most frank of heart. He was the first man for whose society I had found so lively a preference. I used to smile at this delight which I felt, or sometimes weep, for the emotions that agitated me were undefinable; but they were enchanting, and unheedingly I gave them indulgence. The hours of reciprocal sentiments and feelings which we passed together, the kind beaming of his looks, the thousand sighs that

---

* The Arno river flows through Italy's Tuscany region.

he breathed, the half-uttered sentences, all conspired to delude me into confidence.

"Thus were eight months spent. For the last three, doubts and anguish had usurped the fairy reveries of an infant tenderness. An averted glance, a cold answer, or a careless demeanor, would now plunge me into all the horrors of distrust. The attentions of Mr. Sackville died away. From being the constant object of his search, he now sedulously sought to avoid me. When my father withdrew to his closet, he would take his leave, and allow me to walk alone. Solitary and wretched were my rambles. Immured as I had been within the palace of Villanow, watching the declining health of my mother, I had learnt nothing of the real world; the little which I knew of society, being drawn from books, uncorrected by experience, taught me to believe a perfection in man, which to my affliction, I have since found to be a poet's dream. When I came to Italy, I still continued averse to public company. In this seclusion, the presence of Sackville being almost my only pleasure, entirely chaced from my mind its usual reserve, and gradually, and surely, won upon the awakened affections of my heart. Artless and unwarned, I knew not the nature of the feelings I cherished, until they had gained an ascendancy that menaced my life.

"On the evening of one of those days in which I had not seen this too dearly beloved friend, I strolled out, and hardly conscious of my actions, threw myself along the summit of a flight of steps that led down to the Arno. My head rested against the base of a statue, which because of its fancied resemblance to me, Sackville had presented to my father. Every recollected kindness of his, now gave me additional torment; and clinging to its pedestal, as to the altar of my adoration, in the bitterness of disappointment, I addressed myself to the insensible stone; 'O! were I as pale as thou art, and this breast as cold and still, would Sackville when he looked on me, give one sigh to the creature he has destroyed?' My sobs followed this adjuration, and the next moment, I felt myself encircled in his arms. I struggled, and almost fainting, begged to be released. He did release me, and, falling on his knees, implored my pardon for the misery I had endured. 'Now Therese,' cried he, 'all is as it ought to be! you are my only hope. Consent to be mine, else I shall be driven to madness!' His voice was hurried and incoherent. Lifting my eyes to his, I beheld them wild and bloodshot. Terrified at his look, and overcome by my own emotions, my head sunk back on the marble. With encreased violence, he exclaimed, 'have I deceived myself here too? Therese, did you not prefer me? Did you not love me? – Speak now, I conjure you, by your own happiness and mine. Do you reject me?' He clenched my hands in his with a force that made me tremble, and I hardly articulated, 'I will be yours.' At these words, he hurried me down a dark vista, which led out of the gardens to the open country. A carriage stood at the gate. I fearfully asked what he intended. 'You have given yourself to me,' cried he, 'and by the great Lord of Heaven, no power shall separate us until you are mine, out of the reach of man!' Unnerved in body, and weak in mind, I yielded to his impetuosity; and, suffering him to lift me into the chariot, was carried to the door of the nearest monastery, where in a few minutes we were married.

"I am thus particular in the relation of every incident, in the hope that you will, my dear son, see some excuse for my great imprudence, in the circumstances of my youth, and the influence which a man, who seemed all excellence, held over every thought of my heart. However, my fault was not long unpunished.

"The ceremony past, my husband conducted me in silence back to the carriage. My full bosom discharged itself in abundance of tears, whilst Sackville sat by me, unmoved and mute. Two or three times I raised my eyes, in hopes of seeing in his some consolation for my hasty acquiescence. But no; his gaze, vacant and glaring, was fixed on the window; and his brow scowled, as if he had been forced into an alliance with one whom he hated, rather than had just made a voluntary engagement with the woman he loved. My heart sickened at this commencement of a contract, which I had dared to make, unsanctioned by my father's consent. At length, my sighs seemed to startle my husband's ear; and turning suddenly round, 'Therese,' cried he, 'this marriage must not be told to the Count.' – 'Why?' murmured I, hardly able to speak; 'Because I have been precipitate. It would ruin me with my own family. Wait, for only one month; and then I will publickly acknowledge you.' The agitation of his features, the sternness of his voice, and the feverish burning of his hand, which held mine, alarmed me; and trembling from head to foot, I answered, 'Sackville! I have already erred enough in consenting to this stolen union. I will not transgress further by concealing it. I will instantly throw myself at my father's feet, and confess all.' His countenance darkened. 'Therese,' said he, 'I have not married you to be your slave. I am your husband. You have sworn to obey me, and I command your silence. Till I allow you, divulge this marriage at your peril.' This last cruel sentence, and the more cruel look that accompanied it, pierced me to the heart, and I fell senseless on the seat.

"When I recovered, I found myself at the foot of that statue, beneath which my unfortunate destiny had been fixed. My husband was leaning over me. He raised me with tenderness from the ground; and conjured me, in the mildest accents, to be comforted; to pardon the severity of those words which had arisen from fear, that by an imprudent avowal on my part, I should risk both his happiness and my own. He informed me, that, as he was heir to one of the first fortunes in England, he had pledged his honour with his father never to enter into any matrimonial engagement, without first acquainting him with the particulars of the lady and her family. Should he omit this duty, his father declared, that though she were a princess, he would disinherit him, and never again admit him to his presence.

"'Consider this, my dear Therese,' continued he, 'could you endure to behold me a beggar, stigmatized with a parent's curse, when a little forbearance on your side would make all right? I know I have been hasty in acting as I have done, but now I cannot remedy my error. To-morrow I will write to my father, describe your rank and merits, and request his consent for our immediate marriage. The moment his permission arrives, I will cast myself on the Count's friendship and feelings, and reveal all that has passed.' The tenderness of my husband won my affection and reason to his side; and with many tears, I sealed his forgiveness, and pledged my faith on his word.

"My dear deceived parent, little suspected the perfidy of his guest. He detained him as his visitor, and often rallied himself on the hold which his distinguished accomplishments had taken on his esteem. Sackville's manner to me in public was obliging and free: it was in private only, that I found the tender, the capricious, the unfeeling husband. Night after night I have washed the memory of my want of duty to my father, with bitter tears: But my husband was dear to me, was more precious than my life. One kind look from him, one fond word, would solace every pain, and make me wait the arrival of his father's letter, with all the gay anticipations of youth and love.

"A fortnight passed away. A month, a long and lingering month. Another month, and a packet of letters was presented to Sackville. He was at breakfast with us. At the sight of the superscription, he coloured, tore open the paper, ran his eyes over a few lines, and then pale and trembling, rose from his seat, and left the room. My emotions were almost uncontroulable. I had already half risen from my chair to follow him, when the Count exclaimed, 'What can be in that letter? he seems dreadfully shocked.' And without observing me, or waiting for a reply, he hurried out after him. I stole to my chamber, where, throwing myself on my bed, I tried by all the delusions of hope, to obtain some respite from inquietude.

"The dinner bell rouzed me from my fluctuating reverie. Dreading to excite suspicion, and anxious to read in the countenance of my husband the denunciation of our fate, I obeyed the summons, and descended to the dining-room. On entering it, my eyes irresistably wandered round to fix themselves on Sackville. He was leaning against a pillar, his face pale as death. My father looked grave, but immediately took his seat, and tenderly placed his friend beside him. I sat down in silence. Little dinner was eaten, and few words spoken. – As for myself, my agitations almost choked me. I felt that the first word I should attempt to pronounce, must give them utterance, and that their vehemence would betray me.

"When the servants withdrew, Sackville rose, and taking my father's hand, said in a faultering voice, 'My lord, I must leave you.' – 'It is a wet evening;' replied the Count, 'besides, you are disturbed by the shock you have received. To-morrow will do as well for your business.' – 'I thank your lordship,' answered he, 'but I must go to Florence to-night. You shall see me again before to-morrow afternoon: all will then, I hope, be settled to my wish.' – 'Well, if you are resolved,' said my father, 'God bless you! Remember, we shall be anxious to see you again.' Sackville took his hat. Motionless, and incapable of speaking, I sat fixed to my chair, in the direct way he must pass. His eye met mine. He stopped, and looking at me, abruptly caught my hand; then as abruptly quitting it, darted out of the room. I never saw him more.

"I had not the power to dissemble another moment. I fell back, weeping, into the arms of my father. He did not, even by this imprudence, read what I almost wished him to guess; but with all the indulgence of affection, lamented the distress of Sackville, and the sensibility of my nature, which sympathized so painfully with his friend. I durst not ask *what* was the *distress* of his friend: abashed at my duplicity to him, and overwhelmed with a thousand dreads, I obtained his permission to retire to my chamber.

"The next day, I met him with a serene air; for I had schooled my heart to endure with greater composure the sufferings which it had deserved. The Count did not remark my recovered tranquillity; neither did he appear to think any more of my tears; so entirely was he occupied in conjecturing what could be the cause of Sackville's grief, who had only complained of having received a great shock, without revealing the circumstance. This ignorance of my father, surprised me; and to all his suppositions I said little. My soul was too deeply interested in the subject, to trust to the faithfulness of my lips.

"The morning crept slowly on, and the noon appeared to stand still. I anxiously watched the declining sun, as the signal for my husband's return. Two hours had elapsed since his promised time, and my father grew so impatient, that he went out with the view to meet him. I eagerly hoped that they might miss each other. I should then see my Sackville a few minutes alone, and by one word, be comforted, or driven to despair.

"I was listening to every footstep that sounded under the colonade, when my servant brought me a letter, which had just been left by one of Mr. Sackville's grooms. 'Ah!' thought I, 'this will release or confirm my fears! Heaven grant that his father may have consented!' I tore open the seal; and fell senseless on the floor, ere I had read half the killing contents – ."

Thaddeus, with a burning cheek, and a heart all at once robbed of that elastic spring, which till now had ever made him feel the happiest of the happy, took up the letter of his father. The paper was worn, and blistered with his mother's tears. His head seemed to swim, as he contemplated the hand-writing, and he said to himself, "Am I to respect or to abhor him?" He proceeded in the perusal.

"To Therese, Countess Sobieski.

"How, Therese, am I to address you? But an attempt at palliating my conduct, will be of no use. It is impossible. You cannot conceive a viler opinion of me, than I hold of myself. I know that I deserve to be called a villain; that I have sacrificed your tenderness to my distracted passions. But you shall no more be subject to the caprices of a man who cannot repay your love with his own. – *You* have no guilt to torture you; and you possess virtues that will render you tranquil under every calamity. I leave you to your own innocence. Forget the ceremony which has passed between us: my wretched heart disclaims it for ever. Your father is happily ignorant of it; pray spare him the anguish of knowing that I was so completely unworthy of his kindness! I feel that I am more than ungrateful to you, and to him. Therese, your most inveterate hate, cannot more strongly tell me, than I tell myself, that I have treated you like a scoundrel. But I cannot retract. I am going where all search will be vain; and I now bid you an eternal farewel. May you be happier than ever I can be!
"*Florence.*   "R. S – ."

Thaddeus went on with his mother's narrative.

"When my senses returned, I was on the ground, holding the half-perused paper in my hand. Grief and horror had locked up the avenues of complaint, and I sat as one petrified to stone. My father entered. At the sight of me, he started as if he had seen a spectre. His well known features, opened at once my agonized heart. With fearful cries, I cast myself at his feet, and putting the letter into his hand, clung, almost expiring, to his knees.

"When he had read it, he flung it from him, and dropping into a chair, covered his face with his hands. I looked up imploringly, for I could not speak. My father stooped forward, and raising me in his arms, pressed me to his bosom. 'My Therese,' said he, 'it is I who have done this. Had I not harboured this villain, he never could have had an opportunity of ruining the peace of my child.' In return for the unexampled indulgence of this speech, I promised to forget a man, who could have so little respect for gratitude, or his own honour. The Count replied, that he expected such a resolution, in consequence of the principles he had taught me; and to shew me how far dearer to him was my real tranquillity, than any false idea of impossible restitution, he would not remove even from one principality to another, were he sure by that means, to discover Mr. Sackville, and avenge himself. My understanding assented to the justice of all his reasoning; but long and severe were the struggles, before I could erase from my soul, the image of that being who had been the lord of all its joys and sorrows.

"It was not until you, my dear Thaddeus, were born, that I could repay the goodness of my father with the smiles of cheerfulness. I christened you Thaddeus Constantine, after himself, and his best-loved friend Kosciuszko.* He would not permit me to give you any name, which could remind him or myself of the cruel parent who gave you being: and on our return to Poland, the story which he related, when questioned about my apparently forlorn state, was simply this, 'My daughter was married and widowed in the course of two months. Since then, to root from her memory, as much as possible, all recollection of a husband who was only given to be taken away, she still retains my name; and her son as my sole heir, shall wear no other.' This reply satisfied every one: the king, who was my father's only confidant, gave his sanction to it, and no further enquiries were ever started.

"You are now, my beloved child, entering on the eventful career of life. God knows, when the venerable head of your grandfather is laid in dust, and I, too, shut my eyes upon you for ever, where destiny may send you! perhaps to the country of your father. Should you ever meet him – but that is unlikely; so, I will be silent on a subject, which eighteen years of reflection, have not yet deprived of its sting.

"Not to imbitter the fresh spring of your youth, my Thaddeus, with the draught that has poisoned mine; not to implant in your breast,

---

* Tadeusz Kościuszko (1746–1817), Poland's greatest military leader of the era. Kościuszko had gained notoriety for his seven years of service in the Continental Army during the American Revolutionary War. In 1784, he returned to Poland and eventually received a position in the Commonwealth Army. He supported the 3 May 1791 Constitution but also believed that the reforms did not go far enough.

hatred of a parent you may never behold, have I written this: but to inform you in fact from whom you sprung. My history is made plain to you, that no unexpected events may hereafter perplex your opinion of your mother; or cause a blush to rise on that cheek for her, which from your grandfather, can derive no stain. For his sake, as well as for mine, whether in peace or in war, may the angels of Heaven guard my boy! This is the everlasting prayer of thy fond mother,
"*Villanow, March*, 1792.   "THERESE SOBIESKI."

When he had finished, Thaddeus held the papers in his hand; and unable to recover from the shock which he had received by their contents, he read them a second time to the end: then laying them on the table, against which he rested his now aching head, he gave vent to the fullness of his heart.

The Countess, anxious for the effect her history might have on her son, at this instant entered the room. Seeing him in so dejected an attitude, she approached him, and pressing him to her bosom, mingled her tears with his. Thaddeus, ashamed of his emotions, yet incapable of dissembling them, struggled a few moments to release himself from her arms. The Countess, mistaking his motive, said in a melancholy voice, "And do you, my son, despise your mother for the weakness which she has revealed? Is this the reception that I expected from a child, on whose affection I reposed my confidence and my comfort?"

"No, my mother:" replied Thaddeus, "it is your afflictions, which have discomposed me. This is the first unhappy hour that I ever endured, and can you wonder that I should be affected? Oh! mother," continued he, laying his hand on his father's letter, "whatever were his rank, had my father been but noble in mind, I would have gloried in bearing his name; but now, I put up my prayers never to hear it more."

"Forget him," cried the Countess, hiding her eyes with her handkerchief.

"I will!" answered Thaddeus, "and allow my memory, to dwell only on the virtues of my mother."

It was impossible for the Countess or her son, to conceal their agitation from the Palatine, who now opened the door. On his expressing alarm at a sight so unusual, his daughter, finding herself incapable of speaking, put into his hand the letter which Thaddeus had just read. Sobieski cast his eye over the first lines; he immediately comprehended their tendency, and seeing that the Countess had withdrawn, looked towards his grandson. Thaddeus was walking up and down the room, striving to command himself for the conversation which he anticipated with his grandfather.

"I am sorry, Thaddeus," said Sobieski, "that your mother has so abruptly imparted to you, the real name and character of your father. I see that his villainy has distressed a heart, which I have sought to make alive to the slightest dishonour. But be consoled, my dear boy! I have prevented the publicity of his conduct, by an ambiguous story of your mother's widowhood. I declared to the world, that you were not only the son of my daughter, but should be the sole heir to my estates and name. Notwithstanding this arrangement, she judged it proper that you ought not to enter general society, without having first been made acquainted with the true events of your birth. I believe my daughter is right. But cheer yourself, my child, now that all is past. You will imbitter the remainder of my days, if you suffer the vices of a worthless man, to prey upon your mind."

"No, my lord;" answered his grandson, "you have been more than a parent to me; and henceforward, for your sake, as well as my own, I shall hold it my duty, to forget that I drew my being from any other source, than the house of Sobieski."

"You are right," cried the Palatine with an exulting emotion, "you have the spirit of your ancestors; and I yet shall live to see you add glory to the name!"

The beaming eyes and smiling lips of the young Count, declared that he had shaken sorrow from his heart. His grandfather squeezed his hand with delight; and saw in his recovered serenity the sure promise of his fond prophecy.

CHAP. II.

The fearful day arrived, when Sobieski and his grandson were to bid adieu to Villanow and its peaceful scenes.

The well-poised mind of the veteran, bade his daughter farewell, with a fortitude which imparted some of its strength even to her. But when Thaddeus, ready habited for his journey, entered the room, at the sight of his military accoutrements she shuddered; and when with a glowing countenance he advanced smiling through his tears towards her, she clasped him in her arms, and rivetted her lips to that face, whose very loveliness added to her affliction. She gazed at him, she wept on his neck, she pressed him to her bosom. "O! how soon may all that beauty be mingled with the dust! how soon may that warm heart, which then beat against hers, be pierced by the sword! be laid on the ground, mangled and bleeding, exposed, and trampled on!" These thoughts thronged upon her soul, and deprived her of sense. She was carried away lifeless by her maids; whilst the Palatine, almost by force, compelled Thaddeus to quit the spot.

It was not until the lofty battlements of Villanow blended with the clouds,* that Thaddeus could throw off his melancholy. The parting agony of his mother hung on his spirits; and heavy and frequent were his sighs, as he gazed on the russet cottages and fertile fields, which reminded him that he was yet passing through the territories of his grandfather. The picturesque mill of Mariemont was the last spot on which his sight lingered. The ivy that mantled over its sides, sparkled with the brightness of a shower which had just fallen; and the rays of the setting sun, gleaming on its shattered wall, made it an object of such romantic beauty, as well as interest, that he could not help pointing it out to his fellow travellers.†

Whilst the eyes of General Butzou,‡ who was in the carriage, fol-

---

* Since Wilanów Palace is in fact on a flat plain, the narrator's description is unlikely.
† Mariemont (or Marymont) was a hilly region north of Warsaw named for Maria Kazimiera, the wife of John III Sobieski. In the eighteenth century, Mariemont was known for its large number of windmills.
‡ General Butzou is a fictional creation, though he was clearly inspired by William Coxe's description of George Henry Butzau, a soldier who was killed defending Stanisław II during the events of 1771 described below. See Coxe, *Travels*, 1. 42. In the 1831 edition, Porter's General Butzou becomes the brother of the historical soldier.

lowed the direction of Thaddeus, the Palatine observed the heightening animation of his features, with that philanthropy which expands the heart of a good man; and recollecting at the same time the feelings he himself enjoyed, when he visited that place one and twenty years ago, he put his hand on the shoulder of Butzou, and said, "General, did you ever relate to my boy the particulars of that mill?"

"No, my lord."

"I suppose," continued the Palatine, "the same reason deterred you from speaking of it uncalled for, as lessened my wish to tell the story? We are both too much the heroes of the tale, to have volunteered the recital."

"Do you mean, my lord," asked Thaddeus, "the rescue of our king* from this place?"

"I do."

"I have a very indistinct knowledge of the affair. I remember it was told me many years since, but I have nearly forgotten it; and can only account for my apparent insensibility in never having enquired any further, to the happy thoughtlessness in which you have hitherto permitted me to live."

"But," said the Palatine, whose only object was to draw his grandson from saddening reflections; "What will you say to me, turning egotist?"

"I now ask the story of you;" returned Thaddeus smiling; "besides, as soldiers are permitted by the fire-side to '*fight their battles o'er again*;'† your modesty, grandfather, cannot object to repeat it to me here, on the way to more."

"As a preliminary," said the Palatine, "to relate our history in form, I must suppose that it is unnecessary to tell you, that General Butzou was the brave soldier, who, at the imminent risk of his own life, saved that of our sovereign?"

"Of course, I know that;" replied the young Count; "and that you, too, had a share in it; for when I was yesterday presented to his majesty, amongst other things which he spoke of, he told me, that he believed, under heaven, he owed his present existence to General Butzou and yourself."

"So very little to me," resumed Sobieski, "that I will to the best of

---

* Stanisław August Poniatowski (1732–98), the last king of Poland. A former lover of Catherine the Great, he became king through the efforts of Russia. Nevertheless, he supported widespread political reform.

† In John Dryden's 'Alexander's Feast' (London: Jacob Tonson, 1697), the bard Timotheus sings of Alexander's victories: 'Sooth'd with the sound, the king grew vain; / Fought all his battles o'er again' (lines 52–3).

my recollection, repeat every circumstance of the affair. Should I err, I must beg of you, General," turning to Butzou, "to put me right?"

Butzou, with the glow of honest exultation still painting his face, nodded assent; and Thaddeus, bowing to his grandfather in sign of his attention, the Palatine began.*

"It was on Sunday night, the third of September, in the year 1771, that this event took place. At that time, instigated by the courts of Vienna and Constantinople, the confederate lords of Poland were laying waste their country from one end to the other, and perpetrating all kinds of outrage on the loyal inhabitants.†

"Amongst their numerous crimes, a plan was laid for surprising, and taking the king's person. Pulaski was one of the most daring of these rebels; and assisted by Lukawski, Strawenski and Kosinski, three Poles of distinction, he meditated at any rate to accomplish his death.‡ Accordingly, the three latter, in obedience to his orders, with forty other conspirators, met at Czetschokow,§ and in the presence of their commander swore, with the most horrid oaths, to deliver Stanislaus alive or dead into his hands.

"About a month after this meeting, these noblemen, at the head of a band of assassins, disguised themselves as peasants; and concealing their arms in waggons of hay which they drove before them, they entered Warsaw unsuspected.

"It was ten o'clock, on the third of September, as I have told you, that they found an opportunity to execute their scheme. They placed themselves under cover of the night, in those avenues of the city, through which they knew his majesty must pass in his way from Villanow, where he had been dining with me. His carriage was escorted by four of his own attendants, myself, and twelve of my guards. We had scarcely lost sight of Villanow, when the conspirators rushed out and surrounded us, commanding the coachman to stop, and beating down the men with the butt end of their musquets. Several shot were

---

* Count Sobieski's account of the abduction and its aftermath closely follows the narrative of the same events published in Coxe's *Travels*, 1. 29–42. Jones repeats Coxe's account almost verbatim (*History*, pp. 313–26). The actual abduction occurred on 3 November 1771.

† In February 1768, a group of Polish noblemen, fearing the influence of Russia in Polish affairs, formed the Confederation of Bar and attempted to overthrow King Stanisław, who at the time was seen as too closely aligned with Russian interests.

‡ Casimir Pulaski (1745–79), later a hero of the American Revolutionary War, was one of the confederates. The other conspirators (also named in Coxe's *Travels*, 1. 42) include Walenty Łukawski (c. 1743–73), Stanisław Strawiński (d. after 1773) and Jan Kuźma (that is, Kosinski, 1742–1822).

§ That is, Częstochowa, a town (now city) in southern Poland.

fired into the coach. One passed through my hat, as I was getting out, sword in hand, the better to repel an attack, the motive of which I could not divine. A cut across my right leg with a sabre, soon laid me under the wheels; and whilst I lay there, I heard the shot pouring into the coach like hail, and felt the villains stepping over my body, to finish the murder of the king.

"It was then that our friend Butzou, (who at that period was a private in my service), stood between his sovereign and the rebels. In one instant he received several balls through his limbs, and a thrust from a bayonet in his breast, which cast him, weltering in his blood, upon me. By this time, all the persons who had formed the escort, were either wounded or dispersed. Being now secure of their prey, one of the assassins opened the carriage door, and with shocking imprecations, seizing the king by the hair, cried, 'Tyrant, we have thee now; thy hour is come!' and discharged his pistol so near his majesty's face, that he felt the heat of the flash. A second villain cut him on the forehead with his sword; whilst a third, who was on horseback, laying hold of his collar, between himself and another, at full gallop, dragged him along the ground, through the suburbs of the city.

"During the latter part of this outrageous scene some of our frighted people returned with a detachment, and seeing Butzou and me apparently lifeless, carried us to the royal palace, where all was commotion and alarm. The foot-guards immediately followed the track that the conspirators had seemed to take. In one of the streets they found the king's hat dyed in blood, and his pelisse perfectly reticulated with bullet holes. This confirmed their apprehensions of his death; and they came back, filling all Warsaw with dismay.

"The assassins meanwhile got clear of the town. Finding, however, that the king by loss of blood, weakness, and wounds in his feet, was not likely to exist much longer in their manner of dragging him towards their employer, they set him on a horse, and redoubled their speed. When they came to the moat which surrounds Warsaw, they compelled him to leap across it. In the attempt his beast fell twice; and, at the second fall, broke its leg: they then compelled him, fainting as he was with pain, to mount another, and spur it over. The conspirators had no sooner passed the ditch, than they threw his majesty down, and held him there, till Lukawski tore from his neck the ribbon of the black eagle, and its diamond cross. Lukawski was so foolishly sure of his prisoner, that he quitted his charge, and repaired with his spoils to Pulaski, meaning to shew them as an incontestable proof of his success. Many of the other plunderers, concluding that they could not do better than follow his example, fled also, and left only seven of the party, with Kosinski at their head, to remain over the unfortunate Stanislaus.

"The night was now grown so dark, that they could not be sure of their way; and their horses stumbling at every step over stumps of trees and hollows in the earth, encreased their apprehensions to such a degree, that they obliged the king to keep up with them on foot: he literally marked his path with his blood, his shoes having been torn off in the struggle at the carriage. Thus they continued, wandering backwards and forwards, and round the outskirts of Warsaw without any exact knowledge of their situation. The men who guarded him, at last became so much afraid of their prisoner taking advantage of these circumstances to escape, that they repeatedly called on Kosinski, for orders to put him to death. Kosinski refused; but their demands growing more violent and imperious, as they found that the intricacies of the forest had involved them completely, the king expected every moment to receive the points of their bayonets in his breast.

"When I recovered from my swoon, and my leg was bound up, I felt myself able to stir; and questioning the officers who stood about my couch, I found that a general panic had seized them. They knew not how to proceed; they shuddered at leaving the king to the mercy of the confederates; and yet were fearful by pursuing them farther, to incense them, through terror or revenge, to massacre their prisoner, if he were still alive. I tried what I could to dispel this last dread. Anxious, at any rate to make another attempt to preserve him, though I could not ride myself, I strenuously advised an immediate pursuit on horseback; and that neither darkness nor danger should be permitted to impede their course. A little spirit on the side of the nobles, soon brought back hope and animation to the terrified soldiers; and my orders were instantly obeyed. But I must add, almost as instantly disappointed: for, in less than half an hour they returned in despair, shewing me his majesty's coat, which they had found in the fosse. I suppose the ruffians tore it off when they rifled him. It was rent in several places, and so wet with blood, that the officer who presented it to me, declared it as his opinion, that they had murdered the king there, and had drawn away the body; for by the light of the torches, he could trace drops of blood to a considerable distance.

"Whilst I was again attempting to combat this new evidence of his majesty being beyond the reach of succour or of insult, he was driven before the seven conspirators, so far into the wood of Bielany, that unknowing whither they went, they came up with one of the guard houses, and to their extreme terror were accosted by a patrole. Four of the banditti immediately disappeared, leaving only two with Kosinski;

who, much alarmed, forced his prisoner to walk faster, and keep a profound stillness. Notwithstanding all this precaution, scarce a quarter
of an hour after, they were challenged by a second watch; and the
other two men, now taking to flight, left Kosinski full of dismay, alone
with the king. His majesty, sinking with pain and fatigue, beseeched
permission to rest for a moment: Kosinski refused, and pointing his
sword towards his breast, compelled him to proceed. The king obeyed
in silence.

"As they walked on, the unfortunate Stanislaus, hardly able to drag
one limb after the other, observed that his conductor gradually seemed
to forget his vigilance, till he appeared at last thoroughly given up to
thought. He took courage at this; and conceiving some hope, from
the manner in which he was agitated, he ventured to say, 'I see, that
you know not how to proceed. You cannot but be aware, that the
enterprise you are engaged in, end how it will, is full of peril to you.
Successful conspirators are always jealous of each other: Pulaski will
find it as easy to rid himself of your life, as it is to take mine. Avoid
this danger; and I will promise you none on my account. Suffer me to
enter the convent of Bielany: we cannot be far from it; and then, do
you provide for your safety.' Kosinski, rendered desperate, by the circumstances in which he was involved, replied, 'No; I have sworn; and I
would rather sacrifice my life, than my honour.'

"The king had neither strength nor spirits to make any answer.
They continued to break their way through the underwood, till they
arrived close to Mariemont. Here Stanislaus, unable to stir another
step, fell back against a tree, and again implored, for one moment's
rest, to recover some power to move. Kosinski now consented. This
unexpected humanity gave his majesty courage to employ the minutes
during which they sat together, in another attempt to soften his heart,
and to convince him that the oath he had taken was atrocious, and by
no means binding, to a brave and virtuous man.

"Kosinski, heard him with attention, and exhibited strong symptoms of being affected. 'But,' said he, 'if I should assent to what you
propose, and re-conduct you back to Warsaw, what will be the consequence to me? I shall be taken, and executed.' – 'I give you my word,'
answered the king, 'that you shall not suffer any injury. But if you
doubt my honour, escape while you can. I shall find my way to some
place of shelter, and will direct your pursuers to take the opposite
road to that which you may chuse.' Kosinski entirely overcome, threw
himself on his knees before his majesty; and, imploring pardon for
what he had done, swore, that from this hour he would defend his king
against all the conspirators, and would trust confidently on his word,

for future preservation. Stanislaus repeated his promise of forgiveness and protection; and directing him to seek refuge for them both, in the mill near which they were discoursing, Kosinski obeyed, and knocked, but no one gave answer. He then broke a pane of glass in the window, and through it, begged succour for a nobleman, who had been way-laid by robbers. The miller refused to come out, or let them in; telling them it was his belief, they were robbers themselves, and if they did not go away he would fire on them.

"This dispute had continued for near an hour when the king con-trived to crawl up close to the window, and said, 'My good friend, if we were banditti as you suppose, it would be as easy for us, without all this parley, to break into your house, as to break this pane of glass; there-fore if you would not incur the shame of suffering a fellow-creature to perish for want of assistance, let us in.' This argument had its weight with the man, and opening the door, he admitted them. After some trouble, his majesty procured pen and ink, and immediately addressing a few lines to me, at the palace, with more difficulty he prevailed on one of the miller's sons to carry it; so fearful were they of falling in with any of the troop, whom they understood had plundered their guests.

"The joy I experienced at the sight of this note, I cannot describe. I well remember the contents; they were literally these:

'By the miraculous hand of providence, I am escaped from the hands of assassins. I am now at the mill of Mariemont. Send as soon as possi-ble, and take me away. I am wounded, but not dangerously.'

"Regardless of my condition, I instantly got into a carriage, and followed by a detachment of horse, arrived at the mill. I met Kosinski at the door, keeping guard with his sword drawn. As he knew my person, he admitted me directly. The king had fallen into a sleep, and lay in one corner of the hovel, on the ground, covered with the miller's cloak. To see the most virtuous monarch in the world, thus abused by his ungrateful subjects, pierced me to the heart; and kneel-ing down by his side, I took hold of his hand, and in a paroxism of tears, which I am not ashamed to confess, I exclaimed, 'I thank thee, Almighty God, that I again see my sovereign alive!' It is not easy to say, how these words struck the simple family with amazement. They instantly dropped on their knees before the king, whom my voice had awakened, and beseeched his pardon for all their ill-manners. The good Stanislaus soon quieted their fears; and graciously thanking them for their kindness, told the miller to come to the palace the next day, when he would shew him his gratitude in a better way than by promises.

"Five minutes afterwards, the officers of the detachment assisted his majesty and myself, into the carriage; and, accompanied by Kosinski, we reached Warsaw about six in the morning."

"Yes," interrupted Butzou, "I remember the joy I felt when the news was brought to me, in my bed, that I had not in vain received the wounds intended for my sovereign; and besides, his majesty visited his poor soldier in his chamber. Do you not recollect, my lord, how he was brought into my room in a chair, between two men? and how he thanked me, and shook hands with me? It made me like a child."

"But," enquired Thaddeus, hardly recovering from the deep attention with which he had listened to this recital; "what became of Kosinski? I suppose the king kept his word."

"He did indeed," replied Sobieski; "his word is at all times sacred. Yet I believe Kosinski had his fears that he would not be so generous; for I perceived him look anxious, and change colour very often, whilst he was in the coach. However, he was soon tranquillized by his majesty's manner, who, when he alighted at the palace in the midst of the joyous cries of the people, shouting, 'The king is alive!' leaned upon his arm, in preference to mine, and presented him to the populace, as his preserver. The great gate was ordered to be left open: and never, whilst I live, shall I again behold such a scene! every soul in Warsaw, from the highest to the lowest, came running to catch a glimpse of their rescued sovereign; seeing the doors free, they entered without ceremony, and thronged forward in crowds, to get near enough to kiss his hand, or to touch his clothes; then, elated with joy, they turned to Kosinski, and loaded him with demonstrations of gratitude, calling him the '*Saviour of their good king.*' Kosinski bore all this with surprising firmness; but in a day or two, when the facts of the business became known, he felt that he might meet with different treatment from the people, and therefore petitioned his majesty for leave to depart. Stanislaus consented, and he retired to Semigallia in the papal territories,* where he now lives, on a very handsome pension from the king."

"For me," said the General, "you see how he has rewarded me for that which had I left undone, I should have deserved to have been shot. He put it at my option, to become what I pleased about his person, or hold what rank I liked in the army. Attached as I have ever been to your family, under which all my ancestors have lived and fought, I vowed in my own mind never to quit it; and accordingly only begged

---

* The Duchy of Courland and Semigallia was a region of the Polish–Lithuanian Commonwealth on the Baltic Sea. Today Semigallia is a region of Latvia, southwest of Riga. Porter follows Coxe's *Travels* (1. 58) in incorrectly declaring Semigallia a papal territory.

permission of my sovereign to remain with the Count Sobieski. I did remain: but see," cried he, his voice faultering, "what they have made of me! I command those troops, among whom it was once my greatest glory to be only a private soldier."

Thaddeus pressed the hand of the veteran between both his, and regarded him with respect and affection, whilst the grateful old man wiped off a tear that was trickling down his face.

"How happy ought it to make you, my son," observed Sobieski, "that you are called out to support such a sovereign! He is not merely a king, whom you follow to battle, because he will lead you to honour; the hearts of his people feel him in a different light: they look on him as their friend; as a being delegated by God, to study what is their greatest good, then to bestow it, and, when it is attacked, to defend it. To preserve the life of such a sovereign, who is there that would not sacrifice his own?"

"Yes," cried Butzou; "and how ought we to abhor them who threaten his life! How ought we to estimate those crowned heads, who, under the mask of amity, have, from the year sixty-four when he ascended the throne, till now, been plotting his death! That calamity, O Heaven, avert! Happen when it may, it will I fear, be a prelude to the certain ruin of our country!"

"Not so," interrupted Thaddeus, with eagerness; "not whilst a Polander has power to lift an arm, shall it be quite lost."

Butzou applauded his spirit; and warmly seconded the Palatine, (who, never weary of infusing into every emotion of his grandson an interest for his country,) pursued the discourse, and dwelt minutely on the happy tendency of the glorious constitution of ninety-one, in defence of which they were now going to hazard their lives. As Sobieski pointed out its several excellencies, and described the pure spirit of freedom which animated its laws, the feelings of Thaddeus followed his eloquence; and with the restraintless fervour of youth he branded the names of Catherine, and the faithless Frederick, with some of those epithets, which posterity will not fail to ratify.* During these conversations, Thaddeus forgot his regrets; and the third day, they put themselves at the head of their men, and commenced a regular march.

---

* Catherine II, also known as Catherine the Great, Empress of Russia (1729–96); and Frederick William II (1774–97), King of Prussia.

CHAP. III.

The little army of the Palatine, passed by the battlements of Chelm, crossed the Bug into Volhinia, and impatiently counted the leagues over those vast plains, till it reached the borders of Kiovia.*

When the column, at the head of which Thaddeus was stationed, descended the heights of Lininy,† and the broad camp of his countrymen burst on his sight, he felt his heart swell with an emotion quite new to him. He beheld with admiration, the regular disposition of the entrenchments, the long intersected streets, and the warlike appearance of the soldiers, whom he could descry, even at that distance, by the beams of a bright evening sun which shone on their arms.

In half an hour, his troops descended into the plain, where, meeting those of the Palatine and the General, the three columns again united, and Thaddeus joined his grandfather in the van.

"My lord," cried he, as they met, "can I behold such a sight, and despair of the freedom of Poland!"

Sobieski made no reply; but giving him one of those expressive looks, which immediately makes its way to the soul, he commanded the troops to advance with greater speed. In a few minutes they reached the outworks of the camp, and entered the lines. The eager eyes of Thaddeus wandered from object to object. Thrilling with that delight with which youth beholds wonders, and anticipates more, he stopped with the rest of the party before a tent which General Butzou informed him, belonged to the commander in-chief. They were met in the vestibule, by an hussar officer of a most commanding appearance. Sobieski and he having accosted each other with mutual congratulations the Palatine turned round to Thaddeus, took him by the hand, presented him to his friend, and said with a smile,

"Here, my dear Kosciuszko, this young man is my grandson; he is

---

* Chełm is a city about 250 kilometres southeast of Warsaw. The Bug river flows some 25 kilometres east of Chełm and today separates Poland and Ukraine. Volhinia (Volhynia) and Kiovia (Kiev) refer to regions that were once part of the Polish–Lithuanian Commonwealth but today make up northeast and central Ukraine.

† Unidentified; none of Porter's usual sources refer to a location called Lininy. The following pages make clear that the Polish forces are at Winnica (Vinnytsia), near the Commonwealth's southeast border.

called Thaddeus; and I trust, that he will neither disgrace your name, nor mine."

Kosciuszko embraced the young Count, and with a hearty pressure of his hand, replied; "If you resemble your grandfather, Thaddeus, you will remember, that the only king of Poland who equalled Stanislaus, was a Sobieski: and, as becomes his descendant, you will not spare your best blood in the service of your country."

As Kosciuszko finished speaking, an aid-de-camp came forward, to lead the party into the room of audience. Prince Poniatowski welcomed the Palatine and his suite, with the most lively expressions of pleasure.* He gave Thaddeus, whose figure and manner instantly charmed him, many flattering assurances of friendship; and promised that he would appoint him to the first post of honour which should offer. After detaining them half an hour, on the subject of their march, his highness withdrew, and they rejoined Kosciuszko, who conducted them to the quarter where the Masovian soldiers had already pitched their tents.

The officers who supped with Sobieski, left him at an early hour, that he might retire to rest: but Thaddeus, neither felt able nor inclined to benefit by their consideration. He laid himself down on the bed, shut his eyes, and tried to sleep; but it was all in vain; in vain he turned from side to side, in vain he attempted to restrict his thoughts to one thing at once; his imagination was so roused by anticipating the scenes in which he was to become an actor, that he found it impossible even to lie still. His spirits being quite awake, he determined to rise, and walk himself drowsy.

Seeing his grandfather sound asleep, he got up, and dressed himself quietly; then stealing gently from the marquée, he gave the word in a low whisper to the guard at the door, and proceeded down the lines. The pitying moon seemed to stand in the heavens, watching the awaking of those heroes, who the next day might sleep to rise no more. At another time, and in another mood, such might have been his reflections; but now, he pursued his walk with far different thoughts; no sensations but those of joy moved his breast. He felt what he saw only; the light of that beautiful planet, trailing its long stream of glory across the entrenchments; and a solitary candle here and there, glimmering through the curtained entrance of the tents, shewed that their inmates were probably longing with the same anxiety as himself for the morning's dawn.

---

* Prince Józef Antoni Poniatowski (1763–1813), a nephew of King Stanisław II, commanded the Commonwealth Army in southeast Poland (today Ukraine) during the 1792 Polish–Russian War.

Thaddeus walked slowly on; sometimes pausing at the lonely foot-fall of the centinel; or answering with a start, to the sudden challenge for the parole; then lingering at the door of some of these canvas dwell-ings, he offered up a prayer for the brave inhabitant, who had quitted the endearments of home, to expose his life, and stand on this spot, a bulwark of liberty. Thaddeus knew not what it was to be a soldier from profession; he had no idea of making war a trade, by which a man is at any rate to acquire subsistence and wealth: he had but one motive for appearing in the field, and one for leaving it. The first energy of his mind, was a desire to assert the rights of his country. It had been inculcated into him, from an infant; it had been the subject of his morning thoughts, and nightly dreams; it was now the passion which beat in every artery of his heart: yet, he knew no honour in slaughter; his glory lay in defence; and, when that was accomplished, his sword would return to its scabbard, unstained by the blood, of a vanquished or an invaded people. On these principles, he was at this hour full of enthusiasm; a glow of triumph flitted over his cheek, for he had left the indulgences of his mother's palace, had left her maternal arms, to take upon him the toils of war, and risk an existence just blown into enjoy-ment. He felt a proud satisfaction, as this passed in his mind; and with all that animation which an inexperienced and raised fancy, imparts to that age when boyhood breaks into man, his soul grasped at every show of creation with the confidence of belief. Pressing the sabre which he held in his hand, to his lips, he half uttered, "Never will I suffer this sword to leave my arm, but at the command of mercy; or when death shall deprive my nerves of their strength."

Morning was tinging the hills that bound the eastern horizon of Winnica, before Thaddeus found that his pelisse was wet with dew, and that he ought to return to his tent. He had hardly laid his head upon the pillow, and *"lulled his senses in forgetfulness,"** when he was dis-turbed by a confused noise, and the drum beating to arms. He opened his eyes; seeing that Sobieski was out of bed, he sprung from his own, and asked what was the matter?

"Only follow me directly," answered his grandfather, as he quitted the tent.

Whilst Thaddeus was putting on his clothes, and buckling on his arms, with a trembling eagerness that almost defeated his haste, an aid-de-camp of the Prince's entered. He informed him, that, an advanced guard of the Russians, about three hundred piquets, had attacked

---

* *Henry IV, Part 2*: 'That thou no more wilt weigh my eyelids down, / And steep my senses in forgetfulness?' (III, i, 7–8).

one of the Polish out-posts, to which Lieutenant Lomza* had been commanded the evening before; and that his Highness had ordered a detachment from the Palatine's brigade to march immediately to its relief. Before Thaddeus had time to reply, Sobieski sent in, to apprise his grandson that the Prince had appointed him to be second in command, over the troops which were turning out to assist the lieutenant.

Thaddeus heard this message with delight; yet fearful how the event might answer the expectations which this high distinction declared, he issued from his tent, like a youthful Mars, or rather like the young Isadas,† trembling at the dazzling effects of his temerity, and hiding his valour and his blushes, beneath the waving plumes of his helmet. Kosciuszko, who was to head the party, observed this modesty with pleasure, and shaking him warmly by the hand, "Go Thaddeus," said he, "take your station on the left flank; I shall require your fresh spirits to lead the charge I intend it to make, and to ensure its success." Thaddeus bowed to these encouraging words, and took his place according to order.‡

Every thing being ready, the detachment quitted the camp, and dashing through the dews of a sweet morning, for it was yet May, in a few hours, arrived in view of the Russian battalions. Lomza, who from the only redoubt now in his possession, first caught a glimpse of this welcome reinforcement, rallied his few remaining men, and by the time that Kosciuszko came up, contrived to join him in the van. The fight re-commenced. Thaddeus, at the head of his hussars, in full gallop, bore down upon the enemy. They received the charge with firmness; but the young leader, perceiving that extraordinary means were necessary, exerted his voice to the utmost; calling on his men to follow him, he put spurs to his horse, and rushed into the thickest of the battle. His soldiers did not shrink; they pressed on, mowing down the foremost ranks, whilst he, by a lucky stroke of his sabre, disabled the sword arm of the Russian standard-bearer, and seized the colours. His own troops seeing the standard in his hand, with one accord, in loud and repeated cries, shouted victory. The reserve of the enemy, alarmed at this outcry, instantly gave way, and retreating with precipitation,

---

* Unidentified; perhaps borrowed from the town Łomża in northeastern Poland. In later editions, Porter revised his name and rank to Colonel Lonza.

† According to Plutarch's *Life of Agesilaus*, Isadas (or Isidas) was a young Spartan warrior who fought against the Theban army in 362 BCE. Armed with a spear in one hand and a sword in the other, Isadas brought down numerous soldiers without sustaining any injuries himself.

‡ Jones identifies the skirmish that follows as occurring on 26 May 1792 (*History*, pp. 415–16).

was soon followed by the rear ranks of the center, where Kosciuszko had already slain the commander of the attack. The flanks next gave ground; and after holding a short stand at intervals, at length fairly turned about, and fled, panic-struck, across the country.

The conquerors, elated with so sudden a success, put their horses on full speed, and without order or attention, pursued the fugitives with the noise of thunder, till they were lost amidst the trees of a distant wood. Kosciuszko now called on his men to stop; but he called in vain: they continued their career, animating each other, and with redoubled shouts drowning the voice of Thaddeus, who galloped forwards, repeating the command till they* were met at the entrance of the wood, by a few stragglers who had formed themselves into a body. These men withstood the first onset of the Poles with considerable steadiness: But after a skirmish of ten minutes, they fled a second time; and took refuge in the bushes, where, still regardless of orders, their enemies followed. Kosciuszko foreseeing the consequence of this rashness, ordered Thaddeus to dismount part of his squadron, and march after these headstrong men, into the forest. He came up with them on the edge of a heathy tract of land, just as they were extending their lines to surround a band of arquebusers, who, having kept up a quick running fire as they retreated, had drawn their pursuers thus far into the thickets. Heedless of any thing but giving their enemy a complete defeat, the Polanders went on, never looking to the left nor to the right, till, all at once, they found themselves encompassed by two thousand Muscovite horse, several battalions of chasseurs, and in front of fourteen pieces of cannon, which this dreadful ambuscade fired upon them, with instant and unremitted violence.

Thaddeus threw himself into the midst of his countrymen, and taking the place of their unfortunate conductor, who had been killed in the first sweep of the artillery, prepared the men for a desperate stand. He gave his orders with intrepidity and coolness, though under a heavy shower of musquetry, and a cannonade, which carried death in every round: for himself, he had no thought; it was only how to relieve the unlucky Poles from the dilemma into which they had plunged themselves, that occupied his mind. In a few minutes, the scattered soldiers were consolidated into a close phalanx, flanked and reared with the pikemen; "who stood like a grove of pines in a day of tempest, only moving their heads and arms."† Many of the Russian horse impaled themselves on

---

* 'They' refers to the overenthusiastic Polish soldiers who here encounter Russian 'stragglers'. Porter's syntax is out of control, like the soldiers.

† A quotation from Robert Codrington's 'Life and Death of Robert, Earl of Essex',

the sides of this little phalanx, which they vainly attempted to shake, though the ordnance was rapidly weakening its strength. File after file, the men were swept down, their bodies making a horrid rampart for their brave comrades, who, rendered desperate by slaughter, threw away their most cumbrous accoutrements, and crying to their leader, "Let us escape or die!" followed him sword in hand; and bearing like a torrent upon the enemy's ranks, who expected nothing less, cut their way right through the forest. The Russians, exasperated that their prey should not only escape, but escape by such dauntless valour, hung closely on their rear, goading them with musquetry, whilst they, (like a wounded lion, hardly pressed by the hunters, who retreats, and yet stands proudly at bay) gradually retired towards the camp, moving with a backward step, their faces towards the foe.

Meanwhile, Sobieski, anxious for the fate of the day, had mounted the dyke, and looked eagerly around, for the arrival of some messenger from the little army. As the wind blew strongly from the south, a cloud of dust precluded his view; but from the nearer approach of the firing, and the clashing of arms, he was led to fear that his friends had been defeated, and were retreating towards the camp. He quitted the lines instantly, to call out a fresh reinforcement, when the enemy, at the sight of Kosciuszko and his squadron on full charge, suddenly halted, and wheeling round, left the harassed Polanders to enter the trenches in quiet.

Thaddeus, covered with dust and blood, flung himself into his grand-father's arms. In the heat of action, his left arm had been wounded by a Cossac:* fearful that the bleeding might disable him from further service, at the moment it happened, he bound it up in his sash, and had thought no more of it, until the Palatine, now remarked the stains on his cloak and the bosom of his shirt.

"My hurt is slight, my dear sir;" said he, "I wish to heaven, it were all the evil that has befallen us to-day! Look at the remnant of our brave comrades."

Sobieski turned his eyes on the panting soldiers, and on Kosciuszko, who was inspecting them. Some, no longer upheld by desperation, were sinking with wounds and fatigue; these the good General, ever mindful of the comfort of his men, was sending off in litters to the medical department: and others, who had sustained the conflict of

in *A Selection from the Harleian Miscellany of Tracts* (London: C. and G. Kearsley, 1793), p. 166.
* Cossacks, from southern Russia and Ukraine, were renowned for their horsemanship and military skills.

the day without meeting any personal harm, after having received the praise and admonition of their commander, were dismissed to their quarters.

Before this inspection was half over, the Palatine found it necessary to assist Thaddeus to his tent, who, in spite of his exertions to the contrary, had become so faint, that he staggered rather than walked, as he was led off the ground.

A very short time perfectly restored him; and with his arm in a sling, he joined his brother officers on the fourth day, at the parade. After the duty of the morning, he heard with concern, that during his confinement, frequent skirmishes had taken place between his countrymen and their adversaries, in which they found, that the Russians had augmented their force to such a tremendous strength, that it would be impossible for the Poles to remain longer at Winnica, without incurring the danger of being surrounded, and cut to pieces. In consequence of this, the Prince held a council late the preceding night, in which it was determined that the camp should be immediately razed and removed towards Zielime.

This news displeased Thaddeus, who in his fairy dreams of war, always added conquest, as the sure end of his battles; and many were the sighs he drew, when next day, at an hour before dawn, he witnessed the striking of the tents, which he thought to be only the prelude to a shameful flight from the enemy. While he was standing by the sides of the busy people, and musing on the nice line which divides prudence from pusillanimity, his grandfather came up, and desiring him to mount his horse, told him, by reason of the unhealed state of his wound, that he was not to take his appropriate place in the vanguard, but to march in the center, along with the Prince and his suite. Thaddeus very warmly remonstrated against this arrangement: he called his hurt a mere scratch; and almost reproached the Palatine for forfeiting his promise, that he should always be stationed near him. Sobieski would not be moved, either by argument or entreaty; Thaddeus, finding that he neither could, nor ought to oppose him, obeyed, and followed an aid-de-camp to his highness.

After a march of three hours, the army came in sight of Volunna, when the advanced column suddenly halted. Thaddeus, who was about half a mile to its rear, with a throbbing heart, heard that a momentous pass must be disputed before they could proceed. He curbed his horse; then almost gave it the spur, so eagerly did he wish to penetrate the cloud of smoke which rose in volumes from the discharge of musquetry, on whose wing, at every round, he dreaded might be carried the fate of his grandfather. At last the firing ceased, and the troops were commanded to go forward. On entering the contested defile, Thaddeus shuddered; for at every step the heels of his charger struck upon the wounded or the dead. There lay his enemies, here lay his friends: his respiration felt suffocated; his eyes clung to the ground, expecting at each moment, to fasten themselves on the breathless body of his grandfather.

Again, the tumult of battle presented itself. About a hundred soldiers, in one firm rank, stood at the end of the pass, firing on the rear-guard of the Russians which was rapidly dispersing. Thaddeus checked his horse. Five hundred had been detached to this post; how few remained! Could he hope Sobieski had escaped such a desperate rencontre? Fearing the worst, and dreading to have those fears confirmed, his heart sickened when he received the orders of Poniatowski, to examine the extent of the loss. He rode up close to the mouth of the defile. He could no where see the Palatine. A few of the hussars, a little in advance, were engaged over a heap of the killed, as if defending it from a troop of chasseurs, who appeared fighting for the barbarous privilege of trampling on the bodies. Thaddeus at this sight, and impelled by despair, called out, "Courage soldiers! the Prince is here." The chasseurs looking forward, saw that the information was true, and took to flight. Poniatowski, almost at the word, was by the side of his young friend, who unconscious of any thing but filial solicitude, had immediately dismounted.

"Where is the Palatine?" cried he to a soldier, who was stooping towards the slain he had attempted to defend. The man made no answer, but lifted from the heap, the bodies of two soldiers, which lay at the top; beneath these, Thaddeus saw the pale and deadly features of his grandfather. He staggered a few paces back, when the Prince thinking that he was falling, put out his arm to catch him; but he recovered himself, and flew forwards to assist Kosciuszko, who had raised the head of the Palatine upon his knee.

"Is he alive?" cried Thaddeus.

"He breathes."

Hope was now as warm in his breast, as it had before been cold: they soon released Sobieski from the surrounding dead; but his swoon continuing, the Prince desired him to be laid on a bank, until a litter could be brought from the rear ranks, to convey him to a place of security. Meantime, Thaddeus and the General bound up his wounds, and poured some water into his lips. The effusion of blood being stopped, the brave veteran opened his eyes; and in a few minutes, whilst he leaned on the bosom of his grandson, was so far recovered, as to receive, with his usual modest dignity, the thanks of his Highness for the intrepidity with which he had preserved a passage that ensured the safety of the whole army.

Two surgeons arrived with the litter, and relieved the anxiety of the by-standers, with the assurance that the wounds which they had re-examined, did not appear to be dangerous. Having laid their patient on the vehicle, they were preparing to retire with it into the rear, when Thaddeus petitioned the Prince to grant him permission to take the command of the guard that was appointed to attend his grandfather. His Highness consented; but Sobieski positively gave his negative.

"No, Thaddeus;" said he, "you forget the effect that all this solicitude about so trifling a matter might have on the men. Remember, that he who goes into battle, only puts his own life to the hazard; but he who abandons the field, sports with the lives of his soldiers. Do not give them leave to suppose, that even your dearest interests could tempt *you* from the front of danger, when it is your duty to remain." Thaddeus obeyed his grandfather in silence; and at seven o'clock the army resumed their march.

Near Zielime, the Prince was saluted by Count Potocki, at the head of some fresh troops which he had collected at Zaslow.* This succour appeared very seasonably. The scouts had brought information, that, directly across the plain, the Russians, under the command of General Branicki,[†] had doubled their numbers, and were drawn up in order of battle, to dispute their progress.

Thaddeus, for the first time, shuddered at the sight of the enemy. Should his friends be defeated, what might be the fate of his grandfather, now rendered helpless by his wounds! Occupied by these fears, with anxiety in his heart and looks, he kept his place at the head of the light horse, close to the hill.[‡]

Prince Poniatowski ordered the lines to extend themselves, that the right should reach to the river, and the left be covered by a rising ground, on which were mounted seven pieces of ordnance. Immediately after these dispositions, the battle commenced. It continued with violence

* Count Ignacy Potocki (1750–1809) supported the reformers but did not participate in any battles. Count Stanisław Potocki (1751–1805) was in fact an opponent of Poland's constitutional reforms and did not fight with Poniatowski and Kościuszko. This opening sentence was revised in the second edition to read simply, 'Near Zielime, the Prince was saluted by a reinforcement of fresh troops.'

† Franciszek Ksawery Branicki (1730–1819), a Polish nobleman and (along with Count Stanisław Potocki) a key member of the Targowica Confederation, which opposed Poland's constitutional reforms. In the first edition, the name is spelled 'Brinicki' here and in the following paragraph but correctly elsewhere.

‡ The Battle of Zieleńce occurred on 18 June 1792. Porter follows Stephen Jones and other British sources in calling the battle site Zielime (*History*, p. 416).

and unabating fury, from eight in the morning, until sunset. Several times, during the contest, the Poles were driven from their ground; but recovering themselves, and animated by their commanders, they prosecuted the fight with advantage. General Branicki perceiving that the fortune of the day was going against him, called up the body of reserve, consisting of four thousand men besides several cannon, for which they erected temporary batteries in a few minutes; with this unexpected addition of new forces, he opened a rapid and destructive fire on the Polanders, who, already sinking with the fatigue of marching, and the heat of the sun, were now on the point of giving way. Kosciuszko, alarmed at the retrograde motion of the troops, gave immediate orders for a close attack on the enemy in front, whilst Thaddeus, at the head of his hussars, should wheel round the hill of artillery, and with loud cries, charge the opposite flank. This stratagem succeeded. The Cossacs who were posted on that spot, seeing the impetuosity of the Poles, and the quarter from whence they came, supposing them to be a fresh squadron, gave ground, and opening in all directions, threw their own people into a confusion that completed the defeat. Kosciuszko and the Prince were equally successful, where they attacked; and a general panic amongst their adversaries was the consequence. The whole of the Russian army now took to flight, except a few regiments of carabiniers,* who were entangled between the river and the Poles. These were immediately surrounded by a battalion of Masovian infantry, which, enraged at the loss its body had sustained the preceding day, was answering their cries for quarter, with reproach and derision. At this instant, the Sobieski squadron, who were scouring the field, came up, and Thaddeus, who saw the perilous situation of these regiments, directly ordered that they might be taken prisoners, and the slaughter cease. The Masovians exhibited strong signs of dissatisfaction at these commands; but the young Count, charging through them, ranged his troops before the Russians, and threatened that the first man who would dare to lift a sword against his order, should be shot. The Poles dropped their arms. The poor carabiniers fell on their knees to thank his mercy; whilst their officers, in a sullen silence, which seemed ashamed of gratitude, surrendered their swords into the hands of their deliverers.

During this scene, only one very young Russian, appeared wholly refractory. He held up his sword in a menacing posture, when Thaddeus, who was approaching, drew near; and before he had time to speak, the young man made a longe at his breast, which one of

---

* Soldiers armed with carbines.

his hussars parrying with great dexterity, struck him to the earth: he would have killed him on the spot, had not Thaddeus caught the blow on his own sword, and instantly dismounting, raised the officer from the ground, apologising for the too hasty zeal of his soldier. The youth blushed, and, bowing, presented his sword, which was received, and directly returned.

"Brave sir," said he, "I feel myself ennobled in restoring this sword to one, who so courageously defended it."

The Russian made no other reply, but by a second bow, and put his hand on his breast, which was wet with blood. Ceremony was now at an end. Thaddeus never considered the unfortunate as strangers: accosting the wounded young soldier with a friendly voice, he assured him of his services, and made him lean on his shoulder. The officer incapable of speaking, accepted the assistance of his enemy; but before the conveyance arrived for which two men had been dispatched, he fainted in his arms. Thaddeus, who was obliged to join the Prince with his prisoners, very unwillingly left the young Russian in this situation. Before he did so, he directed one of his lieutenants to stay behind, and take care that the surgeons should pay attention to the officer, and have his litter carried next to the Palatine's during the rest of the march.

When the army halted at nine o'clock, preparations were made to fix the camp; and in case of a surprisal from any part of the dispersed enemy which might have rallied, orders were delivered for throwing up a dyke. Thaddeus, having been assured that his grandfather and the wounded Russian were comfortably stationed together, did not hesitate to accept with alacrity the command of the entrenching party; to that end, he wrapped himself loosely in his pelisse, and prepared for a long watch. The night was beautiful. It being the month of June, a softening warmth still floated through the air, as if the moon which shone over his head, emitted heat, as well as splendour. His mind was in unison with the season. He rode slowly round, from bank to bank, sometimes speaking to the workers in the fosse; sometimes lingering for a few minutes, looking on the ground, he thought on the element of which he was composed, to which he might so soon return; then gazing upwards, he observed the silent march of the stars, and the moving scene of the heavens! On whatever he cast his eyes, his soul, which the recent events had dissolved into a temper not the less delightful for being tinged with melancholy, dwelt with intense feeling on the littleness of human pride, when opposed to the grandeur of eternity. He looked with pity over that wide tract of land, which now lay betwixt him and the remains of those four thousand Russians who had fallen a sacrifice to the insatiate desires of ambition. He well knew the difference between a defender of his own country and the invader of another's. He felt his heart beat, his soul expand, at the prospect of securing liberty and life to a virtuous people; while he could only imagine, how that spirit must shrink from reflection, which would animate the head and hands of a self-condemned slave, to fight, not merely to fasten chains on others, but to rivet his own still closer. The best affections of man having put the sword into the hand of Thaddeus; his principles, as a philosopher, did not rebel in the smallest degree against his passion for arms. When he was told that the fortifications were finished, he retired with a tranquil step and smiling conscience, towards the Masovian quarters. He found the Palatine awake, and eager to welcome him with the joyful reply to his anxious enquiries, that his wounds were so slight, as to promise a speedy amendment. Thaddeus asked for his prisoner. The Palatine said, "he is in the next tent, where, according to your desire, the surgeon never leaves him; and he has given a very favourable opinion of the wound, which was a shot through the muscles of the breast."

"Have you seen him, my dear Sir?" asked Thaddeus, "Does he express himself, as if he felt at ease, and thought himself well treated?"

"Yes;" replied the Palatine, "I was supported into his marquée, before I retired to my own. I told him who I was, and repeated your offers of service. He received what I said, with lively expressions of gratitude; and at the same time declared that he had nothing to blame, but his own folly, in bringing him to the state in which he then was."

"How, my lord!" asked Thaddeus, rather surprised, "Does he repent of being a soldier? or is he ashamed of the cause for which he fought?"

"Both, Thaddeus; he is not a Russian, but a young Englishman."

"An Englishman! and raise his arm against a country struggling for liberty!"

"It is very true;" returned the Palatine, "but as he confessed, that it was his folly, and the persuasions of others, which impelled him, he merits pardon; he is a mere youth; I think hardly your age. I understand that he is of rank; and having undertaken the tour of Europe under the direction of a travelling governor, he took Russia in his map of route. At Petersburgh he became intimate with many of the nobility, particularly with Count Branicki, at whose house he resided; and when his lordship was named to the command of the army in Poland, Mr. Somerset, (for that is your prisoner's name), instigated by his own volatility, and the arguments of his host, volunteered with him; and so followed his friend, to oppose that freedom here, which he would have asserted in his own nation."

Thaddeus thanked his grandfather for this information; and pleased that the young man who had so much interested him, was any thing but a Russian, he instantly repaired to his tent.

A generous heart is as eloquent in acknowledging benefits, as it would be bounteous in bestowing them; and Mr. Somerset received his preserver with the warmest demonstrations of gratitude. Thaddeus begged him not to consider himself as particularly obliged, by a conduct which every soldier of honour has a right to expect from another. The Englishman bowed his head, and Thaddeus sat down by his bed-side, where he remained conversing, for near an hour.

Whilst he gathered from his own lips a corroboration of the narrative of the Palatine, he could not forbear enquiring, how a person of his apparent candid nature, and who was also the native of a soil where liberty had so long been the palladium of its happiness, could volunteer in a cause, the end of which was to make a brave people slaves?

Somerset listened to these questions with blushes; and they did not leave his face, when he confessed, that all he could say in extenuation of what he had done, was to plead his youth, and having thought little on the subject.

"I was wrought upon," continued he, "by a variety of circumstances; first, the principles of Mr. Loftus, my governor, are strongly in favour of the court of Petersburgh: secondly, my father disliked the army, and I adored it; this was the only opportunity in which I might ever satisfy my passion: and lastly, I believe I was dazzled by the picture which the young men about me, drew of the campaign. I longed to be a soldier; they persuaded me; and I followed them to the field, as I would have done to a ball-room, heedless of the consequence."

"Yet," replied Thaddeus, smiling, "from the intrepidity with which you maintained your ground when your arms were demanded, any one might have thought, that your whole soul, as well as your body, was engaged in the cause."

"To be sure," returned he, "I was a blockhead to be there; but when there, I should have despised myself for ever, had I given up my honour into the hands of those ruffians, who would have wrested my sword from me! But when you came, noble Sobieski, it was the fate of war, and I confided myself to a brave man."

CHAP. IV.

Each succeeding morning not only brought fresh symptoms of recovery, to the two invalids, but condensed the interest and admiration of the young men, into an ardent esteem.

It is not the disposition of youthful minds to weigh for months and years, the sterling value of those qualities which attract them. As soon as they see virtue, they respect it; as soon as they meet kindness, they believe it; and as soon as a union of both presents itself, they love it. Not having passed through the disappointments of a delusive world, they grasp, for reality, every pageant that appears. They have not yet admitted that cruel doctrine, which, when it takes effect, creates and extends the misery it affects to cure. Whilst we give up our souls to suspicion, we gradually learn to deceive; whilst we repress the fervours of our own hearts, we freeze those which approach us; whilst we cautiously avoid occasions of receiving pain, we at every remove acquire an unconscious influence to inflict anguish on those who follow us. They again meet from our conduct and lips, the reason and the lesson, to obliterate the expanding sensibilities of their nature; and thus the tormenting chain of deceived and deceiving characters is lengthened to infinitude.

About the latter end of the month, Sobieski received a summons, desiring his immediate attendance at court, where a Diet* was to be held in consequence of the victory at Zielime, to consider of future proceedings. With this letter, his Majesty enclosed a collar and investiture of the order of St. Stanislaus,† as an acknowledgment of service to the young Thaddeus, with a note from himself, expressing his commands, that he would return with the Palatine and the other generals, to receive thanks from the throne.

Thaddeus, half wild with delight at the thoughts of so soon meeting his mother, ran to the tent of his British friend to communicate to him the tidings. Somerset participated in all his pleasure; and, with sensations equally warm, accepted the invitation to go with him to Villanow.

---

* An assembly of political leaders.
† Porter (or her source) seems to have named the wrong award. The Order of Saint Stanislaus was a Polish order of knighthood, founded by Stanisław II in 1765. Stanisław created the War Order of Virtuti Militari in June 1792 to honour soldiers who fought at the Battle of Zieleńce.

"I would follow you, my friend," said he, squeezing the hand of Thaddeus, who was eagerly describing the merits of the Countess and the beauties of his home; "all over the world."

"Then I will take you, to the most charming spot in it!" cried he, "Villanow is a perfect paradise; and my mother, the dear angel, that would make a desert so to me."

"You speak so rapturously of your *enchanted castle*, Thaddeus," returned his friend, "that I do believe I shall have to consider my knight-errantry, in being fool enough to thrust myself amid a fray in which I had no business, as one of the wisest decisions of my life!"

"I consider it," replied Thaddeus, "as one of the luckiest events in mine."

Before the Palatine quitted the camp, Somerset thought it proper to acquaint Mr. Loftus, who was yet at Petersburgh, of the particulars of his late danger; and that he was going to Warsaw with his new friends, where he should remain for several weeks. He also added, that as the court of Poland, through the intercession of the Palatine, had generously given him his liberty, he should be able to see every thing in that country worthy of investigation; and that he would write to him again, enclosing letters for England, soon after his arrival at the Polish capital.

The weather continuing fine, the party left Zielime in a few days; and the Palatine and Somerset, being so far restored from their wounds, that they could walk about, the one, with a crutch, and the other, by the support of his friend's, or a servant's arm: they went through the journey with animation and pleasure. The benign wisdom of Sobieski, the intelligent enthusiasm of Thaddeus, and the playful vivacity of Somerset, all mingling together, made the minutes fly even as fast as their wishes, till a week more, carried them into the Palatinate of Masovia, and soon after within the walls of Villanow.

Every thing that presented itself to Mr. Somerset was new and fascinating. He saw, in the domestic felicity of his friend, scenes which reminded him of the social harmony of his own home. He beheld, in the palace and retinue of Sobieski, all that magnificence which bespoke the descendant of a great king, who even now wanted nothing of royal grandeur but the crown, which he had the magnanimity to think and to declare was then placed upon a more worthy brow. Whilst Somerset venerated this true patriot, the high tone which his feelings acquired, was not lowered by associating with characters who were nearer the common standard. The friends of Sobieski were men of tried probity: Men, who at all times preferred their country's welfare, before their own particular interest. The most distinguished amongst them, were the Counts Malachowski, Potocki, Puchala, and the Prince Cassimer Sapieha.* Mr. Somerset, day after day, listened with deep attention to these virtuous and energetic noblemen. He saw them full of fire and personal courage, when the affairs of Poland were the subject of discourse; and he beheld, with amaze and admiration, their perfect forgetfulness of their own individual safety, in their passion for the general good. In these moments, he felt his heart bowing down before them; and all the ancient pride of a Briton distended his breast, when he thought, that such men as these are, his ancestors were. He remembered how often their almost chivalric virtues used to occupy his reflections, in the picture-gallery at Somerset Castle; and his doubts, when he compared what is with what was, that history had glossed over the actions of past centuries; or else, that a different order of men lived then, from those which now inhabit the world. Thus, studying the sublime characters of Sobieski and his friends; and enjoying the endearing kindness of Thaddeus and his mother, did a fortnight pass away, without his even recollecting the promise of writing to his governor. At the end of that period, however, he stole an hour from the Countess's society, and enclosed, in a short letter to Mr. Loftus, the following epistle to his mother.

"*To Lady Somerset, Somerset Castle, Leicestershire.*

"Many weeks ago, my dearest mother, I wrote a letter of seven sheets from Petersburgh, which long ere this you and my dear father must have received. I there attempted to give you some idea of the manners of Russia, with the face of the country; and my vanity whispers, that I succeeded tolerably well. The court of the famous Catherine, and the attentions of the hospitable Count Branicki, were then the subjects of my pen.

"But, how shall I account for my being here? How shall I allay your surprise and displeasure, on seeing that this letter is dated from Warsaw! I know that I have acted against the wish of my father, in visiting one of those countries which he had interdicted. I know that I have disobeyed your commands, in ever having at any period of my life taken up arms without an indispensable necessity: but I have nothing to allege in my defence. I fell in the way of temptation, and I yielded to it. I really cannot enumerate all the things which induced me

---

* Count Stanisław Malachowski (1736–1809), Count Ignacy Potocki (1750–1809) and Prince Kazimierz Nestor Sapieha (1757–98) were all supporters of the 3 May 1791 Constitution. Porter may have borrowed the list from William Thomson's *Letters from Scandinavia* (London: G. G. and J. Robinson, 1796), where all four surnames appear as supporters of reform (2. 431).

to volunteer with the Russians; suffice it to say, that I did so, and that we were defeated by the Poles at Zielime: and as Heaven has rather rewarded your prayers than punished my imprudence, I trust you will do the same, and pardon an indiscretion that I will never repeat.

"Notwithstanding all this, I must have lost my life through my folly, had I not been preserved, even in the moment when death was pending over me, by a young officer, with whose family I now am. The very sound of their title will create your respect; for *we* of the *Patrician order*, have a strange tenacity in our belief, that virtue is hereditary, and in this instance our creed is duly honoured. The title is Sobieski: the family which bears it, is the only remaining posterity of the great monarch of that name; and the Count, who is at its head, is Palatine of Masovia, which next to the throne, is the first dignity in the state. He is one of the warmest champions in favour of the invaded rights of his country; and though born to command, he has so far trans-gressed that golden law of despotic rulers, '*Ignorance and subjection,*' that throughout his territories every man is taught to worship his GOD, with his heart as well as his knees. The understandings of his peas-ants are awakened to all useful knowledge: he does not put books of science and speculation into their hands vainly to consume their time in idleness. He gives them the Bible, and implements of industry, to afford them the means of knowing, and of practising their duty. All Masovia, around his palace, blooms like a garden. The cheerful faces of the farmers, and the blessings which they implore on the family, as I walk in the fields with the young Count, (for in this country, the sons bear the same title with their fathers;) have even drawn a few delighted drops from the eyes of your '*thoughtless son!*' I know, mother, that you think I have nothing sentimental about me; else you would not so often have poured into my *not inattentive ears*, that it is by the feelings of the heart, we are to estimate the pleasures of earth and heaven: shut our eyes against them, and we are merely nicely constructed speculums, which reflect the beauties of nature, but enjoy none. You see, mama, that I both remember and adopt your lessons.

"Thaddeus Sobieski is the grandson of the Palatine, and the last of his illustrious race. It is to him that I owe the preservation of my life at Zielime, and much of my happiness since; for he is not only the bravest, but the most amiable young man in the kingdom; and he is my friend. Indeed, as things have happened, you must think that out of evil has come good: though I have been disobedient, my fault has introduced me to the affection of people, whose friendship henceforward will prove the greatest pleasure of my days. The mother of Thaddeus is the only daughter of the Palatine; and of her, I can only sum up, that nothing on earth can more remind me of you; she is equally charming, equally tender to your son.

"Whilst the Palatine is engaged at the Diet, her ladyship, Thaddeus, and myself, with now and then a few visitors from Warsaw, form the most agreeable parties you can imagine. We walk together, we read together, we converse together, we sing together: at least, the Countess sings to us; which is all the same: and you know, that time flies swiftly on the wings of harmony. She has an uncommonly sweet voice, and a taste, which I never heard paralleled. By the way, you cannot imagine any thing more beautiful than the Polish music. It partakes much of that delicious langour, so distinguished in the Turkish airs; with a mingling of those wandering melodies, which the now-forgotten composers must have caught from the Tartars. In short, whilst the Countess is singing I hardly suffer myself to breathe; and I feel, just what our poetical friend William Scarsdale, said a twelve month ago, at a concert of yours, 'I feel, as if love sat upon my heart, and flapped it with his wings.'*

"I have tried all my powers of persuasion to prevail on this charming Countess to visit our country. I have over and over again told her of you, and described you to her; that you are near her own age; (for this lovely woman, though she has a son near nineteen, is not more than forty;) that you are as fond of your *ordinary* boy, as she is of her *peerless* one; that, in fine, you and my father will receive her, and Thaddeus, and the Palatine, with open arms and hearts, if they will condescend to visit our humble home, at the end of the war. I believe, that I have repeated my entreaties, both to her ladyship and my friend, regularly every day, since my arrival at Villanow; but always with the same ill success: She smiles, and refuses: and Thaddeus *'shakes his ambrosial curls'* with a very *'godlike frown'* of denial;† I hope, self-denial in compliment to his mother's cruel and unprovoked negative.

"Before I proceed, my dear mother, I must give you some idea of the real appearance of this palace. I recollect your having read a superficial account of it in the few slight sketches that have been published in England, of Poland; but the pictures which they exhibit are so faint, that they hardly resemble the original. Pray do not laugh at me, if I begin in the true descriptive stile! you know, that there is only one way

---

* Possibly an inside joke; Jane Porter mentions a 'Raphael Scarsdale' in a c. 1802 letter to her sister (Huntington POR 1472).
† In Alexander Pope's translation of Homer's *Iliad* (London: W. Bowyer, 1715–20), Jove 'Shakes his ambrosial curls, and gives the nod' to Thetis's request on behalf of her son Achilles (1. 584).

to draw houses, and lands and rivers; so that no blame can be attached to me as, *will'e nill'e'*,* I take the beaten path. To commence –

"When we left Zielime, and advanced into the Province of Masovia, the country around Prague† rose at every step in fresh beauty. The numberless chains of gently-swelling hills, which encompass it on each side of the Vistula, were in some parts, chequered with corn fields, meadows and green pastures, covered with sheep, whose soft bleatings thrilled in my ears, and transported my senses into new regions; so different were my charmed and tranquilized feelings, from that tossing of mind, attendant on the horrors I had recently witnessed. Surely, there is nothing in the rational world, short of the most undivided reciprocal attachment, that has such power over the workings of the human heart, as the mild sweetness of nature. The most ruffled temper, when emerging from the town, will subside into a perfect calm, at the sight of a wide stretch of landscape reposing in the twilight of a fine evening. It is then, that the balm of peace settles upon the heart, unfetters the spirit, and elevates the soul to the creator. It is then, that we behold the parent of the universe in his works; when *we see* his grandeur, in earth, sea, and sky; feel his affection, in the emotions which they raise; and, half mortal, half etherialized, forget where we are, in the anticipation of what that world must be, of which this lovely earth is merely the shadow.

"Autumn seemed to be unfolding all her beauties, to greet the return of the Palatine. In one part, the haymakers were mowing the hay, and heaping it into stacks; in another, the reapers were gathering up the wheat, with a troop of rosy little gleaners behind them; each of whom might have tempted the proudest Palemon in Christendom, to have changed her toil into '*a gentler duty.*'‡ Such a landscape, intermingled with the little farms of these honest people, whom the philanthropy of Sobieski had rendered free, (for it is a tract of his extensive domains that I am describing), gave me sensations that reminded me of Somerset. These cottages are dispersed among the deep hollows of the vales, and are seen peeping from amid the thick umbrage of the woods, which cover the face of the hills. Their irregular forms, and thatched roofs, with many of their infant inhabitants playing at the doors, compose

---

* willy nilly, 'whether one likes it or not; willingly or unwillingly' (*OED*).

† Prague, more often written Praga, is a district of Warsaw on the eastern bank of the Vistula river. Porter added a note to the second edition defending her use of Prague (which then, as now, was more commonly used to refer to the Bohemian city). See also Appendix D.

‡ The story of the gentleman Palemon who falls in love with the gleaner Lavinia appears in James Thomson's *The Seasons: Autumn* (lines 177–310).

such lovely groupes, that I could only wish for our dear Mary's pencil, and fingers, (for alas! that way mine are motionless!) to transport them to your eyes.

"The palace of Villanow, which is castellated, and stands in the midst of a fortress, now burst upon my view. It rears its embattled head from the summit of a hill, that gradually slopes down towards the Vistula, and borders, to the south, the plain of Vola; a spot, so long famous for the election of the kings of Poland.* On the north of the building, the earth is cut into natural ramparts, which rise in high succession, till they reach the foundations of the palace, where they terminate, in a noble terrace. These ramparts, covered with grass, overlook the stone-outworks, and spread down to the bottom of the hill, which being cloathed with fine trees and luxuriant underwood, forms such a rich and verdant base to the fortress, as I have not language to describe; were I privileged to be poetical, I would say, that it reminds me of the god of war, sleeping amid roses in the bower of love.† Here, the eye may wander over the gifts of bounteous nature arraying hill and dale in all the united treasures of spring and autumn. The forest stretches its yet unsunned arms to the breeze; whilst that breeze comes laden with the fragrance of the tented hay, and the thousand sweets breathed from those flowers which in this delicious country, weep honey.

"A magnificent flight of steps led us from the foot of the ramparts up to the gate of the palace. We entered it; and were presently surrounded by a train of attendants, in such sumptuous liveries, that I found myself all at once carried back into the fifteenth century; and might have fancied myself within the courtly halls of our Tudors and Plantagenets. You can better conceive, than I can recapitulate, the scene which took place, between the Palatine, the Countess, and her son. I can only repeat, that from that hour I have experienced no default of happiness, but what arises from regret that my dear family are not partakers with me.

"You know, that this stupendous building was the favourite residence of John Sobieski; and that he erected it, as a resting place from the labours of his long and glorious reign. I cannot move, without meeting some vestige of that truly great monarch. I sleep in his bed-chamber:

---

* Poland had a long history of elective rather than hereditary monarchy. During the period of the Polish–Lithuanian Commonwealth, thousands of nobles would gather on the field at Wola to elect a new king. The 3 May 1791 Constitution removed elective monarchy, in order to stop the interference of foreign powers at each election (such interference allowed Catherine to elect Stanisław as ruler).

† In European art, Ares/Mars, the god of war, is often depicted at ease or asleep in the presence of his lover Aphrodite/Venus, goddess of love.

there hangs his portrait, dressed in the robes of sovereignty; here, are suspended the arms, with which he saved those kingdoms, which are now coalescing to the destruction of Poland. On one side, is his library; on the other, the little chapel, in which he used to pay his morning and evening devotions. Wherever I look, my eye finds some object, to excite my reflections and emulation. The noble dead appear to address me from their graves, and I blush, at the inglorious life I might have pursued, had I never visited this house, and its inhabitants: yet, my dearest mother, I do not mean to reproach you; nor to insinuate that my revered father, and brave ancestors, have not set me examples as bright, as man need follow; but human nature is capricious; we are not to be stimulated so much with what is always in our view, as by sights, which rising up, when we are removed from our customary associations, surprise and captivate our attention. Villanow has only awakened me to the same lesson, which I have conned over in drowsy carelessness at home. Thaddeus Sobieski is hardly one year my senior; but good heaven! what has he not done? What has he not acquired? Whilst I abused the indulgence of my parents, and wasted my days in riding, shooting, and walking the streets, he was learning to act, as a man of rank ought to act; and by seizing every opportunity to serve the state, he has obtained a rich reward, in the respect and admiration of his country. I am not envious, mother, but I now feel the truth of Cæsar's speech, when he declared, '*that the reputation of Alexander would not let him sleep.*'* Nevertheless, I dearly love my friend; I murmur at my own demerits, not at his worth.

"I have scribbled out all my paper, otherwise I verily believe that I would write more; however, I promise you another letter, in a week or two. Meanwhile I shall send this packet to Mr. Loftus, who is at Petersburgh, to forward to you. Adieu, my dear mother; I am, with reverence to my father and yourself,

Your truly affectionate son,
PEMBROKE SOMERSET."

"*Villanow, August*, 1792."

"To Lady Somerset, Somerset Castle, England.
(Written three weeks after the preceding.)

"You know, my dear mother, that your Pembroke is famous for his ingenious mode of shewing the full value of every favour he confers:

---

* Unidentified. In his life of Caesar, Plutarch reports that Caesar burst into tears upon learning that, at his age, Alexander had already conquered many nations. A similar anecdote appears in Suetonius's *Twelve Caesars*.

Can I then lose the opportunity of telling you, what I have left, to make you happy with this epistle?

"About five minutes ago, I was sitting on the lawn at the feet of the Countess, reading to her and the Princess Sapieha, the charming poem of '*The Pleasures of Memory*;'* as both these ladies understand English, they were admiring it, and paying many compliments to the *graces* of my delivery, when the Palatine presented himself, and told me, that if I had any commands for Petersburgh, I must prepare them, for a messenger was to set off to-morrow morning by day-break. I instantly sprang up, threw my book into the hand of Thaddeus; and here I am, in my own room, scribbling to you.

"Even at the moment in which I dip my pen in the ink, my hurrying imagination paints on my heart, the situation of my beloved home, when this letter reaches you. I think I see you, and my good aunt, seated on the blue sofa in your dressing-room, with your needle work on the little table before you; I see Mary, in her usual nook, the recess by the old harpsichord; and my dear father, bringing in this happy letter from your son! I must confess, that this romantic kind of fancy-sketching makes me feel rather oddly; very unlike, indeed, from what I felt a few months since, when I was a mere, indifferent, unreflecting, unappreciating coxcomb. Well, it is now made evident to me, that we never know the blessings of existence, till we are separated from the possession of them. Absence tightens the string that unites friends, as well as lovers; at least, I find it so; and though in the fruition of every good on this side the ocean, yet my happiness renders me ungrateful, and I repine, that I enjoy it alone. Positively, I must bring you all here to pass a summer; or come back at the termination of my travels, and carry away this dear family by main force to England.

"Tell my cousin Mary, that, either way, I shall present to her esteem the most accomplished of human beings; but I warn her not to fall in love with him, neither in *propria personæ*,† nor by his public fame, nor with his private character. Tell her, that '*he is a bright and particular star*,'‡ neither in her sphere, nor in any other woman's. In this way he is as cold as '*Dian's crescent*;' and to my great amazement too: for, when I throw my eyes over the many lovely young women, who at different times fill the drawing-room of the Countess, I cannot but wonder at

---

* Samuel Rogers, *The Pleasures of Memory, a Poem* (London: T. Cadell, 1792).
† Latin, 'for his own character'.
‡ Pembroke refers to Helena's love for Bertram in *All's Well That Ends Well*: ''Twere all one / That I should love a bright particular star / And think to wed it, he is so above me' (I, i, 85–7).

the perfect indifference with which he views their (to me) irresistible attractions.

"He is polite and attentive to them all; he talks with them, smiles with them, and treats them with every active complacency; but they do not live one instant in his memory. I mean, they do not occupy his particular wishes; for with regard to every respectful sentiment towards the sex in general, and esteem to some amiable individuals, he is as lively, as in the other case he is dead. The fact is, he never casts one thought upon himself: kindness is spontaneous to his nature; his sunny eyes shine over all, with modest benignity; and his frank and glowing conversation, is directed to every rank of people; who imbibe it with an avidity and love, which makes its way to his heart without awakening his vanity. Thus, whilst his fine person, and splendid actions, fill every eye and bosom, I see him moving in the circle, unconscious of his eminence, and the interest he excites.

"Instigated by such an example, to which his high quality, as well as extraordinary merit, gives so great an influence, many of the younger nobility have been led to enter the army. This circumstance, added to the detail of his bravery and uncommon talents in the field, has made him an object of universal regard; and, in consequence, where ever he is seen, he meets with applause and acclamations: nay, even at the appearance of his carriage in the streets of Warsaw, the passengers take off their hats, and pray for him till he is out of sight. It is only then that I perceive his cheek flushed with the conviction that he is adored.

"'It is this, Thaddeus;' said I to him one day, when walking out together, we were obliged to retire into the royal palace, from the crowds who followed him; 'It is this, my dear friend, that shields your heart against the arrows of love. You have no place for that passion; your mistress is glory, and she courts you.'

"'My mistress is my country,' replied he; 'at present, I desire no other. For her, I would die; for her only, I would wish to live.' While he spoke, the energy of his soul blazed in his eyes; I smiled.

"'You are an enthusiast, Thaddeus.'*

"'Pembroke!' returned he, in a surprised and reproachful tone.

"'I do not think you one,' resumed I laughing; 'but there are many in my country, who, hearing these sentiments, would not scruple to call you mad.'

"'Then I pity them,' returned Thaddeus. 'Men who cannot ardently feel, cannot taste supreme happiness. My grandfather educated me at

* Pembroke uses 'enthusiast' in the sense of a zealous, self-deluded person.

the feet of patriotism; and when I forget his precepts and example, may my guardian angel forget me!'

"'Happy, glorious, Thaddeus!' cried I grasping his hand, 'how I envy you your destiny! To live as you do, in the lap of honour; virtue and glory, the aim and end of your existence!'

"The animated countenance of my friend changed at these words, and laying his hand on my arm, he said, 'Do not envy my destiny; Pembroke, you are the citizen of a free country, at peace with itself. Insatiate power has not dared to invade its rights. Your king, in happy security, reigns in the hearts of his people; whilst our anointed Stanislaus, is baited and insulted by oppression from without, and ingratitude within. Do not envy me! I would rather live in obscurity all my days, than have the means which I have, of acquiring celebrity over the ruins of Poland. O! my friend, the wreath that crowns the head of conquest, is thick and bright; but that which binds the olive of peace, on the bleeding wounds of my country, will be the dearest to me.'

"Such sentiments as these, my dear madam, have opened new lights upon my poor mistaken faculties. I had not considered the subject so maturely as my friend; victory and glory were with me synonimous words: I had not learnt, till frequent conversations with the young and ardent Sobieski taught me, how to discriminate between ferocity and valour; between the patriot and the assassin; between the defender of his country, and the ravager of other states. In short, I see in Thaddeus Sobieski, all that my fancy hath ever pictured of the heroic character. Whilst I contemplate the sublimity of his nature, and the tenderness of his soul, I cannot help thinking, how few would believe, that all these amazing qualities could belong to one mind, and it remains unacquainted with the throes of ambition, and the taints of vanity."

Pembroke judged rightly of his friend; for if ever the real disinterested *amor patriæ** glowed in the breast of a man, it animated the heart of the young Sobieski. Pembroke laid down his pen, at the termination of the foregoing sentence in the letter to his mother, on the entrance of a servant, who presented him with a packet which had that moment arrived from Petersburgh. He took it, and laying his writing materials back into the desk, read the following epistle from his governor.

"*To Pembroke Somerset, Esq.*
"My dear sir,
"I have this day received your letter, enclosing one for Lady Somerset. You must pardon me, that I have detained it, and will continue to do

* Latin, 'love of one's country; patriotism'.

so, till I am favoured with your answer to this; for which I shall most anxiously wait.

"You know, Mr. Somerset, my reputation in the sciences; you know my depth in the languages; and besides, the Marquis of Inverary, with whom I travelled over the Continent, offered you sufficient credentials respecting my knowledge of the world, and the honourable manner in which I treat my pupils. Sir Robert Somerset, and your lady mother, were amply satisfied with the account, which his lordship gave of my character; but with all this, in one point every man is vulnerable. No scholar can forget those lines of the poet,

> Felices ter, & amplius,
>> Quos irrupta tenet capula; nec malis
> Divulsus quærimoniis,
>> Supremâ citius solvet amor die.*

It has been my misfortune that I have felt them.

"You are not ignorant, that I was known to the Branicki family, when I had the honour of conducting the Marquis through Russia. The Count's accomplished kinswoman, the amiable and learned widow of Baron Surowkoff,† even then took particular notice of me; and when I returned with you to Petersburgh, I did not find that my short absence had obliterated me from her memory.

"You are well acquainted with the dignity of that lady's opinions, on political subjects: She and I coincided in ardour for the cause of insulted Russia, and in hatred of that levelling power which pervades all Europe.‡ Many have been the long and interesting conversations we have held on the prosecution of those schemes, which her late husband had so principal a hand in laying, for the subversion of that miserable kingdom in which you now are.

"The Baroness, I need not observe, is as handsome as she is ingenuous; her understanding is as masculine, as her person is lovely; and I had been more, or less than man, if I had not understood that my figure and talents were agreeable to her. I cannot say that she has

---

* Horace, Ode 1.13. 'Thrice happy They, in pure Delights, / Whom Love with mutual Bonds unites, / Unbroken by Complaints or Strife, / Even to the latest Hours of Life.' *The Odes, Epodes, and Carmen Seculare of Horace*, trans. Philip Francis (London: A. Millar, 1743).

† Baroness Surowkoff is apparently a fictional figure, though her name approximates the Russian General Alexander Suvorov (or Suwarrow, as Porter has it below). Loftus's characterisation of her brings to mind contemporary descriptions of Catherine the Great.

‡ Loftus refers to the spirit of democratic change that spread across Europe in the 1790s, in the wake of the American and French Revolutions.

absolutely promised me her hand, but she has gone as far that way, as delicacy would permit. I am thus circumstantial, Mr. Somerset, to shew you that I never proceed without proof. She has repeatedly said in my presence, that she would never marry any man, unless he were not only well-looking, but of the profoundest erudition, united with an acquaintance with men and manners, which none could dispute. 'Besides,' added she, 'he must not differ with me one tittle in politics, for on that head I hold myself second to no man nor woman in Europe.' And then she has complimented me, by declaring, that I possessed the most judicious sentiments on government she had ever met with; that she should consider herself happy, on the first vacancy, to introduce me at court, where she was sure the Empress would at once discover the value of my talents; but she continued, 'In such a case, I will not allow, that even her majesty shall rival me in your esteem.' The modesty natural to my character, told me, that these praises must have some other source, than my comparatively unequal abilities; and I unequivocally found it, in the partiality with which her ladyship condescended to regard me.

"Was I to blame, Mr. Somerset? Would not any man of sensibility and honour have immediately comprehended such advances from a woman of her rank and reputation? I could not be mistaken; her looks and words needed no explanation which my judgment could not pronounce. Though I am aware that I do not possess that *lumen purpureum juventæ*,* which attracts very young uneducated women, yet I am not fifty; and from the Baroness's singular behaviour, I had every reason to expect handsomer treatment than she has been pleased to dispense to me since my return.

"But to proceed regularly; (I must beg your pardon for the warmth which has carried me to this digression) you know, sir, that from the hour in which I had the honour of taking leave of your noble family in England, I strove to impress upon your rather volatile mind, a just and accurate conception of the people amongst whom I was to conduct you. When I brought you into this extensive empire, I left no pains of mine unexerted, to heighten your respect, not only for its amiable sovereign, but for all regal powers. It is the property of genius to be zealous: I was so in favour of the pretensions of the great Catherine to that paltry country, to which she deigned to offer her protection.

---

* 'The glowing light of youth'. Edmund Burke popularised the phrase (a misquotation from Virgil's *Aeneid* (i. 590–1)) in his influential treatise, *A Philosophical Enquiry into the Origin of our Ideas of the Sublime and Beautiful* (London: R. and J. Dodsley, 1757).

To this zeal, and my unfortunate, though honourable devotion to the wishes of the Baroness, I am constrained to date my present dilemma.

"When Poland had the insolence to rebel against its illustrious mistress, you remember that every man of rank in Petersburgh was highly incensed. The Baroness Surowkoff declared herself frequently and with vehemence: she appealed to me; my veracity and my principles were called forth, and I confessed, that I thought every friend to the Zsarina* ought to take up arms against that ungrateful people. The Count Branicki was then appointed to command the Russian forces; and her ladyship, very unexpectedly on my part, answered me, by approving what I said; and saying, that of course I meant to follow her cousin into Poland; for that even she, as a woman, was so earnest in the cause, that she would accompany him to the frontiers, and there await the result.

"What could I do? How could I withstand the expectations of a lady of her quality, and one whom I believed loved me? However, for some time I did oppose my wish to oblige her; I urged my cloth, and how I should be able to account for such a line of conduct, to the father of my pupil? The Baroness ridiculed all these arguments, as mere excuses; and ended with saying, 'Do as you please, Mr. Loftus. I have been deceived in your character; the friend of the Baroness Surowkoff must be consistent: he must be as willing to fight for the cause he espouses as to speak for it; in this case, the sword must follow the oration, else we shall see Poland in the hands of a rabble.'

"This decided me. I offered my services to the Count, to attend him to the field. He, and the young lords, persuaded you to do the same; and as I could not think of leaving you, when your father had placed you under my charge, I was pleased to find that my approval confirmed your wish to turn soldier. I was then unacquainted, Mr. Somerset, (for you did not tell me of it, till we were far advanced into Poland;) with Sir Robert's and my lady's dislike of the army. This has been a prime source of my error; and had I known their repugnance to your taking up arms, I do believe that my duty would have triumphed even over my devotion to the Baroness: But I was born under a melancholy horoscope; nothing happens, as any one of my humblest wishes might warrant.

"At the first onset of the battle, I became so suddenly ill, that I was obliged to retire, or swoon upon the ground; and on this unfortunate event, which was completely unwilled on my part, (for no man can command the periods of sickness) the Baroness has founded a contempt which has disconcerted all my schemes. Besides, when I

---

* Catherine the Great; corrected to read 'Czarina' in the second edition.

attempted to remonstrate with her ladyship, on the promise, which, if not directly given, was implied, she laughed at me; and when I persisted, all at once, like the rest of her ungrateful undistinguishing sex, she burst into a thousand invectives, and forbade me her house.

"What am I now to do, Mr. Somerset? This inconsistent woman has betrayed me into conduct diametrically opposite to the commands of your family. Your father particularly desired, that I would not suffer you to go either into Hungary or Poland. In the last instance, I have permitted you to disobey him. And my Lady Somerset, who lost both her father and brother in different engagements, you tell me, hath declared, that she never would pardon the man who should put military ideas into your head.

"Therefore, sir, though you are my pupil, I throw myself on your generosity. If you persist in acquainting your family with the late transactions at Zielime, and your present residence in Poland, I shall finally be ruined. I shall not only forfeit the good opinion of your father and mother, but, through their means, lose all prospect of any establishment, in the rich living of Somerset, which Sir Robert was so gracious as to promise me, on the demise of the present incumbent. You know, Mr. Somerset, that I have a mother and six sisters in Wales, whose entire support depends on my success in life; if my promotion be stopped now, they must necessarily be involved in a distress that makes me shudder.

"I cannot add more, sir; I know your generosity; and I therefore rest upon it. I shall detain the letter, which you did me the honour to enclose for my Lady Somerset, till I receive your decision; and ever, whilst I live, shall I henceforth remain firm to my old and favourite maxim, which I have adopted from the glorious epistle of Horace to Numicius. Perhaps, you may not recollect the lines? They run thus.

>Nil admirari, prope res est una, Numici,
>Solaque, quæ possit facere & servare beatum.*

"I have the honour to be,
Dear sir,
Your most obedient servant,
ANDREW LOFTUS.

"*Petersburgh, September,* 1792.

"P.S. Just as I was sealing this packet, the English ambassador forwarded to me a short letter from your father, wherein he desires us to

---

* Horace, Epistle 6. 'To admire nothing, Numicius, is almost the only way to make and continue us happy.' *The Works of Horace*, trans. David Watson (London: Longman, 1792).

quit Russia immediately; and to make the best of our way to England, where you are wanted on a most urgent occasion. He explains himself no farther; only repeating his orders in express commands, that we set off instantly. I therefore wait your directions."

The whole of this epistle very much disconcerted Mr. Somerset. He had always guessed, that the Baroness Surowkoff was amusing herself with his vain and pedantic preceptor; but he had never entertained a suspicion that her ladyship would have carried her pleasantry to so cruel an excess. He saw clearly, that the fears of Mr. Loftus, with regard to the displeasure of his parents, were far from groundless; and therefore, as there was a probability from the age of Dr. Manners, who was upwards of eighty, and afflicted with the dropsy, that the rectory of Somerset would soon become vacant; he thought that he had better oblige his poor governor, and preserve the secret for a month or two, than give him up to the chance of Sir Robert's indignation, which, (he had reason to believe, from the resolution with which he carried through all his determinations,) would not much favour the side of lenity. On these grounds, Pembroke resolved to write to Mr. Loftus, and ease the anxiety of his heart: although he ridiculed his vanity, he could not help feeling some compassion for the affectionate solicitude of a son and a brother; and, as this last plea had won him; half angry, half grieved, and half laughing, he scribbled these hasty lines, which he immediately dispatched by the courier.

"To the Reverend Andrew Loftus, Petersburgh.
"Upon my soul, sir, it is too bad! I am to burn my letters, and go home! what can be the matter? what whimsical fit has seized my father, that I am recalled at a moment's notice? Faith, I am so mad at it; and at his not chusing to assign any reason, but that he '*desires me to make the best of my way directly to England,*' that I do not know how I may be tempted to act.

"Another thing! you beg that I will not say a word of my having been in Poland; and for that purpose, you have withheld the letter which I sent to you to forward to my mother! One cause of my being here, you say, was your '*ardour in the cause of insulted Russia; and your hatred of that levelling power which pervades all Europe.*'

"Well I grant it. I understood from you and Branicki, that you were leading me to march against a set of violent, discontented men of rank, who in proportion as they were inflated with personal pride and insolence, despised their own order; and under the name of freedom, were introducing anarchy throughout a country, which Catherine would graciously have protected. All this I find is false. But you both, may have been misled; the Count, by interest; and you, by misrepresentation; therefore I do not perceive why you should be in such a terror. The wisest man in the world may see through bad lights; and, why should you think, my father would never pardon your having been so unlucky?

"Yet, to satisfy your dreads of such tidings ruining you with Sir Robert, I will not be the first to tell him of our quixoting. Only remember, my good sir, though to oblige you, I withhold all my letters to my mother, and when I arrive in England, shall lock up my lips from mentioning Poland; yet positively, I will not be mute one day longer than that in which my father presents you with the living of Somerset: then, you will be independent of his displeasure; and I may and will, declare my everlasting gratitude to this illustrious family.

"Heigho! I am half crazy when I think of leaving them. I must tear myself from this heaven on earth! The days have passed with me as minutes. Alas, Alas! that I quit this mansion of comfort and affection, to wander with you, in some rumbling old coach, *'over brake and through briar!'** Well, patience, patience! Another such a drubbing given to my quondum friends the Russians, and with *'victory perched like an eagle on their laurelled brows,'*† I may have some chance of wooing the Sobieski's to the banks of the Thames. At present, I have not sufficient patience to keep me in good humour.

"Meet me this day week at Dantzic:‡ I shall there embark for England. You had better not bring any of the servants with you; they might blab; discharge them at Petersburgh, and hire others for yourself and me when you arrive at the sea-port.

"I have the honour to remain,

Dear sir,

"Your most obedient servant,

"PEMBROKE SOMERSET."

"*Villanow, September* 1792."

When Somerset joined his friends at supper, and imparted to them the commands of his father, an immediate change was produced in the spirits of the party. During the lamentations of the ladies and the murmurs of the young men, the Countess tried to dispel the effects of the information, by addressing Pembroke with a smile, and saying,

---

* This phrase is reminiscent of Puck in *A Midsummer Night's Dream*: 'I'll follow you, I'll lead you about a round, / Through bog, through bush, through brake, through brier' (III, i, 106–7).
† Unidentified.
‡ Gdańsk, Poland's principal seaport on the Baltic coast.

"But we shall hope that you have seen enough at Villanow, to tempt you back again at no very distant period? Tell Lady Somerset, that you have left a second mother in Poland, who will long to receive another visit from her adopted son."

"Yes, my dear madam," returned he, "and I shall hope, before a very distant period, to see those two kind mothers, united as intimately by friendship, as they now are in my heart."

Thaddeus listened to all this with a saddened countenance. He had not been accustomed to much disappointment, and his feelings when disturbed, hardly knew how to proportion the uneasiness to the privation. Hope, and all the hilarities of youth flourished in his soul; his features continually glowed with animation, while the gay beaming of his eyes, ever answered to the smile on his lips. Hence, the slightest veering on his mind was perceptible to the Countess, who turning round, saw him leaning back in his chair, with his arms folded, and his colour heightened, whilst Pembroke, with greater force and vociferation, was running through various invectives against the hastiness of his recall.

"Come, come, Thaddeus!" cried she to him, and parting the thick auburn curls on his forehead, "let us think no more of this separation until it arrives. You know that anticipation of evil is the death of happiness; and it will be a kind of suicide, should we destroy the hours which we may yet enjoy together, in vain complainings that they are so soon to terminate."

A little more exhortation from the Countess, and a maternal kiss, which she imprinted on his cheek, restored him to cheerfulness; and the evening past away, pleasanter than it had portended.

Much as the Palatine esteemed Pembroke Somerset, his mind was too deeply absorbed in the losses of his country, to attend to less considerable cares. He beheld the republic on the verge of destruction, with firmness and indignation, awaiting the earthquake which was to ingulph it in the neighbouring nations. He saw the storm approaching; but he determined, whilst there remained even one spot of vantage ground above the general wreck, that Poland should yet have a name and a defender. These thoughts possessed him, these plans engaged him; and he had not leisure to regret pleasure, when he was struggling for existence.

The Empress continued to pour her armies into the heart of the kingdom. The king of Prussia boldly flying from his treaties, refused his succour; and the emperor of Germany, following the example of so great a prince, did not blush to shew that his word was equally contemptible.*

* Frederick William II (1774–97) ruled Prussia from 1786 until his death; Francis II

Whilst the Russians were marking their advances with sword and rapine, Frederick openly avowed his designs to be in concert with Petersburgh; and Poland, accordingly, was attacked on every quarter. Continual dispatches arrived, that the villages were daily laid waste; that neither age nor sex, nor situation, prevented their unfortunate inhabitants from becoming the victims of cruelty; and that all the frontier provinces were in flames.

The Diet was called, and the debates agitated with all the anxiety of men, who were met to decide on their dearest interests. The feelings of the benevolent Stanislaus, bled at the dreadful picture of his people's sufferings; and hardly able to restrain his tears, he answered the animated exordiums of Sobieski for resistance to the last, with an appeal immediately to his heart.

"What is it that you urge me to do, my lord?" said he. "Was it not, to secure the happiness of my subjects, that I laboured? and finding that impracticable, what advantage would it be to them, should I pertinaciously oppose their small numbers against the accumulated hordes of the north? What is my kingdom, but the comfort of my people? What will it avail me, to see them fall around me, man by man, and the few that remain hanging in speechless sorrow over their graves? Such a sight would break my heart. Poland without its people, would be a desart; and I, rather a hermit than a king."

In vain the Palatine combated this argument, and the quiet that a peace would now afford, by declaring it could only be temporary. In vain he told his majesty, that he would purchase safety for the present race, at the vast expense, of not only the liberty of posterity, but of its probity and happiness.

"However you disguise slavery," cried he, "it is slavery still. Its chains, though wreathed with roses, not only fasten on the body but rivet on the mind. They bend it from the proudest virtue, to a debasement beneath calculation. They disgrace honour; they trample upon justice. They transform the legions of Rome into a band of singers. They prostrate the sons of Athens and of Sparta at the feet of cowards. They make man abjure his birthright, bind himself to another's will, and give that into a tyrant's hands, which he received as a deposit from heaven, his reason, his conscience, and his soul. Think on this, and then, if you can, subjugate Poland to her enemies."

Stanislaus, weakened by years, and impelled by disappointment,

(1786–1835) was the last Holy Roman Emperor, ruling from July 1792 to August 1806. Both rulers refused to honour previous treaties with Poland that required Prussia and Austria to come to Poland's defence.

now only wished to save his subjects from immediate outrage. He returned no answer, but with streaming eyes, bent over the table, and annulled the glorious constitution of 1791; then with emotions hardly short of agony, he signed the order presented by the Russian officer, which directed Prince Poniatowski to deliver the army under his command into the hands of General Branicki.*

As the king put his signature to these papers, Sobieski, who had so strenuously withstood each decision, started from his chair, bowed to his sovereign, and in silence left the apartment. Prince Sapieha and several other noblemen followed him.

These pacific measures did not meet with better treatment from without. When they were noised abroad, an alarming commotion arose amongst the inhabitants of Warsaw; and nearly four thousand men, of the first families in the republic, assembled themselves in the park of Villanow, where they immediately resolved, that if necessary, they alone would resist the power of their combined ravagers to the utmost. The Prince Sapieha, Kosciuszko, and Sobieski, were the first who took the oath of *eternal fidelity to Poland*; and they administered it to Thaddeus, who kneeling down, called on Heaven to hear him, as he swore, to assert the freedom of his country to the last gasp of its existence.

In the midst of these momentous affairs, Pembroke Somerset bade adieu to his friends; and set sail with his governor from Dantzic, for England.

* Stanisław capitulated to the demands of Russia and the Targowica confederates on 23 July 1792, thus bringing the Polish–Russian War of 1792 to an end. See Jones, *History*, pp. 417–18.

CHAP. V.

Those winter months, which before this year, had been at Villanow the season for cheerfulness and festivity, now rolled away in the sad pomp of national debates and military assemblies.

Prussia usurped the best part of Pomerelia, and garrisoned it with troops; Catherine declared her dominion over the vast tract of land that lies between the Dwina and Borystenes: and Frederick-William marked down another sweep of Poland, to follow the fate of Dantzic and Thorn.*

Calamities, and insults, and robberies, were heaped, day after day, on the defenceless Poles. The deputies of the provinces were put into prison; and the Russian ambassador† had the insolence even to interrupt provisions intended for the King's table, and appropriate them to his own. Sobieski remonstrated with *his Excellency* on this outrage, who incensed at the reproof, and irritated at the sway which the Palatine still held at court, ordered that his extensive estates in Lithuania and Podolia should be sequestered, and divided between four of the Russian Generals.

In vain the Villanow confederation endeavoured to remonstrate with the Empress. Her ambassador, not only refused to forward the dispatches, but threatened the nobles, that, "if they did not comply with every one of his demands, he would lay all the estates, possessions, and habitations, of the members of the Diet under an immediate military execution. Nay, punishment should not stop there, for should the king continue (as he now appeared so much inclined) to join the Sobieski party, the royal domains should not only be treated with the same rigour, but some harsher means, were already devised to bring them and their proud sovereign into subjection."

These menaces were of a nature too degrading to have any other effect on the Poles, than that of giving them a fresh spur to be resolute. With the same firmness, they repulsed similar fulminations from the Prussian ambassador;‡ and with a coolness, that

---

* These developments describe the second partition of Poland by Russia and Prussia in 1793.
† Count Jacob Sievers (1731–1808), Russian ambassador to Poland from 1792 to 1794.
‡ Ludwig Heinrich von Buchholtz (1740–1811), Prussian ambassador to Poland from 1780 to 1789 and again from 1792 to 1794.

was only equalled by their intrepidity, they prepared to resume their arms.

The insolent Russian, finding his threats unheeded, next morning surrounded the building where the confederation sat, with two battalions of grenadiers and four pieces of cannon: the disposition made, he issued orders, that no Pole should be permitted to go out on pain of instant death. General Rautenfeld, with the officers of the division, were set over the person of the king, who was present; they declared, that they would not stir, till his majesty, and the Diet, had given an unanimous consent to the full length of the Empress's commands.*

The Diet set forth the unlawfulness of signing any treaty, when they were thus withheld from the freedom of will and debate, by the presence of an intimidating force. They urged, that it was not legal to enter into deliberation, when any violent act had recently been exerted against an individual of their body; and how could they do it now, when they were deprived of five of their principal members, whom the ambassador well knew he had ordered to be arrested in their way to the senate? Sobieski and four of his friends, as the members most inimical to the wishes of Russia, were these five. In vain their liberation was required: Rautenfeld, enraged by the pertinacity of this opposition, repeated the former threatenings, with the addition of more, and declared that they should certainly take place, if the Diet did not directly and unconditionally, sign the pretensions both of his court, and that of Prussia.

After a hard contention of many hours, the members at last agreed amongst themselves, to make a solemn public protest against the present tyrannous measures of the Russian Ambassador; and, seeing that any attempt to inspire him even with decency was useless, they determined to cease all debate, and keep a profound silence, when the Marshal should propose the project in demand.

This sorrowful silence was commenced in resentment, and retained through despair; this sorrowful silence was called, by their usurpers, a consent: this sorrowful silence is held up to the world, and to posterity, as a free cession by the Poles, of all those rights which they had received from nature, and defended with their blood.

The morning after this dreadful day, the Senate met at one of the

---

* Johann von Rautenfeld (1741–1805), a Major General in the Army of the Russian Empire. The following pages describe the Grodno Diet (or Grodno Seym), the final assembly of the Polish–Lithuanian Commonwealth's parliament, in which the Diet, under duress, ratified the second partition of Poland in November 1793. Porter's account shares many details with Jones's *History* (especially pp. 452–8), though it is likely that she consulted other works as well.

private palaces, and, indignant and broken-hearted, delivered the following declaration to the people:

"The Diet of Poland, hemmed in by foreign troops, and menaced with an invasion from the Prussian army, which is to be attended with universal devastation and ruin; finally, insulted by a thousand outrages, have been forced to witness the signing of a treaty with Prussia.

"They did endeavour to have added to the treaty some conditions, to which they supposed the lamentable state of this country, would have extorted an acquiescence even from the heart of power: but the Diet was deceived; they found, that power was unaccompanied by humanity; and that Prussia, having thrown his victim to the ground, would not refrain from enjoying the miserable satisfaction of trampling upon her neck.

"The Diet confides in the justice of Poland; confides in her belief, that they would not abandon the citadel which she has reposed in their keeping: her preservation is dearer to them than their lives; but fate seems to be on the side of their destroyer. Fresh insults have been heaped upon their heads, and new hardships have been imposed upon them. To prevent all deliberations on this debasing treaty, they are not only surrounded by foreign troops, and dared with hostile messages, but they have been violated by the arrest of their prime members, whilst those who are still suffered to possess a personal freedom, have the heaviest shackles laid on their minds.

"Therefore, I, the King of Poland, enervated by age, and sinking under the accumulated weight of so many afflictions; and also, we, the members of the Diet, declare, that being unable, even by the sacrifice of our existence, to relieve our country from the yoke of its oppressors, we consign it to posterity.

"In another age, means may be found to rescue it from chains and misery; but such means are not put in our power: other countries neglect us. Whilst they reprobate the violations which a neighbouring nation is alleged to have committed against rational liberty, they behold not only with apathy, but with approbation, the ravages which are now desolating Poland. Posterity must avenge it; we have done. We accede, for the reasons above mentioned, to the treaty laid before us; though we declare, that it is contrary to our wishes, to our sentiments, and to our rights."

Thus, in November, 1793, compressed to one fourth of her dimensions, within the lines of demarcation drawn by her enemies, Poland was stripped of her rank in Europe: the lands of her nobles given to strangers, and her citizens left to starve for want of bread. Ill-fated nation! Posterity will weep over thy wrongs; whilst the burning blush of shame, that their fathers witnessed such wrongs unmoved, shall cause the bitter tears to blister as they fall.

During these transactions, the Countess Sobieski continued in solitude at Villanow, awaiting with awful anxiety the termination of those portentous events, which so deeply involved her own comforts with those of her country. Her father was in prison; her son at a distance with the army. Sick at heart, she saw the opening of that spring which might be the commencement only of a new season of injuries: and her fears were prophetic.

Those soldiers who had dared to retain their arms in their hands, were again ordered by the Russian Ambassador to lay them down. Some few, thinking denial vain, obeyed; but those of bolder spirits followed Thaddeus Sobieski into South Prussia, whence he had directed his steps on the arrest of his grandfather, and had gathered, and kept together, a handful of brave men still faithful to their liberties.* Indeed his name alone collected numbers around him in every district through which he marched. Persecution from their adversary, as well as admiration of Thaddeus, gave a resistless power to his appearance, look, and voice; all which, had such an effect on this afflicted people, that they crowded to his standard by hundreds: whilst their lords, having caught a similar fire from the blazing ardour of the young Count, committed themselves, without reserve to his sole judgment and command. The Empress, hearing of this, ordered Stanislaus to command him directly to disband his troops: but the King refusing, she augmented the strength of her own forces; and, enraged at such stubborn resistance, renewed the war with redoubled horrors.

The Palatine remained in confinement, hopeless of obtaining release without the aid of stratagem. The emissaries of Catherine were too well aware of their interest, to give freedom to so active an opponent: however, this patriotic victim to vindictive tyranny, received every consolation which a brave man can feel, (his own arms being tied from serving his country,) in the information which he hourly learnt of his jailors, "that his grandson was continuing to carry himself with such insolent opposition in the south, that it would be well if the Empress, at the termination of matters, allowed him to escape with his life." Every reproach which was levelled at the Palatine, he found was bought by some new conquest of Thaddeus; and instead of permitting their premeditated malice to take effect by intimidating his age or alarming

---

* Thaddeus's fictional activities mirror the historical activities of Kościuszko, who, after the second partition, spent time in Leipzig planning the uprising that would begin in March 1794.

his affection, he told the Russian officer, (whose daily office it was to attend and to torment him,) that if his grandson were to lose his head for fidelity to Poland, he would almost as readily follow him to the scaffold, as witness him entering the streets of Warsaw with all Russia at his chariot wheels; "the only difference in my emotions would be," continued Sobieski, "that as the first cannot happen till all virtue be dead in this land, I should feel his last gasp, as the last sigh of that virtue which found a triumph even under the axe. For the second, it would be joy unutterable to behold the victory of justice over rapine and murder! But, either way, he is still the same; ready to die, or ready to live, for his country; and equally worthy of the eternal halo with which posterity will encircle his name."

Indeed the accounts which arrived from this young soldier, who had lately formed a junction with General Kosciuszko, were in the highest degree formidable to the coalesced powers. They had gained a considerable advantage over the Prussians in several places, and were advancing towards Inowlotz, when a large and fresh body of the enemy unexpectedly appeared in their rear. The troops who were on the opposite bank of the river, (whom the Poles were driving before them) on sight of this reinforcement, suddenly rallied; and, as a mean of retarding the approach of the pursuers, and ensuring their probable defeat from the army in view, they broke down the wooden bridge which might have brought them over. The Poles were for some time at a stand. Kosciuszko proposed swimming the river; but, owing to the recent heavy rains, it was so swoln and rapid, that the young men to whom he mentioned it, terrified by the blackness and dashing of the water, drew back. The General perceiving their panic, called Thaddeus to him, and both together they plunged into the stream. The rest, now ashamed of their hesitation, tried who could first follow this example; and after hard buffeting with the waves, the whole army gained the opposite shore. The Prussians in the rear, incapable of the like intrepidity, halted; and those in the van, intimidated at the dauntless courage of their adversaries, concealed themselves amidst the thickets of an adjoining valley.*

The Poles proceeded towards Cracow, carrying redress and protection to the provinces through which they marched. But they had barely rested two days in that city, before dispatches were received, that Warsaw was lying at the mercy of General Branicki.† No time

---

* See Jones, *History*, pp. 469–70 for a shorter version of this episode, which he dates to February 1794.
† In fact, Iosif Igelström (1737–1823) served as both ambassador (replacing Jacob Sievers) and commander-in-chief of the Russian forces in Poland.

could be lost; officers and men had set their lives on the cause; and they re-commenced their toils, with a perseverance which brought them before the capital, on the sixteenth of April.*

Things were even in a worse state than Kosciuszko had expected. The Russian Ambassador, with his usual arrogance had demanded the surrender of the national arsenal, subscribing his orders with a threat, that whichever of the nobles should presume to dispute his authority, should be arrested and put to death; and, as to the people, if they dared to murmur, he would immediately command General Branicki to lay the city in ashes. None doubted the sincerity of this barbarian; for there were many in the senate who recollected, that when the nation was at war with them, two-and-thirty years ago, nine Polish Lords were sent into Warsaw with both hands lopped off; and, that for this mutilation, they had to accuse the Russian General, who had acted the double part of judge and executioner. When the Poles remembered this instance of cruelty, which the court of Petersburgh had heard of without condemning it, they could not anticipate any humanity for themselves.†

The King remonstrated against these oppressions; and to "*punish his presumption,*" this proper representative of the Imperial Catherine, commanded that his Majesty's garrison and guards should be instantly broken and dispersed. At the first attempt to execute this mandate, the people flew in crowds to the palace, and on their knees implored Stanislaus for permission to avenge the insult offered to his troops. His Majesty looked at them with pity, gratitude, and anguish; at last, in a voice of agony, that was wrung from his tortured heart, he answered, "Go, and defend your honour!"

The army of Kosciuszko marched into the town time enough to join the armed citizens: and that day, after a dreadful conflict, in which the streets were strewed with the killed, Warsaw was rescued from the immediate grasp of Russia. During the fight, the King who was alone in one of the rooms of his palace, sunk almost fainting on the floor; he heard the mingling clash of arms, the roar of musquetry, and the cries, and groans of the combatants; ruin seemed no longer to hover over his kingdom, but to have pounced at once upon her prey. At every renewed shout, which followed each pause in the firing, he expected

---

* Though Porter does not mention it, it was on 24 March 1794 in the Kraków town square that Kościuszko declared the start of the uprising that today bears his name.
† The second half of this paragraph (from 'None doubted ...') was removed from later editions. Since this gruesome event does not seem to appear in any histories of Poland, Porter perhaps discovered that her source was incorrect.

the next moment to see his palace gates burst open, and himself, then indeed, made a willing sacrifice to the fury of his enemies.

Whilst he was yet upon his knees, petitioning the god of battles, for a little longer respite from the last calamity which was doomed to overwhelm devoted Poland, Thaddeus Sobieski, panting with heat and toil, flew into the room, and, before he could speak a word, was clasped in the arms of the agitated Stanislaus.

"Are my people safe?" asked the King.

"Yes, my liege;" returned Thaddeus, "and victorious. The foreign guards are beaten from the palace; your own have resumed their station at the gates."

At this assurance, tears of joy ran over the venerable cheeks of his Majesty; and again embracing his young deliverer, he said, "I thank Heaven, that my unhappy country is not bereft of all hope. Whilst Kosciuszko and a Sobieski live, she will not quite despair."

CHAP. VI.

Thaddeus was not less eager to release his grandfather, than he had been to relieve the anxiety of his sovereign. He hastened at the head of a few troops, to the place which was the prison of Sobieski; and gave him liberty, amidst the acclamations of his soldiers, who united in general demonstrations of joy at the sight of their veteran commander.

The universal gladness at these prosperous events, did not last many days: it was speedily terminated, by the information that Cracow had surrendered to a Prussian force under General Van Elsner;[*] that the King of Prussia was advancing towards the capital; and that the Russians, more implacable in consequence of the late treatment which their garrison had received at Warsaw, were pouring into the country like a deluge.

At this news the consternation became dreadful. The Polenese[†] army, worn with fatigue and long services, were without cloathing, ammunition, or in any way, excepting courage, fitted for the field.

The treasury was exhausted, and no means of raising a supply seemed practicable. The provinces were laid waste, and the city had been already drained of its last ducat. In this exigency, hopeless of devising any expedient for even a temporary succour, a council met in his Majesty's private cabinet, to consult about obtaining resources. The debate was as desponding as their situation, till Thaddeus Sobieski, who had hitherto been a silent observer, rose from his seat; and whilst the blushes of awe and eagerness crimsoned his cheek, he advanced towards Stanislaus, and taking from his neck and other parts of his dress, those magnificent jewels which it was customary always to wear in the presence of the king, he knelt down, and laying them at the feet of his Majesty, said, in a suppressed voice, "These are trifles; but such as they are, and all of the like kind which I possess, I beseech your Majesty to appropriate to the public service."

"Noble young man!" cried the king, lifting him from the ground; "you have indeed taught me a lesson: I accept these jewels with gratitude. Here," said he, turning to the treasurer, "put them into the national fund; and let them be followed by my own, with my plate,

* Karl Friedrich von Elsner (1739–1808) took Kraków on 15 June 1794.
† A now obsolete term for Polish (more often written 'Polonese').

which I desire may be instantly sent to the mint. One half of it the army shall have; the other, we must expend in giving some little support to the surviving families of those who have fallen in our defence."

The Palatine, who thanked his grandson for his generous warmth, readily united with him, in the surrender of all their personal property, for the benefit of their country. According to their example, the treasury was filled with gratuities from the nobles; and the army, newly equipped, marched out in high spirits.

The Countess had a third time to bid adieu to a son, who was become as much the idol of her reason, as before he had been of her love; in proportion as glory surrounded him, and danger courted his steps, the strings of affection drew him closer to her soul: the *"aspiring blood"** of the Sobieskis, which beat in her veins, could not dull the feeling that she was a parent; that the spring of her existence now flowed from that fountain, which had drawn its source from her. Her anxious, and waiting heart, paid dearly in tears and sleepless nights, for the honour with which she was saluted at every turning, as the mother of Thaddeus: that Thaddeus, who was not more the soul of council, and the sinew of war, than he was to her, the gentlest, the dearest, the most amiable of sons. It matters little to the undistinguishing bolt of carnage, whether it strike common breasts, or those rare hearts, whose course is usually as brief as it is dazzling; this leaden messenger of death banquets as sullenly on the bosom of a hero, as if it had lit upon more vulgar prey: all is levelled to the chance of war, which comes like a whirlwind of the desart, scattering man and beast in one wide ruin.

Such thoughts as these, possessed the melancholy reveries of the Countess Sobieski, from the hour in which she saw Thaddeus and his grandfather depart for Cracow, until she heard it was retaken, and the enemy defeated in many battles.

Warsaw was again bombarded; and again Kosciuszko, with the Palatine and Thaddeus, preserved it from destruction. In short, wherever they moved, this dauntless little army carried terror to their adversaries, and diffused hope amongst the homes and hearts of their countrymen.

They next turned their course to the relief of Lithuania; but whilst they were on their route thither, they received intelligence that a detachment from their body having been beaten by the Russians under Suwarrow,[†] that General, elated with his success, was hastening forward to attack the capital.

---

* *Henry VI, Part 3*, V, vi, 61.
† Alexander Suvorov (c. 1729–1800), Russian military leader.

Kosciuszko resolved to prevent him; and as a mean, he prepared to give immediate battle to Fersen,* another commander, who was on his march to form a junction with the victorious Russian. To this effect, Kosciuszko divided his forces; half of them, under the command of Prince Poniatowski, were to pursue Suwarrow, and keep a watchful eye over his motions; whilst he, with the remainder, to the amount of six thousand men, accompanied by the two Sobieskis, should proceed towards Brzesc.†

It was the tenth of October. The weather being fine, a cloudless sun diffused life and brilliancy through the pure air of a keen morning. The vast green plain before them, glittered with the troops of General Fersen, who had already arranged them in order of battle.

The word was given. Thaddeus, as he drew his sabre from its scabbard, raised his eyes, to implore the justice of Heaven on that day's events. The attack was made. The Poles kept their station on the heights. Twice the Russians rushed on them like wolves, and twice they repulsed them by their steadiness. Conquest declared for Poland. Thaddeus was seen in every part of the field. But reinforcements poured in to the support of Fersen, and war raged in new horrors. Still the courage of the Poles was unabated. Sobieski, fighting at the head of the infantry, would not recede one foot; and Kosciuszko, exhorting his men to be resolute, appeared in the hottest places of the battle.

At one of these portentous moments Thaddeus saw the General struggling with his charger, which had been shot under him: he immediately galloped to his assistance, and, giving him another, remained and fought by his side, till he beheld two more horses share the same fate; and, on the next charge, Kosciuszko himself drop back on his saddle. Thaddeus caught him in his arms, and finding that a Cossac had stabbed him in the back, he unconsciously uttered a groan of dismay. The surrounding soldiers took the alarm, and, "Kosciuszko, our General is killed!" was echoed from rank to rank with such piercing shrieks, that the wounded hero opened his eyes, and was preparing to speak to his young friend, when two Russian chasseurs, in the same moment made a cut at them both. The sabre struck the exposed head of Kosciuszko, who fell almost lifeless to the ground; and Thaddeus received a gash in his shoulder, which knocked him off his horse.

The conflict thickened over the fallen General: the consternation

---

* Ivan Fersen (d. 1801), Infantry General in the Russian army. 'Ferfen' appeared in the first edition and remained uncorrected in Porter's lifetime, but it is corrected here.
† Brzesc or Brest, today a city in Belarus on the border with Poland. Though the Russians defeated a Polish army at Brest on 19 September 1794, the events described in the following paragraphs actually refer to the 10 October 1794 Battle of Maciejowice.

now becoming universal, for groans of despair seemed to issue from the whole army, Thaddeus with difficulty extricated himself from the bodies of the slain; and fighting his way through the throng of the enemy which pressed around him, he joined his terror-stricken comrades, who, in the wildest confusion, were dispersing under a heavy fire, to the right and left, and flying like frighted deer. In vain he called to them, in vain he urged them to avenge Kosciuszko, the panic was complete, and they fled.

Almost alone in the rear of his soldiers, he opposed with his single and desperate arm, party after party of the enemy, till a narrow stream of the Muchavez* stopped his retreat. The waters were crimsoned with blood. He plunged in, and, beating the blushing wave with his left arm, in a few seconds gained the opposite bank; where, fainting from fatigue and loss of blood, he sunk, almost deprived of sense, amidst a heap of the killed.

When the pursuing squadrons had galloped by him, he again summoned strength to look around. He raised himself from the ground, and by the help of his sword, on which he leaned, supported his steps a few paces farther: but, good God! What was the shock he received, when the bleeding and lifeless body of his grandfather lay before him? He stood, for a few moments, motionless, and without sensation; then, kneeling down by his side, whilst his heart felt as if it were palsied with death, he searched for the wounds of the Palatine. They were numerous and deep. He would have torn away the handkerchief with which he had staunched his own blood, to have applied it to that of his grandfather, but by so doing he must have disabled himself from giving him further assistance; he took his sash and neck-cloth, and when they were insufficient, he rent the linen from his breast; then hastening to the river, brought a little water in his cap, and threw some of its stained drops on the pale features of Sobieski.

The venerable hero opened his eyes; in a minute afterwards he recognised that it was his grandson who knelt by him. The Palatine pressed his hand, which was cold as ice: the marbled lips of Thaddeus could not move.

"My son," said the veteran in a low voice, "Heaven hath led you here, to receive the last sigh of your grandfather." Thaddeus trembled; the Palatine continued, "Carry my blessing to your mother; and bid her seek comfort in the consolations of her God. May that God preserve you; ever remember, that you are his servant; be obedient to him: and as I have been, be faithful to your country."

* The Mukhavetz river feeds into the Bug river at Brest.

"May God so bless me!" cried Thaddeus, lifting his eyes to Heaven.

"And ever remember," said the Palatine, raising his head which had dropped on the bosom of his grandson, "that you are a Sobieski! It is my dying command, that you never take any other name."

"I promise."

Thaddeus could say no more, for the countenance of his grandfather became altered; his eyes closed. Thaddeus caught him to his breast. No heart beat against his; all was still, and cold. The body dropped from his arms, and he sunk senseless by its side.

When sensation returned to him, he looked up. The sky was shrouded in clouds, which a driving wind was blowing from the orb of the moon, as a few of her white rays, here and there, gleamed on the weapons of the slaughtered soldiers.

The scattered senses of Thaddeus slowly recollected themselves. He was now lying, the only living creature, amidst thousands of the dead, who, the preceding night, had been like himself, alive to all the consciousness of existence. His right hand rested on the chilled face of his grandfather; it was wet with dew; he shuddered; and taking his own cloak from his shoulders, laid it over the body. He would have said, as he did it, "So, my father, I would have sheltered thy life, with the sacrifice of my own;" but the words choaked in his throat; and he sat watching by the corse, till the day dawned, and the Poles returned to bury their slain.

The wretched Thaddeus was discovered by a party of his own hussars, seated on a little mound of earth, with the cold hand of Sobieski grasped in his. At this sight, the soldiers uttered a cry of horror. Thaddeus rose up; "my friends," said he, "I thank God that you are come! Assist me to bear my dear grandfather to the camp."

Astonished at his composure, but distressed at the deathful hue of his countenance, they obeyed him in mournful silence, and laid the remains of the Palatine upon a bier, which they formed with their sheathed sabres; then gently raising it, they retrod their steps to the camp; having left a detachment to accomplish the duty for which they had quitted it. Thaddeus, hardly able to support his weakened frame, mounted a horse, and followed the melancholy procession.

General Wawrzecki,* on whom the command had devolved, seeing the party returning so soon, and in such an order, sent an aid-de-camp to enquire the reason. He came back, with dejection in his face; and informed the commander, that the brave Palatine of Masovia,

---

* Tomasz Wawrzecki (1753–1816), General of the Polish army and second-in-command to Kościuszko during the Uprising.

whom they supposed had been taken prisoner with his grandson and Kosciuszko, had been killed, and was approaching the lines on the arms of his soldiers. Wawrzecki, though glad to hear that Thaddeus was alive and at liberty, turned round to conceal his tears; then calling out a guard, he marched at their head, to meet the corpse of his illustrious friend.

The bier was carried into the General's tent. An aid-de-camp, with some gentlemen of the faculty, were ordered to attend Thaddeus to his quarters; but the young Count, though scarcely able to stand, appeared to linger; and holding fast by the arm of an officer, he looked stedfastly on the body. Wawrzecki understood his hesitation. He pressed his hand; "Fear not, my dear Sir," said he, "every honour shall be paid to the remains of your noble grandfather." Thaddeus bowed his head, and was supported out of the tent to his own.

His wounds, of which he had received several, were not deep; and might have been of little consequence, had not his thoughts continually hovered about his mother, and painted her afflictions, when she should be informed of the lamentable events of the last day's battle. These reflections, awake, or in a slumber (for he never slept), possessed his mind; and even whilst his wounds were healing, produced such an irritation in his blood, as hourly threatened a fever.

Things were in this situation, when the surgeon, with a hesitating countenance, put a letter from the Countess into his hand. He opened it, and read with breathless anxiety, these lines:

"To Thaddeus, Count Sobieski.

"Console yourself, my most precious son, console yourself for my sake. I have seen Colonel Lomza, and I have heard all the horrors which took place on the tenth of this month. I have heard them, and I am yet alive; I am resigned: but he tells me, that you are wounded. Oh! do not let me be also bereft of my son! Remember, that you were my dear sainted father's darling; remember, that as his representative, you are to be my consolation: in pity to me, if not to our suffering country, preserve yourself, to be at least the last comfort that Heaven will spare to me. I find, that all is lost to Poland, as well as to myself; that when my glorious father fell, and his friend with him, the republic became extinct. The Russian army is now on its march towards Masovia; and I am too weak to come to you. Let me see you soon, very soon, my beloved son; I beseech you, come to me! You will find me more feeble of body, than of mind; for there is a holy comforter, that descends on the bruised heart, which none other than the unhappy have conceived or felt. Farewell, my dear, dear Thaddeus! Let the memory, that you have a mother, check your too ardent courage. God for ever guard you. Live for your mother, who has no stronger words to express her affection for you, than that she is thy mother, thy

"THERESE SOBIESKI.

"*Villanow, October,* 1794."

This letter was indeed a balm to the soul of Thaddeus. That his adored mother had received the cruel event with such resignation, was the best medicine which could now be applied to his wounds, both of mind and body; and when he was told, that on the succeeding morning, the body of his grandfather should be removed to the convent near Biala, he declared his resolution to attend it to the grave.

In vain his surgeons and General Wawrzecki remonstrated against the danger of this project; for once, the gentle, and yielding spirit of Thaddeus, seemed inexorable. He had fixed his determination, and it was not to be shaken.

Next day, being the seventh from that in which the fatal battle had been decided, Thaddeus, at the first beat of the drum, rose from his bed, and, almost unassisted, put on his cloaths. His uniform being black, he needed no other index than his pale and mournful countenance, to announce that he was chief mourner.

The procession began to form, and he walked from his tent. It was a fine morning; Thaddeus looked up, as if to upbraid the sun for shining so brightly. Lengthened and repeated rounds of cannon rolled along the air. The solemn march of the dead, was moaning from the muffled drum, interrupted at measured pauses, by the shrill tremor of the fife. The troops, preceded by their General, moved forward with a decent and melancholy step. The Bishop of Warsaw followed, bearing the sacred volume in his hands: and next, borne upon the crossed pikes of his soldiers, and supported by twelve of his most veteran companions, appeared the body of the brave Sobieski. A velvet pall covered it, on which were laid those arms, with which for fifty years, he had asserted the liberties of his country. At this sight, the sobs of the men became audible. Thaddeus followed, with a slow but firm step, his eyes bent to the ground, and his arms wrapped in his cloak: it was the same which had shaded his beloved grandfather from the dews of that dreadful night. Another train of solemn music succeeded; and then the squadrons, which the deceased had commanded, dismounted, and leading their horses, closed the procession.

On the verge of the plain that borders Biala, and within a few paces of the convent gate of St. Francis, the bier stopped. The monks saluted its appearance with a requiem, which they continued to chant till the coffin was lowered into the ground. The earth received its sacred deposit.

The anthems ceased: and the soldiers kneeling down, discharged their musquets over it; then, with streaming cheeks, rose, and gave place to others. Nine vollies were fired, and the ranks fell back. The bishop advanced to the head of the grave; all was hushed; he raised his eyes to Heaven, then, after a pause, in which he seemed to be communing with the regions above him, he turned to the silent assembly, and in a voice, collected and impressive, addressed them in a short, but affecting oration, in which he set forth the brightness of Sobieski's life; his noble forgetfulness of self, in the interests of his country; and the dauntless bravery which had laid him in the tomb. A general discharge of cannon and musquetry was the awful response to this appeal. Wawrzecki took the sword of the Palatine, and breaking it, dropt it into the grave. The aid-de-camps of the deceased did the same by theirs, shewing, that by so doing they resigned their offices; and then, covering their faces with their handkerchiefs, they turned away with the soldiers, who filed off. Thaddeus sunk on his knees; his hands were clasped, and his eyes for a few minutes fixed themselves on the coffin of his grandfather; then rising, he leaned on the arm of Wawrzecki, and with a tottering step, and pallid countenance, mounted his horse, which had been led to the spot, and returned with the scattered procession to the camp.

The cause for exertion being over, his spirits fell with the rapidity of a spring too highly wound up, which snaps, and runs down to immobility. He entered his tent, and threw himself on the bed, from whence he did not arise, during five days.

CHAP. VII.

At a time, when the effects of these sufferings and fatigues had brought him very low, the young Count Sobieski was arouzed by the information that the Russians had already planted themselves before Prague, and were threatening to bombard the town.* This news rallied the spirits of his depressed soldiers, who readily obeyed their commander, to put themselves in order of march the next day. Thaddeus felt that the decisive blow was pending; and though hardly able to sit his horse, he refused the indulgence of a litter; determining, that no illness, however severe, should make him flag one hour from the active exercise of duty.

Devastation was spread over the face of the country. As the troops moved, the unhappy and houseless villagers presented an agonizing picture to their view. Old men stood amongst the ashes of their homes, deploring the cruelty of power; children and women sat by the way side, weeping over the last sustenance which the wretched infant drew from the breast of its perishing mother.

Thaddeus shut his eyes on the scene.

"O, my country! my country!" exclaimed he, "what are my personal griefs to thine? Nothing, nothing. It is your wretchedness that barbs me to the heart! Look there," cried he to the soldiers, pointing to the miserable spectacles before him, "look there, and carry vengeance into the breasts of their destroyers. Let Prague be the last act of this tragedy!"

Unhappy young man, unfortunate country! It was indeed the last act of a tragedy, to which all Europe were spectators; a tragedy, which the nations witnessed, without one attempt to stop or delay its dreadful catastrophe! O! how must virtue be lost, when it is no longer an article of policy even to assume it.

After a long march, through a dark and dismal night, the morning began to break; and Thaddeus found himself on the southern side of that little river, which divides the territories of Sobieski from the woods of Kobylka.† Here, for the first time, he endured all the torturing varieties of despair.

The once fertile fields were burnt to stubble; the cottages were yet smoking, from the ravages of the fire; and in place of smiling eyes

---

* That is, Praga. See note on page 45.
† Kobylka was a village (now town) northeast of both Warsaw and Praga.

and thankful lips, the dead bodies of his peasants were stretched on the high roads, mangled, bleeding, and stripped of that decent covering, which humanity would not deny even to guilt.

Thaddeus could bear the sight no longer; but setting spurs to his horse, fled from the contemplation of scenes which harrowed up his heart.

At night-fall, the army halted under the walls of Villanow. The Count looked towards the windows of the palace, and by the glare of light shining through the half-drawn curtains, soon distinguished his mother's room. He then turned his eyes on that sweep of building appropriated to the Palatine; but not one solitary lamp illumined its gloom; the moon alone glimmered on the battlements; silvering the painted glass of the study window, where with that beloved parent, he had so lately gazed upon the stars; and anticipated a campaign, which had now so fatally terminated.

These thoughts, with his grief, and his forebodings, were buried in the depths of his soul. Addressing General Wawrzecki, he bade him welcome to Villanow; requesting at the same time, that the men might be directed to rest till the morning; and that he, and the officers, would partake of their refreshment within the palace.

As soon as Thaddeus had seen his guests seated at different tables in the eating-hall, and had given orders for the soldiers to be served from the cellars, he withdrew to seek the Countess. He found her in her dressing-room, surrounded by the attendants, who had just informed her of his arrival. The moment he appeared at the door, the women went out at an opposite passage, and Thaddeus, with an anguished heart, threw himself on the bosom of his mother. They were silent for some time. Poignant recollection stopped their utterance; but neither tears nor sighs filled up its place, until the Countess, who felt the full tide of maternal affection press upon her soul and mingle with her grief, raised her head from her son's neck, and said, whilst she strained him close in her arms: "Receive my thanks, O! Father of Mercy, that thou has yet spared to me this blessing!"

Sobieski breathed a response to the address of his mother; and drying her tears with his kisses, dwelt upon the never-dying fame of his beloved grandfather; upon his preferable lot to that of their brave friend Kosciuszko, who was doomed, not only to survive the liberty of his country, but to pass the residue of his life, within the dungeons of a Russian prison.* He then tried to re-animate her spirits with hope. He

---

* Kościuszko was released in 1796 by Catherine's successor, Tsar Paul I. The statement seems to reflect Thaddeus's fears rather than the narrator's knowledge.

spoke of the approaching battle, without expressing any doubt of the valour and desperation of the Poles rendering it successful. He talked of the firmness of the king, of the courage of the General, of his own resolution. His discourse began in a wish to cheat her into tranquillity, but as he advanced on the subject, his soul took fire at its own warmth, and he half believed the probability of his anticipations.

The Countess looked on the honourable glow that crimsoned his harrassed features, with a pang at her heart.

"My heroic son!" cried she, "my darling Thaddeus! what a vast price do I pay for all this excellence! I could not love you, were you otherwise than what you are; and being what you are, O! how soon may I lose you! Already has your noble grandfather paid the debt that he owed to his glory: he promised, to fall with Poland; he has kept his word; and now, all that I love on earth is concentrated in you." The Countess paused, and pressing his hand almost wildly on her heart, she continued, in a hurried voice, "The same spirit is in your breast; the same principle binds you; and I may at last be left alone. Heaven, have pity on me!"

She cast her eyes upwards, as she ended. Thaddeus, sinking on his knees by her side, implored her with all the earnestness of piety and confidence, to take comfort. Her ladyship embraced him with a forced smile, and said, "You must forgive me Thaddeus, I have nothing of the soldier in my heart; it is all woman. But, I will not detain you longer, my dear boy, from that rest which you require; go to your room, and try and recruit yourself for the fatigues, which I expect to-morrow will bring forth."

Sobieski, consoled to see any composure in his mother, withdrew; and after having heard that his numerous guests were properly lodged, went to his own chamber.

Next morning, at sun rise, the troops prepared to march. General Wawrzecki with his officers, begged permission to pay their personal gratitude to the Countess, for the hospitality of her reception: she declined that honour, on the plea of indisposition; and in the course of an hour, the Count appeared from her apartment, and joined the General; his cheeks were flushed with the struggles of parting; and he was so shaken by emotion, that his steps were irregular, and his manner confused, till he entered the court yard.

The soldiers filed off through the gates, crossed the bridge, and halted under the walls of Prague. The lines of the camp were drawn and fortified before the evening; when they found full leisure, to observe the enemy's strength.

Russia seemed to have exhausted her wide regions, to people the narrow shores of the Vistula; from east to west, as far as the eye could reach, her armies were stretched to the horizon. Sobieski looked at them, and then on the handful of dauntless hearts, contained in the small circumference of the Polish camp, and sighing heavily, retired into his tent; where he mixed his short, and startled slumbers, with frequent prayers for the preservation of these last victims of their country.

The hours appeared to stand still. Several times he rose from his bed, and went to the door, to see whether the clouds were tinged with any appearance of dawn. All continued dark. He again returned into his marquée, and standing by the lamp, which was nearly exhausted, took out his watch, and tried to distinguish the points; but finding that the light burnt too feebly he was pressing the repeating spring, which struck five, when the report of a single musquet made him start.

He flew to his tent door, and looking about him, saw that all in that quarter was at rest; then suspecting that it might be a signal of the enemy, he hurried towards the entrenchments, where he found the centinels in perfect security from any fears respecting the sound, as they supposed it to have proceeded from the town.

Sobieski paid little attention to their opinions, but ascending the nearest bastion to take a wider survey, in a few minutes he discerned, though obscurely, through the faint gleams of morning, the whole host of Russia advancing in profound silence towards the Polish lines. The instant he made this discovery, he came down, and lost no time in giving orders for a defence; then flying to other parts of the camp, he awakened the commander in chief, encouraged the men, and saw that the whole encampment was not only in motion, but prepared for the assault.

In consequence of these prompt arrangements, the Russians were received with the cross fire of the batteries, and case-shot and musquetry, from several redoubts, which raked their flanks as they approached; however, in defiance of this shower of bullets, they pressed on with an intrepidity worthy of a better cause, and overleaping the ditch by squadrons, entered the camp. A passage once secured, the Cossacs rushed in by thousands, and spreading themselves in front of the storming party, put every soul to the bayonet who opposed their way.

The Polish works gained, the Russians turned the cannon on its former masters; and as these rallied to the defence of what remained, swept them down, by whole regiments. The noise of artillery thundered from all sides of the camp; the smoke was so great that, it was hardly possible to distinguish friends from foes; nevertheless, the spirits of the Poles, flagged not a moment: as fast as one rampart was wrested from them, they threw themselves within another; which was as speedily taken, by the help of hurdles, fascines, ladders, and a courage engendered by ferocity. Every spot of vantage ground was at length lost; and yet, the Poles fought like lions; quarter was neither offered to them, nor required; they disputed every inch of way, till they fell upon it in heaps; some, lying before the parapets; others, filling the ditches; and the rest, covering the ground for the enemy to tread on, as they cut their passage to the heart of the camp.

Sobieski, almost maddened by the scene, dripping with his own blood, and that of his brave friends, was seen in every part of the action; he was in the fosse, defending the trampled bodies of those who were dying; he was on the dyke, animating the few who remained; Wawrzecki was slain,* and every hope hung on Thaddeus; his presence and voice infused new energy into the arms of his almost fainting countrymen; they kept close to his side, till the Russians, enraged at the dauntless intrepidity of this young hero, uttered the most unmanly imprecations, and rushing on his little phalanx, attacked them with redoubled numbers and fury.

Sobieski sustained the shock with firmness; but wherever he turned his eyes, they were blasted with some object which made them recoil; he beheld his companions, and his soldiers, strewing the earth, and their barbarous adversaries mounting their dying bodies as they hastened with loud huzzas, to the destruction of Prague, whose gates were now burst open. His eyes grew dim at this sight; and at the very moment in which he tore them from spectacles so deadly to his heart, a Livonian officer struck him with a sabre, to all appearance dead upon the field.

When Thaddeus recovered from the blow, which having lit on the steel of his cap, had only stunned him, he looked round and found that all near him was quiet; but a far different scene presented itself from the town. The roar of cannon, and the bursting of bombs, thundered through the air rendered livid and tremendous, by long spires of fire streaming from the burning houses and mingling with the volumes of smoke which rolled from the guns. The dreadful tocsin, and the hurras of the victors, pierced the soul of the Count; springing from the ground, he was preparing to rush forward to the gates, when loud outcries of distress issued from the interior of the place; and a moment after, the grand magazine was blown up, with a horrible explosion.

---

* In reality, General Wawrzecki surrendered to the Russians after the Battle of Praga and was taken prisoner. In the 1831 edition of *Thaddeus*, Porter allows her Wawrzecki to mirror more closely his historical namesake, being wounded rather than slain in this skirmish.

In an instant, the front of Prague was filled with women and children, flying in all directions, and rending the sky with their shrieks. "Father Almighty!" cried Thaddeus, wringing his hands, "canst thou suffer this?" Whilst he yet spake, some straggling Cossacs, from the town, who were prowling about, glutted, but not sated with blood, seized the poor fugitives, and with a ferocity as wanton as unmanly, released them at once from life and affliction.

This hideous spectacle brought his mother's defenceless state before the eyes of Sobieski. Her palace was only four miles distant; and whilst the barbarous avidity of the Russians, sparing neither age, nor sex, nor infancy, was too busily engaged in sacking the place, to permit them to perceive a solitary individual hurrying away amidst heaps of dead bodies, he flew across the few fields which intervened between Prague and Villanow.

Thaddeus was met at the gate of the palace, by General Butzou; who having already learnt the fate of Prague, from the noise and flames in that quarter; anticipated the arrival of some part of the victorious army before the walls of Villanow. When the Count crossed the draw-bridge, he saw that the worthy veteran had prepared every thing for a stout resistance; the ramparts were lined with soldiers, and well mounted with artillery.

"Here, my dear lord," cried he, as he led the Count up to the keep, "let the worst happen, here I am resolved to dispute the possession of your grandfather's palace, till I have not a man to stand by me!"

Thaddeus strained him in silence to his breast; and then, after examining the force, and giving further orders for more commanding dispositions, he went to the apartments of his mother.

The Countess's women who met him in the vestibule, begged him to be careful how he entered her ladyship's room; she had but recently recovered from convulsions, into which she had been thrown, on hearing the cannonade against the Polish camp. Thaddeus waited for no more; but, regardless of their caution, threw open the door of the chamber, and hastening up to his mother's couch, cast himself into her arms. She clung round his neck; and for a while, joy stopped her respiration, till bursting into a flood of tears, she wept over him, incapable of expressing by words, her tumultuous gratitude at again beholding him alive. He looked on her altered and pallid features.

"O! my mother," cried he, clasping her to his breast, "you are ill; and what will become of you?"

"My beloved son," replied she, kissing his forehead, through the clotted blood which oosed from a cut above his temple; "my beloved son, before our cruel murderers can arrive, I shall have found a refuge in the bosom of my GOD."

Thaddeus could only answer with a groan. She resumed. "Give me your hand. I must not witness the grandson of Sobieski, given up to despair: let your mother incite you to resignation. You see, I have not breathed a complaining word, although I behold you covered with wounds." As she spoke, she pointed to the sash and handkerchief, which were bound round his thigh and left arm. "Our separation will not be long; a few short years, perhaps hours, may unite us for ever in a better world."

The Count was still speechless; he could only press her hand to his lips. After pausing a moment, she proceeded. –

"Look up, my dear boy! and attend to me. Should Poland become the property of other nations, I conjure you, if you survive its fall, to leave it. When reduced to slavery, it will be no longer an asylum for a man of honor. I beseech you should this happen, go that very hour to England: That is a free country; and I have been told, the people are kind to the unfortunate. Thaddeus! Why do you delay to answer me? Remember, these are your mother's dying prayers."

"I will obey you."

"Then," continued she, taking out of her bosom a picture, "Let me tie this round your neck? It is the portrait of your father." Thaddeus bent his head forward, and the Countess fastened it under his waist-coat: "Prize this gift, my child; it is likely to be all that you will now inherit either from me, or that father. Try to forget his injustice my dear son; and in memory of me never part with it. O! Thaddeus, since the moment in which I first received it, till this instant, it has never been from my heart!"

"And it shall never leave mine," answered he in a stifled voice, "whilst I have being."

The Countess was preparing to reply, when a sudden volley of fire arms made Thaddeus spring upon his feet. Loud out-cries succeeded. The women rushed into the apartment, screaming, "The ramparts are stormed!" and the next moment, that quarter of the building rocked to its foundation. The Countess clung to the bosom of her son; Thaddeus clasped her close to his breast, and casting up his petitioning eyes to Heaven, "O GOD!" cried he, "can I not find shelter for my mother!"

Another burst of cannon was followed by a heavy crash, and the most piercing shrieks, echoed through the palace. "All is lost!" cried a soldier, who appeared for an instant at the room door, and vanished.

Thaddeus, overwhelmed with despair, grasped his sword, which had fallen to the ground, and crying, "Mother, we will die together!"

would have given her one last and assuring embrace, when his eyes met the dreadful sight of her before anxious features, now tranquilized in death. She fell from his palsied arms back on the sofa, and he stood gazing on her, as if struck by a power which had benumbed all his faculties.

The tumult in the palace encreased every moment; but he heard it not, till Butzou, followed by two or three of his soldiers, ran into the apartment, calling out, "Count, save yourself!"

Sobieski still remained motionless. The General caught him by the arm, and throwing his mantle over the dead Countess, hurried him almost unconscious, by an opposite door, through the state-chambers, into the gardens.

Thaddeus did not recover his recollection, till he reached the outward-gate; then, breaking from the hold of his friend, was returning to the sorrowful scene he had left, when Butzou, aware of his intentions, just stopped him time enough, to prevent his rushing on the bayonets of a party of Russian Infantry which was pursuing them at full speed.

The Count now rallied his distracted energies; and making a stand with the General and his three Poles, they compelled this merciless detachment to seek refuge among the arcades of the building.

Butzou would not allow his young lord to pursue these wretches; but hurried him across the park. He looked behind him; a long column of fire issued from the south towers. Thaddeus groaned, "All is indeed over!" and pressing his hand on his forehead, in that attitude, followed the steps of the General towards the Vistula.

From the wind being very high, the flame spread itself over the roof of the palace, and catching at every combustible in its way, the Russians became so terrified at the quick progress of a fire, which threatened to consume themselves as well as their plunder, that they quitted it with precipitation; and decrying the Count and his soldiers at a little distance, directed all their malice to that point: speedily overtaking him, they blocked up the bridge by a file of men with fixed pikes, and not only menaced the Polanders as they advanced, but derided their means of defence.

Sobieski, indifferent alike to danger and to insults, stopped short to the left, and followed by his friends, plunged into the stream, amidst a shower of musquet balls from the enemy. In a few minutes he reached the opposite bank; where he was assisted out of the river, by some of the weeping inhabitants of Warsaw, who had been watching the expiring ashes of Prague, and the flames which were feeding on the boasted towers of Villanow.

Emerged from the water, Thaddeus stood to regain his breath; and leaning on the shoulder of Butzou, he pointed to his burning palace, and said, with a smile of agony, "See what a funeral pile, Heaven has given to the manes of my dear mother!"

The General did not speak; for his emotions choaked him; but motioning the two soldiers to proceed, he supported the Count into the citadel.

CHAP. VIII.

From the termination of this awful day, in which a brave and unhappy nation was consigned to slavery, Thaddeus had been confined to his apartment in the garrison.

It was now the latter end of November. General Butzou, supposing that the illness of his lord might continue some weeks, and feeling that no time ought to be lost; obtained his permission, and quitting Warsaw, joined Prince Poniatowski, who was yet under arms, at the head of a few troops near Sachoryn.[*]

Meanwhile, the Count Sobieski, finding himself tolerably well restored, except in those wounds of the heart, which only time can heal, was enabled to leave his room, and breathe a little fresh air on the ramparts. His first appearance was greeted by the officers, with melancholy congratulations; but their replies displaced the faint smile which he tried to spread over his countenance; and with a contracted brow, he listened to the following information.

Prague had not only been razed to the ground: but upwards of thirty thousand persons, besides old men, women, and defenceless infants, had either perished by the sword, or had been cast into the river, or into the flames. All the horrors of Ismail had been re-acted by Suwarrow on the banks of the Vistula.[†] The citizens of Warsaw, intimidated by such a spectacle, had assembled in a body, and, driven to desperation, repaired to the foot of the throne; on their knees, they implored his Majesty to forget the contested rights of his subjects; and, in pity to their wives and children, allow them by a timely submission, to save those dear relatives from the ignominy and cruelty which had been wreaked upon the inhabitants of Prague. Stanislaus saw that opposition would be fruitless; the walls of his capital were already surrounded by a train of artillery, prepared to blow the town to atoms on

---

[*] Poniatowski commanded a modest party at Sachorzyn (Zagorzyn) in southern Poland in October 1794. He had intended to surrender to Suvorov, but before this could be negotiated, Prussian forces dispersed Poniatowski's troops. Anthing, Frederic, *History of the Campaigns of Count Alexander Suworow Rymnikski*, 2 vols (London: J. Wright, 1799), 2. 353–4.

[†] On 22 December 1790, Suvorov stormed and captured the Ottoman fortress at Izmail on the Danube river in modern Ukraine. After the battle, in which the Ottoman forces lost more than 25,000 men, Suvorov allowed his army three days of looting.

the first command of the Russian General; therefore, with a deep sigh, he assented to the petition, and sent deputies to the enemy's camp.

"And," continued the officer, "Suwarrow, in reply, demands, that every man in Poland, shall not only surrender his arms, but shall sue for pardon for the past; and these conditions are consented to."

"They never shall be, by me," said Sobieski; and turning from his informer, he walked towards the royal palace, hardly knowing what were his intentions or what he had else, to hope or fear.

When his Majesty was apprized, that the young Count Sobieski awaited him in the audience-chamber, he left his closet, where he had been musing alone, and entered the room. Thaddeus, with a swelling heart, would have thrown himself on his knee, but the king prevented him with emotion, and pressed him in his arms.

"Brave young man!" cried he, in a faltering voice, "I embrace, in you, the last of those Polish youth, who were so lately the brightest jewels in my crown."

Tears stood in the monarch's eyes, as he spoke; and Sobieski, with hardly a steadier utterance, answered, "I come to receive your Majesty's commands. I will obey them in all things, but in surrendering this sword (which my grandfather bequeathed,) into the hands of your enemies."

"I will not desire you, my noble friend," replied Stanislaus; "by my acquiescence with the terms of Russia, I only comply with the earnest prayers of my people; I do not compel any. I shall not ask you to betray your country; but alas! you must not throw away your life in a now hopeless cause. Fate has consigned Poland to subjection; and when Heaven, in its all-wise, though mysterious decrees, confirms the destruction of kingdoms, man has no further duty than resignation. For myself, I am ordered by our conqueror, to bury my griefs and indignities in the castle of Grodno."*

The blood rushed over the cheek of Thaddeus, at this meek declaration of his Majesty, to which the proud indignation of his soul could in no way subscribe; with a heated and agitated voice, he exclaimed, "If my sovereign be already at the command of our oppressors, then indeed is Poland no more! and I have nothing to do, but to perform the dying will of my mother. Will your Majesty grant me permission to set

---

* In December 1794, Catherine ordered Stanisław to depart Warsaw for Grodno, today in western Belarus. He remained in Grodno for more than two years, signing the final partition of Poland on 24 October 1795 and abdicating the Polish throne on 25 November 1795. He died in St Petersburg on 12 February 1798.

off for England, before I can be obliged to witness this last calamity of my wretched country?"

"I would to Heaven," replied the king, "that I, too, might repose my age and sorrows in that happy kingdom! Go, Sobieski; my prayers and blessings shall follow you."

Thaddeus pressed his Majesty's hand to his lips.

"Believe me, my dear Count," continued Stanislaus, "my soul bleeds at this parting. I know the treasure which your family has always been to this nation: I know your own individual merit: I know the wealth which you have sacrificed for me, and my subjects; and I am powerless to express my gratitude."

"Had I done any thing more than my absolute duty," replied he, "such words from your Majesty's lips, would have been a reward adequate to every deprivation: but, alas, no! I have perhaps performed less than my duty; the blood of a Sobieski ought not to have been spared one drop, when the liberties of his country perished!" Thaddeus blushed whilst he spoke; and almost repented the too ready zeal of his friends, in having saved him from the general slaughter at Villanow.

The voice of the venerable Stanislaus became fainter, as he resumed –

"Perhaps, had a Sobieski reigned at this time, these horrors might not have been accomplished! That tyrannous power which has crushed my people, I cannot forget, was the same which put the sceptre into my hand.* Catherine misunderstood my principles: She calculated on giving a traitor to the Poles; but, when she made me a king, she could not obliterate that stamp which the KING OF KINGS had graved upon my heart: I believed myself to be HIS Vicegerent; and, to the utmost, I have struggled to fulfil my trust."

"Yes, my sovereign!" cried Thaddeus, "and whilst there remains one man on earth, who has drawn his first breath in Poland, he will bear witness in all the lands through which he may be doomed to wander, that he has felt from you the care and affection of a father. O! sir, how will future ages believe, that, in the midst of civilized Europe, a brave people and a virtuous monarch, were suffered unaided, undeplored, to fall into the grasp of usurpation and murder?"

Stanislaus laid his hand on the arm of the Count, and with a languid smile gleaming from his eyes, which still shed benign lustre, through his grey locks, he said, –

"Man's ambition and baseness are monstrous, only to the contemplation of youth. You are learning your lesson early: I have studied

---

* It was through Catherine's efforts that Stanisław, a former lover, was elected King of Poland in 1764.

mine for many years; and with a bitterness of soul, which in some measure prepared me for the completion. My kingdom has passed from me, at the moment you have lost your country. Before we part for ever, my dear Sobieski, take with you this assurance, that you have served the unfortunate Stanislaus, to the latest hour in which you beheld him: what you have just said, relative to the sentiments of those who were my subjects, is indeed a balm to my heart, and I will carry its consolation with me to my prison."

The king paused; Sobieski, agitated and incapable of speaking, threw himself at his majesty's feet, and pressed his hand with fervency and anguish, to his lips. The king looked down at his graceful figure; and pierced to the soul, by the more graceful feelings which dictated the action, the tear which stood on his eye-lid rolled over his cheek, and was followed by another, before he could add,

"Rise, my young friend, and take this ring. It contains my picture; wear it in remembrance of a man who loves you, and who never can forget your worth, or the loyalty and patriotism of your house."

The Chancellor, at that moment being announced, Thaddeus rose from his knee, and was preparing to leave the room, when his Majesty perceiving his intention, desired him to stop.

"Stay, Count!" cried he, "I will burthen you with one request. I am now a king without a crown, without subjects, without a foot of land to bury me when I die; I cannot reward the fidelity of even one of the few friends of whom my enemies have not deprived me; but you are young, and Heaven may yet smile upon you in some distant nation. Will you pay a debt of gratitude for your poor sovereign? Should you ever again meet with the good old Butzou, who rescued me when my life lay on the fortune of a moment, remember, that I regard him as the preserver of my existence! He was then a private soldier in the Sobieski guards; and when I offered to recompense him by riches and honours, he only prayed to remain with his first patron. I committed him to the friendship of your grandfather, who immediately promoted him to the rank of General over that battalion. This brave man, I was told this morning, directly on the destruction of Prague, joined the army of my brother; which being now disbanded, with the rest of my faithful soldiers he is cast forth in his old age, on the bounty of a pityless world. Should you ever meet with him Sobieski, succour him for my sake."

"As Heaven may succour me!" cried Thaddeus; and putting his Majesty's hand a second time to his lips, he bowed to the Chancellor, and passed into the street.

When the Count returned to the citadel, he found that all was as the king had represented. The soldiers in the garrison were reluctantly preparing to give up their arms; and the nobles, in compassion to the cries of the people, were proudly trying to humble their necks to the yoke of the ravager. The magistrates lingered, as they went to take the city keys from the hands of their good king, who had so faithfully protected them; and anticipated, with bitter sighs, the moment in which they should surrender them and their rights into the power of Suwarrow, and that *"foul woman of the North,"** who exulted in nothing more than devastation.

Poland was now no place for Sobieski. He had survived all his kindred. He had survived the liberties of his country. He had beheld his king a prisoner; and his countrymen trampled on by deceit and cruelty. As he walked on, musing over these circumstances, he met with little interruption; for the streets appeared deserted. Here and there, a poor miserable wretch passed him, who seemed by his wan cheeks and haggard eyes, already to repent the too successful prayers of the deputation. The shops were shut. Thaddeus stopped a few minutes, in the great square, which used to be crowded with happy citizens, but not one man was now to be seen. An awful and expecting silence reigned over all. He sighed, and walking down the east-street, ascended that part of the ramparts which covered the Vistula.

He turned his eyes to the spot, where once stood the magnificent towers of his paternal palace.

"Yes," cried he, "it is now time for me to obey the last command of my mother! There is nothing remains of Poland, but its soil! nothing of my home, but its ashes!"

The Russians had pitched a detachment of tents amidst the ruins of Villanow; and were at this moment, busying themselves in searching amongst the stupendous fragments, for what plunder the fire might have spared. Thaddeus gazed on the place, for nearly an hour.

"Insatiate robbers!" exclaimed his tortured heart, his lips could only faulter with emotion; "Heaven will requite this sacrilege." He thought on the Countess, who lay beneath the ruins, and tore himself from the sight, whilst he added "Farewell for ever; farewell, thou beloved Villanow, in which I have spent so many blissful years! I quit you, and my country, for ever!" As he spoke, he raised his hands and eyes to Heaven, and pressing the picture of his mother to his lips and bosom, turned from the parapet against which he had been leaning, and walked

---

* Catherine the Great; see Coleridge, Samuel Taylor, 'Religious Musings' (in *Poems on Various Subjects*, London: C.G. and J. Robinsons, 1796): 'From all sides rush the thirsty brood of War!— / Austria, and that foul Woman of the North, / The lustful murderess of her wedded lord!'

back to his chamber, determining to prepare that night, for his departure the next morning.

He arose by day break: and, having gathered together all his little wealth; which consisted merely of the Hussar uniform that he wore, a few rings, and pieces of gold, which he concealed with his linen in the portmanteau that was buckled on his horse; precisely two hours before the triumphal car of General Suwarrow entered Warsaw, Sobieski left it; bedewing its stones, as he rode over the streets, with his tears. They were the first that he had shed, during the long series of his misfortunes; and they now flowed so fast from his eyes, that he could hardly discern his way out of the city.

At the great gate his horse stopped.

"Poor Saladin!" said Thaddeus, stroking his neck, "are you so sorry at leaving Warsaw, that, like your unhappy master, you linger to take a last look!"

His tears redoubled; and the warder as he opened the gate, and closed it after him, implored permission to kiss the hand of the noble Count Sobieski, before he turned his back on Poland, never to return. Thaddeus looked kindly round, and shaking hands with the honest man, after saying a few friendly words to him, rode on with a loitering step, until he reached that part of the river which divides Masovia from the Prussian dominions.

Here he flung himself off his horse, and standing for a moment on the hill that rises near the bridge, retraced, with his almost blinded eyes, the long and desolated lands through which he had passed; then involuntarily dropping on his knees, he plucked a tuft of grass, and pressing it to his lips, exclaimed, "Farewell, Poland! Farewell all my hopes of happiness!"

Almost stifled by regrets, he put this poor relic of his country into his bosom; and remounting his horse, crossed the bridge.

As one, who in flying from any particular object, thinks to lose himself and his sorrows, when it lessens to his view, Sobieski pursued the remainder of his journey with a speed, which soon brought him to Dantzic.

After having spent a few days in this town, by the help of much mental exertion, he regained some firmness of mind. It was a calm, arising from the conviction that his afflictions had gained their summit, and that, however heavy they were, Heaven had laid them on him, as a trial of faith and virtue. Under this belief, he ceased to weep; but he never was seen to smile.

When he had entered into an agreement with the master of a vessel, to carry him across the sea; he found, from calculating the strength of his finances, that they would barely defray the charges of the voyage. Considering these circumstances, it struck him, how impossible it would be, to take his horse with him to England.

The first time this idea presented itself, it almost overset his new arranged philosophy. Tears would have started into his eyes, had he not by force withheld them.

"To part from my faithful Saladin," said he to himself, "that has borne me since I first could use a sword; that has carried me through so many dangers; and has even come with me into exile; it is painful, it is ungrateful!" He was in the stable when this thought assailed him; and as the reflections followed each other, he again turned to the stall; "But, my poor fellow, I will not barter your services for gold. I will seek for some master, who may be kind to you in pity to my misfortunes."

He re-entered the hotel where he lodged, and calling a waiter, enquired who it was that occupied the fine mansion and park, on the east of the town. The man replied, "A Mr. Hopetown, an eminent British merchant, who had been settled at Dantzic for near forty years."

"I am glad he is an Englishman!" was the sentiment which succeeded this information, in the Count's mind; who immediately taking his resolution, had hardly prepared to put it in execution, when he received a summons from the captain, to be on board in half an hour, as the wind had set fair.

Thaddeus, rather disconcerted by this hasty call, with a depressed heart, wrote the following letter.

"To John Hopetown, Esq.

"Sir!

"A Polish officer, who has sacrificed every thing but his honour to the last interests of his country, now addresses you.

"You are an Englishman; and of whom can a victim to the cause of freedom, with less debasement solicit an obligation?

"I cannot afford support to the horse, which has carried me through the battles of this fatal war. I disdain to sell him; and therefore, I implore you by the respect that you pay to the memory of your ancestors, who struggled for, and retained that liberty, in whose defence we are thus reduced! I implore you, to give him an asylum in your park, and to protect him from injurious usage.

"Perform this benevolent action, sir, and you shall ever be remembered with gratitude, by an unfortunate

"POLANDER."

"Dantzic, November, 1794."

The Count having sealed and directed this letter, went to the hotel-yard, and ordered that his horse might be brought out. These few days of rest had restored him to his former mettle, and he appeared from the stable, prancing, and pawing the earth, as he used to do, when Thaddeus was going to mount him for the field.

The groom was in vain striving to restrain the spirit of the horse, when the Count took hold of his bridle. The noble animal immediately knew his master, and became gentle as a lamb. After stroaking him two or three times, with a bursting heart he returned the reins into the man's hand, and at the same time gave him the letter.

"There," said he, "take that note, and the horse, directly, to the house of Mr. Hopetown. Leave them; for the letter requires no answer."

So saying, he walked out of the yard, towards the quay. The wind continuing fair, he entered the ship; and, within an hour, set sail for England.

Sobieski passed the greater part of each day, and the whole of each night, on the deck of the vessel. He was too much absorbed in himself to receive any amusement from the passengers, who observing his melancholy, thought to disperse it by their everlasting company and conversation.

When any of those officious people came upon deck, he walked to the head of the ship, took his seat upon the cable which bound the anchor to the forecastle; and while their fears rendered him safe from their attacks, by pondering with an aching heart upon what might be the consequence of his voyage, he gained some respite from vexation, though none from misery.

The ship having passed through the Baltic, and entered on the British sea, the passengers running from side to side of the vessel, pointed out to Thaddeus, the distant shore of England lying like a hazy ridge along the horizon: the happy people, whilst they strained their eyes through glasses, desired him to observe different spots on the hardly perceptible line, which they called Flamborough Head, and the hills of Yorkshire. He turned sick at all these objects of pleasure, for not one of them, had a corresponding feeling in his breast. England could be nothing to him; if any thing, it would prove only a desart, which contained no one object for his regrets or wishes.

The image of Pembroke Somerset rose in his mind, like the dim recollection of one who has been a long time dead. Whilst he was with him at Villanow, he loved him warmly; and when they parted, they promised to correspond. One day, in pursuit of the enemy, Thaddeus had been so unlucky as to lose his friend's address, which was in his pocket-book; but yet, uneasy at his silence, he had ventured two letters to him, directed merely to Sir Robert Somerset's, England. To these, he received no answer; and the Palatine, and the Countess, became so displeased with such neglect and ingratitude, that they would not suffer him to be mentioned in their presence; and indeed Thaddeus, from disappointment and regret, felt no inclination to do so.

When the Count remembered these things, he found little comfort in recollecting the name of that young Englishman at this period; and now that he was visiting England, rather as a poor exile, than as a powerful lord, half indignant, but more grieved, he almost gave up the wish with the hope, of meeting Mr. Somerset. He felt, that Somerset had not acted as the man must act, to whom he could apply in his distress; and he resolved, unfriended as he was, to think no more about him. With a bitter sigh, he turned his back on the land to which he was going, and fixed his eyes on that track of sea, which divided him from all that had ever given him delight.

"Father of Heaven!" murmured he, in a suppressed voice, "What have I done, to deserve this misery? Why have I been, at one stroke, deprived of all that rendered existence estimable? Two months ago, I had a mother, a more than father, to love and cherish me; I had a country, that looked up to them and to myself, with veneration and confidence: now, I am bereft of all; I have neither father, mother, nor country, but am going to a land of strangers!"

Such impatient adjurations were never wrung from Sobieski by the anguish of sudden torture, without his ingenuous and pious mind reproaching itself for repining. His soul was as soft as a woman's; but it knew neither effeminacy, nor despair. Whilst his heart bled, his countenance retained its serenity. Whilst affliction crushed him to the earth, and nature paid a few hard wrung drops to her expected dissolution, he contemned his tears, and raised his fixed and confiding eye to that Power which poured down its tempests on his head. Thaddeus felt as a man, but received consolation as a christian.

When the ship arrived at the mouth of the Thames, the eagerness of the passengers encreased to such an excess, that they would not stand still, nor be silent a moment; and when the vessel, under full sail, passed Sheerness, and the dome of St. Paul's appeared before them, their exclamations were loud and incessant.* "My home! my parents! my wife! my friends!" were the burthen of every tongue.

Thaddeus found his irritable spirits again disturbed; and rising from his seat, he retired unobserved by the people, who were too happy to attend to any thing foreign to their own transports. The cabin was as deserted as himself. Feeling that there is no solitude like that of the heart, when it looks around, and sees in the vast concourse of human beings, not one to whom it can pour forth its sorrows or receive the answering sigh of sympathy, he threw himself on one of the lockers, and with difficulty restrained the tears from gushing out of his eyes. He held his hand over them, and condemned himself for a weakness so unbecoming his character.

He despised himself: but let not others despise him. It is difficult for

---

* Sheerness is a port town near the Thames estuary; the dome of St Paul's Cathedral was once the dominant feature of the London cityscape.

those who are in prosperity, who lie morning and evening in the lap of indulgence, to conceive the misery of being thrown out into a bleak and merciless world: it is impossible for the happy man, surrounded by luxury and gay companions, to figure to himself the reflections of a fellow creature, who has been fostered in the bosom of affection and elegance, cast at once from society, bereft of home, of comfort, of *"every stay, save innocence and heaven."** None but the wretched can imagine what the wretched endure, from actual distress, from apprehended misfortune, from outraged feelings, and ten thousand nameless sensibilities to injury, which only the unfortunate can conceive, dread, and experience.

Such were the anticipating fears of the Count. Books, and report, had led him to respect the English: Pembroke Somerset at one time, would have taught him to love them; but the nearer he advanced towards the shore, the remembrance that it was from this country his father came; (an idea of whom never crossed him, that he did not banish it with horror;) this thought, made him doubt the humanity of a people, of which his own parent, and forgetful friend, were so detestable a specimen.

The noise redoubled above his head; and in a few minutes afterwards, one of the sailors came rumbling down the stairs.

"Will it please your honour," said he, "to get up? That be my chest, and I want my cloaths to clean myself before I go on shore: Mother, I know, be waiting for me at Blackwall."

Thaddeus rose, and seeing that quiet was not to be found any where, again ascended to the deck.

On coming up the hatchway, he saw that the ship had cast anchor in the midst of a large city, environed by myriads of vessels, from every quarter of the globe. Sobieski leaned over the railing, and in silence looked down on the other passengers, who were bearing off in boats and shaking hands with the people that came to receive them.

"It is near dark, sir;" said the captain, "mayhap you would like to go on shore? There is a boat just come round, and the tide won't serve much longer; and as your friends don't seem to be coming for you, you are welcome to a place in it with me."

The Count thanked him; and after defraying the expences of the voyage, and giving half-a-guinea amongst the seamen, he desired that his portmanteau might be put into the wherry. The honest fellows, in gratitude to the bounty of their passenger, struggled who should obey his commands; when, during their contention and pulling at the

---

* James Thomson, *The Seasons: Autumn* (line 180).

baggage, the captain, angry at being detained, snatched it from between two of them, who in kindness to its master, were almost tugging it asunder, and flinging it into the boat, leaped in after it, and was followed by Thaddeus.

The taciturnity of the sailor, and the deep melancholy of his guest, did not break the silence till they had reached the Tower-stairs.

"Go Ben, fetch the gentleman a coach."

The Count bowed to the captain, who gave the order; and in a few minutes, the boy came back with the intelligence that there was one in waiting; he took up the portmanteau, and Thaddeus followed him to the Tower-gate, where the carriage stood. Ben threw in the baggage: the Count put his foot on the step.

"Where must the man drive to?"

Thaddeus drew it back again.

"Yes, sir;" continued the lad; "where is your honour's home?"

"In my grave," was the response his aching heart made to this question. He hesitated before he spoke. "An hotel," said he, flinging himself on the seat, and throwing some silver into the sailor's hat.

"What hotel, sir?" asked the coachman.

"Any."

The man closed the door, mounted his box, and drove off.

It was now near seven o'clock, of a dark December evening. The lamps were lit; and it being Saturday night, the streets were crowded with people. Thaddeus looked at them, as he drove along; "Happy creatures!" thought he, "you have each a home to go to; you have each, expecting friends to welcome you: every one of you, knows some fellow being in the world, that will smile when you enter; whilst I, unhappy man! am insulated from every social comfort. Wretched, wretched Sobieski! where are now all thy highly prized treasures? Thy boasted glory? and those beloved friends, who rendered that glory most precious to thee? Alas! all are withdrawn; vanished, like a dream of enchantment, from which I have awakened to a frightful solitude."

His reflections were broken, by the stopping of the carriage. The man opened the door.

"Sir, I have brought you to the Hummums, Covent Garden; it has as good accommodations as any in town. My fare is five shillings."*

Thaddeus gave the demand, and followed him and his baggage into

---

* The Hummums was a prominent hotel established in southeast Covent Garden in the late seventeenth century. Thaddeus is likely overcharged here; average coach fare from the Tower of London to Covent Garden would have been approximately 2s.6d. See *New Guide for Foreigners* (London: S. W. Fores, [?1789]), p. 46.

the coffee-room. At the entrance of a man of his figure, several waiters presented themselves, begging to know his commands.

"I want a chamber."

He was immediately ushered into a very handsome dining-room, where one of them laid down the portmanteau, and then bowing low, enquired whether he had dined.

The waiter having received his orders, (for the Count saw that it was necessary to call for something,) hastened into the kitchen to communicate them to the cook.

"Upon my soul, Betty," cried he, "you must do your best to-night; for the chicken is for the finest looking fellow you ever set your eyes on. By heaven, I believe him to be some Russian nobleman; perhaps the great Suwarrow himself."

"A prince you mean, Jenkins!" said a pretty girl, who entered at that moment; "since I was born, I never see'd any English lord walk up and down a room with such an air; he looks like a king: for my part, I should not wonder if he was one of the emigrant kings, for they say, there is a power of them now wandering about the world."*

"You talk like a fool Sally;" cried the sapient waiter. "Don't you see that his dress is military? Look at his black cap, with its long bag and great feather, and the monstrous sabre at his side; look at them, and then if you can, say I am mistaken in pronouncing that he is some commander in the Russian army, most likely come over as ambassador!"

"But he came in a hackney coach;"† cried a little dirty boy in the corner. "As I was running up stairs with Colonel Leeson's shoes, I see'd the coachman bring in his portmanteau."

"Well, Jack-a-napes, what of that?" cried Jenkins, "is a nobleman always to carry his equipage about with him, like a snail with its shell on its back? To be sure, this Russian lord, or prince, is only come to stay here, till his own house is fit for him. I will be civil to him."

"And so will I, Jenkins;" rejoined Sally, smiling, "for I never see'd such handsome blue eyes in my born days; and they turned so sweet on me, and he spoke so kindly, when he bade me stir the fire; and when he sat down by it, and throw'd off his great fur cloak, he shewed a glittering star, and a figure so noble, that indeed, cook, I do verily believe he is, as Jenkins says, an enthroned king!"

"You and Jenkins be a pair of fools;" cried the cook, who without

---

* In the aftermath of the French Revolution, many members of the French nobility and clergy lived in exile. They were joined by Polish exiles after the final partitions.
† A four-wheeled carriage for hire drawn by two horses. This modest form of mobility would not suit a wealthy visitor to London.

noticing their description, had been sulkily basting the fowl; "I will be sworn, he's just such another king, as that palavering rogue was a French duke, who got my master's watch, and pawned it! As for you, Sally, you had better beware of hunting after foreign men folk; it's not seemly for a young woman, and you may chance to rue it."

The moralizing cook, had now brought the whole kitchen on her shoulders. The men abused her for a surly old maid; and the women tittered, whilst they seconded her censure, by cutting sly jokes on the blushing face of poor Sally, who stood almost crying, by the side of her champion Jenkins.

Whilst this hubbub was going forward below stairs, its unconscious subject, was, as Sally had described, sitting in a chair close to the fire with his feet on the fender, his arms folded, and his eyes bent on the flames. He mused; but his ideas followed each other in such quick and confused succession, that it hardly could be said he thought of any thing.

The entrance of dinner roused him from his reverie. It was carried in by at least half a dozen waiters. The Count had been so accustomed to a numerous suite of attendants, that he did not observe the parcelling out of his temperate meal; one bringing in the fowl, another the bread, his neighbour, the solitary plate; and the rest in like order: so solicitous were the male listeners in the kitchen, to see this wonderful Russian.

Thaddeus partook but lightly of the refreshment. Being already fatigued in body, and dizzy with the motion of the vessel, as soon as the cloth was withdrawn, he ordered a night candle, and desired to be shewn to his chamber.

Jenkins, whom the sight of the embroidered star had confirmed in his decision that the foreigner must be a person of consequence, with encreased agility whipped up the portmanteau, and led the way to the sleeping rooms. Here, curiosity put on a new form; the women serv- ants, determined to have their wishes gratified as well as the men, had arranged themselves on each side of the passage through which the Count must pass. At so strange an appearance, Thaddeus drew back; but supposing that it might be a custom of the country, he proceeded through this fair bevy, and bowed as he walked along, to the low curt- sies which they continued to make, till he entered his apartment, and closed the door.

The unhappy are ever restless: They hope in every change of situ- ation, to experience some alteration in their feelings. Thaddeus felt too miserable awake, not to view with eagerness, the bed, whereon he trusted that, for a few hours at least, he might lose his consciousness to suffering, with its remembrance.

When he awoke in the morning, his head ached, and he opened his eyes as unrefreshed as when he had lain down; he undrew the curtain, and saw from the strength of the light, that it must be midday. He got up, and, having dressed himself, descended to the sitting room, where he found a good fire, and the breakfast things already placed; he rang the bell, and walked to the window to observe the appearance of the morning: a heavy snow had fallen during the night; and the sun, ascended to its meridian, shone through the thick atmosphere, like a ball of fire. All seemed comfortless without; and turning back to the warm hearth that was blazing at the other end of the room, he was reseating himself, when Jenkins brought in the tea-urn.

"I hope, my lord," said the waiter, "that your lordship slept well last night?"

"Perfectly, I thank you," replied the Count, unmindful that the man had addressed him according to his rank; "when you come to remove these things, bring me my bill."

Jenkins bowed and withdrew, congratulating himself on his dexterity in having saluted the Russian nobleman according to his title.

During the absence of the waiter, Thaddeus thought it time to examine the state of his purse: He well recollected how he had paid at Dantzic; and from the stile in which he was served here, he did not doubt, but that to defray what he had contracted, would nearly exhaust his all. He emptied the contents of his pocket, into his hand; a guinea, and nineteen shillings, were all that he possessed: a flush of terror suffused itself over his face; he had never known the want of money before, and he trembled now, for fear the charge should exceed his means of payment.

Jenkins entered with the bill. On the Count's examining it, he was pleased to find, that it amounted to no more than the only piece of gold which his purse contained. He laid it upon the tea-board, and putting half-a-crown into the hand of Jenkins who appeared waiting for something, wrapped his cloak round him, and was walking out of the room.

"I suppose my lord," cried Jenkins pocketing the money with a smirk, and bowing with the things in his hands; "we are to have the honour of seeing your lordship again, as you leave your portmanteau behind you?"

Thaddeus hesitated a few seconds, then again moving towards the door, said, "I will send for it."

"By what name, my lord?"

"The Count Sobieski."

Jenkins immediately set down the tea board, and hurrying after Thaddeus, along the passage and through the coffee-room, darted before him, and opening the door for him to go out, exclaimed loud enough for every body to hear, "Depend upon it Count Sobieski, I will take care of your lordship's baggage."

Thaddeus, rather displeased at his noisy officiousness, only bent his head, and proceeded into the street.

The air was piercing cold; and on his looking around, he perceived by the disposition of the square in which he was, that it must be a market place. The booths and stands were covered with snow; whilst parts of the pavement were rendered nearly impassable, by heaps of black ice, which the market people of the preceding day, had shoveled up out of their way. He now recollected that it was Sunday, and consequently, the improbability of finding any lodgings on that day.

He stood under the piazzas for two or three minutes, bewildered on the plan he should adopt; to return to the hotel for any purpose but to sleep, in the present state of his finances would be impossible: he therefore gave himself up, inclement as the season was, to walk about the streets till night; when he would go back to the Hummums to his bed-chamber; and in the morning, quit it for a residence more suitable to the reduction of his fortunes.

The wind blew a keen north-east, with a violent shower of sleet and rain; yet such was the abstraction of his mind, that he hardly observed its bitterness, but walked on, careless whither his feet led him, till he stopped opposite to St. Martin's church.*

"God is my only friend;" said he to himself, "and in his house, I shall surely find shelter!"

He turned up the steps, and was entering the porch, when he met the congregation thronging out of it.

"Is the service over?" he enquired of a decent old woman who was passing him down the stairs. The woman started at this question asked her in English, by a person whose dress was so completely that of a foreigner. He repeated it; and she, smiling and curtseying replied –

"Yes sir, and I am sorry for it. Lord bless your handsome face, though you be a foreign gentleman, it does one's heart good to see you so devoutly given!"

Thaddeus blushed at this personal compliment, though it came from the lips of a wrinkled old woman, and begging permission to assist her down the stairs, he asked when service begun again.

"At three o'clock, sir; and may heaven bless the mother who bore so pious a son!"

---

* Thaddeus has presumably walked the short distance from Covent Garden to St Martin-in-the-Fields.

As the poor woman spoke, she raised her eyes with a melancholy resignation. The Count, touched with her words and manner, almost unconsciously to himself, continued by her side as she hobbled down the street.

His eyes were fixed on the ground till as he walked forward, somebody pressing against him, made him look round; he saw that his aged companion had just knocked at the door of a mean-looking house, and that he and she were surrounded by nearly a dozen people, besides boys, who, through curiosity, had followed them from the church porch.

"Ah! sweet sir;" cried she, "these folks are staring at so fine a gentleman taking notice of age and poverty."

Thaddeus felt uneasy at the inquisitive gaze of some of the bye-standers; and his companion observing it by the fluctuations of his countenance, added as the door was opened by a little girl;

"Will your honour walk in out of the rain, and warm yourself by my poor fire?"

He hesitated a moment; then, accepting her invitation, bent his head to get under the humble door-way; and following through a neatly sanded passage, entered a small but clean kitchen. A little boy, who was sitting on a stool near the fire, uttered a scream at the sight of a stranger; and running up to his grandmother, rolled himself round in her cloak, crying out;

"Mammy, mammy, take away that black man!"*

"Be quiet William; it is a gentleman, and no black man. I am so ashamed, sir; but he is only three years old."

"I should apologize to you," returned the Count smiling, "for introducing a person so hideous as to frighten your family."

By the time he finished speaking, the good dame had pacified the screaming child, who still stood trembling and looking askance at the tremendous black gentleman, as he stroked the head of his pretty sister.

"Come here, my dear!" said Thaddeus, seating himself by the fire and stretching out his hand to the child. It instantly buried its head in its grandmother's apron.

"William! William!" cried his sister, pulling him by the arm, "the gentleman will not hurt you."

The boy again lifted up his head. Thaddeus threw back his long sable cloak, and taking off his cap, whose hearse-like plumes, he thought, might have terrified the child, he laid it on the ground, and again stretching forth his arms, called to the boy to come to him. Little

* black man, 'the devil' or 'a bogeyman invoked to frighten children' (OED).

William now looked steadfastly in his face, and then on the cap, which he had laid beside him; and then, whilst he grasped his grandmother's apron with one hand, he held out the other, half assured, towards the Count. Thaddeus immediately took it, and pressing it softly, pulled him gently to him, and placing him on his knee, "My little fellow," said he, kissing him, "you are not frightened now?"

"No;" said the child, "I see you are not the ugly black man that takes away naughty boys. The ugly black man has a black face, and snakes on his head; but these are pretty curls!" added he laughing, and putting his little fingers through the thick auburn hair, which hung in neglected masses over the forehead of the Count.

"I am ashamed your honour should sit in a kitchen;" rejoined the old lady; "but I have not a fire in any other room."

"Yes," said her grand-daughter, who was about twelve years old, "grandmother has a nice first floor up stairs; but because we have no lodgers, there be no fire there."

"Be silent, Nanny Robson," said the dame, "your pertness teazes the gentleman."

"O, not at all;" cried Thaddeus, "I ought to thank her, for she informs me that you have lodgings to let; will you allow me to engage them?"

"You, sir," cried Mrs. Robson, thunderstruck, "for what purpose? Surely so noble a gentleman would not live in such a place as this?"

"I would, Mrs. Robson; I know not where I could live with more comfort; and where comfort is, my good madam, what signifies the costliness or plainness of the dwelling."

"Well, sir, if you be indeed serious? but I cannot think you so: you are certainly making a joke of me, for my boldness in asking you into my poor house."

"Upon my honour, I am not, Mrs. Robson. I would gladly be your lodger, if you will admit me; and to convince you that I am in earnest, my portmanteau shall this moment be brought here."

"Well, sir," resumed she, "I shall be honoured in having you in my house; but I have no room for any one but yourself, not even for a servant."

"I have no servant."

"Then, I will wait on him grandmother;" cried the little Nanny, "do let the gentleman have them, I am sure he looks honest."

The woman coloured at this last observation of the child, and proceeded.

"Then sir, if you should not disdain the rooms when you see them, I shall be too happy in having so good a gentleman under my roof.

Pardon my boldness, sir; but may I ask? I think by your dress, you are a foreigner?"

"I am;" replied Thaddeus, the sweetness which played over his features contracting into a gloom; "if you have not an objection to take a stranger within your doors, from this hour I shall consider it as my home?"

"As your honour pleases;" said Mrs. Robson, "my terms are half a guinea a week, and I will attend on you as though you were my own son; for I cannot forget, excellent young gentleman! the way in which we first met."

"Then I will leave you for the present;" returned he, rising, and putting down the little William, who had been amusing himself with examining the silver points of the star of St. Stanislaus, and would hardly now quit his knee: "In the mean while," said he, "my pretty friend," stooping to the child, "let this bit of silver," was just mounting to his tongue, as he had already put his hand in his pocket to take out half a crown; when he recollected that his necessities would no longer admit of such gifts, and drawing his hand back with a deep and bitter sigh, he touched the boy's cheek with his lips, and added, "let this kiss remind you of your new friend."

This was the first instance in the life of Sobieski, that his generous spirit had ever been restrained; and he felt it with a pang, for the poignancy of which he could not account.

He had been accustomed to an existence spent in acts of munificence. His grandfather's palace was the asylum of the unhappy; his grandfather's purse, a treasury for the unfortunate. The soul of Thaddeus, did not degenerate from his noble relative: his generosity, begun in inclination, was nurtured by reflection, and strengthened with a daily exercise, that rendered it a habit of his nature. Want never appeared before him, without imparting such sympathetic emotion to his excellent heart, that he rested not till he had administered every comfort in the power of wealth to bestow. His compassion and his purse were the substance and shadow of each other. The poor of his country thronged from every part of the kingdom, to receive pity and relief at his hands. With these houseless wanderers, he peopled the new villages which his grandfather had caused to be erected in the midst of lands, which in former times had been given up to wild beasts and desolation. Thaddeus participated in the happiness of these grateful tenants; and many were the old men, whose eyes he had seen closed, in thankfulness and peace. These honest peasants, even in their dying moments, wished to give up that life in his arms, which he had rescued from misery. He has visited their cottage, he has smoothed their pillow, he has joined in their prayers, and when their last sigh came to his ear, he has raised the weeping family from the dust, with pious exhortations, and his kindest assurances of protection. How often has the Countess clasped her godlike-son to her breast, when after a scene like this, he has returned home, the tears of the dying man and his children yet wet upon his hand! how often has she strained him to her heart, whilst floods of rapture have poured from her own eyes! Heir to the first fortune in Poland, he scarcely felt the means by which he bestowed all these benefits; and with a soul as bounteous as heaven had been munificent to him, wherever he moved, he shed smiles and gifts around him. How frequently has he said to the Palatine, when his carriage wheels were chaced by the thankful multitude; "O, my father! How can I ever be sufficiently grateful to GOD, for the happiness which he hath allotted to me, in making me the dispenser of so many blessings! The gratitude of these people, overpowers and humbles me in my own eyes: what have I done, to be so eminently favoured of Heaven? I tremble, when I ask myself the question." "You may tremble, my dear boy;" replied his grandfather, "for indeed the trial is a severe one: prosperity, like adversity, is an ordeal of our conduct. Two roads are before the rich man; vanity or virtue: You have chosen the latter, and the best; and may Heaven ever hold you in it! May Heaven ever keep your heart generous and pure! Go on, my dear Thaddeus, as you have commenced, and you will find that your Creator hath bestowed wealth upon you, not for what you have done, but as the means of evincing how well you would dispense the gift."

This *was* the fortune of Thaddeus; and now, he who had scattered thousands without counting them, drew back his hand with something like horror at his own injustice, when he was going to give away one little piece of silver, which he might want in a day or two, to defray some indispensible debt.

"Mrs. Robson," said he, as he replaced his cap upon his head, "I shall return before it is dark."

"Very well, sir," and opening the door for him, he went out into the lane.

Ignorant of the town, and thanking Providence for having prepared him an asylum, he directed his course towards Charing Cross.* He looked about him, with a deepened sadness; the wet and

---

* By the 1790s, Charing Cross was regarded as the epicentre of political, social and economic life in London, combining 'the politeness of St. James's with the squalor of the alleys of St Giles's or St Martin's' from which Thaddeus had walked. Barrell, John, *The Spirit of Despotism: Invasions of Privacy in the 1790s* (Oxford: Oxford University Press, 2006), p. 34.

plashy* state of the streets, gave to every object so comfortless an appearance, that he could scarcely believe he was in that London, of which he had read with so much delight. Where were those magnificent buildings, he expected to see in the emporium of the world? Where, that cleanliness, and those tokens of greatness and splendour, which had been the admiration and boast of travellers? He could no where discover them; all seemed to him, like a dark, gloomy, mean looking city.

Hardly heeding whither he went, he approached the Horse-Guards; a view of the park, as it appears through the wide porch, promised him less unpleasantness than the dirty pavement, and he turned in, taking his way along the Bird-cage Walk.†

The trees, stripped of their leaves, stood naked and dripping with melted snow. The season was in unison with the Count's fate. He was taking the bitter wind for his repast, and quenching his thirst with the rain that fell on his pale and feverish lip: he felt the cutting blast enter his breast; and shutting his eye-lids to repel the tears which were rising from his heart, he walked faster, but in spite of himself, the drops mingled with the wet that trickled from his cap down on his face. One melancholy thought introduced another, till his agitated soul lived over again, in memory, every calamity which had reduced him from happiness to misery. Two or three heavy and convulsed sighs followed these reflections; and quickening his pace, he walked once or twice quite round the park: the rain had now ceased, and hardly observing any body that passed, he threw himself down upon one of the chairs, and sat in a musing posture, with his eyes fixed on the opposite tree.

A sudden sound of voices approaching, rouzed him; and turning his eyes, he saw that the speakers were two young men whom he judged by their dress, must belong to the regiment of the centinel who was patroling at the end of the mall.

"By Heavens, Berrington," cried one, "it is the best shaped boot I ever beheld! I have a good mind to ask him whether it be English make?"

"And if it be," replied the other, with a sneer, "you must ask him who made his legs, that you may send yours to be mended."

"Who the devil can see my legs through that boot?"

---

* plashy, 'characterized by shallow pools or puddles' (*OED*).
† Thaddeus walks south from Charing Cross to the Horse Guards (a building that served as army barracks and stables, though at the time of Thaddeus's arrival it was increasingly used as a military headquarters) and then east along Birdcage Walk, named for the royal aviary in the seventeenth century, which runs along the southern side of St James's Park.

"Oh, if to hide them, be your reason, pray ask him immediately."

"And so I will, for I think the boot damned handsome."

At these words, he was making up towards Sobieski with two or three long strides, when his companion pulled him back.

"Surely, Harwold, you will not act so ridiculously? He appears to be a foreigner of rank, and he may take affront and knock you down."

"Curse him and his rank too; he is some paltry emigrant, I warrant, and may the devil fly away with my legs, if I don't ask him who made his boots!"

As he spoke, he would have dragged his companion along with him, but Berrington broke from his arm, and the fool, who now thought himself dared to it, hustled up close to the chair, and bowed to Thaddeus, (who hardly crediting that he could be the subject of this dialogue) returned the salutation with a cold bend of his head.

Harwold looked a little confounded at this haughty demeanor, and whilst his face for once in his life blushed at his own insolence, he roared out as if in defiance of all shame;

"Pray, sir, where did you get your boots?"

"Where I got my sword, sir," replied Thaddeus calmly; and, rising from his seat, he darted his eyes disdainfully on the coxcomb, and walked slowly down the mall. Surprised and shocked at such behaviour in a British officer, as he moved away, he distinctly heard Berrington laughing aloud, and ridiculing the astonishment and set-down air of his impudent associate.

This incident did not so much ruffle the temper of Thaddeus, as it amazed and perplexed him.

"Is this a specimen," thought he, "of a nation, which on the continent is venerated for courage, manliness, and generosity! Well, I find I have much to learn. I must go through the ills of life, to estimate myself thoroughly; and I must study mankind in themselves, and not in their history, to have a true knowledge of what they are."

This strange rencontre was of service to him, by diverting his mind into another channel, than the intense contemplation of his situation; and as the dusk drew on, he turned his steps towards the Hummums.

On entering the coffee-room, he was met by the obsequious Jenkins, who being told by Thaddeus that he wanted his baggage and a carriage to be sent for, went for the things himself, and sent a boy for a coach.

A man dressed in black, was standing by the chimney, and seemed to be eyeing Thaddeus, as he walked up and down, with great attention. Just as he had taken another turn, and drew near him, the stranger accosted him rather abruptly.

"Pray, sir, are there any news stirring abroad? you seem, sir, to be come from abroad?"

"None, that I know, sir."

"Bless me, that's strange. I thought, sir, you came from abroad, sir; from the Continent, from Poland, sir? at least the waiter said so, sir."

Thaddeus coloured; "The waiter, sir?"

"I mean sir," continued the gentleman, visibly confused at the dilemma into which he had brought himself, "the waiter said you were a Count, sir; a Polish Count, at least the Count Sobieski! Hence I concluded that you are from Poland. If I have offended, I beg pardon sir; but in these times we are anxious for every intelligence."

Thaddeus made no other reply, than by a slight inclination of his head; and walking forward to see whether the coach were arrived, he thought, whatever travellers had related of the English, they were the most impertinent race of people in the world.

The stranger would not be contented with what he had already said, but plucking up new courage, pursued the Count to the glass door through which he was looking, and resumed.

"I believe, sir, I am not wrong? you are the Count Sobieski; and I have the honour to be now speaking with the bravest champion of Polish liberty?"

Thaddeus again bowed; "I thank you sir, for the compliment you intend me; but I cannot take it to myself; all the men of Poland, old and young, nobles and peasants, were her champions, equally sincere, equally brave."

Nothing could silence the inquisitive stranger: the coach drew up, but he went on.

"Then I hope, that many of these patriots, besides your lordship, have taken care to bring away their wealth from a land now abandoned to destruction?"

For a moment Thaddeus forgot himself in his country, and all her rights, and all her sufferings, rose in his countenance.

"No, sir! Not one of those men; and least of all, would I have drawn one vital drop from her heart! I left in her bosom, all that was dear to me, all that I possessed; and not until I saw the chains brought before my eyes, that were to lay her in irons, did I turn my back on calamities, which I could no longer avert or alleviate."

The ardour of his manner, and the elevation of his voice, had drawn the attention of every person in the room upon him, when Jenkins entered with his baggage. The door being opened, Sobieski got into the coach, and gladly hastened from a conversation which awakened all his griefs.

"Ah, poor enthusiast!" exclaimed his inquisitor, as the carriage drove off, "It is a pity that so fine a young man should have made so ill a use of his birth and other advantages!"

"He appears to me," observed an old clergyman, who sat in an adjoining box; "to have made the best possible use of his talents; and had I a son, I would rather hear him utter such a sentiment, as that with which he quitted the room, than see him master of millions."

"May be so," cried the questioner with a disdainful and angry glance, "'*different minds incline to different objects!*' His has decided for the '*wonderful, the wild*,' and a pretty end he has made of his choice!"*

"Why to be sure," observed another hearkener, "young people should be brought up with reasonable ideas of right and wrong and prudence: Nevertheless I should not like a son of mine to run harem scarem through my property and his own life; yet one cannot help, when one hears such a brave speech as that from yon foreigner, just gone out, – I say, one cannot help thinking it very fine."

"True, true;" cried the inquisitor, "you are right, sir; very fine indeed, but too fine to wear; it would soon leave us naked, as it has done him; for it seems, by his own confession, he is pennyless; and I know, a twelvemonth ago, he was master of a fortune which, however incalculable, he has managed with all his talents to see the end of."

"Then he is in distress?" exclaimed the clergyman, "and you know him?"

The man coloured at this unexpected inference, and stammering some words, which no one could make out, took up his hat, and looking at his watch, said, "I beg pardon, gentlemen, I have an appointment." And hurried out of the room without speaking farther, notwithstanding that the good clergyman, whose name was Blackmore, hastened after him requesting to know where the young foreigner lived.

"Who is that coxcomb?" cried the disconcerted doctor, as he returned from his unavailing application.

"I don't know sir," replied the waiter: "I never saw him in this house before last night, when he came in late to sleep; and this morning, he was in the coffee-room at breakfast, just as that foreign gentleman walked through; and Jenkins, bawling his name out very loud, as soon as he was gone, this here gentleman in the powdered hair asked him who that Count was. I heard Jenkins say some Russian name, and tell him he came last night, and likely would come back again; and so that

---

* Mark Akenside, *The Pleasures of Imagination* (London: R. Dodsley, 1744): 'Diff'rent minds / Incline to diff'rent objects: one pursues / The vast alone, the wonderful, the wild; / Another sighs for harmony, and grace, / And gentlest beauty' (lines 546–50).

there gentleman has been loitering about all day till now, when the foreign gentleman coming in, he spoke to him."

"And don't you know any thing further of this foreigner?"

"No, sir."

"I am sorry for it. Poor fellow!" sighed the old man, "he has been unfortunate, and I might have befriended him."

"Yes, to be sure doctor," cried the speaker, who now rose to accompany him out, "it is our duty to befriend the unfortunate; but charity begins at home, and as all's for the best, perhaps it is lucky we did not hear any more about this young fellow. We might have involved ourselves in a vast deal of unnecessary trouble, and, you know, the people of Poland have no claims upon us."

"Certainly," replied the doctor, "none in the world, more than those which no human creature can dispute; the claims of nature. All mankind are born heirs of suffering; and as joint inheritors, if we do not wipe away each other's tears, it will prove but a comfortless portion."

"Ah! doctor," cried his companion as they separated at the end of Charles-street,* "you have always the best of the argument; you have logic and Aristotle at your finger ends."

"No, my friend; my arguments are purely christian. Nature is my logic, and the bible my teacher."

"Ah, there you have me again. You parsons are as bad as the lawyers; when once you get a poor sinner among you, he finds it as hard to get out of the church as out of the chancery.† However, have it your own way; charity is your trade, and I won't be in a hurry to dispute the monopoly. Good day. If I stay much longer, you'll make me believe that black is white."

Dr. Blackmore shook him by the hand, and wishing him a good morning, returned home, pitying the worldliness of his friend's mind; and pondering on the interesting stranger, whom he admired and compassionated to absolute pain; because he believed him to be unfortunate, and out of the reach of his services.

END OF THE FIRST VOLUME.

---

* Charles Street (today the northern part of Wellington Street) ran between Russell Street and Tavistock Street, west of Covent Garden.
† The Court of Chancery was notorious for its slow proceedings and backlog of cases.

VOLUME II.

CHAP. I.

The Count Sobieski was cordially received by his worthy landlady: indeed he never stood in more need of kindness. A slow fever, which had been gradually creeping over him since his quitting Poland, had settled on his lungs, and excited a cough that kept him awake all night, and reduced him to such weakness in the day, that he neither had strength nor spirits to stir abroad.

Mrs. Robson was greatly distressed at this sudden and violent illness of her guest. Her own son, the father of the orphans whom she protected, had died a victim to a consumption, brought on by his excesses.

Thaddeus gave himself up completely to her management: he had no money for medical assistance; and to please her, he took what little medicines she prepared. According to her advice, he remained for several days closed up in his chamber, with a large fire, his curtains drawn, and the shutters shut, to exclude the smallest portion of that air, which, the good woman thought, had already stricken him with death.

But all would not do; her patient became worse and worse. Frightened at the symptoms, Mrs. Robson begged leave to send for the apothecary who had attended her deceased son. In this instance only, she found the Count obstinate: no arguments, nor even her tears, could move him. When she stood weeping, holding his burning hand, his answer was constantly of this kind:

"Do not, my excellent Mrs. Robson, grieve yourself on my account; I am not in the danger you think; I shall do very well with your assistance."

"No, no; I see death in your eyes. Can I feel this hand, and see that hectic cheek, without beholding your grave, as it were, opening before me?"

She was not much mistaken; for, during the night after this debate, Thaddeus grew so delirious, that, no longer able to subdue her terrors, she sent for the apothecary to come instantly to her house.

"O! doctor," cried she, as the man ascended the stairs, "I have the best young gentleman that ever the sun shone on, dying in that room!

He would not let me send for you; and now he is raving like a mad creature."

Mr. Vincent entered the Count's humble apartment, and undrew the curtains of the bed. Thaddeus, exhausted by his delirium, had sunk back, almost senseless on the pillow. Mrs. Robson, at this sight, supposing him dead, uttered a shriek that was in a moment echoed by the cries of the little William, who stood near his grandmother.

"Hush, my good woman," said the doctor, in a low voice, "the gentleman is not dead; leave the room till you have recovered yourself, and I will engage that you shall see him alive when you return."

Mrs. Robson, considering all his words as oracles, quitted the room with her grandson.

Mr. Vincent had felt, on entering the chamber, that the fever of his patient must be augmented by the hot and stifling state of the room; and, before he attempted to disturb him from the temporary rest which his senses found in insensibility, he opened the window-shutters, damped the raging of the fire with ashes and water, and then, unclosing the room door wide enough to admit the air from the adjoining apartment, undrew all the curtains of the bed, and pulling the heavy clothes down from the Count's bosom, raised his head on his arm, and poured some drops into his mouth. In a moment he opened his eyes, and uttered a few wild and incoherent words; but he did not rave, he only wandered, and appeared to know that he did so; for when he had quite recovered his powers, he every now and then stopped in the midst of some confused speech, and, laying his hand on his forehead, strove to recollect himself.

Mrs. Robson soon after entered the room, and poured out her thanks to the apothecary, whom she regarded as almost a worker of miracles.

"I must have him bled, Mrs. Robson," continued he; "and for that purpose shall go home for my assistant and lances:* but, in the mean while, I charge you to let every thing remain in the state I have left it. The heat alone would have been enough to have given a fever to a man in health."

When the apothecary returned, he saw that his commands had been strictly obeyed; and finding that the change of atmosphere had wrought some alteration in his patient, he took his arm without any difficulty, and bled him. At the end of the operation Thaddeus again fainted.

"Poor gentleman!" cried Mr. Vincent, binding up the wound before

---

* Bloodletting (usually at the elbow) remained a popular medical treatment in the nineteenth century for a wide variety of illnesses.

he tried to recover him: "look here, Tom," pointing to the scars in his arm and breast; "see what terrible cuts have been made there! This has not been playing at soldiers! Who is your lodger, Mrs. Robson?"

"A Mr. Constantine, Mr. Vincent. But, for heaven's sake! restore him out of that swoon."

Mr. Vincent poured more drops into his mouth; and a minute afterwards, he opened his eyes, divested of their feverish glare, but looking dull and heavy. He spoke to Mrs. Robson by her name; which gave her such delight, that she caught his hands to her lips, and burst into tears. The action was so instantaneous and violent, that it made him feel the stiffness of his arm; and, casting his eyes towards the men near his bed, he conjectured what had been his state, and what the consequence.

"Come, Mrs. Robson," said the apothecary, "you must not disturb the gentleman. How do you find yourself, Sir?"

Thaddeus having regained his perfect recollection, felt uneasy: but, as the deed could not be recalled, he thanked the doctor for the service he had received; and said a few kind and grateful words to his good hostess.

Mr. Vincent was glad to see so promising an issue to his proceedings, and soon after retired with his assistant and Mrs. Robson, to give further directions.

On entering the kitchen, she threw herself into a chair and broke into a paroxysm of lamentations.

"My good woman, what is all this about?" enquired the doctor. "Is not my patient better?"

"Yes," cried she, drying her eyes; "but the bed in which he lies, the whole scene, puts me so in mind of the last moments of my poor unfortunate misguided son, that the very sight of it goes through my heart like a knife. Oh! had my boy been as good as that dear gentleman, had he been as well prepared to die, I think I would scarcely have grieved! Yet, heaven spare Mr. Constantine. Will he live?"

"I hope so, Mrs. Robson; his fever is inveterate; but he is young, and, with extreme care, we may preserve him."

"The Lord grant it!" cried she, "for he is the best gentleman that I ever beheld. He has been above a week with me; and till this night, in which he lost his senses, though hardly able to breathe or see, he has read out of books that he brought with him; and good books too: for it was but yesterday morning I saw the dear soul sitting by the fire with a book on the table, which he had been studying near an hour; and as I was dusting about, I saw him lay his head down on it, and put his hand to his temples. 'Alas! Sir,' said I, 'you teize your brains with these books of learning, when you ought to be taking rest.' – 'No, Mrs.

Robson,' returned he, with a sweet smile, 'in this book I am seeking rest; it is the best soother of human affliction.' He closed it, and put it on the chimney-piece; and when I looked at it afterwards, I saw it was the Scriptures. – Can you wonder I should love so excellent a gentleman?"

"It is a strange account you have given of your lodger," replied Vincent: "I hope he is not a methodist; for if so, I shall despair of his cure, and think his delirium had another cause besides fever."

"A methodist! No, Sir: he is a christian; and as good a reasonable sweet-tempered gentleman, as ever came into a house. Alas! I believe he is more like a papist; though they say papists don't read the bible, but worship images."*

"Why, what reason have you to suppose that? He's an Englishman, is he not?"

"O no, he is an emigrant."

"An emigrant! O, ho!" cried Vincent, with a discontented and contemptuous raise of his eye-brows and voice; "what, a poor Frenchman! Good Lord! how this town is over-run by these fellows!"†

"No, doctor;" exclaimed Mrs. Robson, much hurt in pride and feeling at this affront to her lodger, whom she really loved; "whatever he be, he is not *poor*, for he has a power of fine things; he has got a watch all over diamonds, and diamond rings, and diamond pictures without number. So, doctor, you need not fear that you are attending him for charity; no, I would sell my gown first."

"Nay, don't be offended, Mrs. Robson! I meant no offence," returned he, much mollified by this explanation of hers; "but really, when we see the bread that should feed our children, and our own poor, eaten up by a parcel of lazy French drones;‡ who have covered our land, and destroyed its produce, like a swarm of filthy locusts, we should be fools

---

* Methodism, a denomination in the Protestant church closely associated with John Wesley, began as a mid-eighteenth-century movement for reform within the Church of England. For many Anglicans, it represented excess and a dangerous religious zeal. 'Papist' is a chiefly derogatory term for Roman Catholics.

† Most sources suggest that between 10,000 and 20,000 French *émigrés* lived in London at any given time in the decade following the onset of the French Revolution in 1789. Some settled permanently in Britain, while others passed through the country on their way to the Americas or French colonies. Carpenter, Kirsty, *Refugees of the French Revolution: Emigrés in London, 1789-1802* (New York: St Martin's Press, 1999), pp. 39–43.

‡ The phrase 'a parcel of lazy drones' appears occasionally in eighteenth-century writing. An early example appears in the pamphlet *Hannibal Not at Our Gates* (London: Thornhill, 1714): 'when our Estates must return to *Abbies*, and only serve to fatten a parcel of lazy Drones' (p. 6).

not to murmur. But Mr. Mr., what do you call him, Mrs. Robson? is a different sort of body."

"Mr. Constantine," replied she, "and indeed he is; and no doubt, when you recover him, he will pay you as though he were in his own country."

This last assertion of hers, banished all remaining suspicion from the apothecary's face; and after giving her what orders he thought requisite, he returned home, promising to call in the evening.

Mrs. Robson went up stairs to the Count's chamber, with other feelings towards her infallible doctor than those with which she came down. She well recollected the substance of his discourse; and she gathered from it, that however clever he might be in his profession, he was a hard-hearted man, who would rather see a fellow creature perish, than administer relief to him without a reward.

But here Mrs. Robson was mistaken. She did him justice in esteeming his medical abilities, which were great: he had made medicine the study of his life; and, not allowing any irrelevant occupation to disturb his attention, he became master of that science, while ignorant of every other with which it had no connection. He was the father of a family, and, in the usual acceptation of the term, a very good sort of a man; he preferred his country to every other, because it was his country; he loved his wife and his children: he was kind to the poor, to whom he gave his advice gratis, and letters to the dispensary for drugs; and when he had any broken victuals to spare, he desired it to be divided amongst them; but he seldom caught his maid obeying this part of his commands, without reprimanding her for her extravagance in giving away what ought to be eaten in the kitchen – "in these times it was a shame to waste a crumb; and the careless hussey would come to want, for thinking so lightly of other people's property."

Thus, like many in the world, he was a loyal citizen by habit, an affectionate father from nature, and a man of charity, because he now and then felt pity, and now and then heard it preached from the pulpit. He was exhorted to be pious, and to pour wine and oil into the wounds of the stranger;* but it never once struck him, that piety extended farther than going to church, mumbling his prayers, and forgetting the sermon, through most of which he generally slept: and his commentaries on the Good Samaritan were not more extensive; for the stranger, to him, was like the Canaanite Embassy that cheated the host

---

* Luke 10: 34. The Parable of the Good Samaritan (Luke 10: 25–37) encourages mercy and kindness to all those in need, friend and stranger alike.

of Israel, his nearest neighbour.* To have been born on the other side
of the British channel, spread an ocean between the poor foreigner,
and Mr. Vincent's purse, which, to this hour, the swiftest wings of
charity could never cross. "He saw no reason," he said, "for feeding
the natural enemies of our country. Would any man be mad enough to
take the meat from his children's mouths, and throw it to a swarm of
wolves just landed on the coast?" These wolves were his favorite met-
aphors, when he spoke of the unhappy French; or any other pennyless
foreigners, who came in his way.

After this explanation, it will appear paradoxical, to mention an
inconsistency in the mind of Mr. Vincent, which would never permit
him to discover the above Cainish mark of vagabondism,† upon the
wealthy stranger of whatever country. Somehow or other, it was with
him as with many: riches were a splendid and thick robe that concealed
all blemishes; take it away, and probably the poor stripped wretch
would be treated, even worse than his crimes deserve.

That his new patient possessed some property, was sufficient to
ensure the respect and medical skill of Mr. Vincent; and when he
entered his own house he told his wife, that he had found "a very
good job at Mrs. Robson's, in the illness of a Mr. Constantine, her
lodger."

When the Count Sobieski quitted the Hummums, the evening on
which he brought away his baggage, he had been so disconcerted by
the impertinence of the man who accosted him, that he determined no
longer to expose himself to insult, by retaining a title which rendered
him obnoxious to‡ the curiosity of the insolent and insensible; and
therefore, when Mrs. Robson asked him how she should address him,
as he was averse to assume a feigned name, he merely mentioned, *Mr.
Constantine*.§

Under that unobtrusive character, he hoped in time to accommodate
his feelings to the change of fortune which providence had allotted to
him. He must forget his nobility, his pride, and his sensibility; he must
earn his subsistence. But, by what means? He was ignorant of business;
and he knew not how to turn his accomplishments to account. – Such
were his meditations; till illness and delirium deprived him of these,
and of reason, together.

---

* The Canaanites of Gibeon, fearing the wrath of the Israelites, sent ambassadors who
  tricked Joshua into making a treaty with them. See Joshua 9.
† After denying the murder of his brother Abel, Cain was sent into exile by God
  (Genesis 4: 1–18).
‡ obnoxious to, 'exposed to or subject to' (*OED*).
§ As noted in the novel's opening chapter, Constantine is Sobieski's middle name.

At the expiration of a week, in which Mr. Vincent attended his patient very regularly, Sobieski was able to remove into the front room, and leave that gloomy chamber where he had endured so much anguish of body and mind. Uneasiness about how he should discharge the debts he had incurred, retarded his recovery, and made his hours pass away in cheerless meditation on the scanty means he possessed to repay the good widow and satisfy the avidity of the apothecary; who, in proportion as his patient could bear the addition, had sent in phials of medicines by dozens. Pecuniary obligation was a load to which he was unaccustomed; and, once or twice, the wish almost escaped his heart, that he had died.

Whenever he was left to think, such were always his reflections; but Mrs. Robson, who discovered that he appeared more feverish, and had worse nights after being much alone during the day, contrived, though she was obliged to be in her little shop, to leave either Nanny to attend his wants, or little William to amuse him.

This child, by its uncommon quickness and artlessness of manner, gained upon the Count, who was ever alive to helplessness and innocence. Children and animals, always found a friend and protector in him. From the *"majestic war-horse with his neck clothed in thunder,"** to *"the poor beetle that we tread upon,"*† every creature of creation, met an advocate of mercy in his breast: and, as human nature is prone to love what it has been kind to, Thaddeus never saw either children, dogs, or even that poor slandered and abused animal the cat, that he did not by some spontaneous act, shew it attention.

The little William now possessed what affection he could spare from memory. He hardly ever left his side, where he sat on a stool, prattling about any thing that came into his head; or seated on his knee, followed with his eyes and playful fingers, the Count's hand, as he sketched a horse or a soldier for his pretty companion.

In this way, he slowly acquired sufficient strength to allow him to quit his dressing-gown, and prepare for a walk.

A hard frost had succeeded to the chilling damps of November; and, looking out of the window, he longed, with almost sensations of eagerness, again to inhale the fresh air. After some tender altercations with Mrs. Robson, who feared to trust him even down the stairs, he at length conquered; and taking the little William in his hand, folded his

---

* 'Hast thou given the horse strength? hast thou clothed his neck with thunder?' (Job 39: 19).
† *Measure for Measure*, III, i, 78.

pelisse round him, and promising to venture no farther than the King's Mews,* was suffered to go out.

As he expected, he found the keen breeze act like a charm on his debilitated frame; and with braced nerves and exhilarated spirits, he walked twice up and down the place, whilst his companion played before him, throwing stones, and running to pick them up. At this moment, one of the King's carriages, pursued by a concourse of people, suddenly drove in at the Charing-cross gate. The frightened child screamed and fell. Thaddeus, seeing its danger, darted forward, and seizing the heads of the horses, which were within a yard of the boy, stopped them; meanwhile, the mob gathering about, one of them lifted up William, who continued his cries. The Count now let go the reins, and for a few minutes tried to pacify his little charge: but finding that his alarm and shrieks were not to be quelled, and that his own figure, from its singularity of dress, (his high cap and feathers adding much to his height,) had drawn on him the whole attention of the people, who quitted the carriage, and collected round him; he took the trembling child in his arms, and, walking through the Mews, was followed by some of the by-standers almost to the very door of Mrs. Robson's shop.

Seeing the people, and her grandson sobbing on the breast of her guest, she ran out, and hastily asked what had happened. Thaddeus simply answered, that the boy had been frightened. But when they entered the house, and he had thrown himself, exhausted, on a seat, William, as he stood by his knee, told his grandmother, that if Mr. Constantine had not stopped the horses, he must have been run over. The Count was now obliged to relate the whole story; which ended with the blessings of the poor woman for his goodness, to risk his own life in such a weak state, for the preservation of her darling child.

Thaddeus in vain assured her, that the action deserved no thanks, as it was spontaneous, and merely his duty.

"Well," cried she, "it is like yourself, Mr. Constantine; you think all your good deeds nothing: and yet any little odd thing I can do out of pure love to serve you, you cry up to the skies. However, we won't fall out; I say, Heaven bless you, and that is enough! – Has your walk refreshed you? But I need not ask; you have got a colour."

"Yes," returned he, rising and taking off his cap and cloak, "it has put me in a glow, and made me quite another creature." As he finished

* The King's Mews, housing the royal carriages and stables, stood near Charing Cross on the present site of the National Gallery. It would have been a very short distance from Mrs Robson's shop on St Martin's Lane.

speaking, he dropped the things from the hand that held them, and staggered back a few paces against the wall.

"Good Lord! what is the matter?" cried Mrs. Robson, alarmed, and looking in his face, which was now pale as death, "what is the matter?"

"Nothing, nothing," returned he, recovering himself, and gathering up the cloak he had let fall, "don't mind me, Mrs. Robson; nothing," and he was leaving the kitchen to go up stairs; but she followed him, terrified at his look and manner.

"Pray, Mr. Constantine!"

"Nay, my dear Madam," said he, leading her back again, "I am not well; I believe my walk has overcome me. Let me be a few minutes alone, till I have recovered myself. It will oblige me."

"Well, Sir, as you please!" and she curtseyed; then laying her withered hand fearfully upon his arm, as he was quitting the room, "forgive me, dear Sir," said she, "if my attentions are troublesome? Indeed, I fear, that sometimes great love appears like great impertinence; I would always be serving you, and therefore I often forget the wide difference that there is between your honour's station and mine."

The Count could only press her hand gratefully, and with an emotion that made him hurry up stairs. When in his own room, he shut the door, and cast a wild and inquisitive gaze around the apartment; then throwing himself into a chair, he struck his head with his hand, and exclaimed, "It is gone! What will become of me? of this poor woman, whose substance I have consumed?"

It was true, the watch, by the sale of which he had calculated to defray the charges of his illness, and the sum that he was conscious he must owe Mrs. Robson, was indeed lost. A villain in the crowd, having perceived the sparkling of the chain to which it was united, had taken it unobserved from his side; and he knew nothing of his loss, till feeling for it, to see the hour, he discovered his misfortune.

The shock went like a stroke of electricity through his frame; but it was not till the last glimmering of hope was extinguished, on his examining his room, where he thought he might have left it, that he felt the full horror of his situation.

He sat for some minutes, absorbed, and almost afraid to think. It was not his own, but the necessities of the poor woman, who had perhaps incurred debts on herself to afford him comforts, that bore so hard upon him. At last, rising from his seat, he exclaimed,

"I must determine on something. Since this is gone, I must seek what else I have to part with, for I cannot long bear such suspense."

He opened the drawer into which he had locked the few valuables he had preserved.

With a trembling hand he took them out one by one. There were several trinkets which had been given to him by his mother; and a pair of inlaid pistols that his grandfather had put into his belt on the morning of the dreadful tenth of October;* his miniature lay beneath; the mild eyes of the Palatine seemed beaming with affection upon his grandson: Thaddeus snatched it up, kissed it fervently, and then laid it back into the drawer, whilst he hid his face with his hands.

When he recovered himself, he replaced the pistols, feeling that it would be almost sacrilege to part with them. Without allowing himself time to think, he put a gold pencil-case and a pair of brilliant sleeve buttons into his waistcoat pocket.

He descended the stairs with a soft step, and passing the kitchen door unperceived by his landlady, crossed through a little court; and then anxiously looking from right to left, to find any place in which he might probably dispose of the trinkets, he took his way up Castle-street, and along Leicester-square.†

When he turned up the first street to his right, he was impeded by two persons who stood in his path, the one selling, the other buying, a hat. The thought immediately struck Thaddeus, of asking one of these men (who appeared to be a Jew and a vender of clothes) to purchase his pelisse. By parting with a thing to which he annexed no more value than the warmth it afforded him, he should possibly spare himself the pain, for this time at least, of sacrificing those gifts of his mother, which had been bestowed upon him in happier days and hallowed by her caresses.

He did not permit himself to hesitate a moment, but desired the Jew to follow him into a little court that was nigh. The man obeyed directly; and having no ideas independent of his trade, asked the Count what he wanted to buy.

"Nothing: I want to sell this pelisse," returned he, opening it. The Jew, without any ceremony, inspected the covering and the fur.

"Aye, I see it is black, lined with sable; who would buy it of me? It is embroidered, and nobody wears such things here."

"Then I am answered," replied Thaddeus.

"Stop, Sir," cried the Jew, pursuing him; "what will you take for it?"

"What would you give me?"

---

* 10 October 1794, date of the Battle of Maciejowice.
† Castle Street ran just west of and parallel to St Martin's Lane, along what is now Charing Cross Road. The nearby Leicester Square was once an area of fashionable residences, but by the 1790s it was increasingly turning to entertainment and retail.

"Let me see. It is very long and wide. At the utmost, I cannot offer you more than five guineas."

A few months ago, it had cost the Count twelve times as much; but glad to get any money, however small, he readily closed with the man's price; and taking off the cloak without a sigh, he gave it to him, and put the guineas into his pocket.

He had not walked much farther, before the piercing cold of the evening, and a shower of snow which began to fall, made him feel the effects of his loss: however, that did not annoy him; he had been too heavily assailed by the pitiless rigours of misfortune, to regard the pelting of the elements. Whilst the wind blew in his face, and the sleet, falling on his dress, lodged in its embroidered lapels, he went forward, calculating whether it were likely that this money, with the few shillings he yet possessed, would be sufficient to discharge what he owed. Unused as he had been to all kinds of expenditure that required attention, he supposed, from what he had already seen of a commerce with the world, that the sum he had received from the Jew, was not above half what he wanted; and, with a beating heart, he walked towards one of those shops, which he had heard Mrs. Robson describe when she spoke of the irregularities of her son, who had nearly reduced her to beggary.

The candles were lit. And as he hovered about the door, he distinctly saw the master through the glass, assorting some parcels on the counter. He was a gentleman-like man; and the Count's feelings took quite a different turn from those with which he had accosted the Jew, who was a low sordid wretch, looking upon the people with whom he trafficked, as pieces of wood; therefore few unpleasant sensations assailed his breast when bargaining with him: but the sight of a respectable person, before whom he was to present himself as a man in poverty, as one who in a manner appealed to charity, all at once overcame the resolution of Sobieski, and he debated whether he should return. Mrs. Robson, and her probable distresses, rose before him; and, fearful of trusting his pride any farther, he pulled his cap over his face, stepped up the step, and entered the shop.

The man bowed very civilly on his entrance, and requested to be honoured with his commands. Thaddeus felt his face glow; but, indignant at his own weakness, he walked up to the counter, and laying down the gold case, said in a voice, which notwithstanding his emotion he compelled to be without appearance of confusion, "I want to part with this."

The man, astonished at the dignity of his air, and the nobility of his dress, (for the star did not escape his eye,) looked at him for a moment, holding the case in his hand. The Count, hurt by the steadiness of his gaze, rather haughtily repeated what he had said. The man hesitated no longer. He had been accustomed to similar requests from the emigrant French *noblesse*: but there was a loftiness, and an air of authority, in the countenance and mien of this person, that surprised and awed him; and with a respect, which even the application could not counteract, he opened the case, and enquired of Thaddeus; what was the price he had affixed to it.

"I leave that to you," replied the Count; "you see the gold is solid."

"Yes," returned the man, laying it down, "but I cannot give more than three guineas. It is very thin; and though the workmanship be fine, it is not the fashion of England, and will be of no benefit to me till melted."

"You may have it," said Thaddeus, hardly able to articulate, as he again laid the gift of his mother out of his hand.

The man directly paid him down the money, and the Count, with a bursting heart, darted out of the shop.

Mrs. Robson was shutting up the windows of her little parlour, when he hastily passed her, and glided up the stairs. Hardly believing her senses, she hastened after him, and just got into the room as he swallowed a glass of water.

"Good lord, Sir" cried she, "where has your honour been? I thought you had been all the while in the house, and I would not come near, though I was very uneasy; and there has been poor William crying himself blind, because you had desired to be left alone."

Thaddeus was not prepared to make an answer. He had been in hopes to have gotten in as he had stolen out, undiscovered; for he had determined not to agitate her good mind, by the history of his loss. He would not allow her to know any thing of his embarrassments, from sentiments of justice, as well as of that pride which all his sufferings and philosophy could not wholly subdue.

"I have been taking a walk, Mrs. Robson."

"Dear heart! I thought when you staggered back, and looked so ill, after you brought in William, that you had over-walked yourself!"

"No; I fancy my fears had a little discomposed me, and I hoped more air might do me good; I tried it, and it has: but I am grieved that I have alarmed you."

This ambiguous speech perfectly satisfied his kind landlady. Thaddeus, much fatigued by a bodily exertion, which nothing less than the perturbed state of his mind, could have carried him through in the present feebleness of his frame, after he had taken some tea at the earnest request of Mrs. Robson, went directly to bed, where tired nature soon found temporary repose in a profound sleep.

CHAP. II.

When the Count awoke in the morning, he found himself rather better than worse from the exertions of the preceding day. When Nanny appeared as usual with his breakfast, and little William, (who always sat on his knee and shared his bread and butter,) he desired her to beg that her grandmother would send to Mr. Vincent with his compliments, and tell him, that he was so well at present, as to decline any farther medical aid and, therefore requested to have his bill.

Mrs. Robson, who could not forget the behaviour of the apothecary, undertook to deliver the message herself, happy in the triumph she should experience over the littleness of Mr. Vincent's suspicions.

After the lapse of a quarter of an hour, she re-appeared in the Count's room with the apothecary's assistant; who, with many thanks, received the sum total of the accompt, which amounted to three guineas for ten days' attendance.

The man having withdrawn, Thaddeus told Mrs. Robson, that he must next defray the smallest part of that vast debt, which his heart should ever owe to her parental care.

"O, bless your honour; it goes to my heart to take a farthing of you! but these poor children," cried she, laying a hand on each, and her eyes glistening; "they look up to me as their all here; and my quarter-day was due yesterday, else, dear Sir, I should have scorned to have been like Doctor Vincent, and have taken your money the moment you offered it."

"My good madam," returned Sobieski, giving her a chair, "I am sensible of the kindness of your nature; but it is your just due, and the payment of it can never lessen my gratitude for the friendship that you have shewn to me, a stranger."

"Then there Sir;" said she, looking almost as ashamed as if she were robbing him when she laid it on the table, "there is my bill. I have regularly set down every thing. Nanny will bring it to me." And the good woman, quite disconcerted, hurried out of the room.

Thaddeus looked after her with sensations of admiration and reverence.

"There goes," thought he, "in that lowly and feeble frame, as generous and noble a spirit as ever animated the breast of a princess! – Here, Nanny," said he, glancing his eye over the paper, "there are the two guineas and a half with my thanks; and tell your grandmother that I am astonished at her economy."

This affair over, the Count found himself relieved of a grievous load; and turning the remaining money in his hand; how he might replenish the little stock before it were expended, next occupied his attention. Notwithstanding the pawn-broker's civil treatment, he recoiled at again presenting himself at his shop. Besides, should he dispose of all that he possessed, it would not be of sufficient value to subsist him for a month. He must think of some source within himself not likely to be so soon exhausted. To be reduced a second time to the misery of mind that he had experienced yesterday, from suspense and wretchedness, appeared too dreadful to be hazarded; and he ran over in his memory the merits of his several accomplishments.

He could not make any use of his musical talents, for at public exhibitions of himself his soul revolted; and as to his literary acquirements, he supposed that his youth, and being a foreigner, would preclude all hope on that head. At length he found, that his sole dependence must rest on his talents for painting. Of this art he had always been remarkably fond; and his taste easily perceived, when he passed by several of the print-shops in town, that there were many drawings exhibited for sale, much beneath those which he had executed for mere pastime.

He decided at once; and sending Nanny to purchase pencils and Indian ink, set to work.

When he had finished half a dozen drawings, and was considering how he might find the street wherein he had seen the print-shops, the recollection occurred to him of the impression that his appearance had made on the pawn-broker. He perceived the wide difference between his apparel and the fashion of England; and, seeing with what better security from impertinence he might walk about, if he could so far cast off the relics of his former rank as to change his dress, he got up with an intention to go out, and purchase a surtout coat, and hat, for that purpose: but catching an accidental view of his figure and the star of St. Stanislaus, as he passed the glass to the door, he no longer wondered at the curiosity which such an appendage, united with poverty, had attracted. Rather than again subject himself to a similar situation, he summoned his young messenger; and through her means, furnished himself with an English hat and coat, whilst with his pen-knife, he cut away the embroidery of the order, from the cloth to which it was affixed.

Thus accoutred, with his hat flapped over his face, and his great coat wrapped round him, he put his drawings in his bosom, and about eight o'clock, walked out on his disagreeable errand. After some wearying search, he at last found Great Newport Street,* the place he wanted; but as he advanced, his hopes died away, and his fears and reluctance awakened.

He stopped at the door of the nearest print-shop. All that he had experienced at the pawn-broker's, re-assailed him if possible with redoubled violence. What he had presented there, possessed a fixed value, and was at once to be taken or refused; but now, he was going to offer things of mere taste, and he might meet not only with a flat denial, but affronting remarks.

He walked to the threshold of the door, then as hastily withdrew again, and hurried two or three paces down the street.

"Weak, contemptible, that I am!" said he to himself as he again turned round, "where is all my reason and rectitude of principle, that I would rather endure the misery of dependence and self-reproach, than face the attempt to seek support from the fruits of my own industry?"

He quickened his step, and darted into the shop, almost fearful of his former irresolution. He threw his drawings instantly upon the counter.

"Sir, you purchase drawings. I have these to sell. Will they suit you?"

The man took them up, without deigning to look at the person who had accosted him, and turning them over in his hand, "One, two, three, hum! there is half a dozen of them. What do you expect I will give you for them?"

"I am not acquainted with the prices of these things."

The printseller hearing this, thought, by managing well, to get them for what he liked, and, throwing them over with an air of contempt, resumed,

"And pray, where may the views be taken?"

"They are recollections of scenes in different parts of Germany."

"Ah!" replied the man, "mere drugs!† I wish, my honest friend, that you could have brought subjects not quite so threadbare, and a little better executed; they are but poor things at best!"

Thaddeus, insulted by the speech, and above all, the manner of the print-seller, was snatching up the drawings to leave the shop without a word, when the man observing his design, and, afraid to lose them, laid his hand on the heap, exclaiming;

"Let me tell you, young man, it does not become a person in your

---

* Great Newport Street, northeast of Leicester Square, was a centre for artists, print sellers and art dealers in the 1790s. The Porters lived at 16 Great Newport Street from 1796 to 1799.

† drugs, 'A commodity which is no longer in demand, and so has lost its commercial value or has become unsaleable' (*OED*).

situation to be so huffy to their employers. I will give you a guinea for the six, and you may think yourself well paid."

Without farther hesitation, whilst the Count was striving to subdue the choler that was urging him to knock him down, he had laid the money on the counter, and was slipping the drawings into a drawer; when Thaddeus, snatching them out again, suddenly rolled them up, and turning to the confounded print-seller, walked out of the shop as he said:

"Not all the wealth you may possess, would tempt an honest man to pollute himself by exchanging a second word with one so contemptible."

Irritated and vexed, he returned home too much provoked, to think much of the consequence that might follow a similar disappointment.

The widow, who had become in some measure used to the fluctuations of the Count's looks and behaviour, ceased altogether to teize him with inquiries which she saw he was loth to answer. She now allowed him to walk in and out without a remark; and silently contemplated his pale and melancholy countenance, when after a ramble of the greatest part of the day, he returned home exhausted and dispirited.

William was always the first to welcome his friend at the threshold, by running to him, taking hold of his coat, and asking to go with him up stairs. The Count usually gratified him; and unclouding his mind of the gloom that nearly obscured it, to devise any little plays which could produce pleasure, where he now found that he felt so much affection, he brightened many dull hours with his innocent caresses.

This child was literally his chief comfort; for, he saw, that in him, he could still raise those emotions of happiness, which had once afforded him his sweetest joy. William ever greeted him with smiles; and when he entered the kitchen, sprang to his bosom, as if that were the seat of peace, as it was of virtue. But, alas! fortune seemed averse to lend any thing long to the unhappy Thaddeus, which might render his desolate state more tolerable.

Just arisen from the bed of sickness, he rather required the hand of some tender nurse to restore his wasted vigour, than be reduced to sustain the hard vigils of poverty and want. His recent disappointment, and a cold that he caught, increased his fever and debility; yet he kept firm to the determination, not to appropriate to his own subsistence, the sale of the few valuables which he had assigned as a deposit for the charges of his rent; and accordingly, during a fortnight, he never tasted any thing better than bread and water, accompanied by the thought, that if it ended in his death, his sufferings would then be over, and the widow remunerated by what little of his property might remain.

In this state of body and mind, he received a most painful shock, when, one evening, returning from a walk, in the place of his little favourite, he met Mrs. Robson in tears at the door. She told him that William had been sickening all the day, and was now so delirious, that neither she nor his sister could hold him quiet.

Thaddeus went to the side of the child's bed, where he lay gasping on the pillow, with his little face the colour of scarlet, and held down by the crying Nanny. The Count touched his cheek.

"Poor child," exclaimed he, "he is in a high fever. Have you sent for Mr. Vincent?"

"O no, I had not the heart to leave him."

"Then I will go directly," returned Thaddeus; "there is not a moment to be lost."

The poor woman thanked him. Hastening through the streets with a velocity and eagerness that nearly overset many of the foot passengers, he arrived at Lincoln's Inn Fields;* and in less than five minutes after he quitted Mrs. Robson's door, he brought back the apothecary.

On Mr. Vincent's examining the pulse and countenance of his little patient, he declared the symptoms to be the small pox, which some casualty had repelled, but must be brought out, else the boy's life might be endangered.†

Mrs. Robson, in a paroxysm of distress, now recollected that a girl had been brought into her shop three days ago, just recovered from that frightful malady.

Thaddeus tried to subdue the fears of the grandmother; and at last succeeded in persuading her to go to bed, whilst he and Nanny would watch by the pillow of the invalid.

Towards morning, the disorder broke out in the child's face, and he recovered his recollection. The moment he fixed his eyes on the Count, who was leaning over him with parental solicitude, he stretched out his little arms, and begged to lie on his breast. Thaddeus refused him gently, fearful that by any change of position, he might catch cold, and so again retard what had now so fortunately appeared; but the poor child felt the denial unkind, and began to weep so violently, that his anxious friend thought it better to gratify him, than hazard the irritation of his fever by agitation and crying.

Thaddeus took him out of bed, and rolling him in one of the blankets, laid him in his bosom, and drawing his dressing-gown round him

---

* A large public square named for the adjacent Lincoln's Inn, just over a kilometre northeast of Mrs Robson's abode.

† casualty, 'chance, accident (as a state of things)' (*OED*). The apothecary hopes to induce ('bring out') the characteristic pustules of smallpox in order to rid William's body of the virus.

to shield his face from the fire, held him in that situation asleep for nearly two hours.

When Mrs. Robson came down stairs at six o'clock in the morning, she kissed the hand of the Count as he sustained her grandson in his arms, and, almost speechless with gratitude to him, and solicitude for the child, waited the arrival of the apothecary.

On his second visit, he said a few words to her of comfort; but whispered to the Count, as he was feeling William's pulse, that nothing short of the strictest care could save the boy, the infection he had received having been of the most malignant sort.

These words of Mr. Vincent, fell like an unrepealable sentence on the heart of Thaddeus. They seemed prophetic. Casting his eyes down on the discoloured features of the patient infant, he fancied that he already beheld its clay-cold face, and its little limbs stretched out in death. The idea was bitterness to him; and, pressing the boy to his breast, he resolved that no attention should be wanting on his part, to preserve him one moment from the grave. And he kept his promise.

From that hour, till the day on which the poor babe expired in his arms, he never laid him out of them for ten minutes together: and when he did breathe his last sigh, and raised up his little eyes, Thaddeus met their dying glance with a pang, which he thought his soul had long lost the power to feel. His heart appeared to stop: and, covering the motionless face of the dead child with his hand; unable to speak, he made a sign to Nanny to leave the room.

The girl, who, from respect, had been accustomed to obey even his slightest nod, went to her grandmother, who was in the shop serving a customer.

The instant the girl quitted the room, the Count, with mingled awe and grief, lifted the little corpse from his knee; and without allowing himself to cast another glance on the face of the poor little thing now released from suffering, he put it on the bed, and, throwing the sheet over it, sunk into a chair, and burst into tears.

The entrance of Mrs. Robson, in some measure restored him; for, the moment she perceived her guest with his handkerchief over his eyes, she judged what had happened, and, with a piercing scream, flew forward to the bed, where, pulling down the covering, she uttered another shriek, and must have fallen on the floor, had not Thaddeus and little Nanny, who ran in at her cries, caught her in their arms, and bore her to a chair.

Her feelings were too much agitated to allow her to continue long in a state of insensibility; and when she recovered she would have again approached the dead child; but the Count held her down, and, trying by every means in his power to soothe her, so far succeeded as to subdue her agonies into tears.

Whilst she concealed her venerable head in the bosom of her grand-daughter, he once more lifted the remains of the little William; and, thinking it best for the tranquillity of the unhappy grandmother, to take him out of her sight, carried him up stairs, and laid him on his own bed.

By the time that he returned to the kitchen, one of the female neighbours having heard an unusual out-cry, and suspecting the cause, had kindly stepped in to offer her consolation and services. Mrs. Robson could only reply by groans, which were answered by the sobs of poor Nanny, who lay weeping with her head against the table.

When the Count came down, he thanked the good woman for her benevolent intentions, and, immediately accepting them, took her up stairs into his apartments. Pointing to the open door of the bed-room, "There, Madam," said he, "you will find the remains of my dear little friend. I beg that you will direct every thing for his interment, as you think would give satisfaction to Mrs. Robson. I would spare that excellent woman every pang in my power."

All was done according to his desire; and Mrs. Watts, the charitable neighbour, both from her own tenderness of disposition, and a reverence for "the extraordinary young gentleman who lodged with her friend," performed her task with kindness and activity.

"O! Sir," cried Mrs. Robson, weeping afresh, as she entered the Count's room, "O! Sir, how shall I ever repay all your goodness? and Mrs. Watts! good soul! she has acted like a sister to me. But indeed, indeed, I am yet the most miserable woman that lives. I have lost my dearest child, and must strip his poor sister and myself to bury him. That cruel Dr. Vincent, though he might have imagined my distress, sent his accompt late last night, saying he wanted to make up a large bill, and he wished I would let him have all, or a part of the payment. Heaven knows, I have not a farthing in the house: but I will send poor little Nanny out to pawn my silver spoons; for, alas! I have no other means of satisfying the cruel man."

"Rapacious wretch!" cried Thaddeus, rising indignantly from his chair, and for a moment forgetting how incapable he was to afford relief, "You shall not be indebted one instant to his mercy. *I* will pay him."

The words had passed his lips: he could not retract; though conviction immediately followed, that he had not the means: and he would not have retracted, even should he be necessitated to sell all that he possessed.

Mrs. Robson was overwhelmed by this generous promise, which indeed saved her from ruin. Had her little plate been sold, it could not have covered one half of Mr. Vincent's demand: who, to do him justice, would as soon have swallowed the bitterest drug in his shop, as have done any thing intentionally to cause the distress that he had occasioned. But, having been so readily paid by Thaddeus for his own illness; and observing his great care and affection for the deceased child, he did not doubt, that rather than allow Mrs. Robson a minute's uneasiness, her lodger would likewise defray that bill. So far he calculated right; but he had not sufficient sagacity to prognosticate, that in getting his money this way, he should directly lose the respect of Mrs. Robson and her friend.

The child was to be buried to-morrow; the expenses of which, Thaddeus foresaw that he must discharge also; and he had engaged to pay Mr. Vincent to-night. He had not a shilling in his purse. Over and over, he contemplated the impracticability of answering these debts; yet he could not for an instant repent of what he had undertaken: he thought he was amply recompensed for bearing so heavy a load, in seeing that he had taken it off the worn-down heart of another.

Since his unmannerly treatment at the printseller's, he had never sufficiently conquered his pride, to attempt an application to another. Hence he had no prospect now, but to collect the money by selling some more things to the pawnbroker, – who had behaved at least with civility.

For this purpose, he took his sabre, his pistols, and the fated brilliant buttons which he had brought back on a similar errand. He lifted them out of their deposit with less reluctance than before. They were now going to be an offering of gratitude and benevolence; an act, which he knew his parents,* were they alive, would warmly approve; and he felt, that the end sanctified the means.

It was about half after six in the evening, when he prepared himself for his task. Whether it be congenial with melancholy to seek the gloom, or whether the Count found himself less observed under the shades of night, is not evident; but since his exile, he preferred the dusk to any other part of the day.

Before he went out, he asked Mrs. Robson for Mr. Vincent's bill. Almost sinking with obligation and shame, she put it into his hand, and he left the house. When he approached a lighted lamp, he opened the paper to see the amount; and finding it was near two pounds, he hastened forwards to the pawnbroker's.

---

* That is, his mother and grandfather.

The man was in the shop alone. Thaddeus thought himself fortunate; and after subduing a few qualms, immediately entered the door. The moment he laid his sword and pistols on the counter, and declared his wish, the man, even through the disguise of a large coat and slouched hat, recollected him. This honest money-lender carried sentiments in his breast above his occupation. He did not feel for all the people that presented themselves before him, because many bore about them too evident tokens of the excesses which brought them to his shop; but there was something in the figure and manner of the Count Sobieski, that struck him at first sight; and by keeping its station in his thoughts, had excited so much interest in his mind, that he felt a sensation of pleasure when he discerned the noble foreigner, in the person before him.

Mr. Burnet (for so this money-lender was called) asked him what he demanded for the arms.

"I want, perhaps more than you would give. But I have something else here," laying down the diamonds: "I want eight guineas."

Mr. Burnet looked at them, and then at their owner, hesitated, and then spoke.

"I beg your pardon, Sir; I hope that I shall not offend you, but these things appear to have a value annexed to them, independent of their price – they are inlaid with crests and cyphers!"

The blood flushed over the cheeks of the Count. He had forgotten this circumstance; unable to answer, he waited to hear what the man would say.

"I repeat, Sir, I mean not to offend, but you appear a stranger to these transactions. I only wish to suggest, that in case you should ever like to re-possess these things, had you not better pledge them?"

"How?" asked Thaddeus, irresolutely, and not knowing what to think of the man's manner.

At that instant some other people came into the shop; and Mr. Burnet gathering up the diamonds and the arms in his hand, said, "If you do not object, Sir, we will settle this business in my back parlour?"

The delicacy of his behaviour, penetrated the mind of Thaddeus; and without further demurring, he followed him into a room. As Mr. Burnet offered his guest a chair, the Count spontaneously took off his hat, and laid it on the table. Burnet contemplated the saddened dignity of his countenance, with renewed interest and respect; and, entreating him to be seated, resumed the conversation.

"I see, Sir, that you do not understand the meaning of pledging, or pawning, for it is one and the same thing: but I will explain it in two words. If you leave these things with me, I will give you a paper in acknowledgment, and *lend* on them the eight guineas you request; which, when you return to me again, with a stated interest, you shall have your deposit in exchange."

Sobieski received this offer with pleasure and thanks. He had entertained no idea of any thing more being meant by the trade of a pawnbroker, than a man who bought what others wished to sell.

"Then, Sir," continued Burnet, opening an escrutoire, "I will give you the money, and write the paper I spoke of."

As he put his hand to a drawer, he heard voices in an adjoining passage; and instantly shutting up the desk, caught up the things on the table, threw them behind a curtain, and hastily taking the Count by the hand, "My dear Sir," cried he, "do oblige me and step into that closet! you will find a chair. A person is coming, whom I will dispatch in a few seconds."

Thaddeus, rather surprised at such hurry, did as he was desired; and the door was closed on him, just as the parlour door opened. Being aware, from the concealing him,* that the visitor came on secret business, he found his situation not a little awkward. Seated behind a curtained window, which the lights in the room made transparent, he could not avoid seeing, as well as hearing every thing that passed.

"My dear Mr. Burnet," cried an elegant young creature, who ran into the apartment, "positively without your assistance I shall be undone."

"Any thing in my power, Madam," returned Mr. Burnet, in a distant, respectful voice; "will your ladyship sit down?"

"Yes; give me a chair: I am half dead with distraction. Mr. Burnet, I must have another hundred upon those jewels."

"Indeed, my lady, it is not in my power; you have already had twelve hundred, and upon my honour that is a hundred and fifty more than I ought."

"Pugh, who minds the honour of a pawnbroker!" cried the lady, laughing; "you know very well you live by cheating."

"Well, Ma'am," returned he, with a good natured smile, "as your ladyship pleases."

"Then I please that you let me have another hundred. Why man, you know you lent Mrs. Hinchinbroke two thousand upon a case of diamonds not a quarter so many as mine."

"But consider, Madam, Mrs. Hinchinbroke's were of the best water."†

---

* Revised to the clearer 'from such concealment' in the second edition.
† water, 'the transparency and lustre characteristic of a diamond' (*OED*). Diamonds are valued in part by their transparency.

"Positively, Mr. Burdet," exclaimed her ladyship, purposely miscalling his name, "not better than mine! The king of Sardinia gave them to Sir Charles when he knighted him. I know mine are the best, and I must have another hundred. Upon my soul, my servants have not had a guinea of their board wages these four months, and they tell me they are starving! Come, make haste, Mr. Burnet; you cannot expect me to stay here all night."

"Indeed, my lady, I cannot."

"Heavens, what a brute of a man you are! There," cried she, taking a string of pearls from her neck, and throwing it on the table; "lend me some of your trumpery out of your shop, for I am going immediately from hence to take up the Miss Dundas's to the play; and so give me the hundred on that, and let me go."

"This is not worth a hundred."

"What a teizing man you are!" cried her ladyship angrily. "Well, let me have the money now, and I will send you the bracelets that belong to the necklace to-morrow."

"Upon those conditions, I will give your ladyship another hundred."

"O, do; you are the veriest miser I ever met with. You are worse than Shylock, or, – Good lord! what is this?" exclaimed she, interrupting herself, and taking up the draught he had laid before her; "And have you the conscience to think, Mr. Pawnbroker, that *I* will offer this at your banker's? that I will expose myself so far? No, no; take it back, and give me gold. Come, dispatch! else I cannot go to the play. Look, there is my purse," added she, shewing it, "make haste and fill it."

After satisfying her demands, Mr. Burnet handed her ladyship out the way she came in, which was by a private passage; and having seated her in her carriage, made his bow.

Meanwhile, the Count Sobieski, wrapped in astonishment at the profligacy which the scene he had witnessed implied, remained in his concealment, till the pawnbroker returned and opened the closet door.

"Sir," said he, colouring, "you have, undesignedly on your part, been privy to a very delicate affair; but my credit, Sir, and your honour – "

"Shall both be sacred," replied the Count, anxious to relieve the poor man from the perplexity in which he seemed to think himself involved, and therefore forbearing to express any surprize. But Burnet perceived it in his look; and before he proceeded to fulfil his engagement with him, stepped half way to the escrutoire, and resumed.

"You appear amazed, Sir, at what you have seen. And if I am not mistaken, you are from abroad."

"Indeed I am amazed," replied Sobieski; "and I am from a country where the slightest suspicion of a transaction such as this, would brand the woman with infamy."

"And so it ought," answered Burnet: "though by that sentiment I speak against my own interest; for it is by such ladies as Lady Villiers that we make our money. Now, Sir," continued he, drawing nearer to the table, "perhaps, after what you have just beheld, you will not hesitate to credit what I am going to tell you. I have now in my hands the jewels of one dutchess, three countesses, and women of fashion without number. When they have an ill run at play, they apply to me in their exigencies; first, by bringing their diamonds here, when their husbands suppose them at their bankers', or in their own house; and as their occasions require, on this deposit I lend them money; for which they make me a handsome present when they are released."

"Gracious Heaven!" exclaimed Thaddeus, "what a degrading system of deceit must be the whole lives of these women!"

"It is very lamentable," returned Burnet, "but so it is. And they continue to manage matters very cleverly. By giving me their note or word of honour (for if these ladies are not honourable with me, I have their reputations so much in my power, that I could destroy them at once: therefore I hold them in awe; and whatever be their characters, I have no fears on that head), I allow them to have the jewels out for the birth-days, and receive them again when their exhibition is over. As a compensation for these little indulgences, I generally have additions to the present at the end."

Thaddeus could hardly believe such a history of those women, whom travellers mentioned, as not only the most lovely, but the most amiable creatures in the world.

"Surely, Mr. Burnet," cried he, "these women must despise each other; and become contemptible even to our sex?"

"O, no," rejoined the pawnbroker; "they seldom trust each other in these affairs. All my fair customers are not so silly as that pretty little lady who just now left us. She, and another woman of quality, have made each other confidants in this business. And Lord have mercy upon me when they come together! They are as ravenous of my money as if it had no other use than to supply them. As to their husbands, brothers, and fathers, they are usually the last people who suspect or hear of these matters. Their applications, when they run out, are made to Jews and professed usurers, a race completely out of our line."

"But, are all English women of quality of this disgraceful stamp?"

"No, Heaven forbid!" cried Burnet; "if these spendthrift madams were not held in awe by their dread of superior characters, we should have no dependence whatever on their promises. O, no; there are ladies about court, whose virtues are as eminent as their rank: women, whose actions might all be performed in mid-day, before the world; and them, I never see within my doors."

"Well, Mr. Burnet," rejoined Thaddeus, smiling, "I am glad to hear that. Yet I cannot forget the unexpected view of the so famous British fair, which this night has offered to my eyes. It is strange!"

"It is very bad, indeed, Sir," returned the man, giving him the money and the paper that he had been preparing; "but if you should have occasion to call again upon me, perhaps you may be astonished still farther."

The Count bowed; and thanking him for his kindness, wished him a good evening and left the shop.

It was about seven o'clock when Thaddeus arrived at the apothecary's. Mr. Vincent was from home. To say the truth, he had purposely gone out of the way. For though he did not hesitate to commit a shabby action, he had not courage to face its consequence; and, to avoid the probable remonstrances of Mrs. Robson, he had commissioned his assistant to receive the amount of the bill. The Count, without making an observation, having paid the man, was returning homeward, along Duke's-street and the Piazzas of Drury-lane Theatre,* when the crowd that was pressing round the doors, constrained him to stop.

After two or three ineffectual attempts to get through the bustle without throwing himself into the midst of the splendid groupes, that were passing from their carriages to the doors, he retreated a little behind the mob, at the moment when a chariot drew up, and a gentleman stepping out with two ladies, darted with them into the house. One glance was sufficient for the Count, who recognized his friend Pembroke Somerset, in high dress, gay, and laughing. The heart of Thaddeus sprang to him at the sight; and forgetting his neglect and his own misfortunes, he ejaculated,

"Somerset!"

Trembling with eagerness and pleasure, he pressed through the crowd, and entered the passage, at the instant a green door shut in upon his friend.

The disappointment was dreadful. To be so near Somerset and to lose him, was more than he could sustain. His bounding heart recoiled; and the chill of despair running through his veins, turned him almost

---

* Duke Street formerly ran from the west side of Lincoln's Inn Fields towards Drury Lane. The Theatre Royal, Drury Lane, had been recently rebuilt, reopening in March 1794. Along with the Theatre Royal, Covent Garden, it was one of the city's patent theatres, and therefore able to perform spoken drama.

faint. Leaning against the door, he took his hat off to give himself a little air. He had scarcely stood a minute in this situation, revolving whether he should follow his friend into the house or wait till he came out again, when a gentleman begged him to make way for a party of ladies that were entering. Thaddeus moved on one side; but the opening of the green door casting a strong light, both on his face and the groupe behind, his eyes and those of the impertinent inquisitor of the Hummums met each other.

Whether the man were conscious that he deserved chastisement for his former insolence, and dreaded to meet it now, cannot be explained; but he turned pale and shuffled by Thaddeus, as if he were fearful to trust himself a second time within reach of his grasp. For the Count, he was too deeply interested in his own pursuit, to waste one surmise upon him.

He continued to ponder on the sudden and unexpected sight of Pembroke Somerset, which had conjured up ten thousand fond and distressing recollections; and with impatient anxiety determining to watch till the performance was over, he thought of enquiring his friend's address of the servants; but on looking round for that purpose, perceived that the chariot had driven away.

Thus foiled, he returned to his post near the green door; where he soon saw it opened several times by footmen passing and repassing. Judging that the chamber within might be a lobby, in which he would be less likely to miss his object, he entered with the next person that approached; and seeing seats along the sides of the place, he sat down on the one nearest to the stairs.

His first idea was to proceed into the play-house. But on reflection, he considered the little chance of finding any particular individual in so vast a building, as not equal to the expence he should incur. Besides, from the dress of the gentlemen who entered the box door, he was sensible that a great coat and round hat were not admissible.

Having remained near an hour, with his eyes invariably fixed on the stairs; he observed that same curious person who had passed almost directly after his friend, come down the steps and walk out of the door. In two minutes he was returning with a smirking countenance, and alert steps; when his eyes accidentally falling on the Count, (who sat with his arms folded and himself almost hidden by his hat and the shadow of the wall,) he appeared to faulter in his walk; and stretching out his neck towards him, the gay grin left his features; and exclaiming in an impatient voice, "Confound him!" he hastened once more into the house.

This rencontre with his Hummums acquaintance, affected Thaddeus as slightly as the former; and without even annexing a thought to his figure, as it flitted by him, he remained, watching the passage till half after eleven. At which hour the doors being thrown open, the company began to pour forth.

The Count's hopes were again on his lips, and in his eyes. With the first party that came down the steps, he immediately rose; and planting himself close to the bottom stair, drew his hat over his face, and narrowly examined each groupe as it descended. Every fresh set that he heard approach, made his breast palpitate. How often did his heart rise and fall during the long succession which continued moving for near half an hour!

By twelve, the house was completely cleared. He saw the middle door locked; and motionless with disappointment, did not attempt to stir, till the man who held the keys told him to go, as he was about to fasten the other doors.

This roused Thaddeus. And as he was preparing to obey, he asked the man if there were any other passage from the boxes.

"Yes," cried he, "there is one that goes into Drury-lane."

"Then, by that I have lost him!" was the reply which he made to himself. And returning homewards, he arrived there a few minutes after twelve.

CHAP. III.

Thaddeus awoke in the morning with his heart full of the last night's rencontre. One moment, he regretted that he had not been seen by his friend; and in the next, when he surveyed his altered state, was almost reconciled to the disappointment: then reproaching himself for a pride so unbecoming his principles and dishonourable to friendship, he asked, if he were in Somerset's place and Somerset in his, whether he could ever pardon that morose delicacy, which would prevent the knowledge of his friend's misfortunes and arrival in the same kingdom?

These reflections soon persuaded his judgment to what he was so much inclined, determining him to enquire Pembroke's address of every one likely to know a man of Sir Robert Somerset's consequence; and then to venture a letter.

In the midst of these meditations, the door opened, and Mrs. Robson appeared before him drowned in tears.

"My dear, dear Sir!" cried she, "my William is going; I have just taken my last look of its sweet face.* Will you go down, and say farewell to the poor child you loved so dearly?"

"No, my good madam;" returned Thaddeus, his straying thoughts at once gathering round this sad center, "I will rather retain you here until the melancholy task be entirely accomplished."

With gentle violence he forced her upon a seat, and in silence supported her head on his side, against which she unconsciously leaned and wept. He listened with a painful melancholy to the removal of the coffin; and at the closing of the street-door, which for ever shut the little William from that house in which he had been the source of pleasure. A tear trickled down the cheek of Thaddeus, and the groans of the poor grandmother were audible.

The Count, incapable of speaking, squeezed her hand in his.

"O, Mr. Constantine!" cried she, "see how my supports, one after the other, are taken from me! first my son, and now his infant! To what shall I be at last reduced?"

"You have still, my good Mrs. Robson, a friend in heaven, that will supply the place of all that you have lost on earth."

* Later changed to 'his sweet face', though 'its' remained through at least four editions.

"True, dear Sir; I am a wicked creature to speak as I have done: but it is hard to suffer; it is hard to lose all we loved in the world!"

"It is," returned the Count, greatly affected at her grief. "But you are not yet deprived of all; you have a grand-daughter."

"Ah, poor little thing! what will become of her when I die? I used often to think what a precious brother my darling William would have proved to his sister, when I should be no more."

This additional distress which her fancy had conjured up, augmented the affliction of the good old woman. And Thaddeus, looking on her with his compassionate soul beaming in his eyes, exclaimed,

"Mrs. Robson, the same almighty being that protected me, the last of my family, will protect the orphan offspring of so excellent a woman as yourself."

Mrs. Robson lifted her head for a moment. She had never before heard him utter a sentence of his own history; and what he had now let drop, added to the tender solemnity of his manner, for an instant arrested her attention. – He went on.

"In me, you see a man, who within the short space of three months, has lost a grandfather that loved him as fondly as you did your William; a mother, whom he saw expire before him, and whose sacred remains he was forced to leave in the hands of her murderers! Yes, Mrs. Robson, I have neither parents nor a home. *I was a stranger, and you took me in*;* and heaven will reward your family in kind. At least I promise that, whilst I live, whatever be my fate, should you be called hence, I will protect your grand-daughter with a brother's affection."

"May heaven in its mercy bless you!" cried Mrs. Robson, dropping on her knees. Thaddeus raised her with gushing eyes; and having replaced her in a seat, left the room for a few minutes to recover himself.

In the evening, Mrs. Watts, according to the Count's desire, called with an estimate of the expences attending the child's interment. Fees and every thing collected, the demand on his benevolence was six pounds. The sum proved rather more than he had expected, but he paid it without a demur; leaving himself only a few shillings.

He considered what he had done as the fulfilment of a duty so indispensable, that it must have been accomplished even by the sacrifice of his uttermost farthing. Gratitude and distress held claims upon him which he would never allow his necessities in the smallest instance to transgress. All gifts of mere generosity were beyond his power, and consequently in a short time beyond his wish; but to the cry of want

---

* 'For I was an hungred, and ye gave me meat: I was thirsty, and ye gave me drink: I was a stranger, and ye took me in' (Matthew 25: 35).

and wretchedness, his hand and heart were ever open. Often has he in the street given away to a starving child, that pittance which was to purchase his own hard meal; and never felt such neglect of himself a privation. To have turned his eyes and ears from the little mendicant, would have been the hardest struggle; and the remembrance of such inhumanity would have haunted him to his pillow. This being the natural disposition of the Count Sobieski, it had been so fostered and directed by the venerable Palatine, that he now found it more difficult to bear calamity when viewing another's poverty, whom he could not relieve, than when penury assailed himself in all its shapes of desolation.

Towards night the idea of Somerset again presented itself. When he fell asleep, his dreams repeated the scene at the play-house; again he saw him, and again he eluded his grasp.

His waking thoughts were not less true to their object; and next morning he went to a coffee-house in the lane,* where he called for breakfast, and inquired of the master if he knew any thing of Sir Robert Somerset. The question was no sooner asked than it was answered to his satisfaction. The Court Guide† was examined, and he found this address, "*Sir Robert Somerset, Bart. Grosvenor Square, – Somerset Castle L – shire, – Deerhurst, C – shire.*"

Gladdened by the discovery, Thaddeus hastened home; and unwilling to affect the feelings of his friend by a sudden appearance, with an overflowing heart he wrote the following letter.

"To Pembroke Somerset, Esq. Grosvenor Square.
"Dear Somerset!

"Will the name at the bottom of this paper surprise you? Will it give you pleasure? I cannot suffer myself to retain a doubt, although you have by the silence of two years almost convinced me that I am forgotten. In truth, Somerset, I had resolved never to obtrude myself and my misfortunes on your knowledge, until last Wednesday night, when I saw you going into Drury-lane Theatre; the sight of you quelled all my resentment, and I called after you, but you did not hear. Pardon me, my dear friend, that I speak of resentment. It is a hard lesson to learn, that of being resigned to the forgetfulness of them we love.

---

* Identified in the third volume as Old Slaughter's Coffee House at 74–5 St Martin's Lane. Slaughter's hosted eminent writers and artists, including Samuel Johnson, Henry Fielding and William Hogarth. For patrons like Porter's Thaddeus, who lodged in boarding houses or had no fixed address, coffee houses served as a reliable place to send and receive mail.
† In 1792, Patrick Boyle began publishing the yearly *Fashionable Court Guide*, which was the first directory to consist entirely of private residents.

"Notwithstanding that I lost my pocket-book with your direction, in a skirmish soon after your departure, I have written to you frequently at a venture; and yet, though you knew in what spot in Poland you left Thaddeus and his family, I have never heard of you since the day of our separation. Yet, you must have some good reason for your silence; at least I will hope so, – and let me beg that I may either hear from or see you directly you receive this.

"Doubtless, public report has afforded you some information relative to the destruction of my ever-beloved country! I bear its fate on myself. You will find me in a poor lodging at the bottom of St. Martin's Lane. You will find me changed in every thing. The first horrors of grief have subsided, and my dearest consolation rises in the midst of my affliction, out of what was its bitterest cause: I thank heaven, that my revered grandfather and mother were taken from a consummation of ills, that would have reduced them to a misery which I am content to endure alone.

"Come to me, dear Somerset. To look on you, to press you to my heart, will be a happiness, that even in hope makes my heart throb with pleasure.

"I will remain at home all day to-morrow in the expectation of seeing you; mean while adieu, my dear Somerset! you will find, at No. 5, St. Martin's Lane, your very affectionate
                                        "Thaddeus Constantine Sobieski.
"*Friday noon.*
"P.S. Inquire for me by the name of Mr. Constantine."

With the most delightful emotions Thaddeus sealed this letter, and gave it to Nanny, with orders to inquire at the post-office when he might expect an answer. The child returned with the information that it would reach Grosvenor Square in an hour, and therefore he could have the reply by three o'clock.*

Three o'clock arrived, but no letter. Thaddeus counted the hours till midnight, which brought him nothing but disappointment. The whole of the succeeding day wore away in the same uncomfortable manner. His heart bounded at every step that sounded in the passage, and, throwing open his room door, he listened to every person that spoke, but none bore any resemblance to the voice of Somerset.

---

* Eighteenth-century London had a highly developed postal service, with over 300 offices in London and Westminster providing deliveries three times each day. Olsen, Kirstin, *Daily Life in 18th-Century England* (Santa Barbara, CA: Greenwood Press, 2017), p. 292.

Night again shut in, and the Count, overcome by a train of doubts, in which despondence had now the greatest share, threw himself on his bed unable to close his eyes.

Whatever be our afflictions, not one human creature, who has endured misfortune, will hesitate to aver, that, of all the tortures incident to mortality, there are none like the rackings of suspense. It is the hell which Milton describes with such horrible accuracy;* in its hot and cold regions the anxious soul of man is alternately tossed from the ardours of hope, to the petrifying rigours of doubt and dread. Men who have not been suspended between confidence and fear, in the faith of a beloved friend, are ignorant of "*the nerve whence agonies are born.*"† It is, when sunk in sorrow, when adversity loads us with divers miseries, and our wretchedness is complete; it is then we feel, that though life is brief, there are few friendships which have strength to follow it to the end.

Such were the reflections of the Count Sobieski, when he arose in the morning from his sleepless pillow. The idea that the letter might have been delayed, afforded him a faint hope, which he cherished all day, clinging to the expectation of seeing his friend before sunset. But Somerset did not appear; and Thaddeus, obliged to seek an excuse for his absence in the supposition that his application had miscarried, rather than hastily abandon himself to the belief that he was treated with cruelty and ingratitude, determined to write once more, and deliver the letter himself at his friend's door. Accordingly, with different sensations from those with which he had addressed him a few days before, he wrote these lines.

"To Pembroke Somerset, Esq.

"If he, who once called Thaddeus Sobieski his friend, have received a letter which that exile addressed to him on Friday last, this note will meet the same neglect. But if this be the first intelligence that tells Somerset, his friend is in town; though robbed of all that he possessed, he will receive him with open arms at his humble abode in St. Martin's Lane.

"Sunday Evening, No. 5, St. Martin's Lane."

Thaddeus, having sealed the letter, walked out in search of Sir Robert Somerset's habitation. After some inquiries he found

---

* Milton vividly describes hell in the opening two books of *Paradise Lost* (1667).
† See Edward Young, *The Brothers* (London: R. Dodsley, 1753): 'Love only feels the *Marvellous* of Pain; / Opens new Veins of Torture in the Soul, / And wakes the Nerve where Agonies are born' (V, i, 84).

Grosvenor Square; and, notwithstanding the darkness of the night, was directed to the house by the light of the lamps and the lustres that shone through the open windows. He hesitated a few minutes on the pavement, and looked up. An old gentleman was standing with a little boy at the nearest window. Whilst the Count's eyes were fixed on these two figures, he saw Somerset himself come up to the child and lead it away towards a groupe of ladies.

Thaddeus immediately flew to the door with a tremor over his frame which communicated itself to the knocker, for he knocked with such violence that the door was opened in an instant by half a dozen footmen at once. He spoke to one.

"Is Mr. Pembroke Somerset at home?"

"Yes," replied the man, supposing him to be a visitor, and making way for him to pass.

"I do not want to see him now," rejoined the Count: "only, give him that letter directly, for it is of consequence."

"Certainly, Sir," replied the servant; and Thaddeus instantly withdrew.

He now turned homewards, with his mind more than commonly depressed. There was a something in the whole affair that pierced him to the soul. He had seen the house that contained the man he most warmly loved, but he had not been admitted within it. He could not forbear recollecting, that when his gates had opened wide as his heart to welcome Pembroke Somerset, how he had been implored by his then grateful friend, to bring the Palatine and the Countess with their retinue to England, where his father would be proud to entertain them as the preservers of his son. How different did he find the reality, to all these professions. Instead of seeing the doors open to welcome him, he had been allowed to stand like a beggar on the threshold; and had heard them shut against him, whilst the form of Somerset glided above him, even as the shadow of his buried joys.

These discomforting retrospections on the past, and painful meditations on the present, continued to occupy his mind; till, passing over from Piccadilly to Coventry Street, he perceived a wretched looking man, almost bent double, accosting a party of people in broken French, and imploring their charity.

The voice, and the accent being Sclavonian,* arrested the ear of Thaddeus. Drawing close to the man as the party proceeded without taking notice of his application, he hastily asked, "are you a Polander?"

---

* Sclavonia (more often written Scalovia) is a region along the Baltic Sea that neighbours modern Poland and Lithuania.

"Father of mercies!" cried the beggar, catching hold of his hand, "am I so blessed! have I at last met him!" and bursting into tears, he leaned upon the arm of the Count, who, hardly able to articulate from surprise, exclaimed, "dear, worthy Butzou! What a time is this for you and I to meet! But come, you must go home with me."

"Willingly, my dear lord," returned he; "for I have none. I begged my way from Harwich* to this town; and have already spent two dismal nights in the streets."

"O my country!" cried the full heart of Thaddeus.

"Yes," continued the poor old soldier, "it received its death-wound, when Kosciuszko and my honoured master fell."

Thaddeus could make no reply; but, supporting the exhausted frame of his friend, who was hardly able to walk, he gladly descried his own door.

The widow opened it the moment he knocked, and, seeing some one with him, was retreating, when Thaddeus, who found from the silence of Butzou and his increasing feebleness, that he was near fainting, begged her to allow him to take his companion into her kitchen. She instantly made way; and whilst the Count placed him in the arm-chair by the fire, the poor man seemed at once bereft of sensation.

"He is my friend, my father's friend!"† cried Thaddeus, looking at his pale and haggard face, with a strange wildness in his own features, "for heaven's sake give me something to restore him!"

Mrs. Robson, in dismay, and literally having nothing better in the house, gave him a glass of water.

"That will not do;" exclaimed he, still upholding the motionless body on his arm; "have you no wine? nothing? He is dying for want."

"None, Sir; I have none;" answered she, frightened at the violence of his manner; "Run, Nanny, and borrow some of Mrs. Watts."

"Do," said Thaddeus; "and bring me a bottle from the nearest inn." As he spoke, he threw her the only half guinea he possessed, and added, "fly, for he may die in a few minutes."

The child flew like lightning over to the Golden-cross; and brought in the wine just as Butzou had opened his eyes, and was gazing at Thaddeus with a languid agony that penetrated his soul. Mrs. Robson held the water to his lips. He swallowed a little, and scarcely articulated, whilst his head dropped back on the chair, "I am perishing for want of food."

Thaddeus caught the bottle from Nanny, and pouring some wine

---

* A port town in Essex, approximately 120 kilometres from London.
† Thaddeus, of course, refers to his grandfather.

into a glass, made him drink nearly all. This draught appeared to revive him. He raised himself up in his seat, and, though still panting and speechless, leaned his swimming head upon the bosom of his friend, who knelt by his side, whilst Mrs. Robson was preparing some toasted bread and mulled wine.

After much exertion between the good landlady and the Count, they sufficiently recovered the poor invalid to lead him up stairs, and lay him on the bed. The natural drowsiness attendant on debility, aided by the fumes of the wine, threw him into an immediate and deep sleep.

Thaddeus seeing him at rest, thought it proper to go down to Mrs. Robson, and by a partial history of his friend, satisfy her about the cause of the scene that she had just beheld. He found the good woman surprised and concerned, but no way displeased; and in a few words he gave her a summary explanation of the precipitancy with which, without her permission, he had introduced a stranger to her roof.

The substance of what he said, related, that the person up stairs had served with him in the army; that in consequence of the ruin of his country, (which he could no longer conceal was Poland,) he had flown in quest of him to England; and in his journey had sustained those misfortunes which had reduced him to the state she had witnessed.

"I met him," continued he, "as a beggar in the street; and whilst he lives, I shall hold it my duty to protect him. I love him for his own sake, and I honour him for my grandfather. Besides, Mrs. Robson," cried he, with additional energy, "before I left my country I made a vow to my Sovereign, that, where ever I should meet this brave old man, I would serve him to the last hour of his life. Therefore we must part no more. Will you give him shelter?" added he, in a subdued voice, "Will you allow me to retain him in my apartments?"

"Willingly, Sir; but how can I accommodate him? he is already in your bed, and I have got no other."

"Leave that to me, best, kindest of women!" exclaimed the Count; "your permission has rendered me happy."

He then wished her a good night; and returning up stairs, wrapped himself in his dressing gown, and passed the night by the little fire of the sitting room.

CHAP. IV.

Owing to comfortable refreshment, and a night of quiet and undisturbed sleep, General Butzou awoke in the morning much recovered from the weakness which had subdued him the preceding day.

Thaddeus observed this change with pleasure. Whilst he sat by his bed, ministering to him with the care of a son, he dwelt with a melancholy delight on his revered features; and listened to his languid voice, with those tender associations, and sensations of the heart, which are delicious, though they pierce it with anguish.

"Tell me, my dear General," said he, "for I can bear to hear it now; tell me what has befallen my unhappy country since I quitted it?"

"Every calamity," cried the brave old man shaking his head, "that tyranny could devise."

"Well, go on;" returned the Count, with a smile that too truly painted the pretended composure of his air; "we, who have beheld her sufferings and yet live, need not fear hearing them related! Did you see the King before he left Warsaw? He told me, that he was to be banished to Grodno some time in the last month."*

"No," replied Butzou, "our oppressors took care of that. Whilst you, my lord, were recovering of your wounds in the citadel, I set off for Sachoryn to join Prince Poniatowski. In my way thither, I met some soldiers, who informed me that his Highness had been compelled to discharge the troops, and was returning to support his brother under the indignities which the haughtiness of Suwarrow might premeditate. I then directed my steps towards Sendomir, where I hoped to find Wawrzecki with a few faithful followers; but here too I was disappointed.† Two days before my arrival, that General had, according to orders, disbanded his whole party. I now found that Poland was

---

* In 1795, Stanisław II abdicated the throne at the request of Catherine of Russia. He spent the rest of his life under Russian military escort, first in Grodno (in modern Belarus) and then in St Petersburg.

† Sachorzyn (Zagorzyn) is a small village in southern Poland and Sendomir (Sandomierz) is a town in southeastern Poland; both were sites of military outposts and skirmishes during the 1794 Kościuszko Uprising (Anthing, *History*, pp. 199, 262, 353). In the 1831 edition, Porter changes 'Wawrzecki' (who had been captured) to 'Dombrowski'. Following the Uprising, Polish General and national hero Jan Dąbrowski (1755–1818) withdrew to France and organised the Polish Legions during the Napoleonic Wars.

completely in the hands of her ravagers, and I prepared to return. I was shocked and agonized at every step I re-trod. I beheld the shores of the Vistula lined on every side with Russian troops. Ten thousand were posted on her banks, and eighteen thousand amongst the ruins of Prague and Villanow.

"When I approached the walls of Warsaw, imagine, my dear Count, how great was my indignation! How barbarous, how unmanly, the conduct of our enemies! Around the city, batteries of cannon were erected, that on the least symptom of discontent were commanded to level it with the ground.

"On the morning of my arrival, I was hastening to the palace to pay my duty to the King, when a Russian officer intercepted me, and threatened that, if I attempted to pass, my obstinacy would be fatal to myself, and hazardous to his Majesty, whose confinement and suffering should increase in proportion to the adherents he retained amongst the Poles. Hearing this, I was turning away overwhelmed with grief and anger, just as the doors of the audience-chamber opened, and the Counts Potocki, Kilinski, and several others of your grandfather's dearest friends, were led out under a strong guard.* I was standing motionless with surprise, when Potocki, perceiving me, held forth his hand. I took it, and, wringing it, in the bitterness of my heart uttered some words which I cannot remember; but the Russian bade me beware how I again gave way to such injurious warmth.

"'Farewell, my worthy General,' said the Count, 'you see that we are arrested. We have loved Poland too faithfully for her enemies; and for that reason are to be sent out of the way to-morrow to Petersburgh. Though we are prisoners, we shall at least have the consolation of sharing the same fate with Kosciuszko.' – 'Sir, I cannot admit of this conversation,' cried the officer of the guard; who commanding the escort to proceed, I lost sight of these illustrious patriots, probably for ever.

"I understood from the few Poles that remained in the citadel, that the good Stanislaus was to be sent on the same dismal journey to Grodno the next day. And that you had quitted Poland the moment your wounds would allow you to move, that you might at least avoid the sight of Suwarrow's triumphant entry, which happened on the ninth of November last. On the eighth, I believe, you left Warsaw for England."

---

* Count Ignacy Potocki (1750–1809); Jan Kiliński (1760–1819), a military leader who led the uprising against the Russian garrison in Warsaw in 1794. Both were arrested and imprisoned in St Petersburg.

"Yes," replied the Count, who with a breaking heart had listened to this distressing narrative; "and doubtless, I saved myself much misery?"

"You did. One of the magistrates described to me the whole scene, at which I would not have been present for worlds. He told me, that when the morning arrived in which the Russian was to make his public entrée, not a citizen would be seen without compulsion. A dead silence reigned in the streets; the doors and windows of every house remained so closed, that a stranger might have supposed it to be a general mourning; and it was the bitterest that could have fallen upon our souls! At this moment, when Warsaw in a manner lay dying at the feet of her conqueror, the Russian troops marched into the city, and lined the roads, the only spectators of their own horrible tragedy. At length, with eyes that could no longer weep, the magistrates, reluctant, and full of indignation, proceeded to meet Suwarrow and his train on the bridge of Prague. When they came near enough to the procession, they presented the keys of Warsaw on their knees."*

"On their knees!" interrupted Thaddeus, starting up, and the blood flushing over his face.

"Yes," answered Butzou, "on their knees."

"Father of heaven!" exclaimed the Count, walking about the room with emotion, "why did not the earth open and swallow them? Why did not the blood which saturated the spot whereon they knelt, cry out to them? O Butzou, this humiliation of Poland is worse to me than all her miseries!"

"I felt as you feel, my lord;" continued the General, "and I expressed myself with the same resentment; but the magistrate who related to me the circumstance, urged in excuse for himself and his brethren, that such a form was necessary; and had they refused, probably their lives would have been forfeited."

"Well," inquired Thaddeus, resuming his seat, "but where was the King during this transaction?"

"In the castle; where he soon underwent a similar scene, and received orders to be present next day at a public thanksgiving, when all the inhabitants of Warsaw were forced to attend a *te deum*† in gratitude for the destruction of their country. I thank heaven, I was spared from witnessing this monstrous blasphemy; I was then at Sendomir. The day after I heard these horrid accounts, I saw the carriage which contained

---

* Jones's *History*, p. 496, presents a similar description of the Polish magistrates handing over the keys of Warsaw, though not 'on their knees'.
† A Christian hymn of gratitude, sung in Latin, and beginning 'Te Deum Laudamus' ('We Praise Thee, O God').

the good Stanislaus, guarded, like a traitor's, out of the gates; and that very hour I left the country. I travelled towards Hamburgh, where I took my passage to Harwich. From fatigue, one of my old wounds broke out afresh, and, continuing ill a week, I expended the little money I had brought with me. Reduced to my last shilling, and eager to find you, I begged my way from that town to this. I had already spent two miserable days and nights in the open air, with no other sustenance than the casual charity of passengers, when heaven sent you to save me from perishing in the streets."

Butzou pressed the hand of his young friend, as he concluded. Displeasure still kept its station on the Count's features. The good General observed it with satisfaction, well pleased that indignation at the supposed pusillanimity of his countrymen, prevented those bursts of grief, which he had expected from his sensible nature, when he should be informed that the ruin of Poland was confirmed.

Towards evening, General Butzou fell asleep. Thaddeus, leaning back on his chair, fixed his eyes on the fire, and pondered, with amazement and sorrow, on all that had passed. When it was nearly dark, and he was yet lost in his musings, Mrs. Robson gently opened the door with a candle in her hand, and presenting a letter; "Here, Sir," said she, "is a letter a servant has just left; he told me there required no answer."

Thaddeus had sprung from his seat at the sight of the paper, and, almost catching it from her, his former gloomy cogitations dispersed before the hopes and fond emotions of friendship which now lit up in his bosom. Mrs. Robson had withdrawn. He looked at the superscription, it was the hand-writing of his friend. Tearing it asunder, two folded papers presented themselves; he opened them, and they were his own letters, which had been read and returned to him without a word. His beating heart felt suddenly chilled. Letting the papers fall from his hand, he dropped down on a seat, and closed his eyes, as if he would shut them from the world and its ingratitude.

Unable to recover from the astonishment into which this event had thrown him, his thoughts whirled about in a succession of accusations, surmises, and doubts, that seemed for a few minutes to drive him to distraction.

"Was it really the hand of Somerset?"

Again he examined the *envelope*. It was; and the enclosures were his own letters, without one word of apology for such ingratitude.

"Could he make one? No," replied Thaddeus to himself. "Unhappy that I am, to have been induced to apply twice to so despicable a man! Oh, Somerset!" cried he, looking at the papers as they lay before him, "was it necessary that insult should be added to unfaithfulness and ingratitude, to throw me off entirely? Good heaven! did he think, because I wrote twice, that I would persecute him with applications? Well, I have been told that this is mankind; but, that I should find it in him!"

In this way, agitated and muttering, and walking up and down the room, he spent another wakeful and cheerless night.

Next morning, when the Count went down stairs to beg Mrs. Robson to attend his friend till his return, she mentioned what uneasiness he occasioned her the preceding night, as she heard him most of the time moving above her head. He was accounting to her for his restlessness, by complaining of a head-ache that would not allow him to sleep, when she interrupted him by saying, "O no, Sir; I am sure it is the hard boards you lie on to accommodate the poor old gentleman. I am certain you will make yourself ill."

Thaddeus thanked her for her solicitude; but, declaring that nothing of the kind was any hardship to him, he left her; and, with his drawings in his pocket, once more took the path to Great Newport Street.

Indignation against his fickle friend, and anxiety for the tranquillity of General Butzou, whose age, infirmities, and sufferings, threatened a speedy termination of his life, determined the Count to sacrifice all false delicacy and weakness, and to hazard another attempt at acquiring the means of affording those comforts to the sick veteran which his state demanded. Happen how it would, he resolved that Butzou should never know the complete wreck of his property. He shuddered at loading him, with the additional distress, of feeling that he was a burthen on his protector.

Thaddeus passed the door of the print-seller who had behaved so ill to him on his first application; and, walking to the farthest shop on that side, entered it, and, laying his drawings on the counter, requested the master to look at them. The man opened the packet; and the Count, dreading a second repulse, or even more than similar insolence, hastily added:

"They are scenes in Germany. If you like to have them, their price is a guinea."

"Are you the painter, Sir?" asked the man.

"Yes, Sir. Do they please you?"

"Yes;" answered the man, examining them nearer, "there is a breadth and freedom in the style which is novel, and may take. I will give you your demand."

Thaddeus rejoiced that he had succeeded where he really felt no hope; with a bow was leaving the shop, when the man called after him, "Sir! Sir!"

Thaddeus returned, prepared to hear some impertinent remark.

It is a strange thing, but it is true; that those who have been thrust by misfortune to a state beneath their birth and expectations, feel as if they were the object of universal hostility. They see contempt in every eye, they suppose insult in every word; the slightest neglect is sufficient to set the sensitive pride of the unfortunate in a blaze: and, alas! how little is this sensibility respected by the rich and gay in their dealings with the unhappy! To what an addition of misery are the wretched exposed; meeting not only those contumelies which the prosperous are not backward to bestow, but those fancied ills, that, however unfounded, keep the mind in a constant fever with itself and warfare with the surrounding world!

Repeated insults had taught the Count Sobieski to feel much of this anticipating irritability; and it was with a very haughty step that he turned back to hear what the print-seller had to say.

"I only want to ask, whether you follow this art as a profession?"

"Yes."

"Then, I will be glad if you can furnish me with six such drawings every week."

"Certainly," replied Thaddeus, pleased with the probability of securing something towards the support of his friend.

"Then bring me another half dozen next Monday."

Thaddeus promised, and with a more satisfied mind took his way homewards.

Who is there in England that does not remember the dreadful Winter of 1794, when the whole country lay buried in a thick ice that seemed eternal?* Over that ice, and through those snows, the venerable General Butzou had begged his way from Harwich to London; resting at night under the shelter of some shed or out-house. The effect of this, was a painful rheumatism that fixed itself in his limbs, and now rendered them nearly useless.

Two or three weeks passed over the heads of the General and his young protector; Thaddeus, cheering the old man with his smiles; and, he in return, imparting the only pleasure to him that his melancholy heart could receive; the conviction that his attentions and affection were productive of comfort.

In the exercise of these duties, the Count not only felt his health gradually recover its tone, but his mind become more tranquil, and

---

* The winter of 1794–5 was a famously bitter winter in England and across northern Europe, with January 1795 holding long-standing record low temperatures. The River Thames froze over in London.

less prone to those sudden floods of regret and feeling which had been rapidly sapping his life.

By a strict economy on his own part, he managed to pay the widow and support his friend, out of the weekly profits of his drawings, which were now and then augmented, by a commission to do one or two more than the stipulated number.

Thus, conversing with Butzou, reading to him when awake, or pursuing his drawing when he slept, Thaddeus spent the time until the beginning of March.

One fine star-light evening in that month, just before the frost broke up, after painting all day, he put on his hat, and, desiring little Nancy* to take care of the General, he left his work at the print-seller's, and then proceeded through Piccadilly, intending to go as far as Hyde Park Corner, and return.

Much pleased with the beauty of the night, he walked on, not remarking that he had passed the turnpike, until he heard a scream. The sound seemed to come from near the Park-wall. He immediately hurried along, and came up with† a woman who was struggling with a man that was swearing and behaving in a very brutish manner.

Without a moment's hesitation, Thaddeus with one blow of his arm sent the fellow reeling against the wall. But whilst he supported the outraged person, who was fainting, the man recovered himself, and, flying at her champion, aimed a stroke at his head with an immense bludgeon, which the Count catching hold of as it descended, wrenched out of his hand. The horrid oaths of the ruffian, and the hysterical shrieks of the woman, soon collected a mob; when the villain, fearing worse usage, made off, and left Thaddeus to restore the terrified woman at his leisure.

As soon as she was able to speak, she thanked her deliverer in a voice and language that assured him it was no common person he had befriended.‡ Though, in the circumstance of her distress, all would have been the same to him; a helpless female was insulted, and whatever were her rank, he felt that she had an equal claim on his protection.

The mob dispersed; and the Count, finding the lady capable of walking, begged permission to see her safe home.

"I thank you, Sir," replied she; "and I accept your offer with gratitude. Besides, after your generous interference, it is requisite that I

---

* That is, Nanny. Porter uses both names through the rest of the novel.
† That is, 'came upon'.
‡ In the gendered spatial politics of Georgian Britain, middle- and upper-class women were not expected to go out at night without a servant or companion.

should account to you, how a woman of my appearance, came out at this hour without attendance. I have no other excuse to advance for such imprudence, than the declaration that I have often done so with impunity. I have a friend, whose husband being in the guards, lives near the barracks.* We often drink tea with each other, and sometimes my servants come for me; and sometimes, when I am wearied and indisposed, I come away earlier and alone. This happened to-night: and I have to thank your gallantry, Sir, for my rescue from the first outrage of the kind that ever assailed me."

By the time that a few more complimentary words on her side, and a modest reply from Thaddeus, had passed, they stopped before a house in Grosvenor Place.† The lady knocked at the door, and as soon as it was opened, the Count was taking his leave, but she laid her hand on his arm, and exclaimed,

"No, Sir; I must not lose the probability of convincing you, that you have not succoured a person unworthy of your kindness. I entreat you to walk in!"

Thaddeus was too much pleased with her manner, not to accept this invitation. He followed her up stairs into a drawing room, where a young lady was seated at work.

"Miss Egerton," cried the lady, as she entered and introduced the Count, "here is a gentleman, who has this moment saved me from the hands of a ruffian. You must assist me to express my gratitude."

"I would with all my heart," returned she; "but your ladyship confers benefits so well, that you cannot be at a loss how to receive them."

Thaddeus took the chair that a servant set for him, and with mingled pleasure and admiration turned his eyes on the lovely woman whom he had rescued. She threw off her cloak and veil, and displayed a dignity of figure, and pensiveness of countenance, full of such expression and interest, that he felt an irresistable wish to secure her acquaintance.

Her ladyship begged him to lay aside his great-coat, as she must insist upon his supping with her. There was a commanding softness in her manner, and a gentle, yet unappealable decision in her voice, that he could not withstand; and he prepared to obey, although he was aware that the fashion and richness of the military dress concealed under his coat, would give her ideas which his situation could not answer.

---

* The Knightsbridge Barracks, located along the southern end of Hyde Park, were established in 1792 in response to the civil unrest spurred by the French Revolution.
† Grosvenor Place runs from Hyde Park Corner along the west side of Queen's Garden (today Buckingham Palace Gardens).

The lady did not notice that he hesitated, but, ringing the bell, desired the servant to take the gentleman's hat and coat. Thaddeus saw immediately in the looks of both the ladies what he feared.

"I perceive," said the elder, as she took her seat, "that my deliverer is in the army; yet I do not recollect having seen that uniform before."

"I am not an Englishman," returned he.

"Not an Englishman!" exclaimed Miss Egerton, "and speak the language so accurately! You cannot be French?"

"No, madam; I had the honour of serving under the King of Poland."

"Then, his was a very gallant court I suppose," rejoined Miss Egerton with a smile; "for I am sorry to say, that there are few about St. James's, that would have ventured to have done what you did by Lady Tinemouth."

The Count returned the young lady's smile.

"I have seen too little, madam, of Englishmen of rank, to shew any gallantry in defending this part of my sex against so fair an accuser." Indeed, he recollected the officers in the park, and the perfidy of Somerset, and thought, that he had no reason to give them more of his respect, than their countrywoman considered fit to bestow.

"Come, come, Maria," cried Lady Tinemouth; "though no woman has less cause to speak well of mankind than I have, I will not permit my countrymen to be run down *in toto*. I dare say this gentleman will agree with me, that it neither shews a candid nor a patriotic spirit?"

"I dare say he will not agree with you, Lady Tinemouth. No gentleman yet, who had his wits about him, ever agreed with an elder lady against a younger. Now, Mr. Gentleman! for it seems that is the name by which we are to address you: what do you say?"

Thaddeus almost laughed at the singular way she had chosen to ask his name; and, allowing some of the gloom which generally obscured his fine eyes, to disperse, he answered her with a smile,

"My name is Constantine."

"Well, you have replied to my last question first; but I will not let you off about my bearish countrymen. Don't you think, Mr. Constantine, that I may call them so, without any breach of good manners to them, or duty to my country? For you see her ladyship hangs much upon patriotism."

Lady Tinemouth shook her head.

"O Maria, Maria, you are a strange mad-cap."

"I don't care for that; I will have Mr. Constantine's unprejudiced reply. I am sure, if he had taken as long a time in answering your call, as he does mine, the ruffian might have killed, and eaten you too, before he moved to your assistance. Come, Sir, may I not say that they are bears?"

"Certainly. A pretty woman may say any thing."

"Positively, Mr. Constantine, I won't endure contempt! Say such another word, and I will call you as abominable an animal as the worst of them."

"But I am not a proper judge, Miss Egerton. I have never been in company with any of these men; so, to be impartial, I must suspend my opinion."

"And not believe my word!"

Thaddeus bowed.

"There, Lady Tinemouth," cried she, affecting pet,* "take your champion to yourself; he is too great a savage for me."

"Thank you, Maria," returned her ladyship, giving her hand to the Count to lead her to the supper room; "This is the way she quarrels with every man that comes into my house, and then her ill-humour transforms them to its own likeness."

"And where is the man," observed Thaddeus, "that would not be happy under the spells of so beautiful a Circe?"†

"It won't do, Mr. Constantine," cried she, taking her place opposite to him; "my anger is not to be appeased by calling me names; you don't mend the matter much, by likening me to a heathen and a witch."

Lady Tinemouth bore her part in the conversation of the evening, in a strain more in unison with the Count's mind. However he found no inconsiderable degree of amusement, from the unreflecting volubility and giddy sallies of her friend; and on the whole, spent the few hours that he passed there, with some resemblance to his almost forgotten sense of pleasure.

He was in an elegant apartment, he was in the company of two lovely and accomplished women, and he was the object of their entire attention and gratitude. He had been used to such scenes in his days of happiness, when he felt himself "*the expectancy and rose of the fair state, the glass of fashion, and the mould of form, the observed of all observers;*"‡ and its re-appearance, awakened, with tender remembrances, associating feelings, which made him rise with regret when the clock struck one.

Lady Tinemouth bade him good night, with an earnest request that he would shortly repeat his visit. This invitation gratified him much; and they parted, mutually delighted with each other.

---

* Maria is pretending 'offence at being or feeling slighted' (*OED*).
† In Homer's *Odyssey*, the sorceress Circe puts a spell over those who drink from her enchanted cup, transforming the unsuspecting men of Odysseus' crew into swine.
‡ *Hamlet*, III, i, 152–4.

CHAP. V.

Pleased as the Count was with the acquaintance to which his gallantry had introduced him, he did not repeat his call for a long time.

A few mornings after his meeting with Lady Tinemouth, the hard frost broke up. The change in the atmosphere so dreadfully affected the General, by producing a relapse of his rheumatic fever, that his friend had to watch by his pillow night and day for ten days. At the end of this period, he recovered sufficiently to sit up and read, or to amuse himself by registering the melancholy events of the last campaigns, in a large book, with plans of the different battles. The sight of this volume would have distressed Thaddeus, had he not seen that it afforded comfort to the poor veteran, whom it transported back into the midst of scenes, on which he delighted to dwell; yet, he would often lay down his pen, shut the book, and weep like an infant.

The Count left him one morning at this employment, and strolled out, with the intention of calling on Lady Tinemouth. As he walked along by York-house, he perceived Pembroke Somerset with a gentleman leaning on his arm, coming out of Bond Street.

All the blood in the Count's body seemed rushing to his heart. He trembled. The ingenuous smile on his friend's countenance, and his features so sweetly marked with frankness, made his resolution falter.

"But proofs," cried he to himself, "are absolute!" and turning his face to a stand of books that was near him, he stood there till Somerset had passed. He went by him speaking these words:

"I trust, father, that ingratitude is not his vice."

"But it is yours, Somerset!" murmured Thaddeus, as for a moment he gazed after them, and then proceeded on his walk.

When his name was announced at Lady Tinemouth's, he found her ladyship and another lady, but not Miss Egerton. Lady Tinemouth expressed her pleasure at this visit, and her surprise that it had been so long deferred.

"The pain of such an apparent neglect of your ladyship's goodness," replied he, "has been added to my anxiety for the declining health of a friend, whose increased illness is my apology."

"I wish," returned her ladyship, her eyes beaming approbation, "that all my friends could excuse their absence so well!"

"Perhaps they might, if they chose;" observed the other lady, "and with equal sincerity."

Thaddeus understood the incredulity couched under these words. So did Lady Tinemouth.

"However," rejoined she, "be satisfied, Mr. Constantine, that I believe you sincere."

The Count bowed.

"Fie, Lady Tinemouth!" cried the lady, "you are partial; nay, you are absurd; did you ever yet hear a man speak truth to a woman?"

"Lady Sara!" replied her ladyship, with one of those arch glances that seldom visited her eyes, "where will be your vanity if I assent to this?"

"In the moon, with man's sincerity."

Thaddeus paid little attention to this dialogue. His thoughts, in spite of himself, were wandering after the figures of Somerset and his father.

Lady Tinemouth, whose fancy had not been quiet about him since chance had introduced him to her acquaintance, observed his present absence without noticing it. And indeed, the fruitful imagination of Maria Egerton had not lain still. She declared, "he was a soldier by his dress, a man of rank from his manners, an Apollo in his person, and a hero from his gallantry!"

Thus did Miss Egerton describe him to Lady Sara Roos; "and," added she, "what convinces me that he is a man of fashion, he has not been within these walls since we told him that we should take it as a favour."

Lady Sara had been eager to see this handsome stranger. Having previously determined to drop in at Lady Tinemouth's, under some excuse or other, every morning, till her curiosity was gratified, she was not a little pleased when she heard his name announced.

Lady Sara was married; but she was also young and beautiful, and she liked that her power should be felt by others besides her husband. The instant she beheld the Count Sobieski, she formed the wish to entangle him in her chains. She learnt, by his pale countenance and thoughtful air, that he was a melancholy character, and, above all things, she had sighed for such a lover. She expected to receive from one of that cast, a tenderness, a devotedness; in short, a fervent, wild, and romantic passion, which would feed on her sighs and its own fires to eternity. Thaddeus appeared to her to be the very creature of whom she had been in search. His abstraction, his voice and eyes, the one so touching, the other so neglectful of any thing but the ground, all were irresistible, and she resolved from that moment (in her own words) "to make a dead set at him."

Lady Tinemouth, not less pleased with this second view of her new acquaintance than she had been at the first, directed her discourse to him, accompanied by all that winning interest so endearing to a liberal heart. Whilst she was speaking, Lady Sara, who never augured well to the success of her fascinations when the Countess addressed herself to any of her victims, tried every mean in her power to draw aside the attention of the Count. She played with her ladyship's dog; but, that not succeeding, she determined to strike him at once with the elegance of her figure. Complaining of the heat, she threw off a large green velvet mantle which she had on, and, rising from the chair, walked towards the window.

When she looked round to enjoy her victory, she saw that this manœuvre had failed like the rest; for the provoking Countess was still standing between her and Thaddeus. Almost angry, she flung open the sash, and, putting her head out, exclaimed in her best modulated tones:

"How d'ye do?"

"I hope your ladyship is well this fine morning!" was answered in the voice of Pembroke Somerset.

Thaddeus grew pale, and the Countess feeling the cold, turned round to ask Lady Sara to whom she was speaking.

"To a pest of mine, my dear," returned she; and then stretching out her neck she resumed, "But where, in the name of heaven, are you going, Somerset, with all that travelling apparatus?"

"To Deerhurst; we are going to take Lord Arun down. But I keep your ladyship in the cold. Good morning."

"My compliments to Sir Robert. Good bye! Good bye!" and, waving her white hand till his curricle* was out of sight, when she turned round, her desires were gratified, for the elegant stranger was standing with his eyes fixed on that hand. But, had she known, that for any cognizance they took of its beauty, they might as well have been fixed on vacancy, she would not have pulled down the window, and reseated herself, with such an air of triumph.

The Count took his seat with a sigh, and Lady Tinemouth did the same.

"So, that is the son of Sir Robert Somerset?"

"Yes," replied her ladyship, "and what do you think of him? He is called very handsome."

"Your ladyship has forgotten that I am near-sighted," answered the Countess, "I could not discriminate his features, but I think his figure

---

* curricle, 'a light two-wheeled carriage, usually drawn by two horses abreast' (*OED*). It was the typical carriage of a smart young man in the early nineteenth century.

fine. I remember his father was a handsome man, and a man of wonderful talents."

"That may be;" resumed Lady Sara laughing, and anxious to excite some emotion of rivalry in the breast of Thaddeus, "I am sure I ought not to call in question his talents and taste, for he has often wished that fate had reserved me for his son." Her ladyship sighed and looked down.

This sigh and gesture had more effect upon her victim, than all her exhibited graces. So difficult it is to break affection and habit. Any thing relating to Pembroke Somerset, could yet so powerfully interest the Count, as to stamp itself on his features. Besides, the appearance of any latent disquietude, where all seemed splendor and vivacity, reminded him painfully of the chequered lot of man. His eyes were resting upon her ladyship, full of a tender commiseration, pregnant with compassion for her, himself, and all the world, when she raised her head. The meeting of such a look from him, filled her with agitation. She felt something strange at her heart. His eyes seemed to have penetrated to its inmost devices. Blushing like scarlet, she got up to hide an embarrassment not to be subdued; and, hastily wishing the Countess a good morning, curtseyed to him and left the room.

Her ladyship entered the carriage with feelings all in commotion. She could not account for the confusion which his look had occasioned; and, half angry at a weakness so like a raw inexperienced girl, she determined to become one of Lady Tinemouth's constant visitors, until she should have brought him (as she had done most of the men about court), to her feet.

These were her ladyship's cognitions, as she rolled along towards St. James's Place. But she a little exceeded the fact in her statement; for, notwithstanding she could count as many lovers as any woman, both before and after her marriage, yet few would have ventured so far as to trust the consequence of a kneeling petition. Somehow, these worthy lords and gentlemen had all, to a man, adopted the oracle of the poet, that,

> "Love fleet as air, at sight of human ties,
> "Spreads his light wings, and in a moment flies!"*

They all professed to adore Lady Sara; some were caught by her beauty, others by her eclat, but none had the most distant wish to make this beauty and eclat his own legal property.

---

* Alexander Pope, 'Eloisa to Abelard': 'Love, free as air, at sight of human ties, / Spreads his light wings, and in a moment flies' (lines 75–6). *The Works of Mr. Alexander Pope* (London: W. Bowyer, 1717).

The young Marquis of Severn fluttered round her ladyship during the first year of his appearance at court; but at the end of that time, instead of offering her his hand, he married the daughter of a rich city banker.

Lady Sara, who was at her father's house in the country when this intelligence arrived, was so incensed, that, to shew her disdain of this apostate lover, she set off the same evening for Scotland with Harry Roos, a grandson of the Duke of Lincoln. They were married, and her ladyship had the triumph of being presented to her Majesty the same day with the Marchioness of Severn.

When the whirlwind of her resentment subsided, she began most dismally to repent her union. She loved Captain Roos as little as she had loved Lord Severn. She had admired the rank and gallantry of the one; and the profound adoration of the other, had made a complete friend of her vanity. But now, since her revenge was gratified, the homage of Harry Roos ceasing to excite the envy of her companions, from the hour in which he became her husband, she grew weary of his attentions, and was very happy when the admiralty ordered him to take the command of a ship bound to the Mediterranean.

The last fervent kiss which he imprinted on her lips, as they breathed out the cold "Good bye, Roos, take care of yourself!" seemed to her the seal of freedom; and she returned into her dressing-room, not to weep, but to rejoice in the project of a thousand festivities and a thousand lovers.

Left at an early age without a mother, and ignorant of the duties of a wife, she thought that if she kept her husband and herself out of Doctors Commons,* she should do no harm by amusing herself with the hearts of every man that came in her way. Thus, she hardly moved without a train of admirers. She had already attracted every one worth the trouble; and had listened to their compliments and insolent presumptions, till she was nearly tired of both; when Miss Egerton related to her the Countess's rencontre with the gallant foreigner.

As soon as her ladyship heard that he was of rank, (for Miss Egerton had not been backward to affirm the dreams of her own imagination,) she formed an earnest wish to see him: and when, to her infinite satisfaction, he did present himself, in her eyes he exceeded every thing that had been described. To secure such a conquest, she thought would not only raise the envy of the women, but make the men look about them

---

* Doctors' Commons, or College of Civilians, was a London-based society of lawyers practising civil law. Porter here implies that by staying out of Doctors' Commons, Lady Sara and Captain Roos have been able to avoid divorce.

to discover some novel and more attractive way than they had hitherto attempted, to portray the extent of their devotion.

Whilst Lady Sara was meditating on her new plans, the Count and Lady Tinemouth remained alone. Her ladyship talked to him on various subjects; but he answered ill upon them all, and sometimes very wide of the matter. At last, feeling that he must be burthensome, he arose, and, looking paler and more depressed than when he entered, wished her a good morning.

"I am afraid, Mr. Constantine, that you are unwell?"

Thaddeus, like most people who desire to hide what is passing in their minds, gladly assented to this, as an excuse for a taciturnity he could not vanquish.

"Then," cried her ladyship, "I hope you will favour me with your card, that I may know where to send?"

Thaddeus was confounded, and looked down for a moment; then, returning into the room, took up a pen which lay on the table, and said,

"I will write my address to a place from whence any of your ladyship's commands will reach me; but, I will do myself the honour to repeat my call very soon."

"I shall always be happy to see you," replied the Countess, while he was writing; "but, before I engage you in a promise of which you may afterwards repent, I must tell you, that you will meet with dull entertainment at my house. I see very little company; and were it not for the inexhaustible spirits of Miss Egerton, I believe I should become a complete misanthrope."

"Your house will be my paradise!" exclaimed the Count, with an earnestness, to the force of which he did not immediately attend.

Lady Tinemouth smiled.

"I must warn you here, too," cried she; "Miss Egerton must not be the deity of your paradise. She is already under engagements that would preclude all hope on that head."

Thaddeus blushed at being mistaken, and wished to explain himself.

"You misunderstand me, madam. I am not insensible to beauty; but, upon my word, at that moment I had nothing else in my thoughts than gratitude for your ladyship's kindness to an absolute stranger."

"That is true, Mr. Constantine; you are an absolute stranger, if the want of a formal introduction, and an ignorance of your family, constitute that title. But your protection introduced you to me; and there is something in your appearance which convinces me, that I may not be afraid of admitting you into the very scanty number of my friends."

Thaddeus immediately perceived the delicacy of Lady Tinemouth; who wished to know who he was, yet felt so repugnant to give him pain by a question so direct that he must answer. As she had proposed it, she left him entirely to his own discretion; and he determined, as far as he could, without exposing his real name and circumstances, to satisfy her very proper curiosity.

The Countess, whose benevolent heart was deeply interested in his favour, observed the changes of his countenance with an anxious desire that he would be ingenuous. Her solicitude did not arise from any doubts that she entertained of his quality and worth, but she wished to be enabled to reply with promptness to the inquisitive people who might see him at her house.

"I hardly know," said Thaddeus, "in what words to express my sense of your ladyship's generous confidence in me; and that my character is not undeserving of such distinction, time, I trust, will ratify." He paused for a moment, and then resumed: "For my rank, Lady Tinemouth, it is now of little consequence to my comfort; rather, perhaps, a source of mortification; for – ," he hesitated, and then proceeded, with a faint colour tinging his cheek, "exiles from their country, if they would not covet misery, must learn to forget; hence I am no other than Mr. Constantine; though, in acknowledgment of your ladyship's goodness, I deem it only just, that I should not conceal my real quality from you.

"My family was the first in Poland. Even in banishment, the remembrance that its virtues were as well known as its name, affords some alleviation to the conviction, that when my country fell, all my property, and all my kindred, were involved in the ruins. Soon after the dreadful sealing of its fate, I quitted it; and by the command of a dying parent, who expired in my arms, sought a refuge in this island, from degradations, which otherwise, I could neither repel nor avoid."

Thaddeus stopped; and the Countess, struck by the graceful modesty with which this simple account was related, laid her hand upon his.

"Mr. Constantine, I am not surprized at any thing you have said. The melancholy of your air induced me to suspect that you were not happy; and my sole wish, in penetrating your reserve, was to shew you that a woman can be a sincere friend."

Tears of gratitude and respect glistened in the Count's eyes. Incapable of making a suitable reply, he pressed her hand to his lips. She rose; and, willing to relieve a sensibility that delighted her, added, "I will not detain you longer, only let me see you soon."

Thaddeus uttered a few inarticulate words, whose significancy conveyed nothing, but every thing was declared by their confusion. The Countess's eloquent smile, shewed that she comprehended their meaning; and he left the room.

On his return home, he found General Butzou in better spirits, still poring over his journal. This paper seemed to be the representative of all which had ever been dear to him. He dwelt upon it, and talked about it, with a doating eagerness, bordering on insanity.

These symptoms, increasing from day to day, gave his young friend considerable uneasiness. He listened with pain to the fond dreams which had taken possession of the poor old man, who delighted in saying, that much might yet be done in Poland, when he should be recovered, and they enabled to return together to Warsaw, and stimulate the people to revolt.

Thaddeus at first attempted to prove the emptiness of these schemes; but seeing that contradiction on this head threw the General back into deeper despondency, he thought it better to affect the same sentiments; too well perceiving, that death would soon terminate these visions with his life.

Accordingly, as far as lay in the Count's power, he satisfied all the fancied wants of his revered friend; who, on every other subject, was perfectly reasonable; but at last he became so absorbed in this chimerical plot, that even conversation, and his meals, seemed to oppress him with restraint.

When Thaddeus, with sorrow, perceived that his company was rather irksome than a comfort to his friend, he the more readily repeated his visits to Lady Tinemouth. She now looked for his entrance at least once a day. If ever a morning and evening passed away without his appearance, he was sure of being scolded by Miss Egerton, reproached by the Countess, and frowned at by Lady Sara Roos. This lady now contrived, in defiance of all other engagements, to drop in, every night, at Lady Tinemouth's. Her ladyship was not more surprized at this sudden attachment of Lady Sara to her house, than pleased with her society, who she found, on intimate acquaintance, could lay aside that tissue of affectation and fashion which she wore in public, and really become a charming woman.

Though Lady Sara was vain, she had sufficient sense to penetrate with tolerable certainty into the characters of her acquaintance. Most of the men with whom she had hitherto associated, having been jumbled together in those large assemblies where individuality is absorbed in the general mass of insipidity and ceremony, she saw that they were frivolous, or at the least warped in taste and principle; and the fascinations she used to subdue them, were the best suited to their capacity, – her beauty, her thoughtlessness, and her caprice. But on the reverse, when she formed the wish to entangle such a man as Thaddeus, she soon discovered that to engage his attention, she must appear in the unaffected graces of nature. To this end, she took pains to display the loveliness of her person in every movement and position; yet she managed the thing with so inartificial and frank an air, that she seemed the only being present, who was unconscious of the versatility and power of her charms. She conversed with good sense and propriety. In short, she appeared completely different from the gay ridiculous creature whom he had seen some weeks before, in the Countess's parlour.

He now admired both her person and her mind. Her winning softness, the vivacity of Miss Egerton, and the kindness of the Countess, beguiled him many an evening from the contemplation of melancholy scenes at home.

One night, it came into the head of Maria Egerton, to banter him about his military dress. "Do, for Heaven's sake, my dear Don Quixote," cried she, "let us see you out of your rusty armour! I declare, I am tired of the sight. Somehow, I do think you would be merrier out of that *customary suit of solemn black!*"*

This demand was not pleasing to the Count, but he good-humouredly replied, "I knew not till you were so kind as to inform me, that a man's temper depends on his clothes."

"Else I suppose," cried she, interrupting him, "you would have changed yours before? Therefore, I expect that you will do as I bid you now, and put on a christian's coat against the next time you enter this house."

Thaddeus was at a loss what to say; he only bowed; and the Countess and Lady Sara smiled at her nonsense.

When they parted for the night, this portion of the conversation passed off from all minds but that of Lady Tinemouth. She had considered the subject, but in a different way from Maria. Maria supposed that the handsome Constantine wore the dress of his country because it was the most becoming. But as such a whim did not correspond with the other parts of his character, Lady Tinemouth, in her own mind, attributed this adherence to his national habit, to the right cause.

She remarked, that whenever she wished him to meet any agreeable people at her house, he always declined these introductions under the plea of his dress, though he never proposed to alter it. This conduct, added to his perfect silence on every subject that related to the public amusements about town, led her to conclude, that like the banished nobility of France, he was encountering the various inconveniences of poverty in a foreign land. She hoped he had escaped its horrors; but

---

* *Hamlet*, I, ii, 78. Maria Egerton's additional literary reference to the eponymous hero of Miguel de Cervantes' 1615 novel is one of many comparisons between Thaddeus and various literary figures.

she could not be certain, for he always shifted the conversation, when it too closely referred to himself.

These observations haunted the mind of Lady Tinemouth, and made her anxious to contrive some opportunity in which she might have this interesting Constantine alone; and, by a proper management of the discourse, lead to some avowal of his real situation. Hitherto, her benevolent intentions had been frustrated by various interruptions at various times. Indeed, had she been actuated by mere curiosity, she would long ago have resigned the trial as fruitless; but sincere pity and esteem kept her still watchful till the very hour in which her considerate heart was fully satisfied.

One morning when she was writing in her cabinet, a servant informed her that Mr. Constantine was below in the parlour. Pleased at this circumstance, she took advantage of a slight cold that affected her, and, hoping to be able to draw something out of him, in the course of a *tête-à-tête*, begged that he would come up to her room.

When he entered, she perceived that he looked sadder than usual. He sat down by her, and expressed his concern at her indisposition. She sighed heavily, but remained silent. Her thoughts were too much occupied with her benevolent plan, to decide exactly what to answer. She had determined, in her reflections, to give him a cursory idea of her own unhappiness; and thus, by her confidence, attract his.

"I hope Miss Egerton is well?" inquired Thaddeus.

"Very well, Mr. Constantine. A heart at ease almost ever keeps the body in health. May she long continue as happy as at this period, and never know the disappointments of her friend!"

He looked at the Countess.

"It is true, my dear Sir," continued she. "It is hardly probable that the mere effect of thirty-five years could have made the inroads on my person which you see; but sorrow has done it; and, with all the comforts that you behold around me, I am miserable. I have no joy independent of the few friends which heaven has preserved to me; and yet," added she, "I have another anxiety united with those of which I complain: some of my friends, who afford me the consolation I mention, deny me the only return in my power, the office of sharing in their griefs."

Thaddeus felt the expression of her ladyship's eye, and the tenderness of her voice, as she uttered these words. He felt to whom the kind reproach was directed, and he looked down confused and oppressed. The Countess resumed.

"I cannot deny what your countenance declares; you think I mean you. I do, Mr. Constantine; I have marked your melancholy; I have weighed other circumstances; and I am sure that you have many things to struggle with besides those regrets which must ever hang about the bosom of a brave man. Forgive me, if I give you pain, (added she, observing his heightening colour,) I speak from a real esteem, I speak to you as I would to my own son, were he in your situation."

"My dearest Madam!" cried the Count, overcome by her benevolence; "You have judged right; I have many things to struggle with; I have a sick friend at home, whom misfortune hath nearly bereft of reason; and whose wants are now so complicated and expensive, that never till now did I know the complete desolation of a man, without a country or a profession. For myself, Lady Tinemouth, adversity has few pangs; but for my friend, for an old man, whose deranged faculties have forgotten the change in my affairs; he who hangs on me for support and comfort; it is this that must account to your ladyship for those inconsistencies in my manner and spirits, which are so frequently the subject of Miss Egerton's raillery."

Thaddeus, in the course of this short and rapid narrative, gradually lowered the tone of his voice; and, at the close, covered his face with his hand. He had never before confided the history of his embarrassments to any creature; and he felt, (notwithstanding it had almost been petitioned from him,) that he had committed an outrage on the firmness of his character, by in any way acknowledging the weight of his calamities.

Lady Tinemouth considered a few minutes, and then addressed him.

"I should ill repay this generous confidence, my young friend, if I were to hesitate a moment in forming some plan that may prove of service to you. You have told me no more, dear Mr. Constantine, than what I had already suspected. And I had something in view." – Here the Countess stopped, expecting that her auditor would interrupt her. He remained silent; and she proceeded; "you spoke of a profession, of an employment?"

"Yes, Madam," returned he, taking his hand from his eyes; "I should be glad to engage in any profession or employment, that you would recommend."

"I have little interest," answered her ladyship, "with people in power; therefore I cannot propose any thing which will in any way suit with your rank; but, the employment I have in view, several of the most illustrious French nobility have not blushed to execute."

"Do not fear to mention it to me," cried the Count, perceiving her reluctance; "I would attempt any thing that is not dishonourable, to render service to my poor friend."

"Well then, would you have any objection to teach languages?"

Thaddeus immediately answered, "None in the world."

"Then," replied her ladyship, greatly relieved by the manner in which he had received her proposal; "I will now tell you, that about a week ago, I paid a visit to Lady Dundas, the widow of Sir Hector Dundas, the rich East-Indian Director.* Whilst I was there, I heard her talking with her two daughters about finding a proper master to teach them German. That language has become a very fashionable accomplishment amongst literary ladies; and, Miss Dundas being a member of the Blue-stocking Club,† you instantly flashed across my mind. Lady Dundas was making a thousand objections against the vulgarity of various teachers whom the young ladies proposed; and I, deeming it a favourable opportunity, told her ladyship, that if she could wait a few days, I would sound a friend of mine, who I knew, if he would condescend to take the trouble, would be the most eligible person imaginable. Lady Dundas and the girls gladly left it to me, and I now propose it to you."

"And I," replied he, "with a thousand thanks, accept the task."

"Then I will arrange every thing," returned her ladyship, "and send you the result."

After half an hour's farther conversation, Lady Tinemouth became more impressed with the unsophisticated delicacy and dignity of the Count's mind. And he, more grateful than utterance could declare, left his respects for Miss Egerton, and took his leave.

---

* Directors to the East India Company (EIC) were elected by company stockholders and formed the executive body of the company. They benefited from the spectacular sums of money collected by the EIC and were often portrayed as greedy or corrupt.

† The Blue Stockings Society was an eighteenth-century group of educated intellectual women, led by Elizabeth Montagu and with members including Sarah Fielding, Hannah More, Frances Burney and Anna Laetitia Barbauld. The society sought to advance women's rights, both civil and educational.

CHAP. VI.

The next morning, whilst Thaddeus was vainly explaining to his poor old friend, that he no longer possessed a regiment of horse that he could order out to try the success of some manœuvres which he had been devising, little Nanny brought a letter from the coffee-house to which he had given Lady Tinemouth the direction. He opened it, and found these contents:

"My dear Sir! So anxious was I to terminate the affair with Lady Dundas, that I went to her house last night. I affirmed it as a great obligation, that you would undertake the trouble to teach her daughters; and I insist, that you do not, by any romantic ideas of candour, invalidate what I have said: I know the world too well not to be convinced of the truth of Dr. Goldsmith's maxim, '*If you be poor, do not seem poor, if you would avoid insult as well as suffering.*'*

"I told Miss Dundas that you had undertaken the task solely at my persuasion; therefore, I could not propose other terms than a guinea for each two lessons that she and her sister would receive. They are rich enough for any expense; and they made no objection to my demand, besides presenting the inclosed by way of entrance-money. Thus, I have settled all preliminaries, and you are to commence your first lesson on Monday, at two o'clock. But, before then, pray let me see you.

"Cannot you dine with us on Sunday? I have informed Miss Egerton of as much of the affair as I think necessary to account for your new occupation. In short, good girl as she is, I thought it most prudent to set her and Lady Sara on the same scent that I have done the Dundas's; therefore, do not be uneasy on that head.

"Come to-morrow, if not before, and you will give real pleasure to your sincere friend,

"Adeliza Tinemouth.

"Saturday morning, Grosvenor Place."

Truly grateful to the active friendship of the Countess, and looking at the General, who appeared perfectly happy in the prosecution of his wild schemes, Thaddeus exclaimed to himself, "By this means I shall at

---

* 'To be poor, and to seem poor, is a certain method never to rise.' Oliver Goldsmith, 'Essay V', *Essays* (London: W. Griffin, 1765), p. 44.

least have it in my power to procure all the assistance your melancholy state requires!"

On opening the inclosed, which her ladyship mentioned, he found it to be a bank note for ten pounds. He felt uncomfortable both at the present, and its amount; not having done any service to earn it, he regarded the money more as a gift, than as a bond of engagement. However, he found that these feelings, with many other painful repugnancies, must at this moment be laid aside; and, without farther self-torment, he consigned the money to the use for which he was aware the Countess had intended it, namely, to provide himself with an English dress.

During these various reflections, he did not leave Lady Tinemouth's letter unanswered. He thanked her sincerely for her zeal; and declined dining with her the next day, on account of leaving his poor friend so long alone; but promised to come in the evening, when he should be retired to rest.

This excuse was felt by none more than Lady Sara Roos; who, having heard from Lady Tinemouth on Saturday morning, that she expected Mr. Constantine to dine on Sunday, had invited herself to be one of the party. She had now seen him constantly for near a month, and to her amazement found, that in seeking to entrap him, she had only ensnared herself. Every word he uttered, penetrated to her heart; every glance of his eyes, shook her frame like electricity. She had now no necessity to affect softness; a young and seducing passion, imparted to her voice and countenance, all its bewitching pathos.

Thaddeus was not insensible to the enchantment which this intoxicating power threw around her; but it did not reach as far as she intended. He felt that she was a lovely woman, who might have affected his senses, had she been free, and his heart been as in happier days. He knew that she was a married woman; and, as he believed her to be a virtuous one, he could not credit the evidence of his feelings, which would have often whispered to him, the language her ladyship wished to convey.

When Lady Tinemouth mentioned to Lady Sara and Miss Egerton, the great favour she had conferred on the Miss Dundas's, by prevailing on Mr. Constantine to undertake the task of teaching them German, Lady Sara could hardly conceal her vexation. She was angry at the Count for his acquiescence, and hated Lady Tinemouth for having made the proposal.

Miss Egerton laughed at the scrape into which Lady Tinemouth had brought his good nature; and declared, that she would tell him next day at dinner, what a mulish pair of misses he had presumed to manage.

It was the youngest of these misses that excited Lady Sara's displeasure. Euphemia Dundas was very pretty; she had a large fortune at her disposal; and what might not such united temptations, effect on the mind of her favourite? Torn with jealousy, she caught at the mention of his coming to dinner on the morrow; and offering to be one of the party, resolved to put on all her charms, that she might make one more essay on the hitherto insensible soul of Thaddeus, before she beheld him enter scenes so likely to extinguish her hopes. – Hopes, of what? she never allowed herself to inquire. She knew that she never had loved her husband, that now she hated him, and was devoted to another. To be assured of a reciprocal passion from that other, she believed was the extent of her wish. Thinking that she held her husband's honour safe as her life, she determined to do what she liked with her heart. Her former admirers were now neglected; and, to the astonishment and admiration of the graver part of her acquaintance, she relinquished all those dissipated assemblies in which she had so recently been the brightest attraction, to seclude herself whole evenings, by the domestic fire-side of the Countess of Tinemouth.

Thus, whilst the world were admiring a conduct which they supposed would give a lasting happiness to herself and to her husband, she was cherishing a passion in her bosom that might prove the destruction of both.

On Sunday evening, the Count Sobieski entered Lady Tinemouth's drawing-room, just as Miss Egerton had seated herself before the tea equipage. At the sight of him, she nodded her head, and called him to sit by her. Lady Tinemouth returned the grateful pressure of his hand. Lady Sara received him with a palpitating heart; and stooped her head, to remove something that seemed to incommode her foot; but this was only a feint, to hide the blushes which were burning on her cheek. No one observed her confusion; so common it is, for those who are the constant witnesses of our actions, to be the most ignorant of their expression and tendency.

Thaddeus could not be so completely uninformed. The frequent falling of her eye, when it met his; the unequivocal intonation of her voice, and sometimes the framing of her speech, often made him shiver. He gladly obeyed a second summons from the gay Maria, and drew his chair close to hers.

Lady Sara observed his motion with a jealous pang that she could not conceal; and, pulling her seat as far on the opposite side as possible, began in silence to sip her tea.

"Ye powers of gallantry!" suddenly exclaimed Miss Egerton, pushing away the table, and lifting her eye-glass to her eye, "I declare

I have conquered! Look, Lady Tinemouth; look, Lady Sara! If Mr. Constantine do not better become this English dress, than his Polish horribles, drown me for a false prophetess!"

"You see I have obeyed you, Madam," returned Thaddeus, bowing.

"Ah! you are in the right. Most men do it cheerfully, when they know they gain by the bargain. Now, you look like a christian; before, you always reminded me of some stalking hero in a tragedy."

"Yes," cried Lady Sara, forcing a smile, and ready to weep with mortification, "yes, and he now exhibits a striking resemblance to George Barnwell."*

Maria, who did not perceive the anger and sarcasm couched under this remark, good humouredly replied.

"True, Lady Sara; but I don't care for his being in black: obedience was the thing I wanted, and I have it in his present appearance."

"Pray, Lady Tinemouth," asked her ladyship, seeking to revenge herself on his alacrity to obey Miss Egerton, the cause of which her jealousy misapprehended, "What o'clock is it? I have promised to be at Lady Sarum's concert by nine."

"It is not yet eight;" returned the Countess; "besides, this is the first time that I have heard of your engagement. I had hoped, your ladyship would have spent all this evening with us?"

"No," answered Lady Sara, "I cannot." And ringing the bell, she rose.

"Bless me, Lady Sara!" cried Miss Egerton, "you are not going? Don't you hear that it is only eight o'clock?"

Lady Sara, busying herself about tying her cloak, affected not to hear her, and told the servant who opened the door, to order her carriage.

Lady Tinemouth, much surprised at the oddness of this precipitation, but far from guessing the cause, requested the Count to see her ladyship down stairs.

"I would rather not," cried she, in a quick voice; and, darting out of the room, was followed by Thaddeus; who got up with her flying footsteps, just as she reached the street door. He hastened past her, to assist her into the carriage, and saw by the light of the flambeaux her face streaming with tears. He had already extended his hand as she approached, when her ladyship, seeing who he was, instead of

---

* George Barnwell is the tragic protagonist of the seventeenth-century ballad 'George Barnwell' and George Lillo's play, *The London Merchant, or, the History of George Barnwell* (London: J. Gray, 1731). Lillo's tragedy follows the story of a young apprentice, George Barnwell, and the murder of his uncle, prompted by a tryst with a prostitute.

accepting it, struck it down with her left hand, and, whilst he stood motionless with astonishment, jumped into the carriage, and, with an indignant tone, ordered it to drive to Berkley Square. He remained stupefied for a few minutes, looking after her; then returned into the house, too well able to translate the meaning of all this petulance.

When he re-ascended the stairs, Lady Tinemouth expressed her wonder at this whimsical departure of her friend; but, as Thaddeus (whose feelings were really disturbed,) returned a vague reply, the subject ended.

Miss Egerton, who hardly thought two minutes on the same thing, sent away the tea-board, and, sitting down by the Count, exclaimed,

"Mr. Constantine, I hold it right, that no man should be thrown into a den of wild beasts, without knowing what kind of monsters he shall meet there. Hence, as I find that you have undertaken the taming of that savage, Lady Dundas, and her cubs, I must tell you what they are like. Will you hear me?"

"Certainly."

"Will you attend to my advice?"

"If I like it."

"Ha!" replied she, returning his smile with another; "that is just such an answer as I would have made myself, so I won't quarrel with you. Lady Tinemouth, you will allow me to draw your friends' pictures?"

"Yes, Maria, provided you don't make them caricatures. Remember, your candour is at stake; to-morrow, Mr. Constantine will be able to judge for himself."

"And I am sure he will agree with me. Now, Lady Dundas, if you please? I know your ladyship is a great stickler for precedence."

Lady Tinemouth laughed, and interrupted her.

"I declare, Maria, you are a very daring girl. What do you not risk by giving way to this satirical spirit?"

"Nobody's love that I value, Lady Tinemouth. *You* know I never daub a fair character; Mr. Constantine takes me on your credit; and, if you mean Charles Montresor, he is as bad as myself, and dare not for his life have any qualms."

"Well, well, proceed," cried her ladyship, "I will not interrupt you again."

"Then," resumed she, "I must begin with Lady Dundas. In proper historical stile, I shall commence with her birth, parentage and education. For the first, my father told me, that he remembers her the maid of Mrs. Sefton, when her husband went out governor of Surat.* And,

---

* A port town in northwest India, today in the Indian state of Gujarat.

soon after their arrival, this pretty abigail,* by some means cajoled old Hector Dundas, (who was then exercising the same command over some other Indian province,) to marry her. When she came back to England, she coaxed her foolish husband to appropriate some of his ill-gotten riches to the purchase of a baronetcy. I suppose the appellation *Mistress* put her in mind of her *ci-devant* servantship; and, in a happy hour, he complied, and she became my lady. That over, Sir Hector had nothing more to do in this world. He was so good as to think so himself: and, to add to his former obligations, had the civility to walk out of it; for one night, whether he had been dreaming of his feats in India I cannot affirm, but he marched out of his bed-room window and broke his neck. Ever since that fortunate event, Lady Dundas has exhibited the finest parties about town. And, though she is as vulgar as she is rich, some-how every body goes to see her; whether in compliment to their own taste, or her silver muslins, I don't know, for there are half a dozen titled ladies of her acquaintance, who, to my certain knowledge, have not bought a ball-dress this twelvemonth. Well, how do you like Lady Dundas?"

"I do not like your sketch," replied Thaddeus, with a secret sigh, that from such a woman he was to receive any obligation.

"Come, don't sigh about my veracity;" interrupted she, "I do assure you, I should have been more correct, had I been more severe; for, she is as ill-natured as she is vulgar, and as presumptuous as ignorant; in short, she is a fit mother for the delectable Miss Dundas, whose description you shall have in two questions. Can you imagine Socrates in his wife's petticoats? Can you imagine, a pedant, a scold, and a coquette, in one woman? If you can, you have a foretaste of Diana Dundas. She is large and ugly, and thinks herself delicate and handsome; she is self-willed and ignorant, and believes she is wise and learned; for, unhappily, she has wriggled herself in amongst the *Blue stockings*; and, to sum up all, she is the most malicious creature breathing."

"My dear, Maria!" cried Lady Tinemouth, laying her hand on her arm, and alarmed at the effect her high colouring might have on the mind of Thaddeus; "for heaven's sake be temperate! I never heard you so unbecomingly harsh in my life."

Miss Egerton peeped archly in her face.

"Are you serious, Lady Tinemouth? You know I would not look unbecoming in your eyes. Come, shake hands with me, and I will be more merciful to the gentle Euphemia, for I intend that Mr. Constantine shall be her lover. Won't you?" cried she, resigning her

* abigail, 'a lady's maid; a female servant or attendant' (*OED*).

ladyship's hand. Thaddeus shook his head. "I don't understand your Lord Burleigh nods;* answer me in words, when I have finished; for I am sure you will immediately unclasp your heart to receive the sweet creature. She is so tiny, and so pretty, that I never see her without thinking of some gay little trinket, all over precious stones. Her eyes are two diamond sparks, melted into lustre; and her teeth, seed pearl, lying between rubies. So much for the casket; but for the quality of the jewel within, I leave you to make the discovery."

Miss Egerton, having run herself out of breath, suddenly stopped. Thaddeus seeing that he was called on to say something, made an answer that only drew upon him a new volley of raillery; which she continued, with very little interruption, till the party separated for the night.

Now that the Count thought himself secure of the means of payment, he sent the next day to consult a physician, respecting the situation of the General. When Dr. Cavendish had seen and conversed with the venerable Butzou, he gave it as his opinion, that the malady had originated in grief.

"I can too well suppose that," replied Thaddeus.

"Then," rejoined the physician, "I fear, Sir, that unless I know something of its nature, my visits will prove almost useless."

The Count remained silent. The doctor resumed –

"I shall be grieved if his sorrows be of a complexion so secret, as not to be trusted to a man of honour: for in these cases, unless we have some knowledge of the springs of the madness, we lose much time, and perhaps entirely fail of a cure. Our discipline is addressed both to the body and mind of the patient."

Thaddeus perceived the necessity of compliance, and did so without farther hesitation.

"The calamities, Sir, which have occasioned the derangement of my friend, need not be any secret; too many have shared them with him; his sorrows have been public ones. You must learn by his language, Dr. Cavendish, that he is a foreigner and a soldier; he held the rank of General in the King of Poland's service. Since the period in which his country fell, and he followed me to England, his wandering senses have approximated to what you see."

Dr. Cavendish paused for a moment, before he answered the Count; then, fixing his eyes on the veteran, who was sitting at the other end of the room, busily forming the model of a fortified town, he said –

---

* Lord Burleigh was a character in Richard Sheridan's satire *The Critic* (1779), whose wordless nods are explicated at great length by another character, Mr Puff.

"All we can do, at present, Sir, is to permit him to follow his schemes without contradiction, meanwhile, strengthening his system with proper medicines, and lulling its irritation by gentle opiates. We must proceed cautiously; and, I trust in Heaven, that success will crown us at last."

When the doctor had written his prescription, and was preparing to go, Thaddeus offered him his fee; but the good Cavendish taking the hand that presented it, and closing it on the guinea, "No, my dear Sir," said he, "real patriotism is too much the idol of my heart, to allow me to receive payment when I behold her face. Suffer me, Mr. Constantine, to visit you and your brave friend as a friend, or I never come again?"

"Sir, this generous conduct to strangers?"

"Generous to myself, Mr. Constantine and not to strangers; I cannot consider you as such; for men who devote themselves to their country, must find a brother in every honest breast. I will not hear of our meeting on any other terms."

Thaddeus could not immediately form a reply adequate to the sentiment which the generosity and philanthropy of the doctor had awakened. Whilst he stood incapable of speaking, Cavendish, with one glance of his penetrating eye, decyphered his countenance; and, giving him a friendly shake by the hand, disappeared.

The Count now took up his hat; and, musing all the way as he went, on the unexpected scenes we meet in life; disappointment where we expected kindness, and friendship where no hope could arise; he arrived at the door of Lady Dundas, in Harley-street.

He was immediately let in, and with much ceremony ushered into a splendid library, where he remained in expectation of the arrival of his pupils. Before they entered, they allowed him sufficient time to examine its costly furniture; its glittering book-cases, bird-cages, globes, and reading-stands, all shining with burnished gilding; its plaster casts of the nine muses, which stood in nine recesses about the room, draperied with blue net, looped up with artificial roses; and, on each side of a fine cut-steel Rumford stove, were placed, on sandell wood pedestals, two five-feet statues of Apollo and Minerva.*

Thaddeus had twice walked round these fopperies of learning, when the door opened, and Lady Dundas, dressed in a morning wrapper of

---

* The nine muses are the Greek goddesses of science, art and literature; in Porter's time, they were linked to the Blue Stockings via Richard Samuel's oft-engraved 1779 painting, *The Nine Living Muses of Great Britain*. The Rumford stove was a shallow fireplace designed by Sir Benjamin Thompson, Count Rumford (1753–1814), in the mid-1790s. Sandalwood suggests the Dundas family link to India, while Apollo and Minerva represent the Arts and Wisdom.

Indian shawls, swam into the apartment. She neither bowed nor curtsied to the Count, who was standing when she entered, but looking at him from head to foot, said, as she passed, "So, you are come;" and ringing the bell, called to the servant, in no very soft tones, "Tell Miss Dundas, the person that Lady Tinemouth spoke of is here." Her ladyship then sat down close to the fire, in one of the little gilded chairs, leaving Thaddeus still standing on the spot where he had bowed to her entrance.

"You may sit down," cried she, not deigning to look at him, and stirring the fire; "for my daughter may not choose to come this half hour."

"I prefer standing," replied the Count, who could have laughed at the accuracy of Miss Egerton's picture, had he not prognosticated many disagreeables to himself, from the ill manners of which this was a specimen.

Lady Dundas took no farther notice of him. Turning from her bloated countenance, (which pride, as well as high eating, had swoln from prettiness to deformity,) he walked to a window, and stationed himself there, looking into the street, till the door was again opened, and two ladies made their appearance.

"Miss Dundas," cried her ladyship, "here is the young man who is to teach you German."

Thaddeus bowed; the younger of the ladies curtsied; and so did the other, not forgetting to accompany such condescension with a toss of the head, that the effect of undue humility might be done away.

Whilst a servant was setting chairs round a table, on which was painted the judgment of Hercules,* Lady Dundas again opened her lips.

"Pray, Mr. Thingumbob, have you brought any grammars, and primers, and dictionaries, and syntaxes, with you?"

Before he had time to reply to her ladyship in the negative, Miss Dundas, with a frown, interrupted her mother.

"I wish, Madam, you would leave the arrangement of my studies to myself. Does your ladyship think that we would learn out of any book which had been touched by other people? Thomas," cried she, to a servant, "send Stevens here."

Thaddeus silently contemplated this strange mother and daughter, whilst the pretty Euphemia paid the same compliment to him. During his stay, he only ventured to look once at her Sylphid figure. There was

---

* A popular subject in painting, which shows the hero Hercules between two women symbolising Virtue and Vice.

an unreceding* something in her liquid blue eyes, when he chanced to meet them, which displeased him; and he saw, that, from the instant she entered the room, she had never ceased staring in his face.

He was a little relieved by the maid putting the books on the table: and Miss Dundas, taking a seat, desired him to sit down by her, and arrange the lessons. Lady Dundas was drawing to the other side of the Count, when Euphemia suddenly whisking round, pushed before her mother, and actually elbowed her out, with this exclamation –

"Dear Mamma! you don't want to learn!" and she squeezed herself upon the edge of her mother's chair; who, very angrily, getting up, declared that rudeness to a parent, was intolerable from such well bred young women; and left the room.

Euphemia blushed at the reproof, more than at her conduct; and Miss Dundas added to her confusion, by giving her a second reprimand. Thaddeus, who pitied the evident embarrassment of the little beauty; to relieve her, presented to her the page in the German grammar with which they were to begin. This had the desired effect, and for an hour and a half they prosecuted their studies with close attention.

Whilst the Count continued his directions to her sister, and then turned his address to herself, Miss Euphemia, wholly unseen by him, with a bent head, was affecting to hear him, though at the same time she looked obliquely through her thick flaxen ringlets; and, gazing with wonder and admiration on his face, as it inclined towards her, said to herself, "If this man were a gentleman, I should think him the most charming creature in the world."

"Will your task be too long, Madam?" enquired Thaddeus, "will it give you any inconvenience to remember?"

"To remember what?" asked she, for in truth she had neither seen what he had been pointing at, nor heard what he had said about it.

"The lesson, Madam, that I have just been proposing."

"Shew it to me again, and then I shall be a better judge."

He did as he was desired; and was taking his leave, when she called after him,

"Pray, Mr. Constantine, come to-morrow at two. I want you particularly."

The Count bowed, and withdrew.

"And what do you want with him to-morrow, child?" asked Miss Dundas, "you are not accustomed to be so fond of improvement."

Euphemia knew very well what she was accustomed to be fond of;

---

* Unreceding, 'not receding' (*OED*), is apparently a Porter neologism. The *OED* currently lists its first appearance as occurring in Porter's 1810 novel *The Scottish Chiefs*.

but not chusing to let her austere sister into her predilection for the contemplation of superior beauty, she merely answered, "You know, Diana, that you often reproach me for my absurd devotion to novel reading, and my repugnance to graver books; now I want at once to be like you, a woman of great erudition; and, for that purpose, I will study day and night at the German, till I can read all the philosophers, and be a fit companion for my sister."

This speech from Euphemia, (who had always been so declared an enemy to pedantry, as to affirm that she merely learnt German, because it was the fashion,) would have awakened Miss Dundas to some suspicion of a covert design, had she not been in the habit of taking down such large draughts of adulation, that where herself was the subject of encomium she gave it full confidence. Euphemia, who seldom administered these doses but to serve particular views, seeing, in the present case, that a little flattery was necessary, felt no compunction in sacrificing sincerity to the gratification of caprice. Weak of understanding, she had fed on works of imagination, till her mind loathed all other kind of food. Not content with devouring the elegant pages of Burney, Smith, and Gunning, she has flown with voracious appetite to sate herself on the "garbage" of any circulating library that fell in her way.*

The effects of such a taste, were soon exhibited in her manners. Being very pretty, she became very sentimental. She dressed like a wood nymph; and talked, as if her soul were made up of love and sorrow: though neither of these emotions she knew by experience, nevertheless, she was ever the victim of some ill fated passion; at least she fancied herself, at different periods in love with all the fine men about town.

By this management, she kept faithful to her favourite principle, that *"love was a want of her soul!"* As it was the rule of her life, it ever trembled on her tongue; ever introduced the confession of any new attachment, which usually happened three times a year, to her dear friend, Miss Arabella Rothes. Fortunately for the longevity of their mutual friendship, owing to the compulsion of an old uncle, this young lady lived in an ancient house, forty miles to the north of London. This latter circumstance proved a pretty distress for their pens to descant on, and Arabella remained a most charming sentimental writing stock, to receive the catalogue of Miss Euphemia's lovers; indeed, that gentle creature might have matched every lady in Cowley's calendar with a

---

* Novelists Frances Burney (1752–1840), Charlotte Smith (1749–1806) and Susannah Gunning (1740–1800), or her daughter Elizabeth Gunning (1769–1823). Porter was acquainted with the Gunning family. The narrator voices contemporary concerns about the dangers of young women reading popular novels.

gentleman.* Every throb of her heart could have acknowledged a different master. First, the fashionable sloven, Augustus Somers, lounged and sauntered himself into her good graces; but his dishevelled hair, soiled linen, and dirty great coat, not exactly meeting her ideas of an elegant lover, she gave him up at the end of three weeks. The next object that her eyes fell on, as most opposite to her former fancy, was the charming Marquis of Inverary.† But here all her arrows failed, for she never could extract more than a *how d'ye do?* from him, through the long lapse of four months; during which time she continued as constant to his fine figure, and her own folly, as could have fallen to the lot of any poor despairing damsel. However, my Lord was so cruel, so perfidious, as to allow several opportunities to pass, in which he might have declared his passion; and she told Arabella, in a letter of six sheets, that she would bear it no longer.

She put this wise resolution in practice, and had already played the same game with half a score, (the last of whom was a young baronet, who, having just skated himself into her heart, she was forming daily parties to see on the Serpentine,) when Thaddeus made his appearance before her.

The moment she fixed her eyes on him, her inflammable imagination was set in a blaze. She forgot his apparent subordinate quality in the nobleness of his figure; and, once or twice, that evening, whilst she was flitting about the sparkling cynosure of the Duchess of Orkney's masquerade, her thoughts hovered over the handsome foreigner.

She viewed the subject first one way and then another, and in her ever-varying mind, "*he was every thing by turns, and nothing long;*"‡ but at length she argued herself into a belief that he must be a man of rank from some of the German courts, who having seen her somewhere unknown to herself, had fallen in love, and persuaded Lady Tinemouth to introduce him as a language master to her family, that he might be enabled to appreciate properly the disinterestedness of her disposition.

This wild idea having once gotten into her head, received instant credence. She resolved, without seeming to suspect it, to treat him as his

---

* Charlotte Cowley's 700-page *The Ladies History of England* (London: S. Bladon, 1780) includes descriptions of Britain's 'most illustrious women for a long series of ages' (p. iv), from Boadicea to Queen Charlotte. Porter uses 'calendar' in the sense of 'a list or register' (*OED*).

† This same character was last seen touring Europe with Mr Loftus; see Volume I, Chapter IV.

‡ An allusion to John Dryden's *Absalom and Achitophel* (London: J. T., 1681): 'every thing by starts and nothing long' (I. 548).

quality deserved, and to deliver sentiments in his hearing, that should charm him with their generosity and delicacy.

With these chimeras floating in her brain, she returned home, went to bed, and dreamed that Mr. Constantine had turned out to be *Monsieur*, had offered her his hand, and that she was conducted to the altar by a train of princes and princesses, his brothers and sisters.

She awoke the next morning, from these deliriums, in an ecstasy, deeming them prophetic; and, taking up her book, began, with a fluttering attention, to scan the lesson which Thaddeus had desired her to learn.

CHAP. VII.

The following day, at noon, as the Count Sobieski was crossing over Cavendish-square to keep his appointment in Harley-street, he was met by Lady Sara Roos. She had spoken with the Miss Dundas's the night before, at the masquerade; where, discovering the pretty Euphemia through the dress of Eloisa, her jealous and incensed heart could not withstand the temptation of hinting at the captivating Abelard she had elected to direct her studies.* Her ladyship soon penetrated into the situation of Euphemia's heated fancy, and drew from her, without betraying herself, that she expected to see her master the following day. Lady Sara, stung to the soul, immediately quitted the rooms, and, in a paroxysm of disappointment, determined to throw herself in his way as he went to their house.

With this hope she had already been traversing the square upwards of an hour, when her anxious eye at last caught a view of his figure, proceeding along Margaret-street. Hardly able to support her tottering frame, shaken as it was with many contending emotions, she accosted him first; for he was passing strait onwards, without looking to the right or the left. On seeing her ladyship, he stopped, and expressed his pleasure at the meeting.

"If you *really* are pleased to meet me," said she, forcing a smile, "take a turn with me round the square. I want to speak with you."

Thaddeus bowed, and her ladyship put her arm through his, but remained silent for a few minutes, in evident confusion. The Count recollected that it must now be quite two. He felt the awkwardness of making the Miss Dundas's wait; and, notwithstanding his reluctance to appear impatient with Lady Sara, he found himself obliged to say,

"I am sorry that I must urge your ladyship to honour me with your commands, for it is already past the time, when I ought to have been with the Miss Dundas's."

"Yes," cried Lady Sara, angrily, "Miss Euphemia told me as much; but, Mr. Constantine, as a friend, I must warn you against her arts, as

---

* In twelfth-century Paris, student Héloïse d'Argenteuil fell in love with and secretly married her teacher, Peter Abelard. Their sentimental tragedy was made popular in the eighteenth century by John Hughes's 1713 translation of *Letters of Abelard and Heloise*, Alexander Pope's 1717 verse epistle 'Eloisa to Abelard', and Jean-Jacques Rousseau's 1761 novel *Julie, ou la nouvelle Héloïse*.

well as those of another lady, who would do well to correct the boldness of her manner."

"Who do you mean, Madam?" interrogated Thaddeus, surprized at her warmth, and totally at a loss to conjecture to whom she alluded.

"A little reflection would answer you," returned she, wishing to retreat from an explanation, yet stimulated by her double jealousy to proceed; "She may be a good girl, Mr. Constantine; and I dare say she is; but a woman that has promised her hand to another, ought not to flirt with you. What business had Miss Egerton to command you to wear an English dress? But she must now see the danger of her conduct, by your having presumed to obey her."

"Lady Sara!" exclaimed the Count, much hurt at this speech, "I hardly understand you, yet I believe I may venture to affirm, that in all which you have just now said, you are mistaken. Who can witness the general frankness of Miss Egerton, or listen to the candid manner with which she avows her attachment to Mr. Montresor, and conceive that she possesses any thoughts that would not do her honour to reveal? And for myself," added he, lowering the tone of his voice, "I trust the least of my faults is presumption. It never was my character to presume on any lady's condescension; and if dressing as she desired, be deemed an instance of that kind, I can declare upon my word, that had I not felt other motives besides her raillery, my appearance should not have suffered any change."

"Are you sincere, Mr. Constantine?" cried Lady Sara, now smiling with pleasure.

"Indeed, I am; and happy, if my explanation have met with your ladyship's approbation."

"Mr. Constantine," resumed she, "I have no motive but one, in my discourse with you; friendship." And casting her eyes down, she sighed profoundly.

"Your ladyship does me honour."

"I would have you regard me with the confidence that you pay Lady Tinemouth. My father possesses the first patronage in this country; therefore, I have it a thousand times more in my power than she has, to render you a service."

Here her ladyship over-shot herself: she had not calculated well on the nature of the mind that she wished to ensnare.

"I am grateful to your generosity;" replied Thaddeus, "but on this head I must decline your kind offices. Whilst I consider myself the subject of one king, though he be in a prison, I will not accept of any employment under another that is in alliance with his enemies."

Lady Sara discovered her error the moment he had made his

answer; and, in a disappointed tone, exclaimed, "Then you despise my friendship!"

"No, Lady Sara; it is an honour far beyond my merits: and my gratitude to Lady Tinemouth must be doubled, when I recollect that I possess it through her means."

"Well," cried her ladyship, "have that as you will; but I expect, as a specimen of your confidence in me, that you will be wary of Euphemia Dundas. I know that she is artful and vain, and finds her amusement in attracting the affections of different men; and then, notwithstanding her affected sensibility, she turns them into a subject for laughter."

"I thank your ladyship," replied the Count; "but in this respect I think I am safe both from the lady and myself."

"How?" asked Lady Sara, rather too eagerly, "is your heart?" – she paused, and looked down.

"No, Madam;" replied he, sighing as deeply as herself, but with his thoughts far from her and the object of their discourse; "I have no portion of my heart to give to love. Besides, the quality in which I appear at Lady Dundas's, would preclude the vainest man alive, from supposing that such behaviour from any lady to him could be possible. Therefore, I am safe; though I acknowledge my obligation to your ladyship's caution."

Lady Sara was satisfied with the first part of this answer. It declared his heart unoccupied; and as he had admitted her proffered friendship, she doubted not, but that when assisted by more frequent displays of her fascinations, she could destroy its lambent nature, and in the end light up in his bosom a similar fire to that which consumed her own.

The almost unconscious object of all these desires, began internally to accuse his vanity of being too fanciful in forming suspicions, which, on a former occasion, he had believed himself forced to receive; and, blushing at a quickness of perception that his contrition nominated a weakness, he found himself at the bottom of Harley Street.

Lady Sara called her servant to walk nearer to her; and, telling Thaddeus, she should expect to meet him the next evening at Lady Tinemouth's, wished him good morning.

He was certain that he must have staid at least half an hour beyond the time when he had promised to be with the sisters. Anticipating very haughty looks, and, perhaps, a reprimand, he knocked at the door, and was again shewn into the library. Miss Euphemia was sitting alone.

The Count offered some indistinct excuse for having made her wait, but Euphemia, with good humoured alacrity, interrupted him.

"O, pray, don't mind; you have made nobody wait but me, and I can easily forgive it; for Mama and my sister chose to go out at one, it being

May-day, to see the chimney-sweepers dine at Mrs. Montague's.* They did as they liked; and I preferred staying at home to repeat my lesson."

Thaddeus, thanking her for her indulgence, sat down, and, taking the book, began to question her. Not one word could she recollect. She smiled.

"I am afraid, Madam, you have never thought of it since yesterday morning?"

"Indeed I have thought of nothing else; you must forgive me; I am very stupid, Mr. Constantine, at learning languages, and German is so harsh – at least to my ears! Cannot you teach me any other thing? I should like to learn of you of all things, but do think of something else besides this odious jargon! Cannot you teach me how to read poetry elegantly? Shakspeare, for instance; I doat upon Shakspeare!"

"That would be strange presumption, in a foreigner."

"No presumption in the least;" cried she, "if you can do it, pray begin! there is Romeo and Juliet."

Thaddeus pushed away the book with a smile.

"I cannot do it. I understand him with as much ease, as you, Madam, will soon do German, if you apply; but I cannot pretend to read him aloud."

"Dear me, how vexatious! – But I must hear you read something. Do, take up that Werter. My sister got it from the Prussian Ambassador, and he tells me it is sweetest in its own language."

The Count opened the book.

"But you will not understand a word of it."

"I don't care for that; I have it by heart in English, and if you will only read his last letter to Charlotte, I know I can follow you in my own mind."†

To please this whimsical little creature, Thaddeus turned to the letter, and read it forward with a pathos that was natural to his voice and character. When he came to an end, and closed the volume, the cadence of his tones, and the lady's memory, did ample justice to her sensibility. She looked up, and smiling through her watery eyes, which glittered like violets wet with dew, she drew out her perfumed handkerchief, and wiping them, said:

---

* Blue Stocking leader Elizabeth Montagu (1718–1800) is reputed to have hosted a feast for the London chimney sweepers every first of May throughout the 1790s.

† Johann Wolfgang von Goethe, *Die Leiden des jungen Werthers* [*The Sorrows of Young Werther*] (1774). Werther's final letter to Charlotte, set within the closing editorial frame of the novel, is a deeply sentimental confession wherein he reaffirms his love for her and determines that he will die rather than live with the despair of Charlotte being married to another man.

"I thank you, Mr. Constantine. You see, by this irrepressible emotion, that I can feel Goethië,* and did not ask you a vain favour."

Thaddeus bowed, for he was at a loss, as to what kind of a reply could be expected by such a strange a creature.

She continued:

"You are a German, Mr. Constantine. Did you ever see Charlotte?"

"Never, Madam."

"I am sorry for that; I should have liked to have heard what sort of a beauty she was. But, don't you think she behaved cruel to Werter? Perhaps you knew him?"

"No, Madam; this lamentable story happened before I was born."

"How unhappy for him! I am sure you would have made the most charming friends in the world! Have you a friend, Mr. Constantine?"

The Count looked at her with surprise. She laughed at the expression of his countenance.

"I don't mean such friends as one's father, mother, and sister, and relations; most people have enough of them. I mean a tender, confiding friend, to whom you unbosom all your secrets; who is your other self, a second soul! In short, a creature in whose existence you forget your own?"

Thaddeus followed with his eyes the heightened colour of the fair enthusiast; who, accompanying her rhapsody with action expressive as her words, had to repeat her question, "*have you such a friend?*" before he found recollection to answer her in the negative.

The Count, who had never been used to such extravagant behaviour in a woman, would have regarded Miss Euphemia Dundas as little better than insane, had he not been prepared by Miss Egerton's description; and he now acquiesced in her desire, to detain him another hour; half amused, and half wearied with her aimless and wild fancies. But here he was mistaken, her fancies were not aimless; his heart was the game that she had in view, and she determined that a desperate attack should make it hers, in return for the deep wounds which she had received from every tone of his voice, whilst reading the Sorrows of Werter.

Thaddeus spent near a fortnight in the constant exercise of his occupations. In the mornings, till two, he prepared those drawings, by the sale of which, he was empowered to pay the good Mrs. Robson for her care of his friend. And he hoped, that when the ladies in Harley Street should think it time to defray any part of their now large debt to him, he might be enabled to liquidate the very long bill of his friend's

---

* This peculiar misspelling of Goethe reappeared in many early editions of *Thaddeus*.

apothecary. But the Miss Dundas's possessed too much money to
think of its utility; they used it as counters;* for they had no conception, that to other people, it became the source of almost every
comfort. Their comforts came so certainly, that they supposed they
grew of necessity out of their situation; and, that their great wealth
owned no other commission, than to give splendid parties, and buy fine
things. Their golden shower being exhaled by the same power of vanity
by which it had been shed, they as little regarded its dispersion, as they
had marked its source.

Hence, these amiable ladies never once recollected that their master
ought to receive some weightier remuneration for his visits, than the
honour of paying them; and as poets tell that all honours are atchieved
by much hardihood, so these two sisters, though in different ways,
seemed resolved that Thaddeus should purchase his distinction with
adequate pains.

Notwithstanding that Miss Dundas continued very remiss in her
lessons, she unrelentingly required the Count's attendance; and, sometimes, not in the most gentle language, reproached him for a backward-
ness, which she owed entirely to her own inattention and stupidity. The
fair Diana would have been the most learned woman in the world,
could she have found any fine-lady path to the temple of science; but
the goddess who presides there,† being only to be won by arduous
climbing, poor Miss Dundas, like the indolent monarch that made the
same demand of the philosophers,‡ was obliged to lay the fault of her
own slippery feet to the weakness of her conductors.

As Thaddeus despised her most heartily, he bore ill humour from
that quarter with perfect equanimity. But the pretty Euphemia was
not so easily managed: she had now completely given up her fanciful
soul to this prince in disguise; and already began to act a thousand
extravagances. Diana, without suspecting the object, soon discovered
that she was in one of her love fits. Indeed she cared nothing about it;
and leaving her to pursue the passion as she liked, poor Euphemia,
according to her custom when labouring under this whimsical malady,
addicted herself to solitude. This romantic taste she generally indulged,
by taking her footman to the gate of the green in Cavendish Square,
where he stood till she had performed a pensive saunter up and down

---

* counters, 'an imitation coin of brass or inferior metal; a token used to represent real
  coin; hence often rhetorically contrasted with real coins, as being only their temporary representatives or counterfeits' (*OED*).
† Athena/Minerva, goddess of wisdom.
‡ Unidentified; perhaps Nebuchadnezzar, who expected his wise men to interpret his
  dreams (Daniel 2).

the walk. After this, she returned, adjusted her hair in the Madonna fashion, because the Count had one day admired the female head in a holy family, by Guido,* over the chimney-piece; then, seating herself in some becoming attitude, usually waited, with her eyes constantly turning to the door, till the object of all these pains presented himself. She impatiently watched all his motions and looks, whilst he attended to her sister; and the moment he was done, ran over her own lessons with greater volubility than clearness. This finished, she shut the books, and employed the remainder of the time in translating a number of little mottoes into German, which she had composed for boxes, baskets, and other frippery.

One day, when the Count, as usual, was tired to death with making decent sense out of so much nonsense; Euphemia, observing that Diana was at the other end of the room with the Honourable Mr. Lascelles,† (for Miss Dundas, to give an eclat to her new studies, had lately opened her library door to morning visitors,) thought that she might do what she wished without detection; and, hastily drawing a folded paper from her pocket, she desired Thaddeus to take it home and translate it into what language he liked.

The Count, surprised at her manner, held it in his hand.

"Put it in your pocket," added she, in a hurrying voice, "else my sister will see it, and ask what it is!"

Thaddeus, full of wonder, obeyed her; and the little beauty, having executed her scheme, seemed quite intoxicated with delight. When he was preparing to withdraw, she called to him, and asked him when he should see Lady Tinemouth.

"This evening, Madam."

"Then," returned she, "tell her ladyship that I shall come and sit half an hour with her to-night; and here," added she, running up to him, "present her that rose, with my love." Whilst she put it into his hand, she whispered in a low voice: "and you will tell me what you think of those verses I have given you?"

Thaddeus blushed, and bowed. He hurried out of the house into the street, as if by that means he could altogether have gotten out of a dilemma, to which he feared all this foolish mystery of Euphemia was only the introduction.

Though the Count Sobieski was, of all men in the world, perhaps

---

* The Bolognese Baroque artist Guido Reni (1575–1642) was known for his religious paintings.
† Since Lascelles is (as we later learn) a younger son, the prefix 'honourable' implies that his father is an earl.

the least inclined to vanity; yet he must have been also the most stupid, if he had not been convinced, by this time, of the criminal attachment of Lady Sara. Added to this disagreeable certainty, he more than half dreaded a similar folly in Miss Euphemia.

Can a man see himself the daily object of a pair of melting eyes; hear everlasting sighs at his entrance and departure; day after day, receive tender, though covert addresses, about disinterested love; can he witness all this, and be sincere, when he affirms, that it is the language of indifference? If that be possible, the Count Sobieski has no pretensions of modesty. He comprehended the *"discoursing"* of Miss Euphemia's *"eye,"** also the tendency of the love-sick mottoes which, under various excuses, she put into his hand; and, with many a smile, mixed with pity, he contemplated her childish absurdity.

A few days prior to that, in which she made this appointment with the Count, she presented to him another of her devices, which ran thus: – "Frighted Love, like a wild beast, shakes the wood in which it hides."

Thaddeus nearly laughed at the oddity of this conceit.

"Do, dear Mr. Constantine," cried she, "translate it into the sweetest French you can; for I mean to have it put into a medallion, and give it to the person I most value on earth!"

There was something so truly ridiculous in the sentence, that he felt reluctant to allow even Miss Euphemia to expose herself so far; and considering a moment how he should make any thing so bad, better, he said, "I am afraid I cannot translate it literally: but, surely, Madam, you can do it yourself!"

"Yes, but I like your French better than mine; so set about it."

He had done the same kind of thing a hundred times, and, without farther parley, wrote as follows:

"L'amour, tel qu'une biche blessée, se trahit lui même par sa crainte, qui fait remuer le feuillage qui le couvre."†

"Bless me, how pretty!" cried she, and immediately put it into her bosom.

To this unlucky addition of the words *se trahit lui même*, Thaddeus was indebted for the present of the folded paper. The ever-working imagination of Euphemia, in a moment seized the inserted thought as a delicate avowal, that he was the wounded deer which he had substituted in place of the wild beast; and as soon as he arrived at home, he

---

* *Romeo and Juliet*: 'She speaks, yet she says nothing; what of that? / Her eye discourses, I will answer it' (II, ii, 12–13).
† 'Love, like a wounded doe, betrays itself by its fear, which makes the leaves that cover it to shake.'

found the effects of her mistake, in the packet which she had given with so much secrecy.

When he broke the seal, something dropped out and fell on the carpet. He took it up, and blushed like scarlet, on finding a gold medallion, with the words that he had altered for Miss Euphemia, engraved on blue enamel. With an agitated hand, he next looked at the envelope; it contained a copy of verses, with this line written at the top,

"To him who will apply them."

On perusing farther, he found them to be Mr. Addison's beautiful translation of that ode of Sappho which runs:

"Blest as the immortal gods is he,
"The youth who fondly sits by thee,
"And hears and sees thee all the while,
"Softly speak and sweetly smile!

"'Twas this depriv'd my soul of rest,
"And rais'd such tumults in my breast;
"For while I gaz'd, in transport tost,
"My breath was gone, my voice was lost.

"My bosom glow'd; the subtle flame
"Ran quick through all my vital frame;
"O'er my dim eyes a darkness hung;
"My ears with hollow murmurs rung.

"In dewy damps my limbs were chill'd;
"My blood with gentle horrors thrill'd;
"My feeble pulse forgot to play:
"I fainted, sunk, and dy'd away!"*

"EUPHEMIA."

Thaddeus threw both them and the medallion together on the table, and sat for a few minutes, considering how he should extricate himself from an affair so truly farcical.

He was thinking of at once giving up the task of attending either of the sisters, when, his eyes falling on the uncomplaining but melancholy features of his poor friend, he exclaimed, "No; for thy sake, gallant Butzou, I will brave every scene however abhorrent to my feelings!"

Well aware, from observation on Miss Euphemia, that the seeming

---

* Ambrose Philips, 'A Fragment of Sappho', in *The Poetical Works of Ambrose Philips* (Edinburgh: Apollo Press, 1781), p. 135. Philips's translation of Sappho's fragment 2 originally appeared in the 22 November 1711 *Spectator*, with some introductory comments by Joseph Addison.

tenderness, which had prompted an act so wild and unbecoming, originated in mere caprice, he felt no hesitation in determining to return the things in as handsome a manner as possible, and by so doing at once crush the whole affair. He experienced no pain when forming those resolves; because he saw that not one impulse of her conduct had any thing to do with her heart. It was a whim lit up by him to-day, which might be extinguished by another to-morrow.

But how different was the case with regard to Lady Sara! Her uncontrouled nature could not long brook the restraints of friendship. Every attention that he gave to Lady Tinemouth, every civility that he paid to Miss Egerton, or to any other lady whom he met at the Countess's, went like a dagger to her soul; and, whenever she could gain his ear in private, she generally made him sensible of her misery, and his own unhappiness in being its cause, by reproaches which too unequivocally proclaimed their source.

He now saw that her ladyship had given way to a dangerous and headstrong passion; and, allowing for the politeness which is due from his sex, he tried, by an appearance of the most stubborn coldness, and an obstinate perversity in shutting his apprehension against all her speeches and actions, to stem a tide that threatened her with the loss of peace.

Lady Tinemouth at least began to open her eyes to the perilous situation of both her friends. Highly as she esteemed Thaddeus, she knew not the extent of his integrity. She had lived too long about the court of Britain, and seen too many from the courts of the continent, to place much reliance on the honour of a single and unattached young man, when assailed by rank, beauty, and love.

Alarmed at what might be the result of her observations, and fearing to lose any time, she had that very evening, in which she expected the Count to supper, drawn out of Lady Sara, the unhappy state of her heart.

The dreadful confession was made by her ladyship with repeated showers of tears, and in paroxisms of agony, which pierced the Countess to the soul.

"My dear, Lady Sara," cried she, "for heaven's sake, remember your duty to Captain Roos!"

"I shall never forget it!" exclaimed her ladyship, shaking her head mournfully, and striking her breast with her clenched hand; "I never look on the face of Constantine, that I do not execrate from my heart, the vows which I have sworn to him; but I have bound myself his property; and, though I hate him, whatever it may cost me, I will never forget that my faith and honour are my husband's."

Lady Tinemouth, with a countenance bathed in tears, put her arms round the waist of Lady Sara, who now sat motionless, with her eyes fixed on the fire.

"Dear Lady Sara! that was spoken like yourself. Do more, abstain from seeing Mr. Constantine."

"Don't ask me that!" cried her ladyship, "I could easier rid myself of existence. He is the very essence of my happiness. It is only in his company, that I forget that I am a wretch."

"This is obstinacy, my dear Lady Sara! This is courting danger."

"Lady Tinemouth, urge me no more on the subject. Is it not enough," continued she, sullenly, "that I am miserable? Would you drive me to desperation? If there be danger, you brought me into it."

"I!"

"Yes, you, Lady Tinemouth; you introduced him to me."

"But you are married. Handsome and amiable as he is, could I suppose – "

"Nonsense!" cried her ladyship, interrupting her, "you know that I am married to a mere fool! But it is not because Constantine is handsome that I like him. No, though no human form can come nearer perfection, yet it was not that: it was you. You, and Maria Egerton, were always telling me of his bravery; what wealth and honours he had sacrificed in the service of his country; how nobly he succoured the distresses of others; how heedless he was of his own. This fired my imagination, and won my heart. No, it was not his beauty; I am not so despicable!"

"Dear Lady Sara, be calm!" entreated her ladyship, completely at a loss how to manage a spirit, whose violence exceeded her conception; "Think, my dear friend, what horrors you would experience if Mr. Constantine were to discover this predilection of yours, and presume upon it! You know, where even the best men are vulnerable."

The eyes of Lady Sara sparkled with pleasure, at this surmise of the Countess's.

"Why, surely, Lady Sara!" exclaimed Lady Tinemouth, doubtingly.

"Don't fear me, Lady Tinemouth; I know my own dignity too well to do any thing disgraceful; yet I would acquire the knowledge that he loves me, at almost any price. But he is cold," added she, sinking again into despondence, "he is a piece of obstinate petrefaction, which heaven itself could not melt!"

Lady Tinemouth was glad to hear this account of Thaddeus. She began to take a little confidence from his side, just as the drawing-room door opened, and Miss Euphemia Dundas was announced.

Lady Sara gave the little beauty such a withering look, when she expressed her amazement at not seeing Mr. Constantine, who was to have apprised the Countess of her intended visit, that, had her lady-ship's eyes been Medusean for that moment, poor Euphemia would ever after have represented a stone statue of disappointment.*

Mean-while, the Count having seen Dr. Cavendish, and received a favourable opinion of his friend, wrote the following note to Miss Euphemia; and then arranged his dress, before he proceeded to Grosvenor Place.

"To Miss Euphemia Dundas.

"Mr. Constantine very much admires the taste of Miss Euphemia Dundas, in the choice of those verses which she did him the honour of requesting he would translate into the most appropriate language; and he has, to the utmost of his abilities, obeyed her commands in Italian, thinking it the best adapted, both for versification and the subject.

"Mr. Constantine equally admires the stile of the medallion which Miss E. Dundas condescended to enclose for his inspection, and assures her that the letters are perfectly correct."

When the Count entered Lady Tinemouth's drawing-room, he saw that his young *enamorata* had already arrived, and was in close conver-sation with the Countess. Lady Sara, now that the discovery was made, thought it unnecessary to put any restraint on her temper before her ladyship. Seating herself alone on a sofa, she was inwardly upbraiding Constantine for what she had termed an absolute assignation with Euphemia, when his name was announced.

Her half-resentful eyes, yet swimming in the tears her discourse with Lady Tinemouth had awakened, sought his averted face, which was regarding Miss Dundas, with a look of surprise and disgust. This pleased her; and the more so, as he only slightly bowed to her rival, shook the Countess by the hand, and then returning, took his station beside her on the sofa.

She would not trust her triumphant eyes to wander towards Lady Tinemouth, but immediately asked him some trifling question. At the same moment, Euphemia tapped him on the arm with her fan, and inquired how it happened that she had arrived first.

He answered Lady Sara. Euphemia impatiently repeated her demand, "How did it happen that I arrived here first?" "I suppose, Madam," replied he, "because you set out first. I do not believe that

---

* In Greek mythology, the Gorgon Medusa was capable of turning onlookers into stone.

I am ever with Lady Tinemouth much before eight, and it now wants five minutes of the hour. But, had I been so fortunate as to have preceded you, I should certainly have delivered the message with which I was honoured."

The evening passed off more agreeably to the Count, than he had augured from the scene that presented itself on his entrance. Lady Sara always gave him pain; Miss Euphemia teazed him to death; but to-night, the storm which had agitated the breast of her ladyship, having subsided into thoughtfulness, imparted so abstracted an air to her ever lovely countenance, that Sobieski, merely to elude communication with Euphemia, remained near her; and, by paying those attentions, which he could not avoid, he so deluded the wretched Lady Sara, as to subdue her melancholy, into that enchanting softness, which rendered her the most captivating of women.

The only person present who did not approve the change, was Lady Tinemouth. At every dissolving smile of her Circean ladyship, she beheld the intoxicating cup at the lips of Thaddeus, and dreaded its effect.* Euphemia was too busily employed repeating some new poems, and too intensely dreaming of what her tutor might say on the verses and medallion, to observe the dangerous ascendency which the superior charms of Lady Sara might acquire over the breast of Constantine. Indeed, she had no suspicion of finding a rival in her ladyship; and, when a servant announced the arrival of her mother's coach, and she saw by her watch that it was twelve o'clock, she arose reluctantly, exclaiming,

"I dare say, some plaguing people have arrived, who are to stay with us, else Mama would not have sent for me so soon."

"I call it late:" said Lady Sara, who would not lose any opportunity of contradicting her, "So I will thank you, Mr. Constantine," addressing herself to him, "to hand me to my coach at the same time."

Euphemia bit her lip at this movement of her ladyship; and followed her down stairs reddening with anger. She got into her carriage, but would not suffer the servant to close the door till she had seen Lady Sara seated in hers; then, calling to Mr. Constantine, she desired him to come into the coach.

Lady Sara leaned her head out of the window. As she saw the man whom she loved step into Lady Dundas's carriage, she in her turn almost bit her lips through with vexation.

"Home, my Lady?" asked the servant, touching his hat.

"No, not till Miss Dundas's coach drives on."

* Lady Sara is compared to the sorceress Circe; see note on page 155.

Miss Euphemia had desired Thaddeus to come in for a moment; and reluctantly he obeyed.

"Mr. Constantine!" cried the little beauty, trembling with expectation, "have you opened the paper that I gave you?"

"Yes, Madam," returned he, holding the door open, and widening it with one hand as he spoke, whilst with the other he presented his note, "and I have the honour in that paper to have executed your commands."

Euphemia caught it eagerly; and Thaddeus immediately leaping out, wished her a good night; and hurried back into the house. Whilst the carriages drove away, he ascended to the drawing room to fetch his hat, and take leave of the Countess.

Lady Tinemouth had seated herself on the sofa, and was leaning thoughtfully against one of its arms, when he re-entered. He approached her.

"I wish you a good night, Lady Tinemouth."

She turned her head.

"Mr. Constantine, I wish you would stay a little longer with me! My spirits are disturbed, and I am afraid it will be near morning before Maria returns from Richmond. These rural balls are sad dissipated things!"*

Thaddeus laid down his hat, and took his seat by her side.

"I am happy, dear Lady Tinemouth, at all times, to be with you; but I am sorry to hear that you have met with any thing to discompose you. I was afraid, when I came in, that something disagreeable had happened; your eyes – "

"Alas! if my eyes always told when I had been weeping, they might ever be telling tales!" Her ladyship passed her hand across her eyes, as she spoke, and added, "we may think on our sorrows with an outward air of tranquillity; but we cannot always speak of them, without shewing that the subject gives us agitation."

"Ah, Lady Tinemouth!" exclaimed the Count, drawing closer to her, "Could not even your feeling heart escape calamity?"

"To cherish a feeling heart, my young friend," replied she, "is not a very effectual way to oppose the pressure of affliction. On the reverse, such a temper of mind will extract unhappiness from causes which might escape dispositions of less susceptibility. Ideas of feeling, sensibility, and sympathy, are pretty toys for a novice to play with; but change those wooden swords into weapons of real mettle, and you will

* The town of Richmond, though only 13 kilometres west of central London, was still considered rural in the 1790s.

find the points through your heart, before you are aware of the danger. At least, I find it so. Mr. Constantine, I have frequently promised to explain to you the reason of the sadness which so often tinges my conversation; indeed, I know not when I shall be in a fitter humour to indulge myself at your expence, for I never felt more wretched, never stood more in need of the consolation of a friend."

Her ladyship covered her face with a handkerchief, and remained so sometime. Thaddeus pressed her hand several times, and waited in respectful silence till she would recommence. She raised her head.

"Forgive me, my dear Sir; I am very low to-night – very nervous. I have encountered two or three distressing circumstances to-day, and these tears relieve me. You have heard me speak of my son, and my lord; yet I never had resolution to recount how we were separated. This morning I saw my son pass my window, he looked up, but the moment I appeared, he turned away, and hastened down the street. Though I have received many stronger proofs of dislike, both from his father and himself; yet, slight as this offence may seem, it pierced me to the heart. O, Mr. Constantine, to feel that the child to whom I gave life, should regard me with abhorrence, is dreadful – is beyond even the anxious partiality of a mother, either to excuse or to palliate!"

"Perhaps, dear Lady Tinemouth, you misjudge Lord Harwold; he may be under the commands of his father, and yet, inwardly, long to shew you his affection and duty."

"No, Mr, Constantine, your good heart is too young to know what may be the guilt of another. Gracious Heaven! am I obliged to speak so of my own son! He who was my darling! He who once loved me dearer than existence! But, hear me, my dear Sir, you shall judge for yourself; and you will wonder that I am now alive to endure more. I have suffered by him, by his father, and by a dreadful woman, who not only tore my husband and children from me, but stood by till I was beaten to the ground. Yes, Mr. Constantine, any man of feeling would shudder, as you do, at such an assertion; but it is too true. Soon after Lady Sophia Lovel became the mistress of my Lord, and persuaded him to take my son from me, I heard that the poor boy had fallen ill through grief, and lay sick at his lordship's house in Hampshire. I heard that he was dying. Imagine my agonies. Wild with distress, I flew to the lodge, and, forgetful of any thing but my child, was hastening across the park, when I saw this woman, this Lady Sophia, approaching me, followed by two female servants. One of them carried my daughter, then an infant, in her arms; and the other, a child of which this unnatural wretch had recently become the mother. I was flying towards my little Albina to clasp her to my heart, when Lady Sophia caught hold of my arm. Her voice now rings in my ears.

"'Woman!' cried she, 'leave this place, or you shall be compelled to do so.'

"Struggling in vain to break from her, I implored, only to be permitted to embrace my child; but she held me fast, and, regardless of my cries, ordered both the women to return into the house. Driven to despair, I dropped on my knees, conjuring her, by her feelings as a mother, to allow me for one moment to see my dying son; and that I would promise, by my hopes of everlasting happiness, to cherish her child as my own, should it ever stand in need of a friend. The horrid woman only laughed at my prayers, and left me lying in a swoon upon the grass. When I recovered, the first objects I beheld were my Lord and Lady Sophia standing near me, and myself in the arms of a man servant, whom they had commanded to carry me outside of the gate. At the sight of my husband, I sprang to his feet, when, with one dreadful blow of his hand, he knocked me to the ground. Merciful Providence! I wonder I retained my senses! I beseeched him to give me a second blow, that I might suffer no more.

"'Take her out of my sight,' cried he, 'for she is mad.'

"I was taken out of his sight, more dead than alive, and led by his pitying servants to an inn, where I was afterwards confined three weeks with a brain fever. From that hour, I have never known a day of entire health."

Thaddeus was shocked beyond utterance, at this anecdote. The paleness of his countenance, being the only reply that he could make her ladyship, she resumed.

"I have gone out of order. I proposed to inform you clearly of my situation, but the principal sorrow of my heart rose immediately to my lips. I will commence regularly, if I can methodize my recollection.

"The Earl of Tinemouth married me from passion: I will not sanctify his emotions by the name of affection; though," added she, forcing a smile, whilst, turning her head towards the looking-glass, she put aside the crape veil which shaded her face, "These faded features too plainly declare, *that of all mankind, I loved but him alone!** I was just fifteen when he came to visit my father, who lived in Berkshire. My father, Mr. Cumnor, and his father, Lord Harwold, had been friends at college. My lord, then Mr. Stanhope, was young, handsome, and captivating. He remained all the Autumn with us; and at the end of that

---

* Matthew Prior, *Henry and Emma* (Manchester: G. Nicholson, 1793): 'My fate I can absolve if he shall own / That, leaving all mankind, I love but him alone' (pp. 509–10).

period, declared an affection for me, which my own heart too readily answered. About this time he received a summons from his father, and we parted. Like most girls of my age, I felt an unconquerable bashfulness to admit any confidant in my attachment; hence my parents knew nothing of the affair, till it burst upon them in the cruellest shape.

"About two months after Mr. Stanhope's departure, a letter arrived from him, urging me to fly with him to Scotland. He alleged, as a reason for such a step, that his grandfather, the Earl of Tinemouth, insisted on his forming a union with Lady Sophia Lovel, who was a young widow, and the favourite niece of the most powerful nobleman in the kingdom. Upon this demand, he told the Earl, on whom his affections were placed. His lordship, whose passions were those of a madman, broke out into such horrible execrations, of myself and family, as Mr. Stanhope confessed, made him forget his duty; and he peremptorily swore, that no power on earth should compel him either to marry so notorious a woman as Lady Sophia Lovel, or to give up me. He concluded, with repeating his entreaties that I would consent to go with him to Scotland. The subject of this letter alarmed me, and I shewed it to my parents. My father answered it in a manner that befitted his own character, but which irritated the impetuous passion of my lover almost to frenzy. In short, in a paroxism of rage, he flew to his grandfather, upbraided him with the ruin of his happiness; and so tempted the old man, that he drew his sword upon him; and, had it not been for the interference of Lord Harwold, a most fatal catastrophe might have ensued. To end the affair at once, Lord Harwold, whose gentle nature always embraced the mildest measures, obtained the Earl's permission to send Mr. Stanhope abroad.

"Meanwhile, I was upheld by my father, who is now no more, in firmly rejecting all my lover's entreaties for a private marriage. As Stanhope's grandfather was equally deaf to all compromise, he at length was persuaded, by his excellent father, to accompany a relation to France.

"At the end of a few weeks, Mr. Stanhope began to regard his cousin as a spy; and after a violent quarrel they parted, no one knowing to what quarter my lover had directed his steps. I believe I was the first who heard any tidings of him. I remember well, it was in 1771, about three and twenty years ago, that I received a letter from him; (O! how legibly are these circumstances yet written on my heart!) it was dated from Italy, where he told me he had resided in complete retirement during the period of his banishment, under the assumed name of Sackville."

At this name, Thaddeus uttered a groan of horror; and, with every feature of his face fixed in dismay, fell back on the sofa.

The Countess caught hold of his hand.

"What is the matter? For Heaven's sake! what is the matter?"

The bolt of indelible disgrace had struck to his heart; it was some minutes before he could recover; but when he did speak, he said, "Pray go on, Madam. I am subject to these spasms in my breast. Pray, forgive me, and go on; I shall become better as you proceed."

"No, my dear friend; I will quit my dismal story at present, and resume it some other time."

"Pray, continue it now," rejoined Thaddeus; "I shall never be more fit to listen. Do, I entreat you."

"Are you sincere in your request? I fear that I have already tired you."

"No; I am sincere; let me hear it all. Do not hold back any thing which relates to that barbarian Englishman who married *you!*"

"Alas he did," resumed her ladyship, "for when he returned, which was in consequence of the Earl of Tinemouth's death, my father was also dead, who might have stood between me and my inclinations, and so preserved me from many succeeding sorrows. I sealed my fate, and became his wife.

"The father of my husband was now Earl of Tinemouth; and, as he had never been averse to the union, he presented me with a cottage on the banks of the Wye, where I passed three delightful years, the happiest of womankind. My husband, my mother, and my infant son, formed my felicity; and greatly I prized it; too greatly, to be allowed a long continuance!

"At the end of this period, some gay friends came down to visit us. When they returned to town, they persuaded my Lord to be one in the party. He went, after much entreaty, because he expected that I should be confined in the course of three weeks. And from that fatal day, all my sufferings took their rise.

"Lord Harwold, instead of being with me in a fortnight, as he had promised, procrastinated his absence, under various excuses, from week to week, during which interval my Albina was born. Day after day, I anticipated the delight of putting her into the arms of her father; but she was three months old before he appeared; and ah! how changed. He was gloomy to me, uncivil to my mother, and hardly looked at the child."

Lady Tinemouth stopped at this part of her narrative, to wipe away her tears. Thaddeus was sitting forward to the table, leaning on his arm, with his hand covering his face. The Countess felt grateful for an excess of sympathy which she did not expect; and, taking his other hand as it lay motionless on his knee, "What a consolation would it be to me," exclaimed she, "durst I entertain a hope, that I may one day behold but half this pity, in the breast of my son!"

Thaddeus only pressed her hand, he did not venture to reply; he could not tell her that she deceived herself even here; that he did not only deplore her misfortunes, but owed the agonies which were shaking him to the injuries of his own mother, whom the villainous conduct of this very Earl, under the name of Sackville, had devoted to a life of self-reproach. He had derived existence from the husband of Lady Tinemouth! The conviction humbled him, crushed him, and trod him to the earth.

The Countess resumed, –

"It would be impossible, my dear Sir, to describe to you the gradual changes which assured me I had lost the heart of my husband. Before the end of the winter he left me again; and I saw him no more, till that hour when he struck me to the ground.

"Lord Tinemouth came into Monmouthshire, about six weeks after I had taken leave of my Lord. I was surprized and rejoiced to see my good father-in-law; but how soon were my emotions driven into a different course! He revealed to me, in the tenderest manner possible, that, during Lord Harwold's first visit to town, he had, unknown to him, been in the habit of spending entire evenings with Lady Sophia Lovel.

"'This woman,' added he, 'is the most artful creature breathing. In spite of her acknowledged dishonour, you well know that my deceased father would gladly have married her to my son; and now, it seems, actuated by revenge, she resents Lord Harwold's refusal of her hand, by seducing him from his wife. Alas! I am too well convinced that the errors in my son's temper bear a strict analogy to those of his grand-father. Impatient of contradiction, flattery can mould him to what shape it pleases. Lady Sophia has discovered these weak points in his character; and, I am informed by his steward, has persuaded him that you impose on his affection, by detaining him from the world. This argument must have been well seconded by other fascinations, for in regard to beauty she is only moderate; yet she has succeeded, and my deluded son has accompanied her into Spain.'

"You may imagine, Mr. Constantine, my distraction at this intelligence. I was like one frantic; and Lord Tinemouth fearing to trust me in such despair out of his sight, brought us all with him to London. In less than four months afterwards, I was deprived of this inestimable friend by a paralytic stroke. His death summoned the new Earl to England. Whilst I lay on a sick-bed, into which I had been thrown by the shock, my lord and his mistress arrived.

"They immediately assumed the command of my lamented protector's house, and ordered my mother to clear it directly of me. My heart-broken parent obeyed, and I was carried, in a senseless state, to a lodging in the nearest street. But, when this dear mother returned for my children, neither of them were permitted to see her. The malignant Lady Sophia, actuated by an insatiable hatred of me, easily wrought on my frantic husband, (for I must believe him mad,) to detain them entirely. A short time after this, that dreadful scene happened which I have before described.

"Year succeeded year, during which time I received many cruel insults from my husband, many horrible ones from my son; for I had been advised to institute a suit against my lord, in which I only pleaded for the return of my children. I lost my cause, owing I hope, to bad counsel, not to the laws of my country. I was adjudged to be separated from the Earl, with a maintenance of six hundred a-year, which he hardly pays. I was tied down never to speak to him, his son, or his daughter. Though this sentence was passed, I never acknowledged its justice, but wrote several times to my children. Lord Harwold, who is too deeply infected with his father's cruelty, has either returned my letters unopened, or, with insulting replies. For my daughter, she keeps an undeviating silence; and I have not even seen her, since that moment when she was hurried from my eyes, in Tinemouth Park.

"In vain her brother tries to convince me that she detests me; I will not believe it; and the hope, that should I survive her father, I may yet embrace my child, has been, and will be, my source of comfort, till it be fulfilled, or I bury my disappointment in the grave."

Lady Tinemouth put her handkerchief to her eyes, which were again flowing with tears. Thaddeus thought he must speak, if he would not betray an interest in her narrative, which he determined no circumstance should ever humble him to reveal, and raising his head from his hand, unconsciously discovered to the Countess his dry and bloodshot eyes, flushed cheek, and convulsed lip.

"Kind, sympathising Constantine! surely such a heart as thine, never would bring sorrow to the breast of a virtuous husband!"

These were her ladyship's thoughts, though she did not give them utterance. Thaddeus rose from his seat.

"Farewell, Lady Tinemouth," said he, taking his hat, "may heaven bless you, and pardon your husband!"

Then, grasping her hand with what he intended should be a pressure of friendship, but which his internal tortures rendered almost intolerable, he hastened down stairs, opened the outward door, and got into the street.

Unknowing and heedless whither he went, with the steps of a man driven by the furies, he traversed first one street and then another. As he went along, in vain the watchmen reminded him by their cries, that it was past three o'clock;* he still wandered on, forgetting that it was night, that he had any home, any destination.

His father was discovered! That father, who, notwithstanding his guilt, he had entertained a latent hope, should they ever meet, might produce some excuse, for having been betrayed into an act disgraceful to a man of honour. But when all these filial dreams were blasted by the conviction, that he owed his being to the husband of Lady Tinemouth; that his mother was the victim of a profligate; that he had sprung from a man who was not merely a villain, but the most wanton, the most despicable of villains; he saw himself bereft of hope, and overwhelmed with shame and horror.

Full of reflections, which none other than a son in such circumstances can conceive, he was lost amidst the obscure alleys of Tottenham-court-road, when loud and frequent cries recalled his attention. A quantity of smoke, with flashes of light, led him to suppose that they were occasioned by a fire; and, a few steps farther, the tremendous spectacle burst upon his sight.

It was a house, from the windows of which the flames were breaking out with the most alarming rapidity, whilst the people about, were either standing in stupefied astonishment, or uselessly shouting for engines and assistance.

At the moment the Count arrived, two or three naked wretches, just escaped from their beds, were flying from side to side, making the air echo with their shrieks.

"Will nobody save my children?" cried one of them, approaching Thaddeus, and wringing her hands in agony, "Will nobody take them from the fire?"

"Where shall I seek them?" replied he.

"O! in that room," exclaimed she, pointing, "the flames are already there; they will be burnt! they will be burnt!"

The poor woman was hurrying frantically forward, when the Count stopped her, and giving her in charge to a by-stander, "Take care of this woman," cried he; "I will save her children, if possible." Darting through the open door, in defiance of the smoke and danger he made

---

* Porter refers to London's early form of law enforcement that existed until 1820, prior to the establishment of the metropolitan police force. The watchmen, centralised in each parish, would patrol the streets at night with a lantern and would methodically 'call the watch' or cry out the time every hour, on the hour. Ekirch, A. Roger, *At Day's Close: Night in Times Past* (New York: W. W. Norton, 2006), pp. 77–80.

his way to the children's room, where, almost suffocated by the sulphureous cloud that surrounded him, he at last found the bed, but it only contained one of the children. This he instantly caught up in his arms, and was hastening down stairs, when the cries of the other from a distant part of the building, made him hesitate; but thinking it better to secure one, than hazard both by lingering, he got into the street, just as a post-chaise had stopped to enquire the particulars of the accident. The carriage door being open, and Thaddeus seeing people in it, without saying a word, threw the sleeping infant into their laps, and hastened back into the house, where he hoped to rescue the other, before the fire could encrease.

The flames had now made a dreadful progress, and scorched his face, hands, and clothes, as he flew from room to room, following the shrieks of the child, who seemed to change its situation with every exertion that he made to reach it. At length, when every moment he expected the house would sink under his feet, he directed his steps, as a last attempt, along a passage which he had not before observed, and to his great joy beheld the object of his search, flying down a back staircase. The boy immediately sprung into his arms, and Thaddeus turning round, leaped from one landing-place to another, till he found himself in the street, and surrounded by a concourse of people.

He saw the poor mother clasp the rescued child to her breast, and whilst the spectators were loading her with congratulations, he left the crowd; and proceeded homewards, with a warmth at his heart, which made him forget in the joy of a benevolent action, that petrifying shock, occasioned by the vices of one, who was too nearly allied to his being, to be hated without horror.

END OF THE SECOND VOLUME.

VOLUME III.

CHAP. I.

When Thaddeus awoke next morning, he found himself more refreshed and freer from the effects of the last night's discovery, than he could have reasonably hoped. The labour and anxiety which the fire had compelled him to exert, having forced his thoughts into a different channel, afforded his nerves an opportunity to regain some portion of their usual strength. He could now ponder on what he had heard, without suffering the crimes of another to lay him on the rack. The reins were again restored to his hands; and only as much of his mind as he pleased, could now shew itself either in his face or manner.

Though the Count's feelings were very sensible, and when suddenly attacked, it was not always that he could hide the pain he felt; yet he possessed a power of look that immediately repressed any curiosity which might have been impertinent. Indeed, this mantle of repulsion was often proved to be his best friend, for never had man more demands on the dignity of his soul to shine out about his person.

Not unfrequently, when Miss Dundas has been schooling her sister on the absurd civilities which she paid to her language-master; and half a dozen pretty beaux and belles have joined in the ridicule, the appearance of the Count has at once called a natural glow through the ladies' rouge, and silenced the gentlemen.

The morning after the fire, a little bevy of fashionable butterflies were collected in this way, in one corner of Miss Dundas's study, when, during a moment's pause, "I hope Miss Beaufort," cried the Honourable Mr. Lascelles, a young man of a stamp that generally wears the impression of the last speaker, "I hope Miss Beaufort you don't intend to consume the brightness of your eyes over this stupid language?"

"What language, Mr. Lascelles?" inquired she, "I have only this moment entered the room, and I don't know what you are talking about."

"Good Lud, that is very true!" cried he, "I mean a shocking jargon, which a shocking penseroso man* teaches to these ladies. We want to persuade Miss Euphemia that it spoils her mouth."

"You are always misconceiving me, Mr. Lascelles;" interrupted Miss Dundas impatiently, "I did not advance one word against the language; I merely remonstrated with Phemy against her stupid attentions to the man we hire to teach it."

"That was what I meant, Madam," resumed he with a low bow.

"You meant what, Sir?" demanded the little beauty contemptuously, "but I need not ask. You are like a bad mirror that from radical defect always gives false reflections."

"Very good, efaith, Miss Euphemia! I declare, sterling wit! It would do honour to Sheridan† or your sister."

"Mr. Lascelles," cried Euphemia more vexed than before, "let me tell you, such impertinence is very disgraceful in a gentleman."

"Upon my soul, Miss Euphemia!"

"Pray allow the petulant young lady to get out of her airs, (as she has I believe, got out of her senses,) without our help;" exclaimed Miss Dundas, "for I declare to heaven, I know not where she picked up these vile democratic ideas."

"I am not a democrat,‡ Diana;" answered Euphemia, rising from her seat; "and I won't stay to be abused, when I know it is all envy, because Mr. Constantine happened to say that I had a quicker memory than you have."

She left the room as she ended. Miss Dundas, ready to storm with passion, but striving to conceal it, burst into a violent laugh, and turning to Miss Beaufort, "You see, my dear," said she, "a sad specimen of Euphemia's temper; yet I hope you won't think too severely of her, for poor thing! she has been spoilt by us all."

"Pray do not apologize to me in particular!" replied Miss Beaufort, rather coldly; "but as you have done so, I am induced to say, that I think it probable she would have shewn her temper less, had you given

---

* A reference to John Milton's 1645–6 poem 'Il Penseroso', a study of a thoughtful or melancholy personality.
† Richard Brinsley Sheridan (1751–1816), Irish playwright and satirist, whose comedies of manners, including *The Rivals* (1775) and *The School for Scandal* (1777), were widely performed in the late eighteenth and nineteenth centuries.
‡ In the aftermath of the American and French Revolutions, the notion of democracy (government based on equality rather than hereditary privilege) had dangerous and radical connotations for the upper classes of Britain, where voting was largely limited to male property owners. Diana mocks her sister's affection for her 'common' language teacher as democratic but Euphemia denies the charge, since she believes Constantine is of noble birth.

your admonition in private, though I cannot doubt of her having committed something wrong."

"Yes, something very wrong;" exclaimed Miss Dundas, reddening at a rebuke from a quarter whence she so little expected one; "both Mr. Lascelles, and Lord Berrington there – "

"Don't bring in my name, I pray Miss Dundas;" cried the viscount, who had been sitting in a recess looking over an old edition of Massinger's Plays*; "You know I hate being squeezed into squabbles."

Miss Dundas dropped the corners of her mouth in contempt, and went on.

"Well then, Mr. Lascelles, and Miss Poyntz here, have both at different times been present when Phemy has conducted herself in a very ridiculous way towards a young man whom Lady Tinemouth made a great fuss about sending to teach us German. Can you believe it possible, that a girl of her fashion could behave in this stile, without having first imbibed some very dangerous notions? I am sure I am right, for she treats him with three times the politeness she uses to the gentlemen who are now in the room." Miss Dundas, supposing that she had set the business in a light beyond controversy, stopped with an air of triumph. Miss Beaufort perceived that her answer was expected.

"I really cannot discover any thing in the affair so very reprehensible;" observed she, "Perhaps this man you speak of may have talents and worth; he may be above his situation."

"Ah! above it, sure enough!" cried Lascelles, laughing boisterously at his own folly, "he is tall enough to be above every thing, even good manners; for, notwithstanding his plebeian calling, I don't find that he knows how to keep his distance."

"I am sorry for that, Lascelles," cried Berrington, measuring the puppy with his good-natured eye, "for these Magog men† are terrible objects to us of meaner dimensions! '*A substitute shines brightly as a king until a king be by.*'‡

"Why, my lord, you do not mean to compare me with such a low fellow as this? I don't understand, Lord Berrington – "

"Bless me, gentlemen!" cried Miss Dundas, frightened at the angry looks of the little Honourable, "Why, my lord, I thought you hated squabbles?"

---

* The plays of English dramatist Philip Massinger (1583–1640) remained popular in the eighteenth and nineteenth centuries.
† In the Bible, Magog was the land of Gog, a prophesied invader of Israel (Ezekiel 38). Various British legends suggested that Gog and Magog were two giants; their carved wooden images famously stood in the London Guildhall.
‡ *The Merchant of Venice*, V, i, 94–5.

"So I do, Miss Dundas;" replied he, laying down his book and coming forward, "and, upon my honour, Mr. Lascelles," added he, smiling, and turning towards the coxcomb, who stood nidging* his head with anger, by Miss Beaufort's chair; "upon my honour, Mr. Lascelles, I did not mean to draw any parallel whatever between your person and talents, and those of this Mr. – I forget his name, for truly I never saw him in my life; but, I dare swear, that no comparison can exist between you."

Lascelles took the surface of this speech, and bowed; whilst his lordship turning to Miss Beaufort, began to compliment himself on possessing so fair an ally in defence of the absent person.

"I have never seen him;" replied she, "and what is more, I never heard of him, till on entering the room Mr. Lascelles attacked me for my opinion. I only arrived from the country last night, therefore, I am quite at a loss to guess the real grounds of this ill-judged bustle of Miss Dundas's about a man whom she stiles despicable. If he be, why retain him in her service? And what is more absurd, why make a person in that subordinate situation, the subject of debate amongst her friends?"

"You are right, Miss Beaufort," returned Lord Berrington; "But the eloquent Miss Dundas is so kind to her friends, that she lets no opportunity slip of displaying her power, both over the republic of words, and the empire of her mother's family."

"Are you not severe now, Lord Berrington? I thought you merciful to the poor tutor."

"No; I hope I am faithful on both subjects. I know her; and it is true, that I have seen nothing of the tutor; but it is natural to wield the sword in favour of the defenceless, and I always regard the absent in that light."

Whilst these two conversed at one end of the room, the other groupe were arraigning the presumption of the vulgar, and the folly of them who gave it encouragement.

At a fresh burst of laughter from Miss Dundas, Miss Beaufort turned her head as we mechanically do on hearing an unexpected noise: her eye was arrested by the appearance of a gentleman in black, who was standing a few paces within the door. He was regarding the party before him, with that lofty tranquillity which is inseparable from high rank, when accompanied by virtue. His figure, his face, and his air, contained that pure simplicity of contour, which at the same time pourtrays all the graces of youth, with the dignity of manhood.

---

* nidge, 'to shake' (*OED*).

Miss Beaufort in a moment perceived that he was unobserved; and, rising from her seat, "Miss Dundas," said she, "here is a gentleman."

Miss Dundas looked round carelessly.

"You may sit down, Mr. Constantine."

"Gracious Heaven!" thought Miss Beaufort, as he approached, and the ingenuous expression of his fine countenance was directed towards her, "Can this noble creature have been the subject of such impertinence?"

"I commend little Phemy's taste;" whispered Lord Berrington, leaving his seat; "ha! Miss Beaufort, a young Apollo?"

"And not in disguise,"* replied she in the same manner, just as Thaddeus had bowed to her; and, with "*veiled lids*"† was taking up a book from the table, not to read, but literally to have an object to look on, that could not insult him.

"What did Miss Dundas say was his name?" whispered the viscount.

"Constantine, I think."

"Mr. Constantine," said the benevolent Berrington, "will you accept of this chair?"

Thaddeus declined it. But the viscount read in the "*proud humility*"‡ of his bow, that he had not always waited like a dependent on the nods of insolent men and women of fashion; and with a good-humoured compulsion he added, "Pray oblige me, for by that means I shall have an excuse to squeeze into the *Sultane* that is so '*happy as to bear the weight of Beaufort!*'"§

Though Miss Beaufort had only seen his lordship, once before, (and that hardly for ten minutes, with her cousin in Leicestershire,) she smiled at this unexpected freedom, and in consideration of the motive, made room for him on the sofa.

Insult was not swifter than kindness, in its passage to the heart of Thaddeus; who, whilst he received the viscount's chair, raised his face towards him with a look beaming such graciousness and obligation, that Miss Beaufort turned with a renewed contempt on the party which were leaving the study.

The instant Miss Dundas closed the door after her, Lord Berrington

---

* Apollo, the Greek god associated with the arts, occasionally disguised himself as a human. See also *Winter's Tale*, where Florizel notes that 'Golden Apollo' disguised himself as 'a poor humble swain' (IV, iv, 30).

† Gertrude tells Hamlet, 'Do not forever with thy veiled lids / Seek for thy noble father in the dust'. *Hamlet*, I, ii, 70–1.

‡ *All's Well That Ends Well*: 'His humble ambition, proud humility' (I, i, 171).

§ *Antony and Cleopatra*: 'O happy horse, to bear the weight of Antony!' (I, v, 21). A sultane is a small sofa with closed ends.

exclaimed, "Upon my honour, Mr. Constantine, I have a good mind to put that terrible pupil of yours into my next Comedy! Don't you think she would beat Katherine and Petruchio* all to nothing? I declare I will have her."

"In *propria persona*, I hope?" asked Miss Beaufort, with more bitterness than she was accustomed to conceive, much less approve, by giving it expression.

The Count remained silent during these remarks, though he fully appreciated the first civil treatment which had greeted him since his admission within the doors of Lady Dundas. Miss Euphemia's attentions had any other source than benevolence.

Miss Beaufort wished to relieve his embarrassment by addressing him; but the more she thought, the less she knew what to say; and she had just abandoned it as a vain attempt, when Euphemia entered the room alone. She curtsied to Thaddeus, and took her place at the table. Lord Berrington rose.

"I must say good bye, Miss Euphemia; I will not disturb your studies. Farewel Miss Beaufort," added he, addressing her, and bending his lips to her hand, "adieu! I shall look in upon you to-morrow. Good morning Mr. Constantine."

Thaddeus bowed to him, and the viscount disappeared.†

"I am surprised, Miss Beaufort," observed Euphemia pettishly, her temper not having subsided since her sister's lecture, "how you can endure that coxcomb!"

"Pardon me, Euphemia?" replied she, "though I did not exactly expect the ceremony his lordship uses in taking leave, yet I think there is a generosity in his sentiments which deserves a better title."

"I know nothing about his sentiments, for I always run away from his conversation. A better title! I declare you make me laugh. Did you ever see such fantastical dressing? I vow to heaven, I never meet him without thinking of Jemmy Jessamy,‡ and the rest of the gossamer beaux that squired our grandmothers!"

"My acquaintance with Lord Berrington is trifling;" returned Miss Beaufort, withdrawing her eyes from the pensive features of the Count,

---

* David Garrick's *Catharine and Petruchio*, a 1754 reworking of Shakespeare's *The Taming of the Shrew*, was immensely popular in eighteenth- and nineteenth-century theatre.
† Lord Berrington is evidently the sensible companion of Harwold, the foolish man who admired Thaddeus's boots shortly after his arrival in London. Yet he, Thaddeus, and the narrator all seem to have forgotten the earlier encounter.
‡ Titular character of Eliza Haywood's novel *The History of Jemmy and Jenny Jessamy* (1753), which commented on marriage and courtship among Britain's leisured classes.

who was sorting the lessons: "Yet I am so far prepossessed in his favour, that I see little in his appearance to reprehend. However, I will not contest that point, as perhaps, the philanthropy I this morning discovered in his heart, the honest warmth with which he defended a traduced character, after you left the room, might render his person as charming in my eyes, as I certainly found his mind."

Thaddeus had not for a long time heard such sentiments out of Lady Tinemouth's circle, and he now looked up to take a distinct view of the speaker.

In consequence of the established mode, that the presiding lady of the house is to give the tone to her guests, many were the lords and ladies who sat with the Count in Miss Dundas's library, whose faces he was as ignorant of when they went out as when they came in. They took little notice of him; and he, regarding them much less, pursued his occupation without evincing a greater consciousness of their presence than what mere ceremony demanded.

Accordingly, this morning, when, in compliance with Lord Berrington's politeness, he received his chair, and saw him remove to a sofa beside a very beautiful woman, he supposed that she resembled the rest of Miss Dundas's friends, and never directed his eyes a second time to her figure. But when he heard her (in a voice that was melody itself,) defend his lordship's character, on principles which bore the most honourable testimony to her own, his eyes rivetted themselves on her face.

Though a long muslin wrapper involved her fine person, a modest grace was observable in every limb. Her snowy arm, clasped with a loose pearl bracelet, was extended towards Euphemia, in the energy of her defence; her beautiful eyes shone with benevolence, and her rosy lips seemed to breathe balm whilst she spoke.

Thaddeus did not withdraw his fixed eyes till they encountered those of Miss Beaufort, which immediately retreated, with a deep blush covering her face and neck. She had never met such a look before, except from the dark and penetrating glances of her cousin, who had long elected himself the guardian of her heart.

Miss Beaufort was the orphan heiress of Admiral Beaufort, an only brother of the late Lady Somerset's. Her parents dying at an early age, bequeathed her to the care of Lady Somerset, her paternal aunt, and nominated Sir Robert Somerset, her ladyship's husband, to be her sole guardian. When Lady Somerset died, which happened three days before her son's arrival from the Continent, a double portion of Sir Robert's love fell upon this niece. In her society alone, he found comfort; and, relinquishing the splendid scenes of London, he retired into the country; living sometimes at one seat, and sometimes at another, in hopes, by change of place, to dissipate some of the grief that rankled at his heart.

Sir Robert Somerset, from the time that his marriage took place with Miss Beaufort,* to the hour in which he followed her to the grave, had attracted esteem and affection from people of every rank. The fascination of his manners, united with the inflexible probity of his character both as a man and as a senator, drew after him the confidence of all men. The good, and even the bad, looked on him as a pillar of strength, whenever reliance was to be allied with virtue. For instance, the excellent Lord Arun bequeathed his only child to his protection; and the sordid, and peculent† Sir Hector Dundas, when he descended to *Hades*, named Sir Robert Somerset principal trustee over the immense fortunes of his wife and daughters.

This latter circumstance explains the intimacy between two families, the female parts of which might otherwise never have met.

On Sir Robert's last visit to London, Lady Dundas became so urgent in requesting Miss Beaufort might spend the ensuing season with her in town, that he could not, without absolute rudeness, refuse. In compliance with this arrangement, Miss Beaufort, accompanied by Mrs. Dorothy Somerset, a maiden sister of the Baronet's,‡ quitted Deerhurst, and settled themselves in Harley-street for the remainder of the winter; at least, the winter of fashion; which, by a strange effect of her magic finger, in defiance of grassy meadows, leafy trees, and sweet-scented flowers, extends its nominal sceptre over the vernal months of April, May; and even the rich treasures of *"resplendent June."*§

The summer part of this winter, Miss Beaufort reluctantly consented should be sacrificed to ceremony, in the dust and heat of a great city; and if the melancholy which encreased upon Sir Robert, every day since the death of his wife, had not rendered her averse to oppose his wishes, she certainly would have made objections to the visit.

During their journey, she could not refrain from drawing a comparison between the insipid routine of Lady Dundas's way of life, and the rational, as well as splendid arrangement of her late aunt.

Lady Somerset's monthly assemblies were not only the most elegant

---

* That is, Miss Mary Beaufort's aunt.
† That is, peculant or peculative, 'practising embezzlement' (*OED*).
‡ The prefix 'Mrs' was occasionally adopted by older, unmarried women like Dorothy Somerset in the eighteenth and nineteenth centuries.
§ Anna Maria Porter, 'Address to Summer', published in the *Universal Magazine* (May 1795): 'Come, and with all thy bashful-blushing beams, / Weave the rich mantle of resplendent June!' (pp. 20–1).

and brilliant parties about town, but her weekly *conversasiones** surpassed every thing of the kind in the kingdom. On these nights, her
ladyship's rooms used to be filled with the most eminent characters
which England could afford. There, the young Mary Beaufort, whose
ardent disposition, impelled with a comet's velocity to the feet of
Genius, listened to pious divines of every Christian persuasion: there,
she gathered wisdom from real philosophers; and, in the society of
our best living poets, cherished an enthusiasm for all that is great and
good. Sir Robert Somerset's house, on these evenings, reminded the
visitor of what he had read or imagined of the School of Athens.† He
beheld not only sages, soldiers, statesmen, and poets, but intelligent
and amiable women; amongst whom, the beautiful Mary, imbibed that
steady reverence of virtue and talent, which no intermixture with the
common *ephemera* of the day, could either displace or alloy.

Notwithstanding this freedom from the chains with which her fashionable advisers would have shackled her mind, Miss Beaufort possessed too much judgment and delicacy to flash her liberty in their eyes.
Enjoying her independence with meekness, she held it more secure.
Mary was no declaimer; not even in defence of oppressed goodness,
or injured genius. Aware that direct opposition often incenses malice,
she directed the shaft from its aim, if it were in her power; and when
the attempt failed, strove, by respect or compassion, to heal what she
could not prevent. Thus, whatever she said or did, bore the stamp of
her soul, whose leading attribute was modesty. By having learnt much,
and thought more, she proved, in her conduct, that reflection is the
alchemy which turns knowledge into wisdom.

Miss Beaufort had never found herself incapable of attempting
something towards her benevolent intention, till she witnessed the
Count Sobieski, standing under an over-bearing insolence, which his
dignified composure rebounded upon his insulters. The situation was
new to her; and when she dropped her confused eyes beneath his unexpected gaze, she marvelled within herself at the ease with which she
had just taken up the cause of Lord Berrington, and the difficulty she
felt to summon one word as a repellent to the unmerited attack on the
man before her.

---

* More accurately, 'conversazione': a private assembly of 'conversation, social recrea-
tion, and amusement' (*OED*). The word was imported by British travellers from Italy
around the close of the eighteenth century.
† A reference to Plato's Academy, Aristotle's Lyceum and the other schools of ancient
Athens, as described in works like Edward Gibbon's 1776–89 *History of the Decline
and Fall of the Roman Empire* and informed by Raphael's oft-engraved fresco of
1509–11, *The School of Athens*.

Euphemia cared nothing about Sir Harry;* to her his faults or his virtues were alike indifferent; and forgetting that civility demanded some reply to Miss Beaufort's last observation; or rather taking advantage of the tolerated privilege usurped by many high-bred people, that they may be ill-bred, when and how they please; she turned to Thaddeus, and said, with a forced smile,

"Mr. Constantine, I don't like your opinion upon the ode I shewed to you; I think it a very absurd opinion; or perhaps you did not conceive me rightly?"

Miss Beaufort took up a book, that her unoccupied attention might not disturb their studies.

Euphemia resumed, with a more natural dimple, and touching his glove with the rosy points of her fingers,

"You are stupid at translation."

Thaddeus coloured, and sat uneasily; he knew not how to evade this direct, though covered attack.

"I am a bad poet, Madam. Indeed it would be dangerous for a good one, to attempt the same path with Sappho and Addison."

Euphemia now blushed as deep as the Count, but from another motive; and opening her grammar, whispered, "you are either a very dull, or a very modest man!" and sighing, began to repeat her lesson.

Whilst he bent his head over the sheet that he was correcting, she suddenly exclaimed, "Bless me, Mr. Constantine, what have you been doing? I hope you don't read in bed! The top of your hair is burnt to a cinder! Why, you look much more like having been in a fire, than Miss Beaufort does."

Thaddeus put his hand up to his head.

"I did not know that I had carried away any more marks of a fire in which I really was last night, than scorched clothes and hands."

"A fire," interrupted Miss Beaufort, closing her book, "was it not near Tottenham-court-road?"

"It was, Madam," answered he, in a tone almost as surprized as her own.

"Good gracious!" cried Euphemia, exerting her little voice, that she might be heard before Miss Beaufort should have time to reply, "then I vow, you are the gentleman that Miss Beaufort said, ran into the burning house, and, covered with flames saved two children from perishing!"

---

* In the second edition, Porter revised this to read 'Euphemia cared nothing about Lord Berrington' (3. 21), thus removing the only (and potentially confusing) appearance of Berrington's first name.

"Am I so happy as to meet the lady," replied he, turning with an animated air to Miss Beaufort; "in you, Madam, who so humanely assisted the poor sufferers, and received the child from my arms?"

"It was, indeed, myself, Mr. Constantine," returned she, a tear swimming over her eye, which in a moment gave the cue to the tender Euphemia. She drew out her handkerchief; and, whilst her pretty cheeks overflowed, and her sweet voice was rendered sweeter by an emotion raised by ten thousand delightful fancies, she took hold of Miss Beaufort's hand.

"O! my lovely friend, wonder not that I esteem this brave Constantine far beyond his present station!"

Thaddeus drew back. Miss Beaufort looked amazed; but Euphemia had mounted her romantic Pegasus, and the scene was too sentimental to close.

"Come here, Mr. Constantine," cried she, extending her other hand to him. Wondering where this folly would terminate, he gave it to her; when, instantly joining it with that of Miss Beaufort, she pressed them close together, and said, "Sweet Mary! Heroic Constantine! I thus elect you the two dearest friends of my heart. So charmingly associated in the delightful task of compassion, you shall ever be co-mingled in my feeling bosom!"

Then putting her handkerchief to her eyes, she walked out of the room, leaving Miss Beaufort and the Count, confused and confounded, by the side of each other. Miss Beaufort suspecting that some extravagant passion subsisted between Euphemia and her young tutor, declined speaking first. Thaddeus fixing his gaze on her downcast and revolving countenance, perceived nothing like offended pride at his undesigned presumption. He saw that she was only embarrassed; and, after a minute's hesitation, said, –

"I hope that Miss Beaufort is sufficiently acquainted with the romance of Miss Euphemia's character, to pardon the action, unintentional on my part, of having touched her hand? I declare I had no expectation of Miss Euphemia's design."

"Do not make any apology to me, Mr. Constantine," returned she, resuming her seat, whence she had arisen on the abrupt departure of Euphemia; "To be sure, I was a little electrified by the strange situation in which the vivid feelings of Miss Euphemia have just made us actors. But I shall not forego my claim on a share of what she promised – your acquaintance?"

Thaddeus expressed how highly he felt the honour of her condescension.

"I am not fond of fine terms," continued she, smiling; "but I know, time and merit must purchase esteem. I can engage for the first, as I am to remain in town at least three months; but for the last, I fear I shall never have the opportunity of giving such an earnest of my deserving, as you did last night of yours."

Footsteps sounded on the stairs. Thaddeus took up his hat, and bowing, replied to her compliment with such a modest yet noble grace, that she gazed after him with wonder and concern. Before he closed the door he again bowed. Pleased with the transient look of pleasure which at parting beamed from his eyes, through whose ingenuous mirrors she believed every thought of his soul might be read, she smiled a second adieu; and as he disappeared, left the room by another passage.

CHAP. II.

When the Count appeared the succeeding day in Harley-street, Miss Beaufort introduced him to Mrs. Dorothy Somerset, as the gentleman who had so gallantly preserved the lives of the children at the hazard of his own.

Notwithstanding the lofty tossings of Miss Dundas's head, the good old maid paid him several encomiums on such intrepidity; and telling him that the sufferers were the wife and family of a poor tradesman, who was gone into the country, she added, "But we saw them comfortably lodged before we left them; and, all the time we staid, I could not help congratulating myself on the easy compliance of Mary with my whims. I hate to sleep at an inn; and to prevent it then, I had prevailed on Miss Beaufort to pursue our road to town even through the night. It was lucky it happened so, for I am certain that Mary will not allow these poor creatures a long lament over the wreck of their little property."

"How charmingly charitable, my lovely friend!" cried Euphemia, "let us make a collection for this unfortunate woman and her babes. Pray, as a small tribute, take that from me!" she put five guineas into the hand of the blushing Mary.

The ineffable grace with which the confused Miss Beaufort laid the money on her aunt's knee, did not escape the observation of Thaddeus, neither did the words with which it was accompanied.

"There, my dear Madam," said she, "I am only the agent of your wishes; and I beg you will take charge of Miss Euphemia's gift, until we see the poor woman."

When Lady Tinemouth was informed by Thaddeus of the addition to the Harley-street party, her ladyship declared her pleasure at the news, saying that she had been well acquainted with both Mrs. Dorothy and her niece, for some time before Lady Somerset's death.

As the Countess paused, Thaddeus was on the point of expressing his concern that Pembroke had also lost his highly prized mother; but recollecting that Lady Tinemouth was ignorant of their knowing each other, he allowed her to proceed without a remark.

"I have never been in company with her ladyship's son," continued the Countess; "it was during his absence on the Continent that I was introduced to Lady Somerset. She was a woman who possessed the rare talent of conforming herself to all descriptions of people; and whilst the complacency of her attentions surpassed the most refined flattery, she commanded the highest veneration for herself. Hence you may credit my satisfaction in this acquaintance, which it is probable would never have taken place, had I been the happy Countess of Tinemouth, instead of a deserted wife. Notwithstanding the family of the Somersets were related to my lord, they had long treated him with coldness; and now doubly disgusted at his late flagrant behaviour, they commenced a friendship with me, I believe to demonstrate more fully their detestation of him. Indeed my husband is a creature of inconsistency. No man possessed more power to attract friends, than Lord Tinemouth; and no man possessed less power to retain them; as fast as he made one, he offended the other; and, through these means, has at this time deprived himself of every individual out of his own house, who might have esteemed his life of greater utility than his death."

"But Lady Somerset," cried Thaddeus, impatient to change a subject, every word of which went like a dagger to his heart, "I mean, Mrs. Dorothy Somerset, Miss Beaufort – ."

"Yes," returned her ladyship; "I see, kind Mr. Constantine, your friendly solicitude to disengage me from retrospections so painful! Well then, I knew, and very much esteemed the two ladies you mention; but the death of Lady Somerset, and their consequent residing in the country has prevented a renewal of this pleasure. However, as they have again visited town I will thank you to acquaint them with my intention to call on them in Harley-street. I remember thinking Miss Beaufort a very charming girl."

Thaddeus thought so too: he saw that she was beautiful, and he had witnessed instances of her goodness; and the recollection of which, filled his mind with a complacency, that was quickly disturbed by the entrance of Miss Egerton, and Lady Sara Roos.

"I am glad to see you Mr. Constantine;" cried the lively Maria, shaking hands with him, "you are the very man whom I have been plotting against."

Lady Tinemouth felt uneasy at the care with which Lady Sara averted her face; well knowing that it was to conceal that powerful agitation of her features, which always took place at the sight of Thaddeus.

"Well, what is your plot, Miss Egerton?" inquired he, "I shall consider myself honoured by your commands, and do not require a conspiracy to trap my obedience."

"That's a good boy! Then I have only to apply to you Lady Tinemouth. Your ladyship must know," cried she, "that as Lady Sara and I were a moment ago driving up the Hay-market, I nodded to Mr.

Coleman who was coming out of the Play-house.* When he stopped, I pulled the check string,† and we had a great deal of con-fab out of the window. He tells me that a new farce is to come out this day week, and he should hope I would be there! No, says I, I cannot, for I am on a visit with that precise woman the Countess of Tinemouth, who would not, to save you and all your generation, come into such a mob. Her ladyship shall have my box, cried he, for I would not for the world lose the honour of your opinion on the merits of my farce. To be sure not! cries I, so I accepted his box, and drove off, plotting with Lady Sara how to get your ladyship as our chaprone, and Mr. Constantine for our beau. He has promised; so dear Lady Tinemouth don't be inflexible!"

Thaddeus was confounded at the dilemma into which his ready acquiescence had involved his prudence. The Countess shook her head.

"Now, I declare Lady Tinemouth," exclaimed Miss Egerton, "this is an absolute stingy fit! You are afraid of your purse! You know this private box precludes all awkward meetings, and you can have no excuse."

"But it cannot preclude all awkward sights;" answered her ladyship. "You know Maria, I never go into public for fear I should be shocked by the angry looks of my lord or son."

"Plague them both," cried Miss Egerton pettishly, "I wish the Lord would take your lord and son out of the world altogether!"

"Maria!" retorted her ladyship, with a grave air.

"Rebuke me, Lady Tinemouth, if you like; I confess I am no Serena,‡ and these trials of temper don't agree with my constitution. There," cried she, throwing a silver medal on the table, and laughing in spite of herself, "there is our free entrance; but I will send it back, and so break poor Coleman's heart."§

"Fie, Maria;" answered her ladyship, patting her half angry cheek, "would you owe to your petulance, what was denied to your good-humour?"

"Then your ladyship will go!" exclaimed she exultingly, "You have yielded to my good humour; these sullens were a part of my stratagem. I won't let you recede."

---

* Dramatist George Colman the Younger (1762–1836) served as manager of the Haymarket Theatre from 1789 to 1818.

† check string, 'a string by which the occupant of a carriage may signal to the driver to stop' (*OED*).

‡ Serena was the patient and dutiful heroine of William Hayley's popular poem, *The Triumphs of Temper* (London: J. Dodsley, 1781).

§ Metal tokens served as theatre tickets in the eighteenth and early nineteenth centuries. The 'silver medal' would have gained them access to Coleman's private box for the evening.

The idea struck Lady Tinemouth, that this would be a proper opportunity to shew one of the Theatres to her young friend, without involving him in expence or obligation, and accordingly she ratified her consent.

"Do you intend to favour us with your company, Lady Sara?" asked the Countess, with a hope that she would refuse.

Lady Sara, who had been standing during the debate silently at the window, rather proudly answered.

"Yes, Madam, if you will honour me with your protection?"

Lady Tinemouth was the only one present who understood the offended feeling which these words conveyed; and, almost believing that she had insulted her, by implying suspicion, she approached her ladyship with a pleading anxiety of countenance; "Then, Lady Sara, perhaps you will dine with me?" said she, "I mean to call on Mrs. Dorothy Somerset, and invite her to be of the party."

Lady Sara curtsied her acceptance of the invitation, and smiling, appeared to think no more of the matter. But, she neither forgot it, nor found herself able to forgive Lady Tinemouth, for betraying her into a confidence, which her own turbulent passions made too easy of access. She had listened unwillingly to the reasonable declaration of the Countess, that her only way to retreat from an error which threatened criminality, was to avoid the object.

"When a married woman," observed her ladyship, "is so unhappy as to love another man than her husband, her only safety rests in the resolution to quit his society, and to banish his image whenever it obtrudes."

Lady Sara, believing herself incapable of this exertion, hated the woman who thought it expedient. Lady Tinemouth, by letter and conversation, tried to display in every possible light, the enormity of giving encouragement to such an attachment; and ended with urging the consideration of her duty to heaven.

Of this argument, Lady Sara knew little. She had never reflected on the nature of her Creator, though she sometimes went to church, repeated the prayers without feeling their spirit; and, when the coughing, sneezing, and blowing of noses, which commonly accompanies the text, had subsided, she generally called up the remembrance of the last ball, or an anticipation of the next assembly, to amuse her till the prosing business was over. From church she drove to the park, where bowling round the ring,* or sauntering in the gardens, she soon forgot

---

* The Ring was a circular track north of the Serpentine in Hyde Park where fashionable visitors drove their carriages.

that there existed in the universe a Power of higher consequence to please, than her own vanity, and the admiration of the spectators.

Lady Sara would have shuddered at hearing any one declare himself a deist, much more an atheist; but for any influence that her nominal belief had over her desires, she might as well have been either. She never committed an action deserving the name of premeditated injury; nor went far out of her way, to do her best friend a service; not because she wanted inclination, but she ceased to remember both the petitioner and his petition before he had been five minutes from her sight. She had read as much as most fine ladies have read; she had perused a few histories, a few volumes of essays, a few novels, and now and then a little poetry; these, and morning calls, with evening assemblies, filled up the day. This had been the routine of her life, till she met the Count Sobieski at Lady Tinemouth's, which event caused a total revolution in her mind and conduct.

The strength of Lady Sara's understanding might have credited a better education; but her passions bearing an equal power with this vigour, and having taken a wrong direction, she neither felt the will nor the capability to hold the empire of her reason. When Love entered her heart, his first conquest was her vanity; she surrendered all her admirers in the hope of securing the admiration of Thaddeus; his second victory, made him master of her discretion; she revealed her unhappy affection to Lady Tinemouth, and more than hinted it to himself. What had she else to lose? she believed her honour to be safer than her life. *Her honour* was the term. She had no conception, or at best a faint one, that a breach of the marriage vow could be an outrage on the laws of heaven. The word *Sin*, has been gradually banished by the oligarchy of fashion, from the hour in which Charles II and his profligate court, trod down piety along with hypocrisy, to this day, when the new philosophy has accomplished its total outlawry, and denounced it a rebel to decency, and the freedom of man.*

Thus, religion being driven from the haunts of the great, pagan morality is raised from that prostration, where, Dagon-like it fell at the feet of the Scriptures, and is again erected as the idol of adoration.† Guilt against heaven fades before the decrees of man; his law of

---

* Charles II, the 'Merry Monarch', is remembered for the hedonism of his court during his reign from 1660 to 1685, following the marked puritanism of Oliver Cromwell's leadership. This paragraph and the following appear to offer a reaction against the philosophical thought advanced in works like William Godwin's 1793 *Enquiry Concerning Political Justice*.
† Dagon is a Mesopotamian deity, mentioned in the Bible as the god of the Philistines (Judges 16: 23).

ethics reprobates *crime*; but crime is only a temporary transgression in opposition to the general good; it draws no consequent punishment heavier than the anger of the offended parties. Morality neither promises rewards after death, nor chastisement for error. The disciples of this independent doctrine, hold forth instances of the perfectibility of human actions, produced from the unassisted decisions of human intellect on the limits of right and wrong. They admire virtue, because it is beautiful. They practice it, because it is heroic. They do not abstain from the gratification of an intemperate wish, under a belief that it is sinful, but in obedience to their reason which rejects the commission of a vicious act, because it is uncomely. In the first case, God is their judge; in the latter, themselves. The comparison need only be proposed to humble the pride that made it necessary. How do these systemisers refine and subtilize? How do they dwell on the principle of virtue, and turn it in every metaphysical light, till their philosophy rarifies it to nothing! Thus, some degrade, and others abandon the only basis on which an upright character can stand with firmness. The bulwark which Revelation has erected between the passions and the soul, is levelled first; and then that instinctive rule of right which the modern casuist nominates the citadel of virtue, falls of course.

By such gradations is the progress of depravity accomplished; and on such premises, did Lady Sara, (though she might not arrange them so distinctly,) the general leaven having worked to her mind, deduce, that what she called preserving her honour, was a mere establishment of man, and might be extended or limited by him, to any length he liked. For instance, the Turks were not content with one wife, but appropriated hundreds to their possession; and, because such an enlargement was permitted by Mahammed, no other nation presumed to call them culpable.*

Hence she thought, if she could once reconcile herself to believe, that her own happiness was dearer to her than the notice of half a thousand people to whom she was indifferent; that only in their opinion and the world's, her flying to the protection of Thaddeus would be a crime; could she confidently think this, what should deter her from instantly throwing herself into the arms of the man she loved?

"Ah!" cried she one night as she traversed her chamber in a paroxism

---

* Porter draws upon contemporary characterisations of Ottoman men taking multiple wives under the mandate of Islamic tradition; however, she exaggerates the number of wives into the hundreds. Lady Mary Wortley Montagu's *Letters ... Written, during her Travels*, 4 vols (London: T. Becket and P. A. De Hondt, 1763) notes four wives as falling within the legal allowance (2.35–7). See also Dallaway, James, 'Present State of the Turkish Women', *The Monthly Visitor* 1 (June 1797), pp. 518–25 (520).

of tears, "what are the vows I have sworn? How can I keep them? I have sworn, to love, to honour Captain Roos; but, in spite of myself, without any action of my own, I have broken both these oaths. I cannot love him; I hate him, and I cannot honour the man I hate. What have I else to break? Nothing. My nuptial vow is as completely annihilated, as if I had left him never to return. – How?" cried she, after a pause of some minutes, "how shall I know what passes in the mind of Constantine? Did he love me, would he protect me, I would brave the whole universe; oh, I should be the happiest of the happy!"

Fatal conclusion of reflection! It infected her dreaming and her waking fancy. She regarded every thing as an enemy that opposed her passion; and as the first of these enemies, she detested Lady Tinemouth. The Countess's last admonishing letter had enraged her by its arguments, and throwing it into the fire with execrations and tears, she determined to pursue her own will, but to affect being influenced by her ladyship's counsels.

The Count Sobieski, who had never surmised the hundredth part of the love which Lady Sara bore towards him, began to hope that her ardent manner had misled him; or that she had seen the danger of such imprudence.

Under these impressions, the party for the theatre was settled; and Thaddeus, after sitting an hour in Grosvenor Place, returned to his humble home, and attendance on his friend.

CHAP. III.

The addition of Mrs. Dorothy Somerset and Miss Beaufort, to the morning groupe at Lady Dundas's, imparted a less reluctant motion to the before tardy feet of the Count, whenever he turned them towards Harley-street.

Mrs. Dorothy readily supposed him to have been better born than he appeared; and displeased with the treatment he received from Miss Dundas and her guests, behaved to him herself with the most gratifying politeness.

Aunt Dorothy, (for that was the title by which every branch of the baronet's family addressed her;) was full twenty years the senior of her brother Sir Robert Somerset. Having in her youth been thought very like the famous and lovely Mrs. Woffington,* she was considered the beauty of her time; and, as such, for ten years continued the reigning toast. Nevertheless, she arrived at the age of sixty-five, without having been either the object or the subject of a fervent passion.

Possessing a fine understanding, a fine taste, and fine feelings, she had some way escaped love. It cannot be denied, that she was much admired, much respected, and much esteemed; and that she received two or three splendid proposals from men whom she had animated thus far. Some of these men, she admired, some she respected, and some she esteemed, but not one did she love, and she refused them all. Shortly after their discharge, they generally consoled themselves by marrying other women, who perhaps neither possessed the charms nor sense of Miss Somerset, yet she congratulated them on their choice, and frequently became the friend of both wife and husband.

Thus, year passed over year; Miss Somerset continued the esteemed of every worthy heart, though she could not find the embers of a warmer glow in any one of them; and, at the age of sixty-five, she found herself an old maid; but possessing as much good humour and affection towards the young people about her, as if she owned half a dozen of her own offspring to mingle in the circle.

---

* Margaret 'Peg' Woffington (?1720–60), Irish actress and celebrated beauty who maintained romantic relationships with various members of London's elite, including David Garrick.

This amiable old lady usually took her netting* into the library beside the fair students; and, whenever Thaddeus entered the room, (so natural is it for generous natures to sympathise,) his eyes first sought her venerable figure, then glancing round, to catch an assuring beam from the sunny orbs of the lovely Mary, he seated himself with confidence.

The presence of these ladies operated as a more than sufficient antidote to the disagreeables of his situation. To them he directed all the attention that was not required by his occupation; he heard only them speak, when a hundred others were talking; he saw only them, when a hundred others were in company.

In addition to this pleasant change, Miss Euphemia's passion assumed a form less capable of tormenting. She had been reading Madame d'Arblay's Camilla, and becoming so enamoured of the delicacy and pensive silence of the interesting heroine, she immediately determined on adopting the same character; and at the same time, taking it into her ever creative brain, that Constantine's coldness bore a strict affinity to the caution of Edgar Mandelbert:† without further debate, she wiped the rouge off her face, and prepared to "*let concealment, like a worm in the bud, feed on her damask cheek.*"‡

To afford decorous support to this fancy, her gayest clothes were thrown aside, to make way for a negligence of apparel, that cost her two hours each morning to compose. Her dimpling smiles were now quite banished. She was ever sighing, and ever silent, and ever lolling and leaning about, or reclining along the sofa in some pretty disconsolate attitude, just selected from a folio of prints, in which she daily studied her dress and movements.

Thaddeus preferred this pathetic whim to her former lover-like advances; it afforded him quiet, and relieved him from much embarrassment.

Every succeeding visit induced Miss Beaufort to observe him with nicer accuracy, and a more lively interest. The nobleness, yet humility, with which he behaved towards herself and her aunt; and the manly serenity with which he suffered the insulting sarcasms of Miss Dundas,

---

* 'Netting is a form of lace created with a succession of regular loops that form a mesh'. Ledbetter, Kathryn, *Victorian Needlework* (Santa Barbara, CA: Praeger, 2012), p. 48. Items created from netting include shawls, curtains and purses.

† Euphemia is (anachronistically) reading *Camilla: or, a Picture of Youth* (1796) by Frances Burney (known after her 1793 marriage as Madame D'Arblay), in which the well-meaning but judgemental Edgar Mandelbert is eventually united with the shy and sentimental Camilla.

‡ *Twelfth Night*: 'She never told her love, / But let concealment like a worm i' th' bud / Feed on her damask cheek' (II, iv, 109–11).

led her not merely to conceive, but to entertain many doubts that his present situation was far below his birth.

The ladies who dropped in now and then on the sisters, were not backward in espousing this game; as it played away a few minutes to join in a laugh with the *witty Diana*. These gracious beings, from their sex, knew they were privileged to offend; but it was not always that the gentlemen durst venture beyond a shrug of the shoulder, a drop of the lip, a wink of the eye, or a raising of the brows. However, Mary observed with contempt, that they were wise enough to exercise these specimens of hostility only when the Count had turned his back; and regarding him with increased admiration, she first felt indignation, and then perfect disdain, at the motives of envy which actuated these men to insult him under the mask of indifference.

The occasional calls of Lady Tinemouth and Miss Egerton, stimulated the cabal against poor Thaddeus. The sincere sentiment of equality with themselves, which these two ladies evinced by their behaviour to him; and the same conduct being adopted by Mrs. Dorothy and her beautiful niece; besides the evident partiality of Euphemia; altogether inflamed the spleen of Miss Dundas's *coterie* to absolute rudeness.

This little phalanx, at the head of which was the superb Diana, could offer no real reason for disliking a man, not only beneath them, but who had never offended them even by implication. It was a sufficient apology to their easy consciences, that "he gave himself such courtly airs as were quite ridiculous; that his presumption was astonishing. In short, they were all idle, and it was monstrous amusing to lounge a morning with the rich Dundas's and hoax monsieur."

Had Thaddeus known one fourth of the insolent derision with which his misfortunes were treated behind his back; though he considered the very breath he breathed, ought to be sacrificed if conducive to the life of his friend, perhaps even his necessity, could not in this case have detained him in his employment. The brightness of a brave man's name, makes shadows perceptible, which might pass unmarked over a duller surface. Sobieski's nice honour would have supposed itself sullied by enduring such contumely with toleration. But, as was said before, the male adjuncts of Miss Dundas, had received such a prompt warning from an accidental knitting of the Count's brow, that they never after, could muster temerity to sport their wit to his face.

These circumstances were not lost upon Mary; she collected them as part of a treasure, and turned them over on her pillow with the jealous examination of a miser. Like Euphemia, she supposed Thaddeus to be other than he seemed, yet her fancy did not gift him with the blood of the Bourbons; she merely believed him to be a gentleman; and, from the maternal manner of Lady Tinemouth towards him, suspected that her ladyship knew more of his history than she chose to reveal.

Things were in this state, when the Countess requested that Mrs. Dorothy would trust her niece the ensuing evening, with herself and a little party to the Hay-market Theatre. The good lady having consented, Miss Beaufort received the permission with pleasure; and, as she was invited to sup with her ladyship, she formed the hope that something might fall from the Countess or Miss Egerton, which would throw a light on the true situation of Mr. Constantine.

From infancy, Miss Beaufort had loved with enthusiasm all kinds of excellence. Indeed she esteemed no person warmly, whom she did not think eminent in the liberal qualities over the rest of mankind. She sought for something to respect in every character; and when by chance she found any thing to admire, her susceptible soul blazed, and, by its own pure flame, lit her to a clearer examination of the object for whom she felt interested.

When Lady Somerset collected all the virtue and talent in the country around her table, they were not brought there on a vain errand. From them, Miss Beaufort gathered her best lessons in morality and taste; and from them, her earliest perceptions of friendship. Mary was the beloved pupil, and respected friend, of the brightest characters in England; and though they were men, some of whom had not passed the age of forty, she had never been in love, nor had she mistaken the nature of her feelings so far, as to call them by that name. Hence, she neither felt afraid nor ashamed, to acknowledge a correspondence which she knew to be her best distinction. But, had the frank and innocent Mary, exhibited half the like attentions which she paid to these men in one hour when they were present, to the common class of young men through the course of a month, they would have declared, "that the poor girl was over-head in love with them; and have pitied (what they justly denominate) her folly." Foolish must that woman be, who will sacrifice the most precious gift in her possession, to the superficial graces, or empty blandishments of a self-idolized coxcomb.

Such a being was not Mary Beaufort; and, on these principles, she contemplated the extraordinary merits of the exiled Thaddeus, with an interest honourable to her penetration and heart.

When Miss Egerton called in Lady Sara Roos's carriage to take her to the Hay-market, Mary was not displeased at seeing Mr. Constantine step out of the coach to hand her in. During their drive, Miss Egerton informed her, that from Lady Tinemouth's sudden indisposition, Lady Sara had kindly undertaken to be their chaprone; and promised to bring them all back to sup in Grosvenor Place.

Lady Sara had never seen Mary, though she had frequently heard of her beauty and vast fortune; this last qualification, her ladyship hoped, might have given an unmerited *eclat* to the first; therefore, when she saw in the person of Miss Beaufort, the most beautiful creature she had ever beheld, nothing could equal her surprise and vexation.

The happy lustre that beamed in the fine eyes of Mary, shone like a vivifying influence around her; a bright glow animated her cheek, whilst a pleasure for which she did not seek to account, bounded at her heart, and modulated every tone of her voice, to sweetness and enchantment.

"Syren!" thought Lady Sara, withdrawing her large dark eyes from her face, and turning them full of dissolving languor upon Thaddeus, "here are all thy charms directed?" then drawing a sigh so deep, that it made her neighbour start, she fixed her eyes on her fan, and never looked up till they reached the play-house.

The curtain was raised as the little party seated themselves in the box.

"Can any body tell me what the play is?" asked Lady Sara.

"I never thought of inquiring," replied Maria.

"I looked in the paper this morning," said Miss Beaufort, "and I think it is called *Sighs*, a translation from a Drama of Kotzebue's."*

"A strange title!" was the general observation, when Mr. Suett, who personated one of the characters, beginning to speak, their attention was summoned to the stage.

On the entrance of Mr. Charles Kemble in the character of Adelbert, the Count unconsciously turned pale. He perceived by the dress of the actor, that he intended to personate a Pole; and, alarmed at the probability of seeing something to recall recollections which he strove to banish, his agitation did not allow him to hear any thing that passed.

Miss Egerton was not so tardy in the use of her eyes and ears, but stretching out her hand to the back of the box, where Thaddeus was standing by Lady Sara's chair, she caught hold of his sleeve.

"There, Constantine;" cried she, "look at Adelbert! Now, that is exactly the figure *you* cut in your Polish trumpery two months ago."

---

* *Sighs; or, the Daughter* was adapted for the London stage by Prince Hoare from the German original by playwright August von Kotzebue. It premiered at the Haymarket Theatre on 30 July 1799, featuring Richard Suett as the rich merchant Von Snarl, William Barrymore as his brother Leopold, Maria Gibbs as Louisa Rose (here called Rose), John Fawcett as Tilman Totum, and Charles Kemble as Adelbert, a Polish exile. Kemble was a close family friend of the Porters and later travelled in Europe with Robert Ker Porter. Although its performance is anachronistic for Thaddeus's first year in London, its story of a young and honourable Pole living in exile and falling in love has obvious parallels with Porter's plot.

The Count bowed with a forced smile, and glancing at the stage, replied:

"Then, for the first time in my life, I regret having followed a lady's advice; I think I must have lost by the change."

"Yes," rejoined she, "you have lost much fur, and much embroidery; but you look much more like a christian."

The substance of these speeches were not lost on Mary, who continued to mark with redoubling interest, the changes which his countenance underwent along with the scene. As she sat forward, by a slight turn of the head, she could discern the smallest fluctuation of his features; and they were not a few; for, placing himself at the back of Lady Sara's chair, he now leaned over, with his soul set in his eye, watching every motion of Mr. Charles Kemble.

Mary knew that Constantine was a Polander; and the surmise which she had entertained of his being unfortunate, received full corroboration at the scene wherein Adelbert is grossly insulted by the rich merchant; during the whole of which she scarcely dared trust her eyes towards his flushed and agitated face.

The interview between Adelbert and Leopold commenced: when the former was describing his country's miseries with his own, Thaddeus, unable to bear it longer, unobserved by any but Mary, drew back into the box. In a moment or two, Mr. Charles Kemble made the following reply to an observation of Leopold's, that poverty is no dishonour.

"Certainly none to me! To Poland, to my struggling country, I sacrificed my wealth, as I would have sacrificed my life, if she had required it. My country is no more; and we are wanderers on a burthened earth, finding no refuge but in the hearts of the humane and virtuous."*

The passion and force of these words could not fail of reaching the ears of Thaddeus. Mary's attention followed them to their object, by the heaving of whose breast, she plainly discovered the anguish of their effect. Her pitying heart fluttered. How willingly would she have approached him, and said something of sympathy, of consolation! but she might not; and she turned away her tearful eye, and looked again on the stage.

Lady Sara now stood up: hanging over Mary's chair, she listened with congenial emotions to the scene between Adelbert and the innocent Rose. Lady Sara felt it all in her own bosom; and, looking round to catch what was passing in the Count's mind, she beheld him leaning against a corner of the box with his head inclined to the curtain of the door.

---

* Adelbert and Leopold's discussion and the quoted passage appear in III, i.

"Mr. Constantine!" almost unconsciously escaped her lips. He started up immediately, and discovered,* by the humidity of his eyes, why he had withdrawn. Her ladyship's tears were gliding down her cheeks. Miss Egerton, greatly amazed at the oddness of the scene, turned to Miss Beaufort, who a moment before having caught a glimpse of the distressed countenance of the Count, could only smile, and bow her head to Maria's observation.

Who is there that can enter into the bitterness of the heart? Who participate in that joy which dissolves and rarifies man to the essence of heaven? Soul must mingle with soul, and the invisible language of the spirit must speak, before this can be comprehended.

Mary, who felt ready to suffocate with the emotion which she repelled from her eyes, gladly affected to be absorbed in the business of the stage, (not one object of which she now saw,) and with breathless attention, lost not one soft whisper, which Lady Sara poured into the ear of Thaddeus.

"Why?" asked her ladyship, in a tremulous and low voice. "Why should we seek ideal miseries, when those of our own hearts are beyond alleviation? Happy Rose!" sighed her ladyship, "Constantine," continued she, "do not you think that Adelbert is consoled at least by the affection of that lovely woman?"

Like Miss Beaufort, Constantine had hitherto replied only with bows.

"Come," added Lady Sara, laying her soft hand on his arm, and regarding him with a tenderness so unequivocal that he cast his eyes to the ground, though he felt their compassion and sympathy touch his heart; "Come," repeated she, animated by the faint colour which tinged his cheek, "you know I have the care of this party; and I must not allow our only beau to be melancholy."

"I beg your pardon, Lady Sara," returned he, in gratitude to her kind commiseration, pressing the hand that yet rested on his arm, "I am not very well. I wish I had not seen this play!"

Lady Sara sunk into the seat from whence she had arisen. He had never before, taken her hand, except when assisting her to her carriage; this pressure, shook her very soul, and awakened hopes, which rendered her for a moment incapable of sustaining herself, or of venturing a reply.

There was something in the tones of Lady Sara's voice, and in her manner, far more expressive than her words: a mutual sigh which breathed from her ladyship's bosom, and that of Thaddeus, as they

* That is, 'revealed'.

sat down, made a cold shiver run from the head to the foot of Miss Beaufort. The surprize that Mary felt at the meaning of this emotion, caused a second tremor, and with a palpitating heart, she asked herself a few questions.

Could this interesting young man, whom every person of sense appeared to esteem and respect, could he sully his virtues by participating in a passion with a married woman? No; it was impossible.

Notwithstanding this decision, she determined to observe him narrowly; and be well convinced of his worth before she permitted him to augment the share of regard which he already possessed in her bosom.

With her head full of these reflections, she awaited the farce, without observing when it appeared. Indeed none present knew any thing about this piece, (to see which they had professedly come to the theatre,) excepting Miss Egerton, whose ever merry spirits had enjoyed the humour of *Totum* in the play, and now laughed heartily, though unaccompanied, through the ridiculous whims of the farce.

Nothing that passed, could totally disengage the mind of the Count from those remembrances which the recent drama had awakened. When the melting voice of Lady Sara, in whispers, tried to recall his attention; by a start only, he evinced his recollection of not being alone. However, he felt the kindness of her motive; and exerted himself: by the time that the curtain dropt, he had so far rallied his spirits as to attend to the civility of seeing the ladies safe out of the theatre.

Miss Egerton, laughing, as he assisted her into the carriage, said, "I verily believe, Mr. Constantine, had I glanced round during the play, I should have seen as pretty a lacrymal scene between you and Lady Sara, as any on the stage. I won't have this flirting! I declare I will tell Captain Roos – ."

She continued talking; but he, turning about to offer his service to Miss Beaufort, heard no more.

Miss Beaufort felt strangely; she felt cold and reserved; and, undesignedly, she appeared what she felt. There was a grave dignity in her air, accompanied with a collectedness and stillness in her before animated countenance, which astonished and chilled Thaddeus, though she bowed her head, and gave him her hand to put her into the coach.

In their way home, Miss Egerton ran over the merits of the play and farce; rallied* Thaddeus on the "*tall Pole,*" which she threatened should be his epithet whenever he offended her;† and then flying from

---

* rally, 'to make fun of; to tease' (*OED*).
† In II, iii, Totum refers to Adelbert as 'that cursed tall Pole!'

subject to subject, talked herself and her hearers so weary, that they mutually rejoiced when the carriage stopped in Grosvenor-place.

After they had severally paid their respects to Lady Tinemouth, who being indisposed, was lying along the sofa, she desired Thaddeus to draw a chair near to her.

"I want to learn," said she, "what you think of our English theatre?"

"Prithee, don't ask him!" cried Miss Egerton, pouring out a glass of wine, "we have seen a tremendous brother Pole of his, who I believe has '*hopped off*'* with all his spirits! Why, he has been looking as rueful as a half-drowned man, all the night; and, for Lady Sara, and, I could swear, Miss Beaufort too, they have been two Niobe's, '*all tears.*'† So good folks, I must drink better health to you, to save myself from the vapours."

"What is all this, Mr. Constantine?" asked the Countess, addressing Thaddeus, whose eyes were now fixed with grateful surprise on the blushing, though displeased face of Miss Beaufort.

"My weakness," replied he, sighing, and turning to her ladyship: "The play relates to a native of Poland; one, who, like myself, an exile in a strange land, is subjected to sufferings and contumelies, which the bravest spirits may find hard to bear. Any man may combat misery; but even the most intrepid will shrink from insult. This, I believe, is the sum of the story. Its resemblance, in some points to my own, affected me; and," added he, looking gratefully at Lady Sara, and timidly towards Miss Beaufort; "if these ladies have sympathized with feelings, which I strove, but could not entirely conceal, I owe to it, the sweetest consolation, that is now in the power of fate to bestow!"

"Poor Constantine!" cried Maria Egerton, patting his head with one hand, whilst with the other she wiped a tear from her always smiling eye, "forgive me, if I have hurt you. I like you vastly, though I must now and then laugh at you: you know I hate dismals; so let this tune enliven us all!" and flying to her piano, she played and sung two or three merry airs, till the Countess commanded her back to supper.

At this most sociable repast of the whole day, cheerfulness seemed again to disperse the gloom that threatened the circle. Thaddeus set the example. His unrestrained and elegant conversation, acquired renewed interest from the anguish he had driven back to his heart; like

---

* That is, 'departed'.
† Hamlet describes his mother at her husband's funeral as 'Like Niobe, all tears' (I, ii, 149). Niobe, Queen of Thebes, was turned to a stone after her fourteen children were slaughtered by the gods, yet even as a stone she continued to cry.

other beds through which a stream flows, it imparted an undescribable touchingness and poignancy to his sentiments and manner.

Mary now beheld him in his real character. Unmolested by the haughty presence of Miss Dundas, he became unreserved, intelligent, and enchanting. He was master of every subject; and discoursed on all, with a grace which corroborated her "*waking visions*," that he was, as some "*archangel ruined*."*

With the increase of Miss Beaufort's admiration of the Count's fine talents, she gradually lost the recollection of what had occupied her mind relative to Lady Sara; and her own beautiful countenance dilating into confidence and delight, the evening passed away with pleasure, till the little party separated for their several homes.

Lady Tinemouth and Maria were fascinated by the lovely Miss Beaufort. Miss Beaufort was equally pleased with the Countess and her friend; but when she thought on Thaddeus, she was surprized, interested, charmed.

Lady Sara Roos's reflections were not less flattering: she dwelt with redoubled passion on that look from the Count's eyes, that touch of his hand; which she thought were signs of a reciprocal flame. Both actions were forgotten by him the moment they were committed; yet he was not ungrateful, but whilst he acknowledged her attentions, and assented to the loveliness of her form, he felt that she would lead him to the brink of a precipice, where, if he fell, he must sink to a depth, never to rise again.

He sought a refuge from such dangerous meditation, in the idea of the ingenuous Mary, on whose modest countenance Virtue seemed to have "*set her seal*."† Whilst thus recollecting the pitying kindness of her voice and looks, his heart owned the empire of purity; and in the contemplation of her unaffected excellence, he soon forgot the witcheries of Lady Sara and her love.

---

* The phrase 'waking vision' does not seem to have an obvious literary source, though the waking vision or waking dream is a key element in several of Shakespeare's plays. Milton's *Paradise Lost* is the source of 'archangel ruined' (1. 593).
† Hamlet describes a portrait of his father, upon whose face 'every god did seem to set his seal' (III, iv, 61).

CHAP. IV.*

Next morning, when Thaddeus, according to custom, approached the General's bed to give him his coffee, he found him feverish, and his intellects more than usually unsettled.

The Count awaited with anxiety the arrival of the benevolent Cavendish, whom he expected; and when he appeared, he expressed his encreased alarm. Dr. Cavendish having felt the patient's pulse, expressed a wish that he could be induced to take a little exercise. Thaddeus had often urged this necessity to his friend; and having met with constant refusals, he hopelessly repeated the entreaty now; when, to his surprize and satisfaction, the old man instantly consented.

Having seen him comfortably dressed, (for the Count attended to these *minutiæ* with the care of a son) the doctor said, they must ride with him to Hyde Park, where he would put them out to walk till he had performed a visit to a sick person in Piccadilly, after which he would return, and take them home.

The General not only expressed pleasure at the drive; but, as the air felt warm and balmy, (it being about the beginning of June), he made no objection to the proposed walk.

He admired the Park, the Serpentine River, the cottage on its bank, and seemed highly diverted by the horsemen and carriages in the ring. The pertinency of his remarks, affording Thaddeus a ray of hope that his senses had not entirely lost their union with reason, he was contemplating with awakened confidence what might be the happy effects of constant exercise, when the General's complaints of weariness, obliged him to stop near Piccadilly gate, and await the arrival of the doctor's coach.

He was standing against the railing, supporting Butzou; and, with his hat in his hand, shading his friend's face from the sun; when, two or three carriages driving in, he met the eyes of Miss Euphemia Dundas; who, pulling the check-string, cried out, "Bless me, Mr. Constantine! Who expected to see you here? Why your note told us, that you were confined with a sick friend."

Thaddeus bowed to her, and, still sustaining the debilitated frame of the General on his arm, advanced to the side of the coach. Miss

* Misnumbered 'Chap. III' in the first edition.

Beaufort, who now looked out, expressed her hope that his invalid was better.

"This is the friend I mentioned," said the Count, turning his eyes on the mild features of Butzou; "his physician having ordered him to walk, I accompanied him here."

"Dear me! How ill you look, Sir," cried Euphemia, addressing the poor invalid; "but you are attended by a kind friend."

"My dear lord!" exclaimed the old man, not regarding what she said, "I must go home; call the carriage; you know I am wanted."

Euphemia was again opening her mouth to speak, but Miss Beaufort perceiving a look of distress in the expressive features of Mr. Constantine, interrupted her by saying, "Good morning, Mr. Constantine; I know we detain you, and oppress that gentleman, whose pardon we ought to beg." She bowed her head, with an expression of respectful commiseration beaming from her eyes upon the General, whose white hairs were blowing about his face as he attempted to pull the Count back to the pathway.

"My friend cannot thank you, kind Miss Beaufort," cried Thaddeus with a look of gratitude, that made her blush, "but I do from my heart!"

"Here it is! Pray, my Lord, come along!" cried Butzou: Thaddeus seeing that his information was right, bowed to the ladies; and their carriage drove off.

Though the wheels of Lady Dundas's coach rolled away from the retreating figures of Thaddeus and his friend, the images of both, occupied the meditations of Euphemia and Miss Beaufort, whilst *tête-à-tête*, and in silence, they made the circuit of the Park.

When the carriage again passed the spot on which the subject of their thoughts had stood, Mary, almost mechanically, looked out of the window, towards the gate.

"Is he gone yet?" asked Euphemia, sighing deeply.

Mary drew in her head, with the quickness of conscious guilt; and, whilst a colour stained her face, that of itself might have betrayed her prevarication, she asked, "Who?"

"Mr. Constantine," replied Euphemia, with a second sigh. "Did you remark, Mary, how gracefully he supported that sick old gentleman? Was it not the personification of Youth upholding the fainting steps of Age? He put me in mind of the charming young prince, whose name I forget, leading the old Belisarius."*

---

* Flavius Belisarius (c. 500–565) was a Byzantine general of the Roman empire who was supposedly blinded by order of Justinian and became a homeless beggar in

"You are an enthusiast, Euphemia!" returned Mary, striving to smile, and wondering within herself, what could be the meaning of those appellations with which the old man had addressed Thaddeus.

"So all tell me," replied Euphemia; "so all say, who neither possess the sensibility nor the candour to allow, that great merit may exist without being associated with great rank. Yet," cried the little beauty, in a more animated tone, "I have my doubts, Mary, of his being what he seems. Did you observe the sick gentleman call him *my lord?*"

"I did," returned Mary, "and I was not surprised. Such manners as Mr. Constantine's, are not to be acquired in a cottage."

"Dear, dear Mary," cried Euphemia, flinging her ivory arms round her neck; "how I love you for these words! you are generous, you think nobly, and I will no longer hesitate to – to – " and breaking off, she hid her head in Miss Beaufort's bosom.

Mary's heart throbbed, her cheeks grew pale, and she felt a secret wish to stop the tide of Miss Dundas's confidence.

"Dear Euphemia," answered she, "your regard for this interesting exile is very praise-worthy. But beware of – " she hesitated; a conscious twitch in her own breast, stayed the warning that was rising to her tongue; and, blushing at a motive which she could not at the instant assign to friendship, selfishness, or envy, she touched the cheek of Euphemia with her quivering lips.

Euphemia had finished the sentence for her, and raising her head, exclaimed: "What should I fear in esteeming Mr. Constantine? Is he not the most captivating creature in the world? And for his beauty! Oh, Mary, he is so beautiful, that when the library is filled with the handsomest men about town, the moment Constantine enters, their reign is over. I compare them with his godlike figure, and I feel as one looking at the sun; all other objects appear dim and shapeless."

"I hope," returned Mary, rubbing her forehead with her hand, her head beginning to ache strangely, "that Mr. Constantine does not owe your friendship to his fine person? I think his mental qualities are more deserving such a gift."

"Don't look so severe, dear Mary!" cried Miss Dundas, observing that she cast down her eyes, with a contracting brow; "are you displeased with me?"

Mary's displeasure was at the austerity of her own words, and not at

Rome. This legend appeared in various eighteenth-century iterations, including Jean-François Marmontel's 1767 novel, *Bélisaire*. The 'charming young prince' may refer to Marmontel's representation of Tiberius or to Belisarius's young companion. Euphemia's poor memory for the many stories she references is another indication of her shallowness.

her auditor. Raising her eyes with a smile both in them and on her lips, she said, "I do not mean, my dear girl, to be severe; but I would wish, for the honour of my sex, that the objects which attract either our love or our compassion, should have something more precious than mere personal beauty, to engage our interest."

"Well, I shall soon be satisfied!" cried Euphemia in a gayer tone, as they drove through Grosvenor gate; "We all know that Constantine is sensible and accomplished: He writes poetry like an angel, both in French and Italian: I have hundreds of mottoes composed by him; one of them, Mary, is on that work-box I gave you yesterday: and what is more, I will ask him to-morrow, why that old gentleman called him *my lord?* If he be a lord!" exclaimed she.

"What then?" inquired the eloquent eyes of Mary.

"Don't look so impertinent, my dear," cried the now animated beauty, "I positively won't say another word to you to-day."

Miss Beaufort's head-ache had become so painful, that she felt relieved when Euphemia ceased, and the carriage drew up to Lady Dundas's door.

A night of almost unremitted sleep, performed such good effects on the frame and intellects of General Butzou, that the ever-anxious Thaddeus received with pleasure the opinion of Doctor Cavendish, that he was so much better, as to allow them room to hope the best consequences from a constant repetition of the same air and exercise. Accordingly, after the ride and walk had been repeated the following day, the Count left his friend to his maps and little Nanny, and once more took the way to Harley-street.

He found only Miss Dundas and her sister in the study. Mary (against her will, which she opposed because it was her will,) had gone out a shopping with Mrs. Dorothy Somerset and Lady Dundas.

Miss Dundas left the room the moment she had finished her lessons.

Euphemia, delighted at being *tête-à-tête* with Thaddeus, forgot that she was to act the fascinating character of Madame d'Arblay's heroine; and, shutting her book the instant Diana disappeared, all at once opened her attack on his confidence.

To the eager questions, which the few words of the General had excited, the Count afforded no other reply, than the information, that his poor friend knew not what he said, having been a long time in a state of mental derangement.

This explanation caused a momentary mortification in the fanciful Euphemia; but, as it was a property of her mind, to erect a new airy castle immediately on the sinking of the old, she soon rallied, and

embraced the supposition, that he "might be a Duke, which was more
than a Lord!" At any rate, let him be what he would, he charmed her,
and had much ado to parry the increasing boldness of her speeches,
without letting her see that they were understood.

"You are very diffident, Constantine;" cried she, looking down, "If
I consider you worthy of my friendship, why should *you* make disqual-
ifying assertions?"

"Every man, Madam," returned Thaddeus bowing as he rose from
his chair, "must feel himself diffident of deserving the honour of your
notice."

"There is no man living," replied she blushing, "to whom I would
offer my friendship but yourself."

Thaddeus bit his lip; he knew not what to answer; bowing a second
time, he stretched out his hand, and drew his hat towards him.
Euphemia's eyes followed the movement.

"You are in a prodigious haste, Mr. Constantine!"

"I know that I intrude, Madam; and I have promised to be with my
sick friend at an early hour."

"Well, you may go, since you are obliged;" returned the pretty
Euphemia, rising up, and smiling sweetly as she laid one hand on his
arm, and put the other into her tucker:* she drew out a little white
leather *souvenir*, marked on the back in gold letters, with the words
'*Toujour cher*,' and slipping it into his hand, "There, receive that
Constantine; and retain it as the first pledge of Euphemia Dundas's
friendship."

Thaddeus coloured as he took it; and again having recourse to the
convenient reply of a bow, left the room, quite overcome with vexation.

There was an indelicacy in this absolutely wooing conduct of Miss
Euphemia, that, notwithstanding her beauty, and the softness which
was its vehicle, struck him with the deepest disgust. He could not trace
real affection, either in her words or manner; and, that any woman,
instigated by a mere whim, should lay aside the decent reserves of her
sex, and actually court his regard, surprised, whilst it impelled him, to
loath her.

They who adopt Euphemia's sentiments, are little aware of the conclusion which society deduce from such intemperate behaviour. That
mistaken creature, who, either at the impulse of her own disposition,
or the mandates of example, is led to throw off the veil of modesty,

---

* tucker, 'a piece of lace or linen worn in or around the top of a bodice or as an insert
  at the front of a low-cut dress' (*OED*). Contemporary readers would have found
  Euphemia's gesture vulgar.

literally *"forsakes the guide of her youth,"** and leaves herself open to every attack which man can devise against virtue. By levelling the barrier raised by nature, she herself exposes the hold of her peace; and may find too late for recovery, that what modesty has abandoned, is not long held by honour.

Euphemia's affected attachment suggested to the Count a few unpleasant recollections respecting the fervent and unequivocal passion of Lady Sara. Though guilty, it sprung from a head-long ardour of disposition, which formed at once the error and its palliation. He saw that love was not welcomed by her, (at least he thought so,) as a play thing, but struggled with as a foe; he had witnessed her tortures, he pitied them; and, to render her happy, would gladly have made any sacrifice short of his future tranquillity. Too well assured, of being all the world to Lady Sara; the belief, that Miss Euphemia liked him only from idleness, caprice, and contradiction, caused him to repay her overtures, with decided contempt.

When he arrived at home, he threw the pocket-book, whose unambiguous motto made him laugh at her and himself, into a drawer, and looking round his humble room, whose wicker chairs, oil-clothed floor, and uncurtained windows, announced any thing but splendor; "Poor Euphemia!" thought he, "how would you be dismayed, were the indigent Constantine really to take you at your word, and bring you home to such a cheerless habitation!"

The repetition of the late scene, which was communicated to Miss Beaufort from Euphemia, failed in producing a similar effect on her.

Mary could discover no reason why the old gentleman's mental derangement should dignify his friend with titles that he had never borne. She remarked, that his answer to Euphemia appeared evasive; she remembered his emotion and apology on seeing Mr. C. Kemble in *Adelbert*; and, uniting, with these facts, his manners, and acquirements so far beyond the charges of a vulgar education, she could retain no doubt of his being at least well born.

This mysterious Constantine occupied her hourly thoughts during the space of two months; in which time, she had full opportunity to learn much of a character with whom she associated almost every day. At Lady Tinemouth's, (one of whose evening guests she frequently became,) she beheld him disrobed of that armour of reserve, which was his best repellant against the rude attacks in Harley-street.

---

* See Proverbs 2: 17. Proverbs 2 espouses the value of wisdom, prudence and virtue, which Porter echoes throughout this paragraph and contrasts with her descriptions of Euphemia's behaviour.

In the house of the Countess, Mary saw him welcomed like a certain idolized being, before whose cheering influence, all frowns and clouds must disappear. When he entered, the smile resumed its seat on the languid features of Lady Tinemouth; Miss Egerton's eye lighted up to keener archness; Lady Sara's voluptuous orbs floated in pleasure; and for Mary herself, her breast heaved, her cheeks glowed, her hands trembled, a quick sigh escaped her bosom; and whilst she remained in his presence, she believed that happiness had lost its usual evanescent property, and had become tangible, to hold and press upon the heart.

Mary, who questioned the cause of these tremors on her pillow; bedewed it with delicious though bitter tears, when her alarmed soul whispered, that she felt for this amiable foreigner, "*a something than friendship dearer*."*

"Ah! is it come to this?" cried she, pressing down her saturated eyelids with her hand, "am I at last to love a man, who perhaps never casts a thought on me? How despicable shall I become in my own eyes!"

The pride of woman puts this charge to her taken heart: that heart, which seems tempered of the purest clay, and warmed with the fire of Heaven; that tender and disinterested heart, makes as its appeal – What is love? Is it not an admiration of all that is beautiful in nature and morality? Is it not a union of loveliness with truth? Is it not a passion, whose sole object is the rapture of contemplating the supreme beauty of this combined character?

"Where, then," cried the enthusiastic Mary, wiping the tears from her cheek, "where is the shame that can be annexed to my loving Constantine? If it be honourable to love delineated excellence; it must be equally so, to love it when embodied in a human shape. Such it is in Constantine: and if love be the reflected light of virtue, I may cease to arraign myself of what I otherwise would have scorned. Therefore, Constantine," cried she, raising her clasped hands, whilst renewed tears streamed over her face, "I will love thee! I will pray for thy happiness, though its partner should be Euphemia Dundas!"

Mary's eager imagination would not allow her to perceive those obstacles, in the shapes of pride and prudence, which would stand in the way of his obtaining Euphemia's hand; its light shewed to her only a rival, in the person of the little beauty; from whose direct confidence she afterwards retreated with abhorrence.

---

* Perhaps a revision of "Something than Beauty dearer" in James Thomson's *The Seasons: Spring* (line 1141). The quoted phrase, '*friendship dearer*', reappears in Robert Ker Porter's *Travelling Sketches in Russia and Sweden*, 2 vols (London: Richard Phillips, 1809), 2. 297.

Had Euphemia been more deserving of Constantine, Miss Beaufort believed she would have felt less reluctant to hear that she also loved him. But Mary could not avoid seeing, that Miss E. Dundas possessed little to ensure comfort, if mere beauty and accidental flights of good-humour, were not admitted into the scale. She was weak in understanding, timid of principle, absurd in almost every sentiment she adopted; and, as for love, true, dignified, respectable love, she knew nothing of the feeling.

Whilst Miss Beaufort meditated on this meagre schedule of her rival's merits, the probability that even such a man as Constantine might sacrifice himself to flattery and splendour, stung her to the soul.

The more she reflected on it, the more she conceived it likely. Euphemia was considered a beauty of the day; her affectation of refined prettinesses, pleased many, and might charm Constantine: she was mistress of fifty thousand pounds; and did not esteem it necessary to conceal from her favourite, the empire he had acquired. Perhaps there was generosity in this openness? If so, what might it not effect on a grateful disposition? Or rather, (her mortified heart murmured in the words of her aunt Dorothy;) how might it not operate on the mind of one of that sex, which at the best, is equally moved by caprice, as sentiment!

Mary blushed at her appropriation of this opinion; and, angry with herself, for the injustice which a lurking jealousy had induced her to throw on Constantine's noble nature, she resolved, whatever were her struggles, to promote his happiness to the utmost of her power.

The next morning, when Miss Beaufort opened the study door, she found Mr. Constantine at his station, literally baited between Miss Dundas and her honourable lover.* At such moments, Mary always appeared the kindest of the kind. She loved to see Constantine smile; and, whenever she could produce that effect, by turning the spleen of these polite sneerers against themselves, the smiles which entered her heart afforded a banquet for hours, after his departure.

Mary drew out her work, (which was a purse that she was netting for Lady Tinemouth;) and, taking a seat beside Thaddeus, strove, along with Euphemia, to occupy his attention entirely, that he might not catch even one of those insolent glances, which were passing from Lascelles, and a new ally, whom he had obtained in the pretty Lady Villiers.

---

* bait, 'to persecute or harass with persistent attacks' (*OED*). As noted earlier, the prefix 'honourable' implies that Lascelles is the younger son of an earl, though here it is clearly also used to mock him.

This lady seemed to take extreme pleasure in accosting Thaddeus by the appellation of "friend, my good man, Mr. what's your name?" and similar squibs of insult, with which the prosperous assail the unfortunate. Such random shots often inflict the most galling wounds.

However, *friend, my good man*, and *Mr. what's your name*, disappointed this lady's small artillery of effect. He seemed invulnerable, both to her insolence, and to her affectation; for to be admired by even Miss Dundas's contemned tutor, was not to be despised; though at the very moment, she supposed her haughtiness had impressed him with a proper sense of his own meanness, and a high conception of her dignity.

She jumped about the room; assumed infantine airs, played with Euphemia's lap-dog, fondled it, seated herself on the floor, and swept the carpet with her fine flaxen tresses: but she performed the whole routine of captivation in vain: Thaddeus recollected having seen this pretty full-grown baby, in her appropriate character of a profligate wife, pawning her own and her husband's property; he remembered this, and the united shafts of her charms and folly, fell unnoticed to the ground.

When Thaddeus took his leave, Miss Beaufort, as was her custom, retired for an hour to read in her dressing room, before she directed her attention to the toilet. She opened a book, and ran over a few pages of Lord St. Alban;* but his reasoning was too abstracted for her present frame of mind, and she threw the volume down.

She dipped a pen in the ink-stand. Being a letter in debt to her guardian, she thought she could defray it now. She accomplished "Dear Sir," and stopped. Whilst she rested on her elbow, and heedless of what she was doing, bit the feather of her quill to pieces, no other idea offered itself, than the figure of Thaddeus, sitting *"severe in youthful beauty!"*† She saw him surrounded by those contumelies which the unworthy bestow on the merit they can neither emulate nor overlook.

Uneasy with herself, she pushed the table away; and, leaning her cheek on her arm, gazed into the rainbow varieties of a beau-pot‡ of flowers which occupied the fireplace. Even their gay colours appeared to fade before her sight, and present to her vacant eye, the form of Thaddeus, with the melancholy air which shaded his movements. She

---

* Francis Bacon, Viscount St Alban (1561–1626), author of *Essays*. From the third edition, Mary reads from Germaine de Staël's *A Treatise on the Influence of the Passions* (London: George Cawthorn, 1798).
† 'So spake the Cherub, and his grave rebuke / Severe in youthful beauty, added grace / Invincible': John Milton, *Paradise Lost*, 4. 844–6.
‡ beau-pot, 'a large ornamental vase for cut flowers' (*OED*).

turned round, but she could not disengage herself from the spirit that was within her: his half-suppressed sighs, seemed yet to thrill in her ear, and weigh on her heart.

"Excellent young man!" cried she, starting up, "why are you so wretched? O! Lady Tinemouth, why have you told me so much of his virtues? Why have I convinced myself, that what you said is true? Oh! why was I formed to love superior goodness?"

The natural reply to these self-demanded questions suggesting itself, she assented with a tear to the whisperings of her feelings, that when philosophy would banish the affections, it is incapable of filling their place.

She rung the bell for her maid.

"Marshall, who dines with Lady Dundas to-day?"

"I believe, Ma'am," replied the girl, "Mr. Lascelles, Lady Villiers, and the Marquis of Elesmere."

"I detest them all three!" cried Mary, with a petulance to which she was little liable; "dress me how you like, I am indifferent to my appearance."

Marshall obeyed the commands of her lady, who bent her eyes on a little volume of poems written by Egerton Brydges,* till her maid having fixed the last pearl comb in her beautiful hair, exclaimed, "Dear Ma'am, you are so pale to-day! shall I put on the least bit of rouge?"

"No," returned Mary, glancing a look over her languid features, "no, Marshall, I appear as well as I desire. Any chance of passing unnoticed in company I despise, is worth retaining. No one will be here, this evening, that I care to please."

She was mistaken; other company had been invited besides them whom the maid mentioned; and Miss Beaufort continued from seven o'clock till ten, the period at which the ladies left the table, annoyed to death by the insipid and pert compliments of the men.

Sick of their subjectless and dragging conversation, she gladly followed Lady Dundas to the drawing-room; where, opening her netting case, she took her station beneath one of the lustres in a remote corner, hoping to find a retreat from the ceaseless nonsense of her ladyship's guests.

After half an hour had elapsed, the gentlemen from below, recruited by fresh company, thronged in fast; and, notwithstanding it was stiled a family party, Miss Beaufort saw many strange faces, amongst whom she observed an old clergyman, who was looking about for a chair. The

---

* Egerton Brydges, *Sonnets and Other Poems* (London: G. and T. Wilkie, 1785).

yawning Lascelles threw himself along the only vacant sofa, just as the gentleman approached.

Miss Beaufort immediately resigned her place, and was moving on to another room, when the coxcomb springing up, begged permission to admire her work; and taking it from her, pursued her, twisting the purse into a rope round his fingers, declaring how pretty it was, whilst he thrust, (in his own opinion,) his pretty hand into her eyes.

Mary walked forward, smiling with contempt, till they reached the painted saloon; where the Miss Dundas's were closely engaged in conversation with the Marquis of Elesmere.

Lascelles, who trembled for his Golconda, at this sight, stepped briskly up. Mary, who did not wish to lose sight of her purse, whilst in the power of such a *Lothario*, followed him, and placed herself against the arm of the sofa on which Euphemia sat.*

Lascelles now bowed his scented locks to Diana in vain. Lord Elesmere was describing the last heat at Newmarket,† and the attention of neither lady could be drawn aside.

The beau became so irritated by the perfect neglect of Euphemia, and so nettled at her sister's overlooking him, that, assuming a gay air, he struck Miss Dundas's arm a smart stroke with Miss Beaufort's purse; and laughing, to shew the strong opposition between his broad white teeth, and the miserable mouth of his lordly rival; hoped to alarm him by his familiarity, and to obtain a triumph over the ladies, by degrading them in the eyes of the peer.

"Miss Dundas," demanded he, "who the devil was that, your sister walked with the other day in Portland Place?"

"Me!" cried Euphemia, surprized.

"Aye," returned he; "I was crossing from Weymouth-street, when I perceived you accost a strange looking man. You may remember, you sauntered with him as far as Sir William Miller's.‡ I would have joined you, but seeing the family standing in the balcony, I did not chuse them to suppose, that perhaps *I* brought you into such low company."

"Who was it, Euphemia?" enquired Miss Dundas, in a severe tone.

---

* Golconda, 'synonym for a "mine of wealth"' (*OED*), from the Indian mines of Hyderabad, famous for diamonds. Lothario, 'A man who habitually seduces women or is sexually promiscuous; a libertine, a philanderer' (*OED*), from a character in Nicholas Rowe's 1703 play, *The Fair Penitent*.

† Since the seventeenth century, the Newmarket racecourse in Suffolk has hosted some of England's most prominent and valuable horse races.

‡ Likely a fictional character. A William Miller worked as a publisher in London, but according to the *Fashionable Court Guide*, there was no Sir William Miller in London at this time.

"I wonder he affects to be ignorant," answered her sister, angrily, "he knows very well, it was only Mr. Constantine."

"And who is Mr. Constantine?" demanded the marquis. Mr. Lascelles shrugged his shoulders.

"E'faith, my lord! a fellow that nobody knows; a teacher of languages, giving himself the airs of a prince. A writer of poetry; and a man who will draw you, your house, and dogs, if you will pay him for it."

Mary's heart swelled.

"What, a French emigrant?" drawled his lordship, dropping his lip; "and the lovely Euphemia wishes to soothe his sorrows."

"No, my lord," stammered Euphemia, "he is – he is – "

"What!" interrupted Lascelles, with a malicious grin, "a wandering beggar; that thrusts himself into a society, which may some day repay his insolence with chastisement! For those who encourage him, they had better beware of being scouted by the world. I understand that his chief protectress, is Lady Tinemouth; and, by way of an auxiliary, Lady Sara Roos evinces that she is not quite inconsolable at the absence of her husband."

Mary, pale and trembling, at the scandal his last words would have insinuated, had opened her lips to speak, when Miss Dundas (whose angry eyes darted from her sister to her lover), exclaimed, "Mr. Lascelles, I know not what you mean. The subject you have taken up, is below my discussion; yet, I must confess, if Euphemia ever have disgraced herself so far as to be seen walking with a school-master, she deserves all you have said."

"And why might I not walk with him, sister?" asked the poor culprit, suddenly recovering from her confusion, and looking pertly up, "who knew that he was not a gentleman?"

"Every body, ma'am," interrupted Lascelles; "and when a young woman of fashion condescends to be seen equalizing herself with any creature depending on his wits for support, she is very likely to incur the contempt of her acquaintance, and the censure of her friends."

"She is, Sir," said Mary, holding down her indignant heart, and forcing her countenance to appear serene; "for she ought to know, that those men of fashion, who have no wits, either to be their support or ornament, if they did not proscribe talents from their circle, must soon find '*the greater glory dim the less*.'"*

"True, Madam," cried Lord Berrington, who, having entered during the contest, had stood unobserved till this moment; "and that gold and

---

* *The Merchant of Venice*: 'So doth the greater glory dim the less' (V, i, 93).

title, will prove mere dross and bubble, when struck by the Ithuriel touch of Genius."*

Mary turned at the sound of his philanthropic voice, and gave him one of those glances which go immediately to the soul.

"Come, Miss Beaufort," cried he, taking her hand, "I see the young musician, yonder, who has so recently astonished the public. I believe he is going to sing. Let us leave this ill-natured corner, and seek harmony by his side."

Mary obeyed the impulse of his arm, and seating herself a few paces off the musical party, Berrington took his station behind her chair.

When the finest, and most melting voice in the world, had ceased the last stanza of "*From shades of night;*" Mary's eyes, full of admiration, and a feeling which rapid association rendered more intense, remained fixed on the singer:† Lord Berrington smiled at the vivid expression of her countenance; and, as the inimitable Braham moved from the instrument, exclaimed, "Come, come, Miss Beaufort, I won't allow that Orphean boy to run away with all your attention; listen to my merits. Do you know, if it were not for my timely lectures, little Lascelles would grow the most insufferable gossip about town? There is not a match, nor a divorce near St. James's, of which he cannot repeat to you all the whys and wherefores. I call him Sir Benjamin Backbite;‡ and I believe he hates me worse than the devil."

"Such a man's dislike," rejoined Mary, "is the highest encomium he can bestow. I never yet heard him speak well of a person who did not resemble himself."

"And he is not consistently generous even there," resumed the viscount; "I am not sure, that I have always heard him speak in the gentlest terms of Miss Dundas. Yet, on this topic, I cannot quite blame him; for, on my honour, she provokes me beyond any woman I know."

"Many women," replied Mary, smiling, "would esteem that a flattering instance of power."

"And, like every thing that flatters," returned he, "it would tell a falsehood. A shrew can provoke the man who detests her. And for Miss Dundas," continued he, "notwithstanding her parade of learning,

---

* In *Paradise Lost*, the cherub Ithuriel touches the disguised Satan with his spear, causing him to resume his usual appearance (4. 810–13).
† The English tenor John Braham (c. 1774–1856) made his London debut in Stephen Storace's opera *Mahmoud*, which premiered at Drury Lane on 30 April 1796. 'From Shades of Night' is an air sung by Braham's character, Noureddin. Braham was considered one of the great singers of the era: hence the comparison to the legendary Greek musician Orpheus in the following sentence.
‡ Sir Benjamin Backbite is a scandalmongering poet in Richard Sheridan's *The School for Scandal* (1777).

her judgement has not been taught to decide rightly; consequently she generally espouses the wrong side of the argument; and I may say, with somebody whose name I have forgotten, that any one who knows Diana Dundas, never need be at a loss for a woman to call impertinent."

"You are not usually so severe, my lord!"

"I am not usually so sincere, Miss Beaufort," answered he, "but I see that you think for yourself; therefore I make no hesitation in speaking what *I* think – to you."

Mary bowed her head. Lady Dundas at that moment beckoned him across the room. She compelled him to sit down to whist.* He cast a rueful glance at Mary, and took a seat opposite his costly partner.

"That is a very worthy young man," observed the old clergyman, to whom Miss Beaufort, at the beginning of the evening, had resigned her chair; "I presume, Madam, that you have been honouring him with your conversation."

"Yes," returned Mary, noticing the benign countenance of the venerable speaker; "I have not had the pleasure of long knowing Lord Berrington, but what I have seen of his character is highly to his advantage."

"I was intimate in his father's house for years," rejoined the gentleman; "I knew his lordship from a boy. If he have faults, he owes them to his mother, who doated on him, and rather directed his care to the adornment of a really handsome person, than to the cultivation of talents, which he has since learned to appreciate."

"I believe Lord Berrington to be very sensible, and, above all, very humane;" returned Mary.

"He is so," replied the old gentleman; "yet, it was not till he had attained the age of twenty-two, that he appeared to know that he had any thing to do in the world, besides dressing, and attending on the fair. His taste directed the first, whilst the urbanity of his disposition gave birth to the latter. When Berrington arrived at his title, he was about five-and-twenty. Sorrow for the death of his amiable parents, who died in the same month, afforded him leisure to find his reason. He discovered that he had been acting a part beneath him; and he soon implanted on the old stock, those excellent acquirements of the mind, which you see he possesses. In spite of this regeneration," continued he, casting a good-humoured glance on the dove-coloured silk stockings, breeches, and waistcoat of the viscount; "you perceive first

* A game of cards usually played by four people.

impressions will remain. He loves dress, but he loves justice and philanthropy better."

"This eulogy, Sir," said Mary, "affords me real pleasure. May I know the name of the gentleman with whom I have the honour of conversing?"

"My name is Blackmore," returned he.

"Dr. Blackmore?"

"The same."

He was the same Dr. Blackmore, whose humanity had been struck with the appearance of the Count Sobieski at the Hummums; and who, being a rare visitor at Lady Dundas's, had never, by any chance, met a second time with the object of his compassion.*

"I am happy," resumed Miss Beaufort, "in having the good fortune to meet a gentleman, of whom I have so frequently heard my guardian express his sentiments of esteem."

"Ah!" replied he, "I have not seen him since the death of his lady; I hope that he and his son are well?"

"Perfectly," returned she.

"You, Madam, I suppose, are my lady's niece, Miss Beaufort?"

"I am, Sir."

"Well, I rejoice at this incident," rejoined he, pressing her hand; "I knew your mother when she was a lovely girl. She used to spend her summers with the late Lady Somerset, then Miss Beaufort, at the castle. It was there I had the honour of cultivating her friendship."

"I do not remember ever having seen my mother," replied the now thoughtful Mary. Dr. Blackmore, observing the expression of her countenance, smiled kindly, and said, "I fear I am to blame here. This is a sad way of beginning an acquaintance to which I introduced myself. But your goodness must pardon me," continued he, "for I have so long accustomed myself to speak what I like, to them I like, that sometimes, as in this case, I undesignedly inflict pain."

"Not in this case," returned Mary; "I shall always feel pleasure in listening to a friend of my mother's; and particularly so, when he speaks in her praise."

The breaking up of the card tables prevented any further conversation; and Lord Berrington again approaching Miss Beaufort, exclaimed, as he perceived her companion, "Ah! my good doctor;

---

* While the number of unexpected encounters in *Thaddeus* may seem improbable, it is worth noting that London's population was only one million in 1800, and the polite society of people like Mary Beaumont and Dr Blackmore would have made up a small part of that number.

what, you have presented yourself at this fair shrine? I declare, you eccentric folk may dare any thing. Whilst you are free, Miss Beaufort," added he, turning to her, "adopt this bit of advice, which a good lady once gave me, and which I have implicitly followed, 'When you are young, get the character of an oddity, and it seats you in an easy chair for life.'"

Mary was interrupted in her reply, by a general stir amongst the company; who, now that cards were over, like bees and wasps, were swarming about the room, gathering and stinging as they passed.

At two, the house was cleared; and Mary exhausted, threw herself on the pillow, to think, and dream of Thaddeus.

CHAP. V.

If it be true what the vivid imaginations of poets have often asserted, that when the soul dreams, it is in the actual presence of those beings whose images present themselves to its slumbers, then have the spirits of Thaddeus and Mary been commingled at the hour of midnight; then has the young Sobieski again visited his distant country; again seen it victorious; again knelt before his sainted parent.

From such visions as these, did Thaddeus awake in the morning, after having spent the preceding evening with Lady Tinemouth.

He had walked with her ladyship in Hyde Park till a late hour. By the mild light of the moon, which shone brightly through the still, balmy air of a midsummer night, they took their way twice, along the shadowy bank of the Serpentine.

There is a solemn appeal to the soul in the repose of nature, that "makes itself be felt."* No syllable from either Thaddeus or the Countess, broke the universal silence. Thaddeus looked around, on the clear expanse of water overshaded by the long reflexion of the deepening woods: then raising his eyes to that beautiful planet, which has excited the tenderest sensations in every feeling breast, since the beginning of the world; he drew a deep sigh. The Countess echoed it.

"In such a night as this," said Thaddeus, in a low voice, as if afraid to disturb the sleeping deity of the place, "I used to walk the ramparts of Villanow, with my dear departed mother, and gaze on that lovely orb: when I was far distant from her, I have looked at it from the door of my tent, and, fancying that her eyes were then fixed on the same object with my own, I found happiness in the idea."

Thaddeus felt a tear stealing down his cheek. That moon yet shone brightly, but his mother's eyes were closed in the grave.

"Villanow!" repeated the Countess in a tone of surprise, "surely, that was the seat of the brave Palatine of Masovia! You have discovered yourself, Constantine! I am much mistaken, if you be not his grandson, Thaddeus Sobieski?"

Thaddeus had allowed the remembrances pressing on his mind, to draw him into a speech, which he found had disclosed to the quick

* Unidentified.

apprehension of the Countess, what his pride, would for ever have concealed.

"I have indeed betrayed my secret;" cried he, incapable of denying it; "but, dear Lady Tinemouth, as you value my feelings, never let it escape your lips. Having long considered you as my best friend, loved you as a parent, I forgot in the recollection of my beloved mother now no more, that I had withheld any of my history from you."

"Gracious Providence!" exclaimed her ladyship, after a moment's pause, in which ten thousand admiring and pitying reflections thronged on her mind, "Is it possible? Can it be the Count Sobieski, that brave and illustrious youth, of whom every foreigner spoke with wonder? Can it be him, that I behold in the poor unfriended Constantine?"

"Even so;" returned Thaddeus, pressing her hand; "my country is no more. I am now forgotten by the world, as I have been by fortune. I have nothing to do on the earth, but to fulfil the few duties which friendship has enjoined; and then, it will be indifferent to me how soon I am laid in its bosom."

"You are too young, dear Constantine, (for I am yet to call you by that name,) to despair of happiness being reserved for you."

"No, my dear Lady Tinemouth, I do not cheat myself with such hope; I am not so importunate with the gracious Being who gave me life and reason. He bestowed on me for a while, the tenderest connexions; a mother, a grandfather, friends, rank, honours, glory: all these were crushed in the fall of Poland; yet I survive. I only seek resignation, and I have found it: it cost me many a struggle; but the contest was due to the decrees of that all-wise Creator, who gave my first years to happiness."

"Inestimable young man!" cried the Countess, wiping the flowing tears from her eyes, "you teach misfortune dignity! Not when all Warsaw rose in a body to thank you as one of its bravest deliverers; not when the king received you in the senate with open arms; could you have appeared to me so worthy of admiration, as at this moment, when, conscious of having been all this, you submit to the bitterest storms of fate, because you believe them to be the will of your Maker! Ah! little does Miss Beaufort think, when seated by your side, that she is conversing with the very hero whom she has so often wished to see!"

"Miss Beaufort!" echoed Thaddeus, his heart glowing with delight. "Did she ever hear of me by the name of Sobieski?"

"Who has not?" returned the Countess, "every heart that could be interested by suffering virtue, has heard, and must well remember, the calamities of your country. Whilst the newspapers of the day, informed us of the struggles which Poland made for liberty; they noticed amongst the first of her champions, the Palatine of Masovia, Kosciuszko, and yourself. Many an evening have I spent with Lady Somerset and Mary Beaufort, lamenting the fate of that devoted kingdom."

During this declaration, a variety of transporting emotions agitated the mind of Thaddeus; till recollecting with a bitter pang, the shameless ingratitude of Pembroke, and the cruel possibility of being recognized by the Earl of Tinemouth as his son; he exclaimed, "My dearest Madam, I entreat, that what I have revealed to you, may never be divulged! Miss Beaufort's friendship would indeed be happiness; but I cannot purchase even that, at the expence of feelings which are knit with my life."

"How?" cried the Countess, "Is not your name, and all its attendant ideas, an honour that the proudest man might boast?"

Thaddeus pressed her ladyship's hand gratefully to his heart.

"You are kind! very kind! Yet, I cannot retract. Confide, dear Lady Tinemouth, in the justice of my resolution. I could not bear cold pity; I could not bear the heartless comments of people, who, pretending to compassion, would load me with a heavier sense of my calamities. Besides, there are persons in England, who are so much the objects of my aversion, that I would rather die than have them know that I exist. Therefore, on these grounds, let me implore you to preserve my secret."

Lady Tinemouth saw by the earnestness of his manner, that she ought to comply; and, without further hesitation, promised all the silence on the subject which he could require.

This long, moonlight conversation, by awakening those dormant remembrances, which were cherished, though hidden in his bosom, gave birth to an effort of imagination, that painted within the rapid series of his tumultuous dreams, the images of every being whom he had ever loved, or now continued to regard with interest.

Proceeding next morning towards Harley-street, he pondered on what had happened; and pleased that he had though unpremeditatedly, paid the just compliment of his entire confidence, to the uncommon friendship of the Countess; he arrived at Lady Dundas's door, before he was sensible of the ground he had passed over; and, in a few minutes afterwards was ushered into his accustomed purgatory.

When the servant opened the study-door, Miss Euphemia was again alone. Thaddeus recoiled, but he could not retreat.

"Come in, Mr. Constantine," cried the little beauty, in a languid tone; "my sister is gone to the riding-school with Mr. Lascelles. Miss Beaufort wanted me to drive out with her and my mother; but I preferred waiting for you."

The Count bowed; and, almost retreating with fear of what might next be said, he gladly heard a thundering knock at the door, and, a moment after, the voice of Miss Dundas ascending the stairs.

He had just opened his books, when she entered, followed by her lover. Panting under a heavy riding-habit, she flung herself on a sofa, and began to vilify "the odious heat of Fozard's odious place;"* and telling Euphemia she would play truant to-day, ordered her to attend to her lessons.

Owing to the warmth of the weather, Thaddeus came out this morning without boots; and it being the first time that the fine proportion of his limb, had been seen by any of the present company, excepting Euphemia; Lascelles, bursting with a disdain of such insignificant distinctions, (which he would not call envy) measured the Count's beautiful leg with his insolent eyes; then, declaring he was quite in a furnace, took the corner of his glove, and waving it to and fro, half muttered, "*Come, gentle air.*"

"*The fairer* Lascelles *cries!*" exclaimed Euphemia, looking off her exercise.†

"What! does your master teach you wit?" drawled the coxcomb, with a particular emphasis.

Thaddeus affecting not to hear, continued to direct his pupil.

The indefatigable Lascelles having observed the complacence with which the Count always regarded Miss Beaufort, determined the goad should fret; and drawing out of his pocket the netting which he had taken the night before from Mary, exclaimed, "'Fore Heaven, here is my little Beaufort's purse."

Thaddeus started, and unconsciously looking up, beheld the well-known work of Mary, dangling in the hand of Lascelles. He felt sensations unknown to him; his eyes became dim, and hardly knowing what he saw or said, he pursued the lesson with encreased velocity.

The malicious puppy, having found his malice take effect; with a careless air, threw his clumsy limbs on the vacant part of the sofa, which Miss Dundas had quitted to seat herself nearer the window, and cried, in a voice of sudden recollection,

"By the bye, that Miss Mary Beaufort, when she chuses to be sincere, is a sad little aristocrat."

---

* James Fozard (or Fozzard, d. 1838) ran a fashionable riding school in Park Lane in the 1790s.
† Alexander Pope, 'On a Fan of the Author's Design': 'Come, gentle Air, the fairer *Delia* cries' (line 3). *The Works of Mr. Alexander Pope* (London: W. Bowyer, 1717), p. 376.

"You may as well tell me," replied Miss Dundas, with a contemptuous curl of her lip, "that she is the Empress of Russia."

"I beg your pardon," cried he, raising his voice, at his judgment being doubted; "I will prove it to you. When she gave me this gewgaw,"* added he, rumpling the purse in his hand, "she told me an everlasting story about some friend of hers, whose music-master, having mistaken some condescensions on her part, had dared to snatch a kiss from her snowy fingers as they were flying over the strings of her harp. You cannot imagine how Beaufort's pretty eyes blazed as she related this tale; I verily believe, had it been herself, she would have given poor Tweedledum† a flourish across the cheek."

Miss Dundas laughed.

"These energetic young ladies possess not the gentlest passions in the world; and after Miss Beaufort's outrageous sally last night to you, I should not wonder at any indecorum she might commit."

"Outrageous to me!" echoed the fop, dipping the end of the netting into Diana's lavender-bottle and dabbing his temples, "She was always too civil by half. I hate forward girls."

Thaddeus shut the large dictionary that lay before him, with a violence that made the puppy start; and rising hastily from his chair, with a face as red as crimson, was taking up his hat, when the door opened, and Mary appeared.

A white chip hat was resting lightly on the glittering tresses which waved over her forehead; whilst her lace shade, gently discomposed by the air, half veiled, and half revealed, her graceful figure. She entered with a smile, and walking up to the side of the table where Thaddeus was standing, enquired after his friend's health. He answered her in a voice unusually agitated. All that he had been told by the Countess of her favourable opinion of him; and the slander he had just heard from Diana's lover, were at once present to his mind.

He was yet speaking, when Miss Beaufort casually looking towards the other side of the room, saw her purse still acting the part of a handkerchief, in the hand of Mr. Lascelles.

"Look, Mr. Constantine," said she, gaily tapping his arm with her parasol, "how the most precious things may be degraded! There is the netting that you have so often admired, and which I intended for

---

* gewgaw, 'a gaudy trifle, plaything, or ornament' (*OED*).
† Tweedledum and Tweedledee originally were nicknames for the rival composers George Frideric Handel and Giovanni Buononcini: hence its use here to refer to the brazen music master.

Lady Tinemouth's pocket, debased to do the office of Mr. Lascelles's napkin."

"You gave it to him, Miss Beaufort," cried Miss Dundas; "and after that, surely he may use it as he values it!"

"If I could have given it to Mr. Lascelles, Madam, I should hardly have taken notice of its fate."

Miss Dundas, believing what her lover had advanced, was displeased at Mary for having, by presents, interfered with any of her danglers, and rather angrily replied, "Mr. Lascelles said you gave it to him; and certainly you would not insinuate a word against his veracity?"

"No, not *insinuate*," returned Miss Beaufort, "but *affirm*, that he has forgotten his veracity at least in this statement."

Lascelles yawned, – "Lord bless me, ladies, how you quarrel! You will disturb Monsieur."

"Mr. Constantine," returned Mary, blushing with indignation, "cannot be disturbed by nonsense."

Thaddeus again took his hat: bowing to his lovely champion, with an expression of countenance, which he little suspected had passed from his heart to his eyes, he was preparing to take his leave, when Euphemia requested him to inform her whether she had folded down the right pages for the next exercise. He drew near, and was leaning over her chair to look at the book, when she whispered, "Don't be hurt at what Lascelles says; he is always jealous of any body who is handsomer than himself."

Thaddeus bowed to her with a face of scarlet; for, on meeting the eyes of Mary, he saw that she had heard this intended comforter as well as himself; and, uttering a few incoherent sentences to both ladies, he hurried out of the room.

CHAP. VI.

The Count Sobieski was prevented from paying his customary visit, next morning in Harley-street, by the sudden illness of the General, who, at seven o'clock, had been struck with a fit of the palsy.

When Dr. Cavendish beheld the poor old man stretched along the bed, and hardly exhibiting signs of life, he pronounced it to be a death-stroke. At this sentence, Thaddeus turning deathly pale, staggered to a seat, with his eyes fixed on the altered features of his friend. Dr. Cavendish took his hand.

"Recollect yourself, my dear Sir! Happen when it will, his death must be a release. But do not expect it for some time; he may yet linger a week or a fortnight."

"Not in pain, I hope!" said Thaddeus, rising.

"No;" returned the doctor, "probably he will remain as you now see him, and expire like the last glimmer of a dying taper."

The benevolent Cavendish proceeded to give particular directions, to Thaddeus, and Mrs. Robson who promised to act as nurse; and then with regret left the stunned Count to the melancholy task of watching by the bed-side of his venerable friend.

Thaddeus now retained no thought that was not rivetted on the emaciated form before him. Whilst the unconscious invalid struggled for respiration, he listened to his short and convulsed breathing, with sensations which seemed to tear the strings of his own breast. Unable to bear it longer, he moved opposite to the fire, and seating himself, with his pallid face and aching head supported on his arm, which rested on a plain deal table, he remained, meeting no other suspension from deep meditation, than the now and then appearance of Mrs. Robson on tiptoes, peeping in, and inquiring whether he wanted any thing.

From this depressing reverie, he was aroused next morning at nine o'clock, by the entrance of Dr. Cavendish. Thaddeus seized his hand with the eagerness of anxiety, – "he has not been worse, my dear Sir, may I hope that – "

The doctor, not suffering him to finish with what he hoped, shook his head, and waving his hand in sign of the vanity of that hope, advanced to the bed of the General, and felt his pulse. His opinion exactly coincided with what he had declared before, differing only in

one particular, that he now saw no absolute threatenings of an immediate dissolution.

"Poor Butzou!" said Thaddeus, as the doctor withdrew, putting
the General's motionless hand to his quivering lips, "I never will leave
thee! I will watch by thee, thou last relic of my country!"

With anguish at his heart, he wrote a few hasty lines to the Countess:
then addressing Miss Dundas, he offered as the reason for his late and
continued absence, the danger of his friend.

His note found Miss Dundas attended by her constant shadow Mr.
Lascelles, Lady Villiers, and two or three more fine ladies and gentlemen, besides Euphemia and Miss Beaufort, who, with pensive countenances, were waiting the arrival of its writer.

When Miss Dundas had taken the billet off the silver salver on which
her man presented it, and had looked at the superscription, she threw
it into the lap of Lascelles.

"There," cried she, "is an excuse, I suppose, from Mr. Constantine,
for his impertinence in not coming here yesterday. Read it
Lascelles."

"'Fore Gad, I wouldn't touch it for an earldom!" exclaimed the
affected puppy, jerking it on the table. "It might infect me with the
hypochondriacs. Pray, Phemy, do you peruse it."

Euphemia, in her eagerness to learn what had detained Mr.
Constantine, neglected the insolence of the request, and, hastily breaking the seal, read as follows:

"Mr. Constantine hopes that a sudden and dangerous disorder,
which has attacked the life of a very dear friend with whom he resides,
will be a sufficient appeal to the humanity of the Miss Dundases, and
obtain his pardon for relinquishing the honour of attending them yesterday and to-day."

"Dear me!" cried Euphemia, piteously, "how sorry I am! I dare say,
it is that white-haired old gentleman we saw in the Park. You remember, Mary, he was sick?"

"Probably," returned Miss Beaufort, with her eyes fixed on the agitated handwriting of Thaddeus.

"Throw the letter into the street, Phemy!" cried Miss Dundas, affecting sudden terror, "Who knows but what it is a fever the man has got,
and we may all catch our deaths."

"Heaven forbid!" exclaimed Mary, in a voice of real alarm: but it
was for Thaddeus; not fear of any infection which the paper might
bring to herself.

"Lascelles, take away the filthy scrawl from Phemy. How can you
be so headstrong, child?" cried Diana, snatching the letter from her

sister, and throwing it out the window, "I declare you are sufficient to provoke a saint."

"Then, you may keep your temper, Di," returned Euphemia, with a sneer, "you are far enough from that title."

Miss Dundas made a very angry reply, which was retaliated with another; and a still more noisy and disagreeable altercation might have taken place, had not a good humoured lad, a brother-in-law of Lady Villiers, in hopes of calling off the attention of the sisters, exclaimed, "Bless me, Miss Dundas, your little dog has pulled a folded sheet of paper from under that stand of flowers! Perhaps it may be of consequence!"

"Fly! Take it up, George!" cried Lady Villiers, "Esop will tear it to atoms whilst you are asking questions."

After a chace round the room, over chairs, and through tables, George Villiers at length plucked the devoted piece of paper out of the dog's mouth; and, as Miss Beaufort was gathering up her working materials, to leave the room, opened it, and cried, in a voice of triumph, "By Jove! It is a copy of verses!"

"Verses!" demanded Euphemia, feeling in her pocket, and colouring, "Let me see them."

"That you shan't," roared Lascelles, catching them out of the boy's hand, "if they be your writing, we will have them."

"Help me, Mary!" cried Euphemia, turning to Miss Beaufort, "I know that nobody is a poet in this house, but myself. They must be mine, and I will have them."

"Surely, Mr. Lascelles," said Mary, compassionating the poor girl's anxiety, "you will not be so rude as to detain them from their right owner?"

"O! but I will," cried he, mounting on a table, to get out of Euphemia's reach, who now, half crying, tried to snatch at the paper. "Let me alone, Miss Phemy. I will read them; so here goes it."

Miss Dundas laughed at her sister's confused looks, whilst Lascelles prepared to read, in a loud voice, the following verses. They had been hastily scribbled in pencil by Thaddeus, a long time ago; who having put them by mistake, with some other papers, into his pocket, had dropped them next day, in taking out his handkerchief at Lady Dundas's. Lascelles cleared his throat with three hems, then raising his right hand with a flourish of action, in a very pompous tone, began –

> "Like one, whom Etna's torrent fires have sent
> Far from the land, where his first youth was spent;
> Who, inly drooping, on a foreign shore
> Broods over scenes, which charm his eyes no more;

And while his country's ruin wakes the groan,
Yearns for the buried hut, he call'd his own.
So driv'n, O Poland! from thy ravag'd plains,
So mourning o'er thy sad, but lov'd remains,
A friendless wretch, *I* wander through the world,
From Fame, from Grandeur, and from Comfort hurl'd!
O! not, that each long night my weeping eyes
Sink into Sleep, unlull'd by Pity's sighs;
Not, that in bitter tears my bread is steep'd;
Tears drawn by insult on my sorrows heap'd;
Not, that my thoughts recall a mother's grave; –
Recall the sire I would have died to save,
Who fell before me, bleeding on the field,
Whilst I in vain opposed the fruitless shield: –
Ah! not for these I grieve! – Tho' mental woe
More deadly still, scarce Fancy's self could know.
O'er want and private griefs the soul can climb,
Virtue subdues the one, the other Time; –
But, at his country's fall, the patriot feels
A grief, no time, no drug, no reason, heals. –
Mem'ry! remorseless murderer! whose voice
Kills as it sounds; who never says, rejoice!
To my deserted heart, by joy forgot;
Thou pale, thou midnight spectre, haunt me not!
Thou dost but point to where sublimely stands
A glorious temple rear'd by Freedom's hands,
Circled with palms and laurels, crown'd with light,
Darting Truth's piercing sun on mortal sight:
Then, rushing on, leagued fiends of hellish birth,
Levelling the mighty fabric with the earth!
Slept the red bolt of Vengeance in that hour,
When virtuous Freedom fell the slave of Power!
Slumber'd the God of Justice! that no brand
Blasted, with blazing wing, the impious band! –
Dread God of Justice! to thy will I kneel,
Tho' still my filial heart must bleed and feel,
Tho' still the proud convulsive throb will rise,
When fools my country's wrongs and woes despise;
When low-soul'd Pomp, mean Wealth, that pity gives,
Which Virtue ne'er bestows, and ne'er receives, –
That Pity, stabbing where it vaunts to cure,
Which barbs the dart of Want, and makes it sure; –

How far remov'd from what the feeling breast,
Yields boastless, quench'd in sighs, to the distress'd!
Which whispers sympathy, with tender fear,
And almost dreads to pour its balmy tear. –
But such I know not now – unseen, alone,
I breathe the heavy sigh, I draw the groan;
And, madd'ning, turn to days of liveliest joy,
When o'er my native hills I cast mine eye,
And said exulting – 'Free men here shall sow
'The seed, that soon in tossing gold shall glow!
'While Plenty, led by Liberty, shall rove
'Gay and rejoicing, through the land they love;
'And 'mid their loaded vines, the peasant see
'His wife, his children, breathing out – we're free!'
But now, O wretched land! above thy plains,
Half viewless thro' the gloom, vast Horror reigns. –
No happy peasant o'er his blazing hearth,
Devotes the supper-hour to love and mirth;
No flowers on Liberty's pure altar bloom,
Alas! they wither now, and strew her tomb! –
From the great Book of Nations fiercely rent,
My country's page to Lethe's stream is sent –
O! sent in vain! – Th' historic muse shall raise,
O'er wrong'd Sarmatia's* cause, the voice of praise,
Shall sing *her* nobly struggling, e'en in death;
But blast her royal robbers' bloody wreath!"†

"It must be Constantine's!" cried Euphemia in a voice of surprized delight, when the reader had finished, and springing up to take the paper out of his hand.

"I dare say it is," answered the ill-natured Lascelles, holding it above his head, "Come, you shall have it, only first let us hear it again; it is so mighty pretty, so very lackadaisical!"

"Give it me," cried Euphemia, quite angry.

"Don't Lascelles," exclaimed Miss Dundas; "the man must be a perfect ideot to write such rhodomontade."‡

---

* That is, Poland's.
† 'These lines were furnish'd by a friend' [Porter's note, appearing only in the first edition]. The lines were republished in the annual anthology *Flowers of Literature* (London: B. Crosby and Co., 1804) as the work of 'An Exiled Polish Patriot'.
‡ rhodomontade, 'an extravagantly boastful, arrogant, or bombastic speech or piece of writing' (*OED*).

"O! It is delectable!" returned her lover, opening the paper again, "It would make a charming ditty! Come, I will sing it. Shall it be to the tune of *The Babes in the Wood*, or *Chevy Chace*, or *The Beggar of Bethnal Green*?"*

"Senseless, unfeeling wretch!" exclaimed Mary, rising from her chair, where she had been striving to subdue those emotions, with which every line in the poem had possessed her heart.

"Brute!" cried the enraged Euphemia, taking courage at Miss Beaufort's unusual warmth, "I will have the paper."

"You shan't," answered the malicious coxcomb; and, raising his arm higher than her reach, he tore it into a hundred pieces.

At this sight, Mary, no longer able to contain herself, rushed out of the room; and hurrying to her own chamber, threw herself upon the bed, where she gave way to a paroxysm of tears, that shook her almost to suffocation.

During the first burst of her indignation, her agitated spirit breathed every appellation of abhorrence and reproach on Lascelles and his malignant mistress. Then, wiping her flowing eyes, she said, "Yet, can I wonder, when I compare Constantine with what *they* are? The man who dares to be virtuous and great, and appear so, arms the self-love of all common characters against him."

Such being her meditations, she refused to join the family at dinner; and, it was not till evening, that she felt herself at all able to treat the ill-natured groupe with decent civility.

The next morning, Miss Beaufort (to avoid spending more hours than were absolutely necessary in the company of a woman whom she now loathed;) borrowed Lady Dundas's sedan chair, and, ordering it to Lady Tinemouth's, found her ladyship, at home, alone, and evidently much agitated.

"I intrude on you, Lady Tinemouth!" said Mary, observing her looks, and withdrawing from the offered seat.

"No, my dear Miss Beaufort," replied her ladyship, when the servant closed the door, "I am glad you are come. I assure you, I have few pleasures in solitude. Read that letter," added she, putting one into the hand of Mary, "it has just conveyed one of the cruellest stabs that ever was offered from a son to the heart of his mother. Read it; and you will not be surprised at finding me in the state you see."

The Countess looked on her paralysed hands as she spoke; and Mary, taking the paper from her, sat down, and read to herself the following letter:

* Three ballads popular in the eighteenth and nineteenth centuries.

"*To the Right Honourable the Countess of Tinemouth.*

"Madam,

"I am commissioned by the Earl, my father, to inform you, that if you have lost all regard for your own character, he considers that some respect is due to the mother of his son; therefore, he watches your conduct.

"He has been apprised of your frequent meetings during these many months, in Grosvenor Place, and at other people's houses, with an obscure foreigner, your declared lover. The Earl wished to suppose this false, till your shameless behaviour became so flagrant, that he esteems it neither worthy of doubt nor indulgence.

"With his own eyes he saw you, four nights ago, alone with this man in Hyde Park. Such demonstration is dreadful. Your proceedings are abominable; and, if you do not, without further parley, set off either to Craighall in Cornwall, or the Wolds, you shall receive a letter from my sister as well as myself, to tell the dishonoured Lady Tinemouth, how much she merits her daughter's contempt, added to that of

"HARWOLD."

"And what do you mean to do, my dear Madam?" inquired Mary, shocked at this instance of an ingratitude disgraceful to human nature.

"I will obey my Lord and his children," returned the Countess bursting into tears, "My last action shall be in obedience to their will. I cannot live long; and when I am dead, perhaps the Earl's vigilance may be satisfied; perhaps, some kind friend may then plead my cause in my daughter's heart. One cruel line from her would kill me. I will at least avoid the completion of that threat, by leaving town to-morrow night."

"So soon! But I hope not to Cornwall?"

"No," replied her ladyship, "Craighall is too near Plymouth. I shall determine on the Wolds. Yet, why should I have a choice? It is almost a matter of indifference to what spot I am banished; in what place I am to die. Any where, I shall be equally remote from a friend."

Mary's heart was oppressed when she entered the room; Lady Tinemouth's sorrows seemed to give her a license to weep. She took her ladyship's hand, and with difficulty sobbed out this inarticulate offer, "Take me, dear Lady Tinemouth! I am sure my guardian will be happy to permit me to be with you, where, and how long you like."

"Dear Mary," replied the Countess, kissing her wet cheek, "I thank you from my heart; but I cannot take so ungenerous an advantage of your goodness, as to consign your tender nature to the harassing task of attending on sorrow and sickness. How strangely different may even amiable dispositions be tempered! Maria Egerton is better framed for such an office. Kind as she is, the hilarity of her disposition does not allow the sympathy she bestows on others, either to injure her mind or her body."

Mary interrupted her. "I should be grieved, my dear Countess, to believe, that my very aptitude to serve my friends, will prove the first reason why I should be denied that pleasure. It is only in scenes of affliction that friendship is tried and declares its truth. If Miss Egerton were not going with you, I should certainly insist on putting my affection to that ordeal."

"You mistake, my sweet friend," returned her ladyship, "Maria is forbidden to remain any longer with me. You have overlooked the postscript to Lord Harwold's letter, else you must have seen the whole of my cruel situation. Turn over the leaf."

Miss Beaufort opened the sheet, and read these few lines, which being written on the interior part of the paper, had escaped her sight.

"Go where you will, it is our especial injunction that you leave Miss Egerton behind you; whom we hear has been the ambassadress in this shocking intrigue. If we learn that you disobey, and persist in such audacity, it shall be worse for you in every respect; as it will convince us beyond a possibility of doubt, how uniform is the turpitude of your conduct."

Lady Tinemouth grasped Miss Beaufort's hand, as she threw the barbarous scrawl on the table. "And that, Mary, is from the son for whom I felt all a mother's agonies; all a mother's love! Had he died the first hour in which he saw the light, what a mass of guilt might he not have escaped! It is he," added she in a lower voice, and looking wildly round, "that breaks my heart. I could have borne his father's perfidy; but, insult, oppression, from my child! Oh, Mary, you know not its bitterness!"

Mary could only answer with her tears.

After a pause of near a quarter of an hour, in which the Countess strove to tranquillize her spirits, she resumed in a more composed voice.

"Excuse me for an instant, my dear Miss Beaufort; I must write to Mr. Constantine. I have yet to inform him that my absence is to be added to his other misfortunes."

With her eyes raining down upon the paper, she took up a pen, and having hastily written a few lines, was sealing them, when Mary looking up, hardly conscious of the words which escaped her lips, said, with anguished eagerness, "Lady Tinemouth, you know much of that noble and unhappy young man?" Her eyes irresolutely, and her cheek glowing, awaited the answer of the Countess, who for a moment continued to gaze on the letter she held in her hand as if in profound thought; then all at once raising her head, and regarding the now down-cast face of Mary with tenderness, replied in a tone which conveyed the deep interest of her heart.

"I do Mary. He has reposed his griefs in my friendship and honour; therefore, I must hold them sacred."

"I will not ask you to betray them," returned Mary in a faultering voice, "Yet, I cannot help lamenting his sufferings, and esteeming the fortitude with which he supports his fall."

The Countess looked stedfastly on her fluctuating countenance. "Has Constantine, my dear Miss Beaufort, insinuated to you, that he ever was otherwise than as he now appears?"

Mary could not reply. She would not trust her lips with words, but shook her head in sign that he had not. Lady Tinemouth was too well read in the human heart, to doubt for an instant, the cause of Miss Beaufort's question and consequent emotion. Feeling that something was due to an anxiety so disinterested and noble, she took her passive hand, and said, "Mary, you have guessed rightly. Though I am not authorized to tell you the real name of Constantine, nor the particulars of his history; let this satisfy your generous heart, that it can never be more honourably employed, than in compassionating calamities which ought to wreath his young brows with glory."

Mary's eyes streamed afresh, whilst her exulting soul seemed ready to rush from her bosom.

"Mary!" continued the Countess, warmed by the recollection of his excellence; "You have no need to blush at the interest which you take in this amiable Constantine! Every trial of spirit which could have tortured youth or manhood, has been endured by him with the firmness of a hero. Ah, my sweet friend," added the Countess, pressing the hand of the confused Mary, who, ashamed, and conscious that her behaviour betrayed how dearly she considered him, had covered her face with her handkerchief; "when you are disposed to believe that a man is as great as his titles and demands assert, examine with a nice observance, whether his pretensions be real or artificial. Imagine him disrobed of splendor, and struggling with the world's inclemencies. If his character cannot stand this ordeal, he is only a pageant of pomp, inflated and garnished; and it is reasonable to punish his arrogance with contempt. But, on the reverse, when like Constantine, he rises from the ashes of his fortunes in a brighter blaze of virtue; then, dearest girl," cried the Countess encircling her with her arms, "it is the sweetest privilege of loveliness, to console and bless so rare a being."

Mary raised her deluged face from the bosom of her friend; and, clasping her hands together with trepidation and anguish, implored her to be as faithful to her secret, as she had proved herself to Constantine's: "I would sooner die," added the agitated Mary, "than have him know my rashness, perhaps my indelicacy! Let me possess his esteem, Lady Tinemouth! Let him suppose, that I only *esteem* him! More, I should shrink from; I have seen him beset by some of my sex; and to be classed with *them*! To have him imagine that my affection is like *theirs*! I could not bear it – I entreat you, let him respect me!"

The impetuosity, and almost despair, with which Miss Beaufort uttered these incoherent sentences, pierced to the soul of Lady Tinemouth. How different was the spirit of this pure and dignified love, to the wild passion, which she had seen shake the frame of Lady Sara Roos!

They remained silent for some time.

"May I see your ladyship to-morrow?" asked Mary, drawing her cloak about her.

"I fear not," replied the Countess; "I leave this house to-morrow."

Mary rose; her lips, hands, and feet trembled so, that she could hardly stand. Lady Tinemouth threw her arm round her waist, and kissing her forehead, said, "Heaven bless you, my dear Miss Beaufort! May all the wishes of your innocent heart be gratified!"

The Countess supported her to the door. Mary hesitated an instant, then flinging her snowy arms over her ladyship's neck, in a voice scarcely audible, articulated, "Only tell me! Does he love Euphemia?"

Lady Tinemouth strained her to her breast; "No, my dearest girl; I am certain, both from what I have heard him say, and observed in his eyes, that had he dared to love any one, *you* would have been the object of his choice."

How Mary got into Lady Dundas's chair, she had no recollection, so completely was she absorbed in the recent scene. Her mind was perplexed, her heart ached; and she arrived in Harley Street so much disordered and unwell, as to oblige her to retire immediately to her room, with the excuse of a violent pain in her head.

This interview with Miss Beaufort induced Lady Tinemouth to destroy the note that she had written to Thaddeus, purposing before night, to frame another, better calculated to produce comfort to all parties. What she declared to Mary respecting the state of the Count's affections, was sincere.

She had early penetrated through the veil of bashfulness, with which Miss Beaufort had obscured that countenance, so usually the tablet of her soul. The Countess easily translated the quick receding of Mary's eye, whenever Thaddeus turned his attention towards her;

the confused reply that followed any unexpected question from his lips; and above all, the unheeded sighs heaved by her, when he left the room, or when his name was mentioned during his absence. These symptoms too truly revealed to Lady Tinemouth, the state of her young friend's bosom.

But the circumstances being different, her observations on the Count were not nearly so conclusive. Mary had absolutely given the empire of her happiness, with her heart, into his hands. Thaddeus wished that his ruined hopes had not prevented him from laying his, at her feet. Therefore, not having surrendered his imagination to a passion, which, in his situation, he considered as madness, he was unembarrassed in her presence; and, regarding her as a being beyond his reach, conceived no suspicions, that she entertained one dearer thought of him than what mere philanthropy could authorise.

He contemplated her unequalled beauty, graces, talents, and virtues, with an admiration bordering on idolatry; yet his heart flew from the confession that he loved her: and it was not until reason demanded of his candour, why he felt a pang on seeing Mary's purse in the hands of Mr. Lascelles, that with a glowing cheek, he owned to himself, he was jealous: that although he had not presumed to elevate one wish towards the possession of Miss Beaufort; yet, when Lascelles flaunted her name on his tongue, he found how poignant would be the wound in his peace, should she ever give her hand to another.

Confounded at this discovery of a passion, the seeds of which, he supposed had been crushed by the weight of his misfortunes, he proceeded homewards, with sensations not far differing from those of the dreamer, who sinks into a light but harassing slumber, and, full of terror, doubts whether he be sleeping or awake.

The sudden illness of General Butzou having put these ideas to flight, Thaddeus was sitting on the bed-side, with his anxious thoughts fixed on the pale spectacle of mortality before him, when Nancy brought in a letter from the Countess. He took it, and going to the window, undrew the curtain, where he read, with mingled pain and pleasure, the following epistle.

"To Mr. Constantine.

"I know not, my dear Count, when I shall be permitted to see you again; perhaps never on this side of the grave!

"Since heaven has denied me the tenderness of my own children, it would have been a comfort to me, might I have continued to act a parent's part by you. But my cruel lord, and my more cruel son, jealous of the consolation I meet in the society of my few intimate friends, command me to quit London: and as I have ever made it a system to obey their injunctions strictly, I shall go.

"It pierces me to the soul, my *dear son*! (allow my maternal heart to call you by that name!) it distresses me deeply, that I am compelled to leave the place where *you* are: neither can I see you prior to my departure, for I quit town to-morrow afternoon.

"Write to me often, my loved Sobieski: Your letters will be some alleviation during the fulfilment of my hard duty.

"Wear the enclosed gold chain for my sake; it is one of two given me a long time ago by Miss Beaufort. If I have not greatly mistaken you, the present will now possess a double value in your estimation: indeed it ought. Sensibility and thankfulness, being properties of your nature, they will not deny a lively gratitude to the generous interest with which that amiable young woman regards your fate. It is impossible, that the avowed Count Sobieski, (whom a year ago, I remember her animated fancy painted in the most romantic colours,) could excite more of her esteem, than I know she has bestowed on the melancholy, the untitled Constantine.

"She is all nobleness and affection. Although I am sensible that she will leave much behind her in London to regret, she insists on accompanying me to the Wolds. Averse to transgress so far on her goodness, I resolutely refused her offer, till this evening, I received so warm and urging a letter from the kind girl, that I can no longer withhold my consent.

"Indeed, this lovely creature's active friendship proves of high consequence to me now, situated as I am with regard to a new whim of the Earl's. Had she not benevolently presented herself in obedience to my lord's commands I should have been obliged to go alone; he, having taken some wild antipathy to Miss Egerton, whose company he has interdicted. At any rate, her parents would not have allowed me her society much longer, for Mr. Montresor is to return this month.

"I shall not be easy, my dear Count, till I hear from you. Pray write soon: and inform me of every particular respecting the poor General: is he likely to recover?

"In all things, my *loved son*, in which I can serve you, remember, that I expect you will call on me *as a mother*. Your own could hardly have regarded you with deeper tenderness, than does your affectionate and faithful

"ADELIZA TINEMOUTH.

"Grosvenor Place.
"Thursday, midnight.
"Direct to me at Harwold-park, Wolds, Lincolnshire."

Several opposite emotions discomposed the mind of Thaddeus, whilst reading this epistle. Encreased abhorrence of the man, whom he believed to be incontestably his father, united with regret arising from the proposed departure of Lady Tinemouth, could neither subdue the balmy effect of her maternal affection, nor wholly check that thrill, which the unusual mentioning of Miss Beaufort's name, made throb in his heart, and paint his cheeks with crimson. He read the sentence that contained the assurances of her friendship, a third time.

"Delicious poison!" cried he, kissing the paper, "if adoring thee, lovely Mary, be added to my other sorrows, I shall be resigned! There is sweetness even in the thought. Could I credit all which my dear Lady Tinemouth affirms, the conviction that I possess one kind solicitude in the mind of Miss Beaufort, would be ample compensation for – "

He did not finish the sentence, but sighing profoundly, rose from his chair.

"For any thing, except beholding her the wife of another!" was the sentiment with which his heart panted. Thaddeus had never known a selfish feeling in his life; and this first instance of his wishing that good unappropriated, which he might not himself enjoy, made him start.

"There is a fault in my heart, a dreadful one!" Dissatisfied with himself, he was preparing to answer her ladyship's letter, when, turning to the date, he discovered that it had been written on Thursday night; and, in consequence of Nancy's neglect, in not calling at the coffee-house, had been delayed a day and a half before it reached his hands.

His disappointment at this accident was severe. She was gone, and Mary along with her!

"Then indeed I am unfortunate!" said he, holding the chain in his hand, and looking on it; "I am at once deprived of all that rendered my forlorn existence in this town, tolerable!"

He put the chain round his neck; and, with a true lover-like feeling, thought that it warmed the heart, which mortification had chilled; but the fancy was evanescent, and he again turned to watch the fading life of his friend.

During the lapse of a few days, in which the General appeared merely to breathe, Thaddeus, instead of his attendance, dispatched regular notes to Harley-street. In answer to these excuses, he commonly received little tender billets from Euphemia; the strain of which he seemed totally to overlook, by the cold respect that he evinced in his diurnal apologies for absence.

This young lady was so full of lamentation over the trouble which her elegant tutor must endure in watching his sick friend, that she never thought it worth while to mention any creature in the house except herself and her commiseration. Thaddeus longed to inquire about Miss Beaufort; but the more he wished it, the greater reluctance he felt to write her name.

Things were in this situation, when one evening, as he was reading by the light of a solitary candle in his little sitting-room, the door opened, and Nancy stepped in, followed by a person wrapped up in a large black cloak. Thaddeus immediately rose.

"A lady, Sir," said Nancy, curtsying.

The moment the girl withdrew, the visitor cast herself into a chair, and sobbing aloud, seemed in violent agitation. The Count, astonished and alarmed, approached her, and though she was unknown, offered her every assistance in his power.

Catching hold of the hand, which with the greatest respect he extended towards her, she instantly displayed to his dismayed sight, the features of Lady Sara Roos.

"Merciful Heaven!" exclaimed he, involuntarily starting back.

"Do not cast me off, Constantine!" cried she, clasping his arm, and looking up to him, with a face of anguish, bathed in tears, "on you alone, I now depend for happiness! for existence!"

A cold damp stood on the forehead of her auditor. A tremor shook him from head to foot.

"Dear Lady Sara, what am I to understand by this emotion? Has any thing dreadful happened? Is Captain Roos – ?"

Lady Sara shuddered, and, still grasping his hand, answered in words, every one of which palsied the heart of Thaddeus with horror; – "He is coming home. – He is now at Portsmouth. – O Constantine! I am not yet so debased, as to live with him, when my heart is yours."

At this shameful declaration, Thaddeus clenched his teeth in fearful agony; and, striking his hand upon his closed eyes, to shut her from his sight; he turned suddenly round, and walked towards another part of the room.

Lady Sara followed him. Her cloak having fallen off, now displayed her fine form in all the fervour of grief and distraction; she wrung her snowy arms in despair; and, with accents rendered more piercing by the anguish of her mind, exclaimed, "What? You hate me? You throw me from you? Cruel, barbarous Constantine! Can you drive from your feet the woman who adores you? Can you cast her who is without a home into the streets?"

Thaddeus felt his hand wet with her tears; he fixed his eyes upon her with almost delirious horror. Her hat being off, gave a loose to her long black hair, which falling in masses over her shoulders and eyes, gave such additional wildness to the imploring and frantic expression of those eyes, as distracted his soul.

"Rise, Madam! For Heaven's sake, Lady Sara!" and he stooped to support her up.

"Never," cried she, covering her face with her hands, "never! till you promise to protect me. My husband comes home to-night, and I have left his house for ever. You, you?" exclaimed she, extending her hand to his averted face; "O Constantine! you have robbed me of my peace! On your account I have flown from my home. – For mercy's sake, do not abandon me!"

"Lady Sara," cried he, looking wildly round him, "I cannot speak to you in this position! Rise, I implore you!"

"Only," returned she, "only say that you will protect me! That I shall find shelter here! Say this, and I will rise, and bless you for ever."

Thaddeus knew not what to reply. Distressed by her imprudence, terror-struck at the violent lengths to which she seemed determined to carry her unhappy and guilty passion, he in vain sought to evade this direct demand; for Lady Sara, perceiving the reluctance and horror of his looks, sprang from her knees, and, in a more resolute voice, exclaimed, "Then, Sir, you will not protect me? You scorn and desert a woman, whom you well know has long loved you? Whom by your artful behaviour you have seduced to this disgrace!"

The Count, surprized and shocked at this accusation, with respectful gentleness, but resolution, denied the charge.

Lady Sara again melted into tears, and supporting her tottering frame against his shoulder, replied in a stifled voice, "I know it well. I have nothing to blame for my wretched state, but my own weakness. Pardon, dear Constantine, the dictates of my madness! O! I would gladly owe such misery to any other source than myself!"

"Then, dear Lady Sara," rejoined Thaddeus, gaining courage from the mildness of her manner, "let me implore you to return to your own house!"

"Don't ask me," cried she, grasping his hand; "O Constantine! if you knew what it was to receive with smiles of affection, a creature that you loath! you would shrink with disgust from what you require. I hate Captain Roos. Can I open my arms to meet him, when my heart excludes him for ever? Can I welcome him home, when I wish him in his grave?"

The Count extricated his hand from her grasp. Her ladyship perceived the repugnance which dictated this action; and clasping her hands together, ejaculated, "Unhappy woman that I am! to hate, where I am loved! to love, where I am hated! – Kill me, Constantine!"

cried she, turning suddenly towards him, and sinking down on a chair; "but do not give me such another look as that!"

"Dear Lady Sara," replied he, seating himself by her side, "what would you have me do? You see that I have no proper means of protecting you. I have no mother, no sisters, no friends, to receive you. You see that I am a *poor* man. Besides, your character – "

"Talk not of my character!" cried she, "I will have none that does not depend on you! – Cruel Constantine! you will not understand me. I want no riches, no friends, but yourself. Give me *your* home, and *your* arms," added she, throwing herself in an agony on his bosom, "and beggary would be paradise!"

Thaddeus felt a dimness spread over his eyes. So much loveliness, such love, such disinterestedness, for a moment obliterated every other impression on his heart; but, recovering himself in an instant, he tore himself from her clinging arms, and staggering back a few paces, held her off with his hand, and, in a voice of distraction, exclaimed, "Leave me, for pity's sake!"

"No, dearest Constantine!" cried she, aware of her advantage, and again casting herself at his feet, "Never, never, will I leave this spot, till you consent, that your home shall be my home! That I shall serve you for ever!"

"All-powerful Heaven!" exclaimed Thaddeus, in an agony.

Lady Sara redoubled her tears and prayers.

"Seducing, dangerous woman!" cried he, looking at her with wild horror, "what is it you demand? Would you tear from me all that renders life bearable? Would you take from me a blameless conscience, and drive me to end my miserable days by a deed of desperation?"

Despair was in every feature of his countenance, as he uttered the last words, and flew from her, into the apartment where the General lay asleep. Lady Sara, little expecting to see any one but the man she loved, rushed in after him, and was again pressing to throw her imploring arms about her determined victim, when her eyes were suddenly arrested by a livid, and she thought, dead face of a person lying on the bed. Fixed to the spot, she stood for a moment, then putting her spread hand on her forehead, uttered a faint cry, and fell heart-struck and senseless on the floor.

Thaddeus, having instant conviction of her mistake, eagerly seized the moment of her insensibility to convey her home. He hastily went to the top of the stairs, called to Nancy to run for a coach, and then returning to the extended figure of Lady Sara, lifted her in his arms, and carried her back to the room they had left.

By the help of hartshorn and water, he restored her to a sense of existence. She slowly opened her eyes; then raising her head, looked round her with a terrified air, when her eye falling on the still open door of the General's room, she caught Thaddeus by the arm, and said in a trembling voice, "O, take me from hence."

Whilst she yet spoke, a coach stopped at the door. The Count rose, and attempted to support her agitated frame against his shoulders, but she trembled to such a degree, that he was obliged to throw his arm about her waist, and almost carry her down stairs.

When he had placed her ladyship in the carriage, she retained his hand, and said in a faint tone; "You surely will not leave me?"

Thaddeus returned no other answer, than desiring Nancy to sit by the General till she saw him again; and stepping into the coach, Lady Sara immediately snatched his hand, and bathed it with her tears.

"Where are you going to take me?"

"You shall again, dear Lady Sara," replied he, "return to a guiltless and peaceful home."

"I cannot meet my husband;" cried she, wringing her hands, "he will see all my premeditated guilt in my countenance. O! Constantine, have pity on me! Miserable creature that I am!" added she, redoubling her grief, "It is horrible to live with you! It is dreadful to live with him! Take me not home I entreat you!"

The Count took her clasped hands in his.

"Reflect for a moment, my dear Lady Sara. I believe, if you love me, that it was in consequence of virtues, which you thought I possessed."

"Indeed, you do me justice!" cried she.

He continued.

"Think then, should I yield to the influence of your beauty, and plunge you into a situation like that – " and he pointed to a groupe of unhappy women assembled at the corner of Pall-Mall.* Lady Sara drew back with a thrill of horror; "Think, where would be, not only your innocence, but its price? I, being no longer worthy of your esteem, you would hate me; you would hate yourself; and we should continue together, two guilty creatures, abhorring each other."

Lady Sara, drowned in tears, did not articulate any sounds but deep sighs, till the coach stopped in St. James's Place.

"Go in with me," were all the words which she could utter, as pulling her veil over her face, she gave him her hand to assist her down the step.

---

* Pall Mall, a main thoroughfare from Charing Cross to St James's Palace, was known for its appearance of wealth and aristocracy, but also for the many brothels on nearby King's Place.

"Is Captain Roos arrived?" asked Thaddeus of a servant, who, to his great joy, returned a reply in the negative. During his ride, he had alarmed himself, by anticipating the disagreeable suspicions which might arise in the mind of the husband, should he see his wife in her present strange and distracted state.

When Thaddeus had seated Lady Sara in her drawing-room, he prepared to take a respectful leave; but her ladyship getting up, laid one hand on his arm, whilst with the other she covered her convulsed features; and said, "Constantine, before you go; before we part, perhaps eternally; O! tell me, that you do not hate me! That you do not *hate* me!" repeated she, in a firmer tone, "I know too well, how deeply I am despised."

"Cease, my dearest Madam," returned he, tenderly replacing her on the sofa, "cease these vehement expressions. Shame does not depend on possessing passions, but on yielding to them. You have conquered, Lady Sara; and in future, I shall respect and love you as a dear friend. Whoever holds the first place in my heart, you shall always retain the second."

"Noble! generous Constantine!" cried she, straining his hand to her lips, and bathing it with tears; "I can require no more. May heaven bless you wherever you go!"

Thaddeus dropt upon his knee; imprinted on both her hands a compassionate and fervent kiss; and rising hastily, quitted the room without a word.

CHAP. VII.

The dream-like consternation which enveloped the Count's faculties, since the preceding scene, was dissipated next morning by the appearance of Dr. Cavendish. When he saw the General, he declared it to be his opinion, that in consequence of his long and tranquil slumbers, he should suppose some favourable crisis to be near; "probably," added he, "the recovery of his intellects. Such *phenomena* often in these cases, happen immediately before death."

"Heaven grant it!" ejaculated the Count; "to hear his venerable voice again acknowledge, that I have acted by him as became the grandson of his friend, would be a comfort to me."

"But, Sir," said the kind physician, touching his burning hand, "you must not forget the cares which are due to your own life. If you wish well to the General, during the few days he may have to live, you are indispensably obliged to preserve your own strength. You are already ill, and require air. I have an hour of leisure," continued he, pulling out his watch, "I will remain here, till you have taken two or three walks round the park. It is absolutely necessary; in this instance, I must take the privilege of friendship, and insist on obedience."

Thaddeus, seeing that the benevolence of the excellent Cavendish was resolute, took his hat, and with harassed spirits, walked down the lane towards Charing-cross.

On entering Spring-garden gate, to his extreme surprise, the first objects which met his sight, were Miss Euphemia Dundas, and Miss Beaufort.

Euphemia accosted him immediately with ten thousand inquiries respecting his friend, besides congratulations on his own good looks.

Thaddeus bowed; then smiling faintly, turned to the blushing Mary; who, conscious of the recent conversation which had passed between herself and Lady Tinemouth, trembled so much, that fearing to excite the suspicion of Miss E. Dundas by such tremor, she withdrew her arm, and walked forward alone, her feet tottering at every step.

"I thought, Miss Beaufort," said he, addressing himself to her, "that Lady Tinemouth was to have had the happiness of your company to Harwold-park?"

"Yes," returned she, fearfully raising her eyes to his face; the hectic glow of which, conveyed differing sensations to her breast, from those that Euphemia had expressed; "but to my indescribable alarm and disappointment, the morning after I had written to fix my departure with her ladyship, my aunt's foot caught in the iron of the stair-carpet as she was coming down stairs, and, throwing her from the top to the bottom, broke her leg. I could not quit her a moment during her first agonies; and the surgeons expressing their fears that a fever might ensue, I was obliged altogether to decline my attendance on the Countess!"

"And how is Mrs. Dorothy Somerset?" inquired Thaddeus, truly concerned at the accident.

"She is better, though confined to her bed;" replied Euphemia, speaking before her companion could open her lips; "and indeed, poor Mary and myself have been such close nurses, that my mother insisted on our walking out to-day."

"And Lady Tinemouth;" returned Thaddeus, again addressing Mary, "of course she went alone?"

"Alas, yes!" replied Mary, "Miss Egerton was forced to join her family in Leicestershire."

"I believe," cried Euphemia, sighing, "that Miss Egerton is going to be married immediately. It has been a long attachment. Happy girl! I have heard Captain Roos, whose Lieutenant he was, say that he is the finest young man in the Navy. Did you ever see Mr. Montresor?" added she, turning her pretty eyes on the Count.

"I never had that honour."

"Bless me! that is odd, considering your intimacy with Miss Egerton. I assure you he is very charming."

Thaddeus neither heard this, nor a great deal more of the same trifling chit-chat which was slipping from the tongue of Miss Euphemia; so intently were his eyes (sent by his heart,) searching the downcast, but expressive countenance of Miss Beaufort. His soul was full, and the fluctuations of her colour, with the embarrassment of her step, interested and affected him.

"Then you do not leave town for some time, Miss Beaufort?" inquired he, "I may yet anticipate the honour of seeing – – " he hesitated a moment, then added in a depressed tone – "your aunt, when I next wait on the Miss Dundas's."

"Our stay entirely depends on her health;" returned she, striving to rally herself; "and I am sure, she will be equally happy to see you better; for, I am sorry to say, that I cannot agree with Euphemia, in thinking that you look well."

"Merely a slight fever," replied he; "the effect of an anxiety and watching, which I fear will too soon cease, in the death of their cause.

I came out now for a little air only, whilst the physician remains with my friend."

"Poor old gentleman!" sighed Mary, "how venerable was his appearance that morning in which we saw him in the Park! What a benign countenance!"

"His countenance," replied Thaddeus, his eyes turning mournfully towards the lovely speaker, "is the emblem of his character. He was the most amiable of men."

"And you are likely to lose so interesting a friend? dear Mr. Constantine, how I pity you!" As Euphemia uttered these words, she put the corner of her glove to her eye.

The Count looked at her, and, perceiving that her commiseration was affectation, he turned to Miss Beaufort, who was walking pensively by his side, and made further inquiries respecting Mrs. Dorothy. Solicitous to get back to St. Martin's Lane, he was preparing to quit them, when Mary, as with a full heart she curtsied her adieu, at last, in a hurrying and confused manner, said, "Pray, Mr. Constantine, take care of yourself. You have other friends besides the one you are going to lose. I know Lady Tinemouth, I know my aunt – " she stopped short, and, covered with blushes, stood panting for another word to close the sentence; when Thaddeus, forgetting the presence of Euphemia, with delighted precipitancy caught hold of the hand which in the energy of speaking was a little extended towards him, and, pressing it with fervour, relinquished it immediately: overcome by confusion at the presumption of the action, he bowed with agitation to both ladies, and hastened through the Priory passage, into St. James's Street.

"Miss Beaufort!" cried Euphemia, reddening with vexation, and returning a perfumed handkerchief to her pocket; "I did not understand that you and Mr. Constantine were on such intimate terms!"

"What do you mean, Euphemia?"

"That you have betrayed the confidence which I reposed in you;" cried the angry beauty, wiping away the really starting tears with her white lace cloak; "I told you that the elegant Constantine was the lord of my heart, and you have seduced him from me! Till you came, he was so respectful, so tender, so devoted! – But I am rightly used! I ought to have carried my secret to the grave."

In vain Miss Beaufort protested; in vain she declared herself ignorant of possessing any power, over even one wish of Constantine's. Euphemia thought it monstrous pretty to be the injured friend and forsaken mistress; and all along the Park, and up Constitution Hill, until they arrived at Lady Dundas's carriage, which was waiting opposite Devonshire Wall, she affected to weep. When seated, she continued her invectives: She called Miss Beaufort, ungenerous, perfidious, traitor to friendship; and every romantic and disloyal name, which her inflamed fancy could devise, till the sight of Harley-street, checked her transports, and relieved Miss Beaufort from a load of impertinence and abuse.

During this short interview, Thaddeus received an impulse to his feelings, which hurried them forward with an impetuous rapidity, that neither time nor succeeding sorrows could stop or stem.

Mary's heavenly beaming eyes seemed to have encircled his head with love's brightest lustre. The command, "Preserve yourself for others besides your dying friend," yet throbbed at his heart; with ten thousand rapturous visions dancing before his sight, he felt treading in air, till the humble door of his melancholy home presenting itself, at once wrecked the illusion, and offered sad reality, in the person of his emaciated friend.

On the Count's entrance into the sick chamber, Doctor Cavendish gave him a few directions to pursue, when the General should awake from the sleep in which he had been sunk since the preceding night; and Thaddeus, with a heart still more depressed, from the late unusual exaltation of his feelings, sat down on the bed for the remainder of the day.

At five in the afternoon, General Butzou awoke; seeing the Count, he stretched out his withered hand, and as the doctor had predicted, accosted him rationally.

"Come, dear Sobieski! Come nearer, my dear master!"

Thaddeus rose, and throwing himself on his knees, took the offered hand with apparent composure: It was a hard struggle to restrain the emotions which were roused by this awful contemplation; – the return of reason to the soul, on the instant she was summoned into the presence of her Maker!

"My kind, my beloved Lord!" added Butzou, "to me, you have indeed performed a christian's part; you have clothed, sheltered, and preserved me in your bosom. Blessed son of my most honoured master!"

The good old man put the hand of Thaddeus to his lips. Thaddeus could not speak.

"I am going, dear Sobieski," continued the General in a lower voice, "where I shall meet your noble grandfather, your mother, and my brave countrymen: and if heaven grants me power, I will tell them, by whose labour I have lived, on whose breast I have expired."

Thaddeus could no longer restrain his tears.

"Dear, dear General!" exclaimed he, grasping his hand; "my grand-father, my mother, my country! I lose them again in thee! – O! would the same summons take *me* hence!"

"Hush!" returned the dying man, "Heaven reserves you, my hon-oured lord, for wise purposes. Youth and health are the marks of com-mission: *You* possess them, with virtues, which will bear you through the contest. *I* have done; and my merciful judge, has evinced his pardon of my errors, by sparing me in my old age, and leading me to die with you."

Thaddeus pressed his friend's hand to his streaming eyes, and prom-ised to be resigned. Butzou smiled upon him his satisfaction; then, closing his eye-lids, he composed himself to a rest, that was neither sleep nor stupor, but a balmy serenity, which seemed to be tempering his late recovered soul, for its immediate entrance on a world of eternal peace.

At nine o'clock, his breath became broken with quick sighs. The Count's heart trembled, and he drew closer to the pillow. Butzou felt him, and opening his eyes languidly, hardly articulated, (though not a sound escaped the ear of his friend,) "Raise my head."

Thaddeus put his arm under his neck, and lifting him up, reclined him against his bosom. Butzou squeezed his hands, and looking grate-fully in his face, said, "The arms of a soldier, should be a soldier's bed. I am content."

He lay for a moment on the breast of the almost fainting Thaddeus; then suddenly quitting his grasp, he cried, "I lose you, Sobieski!"

"I am here," exclaimed the Count, catching his motionless hand. The dying General murmured a few words of blessing; and, turning his face inwards, breathed his last sigh on the heart of his last friend.

For a minute, Sobieski remained incapable of thought or action. When he recovered recollection, he withdrew from his melancholy station, and, laying the venerable remains of the General on the bed, did not trust his rallied faculties with a second trial, but, hastening down stairs, was met by Mrs. Robson.

"My dear Madam," said he, "all is over with my poor friend. Will you do me the everlasting kindness, to perform those duties to his sacred relics, which I cannot?"

Mrs. Robson, with tears, and expressions of gratitude, for his good-ness, when she was in a similar distress, sent to request the assistance of the charitable neighbour who had succoured her in the case of her lamented little William; and together, they arranged and ordered every thing that was requisite.

Thaddeus would not allow any person to watch by his friend's coffin, besides himself. The meditations of this solitary night, presented to his sound and feeling mind, every argument, rather to induce rejoicing than regret, that the eventful life of the brave Butzou had terminated.

"Yes, illustrious old man!" cried he, gazing on his marble features, "If valour and virtue be the true sources of nobility, thou surely wert noble! Inestimable defender of Stanislaus and thy country! thou hast run a long and bright career; and though thou art fated to rest in the humble grave of poverty, it will be embalmed by the tears of heaven; it will be engraven on my heart."

Thaddeus did not weep whilst he spoke. Nor did he weep, when he beheld the mould of St. Martin's church yard* close from his view the last dwelling of his friend. It began to rain. Doctor Cavendish, putting his arm through the Count's, tried to pull him away; but he lingered a moment, and, looking on the dust as the sexton piled it up, "Wretched Poland!" sighed he, "how far from thee, lies one of thy bravest sons!"

Doctor Cavendish regarded him with pity and admiration; but he vainly attempted to persuade him to return with him to dinner: Thaddeus refused the kind invitation; alleging with a faint smile, that under every misfortune, he found his best comforter to be solitude.

Doctor Cavendish, respecting the resignation and manliness of this answer, urged him no further; but expressed his regret that they could not meet again till the end of the week, he being obliged to hurry down to Stamford next day, on a medical consultation of considerable moment: and, shaking hands with his thoughtful friend at the door of Mrs. Robson's, they parted.

---

* In the second edition, Porter moves Butzou's grave to 'the mould of St Paul's, Covent Garden' (3. 181). This change was necessary, since the novel's final chapter places the tomb at Covent Garden. Furthermore, by the 1790s, St Martin's rarely offered burials in the immediate grounds. Boulton, Jeremy, 'Traffic in Corpses and the Commodification of Burial in Georgian London', in *Continuity and Change* 29.2 (2014), pp. 181–208.

CHAP. VIII.*

Next morning, when the Count Sobieski unfolded the several packets of papers which were put into his hands by little Nancy who brought his breakfast, he laid them, one after the other, on the table, and, sighing heavily, said to himself, "Now comes the bitterness of poverty! Heaven only knows by what means I shall defray these terrific charges!"

The mere personal privations induced by his fallen fortunes, excited few uneasy sensations in the mind of Thaddeus. As he had derived no peculiar gratification from the enjoyment of a magnificent house, splendid table, and numerous attendants; he had felt equal content in the field, where he was often forced to sleep on the bare ground, and snatch his hasty meal at uncertain intervals. Watching, rough fare, and other hardships, were dust in the path of honour; he had dashed through them with light and buoyant spirits: and he repined as little, at the actual wants of his forlorn state in exile; till, compelled by friendship to contract demands that he could not defray, he was plunged at once into the full horrors of poverty and debt.

He looked at the amount of the bills. The apothecary's was fifteen pounds; the funeral, twenty more. Thaddeus turned pale. The value of all he possessed, would not produce one half of the sum; besides he owed five guineas, to his good landlady, for numerous little comforts appropriated to his deceased friend.

"Whatever be the consequence," cried he, "that excellent woman shall not suffer by her humanity! If I have to part with the last memorial of them who were so dear, she shall be repaid."

He had scarcely ceased speaking, when Nancy re-entered the room with a saddened countenance, and told him, that the apothecary's young man, and the undertaker, were both below, waiting for answers to their letters. The Count, reddening with disgust at the unfeeling avidity of these men, desired Nancy to say, that he could not see either of them to-day, but would send to their houses to-morrow.

In consequence of this promise, the men made their bows to Mrs. Robson, (who too well guessed the reason of this message,) and took their leaves.

When Thaddeus put the pictures of his mother and the Palatine,

* Incorrectly titled 'Chap. IX.' in the first edition.

with other trinkets, into his pocket, he could not forbear feeling something like indignation against the thoughtless meanness of the Miss Dundas's; who, since his entrance into their house, had never offered any farther liquidation of the large sum which they now stood indebted to him, than the trifling note which had been transmitted prior to his attendance, through the hands of Lady Tinemouth.

Whilst his necessities reproached them for this illiberal conduct, his proud heart recoiled at making a request to their charity; for he had gathered from the haughty demeanour of Miss Diana, that what he was entitled to demand, would be given not as a just remuneration for labour received, but as alms of humanity to an indigent emigrant.

"I would rather perish," cried he, putting on his hat, "than ask that woman for a shilling."

When the Count laid his treasure on the table of the considerate pawnbroker, he desired to have the value of the settings, and the pictures put into leather cases. Mr. Burnet having examined the gold of the miniatures, with the other trinkets, declared, on the word of an honest man, that he could not give more than fifteen pounds.

With difficulty, Thaddeus stifled as torturing a sigh as ever distended his breast, whilst he said,

"I will take it. I only implore you to be careful of the things! trifling as they are, circumstances with which they were connected, render them valuable to me."

"You may depend on me, Sir," replied the pawnbroker, presenting him the notes and acknowledgment.

When Thaddeus took them, Mr. Burnet's eye was caught by the ring which he wore on his finger.

"That ring seems curious! If you won't consider it impertinent, may I ask to look at it?"

The Count immediately pulled it off, and forcing a smile, replied, "I suppose it is of little intrinsic value. The setting is antique, but the painting is fine."

Burnet breathed on the diamonds. "If you were to sell it," returned he, "I don't think it would fetch more than three guineas. The diamonds are damaged, and the emeralds would be of little use, being out of fashion here; as for the miniature, it goes for nothing."

"Of course," said Thaddeus, putting it on again; "but I shall never part with it." Whilst he drew on his glove, Mr. Burnet asked him, whether the head were not intended for the King of Poland.

The Count, surprized, answered in the affirmative.

"I thought so," answered the man; "it is very like two or three prints which I had in my shop of that king. Indeed I believe I have them some where now: these matters are but a nine days wonder, and the sale is over."

His auditor did not clearly comprehend him, and he told him so.

"I meant nothing," continued he, "to the disparagement of the King of Poland; or of any other great personage, who is much the subject of conversation. I only intended to say, that every thing has its fashion. The ruin of Poland was the fashionable topic for a month after it happened; and now nobody minds it; it is extinct; it is forgotten."

Thaddeus, who felt he had all its miseries written in his bosom, with a clouded brow, bowed to the remarks of Mr. Burnet, and in silence quitted the shop.

Mrs. Robson was standing with a man in the passage, when he arrived at home. Thaddeus saw that the good woman had been weeping; and, from the angry countenance of her companion, easily divined the occasion of the debate. He asked Nancy, whom he found in the kitchen, what was the matter.

"Nothing, Sir," said she, "but Mr. White the baker; he has been twice this week to my grandmother, for four pounds which she owes him, and I know she cannot pay him yet."

"Call her in," returned the Count, glad that he at least possessed the power, by discharging his debt to her, to relieve so much worth from embarrassment.

Whilst Mrs. Robson obeyed the summons of her beloved lodger, he distinctly heard the incorrigible baker cry after her, "Remember, mistress, I will not leave this spot till I am paid."

"Here, my good Mrs. Robson," said Thaddeus, smiling kindly, and putting five guineas into her hand, "here is the money that you have expended for my poor friend; my gratitude will ever be your due."

Mrs. Robson received the gold with a low curtsey, and hastened out of the room elated with honest triumph, at the opportunity of so immediately satisfying the rapacity of her creditor.

Thaddeus, having entered his own room, laid the remainder of his money on the bills of the two claimants. It was unequal to the demands of either; yet, in some measure to be just to both, he determined on dividing it between them; and to promise the liquidation of the rest by degrees.

Surely he might hope, that even should the Miss Dundas's entirely forget his claims on them, his labour could in the course of time, make drawings sufficient to cover the residue of the debt! But he was not permitted to put this calculation to the trial.

When he called on the apothecary, and offered him five guineas, the man refused it with insolence, insisting on the whole. Unused to the language of compulsion and vulgarity, the Count quitted the shop, telling the man that he was at liberty to act as he thought fit; and, with no very serene countenance, he entered the undertaker's warehouse. This man was civil: to him, Thaddeus gave the sum, half of which the apothecary had rejected with so much derision. The politeness of the undertaker a little calmed the irritated temper of the Count; who returned home, pondering on the vile nature of that part of mankind, which can with indifference heap insult on distress.

Judging men by his own disposition, he had seldom given credence to the possibility of such conduct. He had been told of dastardly spirits; but never having seen them, and possessing no prototype within his own breast of what he heard, the repeated relation passed over his mind without leaving an impression. He had sprung into the world, filled with animating hopes of virtue and renown. He was virtuous; he became powerful, great, and renowned. Creation seemed paradise to his eyes: It was the task of adversity, to teach him a different lesson of mankind. Not less virtuous, not less great, his fortunes fell, he became poor; the perfidy, the hard-heartedness of man, made, and kept him friendless. When he wanted succour and consolation, he found the world peopled by a race too mean, even to bear the stamp of the devil.

Whilst Sobieski was employed next morning at his drawing, Mrs. Robson sent Nancy to say, that there were two strange-looking men below, who wanted to speak with him. Not doubting their being messengers from the apothecary, he desired that they might come up stairs. When they entered his room, the Count, with the politeness spontaneous to his ever-wakeful benevolence, rose. One of the men stepped forward, and, laying a slip of paper on the table, said, "I arrest you, Sir, at the suit of Mr. Jackson, the apothecary."

Thaddeus felt his cheek flush; but, suppressing every indignant emotion, he calmly asked the men, where they were going to take him?

"If you like," replied one of them, "you may be well enough lodged. I never heard a word against Clement's in Wych-street."

"Is that a prison?" inquired Thaddeus.

"No, not exactly that, Sir," answered the other man, laughing; "You seem to know little of the matter, which for a Frenchman is odd enough! But mayhap you have never a *lock-up-house* there? *Howsomever*, if you pay well, Mr. Clements will give you lodgings as long as you like. It is only *poor* rogues, who are *obligated* to go to Newgate; such *Gemmen* as you, can live as *ginteelly* in Wych-street as at their own houses."*

---

* Newgate Prison was one of London's oldest prisons, located at the corner of Newgate Street and Old Bailey, where the Central Criminal Court now stands. Notable for

There was such an air of derision about this fellow as he spoke and glanced round the room, that Thaddeus, sternly contracting his brows, deigned to take no farther notice of him; but, turning towards his more civil companion, said:

"Has this person informed me rightly? Am I going to a prison, or am I not? If I do not possess money to pay Mr. Jackson, I can have none to spend elsewhere."

"Then, you must go to Newgate;" answered the man, in as surly a tone, as his comrade's had been insolent.

"I'll run for a coach, Wilson," cried the other, opening the room-door.

"I will not pay for one," said Thaddeus, at once comprehending the sort of wretches into whose custody he had fallen; "follow me down stairs. I shall walk."

Mrs. Robson was in her shop as he passed to the street. She called out, "You will come home to dinner, Sir?"

"No," replied he; "but you shall hear from me before night."

The men, winking at each other, sullenly pursued his steps down the Lane. In the Strand, Thaddeus asked them which way he was to proceed.

"Straight on," cried one of them; "most folks find the road to a gaol easy enough."

Involved in thought, the Count walked forward, unmindful of the stare which the well-known occupation of his attendants attracted towards him. When he arrived at Somerset-house,* one of the men stepped up to him, and said, "We are now nearly opposite Wych-street. You had better take your mind again, and go there instead of Newgate. I don't much think you will like the debtor's hole."

Thaddeus, coldly thanking him, repeated his determination to be led to Newgate. But when he beheld the immense walls, within which he believed he should be immured for life, his feet seemed rooted to the ground: and when the massy gates were opened, and closed upon him, he felt as if suddenly deprived of the vital spring of existence. A mist spread over his eyes, his soul shuddered, and with difficulty he followed the men into the place where his commitment was to be ratified. Here,

---

its unsanitary and unsavoury conditions, the prison housed prisoners convicted of crimes ranging from petty theft to murder. Though Clement's of Wych Street is apparently fictional, there were many lock-up houses in the area, residences where debtors could be held for a fee and thus avoid Newgate.

* Somerset House, a grand building on the south side of the Strand, housed various government offices as well as the Royal Academy. Wych Street ran parallel to the Strand on its north side.

all the proud feelings of his nature, again rallied themselves round his heart.

The brutal questions of the people in office, re-echoed by taunts from the wretches who had brought him to the prison, were of a complexion so much beneath his answering, that he stood perfectly silent during the business; and when dismissed, without evincing any signs of discomposure, followed the turn-key to his cell.

One deal chair, a table, and a miserable bed, were all the furniture it contained. The floor was paved with flags; and the sides of the apartment daubed with discoloured plaster, part of which having been peeled off by the damp, exposed to view large spaces of the naked stones.

Before the turnkey withdrew, he asked Thaddeus whether he wanted any thing?

"Only a pen, ink, and paper."

The man held out his hand.

"I have no money," replied Sobieski.

"Then you get nothing here," answered the fellow, pulling the door after him.

Thaddeus threw himself on the chair, and in the bitterness of the moment, exclaimed, "Can these scoundrels be christians? Can they be men?" He cast his eyes round him with the wildness of despair: "All-powerful Heaven! Can it be possible, that for a few guineas, I am to be confined in this place during life? In these narrow bounds, am I to waste my youth, my existence? Even so; I cannot, I will not, degrade the spirit of Poland, by imploring assistance from any native of a land, in which avarice has choaked the feelings of humanity."

By the next morning, the first paroxysm of indignation having subsided, Thaddeus entertained a cooler and more reasonable opinion of his situation. He considered, that though he was a prisoner, it was in consequence of debts incurred in behalf of a friend, whose latter hours were rendered less wretched by such means. Feeling that, notwithstanding "*all that man could do unto him*,"* he had brought an approving conscience to lighten the glooms of a dungeon, he resumed his wonted serenity, and continued to distance the impertinent freedom of his gaolers, by a stern dignity, which extorted civility, and commanded their respect.

---

* A rewording of Psalm 118: 6: 'The LORD is on my side; I will not fear: what can man do unto me?'

CHAP. IX.*

Several days elapsed, without the inhabitants of Harley-street hearing any tidings of Thaddeus.

Miss Dundas never bestowed a thought on his absence, except when descanting on her favourite subject, the insolence of dependent people, she alleged his daring to withdraw himself as an instance. Miss Euphemia uttered all her complaints to Miss Beaufort; whom she accused, of not being satisfied with seducing the affections of Mr. Constantine, but she must also spirit him away, lest by remorse, he should be induced to renew his former devotion at the shrine of her tried constancy.

Mary found these secret conferences, very frequent and very teizing. She neither believed the Count's past devoirs to Euphemia, nor his present allegiance to herself. With unquiet feelings, she watched the slow decline of every succeeding day, hoping, that each knock at the door, would present either himself, or an apology for his absence.

In vain her reason urged the weakness and folly of giving way to the influence of a passion as violent as it was unforeseen. "It is not his personal graces;" murmured she, whilst her dewy eyes remained rivetted on the floor; "it is not them; they have not accomplished this effect on me! No; matchless as he is; though his countenance expresses godlike beauty, when illumined by the rare splendours of genius yet, my heart tells me, I would rather see all that perfection demolished, than lose one beam of those bright charities which first attracted my esteem. Yes, Constantine!" cried she, rising in agitation; "I could adore thy virtues, were they even in the bosom of deformity. It is them, that I love; it is them, that are thyself! It is thy noble, god-like soul, that so entirely fills my heart; and will, for ever!"

She recalled the hours, which in his society had glided so swiftly by, to pass in review before her. They came, and her tears redoubled. Neither his words, nor his looks, had been kinder to her, than to Miss Egerton or Lady Sara Roos. She remembered his wild action in the Park: it had transported her at the moment; it even now made her heart throb; but she ceased to believe it intended more, than an animated expression of gratitude.

* Incorrectly titled 'Chap. X.' in the first edition.

An adverse feeling seemed to have taken possession of her breast. In proportion to the vehemence of Miss Euphemia's reproaches, (who insisted on the passion of Thaddeus,) she the more doubted the evidence of those delightful emotions which had rushed over her soul, when she found her hand so fervently pressed in his.

Euphemia never made a secret of the *tendresse* she professed: and Miss Beaufort having been taught by her own heart, to read distinctly, the eyes of Lady Sara; the result of her observations, had long acted as a caustic on her peace: it robbed her cheeks of their bloom, and compelled her to number the lingering minutes of the night with sighs. But her deep and modest flame assumed no violence; retreated far from sight, it burnt the more intensely.

Instead of over-valuing the fine person of Thaddeus, the encomiums which it exacted from even the lips of prejudice, occasioned one source of her pain. She could not bear to think it probable, that the man whom she believed and knew to be gifted with every attribute of goodness and of heroism; might one day be induced to sacrifice the rich treasure of his mind, to a creature, who would select him from the rest, merely on account of his personal superiority.

Such was the train of Mary's meditations, when covering her face with her handkerchief, she exclaimed in a hurried and perturbed voice, "Ah! Why did I leave my quiet home, to expose myself to the vicissitudes of society? sequestered from the world, neither its pageants nor its mortifications could have reached me there. I have seen thee, matchless Constantine! Like a bright star, thou hast passed before my eyes! Like a being of a superior order! And, I never, never can debase my nature, to love another. Thy image shall follow me into solitude; shall consecrate my soul, to the practice of every virtue! I will emulate thy excellence, when, perhaps, thou hast forgotten that I exist."

The fit of despondence, which threatened to succeed this last abrupt reflection, was interrupted by the sudden entrance of Euphemia. Miss Beaufort hastily rose, and drew her ringlets over her eyes.

"O, Mary!" cried the little beauty, holding up her pretty hands, "What do you think has happened?"

"What?" demanded she in alarm, and hastening towards the door, "any thing to my aunt?"

"No, no:" answered Euphemia, catching her by the arm; "but could my injured heart feel satisfaction from revenge, I should now be happy. Punishment has overtaken the faithless Constantine."

Mary looked aghast; and, grasping the back of the chair to prevent herself from falling, breathlessly inquired what she meant?

"Oh! He is sent to prison!" cried Euphemia, not regarding the real agitation of her auditor, (so entirely was she occupied in appearing overwhelmed with distress herself,) and wringing her hands, she continued in a whimpering voice; "that frightful wretch, Mr. Lascelles, is just come in to dinner. You cannot think, with what devilish glee he told me, that about a week ago, as he was driving out of town, he saw Mr. Constantine with two bailiffs behind him, walking down Fleet-street! And, besides, I verily believe, he said that he had irons on."

"Father of Heaven!" ejaculated Mary with a cry of terror, at this *ad libitum** addition of Euphemia's, "What can he have done?"

"Bless my soul, Mary!" returned Euphemia, staring at her, as she sat pale and trembling in a chair; "Why, what frightens you so? Does not every body run in debt, without minding it?"

Miss Beaufort shook her head; and, looking distractedly about her, put her hand to her forehead. Euphemia, now quite alarmed, forced her to drink some water; and, whilst the horror-struck Mary, with ten thousand vague and hideous fancies racking her heart, leaned against the wall; the little beauty, unconscious what part of her narrative occasioned these emotions, thought to obliterate what she had said, by saying more; and determining not to be out-done in "*tender woe*,"[†] drew forth her handkerchief, and putting it to her eyes, resumed in a piteous tone.

"I am sure, I shall hate Lascelles all my life, because he did not stop the men, and inquire what jail they were taking him to! You know Mary, you and I might have visited him. It would have been delightful to have consoled his sad hours! We might have planned his escape."

"In irons!" ejaculated Mary, raising her tearless eyes to heaven.

Euphemia coloured at the agonized manner in which these words were re-iterated, and rather confusedly replied, "Not absolutely in irons. You know that is a metaphorical term for captivity."

"Then, he was not in irons?" cried Miss Beaufort, seizing her hand eagerly, "Tell me, for heaven's sake tell me, he was not in irons?"[‡]

"Why then," returned Euphemia, half angry at being obliged to contradict herself; "if you are such a fool, that you cannot understand poetical language, I must tell you he was not."

Mary heard no further; but even at the moment when a bright glow overspread her countenance, fell senseless back into the chair.

Euphemia flew immediately to the top of the stairs, and shrieking

---

* Latin, 'at one's pleasure', usually shortened to 'ad lib'.
† A common poetic phrase; see, for instance, 'a Mother's tender Woe', in James Thomson's *The Seasons: Summer* (line 569).
‡ Being handcuffed ('in irons') would publicly signal the severity of his crime.

violently, stood wringing her hands, till Diana and Lady Dundas, followed by several gentlemen, hastened out of the saloon, and demanded
what was the matter? as soon as Euphemia had pointed to Mary's
dressing-room door, she staggered, and sinking into the arms of Lord
Elesmere, fell into the most outrageous hysterics. The Marquis, who
had just dropt in, on his return from St. James's, became so possessed
with dread of the agitated lady's tearing his point-lace ruffles, that in
almost as trembling a state as herself, he gladly shuffled her into the
hands of her maid; and, scampering down stairs as if all bedlam were at
his heels, sprung into his *vis-a-vis*,* and drove off like lightning.

When Miss Beaufort opened her eyes, at the sight of such a crowd
she had nearly relapsed; but, trying to repel her confusion, she rose,
and supporting herself on the arm of Mrs. Dorothy's maid, thanked
the company for their attention, and desired to be assisted to her
chamber.

Meanwhile, Euphemia, who had been carried down into the saloon,
thought it time to raise her lily head, and utter a few incoherent words:
the instant they were breathed, Miss Dundas and Mr. Lascelles, in one
voice, demanded what was the matter?

"Has not Mary told you?" returned her sister, languidly opening her
eyes.

"No;" answered Lascelles, rubbing his hands with delighted curiosity; "Come, let us have it?"

Euphemia, pleased at this, and loving mystery with all her heart,
waved her hand solemnly, and in an awful tone, replied; "Then, it
passes not *my* lips."

"What Phemy!" cried he, "you want us to believe you have seen a
ghost? But you forget, they don't walk at mid-day."

"Believe what you like," returned she, with an air of consequential
contempt; "I am satisfied to keep the secret."

Miss Dundas burst into a provoking laugh; and calling her the
most incorrigible little idiot she had ever seen, encouraged Lascelles
to join in the ridicule. Determining to gratify his spleen, if he could
not satisfy his curiosity, this witless coxcomb continued the whole
day in Harley-street, for the mere pleasure of tormenting Euphemia.
From the dinner hour until twelve at night, neither his drowsy fancy,
nor wakeful malice, could find one other weapon of assault, than the
stale jokes attending *mysterious chambers*, *lovers incognito*; or the silly
addition of two Cupid-struck sweeps, hopping down the chimney, to
pay their addresses to the fair friends. Diana talked of Jupiter with his

---

* vis-à-vis, 'a light carriage for two persons sitting face to face' (*OED*).

thunder; and, patting her sister under the chin, added, "I cannot doubt that Mary is the favoured Semelé*: But, my dear, you have overacted your character! As confidant, a few tears were enough when your lady fainted." During these attacks, Euphemia reclined pompously on a sofa, and not deigning a reply, repelled them with much conceit and haughtiness.

Miss Beaufort remained above an hour alone in her chamber, before she ventured to go near her aunt. Hurt to the soul, that the idle folly of Euphemia should have aroused a terror which had completely unveiled to the eyes of that inconsiderate girl, the empire which Thaddeus held over her fate; Mary, overwhelmed with shame, and arraigning her easy credulity, threw herself on the bed.

Horror-struck at hearing he was led along the streets in chains, she could have no other idea, but that hurried into the commission of some dreadful deed, he was become amenable to the laws, and might suffer an ignominious death. These thoughts, having rushed at once on her heart, had deprived her of all self-command. In the conviction that he was a murderer, she felt as if her life, her honour, her soul were annihilated. And when, in consequence of her agonies, Euphemia confessed that she had in this last matter, told a falsehood, the tumult of her joy took refuge in insensibility.

Before Miss Beaufort quitted her room, various plans suggested themselves to relieve the unfortunate situation of Thaddeus. She found no hesitation in believing him poor; and perhaps rendered wretchedly so, by the burthen of that sick friend, whom she suspected, might be some near relation. At any rate, she resolved that another sun should not pass over her head, and shine on him in a prison. Having determined to pay all his debts herself; she next thought of how she might manage the affair without betraying the hand from whence the assistance came. Had her aunt been well enough to leave the house, she could not have scrupled at unfolding to her, the recent calamity of Mr. Constantine. But well aware that Mrs. Dorothy's maidenly nicety would be outraged at a young woman appearing the sole mover in such a business, she conceived herself obliged at present, entirely to withhold her confidence, and decide on prosecuting the whole transaction alone.

In consequence of these meditations, her spirits became less discomposed; and, turning towards Mrs. Dorothy Somerset's apartments, she found the good lady sipping her chocolate.

---

* In Greek mythology, the mortal Semelé fell in love with Jupiter; when she asked to see him in all his glory, his divine lightning and thunder killed her.

"What is this that I have just heard, my dear Mary? Williams tells me you have been ill?"

Miss Beaufort returned her aunt's gracious inquiry with an affectionate kiss; and, proceeding to inform her, that she had only been alarmed by an invention of Miss Euphemia's; she begged that the subject might drop, it being merely one out of the many schemes, which she believed that young lady had devised to give her torment.

"Ah!" replied Mrs. Dorothy, "I hope I shall be well enough to travel in the course of a few days! I can now walk with a stick; and, upon my word, I am heartily tired, both of Lady Dundas and her daughters."

Mary expressed similar sentiments with these; but, as the declaration passed her lips, a sigh almost buried the last word. Go when she would, she must leave Constantine behind; leave him, without an expectation of beholding him more; without a hope of penetrating that sensitive care, with which he had ever eluded any attempt to discover his birth or misfortunes. She sighed over this refinement on delicacy, and *"loved him dearer for his mystery."**

When the dawn broke next morning, it shone on Mary's yet unclosed eyes. Sleep could find no languid faculty in her head, whilst her heart was agitated with plans for the relief of Thaddeus. The idea of visiting the coffee-house to which she knew the Miss Dundases directed their letters, and of asking questions about a young and handsome man, made her timidity shrink.

"But," exclaimed she, "I am not going on an errand that need cause a blush on the cheek of prudery itself. I am going to impart some alleviation to the sufferings of the noblest creature that ever walked the earth!"

Perhaps, there are few persons, who, being auditors of this speech, would have decided quite so candidly on the superlative by which it was concluded? Mary herself, was not wholly divested of doubt about the issue of her conduct; but, conscious that her motive was pure, she descended to the breakfast-room with a quieter mind than countenance.

Never before having had an occasion to throw a false gloss on her actions, she scarcely looked up during breakfast. When the cloth was removed, she rose suddenly from her chair, and turning to Mrs. Dorothy, who sat at the other end of the parlour with her foot on a stool, she said, "Good bye, aunt. I am going to make some particular

---

* Perhaps a reference to Robert Southey's 1801 *Thalaba the Destroyer*, in which Thalaba treasures the Green Bird that 'Woke wonder while he gazed / And made her dearer for her mystery' (11. 285–6).

calls, but I shall be back in a few hours." Luckily, no one observed
her blushing face whilst she spoke, nor the manner in which she shook
hands with the old lady, and hurried out of the room.

Breathless with confusion, she could scarcely stand when she arrived
in her own chamber; but feeling that no time could be lost, she tied on
a muslin cloak, covered her head with a large summer bonnet, and put
a long shawl with a veil into her pocket. She hesitated a moment at her
chamber-door; her eyes filled with tears drawn from her heart, by that
keen spirit of truth which had ever been the guardian of her conduct.
Looking up to heaven, she sunk down on her knees, and exclaimed
with impetuosity, "Father of Mercy! it is thou only that knowest my
heart! Direct me, I beseech thee! Let me not commit any thing unworthy of myself, or of the unhappy Constantine – for whom I would
sacrifice my life, but not my duty to thee!"

Re-assured by the confidence which this simple act of devotion had
inspired, she took her parasol, and descended the stairs. The porter
was alone in the hall. She inquired for her servant.

"He is not returned, Madam."

Miss Beaufort, having foreseen the necessity of getting rid of all
attendants, had sent her footman on an errand as far as Cheapside.

"It is of no consequence," returned she to the porter, who was just
going to propose one of Lady Dundas's men; "I cannot meet with any
thing disagreeable at this time of day, so I shall walk alone."

The man opened the door; and Mary, with a bounding heart, has-
tened down the street, across the square, and at the bottom of Orchard
Street, stepped into a hackney coach, which she ordered to drive to
Slaughter's coffee-house, St. Martin's-lane.

She drew up the glasses; then taking the shawl and veil, with trembling hands, covered her graceful figure; hoping, that the metamorphosis might make her pass very well for a servant-maid. With difficulty
she could individualize the many thoughts which agitated her anxious
mind whilst the carriage rolled along; and when it drew up at the
coffee-house, she involuntarily retreated back into the corner. The
coach door was opened.

"Will you alight, Ma'am?"

"No, call a waiter."

A waiter immediately appeared; and Miss Beaufort, in a tolerably
collected voice, inquired if Mr. Constantine lived there?

"No, Ma'am."

A cold dew stood on Mary's forehead; but taking courage from
a latent and last hope, she added, "I know that he has had letters
directed to this place."

"O! I beg your pardon, Ma'am!" returned the man, evidently recollecting himself; "That is true, I remember a person of that name has received letters from hence, but they were always fetched away by a little girl."

"And do you not know where he lives?"

"No, Ma'am;" answered he, "yet some one else may; I will inquire."

Miss Beaufort bowed her head in token of acknowledgment, and sat shivering with suspense, till he returned followed by another man.

"This person, Ma'am," resumed he, "says he can tell you."

"Thank you, thank you!" cried Mary; then blushing at her eagerness, she stopped, and drew back into the carriage.

"I cannot for certain;" said the man, "but I know the girl very well by sight, who comes for the letters; and I have often seen her standing at the door of a chandler's shop, a good way down the lane. I think it is No. 5, or 6. I sent a woman there, who came after the same gentleman, about a fortnight ago. I dare say he lives there."

Mary's expectations sunk again, when she found that she had nothing but a *dare say* to depend on; and, giving half a crown to each of her informers, she desired the coachman to drive as they would direct him.

Whilst the carriage drove down the lane, with a heart full of fears she looked from side to side, almost believing that she would know by intuition, the house which had contained Constantine. When the man checked his horses, and her eyes fell on the little mean dwelling of Mrs. Robson, she smothered a deep sigh.

"Can this be the house in which Constantine has lived? How comfortless! – And should it not," thought she, as the man got off the box to enquire, "where shall I go for information?"

The appearance of Mrs. Robson, and her immediate affirmative to the question, "Are these Mr. Constantine's lodgings?" at once dispelled this last anxiety. Encouraged by the motherly expression of the good woman's manner, Mary begged leave to alight. Mrs. Robson readily offered her arm; and, with many apologies for the disordered state of the house, led her up stairs to the room which had been the Count's home.

Mary trembled violently; but seeing that every thing depended on self-command, with apparent tranquillity, she received the chair that was presented to her, and turning her eyes from the books and drawings which told her so truly in whose apartment she was, she desired Mrs. Robson, who continued standing, to be seated. The good woman obeyed: after some trepidation, Miss Beaufort asked where Mr. Constantine was? Mrs. Robson coloured, and looking at her questioner for some time, as if doubting what to say, burst into tears.

Mary's ready eyes felt much inclined to flow in concert; but subduing the strong emotions which shook her breast, she added, "I do not come here out of an impertinent curiosity. I have heard of the misfortunes of Mr. Constantine. I am well known to his friends."

"Dear lady!" cried the good woman, grasping at any prospect of succour to her benefactor; "If he has friends, who ever they are, tell them, he is the noblest, most humane gentleman in the world. Tell them, he has saved me and mine, from the deepest want; and now he is sent to prison, because he cannot pay the cruel doctor that attended the poor dead General!"

"What, is his friend dead?" ejaculated Mary, unable to restrain the tears which now streamed over her face.

"Yes," replied Mrs. Robson; "Poor old gentleman! he is dead sure enough; and, Heaven knows, many has been the dreary hours the dear young man has watched by his pillow! He died in that room."

Mary's swimming eyes would not allow her to discern objects through the open door of that apartment within which the heart of Thaddeus had undergone such variety of misery. Feeling an irresistible wish to know whether the deceased were any relation of Constantine's, she paused a moment to compose the agitation that might have betrayed her, and then asked.

"I thought ma'am," replied Mrs. Robson, "that you said you knew his friends?"

"Only his English ones," returned Mary, a little confused at the suspicion this answer implied; "I had imagined that this old gentleman might have been his father, or an uncle, or – "

"O no," interrupted Mrs. Robson, sorrowfully; "he has neither father, mother, nor uncle, in the wide world. He once told me they were all dead, and that he saw them die. Alas! Sweet soul! What a power of griefs he must have seen in his young life! But Heaven will favour him at last; for though he is in misfortune himself, he has been a blessing to the widow and the orphan!"

"Do you know the amount of his debts?" asked Mary.

"Only thirty pounds," returned Mrs. Robson; "and for that, they took him out of this room a week ago; and hurried him away without letting me know a word of the matter. I believe, to this hour, I should not have known where he was, if that brute, Mr. Jackson, had not come to demand all that Mr. Constantine left in my care. But I would not let him have it: I told the man, if my lodger had filled my house with bags of gold, *he* should not touch a shilling; and then the ill-natured wretch abused me, and told me Mr. Constantine was in Newgate."

"In Newgate!"

"Yes, Madam. I immediately ran there, and found him more able to comfort me, than I was able to speak to him."

"Then be at rest, my good woman," returned Miss Beaufort, rising from her chair; "when you next hear of Mr. Constantine, he shall be at liberty. He has friends, who will not sleep till he is out of prison."

"May heaven bless you and them, dear lady!" cried Mrs. Robson, weeping with joy, "for they will release the most generous heart alive."

Mary cast a wishful look on the drawings which stood on a bureau; then withdrawing her eyes with a deep sigh, she descended the stairs. At the street-door, she took Mrs. Robson's hand, and not relinquishing it until she was seated in the coach, pressed it warmly, and leaving within it a purse of twenty guineas, ordered the man to return whence he came.

Now that the temerity of going herself to learn the particulars of Mr. Constantine's fate had been atchieved, determined as she was not to close her eyes whilst the man whom she valued above her life remained a prisoner and in sorrow, she thought it best to consult with Mrs. Dorothy respecting the speediest means of compassing his emancipation.

In Oxford-road, she desired the man to proceed to Harley-street. She had alighted at Lady Dundas's door, paid the coach, and stepped into the hall, before she perceived that a travelling carriage belonging to her guardian, had driven away to afford room for her humble equipage.

"Is Sir Robert Somerset come to town?" she hastily enquired of the porter.

"No, Madam; but Mr. Somerset has just arrived."

The next moment Miss Beaufort was in the drawing-room, and clasped within the arms of her cousin.

"Dear Mary!" – "Dear Pembroke!" were the first words which passed between these two affectionate friends.

Mrs. Dorothy, who doated on her nephew, taking his hand fondly, as he seated himself between her and his cousin, said, in a congratulatory voice, "Mary, our dear boy has come to town purposely to take us down."

"Yes, indeed," rejoined he; "my father is moped to death for want of you both. You know that I am a sad run-about. Lord Arun and Mr. Loftus have been gone these ten days to his lordship's aunt's, in Bedfordshire; and Sir Robert is so completely weary of solitude, that he has commanded me," bowing to the other ladies, "to run off with all the fair inhabitants of this house, sooner than leave you behind."

"I shall be happy at another opportunity to visit Somerset Castle," returned Lady Dundas; "but I am constrained to spend this summer in Dumbartonshire: I have not yet seen the estate that my poor dear Sir Hector bought of the Duke of Dumfries."

Pembroke offered no attempt to shake this resolution. In the two or three morning calls which he had made with Sir Robert Somerset on the rich widow, he had seen sufficient to regard her arrogant vulgarity with disgust; and for her daughters, they were of too common a stamp, to occupy his mind any deeper than with a magic lantern impression of a tall woman with bold eyes, and the prettiest little blue-eyed fairy he had ever beheld.

After half an hour's conversation with this family groupe, Miss Beaufort sunk again into abstraction. During the first month of Mary's acquaintance with Thaddeus, she had mentioned, in her correspondence with Pembroke, having met with a very interesting and accomplished emigrant, in the quality of a tutor at Lady Dundas's. But her cousin, in his replies, beginning to banter her on plea of pity being allied to love, she gradually dropped all mention of his name, as she too truly found, by what insensible degrees the union had taken place within her own breast. She remembered these particulars, whilst a new method of attaining the desired end, suggested itself; and determining, (however extraordinary her conduct might seem,) to rest on the rectitude of her motives, she resolved, that as a man must be the properest person to transact such a business with propriety, she would engage Pembroke for her agent, without troubling Mrs. Dorothy about the affair.

So deeply was she absorbed in these reflections, that Somerset observing her vacant eye fixed on the opposite wall, took her hand, with an arch smile, and exclaimed,

"Mary! What is the matter? I hope, Lady Dundas, you have not suffered any one to run away with her heart? You know that I am her cousin, and it is my unalienable right."

Lady Dundas replied, that young ladies best knew their own secrets.

"That may be, Madam," rejoined he, "but I won't allow Miss Beaufort to know any thing that she does not transfer to me. Is not that true, Mary?"

"Yes," whispered she, colouring; "and the sooner you afford me an opportunity to interest you in one, the more I shall feel obliged to you."

Pembroke pressed her hand in token of assent; and a desultory conversation continuing for another half hour, Mary, who dreaded the wasting of one minute in a day, so momentous to her peace, sat uneasily, till her aunt proposed retiring to dress for dinner, and requested Pembroke to assist her up stairs.

When he returned to the drawing-room, to his extreme satisfaction, he found all the party separated, excepting Miss Beaufort, who was standing by one of the windows, evidently lost in thought. He approached her, and taking her hand, led her back to the sofa she had quitted.

"Come, my dear cousin," said he, in an affectionate voice, "how can I oblige you?"

Mary struggled with her confusion. Had she less loved Thaddeus, she found she could with greater ease have related the interest which she took in his fate. She tried to speak distinctly, and she accomplished it; although her burning cheek and downcast look, told to the fixed eye of Pembroke, what she vainly attempted to conceal.

"You can, indeed, oblige me! You must remember a Mr. Constantine! I once mentioned him to you in my letters."

"I do, Mary. You thought him amiable!"

"He was the intimate friend of Lady Tinemouth," returned she, striving to look up, but the piercing expression which she met from the eyes of Somerset, beating hers down again, covered her face and neck with deeper blushes: she panted for breath.

"Dear Mary!" said Pembroke, pitying her embarrassment, whilst he dreaded that her gentle heart had indeed become the victim of some accomplished and insidious foreigner, "Rely on me, my beloved cousin: consider me as a brother. If you have entangled yourself – "

Miss Beaufort guessed what he would say; and, interrupting him, added, with a more assured air, "No, Pembroke, I have no entanglements. I am going to ask your friendly assistance in behalf of a brave and unfortunate Polander." Pembroke reddened, and she went on. "Mr. Constantine is a gentleman. Lady Tinemouth tells me, he has been a soldier, and that he lost all his possessions in the ruin of his country. Her ladyship introduced him here: I have seen him often, and I know him to be worthy the esteem of every honourable heart. He is now in prison, in Newgate, for a debt of thirty pounds, and I ask you to go and release him? That is my request, my secret; and I confide in your discretion, that you will keep it, even from him."

"Dear, generous, lovely Mary!" cried Pembroke, kissing her hand, "it is thus that you always act! Possessed of all the softness of thy sex, dearest girl," added he still more affectionately, "nature has not alloyed it with one particle of weakness!"

Mary smiled and sighed: If to love tenderly, to be devoted, life and soul to one being, whom she considered as the most perfect work of creation, be weakness? Mary felt that she was the weakest of the weak; and with a languid despondence at her heart, was opening her lips to give some directions to her cousin, when the attentions of both were arrested by a shrill noise of speakers talking above stairs. Before the cousins had time to make an observation, the disputants descended towards the drawing-room with a violent clamour, and bursting open the door, presented the enraged figure of Lady Dundas, followed by Diana, who with a no less swollen countenance, was scolding vociferously, and dragging forward the weeping Euphemia.

"Gracious Heaven!" exclaimed Somerset, amazed at so extraordinary a scene, "What is the matter?"

Lady Dundas lifted up her clenched hand in a passion. "A jade! a hussy!" cried she, incapable to articulate more.

Miss Dundas, still grasping the hands of her struggling sister, broke out next, and turning furiously towards Mary, exclaimed, "You see, Madam, what disgrace your ridiculous conduct to that vagabond foreigner has brought on our family! This bad girl has followed your example, and done worse; she has fallen in love with him!"

Mary, pale and trembling at so rude an accusation, was unable to speak. Lost in wonder, and incensed at his cousin's goodness having been the dupe of imposition, Pembroke stood silent whilst Lady Dundas took up the subject.

"Ay," cried she, shaking her daughter by the shoulder, "You little minx! if your sister had not picked up these abominable verses which you chose to write on the absence of this beggarly fellow, I suppose you would have finished the business by running off with him? But you shall go down to Scotland, and be locked up for months. I won't have Sir Hector Dundas's family disgraced by a daughter of mine."

"For pity's sake, Lady Dundas," said Pembroke, stepping between her vulgar ladyship and the trembling Euphemia, "do compose yourself. I dare say your daughter is pardonable. In these cases, the fault in general lies with our sex. We are the seducers."

Mary felt obliged to re-seat herself; and with pale attention, she listened to the reply of the frightened Euphemia; who, half assured that her whim of creating a mutual passion in the breast of Thaddeus was no longer tenable, without either shame or remorse exclaimed, "Indeed Mr. Somerset, you are right. I never should have thought of Mr. Constantine, if he had not teized me every time he came with his violent love."

Mary rose hastily from her chair. Though Euphemia coloured at the suddenness of this motion, and the immediate flash she met from her eye, she went on; "I know Miss Beaufort will deny it, because she thinks he is in love with her; but indeed, indeed, he has sworn a thousand times on his knees, that he was a Russian nobleman in disguise, and adored me above every one else in the world."

"Scoundrel!" cried Pembroke, inflamed with indignation at this double conduct. Afraid to read in the expressive countenance of Mary her shame and horror at this discovery, he turned his eyes on her with trepidation; when, to his surprise, he beheld her standing perfectly unmoved, by the side of the sofa from whence she had arisen. She advanced with a calm step towards Euphemia; and, taking hold of the hand which concealed her face whilst uttering this last falsehood, she drew it away; and regarding her with a serene but penetrating look, "Euphemia!" said she, "you know well, that you are slandering an innocent and an unfortunate man. You know, that never in his life did he give you the slightest reason to suppose that he was attached to you! And as for myself, I can also clear him of making professions to me. – Upon the honour of my word, I declare," added she, addressing herself to the whole groupe, "that he never breathed a sentence to me, beyond mere respect. By this last deviation of Euphemia from truth, you may form an estimate how far the rest she has alleged deserves credit."

The young lady burst into a vehement passion of tears: "I will not be brow-beat and insulted, Miss Beaufort!" cried she, taking refuge in noise, since right had deserted her; "You know you would fight his battles through thick and thin! else you would not have fallen into fits yesterday, when I told you he was sent to jail."

This last assault struck Mary motionless; and Lady Dundas lifting up her hands, exclaimed, "Good Lord, keep me from the forward misses of these times! – As for you, Miss Euphemia," added she, seizing her daughter by the arm, "you shall leave town to-morrow morning. I will have no more tutoring and falling in love in my house; and for you, Miss Beaufort," turning to Mary, who having recovered herself, stood at a little distance, "I shall take care to warn Mrs. Dorothy Somerset to keep an eye over your conduct."

"Madam," replied she, indignantly, "I shall never do any thing which can dishonour either my family or myself; and of that, Mrs. Dorothy Somerset is too well assured, to doubt, for an instant, even should calumny be as busy with me as it has been injurious to Mr. Constantine."

Mary walked towards the door. When she passed Mr. Somerset, who stood bewildered, and frowning beside Miss Dundas, she said, in a collected and decisive voice, "Pembroke, I shall leave the room, but remember I do not release you from your engagement."

Staggered by the open firmness of her manner, he looked after her as she withdrew, and was almost inclined to believe that she possessed the right side of the argument. Malice did not allow him to think so long. The moment the door closed on Miss Beaufort, both the sisters fell on him pell-mell; and the prejudiced illiberality of the one, supported by the ready falsehoods of the other, soon dislodged all favourable impressions from the mind of Somerset, and filled him anew with displeasure.

In the midst of Diana's third harangue, Lady Dundas having ordered Euphemia to be taken to her chamber, Mr. Somerset was left alone more incensed than ever against Thaddeus, whom he now considered in the light of an adventurer, concealing his poverty, and perhaps his crimes, beneath a garb of lies. That such a character could, by means of his fine person, and a few meretricious talents, work himself into the confidence of Mary Beaufort, pierced her cousin to the soul; and as he mounted the stairs with an intent to seek her in her dressing-room, he could not forbear thinking, what satisfaction it would afford him, to hear that Constantine was hanged.*

When he opened the room door, he found Miss Beaufort with his aunt. The instant he appeared, the ever-benevolent face of Mrs. Dorothy contracted into a frown.

"Nephew!" cried she, "I shall not take it well of you, if you give stronger credence to the passionate and vulgar assertions of Lady Dundas and her daughters, than you choose to bestow on the tried veracity of your cousin, Mary?"

Pembroke felt that if his countenance had been a faithful transcript of his mind, Miss Beaufort did not err in supposing that he believed the foreigner to be a villain. Feeling it impossible to relinquish his reason, into what he now denominated the partial hands of his aunt and cousin, he persisted in his opinion to both the ladies, that their unsuspicious natures had been rendered subservient to knavery and artifice.

"I would not, willingly, my dear Madam," said he, addressing Mrs. Dorothy, "think so meanly of your sex, as to imagine that an atrocity can exist in the female heart, which could give birth to cruel and unprovoked calumnies against an innocent man. I cannot suspect the Miss Dundases of such needless guilt; particularly poor Euphemia, whom I

---

* Softened in the second edition to 'he almost resolved to refuse obeying her commands' (3. 235).

pity. Lady Dundas forced me to read her verses; and they were too full of love and regret for this adventurer, to come from the same breast which could wantonly blacken his character. Such wicked inconsistencies in so young a woman, are not half so probable as that you, my dear aunt and cousin, have both been deceived."

"Well nephew," returned the old Lady, "you are very peremptory. Methinks a little more mercy of opinion would better become your youth! *I* knew nothing of this unhappy man's present distress, till Miss Beaufort mentioned it to me; but before she breathed a word in his favour, I had conceived a very high respect for his merits: from the first hour in which I saw him, I gathered by his deportment and conversation, that they were far above his fortunes. I thought so; I still think so; and, notwithstanding all that the Dundases may chuse to fabricate, I am determined to believe the assertions of an honest countenance."

Pembroke smiled, whilst he compelled his aunt's reluctant hand into his, and said, "I see, my dear Madam, that you are bigoted to the idol of your own fancy! I do not in the least doubt this Mr. Constantine's enchantments; but you must pardon me, if I keep my senses at liberty. I shall think of him, as I could almost swear he deserves, although I am aware I hazard your affection by my firmness." He then turned to Mary, who, with a swelling and distressed heart, was standing by the chimney; "Forgive me, my dearest cousin," continued he, addressing her in a softened voice; "that I feel myself forced to appear harsh? It is the first time I ever dissented from you; it is the first time, Mary, I ever thought you prejudiced!"

Mary drew the back of her hand over her glistening eyes. All the tender affections of Pembroke's bosom smote him at once; and throwing his arms around his cousin's waist, he strained her to his breast, and added, "Ah! why, dear girl, must I love you better for thus giving me pain? Every way, my darling Mary is more estimable. Even now, whilst I oppose you, I feel, that though your goodness is abused, it has been cheated into error by the affectation of honourable calamities!"

Mary felt, "that if the prudence of reserve and decorum dictates silence in some circumstances, in others, a prudence of an higher order would justify her in declaring her thoughts."* Accordingly, she withdrew from the clasping arms of Mr. Somerset; and whilst her beautiful figure seemed to dilate into more than its usual dignity, she mildly replied,

---

* Edmund Burke, *Reflections on the Revolution in France* (London: J. Dodsley, 1790): 'If the prudence of reserve and decorum dictates silence in some circumstances, in others prudence of an higher order may justify us in speaking our thoughts' (p. 10).

"Think what you please, Pembroke; I shall not contend with you: Mr. Constantine is of a nature not to be hidden by obscurity; his character will defend itself: and all that I have to add is this, I do not release you from your promise. Could a woman transact the affair with propriety, I should not keep you to so disagreeable an office; but I have passed my word to myself, that I will neither '*slumber* nor *sleep*,'* till he is out of prison." She put a pocket-book into Pembroke's hand, and added, "Take that, my dear cousin; and without suffering a syllable to transpire, by which he may suspect who served him, accomplish what I have desired."

"I will obey you, Mary," returned he, looking gravely; "but I am sorry that such rare enthusiasm was not awakened by a worthier object. When you see me again, I hope I shall be enabled to say, that your ill-placed generosity is satisfied."

"Fie, nephew, fie!" cried Mrs. Dorothy, "I could not have supposed you capable of conferring a favour so ungraciously."

Mr. Somerset, pained at what he nominated the obstinate infatuation of Miss Beaufort; and, if possible, more chagrined, by what he considered the blind and absurd encouragement of his aunt, lost the whole of her last reprimand, in his hurry to quit the room.

Disturbed, displeased, and anxious, he stepped into a hackney-coach. Ordering it to drive to Newgate, he determined to go through the business, without exposing himself to an interview with a man whom he must now condemn as an artful and unprincipled villain.

END OF THE THIRD VOLUME.

---

* Psalm 121: 4: 'Behold, he that keepeth Israel shall neither slumber nor sleep'.

VOLUME IV.

CHAP. I.

The first week of the Count's confinement was rendered less intolerable, by the daily visits of Mrs. Robson; who, having brought his drawing materials, enabled him, through the means of the print-seller, to purchase some civility from the brutal and hardened people who were his gaolers. After the good woman had performed her diurnal kindness, Thaddeus used to turn to the sad circumference of his miserable apartment to seek amusement. When his pencil had accomplished its task, it wearied him: When he took up a book, having read it before, it failed to engage him. He possessed nothing to beguile the tedious day, and more tedious night. His spirit was in solitude; in the most dismal solitude; banished and shut out from all that could render life desirable.

The elasticity and enterprise of soul, inherent in youth, renders no calamity so difficult to be borne, as is the fettering of its best years and most active virtues, within the walls of a prison. Thaddeus felt this benumbing conviction in every pulse of his ardent and energetic heart. He retraced all that he had been. He looked on what he was. Though he had reaped glory when a boy, his "*noon of manhood*,"* his evening sun, was to waste its light, and set, in captivity.

At short and distant intervals, such melancholy reveries gave place to the pitying image of Mary Beaufort. It sometimes visited him in the day, it always was his companion during night. He courted her lovely idea, as a spell that for a while stole him from painful reflections. With an entranced heart, he recalled every lineament of her beautiful face, every dissolving note of that voice, which had hurried him into the rashness of touching her hand. One moment, he pressed her gold chain closer to his heart, almost believing what Lady Tinemouth

---

* See Richard Glover's once-popular poem *London: or The Progress of Commerce* (London: T. Cooper, 1739), which refers to William of Orange's 'glorious noon of manhood'; and Thomas Campbell's *Pleasures of Hope*: 'Shame to the coward thought that e'er betray'd / The noon of manhood to a myrtle shade!' (II. 53–4). Though 'the noon of manhood' is often associated with the riddle of Oedipus, this usage seems to date from later in the nineteenth century.

had insinuated; the next, he would sigh over his credulity, and return with despondent, though equally intense feeling, to her bewitching recollection.

The more he pondered on the purity of her manners, the elevated principles to which he could trace her actions, and, above all, the benevolent confidence with which she had ever treated him, (a man contemned by one part of her acquaintance, and merely received on trust by the remainder,) the more he found reasons to admire her character and adore herself. When he drew a comparison between Miss Beaufort, and women of the same quality, whom he had seen in England and in other countries, he contemplated with delighted wonder that spotless mind, which having passed through the various dangers annexed to wealth and fashion, still bore itself uncontaminated. She was beautiful, and she did not regard it; she was accomplished, but she did not attempt a display: what she had acquired from education, the graces had so incorporated with her native intelligence, that the whole perfection of her character seemed to have been stamped at once by the beneficent hand of Providence.

Thaddeus never felt her numberless attractions so fascinating, as when witnessing the generous eagerness with which, forgetful of her own almost unparalleled talents, she pointed out merit, and dispensed applause to the deserving. Mary's nature was composed entirely of the gentlest elements, unalloyed by indiscrimination or insipidity. Whilst the Count saw that the urbanity of her disposition made her polite-ness universal, he perceived that neither rank, riches, nor splendour, could extract from her bosom, one spark of that lambent flame, which streamed from her heart like fire to the sun, towards the united glory of genius and goodness.

He dwelt on this lovely, unsophisticated character, with an enthusi-asm bordering on idolatry. He recollected that she had been educated by the mother of Pembroke Somerset; and, turning from the double remembrance, with a sigh fraught with all the bitterness and sweet-ness of love, he acknowledged, how much wisdom (which includes virtue) gives spirit and immortality to beauty; "Yes," cried he, "it is the fragrance of the flower, which lives after the bloom of its leaves are withered."

From the like seducing day-dreams, Thaddeus was one evening awakened by the entrance of the jailer into his cell. The man presented a sealed paper, and told him that he had brought it from a stranger, who, having paid the debts for which he was confined, had immedi-ately withdrawn, desiring that the packet might be delivered to Mr. Constantine.

Scarcely crediting this information, Thaddeus hastily opened the letter, hoping that it might throw some light on his benefactor: a blank cover, inclosing notes to the amount of fifty pounds, presented itself. Surprised at this, he told the man to leave him, who, without much ceremony, was staring at the money over his shoulder; and sitting down, he tried to think who could have acted so generously, and yet be so careful to hide their bounty.

He had seen sufficient proofs of a heedless want of charity in Miss Euphemia Dundas, to lead him to suppose that she could not be so munificent and solicitous for concealment. Besides, how could she have learnt his situation? He thought it was impossible: and that impossibility compelled an erratic hope of his present liberty having sprung from the friendship of Miss Beaufort, to pass by him with a painful swiftness.

"Gracious Heaven!" cried he, starting from his chair, "It is the indefatigable spirit of Lady Sara Roos, that I recognise in this deed! The generous, but unhappy interest which she yet takes in my fate, has discovered my last misfortune, and thus seeks to relieve me!"

The moment he had conceived this supposition, he believed it; and, taking up a pen, with a grateful, though disturbed soul, he addressed to her ladyship the following guarded note:

"To the Right Honourable Lady Sara Roos.

"An unfortunate exile, who feels himself already overpowered by the sense of not having deserved the notice which Lady Sara Roos has hitherto deigned to take of his misfortunes, was this morning liberated from prison in a manner so generous and delicate, that he can affix the act to no other than the noble heart of her ladyship.

"The object of this bounty, bending under the weight of obligations which he cannot repay, begs permission to re-inclose the bills which Lady Sara's agent transmitted to him; but, as the deed which procures his freedom cannot be recalled, he accepts, with the most grateful emotions, that new instance of her ladyship's goodness.

"Newgate."

Thaddeus dispatched the letter by a porter, and was preparing another to acquaint Mrs. Robson of his release, when the good woman made her appearance. She hastened up to him with an animated countenance, and exclaimed before he had time to speak, "Dear Sir! I have seen a dear, sweet lady, who has promised not to sleep till you are out of this horrid place!"

The suspicions of the Count, that his benefactress was indeed Lady

Sara Roos, were now confirmed: seating his landlady in the only chair which furnished the apartment; to satisfy her sensitive decorum he took his station on the table, and then said, "the lady has already fulfilled her engagement; I am free; and only wait for an answer to my acknowledgements, before I quit the prison."

At this assurance, the delighted Mrs. Robson, crying and laughing by turns, did not cease her ejaculations of joy, till the messenger, who had taken the letter to St. James's Place, returned with a reply written by her ladyship, and evidently blotted with tears. Thaddeus took out the re-inclosed bills with a flushed cheek, and read as follows:

"I cannot be mistaken in recognising the proud and high-soul'd Constantine, in the writer of the lines which I hold in my hand. Could any thing have imparted to me more comfort, than your generous belief that there is indeed some virtue left in my wretched and repentant heart, it would arise from the consciousness of having been the happy person who has succoured you in your distress. But no; that enjoyment was beyond my deserving. The bliss of being the lightener of your sorrows, was reserved by heaven for a less criminal creature. I did not even know that you were in prison. Since our dreadful parting, I have never dared to inquire after you; and, much as it might console me to serve one so truly valued, I will not insult your nice honour by offering any farther instance of my friendship, than what will evince my soul's gratitude to your prayers, and my acquiescence with the commands of duty.

"My husband is here, without perceiving the ravages which misery and remorse have made in my unhappy heart. Time, perhaps, may render me less unworthy of his tenderness: at present I detest myself.

"I return the bills; you may safely use them, for they never were mine.

S. R."

The generous heart of Thaddeus bled over every line of this letter. He felt that it bore a stamp of truth, which did not leave him a moment in doubt that he owed his release to some other hand. Whilst he folded it up, his suspicions next lighted on Lady Tinemouth. He had received one short letter from her ladyship since her departure, mentioning Maria's staying in town to meet Mr. Montresor; Miss Beaufort's detention on account of Mrs. Dorothy's accident; and closing with the intelligence of her own safe arrival at the Wold. The idea struck him, that as he had delayed answering this letter in consequence of his late embarrassment, she had made some inquiries regarding him, which having led to a discovery of his situation, most probably Miss Egerton had visited Mrs. Robson by the commands of the Countess, and, finding the information true, had proceeded these lengths to obtain his release.

According to these suppositions, he questioned his landlady about the appearance of the lady whom she had seen. Mrs. Robson replied, "She was indifferent tall, but so wrapped up that I could neither see her face nor figure, though I am certain, from the softness of her voice, she must be both young and handsome. Sweet creature! I am sure she wept two or three times. Besides, she is the most charitable soul alive, next to you, Sir, for she gave me a purse with nineteen guineas; and she told me, she knew your honour's English friends."

This narration, substantiating his hope of Lady Tinemouth being his benefactress, that the kind Maria was her agent; and the gentleman who defrayed the debt, Mr. Montresor; he found himself easier under an obligation, which a mysterious liberation would have doubled. He knew the Countess's maternal love for him. To reject her present benefaction, would be to sacrifice gratitude on the altar of morbid delicacy. He felt, that "nothing can be great, that it is great to despise;"* and rather than pain Lady Tinemouth, by relinquishing her bounty, he smothered in his breast the embers of a haughty repulsion, which having burst forth in the first hour of his misfortunes, was ever ready to consume any wish that might engender the weight of obligation.

Thaddeus quitted his cell; and, ordering that a coach might be brought to the great gate of Newgate, he was obeyed; and, with thankfulness to heaven, for again being permitted to taste the wholesome breeze of a free atmosphere, he handed his delighted landlady into the vehicle.

So true it is, that advantages are only appreciated by comparison; when the Count re-entered his humble apartment in St. Martin's-lane, he considered it a palace of luxury, opposed to the dungeon he had left.

"Ah!" cried Mrs. Robson, pointing to a chair, "there is the very seat in which that dear lady sat! Sweet creature! If I had known that I durst believe all that she promised, I would have fallen on my knees, and kissed her feet, for bringing back your dear self!"

"I thank you, my good madam," returned Thaddeus, smiling with a brimming eye at such ardent demonstration of affection; "but where is little Nancy, that I may shake hands with her?"

The child welcomed the Count with those animated expressions of joy, inseparable from a good and inexperienced heart. It being late, he retired at an early hour to his pillow, where he found that repose,

---

* Longinus, *On the Sublime*, 7.1.

which had been sought in vain, within the gloomy and (he supposed) eternal walls of a prison.

In the morning, he was awakened by the light footsteps of his pretty waiting-maid entering the front room. His chamber door being open, he asked her what was the hour? she replied, nine o'clock; adding, that she had brought a letter, which one of the waiters from Slaughter's coffee-house had just left, with the information, that he did so by the orders of a footman in rich livery.

Thaddeus desired it might be given to him. The child obeyed, and quitted the room. He saw that the superscription was in Miss Dundas's hand; and opening it with pleasure, because every thing interested him which came from the house that contained Mary Beaufort, to his amazement and consternation, he read the following passionate and intemperate lines:

"To Mr. Constantine.

"Mr. Constantine,

"By a miraculous circumstance, this morning, your deep and daring plan of villainy has been discovered to Lady D – and myself. The deluded victim, whom your arts and falsehoods, would have seduced to dishonour her family by connecting herself with a vagabond, has at length seen through her error; and now detests you as much as ever your insufferable presumption could have hoped she would distinguish you with her regard. Thank Heaven! you are completely exposed! This young woman of fashion (whose name I will not trust in the same page with yours) has made a full confession of your villainous seductions; of her own reprehensible weakness, in ever having deigned to listen to one so low. She desires me to assure you, that she hates you; and commands you never again to attempt the insolence of appearing in her sight. Indeed, this is the language of every soul in this house, of Lady D – , Mrs. D – S – , Miss B – , besides that of

D – D – ."

Harley street.

Thaddeus read this ridiculous letter twice, before he could perfectly comprehend its meaning. In a paroxysm of indignation at the vile subterfuge under which he did not doubt Euphemia had screened some accidental discovery of her absurd passion, he hastily threw on his clothes, and determined, though in defiance of Miss Dundas's mandates, to fly to Harley-street, and clear himself in the eyes of Mary and her venerable aunt.

Having flown rather than walked, he arrived in sight of Lady

Dundas's house, just as a coach, full of her ladyship's maids and packages drove from the door. Hurrying up the step, he asked the porter who was standing in the hall, if Mrs. Dorothy Somerset were at home.

"No," replied the man; "she and Miss Beaufort, with Miss Dundas and Mr. Somerset, went out of town this morning by eight o'clock; and my lady and Miss Euphemia, about an hour ago, set off for Dumbarton, in Scotland, where they mean to stay all the summer."

At this information, which seemed to be the sealing of his condemnation with Mary, Thaddeus felt his heart pierced to the core. Unacquainted, till this moment, with the torments attending the calumniated, he could scarcely subdue the tempest in his breast, when forced to receive the conviction, that the woman whom he loved above all the world, now regarded him as not merely a villain, but the meanest of villains.

He returned home, indignant and agitated. The knowledge that Pembroke Somerset had probably listened to the falshoods of Euphemia, without suggesting one word in defence of him who had once been his friend, inflicted a pang more deadly than the rest. Shutting himself within his apartment, tossed and tortured in soul, he traversed the room, till, resolving to seek redress from the advice of Lady Tinemouth, he descended the stairs; and telling Mrs. Robson, that he should leave London next morning for Lincolnshire, begged her not to be uneasy on his account, as he went on business, and would return in a few days.

The good woman almost wept at this intelligence; and when she saw him depart, followed the wheels of the stage-coach with sighs and blessings. For the Count, his long journey passed in resentful reveries, or affectionate anticipations of the moment when he should pour out his gratitude to the maternal tenderness of Lady Tinemouth; and learn from her delicacy and experience, how to wipe from the minds of Mrs. Dorothy Somerset and her lovely niece, sentiments of him, so dishonouring, torturing, and false.

CHAP. II.

The porter at Lady Dundas's had been strictly correct in his account respecting the destination of the dispersed members of her ladyship's household.

Whilst Pembroke Somerset was sullenly executing his forced act of benevolence at Newgate, Miss Dundas suddenly took it into her ever scheming head, to compare the merits of Somerset's rich expectancy, with the pennyless certainty of Lascelles. She considered, how high the wife of a baronet stood in the train of precedence over the humble *cara sposa** of a man, owning no other rank, than a reflected lustre, shot from the coronet of an elder brother. Lady Somerset, she thought, would be a prettier salutation, than the empty courtesy of Honourable. Besides, Pembroke was very handsome; Lascelles, only tolerably so: indeed some women had presumed to call him ugly; but they were odd mortals, who, not believing the *metempsychosis* doctrine of the taylor and his decorating adjuncts,† could not comprehend, that although a mere human creature can have no such property, a man of fashion may possess an *elixir vitæ*,‡ which makes age youth; deformity beauty; and even transforms vice into virtue.

In spite of remembrance, which reminded Diana, how often, amidst a little bevy of females, she had contended with acrimony, that all Mr. Lascelles's teeth were his own; that his nose was not a bit too long, being an exact *fac-simile* of the same feature which reared its sublime curve over the capacious mouth of his noble brother Lord Castle-Conway; notwithstanding this, the Pythagorean pretensions of fashion began to lose their ascendency; and, in the recesses of her mind, when Miss Dundas compared the light elegance of Pembroke's figure, with the heavy limbs of her present lover; Pembroke's dark and ever-animated eyes, with the gooseberry orbs of Lascelles; she dropped the parallel; and resolving to captivate the heir of Somerset Castle, admitted no remorse at jilting the brother of Castle-Conway.

To this end, before Pembroke's return from Newgate, Diana had

---

* Italian, 'dear wife'.

† metempsychosis, 'the transmigration of the soul of a human being ... into a new body of the same or a different species' (*OED*). The narrator mocks Diana's belief in the transformative powers of tailors and fashionable dress.

‡ Latin, 'the elixir of life', which supposedly granted eternal youth.

told her mother of her intention to accompany Mrs. Dorothy down
to the baronet's; where she would remain, till her ladyship should
think Euphemia might be trusted to rejoin her in town. Neither Mrs.
Dorothy nor Miss Beaufort liked this arrangement; and, with an
aching heart, the latter prepared to take her seat next morning, at an
early hour, in the travelling equipage which was to convey them all into
Leicestershire.

At supper, Pembroke sullenly informed Mary of the success of her
commands: that Mr. Constantine was free. This assurance, though
imparted with so ungracious an air, laid her head with less distraction
on her pillow: and, as she stepped into Sir Robert's carriage next day,
enabled her with more ease to deck her lips with smiles. She felt that
the penetrating eyes of her cousin were never withdrawn from her
face; offended with his perverseness and their scrutiny, she tried to
baffle their inspection. She attempted gaiety, when she gladly would
have wept. But when the coach mounted the top of Highgate Hill, and
discovered a last view of that city, which contained the being, whose
happiness was the sole object of her thoughts and prayers, she leaned
out of the window, to hide a tear which she could not repress; feeling
that another and another would start, she complained of the dust; and,
pulling her veil over her eyes, drew back into the corner of the carriage.
The trembling of her voice and hands during the performance of this
little artifice, too well explained to Pembroke what was passing in her
mind: at once dispelling the gloom which had shrouded his own countenance, he turned towards her with a compassionate tenderness in his
words and looks, which, gradually softening her displeasure into the
easy conversation of reciprocal affection, rendered the remainder of
their long journey less irksome.

When, at the end of the second day, Mary found herself in the old
avenue leading to the base of the hill that sustains the revered walls of
Somerset Castle,* a mingled emotion took possession of her breast;
and when the carriage had attained the foot of the highest terrace, she
sprung impatiently out of it, and hastening up the stone stairs into the
front hall, met her uncle at the door of the breakfast-parlour, where he
held out his arms to receive her.

"My Mary! My darling!" cried he, embracing her now wet cheek,
and straining her throbbing bosom to his own, "Why, my dear love,"

* Though no Somerset Castle exists in Leicestershire, Porter frequently visited
  Grantham in her youth, and she almost certainly modelled Somerset Castle on
  Belvoir (pronounced 'beaver') Castle, the seat of the Dukes of Rutland. See the
  Introduction.

added he, almost carrying her into the room, "I am afraid this visit to town has injured your nerves! Whence arises this agitation?"

Mary knew that it had injured her peace; and, now that the flood-gates of her long-repelled tears had opened, it was beyond her art, or the soothings of her affectionate uncle, to stay them. A moment after, her cousin entered the room, followed by Mrs. Dorothy and Miss Dundas. Miss Beaufort hastily rose to conceal what she could not check, and, kissing Sir Robert's hand, asked permission to retire, under the pretence of regaining those spirits which had been dissipated by the fatigues of her journey.

In her own chamber, she did indeed struggle to recover herself. She shuddered at the impetuosity of her feelings, when once abandoned of their reins; and, resolved from this hour to hold a stricter guard over the consequences of her ill-fated passion.

She sat down in the window of her apartment, and, looking down the extensive vale of Somerset, watched the romantic wanderings of the Witham* winding its course through the domains of the castle, and nourishing the roots of those immense oaks, which still wave their centential† arms over its quiet stream. Mary reflected on the revolution which had taken place in her mind, since she walked on its banks the evening that preceded her visit to London. Then, she was free as air, and gay as the lark; each object was bright and lovely to her eyes: hope seemed to woo her from every green slope, every remote dingle: all nature breathed of joy, because her own breast was the home of gladness. Now, all continued the same, but she was changed. Surrounded by beauty, she acknowledged its presence; the sweetness of the flowers bathed her senses in fragrance; the setting sun, gilding the heights, shed a yellow glory over the distant hills; the birds were hailing the fallen dew that spangled every leaf; Mary gazed around, and sighed heavily when she said to herself, "Even in this paradise I shall be wretched. Alas! my heart is far away! My soul lingers about one, whom I may never more behold! about one, who may soon cease to remember that such a being as Mary Beaufort is in existence. He will leave England!" cried she, raising her hands and eyes to the glowing heavens, "He will live, he will die, far, far, from me! In a distant land he will wed another, whilst I shall know no wish that strays from him."

Whilst Mary indulged in these soliloquies, she forgot both Sir Robert

---

* The River Witham runs through Lincolnshire; its headwaters are south of Grantham.
† Porter evidently meant 'centenniel'. In the seventh edition (1816), the passage reads 'those immense oaks which for more than a century have waved their branches over its stream' (4. 27).

and her resolution, till he sent her maid to beg, that if she were better, she would come down and make tea for him. At this summons, Miss Beaufort dried her eyes and descended with an assumed serenity to the saloon, where the family were now assembled. The Baronet having greeted Miss Dundas with an hospitable welcome, seated himself between his sister and his son; and, whilst he received his favourite beverage from the hands of the lovely Mary, he found that comfort had once more re-entered his bosom.

Sir Robert Somerset was a man whose appearance alone must have attracted respect. His person bore the stamp of dignity; and his manners, which possessed the exquisite polish of travel, secured him universal esteem. Though little beyond fifty, the various perplexities to which he had been obnoxious in youth, had not only rendered his hair perfectly grey, but by clouding his once brilliant eyes with thoughtfulness, had marked his aspect with old age and melancholy. The baronet's entrance into gay life was celebrated for wit and vivacity: He was the animating spirit of every party; when, strange to tell, an inexplicable metamorphosis took place. Soon after his return from abroad, his marriage with Miss Beaufort (a woman whom he loved to madness) taking place, excess of happiness seemed to change his nature, and gave his character a gradual tinge of sadness. After his ladyship's death, the alteration in his mind, produced still more extraordinary effects, and shewed itself more than once in all the terrors of threatening insanity.

The latest attack of the kind which assailed him, was about the middle of last winter; it seized him under the appearance of a swoon, as he sat reading the newspaper at breakfast; he was carried to bed, and awoke in a delirium, which menaced either immediate death, or the total extinction of his intellects. However, neither of these dreads being confirmed, in the course of several weeks, to the wonder of every body, he recovered both his health and his sound mind. Notwithstanding this happy event, the circumstances of his danger having deeply affected the hearts of his family, he continued to be a very anxious object of attention. Indeed solicitude did not terminate with them: the munificence of his disposition having spread itself through every county in which he owned a rood of land,* as many prayers ascended for the repose of his spirit, as had ever petitioned heaven from the mouths of "*monkish beadsmen*,"† in favour of power and virtue.

---

* rood, 'a unit of land area equal to 40 square rods (a quarter of an acre)' (*OED*).
† beadsman, 'one paid or endowed to pray for others' (*OED*). The unidentified quotation brings to mind a description in Spenser's *Faerie Queene* of 'an holy Hospitall' 'In which seven Bead-men that had vowed all / Their life to service of high heavens king / Did spend their days in doing goodly thing' (I, x, 36).

Since the demise of Lady Somerset, this excellent man drew all his comfort from the amiable qualities of his son Pembroke. Sometimes in his livelier hours, which came *"like angel visits, few and far between,"** he amused himself with the playfulness of the little Earl of Arun, the pompous erudition of Mr. Loftus (who was become his lordship's tutor), and giving occasional entertainments to the gentry of his neighbourhood.

Of all the personages contained within this circle, (which the hospitality of Sir Robert extended to a circumference of thirty miles,) Lord Berrington was the most respected.

The numerous visitants who attended the Somerset-hunt, were too gay to be admitted with intimacy. A son of one of these itinerant families, (which, ever on the full chace of pleasure, had fixed itself at Woodhill Lodge, on the right of the little town of Grantham,) by calling at the castle soon after the arrival of the London party, caused a trifling change in its disposition.

When Richard Shafto was ushered into the saloon, he nodded to Sir Robert, and, turning his back on the ladies, told Pembroke that he had ridden to Somerset on purpose to bring him to Woodhill Lodge.

"Upon my soul," cried he, "if you don't come, I will leave my mother. Would you believe it, that on account of Sir Hallerand having gone out plenipotentiary to some damned place on the continent, she has taken it into her head to rusticate in the country till his return? Upon my soul, I am moped to death! There is not a creature but yourself within twenty miles, that I would speak to; not a man worth a sixpence. I wish to heaven my father had broken his neck before he accepted that rascally embassy, which encumbers me with the charge of an old woman!"

After this dutiful wish, which brought down a weighty admonition from Mrs. Dorothy, the young gentleman promised to beg her pardon for his ill manners, provided she could persuade Pembroke to accompany him to the lodge. Mr. Somerset did not evince much alacrity in his consent; but purposely to rid his family of such a noisy guest, he rose from his chair, and acquiescing in the sacrifice of a few days to good-nature, bade his father farewel, and gave orders for a ride to Grantham.

As soon as the gentlemen had left the saloon, Miss Dundas ran up stairs, and, from her dressing-room window in the west tower, pursued the steps of their horses cantering down the winding steep into the high-road. An abrupt angle of the hill hiding them at once from her

* Thomas Campbell, *The Pleasures of Hope*, II. 378.

view, she turned round with a toss of the head, and, flinging herself into a chair, exclaimed, "Now I shall be bored to death by this abominable prosing family! I wish the devil had taken Shafto, before he thought of coming here!"

In consequence of the humour which engendered the above no very flattering compliment to the society at the castle, Miss Dundas descended to the dining-room, with sulky looks and a chilling air. She swallowed what the baronet laid on her plate, with an indolent appetite, cut her meat into mince, and dragged the vegetables over the table-cloth. Mrs. Dorothy coloured at this indifference to the usual neatness of her damask covers; but Miss Dundas was so completely in the sullens, that, heedless of any other feelings than her own, she continued to pull and knock about the things just as her ill-humour dictated.

The petulance of this lady's behaviour, did not in the least assimilate with the customary tranquillity of Sir Robert's table; and, when the cloth was drawn, he could not refrain from expressing his concern, that Somerset Castle appeared so little calculated to afford satisfaction to a daughter of Lady Dundas's. Miss Dundas attempted some awkward declaration, that she never was more amused, never happier. But the small credit which Sir Robert gave to her assertion, was fully honoured the next morning, by the ready manner in which she accepted a casual invitation to spend the ensuing day and night at Lady Shafto's. Her ladyship called on Mrs. Dorothy, and intending to have a party in the evening, invited the two young ladies to return with her to Grantham, and be her guests for a week. Mary, whose spirits had much to combat, before they could regain their former serenity, declined her civility; while, with a gleam of pleasure, she heard it accepted by Miss Dundas, who departed with her ladyship for the lodge.

Whilst the enraptured Diana, all life and glee, bowled along with Lady Shafto, anticipating the delight of once more seating herself at the elbow of Pembroke Somerset; Mary Beaufort, relieved from a load of ill-requited attentions, walked out into the park, to enjoy, in solitude, the intoxicating sorrow of thinking on the unhappy and far distant Constantine. Regardless of the way, her footsteps, though robbed of elasticity by nightly watching and daily regret, led her beyond the park, to the ruined church of Woolthorpe, its southern boundary.*

---

* The ruins of Woolsthorpe's St James church were near Belvoir Castle, about 10 kilometres southwest of Grantham. The church was destroyed in 1645, during the English Civil War, because of the Duke of Rutland's royalist support; the destruction of Belvoir Castle followed in 1649.

Her eyes were fixed on the opposite horizon. It was the extremity of Leicestershire; and far, far behind those hills, was that London, which contained the object dearest to her soul. The wind seemed scarcely to breathe as it floated towards her; but it came from that quarter; and, believing it laden with every sweet which love can fancy, she threw back her veil, to inhale its balm; then blaming herself for such baby weakness, she turned blushing, homewards, and wept at what she thought, the unreasonable tenacity of her passion.

The arrival of Miss Dundas at the lodge, was communicated to the two young men on their return from a traverse on foot of half the country in quest of game. The news extracted an oath from Shafto; but rather pleased Somerset, who augured some amusement from her attempts at wit and judgment. Tired to death, and dinner being over when they entered, with ravenous appetites they swallowed their uncomfortable meal in a remote room; then throwing themselves along the sofas, yawned and slept for near two hours.

Pembroke waking first, suddenly jumped on the floor, and shaking his disordered clothes, exclaimed, "Shafto! Get up. This is abominable! Efaith, I cannot help thinking, that if we spend one half of our days in pleasure, and the other in lolling off its fatigues, we shall have past through life more to our shame than our profit!"

"Then you take the shame, and leave me the profit;" cried his companion, turning himself round: "so good night to you."

Pembroke rang the bell. A servant entered.

"What o'clock is it?"

"Eight, Sir."

"Who are up stairs?"

"My lady, Sir, and a large party of ladies."

"There now!" cried Shafto, yawning and kicking out his legs. "You surely won't go to be bored with such damned maudlin company?"

"I choose to join your mother," replied Pembroke. "Are there any gentlemen, Stephen?"

"One, Sir; Doctor Denton."

"Confound you!" roared Shafto, "what do you stand jabbering there for? You won't let me sleep. Can't you send away the fellow, and go look yourself?"

"I will, if you can persuade yourself to rise off that sofa, and come with me?"

"May the devil catch me if I do! Get about your business, and leave me to mine."

"You are incorrigible, Shafto!" returned Pembroke, as he closed the door. He ascended the stairs to change his dress, and before he gained the second flight, he had resolved not to spend two other whole days in the company of such an unmannered, unidea'd* cub.

On Mr. Somerset's entrance into Lady Shafto's drawing-room, he saw many ladies, but only one gentleman, who was the before-mentioned Doctor Denton; a poor, shallow headed, parasitical animal. Pembroke, having seen sufficient of him to despise his pretensions both to science and sincerity, passed his wide smirk and eager inquiries, with a distancing bow, and took his seat by the side of the now delighted Miss Dundas. The vivid spirits of Diana, which she managed should be peculiarly sparkling when he made his appearance, entertained him; when compared with the insipid sameness of her ladyship, or the brutal ribaldry of her son, her mirth was wit, and her remarks wisdom.

"Dear Mr. Somerset!" cried she, "how good you are to break this sad solemnity. I vow, until you shewed your face, I thought the days of paganism had revived, and that, lacking of men, we were assembled here to celebrate the mysteries of the *Bona Dea*."†

"Lacking of men!" replied he smiling, "You have overlooked the assiduous Doctor Denton?"

"O, no; that is a cameleon in man's clothing.‡ He breathes air, he eats air, he emits air; and a most pestilential breath it is: only observe how he is pouring nonsense into the ear of yonder sable statue."

Pembroke directed his eyes as Miss Dundas had desired him; they fell on Doctor Denton, who stood whispering, bowing, and pressing his breast, before a lady in black, who sat, almost concealed by the window curtain. The lady put up her lip, the doctor proceeded, she frowned, he would not be daunted, the lady rose from her seat, and, slightly bending her head, crossed the room. Whilst Mr. Somerset was contemplating her majestic figure and fine, though pale features, Miss Dundas touched his arm, and smiling satirically, she repeated in an affected voice:

> "Hail, pensive Nun! devout and holy!
> "Hail, divinest Melancholy!"

"If she be melancholy," returned Pembroke, unconsciously sighing, "I would for ever say,

---

* unideaed, 'not furnished with an idea' (*OED*). Porter follows convention in contracting the ending.
† *Bona Dea*, 'Good Goddess': an ancient Roman divinity associated with women's chastity and fertility.
‡ Chameleons were once thought to subsist only on air. See *Hamlet*: 'Excellent, i' faith, of the chameleon's dish: / I eat the air, promise-crammed' (III, ii, 93–4).

"Hence, unholy Mirth, of Folly born!"*

Miss Dundas reddened. She had never liked this interesting woman, who was not only too handsome for competition, but possessed of an understanding whose temper would not tolerate ignorance and presumption. Diana's ill-natured impertinence having several times received deserved chastisement from that quarter, she was vexed to the soul, when Pembroke closed his animated response with the question, "Who is she?"

Miss Dundas, rather too bitterly for the success of her design on his heart, iterated his words, and then answered: "Why, she is crazed. She lives in a place called Harrowby Abbey, at the top of that hill;" continued she, pointing through the opposite window to a distant rising ground, on which the moon was shining brightly; "and, I am told, frightens the cottagers out of their wits by her midnight strolls."

Hardly knowing how to credit this wild account, Pembroke asked his informer, if she were serious.

"Never more so."

"Her eyes are uncommonly beautiful. You must be jesting," returned he; "they seem perfectly reasonable."

Miss Dundas laughed. "Like Hamlet's, they 'know not seems, but have that within which passeth shew!'† believe me, she is mad enough for bedlam; and of that I could soon convince you. I wonder how Lady Shafto thought of inviting her at all!"

"Well," cried Pembroke, "if those features announce madness, I shall never admire a look of sense again."

"Bless us," exclaimed Miss Dundas, "you are wonderfully struck! Don't you see, she is old enough to be your mother?"

"That may be," answered he, smiling; "nevertheless, she is one of the most lovely women I ever beheld. Come, tell me her name."

"I will satisfy you in a moment," rejoined Diana; "and then away with your rhapsodies! She is the very Countess of Tinemouth, who brought, as her most particular friend, that vagabond foreigner to our house, who would have run off with Phemy."

"Lady Tinemouth!" exclaimed Pembroke, "I never saw her before. My ever lamented mother met her whilst I was abroad, and she esteemed her highly. Pray, present me to her!"

---

* Both characters echo John Milton's 1645–6 poem 'Il Penseroso': 'Hence vain deluding joys, / The brood of folly without father bred ... But hail thou Goddes, sage and holy, / Hail divinest Melancholy ... Come pensive Nun, devout and pure' (lines 1–2, 11–12, 31).
† *Hamlet*, I, ii, 76–7, 85.

"Impossible!" replied Diana, vexed at the turn his curiosity had taken; "I wrote to her about the insidious wretch, and now we don't speak."

"Then, I will introduce myself," answered he: he was moving away, when Miss Dundas (whose delight lay in tormenting those whom she could not subjugate,) caught hold of his arm, and, by some attempts at badinage and raillery, withheld him in his place, till the Countess made her farewel curtsey to Lady Shafto, and the door was closed.

Disappointed at this manœuvre, Pembroke re-seated himself, and pondering on what could be the reason why his aunt and cousin had not heard of her ladyship's arrival at Harrowby, he determined to wait on her next day. Regardless of every word which the provoked Diana addressed to him, he remained silent and meditating, till the loud voice of Shafto roaring in his ear, made him turn suddenly round. Miss Dundas tried to laugh at his reverie, though she knew that such a flagrant instance of inattention was death to her hopes; but Pembroke, not inclined to partake in the jest, coolly asked his bearish companion what he wanted?

"Nothing, upon my soul," cried he, "but to hear you speak. What the devil were you looking at on the carpet? Miss Dundas tells me, you have lost your heart to yonder grim Countess, that my mother wanted me to gallant up the hill?"

"Shafto!" answered Pembroke, rising from his chair, "you cannot be speaking of Lady Tinemouth?"

"Efaith, I am!" roared he: "and if she be such a scamp as to live without a carriage, I won't be her lacquey for nothing. Two miles are not to be tramped over by me, with no better companion than an old painted woman of quality."

"Surely you cannot mean," returned Pembroke, "that her ladyship was to walk from hence?"

"Without a doubt," cried Shafto, bursting into a horse laugh*: "you would be clever to see my Lady Stingy in any other carriage than her clogs."

Irritated at the malice of Miss Dundas, and despising the vulgar illiberality of Shafto, Pembroke, without deigning a reply, abruptly left the room; and, hastening out of the house, ran, rather than walked, in hopes of overtaking the Countess and her servant before they reached Harrowby.

He crossed the little wooden bridge that lies over the Witham; he scoured the fields; and, leaping every stile and gate which impeded

---

* horse-laugh, 'a loud coarse laugh' (*OED*). A hyphen was added in later editions.

his way, gained the inclosure that leads to the top of the hill, where he descried a light moving, and very rightly conjectured it must be the lantern carried by her ladyship's attendant. Another spring over the shattered fence cleared all obstacles; and he found himself close to Lady Tinemouth, who was leaning on the arm of a gentleman. Pembroke stopped at this sight; supposing that she had been met by some person belonging to the town, whose readier gallantry now occupied the place which Miss Dundas had prevented him from filling, he was preparing to retreat, when Lady Tinemouth happening to turn her head, imagined, from the hesitating embarrassment of his manner, that he was a stranger who had lost his way, and accosted him with that inquiry.

Pembroke bowed in some confusion; and related the simple fact, of his having heard that she had quitted Lady Shafto's without any guard but the servant; and, that he had hurried out, the moment he learned the circumstance, to proffer his services. The Countess not only thanked him for such attention, but, constrained by a civility which she would rather at that instant have been excused from, asked him to walk forward with her to the Abbey, and partake of some refreshment.

"But," added she, "though I perfectly recollect having seen another gentleman in Lady Shafto's room, besides Doctor Denton, I have not the honour of knowing your name?"

"It is Somerset," returned Pembroke: "I am the son of that Lady Somerset, who, during the last year of her life, had the happiness of being intimate with your ladyship."

Lady Tinemouth declared her pleasure at this meeting; and, turning to the gentleman who was walking in silence by her side, "Mr. Constantine," said she, "allow me to introduce to you the cousin of the amiable Miss Beaufort."

Thaddeus, who had too well recognised the voice of his false friend, in the first accents which he addressed to the Countess, with a swelling heart, bent his head to the cold salutation of Somerset. Hearing that her ladyship's companion was no other than the same Constantine whom he had liberated from prison, Pembroke was stimulated with a desire to unmask his double villainy to Lady Tinemouth; and, feeling a curiosity to see the man whose person and meretricious qualities had blinded even the judgment of his aunt; he readily obeyed the second invitation of the Countess, and consented to go home and sup with her.

Meanwhile, Thaddeus was agitated with a variety of emotions. Every tone of Pembroke's voice, reminding him of happier days, pierced to his heart, whilst a sense of his ingratitude, awakened all the pride and indignation of his soul. Full of resentment, he determined that whatever might be the result, he would not shrink from an interview the anticipation of which, Pembroke (who had received from himself an intimation of the name he assumed,) seemed to regard with such unfeeling indifference.

Lady Tinemouth, having no conception that Somerset and the Count had any personal knowledge of each other, begged the gentlemen to follow her into the supper-parlour. Pembroke, with no inconsiderable degree of rudeness, pushed by his friend, and arrived at the side of the Countess, before Thaddeus, who felt himself insulted in every nerve, could summon coolness to enter the room with a composed step. He did so; and, taking off his hat, laid it down on the sofa. Lady Tinemouth began to express her joy at his arrival. The eyes of Pembroke now became fixed on the calm but severe countenance, of the man before him: he stood by the table with an air so full of princely greatness, that the candid heart of Pembroke Somerset soon whispered to him, "*Sure, nothing ill, can dwell in such a breast!*"*

Still his eyes followed him, when he turned round, and when he bent his head to answer the Countess, in a voice so low, that it escaped his ear. Pembroke was bewildered. There was a something in the features, in the mien, of this foreigner, so like his friend Sobieski! But then, Sobieski was all frankness and animation; his cheek blazed with the rich colouring of youth and happiness; his eyes flashed pleasure, and his lips were decked with smiles. On the reverse, the person before him was not only considerably taller, and of more manly proportions, but his face was pale, reserved, and haughty: besides, he did not appear even to recollect the name of Somerset; and, what made the supposition at once untenable, his own was Constantine.

These reasonings having passed through the mind of Pembroke in less time than they can be repeated, left his heart unsatisfied. The mounted blood remained on his cheeks; his bosom beat; and, keeping his searching and ardent gaze rivetted on the man who was either his friend or his counterpart, Lady Tinemouth withdrew from the table, and the eyes of the two young men met. Thaddeus turned paler than before: there is an intelligence in the interchange of looks which cannot be mistaken; it is the communication of souls, and there is no deception in their language. Pembroke flew forward, and catching hold of his friend's hand, exclaimed in an impetuous voice, "Am I right? Are you not Sobieski?"

---

* In *The Tempest*, Miranda says of Ferdinand, 'There's nothing ill can dwell in such a temple' (I, ii, 458).

"I am," returned Thaddeus, half choked with emotion, and hardly knowing what to understand by Somerset's behaviour.

"Gracious Heaven!" cried he, still grasping his hand, "and can you have forgotten your friend Pembroke Somerset?"

The ingenuous heart of Thaddeus felt the words and manner of Pembroke to be the language of truth; and, trusting that some mistake had involved his former conduct, he at once cast off all suspicion; and, throwing his arms round him, strained him to his breast, and burst into tears.

Lady Tinemouth, who, during this scene, had stood mute with surprise, now advanced to the friends, who were weeping on each other's necks,* and taking a hand of each, "My dear Sobieski," cried she, "Why did you withhold the knowledge of this acquaintance from me? Had you told me that you knew Mr. Somerset, this happy meeting might have been accomplished sooner."

"Yes," replied Pembroke, turning to the Countess, and wiping away the tears which were trembling on his cheek; "nothing could have given me pain at this moment, but the conviction that he who was the preserver of my life, and my most generous protector, should, in this country, have endured the most abject distress, rather than let me know, that it was in my power to be grateful."

Thaddeus took out his handkerchief, and for a few minutes concealed his face. The Countess looked on him with tenderness; and believing that he would sooner regain composure were he alone with his friend, she stole unobserved out of the room. Pembroke affectionately resumed; "But, I hope, dear Sobieski, that you will never leave me more. I have an excellent father, who, when made acquainted with my obligations to you and your noble family, will glory in loving you as a son."

Thaddeus having subdued "*the woman in his heart*,"† raised his head with an expression in his eyes, far different from that which had chilled the blood of Pembroke on their first encounter.

"Circumstances," said he, "dear Somerset, have made me greatly injure you. A strange neglect on your side since we separated at Villanow, gave the first blow to my confidence in your friendship. Though I lost your direct address, I had written to you often, and yet you persevered in silence. When I came to England, after having

---

* Grammar requires 'neck' but this was never corrected.
† Mary Hayes, *Memoirs of Emma Courtney*, 2 vols (London: G. G. and J. Robinson, 1796), 2. 177: 'I neither trembled, nor shed a tear – I banished the woman from my heart.'

witnessed the destruction of all that was dear to me in Poland, and then of Poland itself, I wished to give your faithfulness another chance; I addressed two letters to you; I even delivered the last at your door myself, and I saw you in the window when I sent it in."

"By all that is sacred," cried Pembroke vehemently, and amazed, "I never saw any letter from you! I wrote you many. I never heard of these you mention. Indeed, I should even now have been ignorant of the Palatine's, and your mother's cruel fate, had it not been too circumstantially related in the newspapers."

"I believe you," returned Thaddeus, drawing an agonizing sigh, at the dreadful picture which the last sentence recalled; "I believe you; though at the time I speak of, I thought otherwise; for, next day, both my letters were re-inclosed in a blank cover, directed as if by your hand, and brought by a servant with a message that there was no answer."

"Powers of Heaven!" exclaimed Somerset, "there must be some villainy in this! Dearest Thaddeus," cried he, breaking off abruptly, and grasping his hand, "I would have flown to you, had it been to meet my death! But why did you not come in yourself? Who prevented you? Then no mistake could have happened. Why did you not come in yourself?"

"Because I was uncertain of your sentiments: my first letter remained unnoticed; and my heart, dear Somerset," added he, pressing his hand, "would not stoop to solicitation."

"Solicitation!" exclaimed Pembroke with warmth, "You have a right to demand my life! But there is some rascally business in this affair; nothing else could have carried it through: if any of my servants have dared to open these letters – Merciful Heaven," cried he, interrupting himself, "how you must have despised me!"

"I was afflicted," returned Thaddeus, "that the man whom my family had so warmly loved, could prove so unworthy; and, afterwards, whenever I met you in the streets, which I think was once or twice, I confess, to pass you cut me to the heart."

"And you have met me!" exclaimed Pembroke, "and I not see you! I cannot comprehend it."

"Yes," answered Thaddeus, "and the first time was going into the playhouse. I believe I called after you."

"It is now ten months since?" returned Pembroke; "I remember very well, that somebody called out my name, while I was handing Lady Coningsby and her sister into the door. I looked about, and not seeing any one I knew, thought I must have been mistaken. But why, dear Sobieski, why did you not follow me into the theatre?"

Thaddeus shook his head, and smiling languidly; "My poverty would not permit me," replied he, "but I waited in the hall till every body had left the house, in hopes of intercepting you as you passed."

Pembroke sprung from his chair at these last words; and, with the most vehement voice and action, exclaimed, "I see it! That rascal Loftus is at the bottom of it all! He followed me into the theatre, he must have seen you, and his cursed selfishness took fright. Yes, it must be him! He would not allow me to return that way; when I said I would, he told me a thousand lies about the carriages coming round; and, like a fool, I went out by another door."

"Who is Mr. Loftus?" inquired Thaddeus, surprised at his friend's suspicion; "I do not know such a man."

"What," returned Pembroke, walking about the room in a heat, "don't you remember, that Loftus is the name of the scoundrel who persuaded me to volunteer against Poland? to screen his baseness, I have brought all this upon myself."

"Now, I recollect it;" replied Thaddeus, "but I never saw him."

"Yet, I am not less certain that I am right," replied Somerset; "I will recount to you my reasons. After I had quitted Villanow, you remember I met him at Dantzic? Before we left that port, he implored, almost on his knees, that in pity to his mother and sisters, whom he supported out of his salary, I would refrain from incensing my parents against him, by relating any circumstance of our visit to Poland. The man shed tears as he spoke; and, like a fool, I consented to keep the secret, till the vicar of Somerset, (a poor soul, ill of the dropsy,) dies, and he be in possession of the living. When we landed in England," continued Pembroke, casting down his eyes, "I found that the cause of my sudden recall, was the illness of my dear mother. But heaven denied me the comfort of beholding her again: she had been buried two days before I reached the shore." He paused for a moment; and then resumed, "For near a month after my return, I could not quit my room; a fever had seized me: but, on my recovery, I immediately wrote both to you and to the Palatine. I repeated these letters at least every six weeks during the first year of our separation; yet you persisted in being silent. Hurt as I was at this neglect, I felt that gratitude demanded some sacrifices from pride, and I continued to write, even into the spring following. Meanwhile, the papers of the day teemed with Sobieski's actions, Sobieski's fame; and, believing that increasing glory had blotted me out of your memory, I resolved, henceforth to regard our friendship as a dream, and never to speak of it more."

Confounded at this double misapprehension, Thaddeus, with

a glowing countenance, expressed his regret for having doubted his friend; and, repeating the assurance of having been punctual to his promise of correspondence, even when he dreamed him inconstant; acknowledged, that nothing short of a premeditated scheme could have wrought such undeviating miscarriage.

"Aye;" returned Pembroke, reddening with awakened anger; "I could swear that Mr. Loftus has all my letters in his bureau at this moment! No house ever gave a man a better opportunity to play the rogue in, than ours. It is a custom with us to lay our letters in a morning on the hall table, whence they are sent to the office; and, in the same way when the post arrives, they are spread out, for their several owners to take as they pass to breakfast. Owing to this management, I cannot doubt the means by which Mr. Loftus, under the hope of separating us for ever, has intercepted every letter to you, and every letter from you. I suppose, the wretch feared that I would repent my engagement, if our correspondence were allowed. He trembled, lest the business should be blown before the vicar died, and he in consequence, lose both the expected living, and his present situation about Lord Arun. A villain! For once he has judged rightly; I will unmask him to my father, and shew him what it is to purchase subsistence at the expense of honour and justice."

Thaddeus, who could not withhold instant credence to these evidences of chicanery, tried to calm the violence of his friend; who only answered, by insisting on his immediate return with him to Somerset castle.

"I long to present you to my father;" cried Pembroke, "when I tell him who you are; of your kindness to me; how rejoiced will he be! How happy, how proud, to have you as his guest; to shew the warm gratitude of a Briton's heart! Indeed Sobieski, you will love him; for he is generous and noble, like your inestimable grandfather. Besides," added he, smiling with a sudden recollection, "there is my lovely cousin Mary; who, I verily believe, will actually fly into your arms!"

Thaddeus felt the blood rush over his cheeks at this speech of his friend's, and half suppressing a sigh, he shook his head.

"Don't look so like an infidel," resumed Somerset. "If you have any doubts of possessing her affections, I can put you out of your pain by a single sentence! When Lady Dundas's houshold, with myself amongst them, (for little did I know that I was joining the cry against my friend!), were asserting the most flagrant instances of your deceit to Euphemia, Mary alone, withstood the whole tide of malice, and compelled me to release you."

"Gracious Providence!" cried Thaddeus, catching Pembroke's hand,

and looking eagerly and agitatedly in his face, "Was it you who came to my prison? Was it Miss Beaufort who visited my lodgings?"

"Indeed, it was," returned his friend, "and I blush for myself, that I quitted Newgate without an interview. Had I followed the dictates of common decency, I should have seen you; and then, what pain would have been spared my dear cousin! What a joyful surprize would have awaited myself!"

Thaddeus could only reply by pressing his friend's hand. His brain whirled. He could not decide on the nature of his feelings; one moment he would have given worlds to throw himself at Miss Beaufort's feet, and the next, he trembled at the prospect of meeting her so soon.

"Dear Sobieski," cried Pembroke, "how strangely you receive this intelligence! Is it possible, that the love of Mary Beaufort can be rejected?"

"No," cried the Count looking up, his fine face flushed with emotion; "I adore Miss Beaufort. Her virtues possess my whole heart. But can I forget, that I have only that heart to offer? Can I forget that I am a beggar? That even now, I exist on her bounty?" The eyes of Thaddeus, and the sudden tremor which shook his frame, finished this appeal to his fate.

Pembroke felt it enter his soul. To hide its effect, he threw himself on his friend's breast; and exclaimed, "Do not injure me and my father, by these sentiments! You are come, dearest Sobieski, to a second home. Sir Robert Somerset will consider himself ennobled in supplying the place of your lamented grandfather! – and my cousin Mary, as you love her, shall bind us still closer; you must be my relation, as well as my friend!"

Thaddeus replied with animated acknowledgements of Pembroke's affection, – "But," added he, "I must not allow the generous spirit of my dear Somerset, to believe, that I can live a dependant on any power but the author of my being. I consider nothing so degrading as an existence wasted in idleness; therefore, if Sir Robert Somerset will assist me to procure some honest means of acquiring support, I shall thank him from my soul. In no other way, my kindest friend, can I ever be brought to tax the gratitude of your father."

Pembroke coloured at this, and exclaimed in a voice of displeasure, "Gracious Heaven, Sobieski, what can you mean? Do you imagine, that ever my father or myself can forget that you were little less than a prince in your own country? That when in that high station, you treated me like a brother? That you preserved me, even when I lifted my arm against your life? Can we be such monsters, as to forget all this? or think that we act justly by you, in permitting you to labour for your bread? No, Thaddeus, my very soul spurns at the idea. Your mother sheltered me as a son; and I insist that you allow my father to perform the same part by you! Besides, you shall not be idle; you may have a commission in the army, and I will follow you."

The Count squeezed the hand of his friend, and looking gratefully in his face whilst he shook his head, replied, "Had I a hundred tongues, my generous Pembroke, I could not express my sense of your friendship; it is indeed a cordial to my heart; it imparts to me an earnest of happiness which I thought had fled me for ever: but, it shall not allure me from my principles. I am resolved not to live a life of indolence; and I am resolved, not at this period, to enter the British army. No," added he, emotion elevating his tone and manner; "rather would I toil for subsistence by the sweat of my brow, than be subjected to the necessity of acting in concert with those ravagers who destroyed my country! I cannot fight by the side of the Russians! I cannot enlist under their allies!* I will not be led out to devastation! Mine was, and ever shall remain, a defensive sword: and, should danger threaten England, I shall be as ready to withstand her enemies, as I ardently, though ineffectually, opposed those of unhappy Poland."

Pembroke recognized the high-souled Thaddeus of Warsaw, in this lofty burst of enthusiasm: aware that his father's munificence, and manner of conferring esteem and obligations, would go farther towards removing these scruples of delicacy than all his arguments, he did not attempt to combat a resolution which he knew he could not subdue; but tried to prevail on him, to become his guest, till something could be arranged to suit his wishes.

Thaddeus consented to accompany Somerset to the castle the day after the one in which Sir Robert should be apprised of his coming. Pembroke perceived that the morning had surprized them; and shaking his friend warmly by the hand, he bade him farewel; then hastening down the hill, he arrived at the lodge, just as the servants were opening the shutters.

Having given orders to the groom whom he met in the passage, he wrote a slight apology to Shafto for his abrupt departure; and, mounting his horse, gallopped full of delight towards Somerset Castle.

---

* Thaddeus's anger is somewhat premature: the governments of Russia and Britain only became allies against France in 1799.

CHAP. III.

Next morning, when the Countess and Thaddeus were seated at break-fast, her ladyship expressed surprize and pleasure at the scene which she had witnessed the preceding night, at the same time intimating some mortification on the discovery, that he had withheld any of his confidence from her. Sobieski soon obtained her ladyship's pardon, by relating the manner of his first meeting with Mr. Somerset, four years ago at the battle of Zielime, and the consequent events of that momentous period.

Lady Tinemouth wept over the distressful fate that marked the residue of his narrative, with a tenderness which endeared her to his soul. But when, in compliance with his enquiries, she informed him how she came to be at Harrowby Abbey when he supposed her on the Wolds; it was his turn to feel pity; and to shrink from himself, that he had drawn existence from the same source with Lord Harwold.

"Indeed," added the Countess, "you must have had a most tedious journey from Harwold Park to Harrowby; and nothing but my pleas-ure could exceed my astonishment, when I met you last night on the hill."

Thaddeus declared that travelling a few miles farther than he had intended, was no fatigue to him; yet had it been otherwise, the happi-ness he then enjoyed would have acted as a panacea for worse ills, could he have seen her ladyship looking as well as when she left London.

Lady Tinemouth smiled. "You are very right, Sobieski; I am worse than when I was in town. My solitary journey to Harwold harassed me much; and when my son sent me orders to leave it, because his father wanted the place for the autumnal months, I was labouring under a severe cold caught in travelling. Nevertheless, I obeyed him; and, heart-broken and in pain, I arrived here last week. How kind you were to follow me. Who informed you of the place of my destination? Hardly any of Lady Sophia's houshold?"

"No," returned Thaddeus; "I luckily had the precaution to inquire at the inn where the coach stopped, what part of Lord Tinemouth's family were at the Park; and when I heard that the Earl himself was there, my next question was, where then is the Countess? The landlord very civilly told me of your having had a carriage from his house a day or two before, to carry you to one of his lordship's seats, within a few miles of Somerset Castle. Hence, from what I had heard your ladyship say of the situation of Harrowby, I judged it must be the abbey; and so I sought you at a venture."

"And a happy issue I hope will arise from your wanderings!" returned her ladyship, "This rencontre with so old a friend as Mr. Somerset, is a pleasing omen. For my part, I was ignorant of the arrival of the family at the castle, till yesterday morning, when I sent off a messenger to apprise my dear Miss Beaufort, that I am in her neighbourhood. To my great dissatisfaction, Lady Shafto found me out immediately; and when, in compliance with her teizing invitation, I walked down to sit an hour with her last night, little did I expect that I should meet the amiable cousin of our sweet friend. So delightful an accident has amply repaid me for the pain I felt in seeing Miss Dundas in her ladyship's house: an insolent and reproachful letter which she wrote to me on your account, has rendered her an object of my most decided dislike."

Thaddeus smiled and bowed. "Since, my dear Lady Tinemouth, her groundless malice, and Miss Euphemia's folly, have failed in estranging either your confidence or the esteem of Miss Beaufort from me, I despise and pardon them both. Perhaps I ought to pity them, for is it not a difficult ordeal, to pass through the enchantments of wealth and adulation, and emerge as pure as when we entered them? Unclouded fortune, is indeed a trial of spirits; and how brightly does Miss Beaufort rise from the blaze! Surrounded by splendour, homage, and indulgence, she is yet all nature, gentleness, and virtue!"

The Countess, who wished to appear cheerful, rallied him on the warmth of his expressions; then rising from her seat, she left him to his meditations, and retired to dress.

The family at Somerset had just drawn round the breakfast table, when Pembroke arrived. During the repast, they expressed their surprise at the suddenness of his return. Mary, after repeating the contents of the note which she had received the preceding day from Lady Tinemouth, requested that her cousin would be kind enough to drive her in his curricle that morning to Harrowby.

"I will, with pleasure," answered he: "I have seen her ladyship, and even supped with her last night."

"How came that?" asked Mrs. Dorothy.

"I shall explain it to my father, whenever he will honour me with an audience," returned he addressing the baronet, with all the joy of his heart looking out at his eyes; "will you indulge me, my dear Sir, by half an hour's attention, any time before noon?"

"Certainly," replied Sir Robert; "at present I am going into my study, where I must settle my steward's books; but the moment I have finished, I will send for you."

Mrs. Dorothy walked out after her brother, to attend to her aviary; and Mary remaining alone with her cousin, made some enquiries about the Countess's reasons for coming to the abbey.

"I know nothing about them," replied he, gayly, "for she went to bed almost the instant I entered her house. Too good to remain where her company was not wanted, she left me to enjoy a most delightful *tête-à-tête* with a dear friend, from whom I parted four years ago. In short, we sat up the whole night together, talking over past scenes, and present ones too, for I assure you, you were not forgotten."

"Me! What had I to do with it?" replied Mary, smiling, "I cannot recollect any friend of yours that you have not seen these four years."

"Well, that is strange!" answered Pembroke, "he remembers you perfectly; but true to your sex, you affirm what you please, though I know that there is not a man in the world whom you prefer before him."

Mary shook her head, laughed, and sighed, and extricating her hand from his, threatened to leave him if he would not be serious.

"I am serious," cried he, catching her arm, and pulling her back to her seat; "Would you have me swear that I have seen him you most wish to see?"

Mary regarded the expression of his countenance with a thrill, which vanished as soon as felt; and resuming her chair, quietly said, "You can have seen no man that is of consequence to me; so, whoever your friend may be, I have only to congratulate you on a meeting which affords you such extreme delight."

Pembroke burst into a laugh at her composure. "So cold, Mary!" cried he, "So cautious! Yet I verily believe you would answer my transports, did I tell you who he is. However, you are such a sceptic, that I won't hint even one of the many fine things he said of you."

Mary smiled incredulously.

"I could beat you cousin," exclaimed he, "for this oblique way of saying that I am telling lies! But I will have my revenge on your curiosity; for on my honour, I declare," added he emphatically, "that last night, I met with a friend at Lady Tinemouth's, who, four years ago saved my life; who entertained me several weeks in his house; and, who has seen, and adores you! 'Tis true, on my hopes of heaven; and I have promised, that you will repay these heavy obligations, by marrying him. What do you say to this, my sweet Mary?"

Miss Beaufort looked anxious at the serious and energetic manner in which these rapid asseverations were uttered: even the sportive kiss that ended the question, did not dispel the gravity with which she prepared to reply.

Pembroke perceiving her intent, prevented her by exclaiming, "Cease, Mary, cease! I see you are preparing a false statement. Let truth prevail, and you will not deny, that I am suing for a plighted faith? You will not deny who it was that subdued your judgment, to any indulgence? You cannot conceal from me, that the wanderer Constantine possesses your affections?"

Mary reddened with pain and displeasure; and, rising from her seat, "I did not expect this cruel, this ungenerous speech from you, Pembroke!" cried she, averting her brimming eyes; "What have I done to deserve so rude, so unfeeling a reproach?"

Pembroke threw his arm round her waist. "Come," said he in a tender voice, "don't be tragical. I never meant to reproach you child: I dare say, if you gave your heart, it was only in return for his. I know you are a grateful girl; and, I verily believe, you won't find much difference between my friend the young Count Sobieski, and the forlorn Constantine."

A suspicion of the truth flashed across Miss Beaufort's mind: unable to speak, she caught hold of her cousin's hands, and looking eagerly in his face, her eyes declared the question she would have asked.

Pembroke laughed triumphantly; but a servant entering to tell him that Sir Robert was ready, he strained her to his breast, and exclaimed, "Now I am revenged! Farewell! I leave you to all the pangs of doubt and curiosity!" He then flew out of the room, with an arch glance at her distressed countenance, and hurried up stairs.

Mary clasped her trembling hands together as the door closed on Pembroke. "O, Gracious Providence!" cried she, "What am I to understand by this mystery, this joy of my cousin's? Can it be possible, that the illustrious Sobieski, and my contemned Constantine, are the same?" A burning blush over-spread her face and bosom at the expression *my* which had escaped her lips.

Whilst the graces, the sweetness, the dignity of Thaddeus, captivated her notice; his sufferings, his virtues, and the mysterious interest which involved his history, had fixed her attention, and awakened her esteem. From these grounds, the step is short to love. "When the soul is conquered, the heart surrenders at discretion."* But Mary knew not that she had advanced farther than what rendered retreat possible, till the last scene at Dundas-house, by forcing her to defend Constantine

---

* Unidentified. A similar expression ('although her heart were surrendered to him at discretion') appears in Tobias Smollett's 1751 *The Adventures of Peregrine Pickle*.

against the charge of loving her, compelled her to feel how much she wished that the truth were otherwise.

Poor and lowly as he seemed, she found that her whole heart and life were wrapped in his remembrance; that his worshipped idea, was her most precious solace, her property, her dear treasure, on which she banqueted in secret. It was the companion of her walks, the monitor of her actions. Whenever she planned, whenever she executed, she asked herself, How would Constantine consider this? and accordingly, did she approve or condemn her conduct.

Though separated far from this idol of her memory, thus was the impression which he had stamped on her heart, ever present. The shade of Laura visited the solitude of Vaucluse; the image of Constantine haunted the walks of Somerset.* The loveliness of nature; its leafy groves, and verdant meadows; its blooming mornings, and luxuriant sunsets; the romantic shadows of twilight, or the soft glories of the moon and stars; all, as they pressed beauty and sentiment upon her heart, awoke it to the remembrance of Constantine: she saw his image in every thing, she felt his soul in all. Subtle, and undefinable, is that ethereal chord, which unites our tenderest thoughts with their chain of association!

Before this conversation, in which Pembroke had mentioned the name of Constantine with such badinage and ambiguity, he had never heard him spoken of by Mary or his aunt, without declaring a displeasure nearly amounting to anger. Hence, when he now so strangely altered his tone, Miss Beaufort could not escape retaining the only conclusion which could be drawn; that he had seen in the person of him she most valued, some one whom he loved. Prior to this time, she had more than once suspected from the opinions which Somerset occasionally repeated respecting the affairs of Poland, that he could only have acquired so nice a knowledge of its events, by having visited the country itself. She proposed her suspicion to Mr. Loftus: he denied the fact; and she thought no more on the subject, till the present ambiguous hints of her cousin, conjured up these doubts anew; and led her to suppose, that if Pembroke had not disobeyed his father so far as to go to Warsaw, he had at least met with the Count Sobieski in some other realm. The possibility that this young hero, of whom fame had spoken so loudly, might be the mysterious Constantine, bewildered and delighted her. The more she compared what she had heard of the one, with what she had witnessed in the other, the more was she

---

* The narrator compares Mary to the poet Petrarch, who was haunted by memories of the beloved but unattainable Laura while he lived in Vaucluse.

reconciled to the probability of so wild a hope. Besides, she could not for a moment believe that her cousin would so cruelly sport with her delicacy and feelings, as to awaken expectations which he could not fulfil.

Agitated by a suspense which bordered on agony, with a beating heart she heard his quick step descending the stairs. The door opened, and Pembroke, flying into the room, caught up his hat: as he was darting away again, Mary, unable to restrain her impatience, with an imploring voice ejaculated his name. He turned round, and displayed to her amazed sight, a countenance in which no vestige of its former animation could be traced; his cheek was flushed; and his eyes full of distraction, shot a wild fire, that immediately struck to her heart. Unconscious what she did, she ran up to him; but Pembroke pushing her back, with parched lips, and in a hurried voice, exclaimed, "Don't ask me any questions, Mary, if you would not drive me to madness."

"O Heaven!" cried she, catching his arm, and clinging to him while the velocity of his motion dragged her into the hall; "tell me! Has anything happened to my guardian? to your friend? to Constantine?"

"No;" replied he, looking at her with a face full of desperation; "but my father commands me to treat him like a villain."

Mary could hardly credit her senses, at this confirmation that Constantine and Sobieski were one: turning giddy with the tumultuous delight which rushed over her soul, she staggered back a few paces, and, leaning against the now open door, tried to recover breath to regain the room she had left.

Pembroke having escaped from her grasp, ran furiously down the hill, mounted his horse, and, forbidding any groom to attend him, galloped towards the high-road with the impetuosity of a madman. All the powers of his soul were in arms. He felt himself wounded, dishonoured, stigmatised with ingratitude, and every baseness, which can degrade the mind of man.

Sir Robert Somerset had founded a hatred of the Poles and Hungarians, on the recollection of an injury which he had received in early youth from some of those people. In this instance his dislike was implacable; and when his son set out for the continent, he positively forbade him to enter either Poland or Hungary. Nevertheless, when Pembroke joined the Baronet in his library, he did it with confidence. With a bounding heart and animated countenance, he recapitulated how he had been wrought up by the Russian noblemen, to take up arms in their cause and march into Poland. At these last words, the brow of his father contracted.

Pembroke, who expected some marks of displeasure, hastened to obliterate his disobedience, by narrating the event which introduced, not only the young Count Sobieski to his succour, but the consequent friendship of the whole of that princely family.

Sir Robert made no other reply to this, than by a deeper frown; and, when Pembroke, with all the ardour of youth, attempted to describe the calamitous death of the Palatine, the horrors that attended the last hours of the Countess, and the succeeding misery of Thaddeus, who was now in England, no language can paint the rage which burst at once from the Baronet. He stamped on the ground, he covered his face with his clenched hands; then turning on his son with the most tremendous fury, he exclaimed, "Pembroke! You have outraged my commands! And never will I pardon you, if this young man be ever brought into my sight."

"Merciful Heaven!" cried Pembroke, thunder-struck at a violence, which he almost wished might proceed from any cause but intention; "Surely something has agitated my father! What has discomposed you, Sir?"

Sir Robert shook his head, whilst his teeth appeared to grind against each other. "Don't mistake me," replied he in a firm voice, "I am perfectly in my senses. It depends on *you* that I shall continue so. You know my oath against these accursed Polanders; and, I repeat again, if you ever bring that young man into my sight, you shall never see *me* more."

A cold dew overspread the body of Pembroke. He would have caught hold of his father's hand, but he held it back. "O, Sir!" said he, "You surely cannot intend that I shall treat with ingratitude the man who saved my life?"

Sir Robert did not vouchsafe him an answer, but continued walking up and down the room, till his agitation seeming to encrease at every step, he opened the door of an interior apartment, and retired, bidding his son remain.

The horror-struck Pembroke waited for near a quarter of an hour before his father re-entered. When he did appear, the deep gloom of his eye gave no encouragement to his son, who, hanging down his head, recoiled from speaking first. Sir Robert approached with a composed but severe countenance, and said, "I have been seeking every palliation that your conduct will admit, but I can find none. Before you quitted England, you knew well my abhorrence of the Polish nation. One of that country, many years ago, wounded my happiness in a way that I shall never recover. From that hour, I took an oath, never to enter its borders; and never to suffer one of its people to come within my doors. Rash, disobedient boy! You know my disposition, and you have seen the emotion with which this dilemma has shaken my soul! But, be it on your own head: you have incurred obligations which I cannot repay. I will not perjure myself to defray a debt contracted against my positive and declared principles. I never will see this Polander you speak of; and, it is my express command, on pain of my eternal malediction, that you break with him entirely."

Pembroke, with a deep groan, fell into a seat. Sir Robert proceeded.

"I pity your distress, Pembroke, but my resolution cannot be shaken. Oaths are not to be broken with impunity. You must either resign him, or resign me. We may compromise your debt of gratitude; I will give you deeds to put your friend in possession of five hundred a year for life, for ever; but, from the hour in which you tell him so, you must never see him more."

Sir Robert was preparing to quit the room; when Pembroke, starting from his chair, threw himself in agony on his knees, and catching by the skirt of his coat, implored him, for God's sake, to recall his words; to remember, that he was affixing everlasting dishonour on his son! "Remember, dear Sir!" cried he, holding his struggling hand, "that the man to whom you offer money as a compensation for insult, is of a nature too noble to receive it. He will reject it, and spurn me; and I shall feel that I deserve his scorn. For mercy's sake, spare me the agony of harrowing up the heart of my preserver; of meeting reproach from his eyes!"

"Leave me!" cried the Baronet, breaking from him; "I repeat, unless you wish to incur my curse, do as I have commanded."

Thus outraged, thus agonized, Pembroke had appeared before the eyes of his cousin Mary, more like a distracted creature, than a man possessed of his senses. Shortly after his abrupt departure, her apprehension was petrified to a dreadful certainty of some cruel ruin to her hopes, by an order which she received in the hand-writing of her uncle, commanding her not to attempt visiting Lady Tinemouth, whilst the Count Sobieski continued to be her guest.

Hardly knowing whither he went, Pembroke did not arrive at the ruined aisle which leads up to the habitable part of the Abbey, till near three o'clock. He inquired of the servant who took his horse, whether the Countess and Mr. Constantine were at home. The man replied in the affirmative; but added with a saddened countenance, that he feared neither of them could be seen.

"For what reason?" demanded Somerset.

"Alas! Sir," replied the servant, "this day at noon, whilst my lady was dressing, she was seized with a violent fit of coughing, which ended in the rupture of a blood vessel. It continued to flow so long, that Mr.

Constantine told the apothecary whom he had summoned, to send for Dr. Cavendish, a physician of his acquaintance, who is now at Stamford. The doctor is not yet arrived, and Mr. Constantine won't leave my lady."

Though Mr. Somerset was truly concerned at the illness of the Countess, the respite it afforded him from immediately declaring the ungrateful message of Sir Robert, gave him no inconsiderable degree of ease. Some little relieved by the hope of being for one day spared the anguish of displaying his father in a disgraceful light, he entered the Abbey; and commissioned a maid-servant to inform Thaddeus that he was below.

In a few minutes the girl returned with the following lines scrawled on a piece of paper.

"I am grieved, that I cannot see my dear Somerset to-day; and more grieved for the cause: I fear my revered friend is on her death-bed. I have sent for Dr. Cavendish, who is now at Stamford; doubtless you know that he is a man of first rate abilities: if human skill could preserve her, I might yet have hopes; but her disorder is a consumption, and its stroke is sure. I am now sitting by her bed-side, and writing what she dictates, to her husband, her son, and her daughter: painful, you may believe is the task! I cannot, my dear Somerset, add more, than my hope of seeing you soon; and that you will join in prayers to heaven for the restoration of my inestimable friend, with your faithful
"SOBIESKI."

"Alas! unhappy, persecuted Sobieski!" thought Pembroke, as he closed the paper; "To what art thou doomed! Some friends are torn from thee by death; others, desert thee in the hour of trouble!"

He took out his pencil, to answer this distressing epistle, but he stopped at the first word; he durst not write that his father would fulfil any one of those engagements which he had so largely promised; and, throwing away the pencil and the paper, he left a verbal declaration of his sorrow at what had happened, and an assurance of calling next day. Turning his back on a house which he had left in the morning with such animating hopes, he re-mounted his horse, and, melancholy and slow, rode about the country till evening; so unwilling was he to return to that home, which now threatened him with the frowns of his father, the tears of Mary Beaufort, and the miserable reflections of his own wretched heart.

CHAP. IV.

Doctor Cavendish not having quitted his friend at Stamford, set off for Harrowby the instant Mr. Constantine's messenger arrived; and, before midnight alighted at the Abbey.

When he entered Lady Tinemouth's chamber, he found her ladyship supported in the arms of Thaddeus, and struggling with a second rupture of her lungs, which seemed to threaten immediate dissolution. As he approached the bed, Thaddeus turned his eyes on him with an expression that powerfully told his fears. Dr. Cavendish silently squeezed his hand; then taking from his pocket some styptic drops* which he brought on purpose, he made the Countess swallow them, and soon saw that they succeeded in stopping the blood.

Thaddeus and his friend remained by the side of the suffering Lady Tinemouth till towards ten in the morning, when she sunk into a gentle sleep. Complete stillness being necessary to continue this repose, the doctor proposed leaving a maid to watch by her ladyship; and, drawing the Count out of the room, descended the stairs.

Mr. Somerset, who had been arrived half an hour, met them in the breakfast-parlour. After a few kind words exchanged between the parties, they all sat down with dejected countenances to their melancholy meal. Thaddeus was too much absorbed in the scene he had left, to swallow any thing but a dish of coffee.

"Do you think Lady Tinemouth is in imminent danger?" inquired Pembroke of the doctor.

Dr. Cavendish sighed, and turning to Thaddeus, directed to him the answer which his friend's question had demanded. "I am afraid, my dear Mr. Constantine," said he, in a reluctant voice; "that you are to sustain a new trial! I really fear, that her ladyship cannot live eight-and-forty hours."

Thaddeus threw down his eyes and shuddered, but made no reply. Further remarks were prevented by a messenger from the Countess, who desired Mr. Constantine's immediate attendance at her ladyship's bed-side. He obeyed. In half an hour he returned with the tears yet wet on his cheek.

"Dear Thaddeus!" cried Pembroke, rising and taking his hand,

* A liquid that halts bleeding by contracting blood vessels.

"I trust the Countess is not worse? This emotion of yours is too distressing: it afflicts my very heart." Pembroke felt that it rent it; for he could not help internally acknowledging, that when Sobieski should close the eyes of Lady Tinemouth, he would be paying the last sad office to his last friend. That dear distinction he durst no longer arrogate to himself. Denied the fulfilment of its duties, he felt, that to retain the title, would be an assumption without a right.

Thaddeus drew his hand over his again brimming eyes; "The Countess herself," said he, "feels the truth of what Dr. Cavendish told us. She sent for me, to beg as I loved her, or would wish to see her die in peace, to devise some means of bringing her daughter to the Abbey to night. As for Lord Harwold, she says, his behaviour since he arrived at manhood, has been of a nature so cruel and unnatural, that she would not draw on herself the misery, or he the added guilt, of a refusal: for Lady Albina, who has been quiescent in all their barbarities, she trusts, she might be prevailed on to seek a last embrace from a dying parent. It is this request," added Thaddeus, "that has thus agitated me. When she pictured to me, with all the fervour of a mother, her doating fondness for this daughter, (on whom, whenever she did venture to hope, all her fairy dreams had rested;) when she wrung my hands, and beseeched me, as if I had been the sole disposer of her fate, to let her see her child before she died; I could only promise every exertion to effect it; and, with an aching heart, I came to consult you."

Dr. Cavendish was opening his lips to speak; but Somerset, in his eagerness to relieve his friend, did not perceive it, and immediately answered: "I will undertake this very hour what you have promised. I know Lord Tinemouth's family are now at the Wold. It is only thirty miles distant. I will send a servant, to have relays of horses ready. My curricle, which is at the door, will be more convenient than a chaise; and I will engage to be back before to-morrow morning. Write a letter, Thaddeus," continued he, "to Lady Albina; tell her of her mother's situation; and, though I have never seen her ladyship, I will give it into her own hand, and carry her off directly, even were it in the face of her rascally father."

The pale cheeks of Thaddeus were flushed with a momentary hectic; turning to Dr. Cavendish, he begged him to write, whilst he walked out with his friend to order the carriage. Pembroke was thanked for his zeal, but it was not by words; they are too weak vehicles to convey strong feelings; Thaddeus pressed his hand, and accompanied the action with a look that spoke volumes. The warm heart of Pembroke expanded under the animated gratitude of his friend: He sprung into his seat, and forgot till he had lost sight of

Harrowby Hill, how soon he must appear to that friend, as the most ungrateful of men.

It was near four in the afternoon, before Mr. Somerset left his curricle at the little inn which skirts the village of Harthorpe. The paling belonging to Lord Tinemouth's park, was only a few yards distant; but, fearful of being observed, Pembroke sought a more obscure part; and, scaling a wall covered by the branches of high trees, he found a way to the house through an almost impassible thicket.

He watched two hours for the appearance of Lady Albina, (whose youth and elegance he thought would unequivocally distinguish her from the rest of the Earl's household,) but in vain. Desponding of success, he was preparing to change his station, when he heard a sound among the withered leaves, and the next moment, a beautiful young creature passed the bush behind which he was concealed. The fine symmetry of her profile, assured him that she must be the daughter of Lady Tinemouth. She stooped to gather a china aster: Pembroke, knowing that no time ought to be lost, gently emerged from his recess; but not so stilly as to escape the ear of Lady Albina, who instantly looking round, screamed, and would have fled, had he not thrown himself before her, and exclaimed, "Stay, Lady Albina! For Heaven's sake, stay! I come from your mother!"

Her ladyship gazed fearfully in his face, and tried to release her hand which he had seized to prevent her flight.

"Do not be alarmed;" continued he, "no harm is intended you. I am the son of Sir Robert Somerset, and the friend of your mother, who is now on the point of death. She implores to see you this night, (for she has hardly an hour to live,) to hear from your own lips, that you do not hate her."

Lady Albina, now wholly given up to his relation, trembled dreadfully; and, with faded cheeks, and quivering lips, replied, "Hate my mother! O, no! I have ever dearly loved her!"

A flood of tears prevented her speaking further; and Pembroke perceiving that he had gained her confidence, put the doctor's letter into her hand. The gentle heart of Lady Albina bled at every word which her almost blinded eyes read over; turning to Pembroke, who stood contemplating her lovely countenance with the deepest interest, she said, "Pray, Mr. Somerset, take me immediately to my mother. If she were to die before I can arrive, I shall be made miserable for life. Alas! alas! I have never been allowed to behold her! Never been allowed to visit London, because my father knew that I believed my poor mother innocent, and would have seen her, if it were possible."

Lady Albina wept violently as she spoke, and giving her hand to

Pembroke, added, timidly looking round to the house, "You must take me now. We must hasten away, in case we should be surprised. If Lady Sophia were to know that I have been speaking with any body out of the family, I should be locked up for months."

Pembroke did not require a second command from his beautiful charge, but conducting her through the unfrequented paths by which he had entered, soon seated her in his curricle; he sheltered her delicate form with his great coat, and tied down her straw hat with his cambric handkerchief; then whipping his horses, set off on full gallop, towards the melancholy goal of his enterprize.

The tender Lady Albina, whose ingenuous mind had ever been proof against the malicious insinuations of Lady Sophia to the prejudice of Lady Tinemouth, sat by the side of Mr. Somerset, sometimes mute with sorrow; sometimes, lamenting, with all the artless eloquence of nature, the injuries of her dying parent, and her own unhappiness, in having been so long withheld from paying duty, where she owed so much affection.

Whilst the two anxious travellers were pursuing their sad journey, the inhabitants of the abbey were distracted with apprehension that the Countess would expire before their arrival. Ever since Lady Tinemouth had been informed that Mr. Somerset was gone to the Wold, hope and fear agitated her almost to suffocation; at length, wearied out with solicitude and expectation, she turned her dim eyes upon Thaddeus, and forcing a smile, said, in a languid voice, "My dear friend, it must be near midnight. I shall never see the morning; I shall never in this world see my child. I pray you, thank Mr. Somerset for all the trouble I have occasioned; and my daughter, my Albina!" added her ladyship, hardly able to articulate. "Oh! Father of mercies!" cried she, holding up her clasped hands, "pour all thy blessings on her head, she has never wilfully given this broken heart a pang!"

The Countess had hardly ended speaking, when Thaddeus heard a bustle on the stairs; suspecting that it might be the arrival of his friend, he made a sign to Dr. Cavendish to go and enquire. His heart beat violently, whilst he kept his eye fixed on the door, and held the fainting pulse of Lady Tinemouth in his hand. The doctor re-entered, and, in a low voice, whispered, "Lady Albina is here."

The words acted like magic on the fading senses of the Countess; with preternatural strength she started from her pillow, and catching hold of Sobieski's arm with both hers, cried, "O! give her to me, whilst I have life!"

Lady Albina appeared, led in by Pembroke, but instantly quitting his hand, with an agonizing shriek she rushed towards the bed, and flung herself into the extended arms of her mother. Those arms closed on her, and the head of the Countess rested on her bosom.

Dr. Cavendish soon perceived, by the struggles of the young lady, that she was in convulsions; taking her off the bed, he consigned her to Pembroke and Thaddeus, who carried her into another apartment: he remained to assist the Countess.

Albina was removed; but the eyes of her amiable and injured mother, were never again unclosed: she had breathed her last sigh in grateful exstacy on the bosom of her daughter; and Heaven had taken her spot-less soul to itself.

Being convinced that the Countess was indeed no more, the good doctor left her remains in charge with the women, and repairing to the adjoining room, found Lady Albina yet senseless, in the arms of his two friends. She was laid on a sofa, and Cavendish was pouring some drops into her mouth, when he descried Thaddeus gliding out of the room: desirous to spare him the shock of suddenly seeing the corpse of one whom he loved so dearly, he said, "Stop, Mr. Constantine! I conjure you, do not go into the Countess's room!"

The eyes of Thaddeus turned with quickness on the distressed face of the physician; one glance explained what the doctor durst not speak; and hastily saying, "I shall obey you," he hurried from the chamber.

In the Count's rapid descent from Lady Albina's room, to the break-fast-parlour, he too plainly perceived, by the tears of the servants, that he had now no sorrows to regret but his own. He darted from the clam-orous laments of these honest people into the parlour, and shutting the door, threw himself down on a sofa; but rest induced thought, and thought harrowed up his soul. He started from his position; he paced the room in a paroxysm of anguish; he would have given worlds for one tear to relieve his oppressed heart. Ready to suffocate, he threw open a window, and leaned out. Not a star appeared to light the sky; the wind blew freshly; and, with parched lips, he inhaled it, as the reviv-ing breath of heaven.

He was sitting on the window-seat, with his head leaning against the casement, when Pembroke entered unobserved: walking up to him, he laid his hand upon his arm, and ejaculated, in a tremulous voice, "Thaddeus, dear Thaddeus!"

Thaddeus rose at the well-known sounds; they reminded him that he was not yet alone in the world; and throwing himself upon the bosom of Mr. Somerset, he exclaimed, "Heaven has still reserved thee, my dear Pembroke, to be my comforter! In thy friendship," added he, wiping away the tears which relieved his bursting heart; "I shall find an affection similar with those which are gone for ever: my friend, my brother! you are the last cord that binds me to the world."

Pembroke received the embrace of his friend; he felt his tears upon his cheek; but he could neither return the one, nor sympathize with the other. The conviction, that he was soon to sever that cord which bound them to each other; that he was to cut asunder that knot which ought to have united them for ever; that he was to deprive the man who had preserved his life, of the only stay of his existence, and abandon him to despair! all these ideas struck to his soul; and, grasping the hand of his friend, he gazed at his averted and dejected features, with a look of desperate horror. "Sobieski," cried he, "whatever may happen, never forget, that I swear, I love you dearer than my life! And, when I am forced to abandon my friend, I shall not be long of abandoning what will then be worthless to me."

Not perceiving the phrenzy of eye which accompanied this energetic declaration, Thaddeus gave no other meaning to the words, than believing it to be the most expressive assurance of affection that the forceful nature of his friend could devise.

The entrance of Dr. Cavendish disturbed the two young men, to whom he immediately communicated the encreased indisposition of Lady Albina.

"The shock," said he, "which she has received from the meeting, and death of her mother, has so materially shaken her delicate frame, that I have ordered her to bed, and administered an opiate, which I hope will procure her some repose: and you, my dear Sir," added he, addressing the Count, "you had better seek a little rest! The stoutest constitution might sink under what you have lately endured. Pray, allow Mr. Somerset and myself to prevail on you, on our accounts, if not on your own, to retire for half an hour!"

Thaddeus, in disregard of his personal comfort, never infringed on that of others; he felt that he could not sleep: but he knew it would gratify his benevolent friends, to suppose that he did; and accordingly, without opposition, he went to a room, and throwing himself on a bed, lay for near an hour, ruminating on what had passed. There is an omnipresence in thought, or a velocity producing nearly the same effect, which brings within the short space of a few minutes, the images of many foregoing years. In almost the same moment, Thaddeus pondered on his strange meeting with the Countess, her melancholy story, her forlorn death-bed, the fatal secret that her vile husband and son were his father and brother; and that her daughter, whom his warm heart acknowledged as a sister, was with him under the same roof, and, like him, the innocent inheritor of her father's shame.

Whilst these multifarious and painful meditations were agitating his perturbed mind, Dr. Cavendish found repose on a couch, and Pembroke Somerset, every instant feeling greater abhorrence to his ungrateful talk, resolved once more to try the influence of entreaty on the otherwise generous spirit of his father. With a half hoping, half desponding heart, he commenced this last attempt, to shake, if possible, so fatal a resolution:

"*To Sir Robert Somerset, Bart. Somerset Castle.*

"I have not ventured into the presence of my dear father, since he uttered those dreadful words, which I would give up my existence to believe I had never heard. You denounced a curse upon me, if I opposed your will to immediately break all connexion with the man who preserved my life. When I think on this; when I remember that it was from *you* I received a command so inexplicable in yourself, so disgraceful to me, I am nearly mad: and what I shall be, should you, by repeating your injunctions, force me to obey them, Heaven only knows! but I feel that I cannot survive the loss of my honour, and the sacrifice of my character for every principle of virtue, which such conduct must forever destroy.

"O, my father! I conjure you! reflect, before, in compliance with an oath, which it was almost guilt to make, you decree your only son to everlasting shame and remorse! Act how I will, I shall never be happy more. I cannot live under your malediction; and should I give up my friend, my conscience will reproach me at every instant of my existence. Can I draw that breath which he prolonged, and cease to remember, that I have abandoned him to want and misery? It were vain to flatter myself, that he will condescend to escape either, by the munificence which you offer as a compensation for my friendship. No; I cannot believe that his sensible and independent nature is so changed: circumstances never had any power over the nobility of his soul.

"The hand of misfortune, which threw Count Sobieski friendless on the bounty of England, cannot make him appear otherwise in my eyes, than as that idol of Warsaw, whose smile was honour, whose friendship conferred distinction.

"Though deprived of the splendour of command; though the eager circle of friends no longer cluster round him; though a stranger in this country, and without a home; though in place of an equipage and retinue, he is followed by calamity and neglect; yet, in my mind, I still see him in a car of triumph: I see not only the opposer of his nation's enemies, but the vanquisher of his own desires; I see the heir of a princely house, even when deserted by mankind, yet encompassed by his virtues; I see him, though cast out from a hardened and unjust society, still surrounded by the lingering spirits of those who have fled to better worlds!

"And this is the man, my dear father, (whom I am sure, had he been of any other country than Poland, you would have selected from all other men, to be the friend and example of your son;) this is he, whom you command me to thrust away!

"I beseech you, to reconsider this injunction! I am now writing under the same roof with him: it depends on you, my ever revered father, whether I am doing so for the last time; whether this is the last day in which your son is to feel himself a man of honour; whether he is henceforth to be a wretch overwhelmed with shame and sorrow!

"I have not yet dared to utter one word of what your cruel orders dictated, to my unhappy friend; he is now retired to a room to obtain some rest, after the anguish of witnessing the death of Lady Tinemouth who died this night, in consequence of an illness which only lasted eight-and-forty hours. Should I have to tell him, that he is to lose me too, – but I cannot add more. Your own heart, my dear father, must tell you, that my soul is on the rack, till I have an answer to this letter."

"Before I shut my paper, let me implore you on my knees! whatever you may decide, do not hate me; do not load my breaking heart with a parent's curse! Whatever I may be, however low and degraded in my own eyes, still, that I have sacrificed what is most precious to me, to my father, will impart the only consolation that will then have power to reach your dutiful son,

"Pembroke Somerset."

"*Harrowby Abbey,*
Five o'clock on the morning."

Dr. Cavendish remained in a profound sleep, whilst Pembroke, with an aching heart, having written the above letter, and dispatched it with a man and horse, tried to compose himself, to half an hour's forgetfulness of life and its turmoils; but he found his attempts as ineffectual as those of his friend.

Thaddeus tossed and tumbled on his restless pillow. Reluctant to disturb the doctor and Somerset, whom he hoped, having less cause for regret, had found that repose which he sought in vain, he remained in bed. He longed for morning. Any change of situation seemed to his irritated nerves, better than the state he was in; and, with some gleams of pleasure, he watched the dawn break, and the sun rise behind the opposite hill. He got up, opened the window, and looking out, saw a man throw himself off a horse that was all in foam, and enter the house. The next minute the clock struck eight.

Surprised at this circumstance, Thaddeus descended to the parlour, where he found the man; who, being Pembroke's messenger, had returned express from the castle, bearing an order from Sir Robert, (who was seized alarmingly ill,) that his son should come back immediately.

Dismayed to the soul with this new distress, Mr. Somerset gave the Count such a strain to his breast when he bade him farewel, as might have informed a more suspicious person, that it was intended for a final parting; but Thaddeus discerned nothing more in the anguish of his friend's countenance, than fear for the safety of Sir Robert; and, fervently wishing his recovery, he bade Pembroke remember, that should more assistance be necessary, Dr. Cavendish would remain at the Abbey till Lady Albina's return to the Wold.

Mr. Somerset being gone; towards noon, when the Count was anxiously waiting the appearance of the physician from the room of his sister, he was surprised by the abrupt entrance of two gentlemen. He rose, and bowing, inquired what were their business? The elder of the men, with a fierce countenance, and in a voice of thunder, announced himself to be the Earl of Tinemouth, and the other as his son.

"We are come," continued he, standing at a haughty distance, "we are come, to carry from this nest of infamy, Lady Albina Stanhope, whom some one of her mother's paramours, – perhaps you, Sir? dared to steal from her father's house, yesterday evening. Tell me, if you do not wish to meet the chastisement due to your situation, where my daughter is?"

With difficulty the Count Sobieski could suppress the passions that were rising in his breast. He turned a scornful glance on the person of Lord Harwold, (who, with an air of insufferable derision, was coolly measuring his figure through an eye-glass;) and then replying to the Earl, said in a firm voice; "My lord, whoever you suppose me to be, it matters not; I now stand in the place of Lady Tinemouth's executor; and, to my last gasp, I will prove myself the defender of her injured name."

"Her lover!" interrupted Lord Harwold, turning on his heel.

"Her defender, Sir!" repeated Thaddeus, with a tremendous frown; "and shame and sorrow will pursue that son, that requires a stranger to supply his duty."

"Wretch!" cried the Earl, forgetting his assumed loftiness, and advancing passionately towards Thaddeus, with his stick held up; "How dare you address such language to an English nobleman?"

"By the right of Nature, which holds her laws over all mankind:" returned he, calmly looking on the raised stick, "When an English nobleman forgets that he is a son, he is amenable to meet reproach from the meanest vassal he commands."

"You see, my lord," cried Harwold, sliding behind his father, "what we bring on ourselves by harbouring these democratic foreigners! Sir," added he, addressing himself to Thaddeus; "your dangerous principles shall be communicated to the Alien-office!* Such fellows ought to hanged."†

Sobieski eyed the enraged little lord, with contempt; and, turning to the Earl, who was again opening his lips to speak, he said in an unaltered tone, "I cannot guess, Lord Tinemouth, what is the reason of this attack on me. I came here by mere accident; I found the Countess ill; and, from respect to her excellent qualities, I remained with her till her eyes were closed for ever. She prayed to see her daughter before she died. What human heart could deny a mother such a request? and my friend Pembroke Somerset undertook to bring Lady Albina to the Abbey."

"Pembroke Somerset!" echoed the Earl, "A pretty guard for my daughter truly! I make no doubt, he is just such a rascal as his father; just such another as yourself! I am not to be imposed on by your falsehoods: I know Lady Tinemouth to have been a disgrace to me; and you, to be that German adventurer, on whose account I sent her from London."

Surprised at this unexpected calumny on the memory of a woman, whose fame, from any other mouth, came as unsullied as purity itself, Thaddeus gazed with horror at the furious countenance of the man whom he believed to be his father. His heart swelled, his temples throbbed; and, not deigning to reply to a charge as unmanly as it was false, he quietly took out of his pocket the two letters which the Countess had dictated to her husband and her son.

Lord Harwold tore his open, cast his eyes over the first words, then crumpling it up in his hand, threw it from him, exclaiming, "I am not to be frightened, either by her arts, or the lies of her fellows."

Thaddeus, no longer master of himself, sprung towards this unnatural son, and, seizing his arm with the strength of a Hercules; "Lord Harwold!" cried he, in a dreadful voice, "If it were not that I have some

---

* The Alien Office was created in 1793 to regulate the high volume of migrants entering Britain after the French Revolution.
† The younger Harwold is surely the foolish man of the same name who admired Thaddeus's boots shortly after his arrival in London. Yet, as with his former companion Berrington, neither Thaddeus nor the narrator mentions the earlier encounter.

mercy on you for that parent's sake, whom like a parricide, you are giving a second death by such murderous slander, I would resent her wrongs at the hazard of your worthless life!"

"My lord! my lord!" cried the trembling Harwold, quaking under the gripe of Thaddeus, and shrinking from the terrible brightness of his eyes; "my lord! my lord, save me!"

The Earl, almost suffocated with rage, called out, "Ruffian! Let go my son!" and again raising his arm, aimed a blow at the head of Thaddeus, who, wrenching the stick out of the foaming lord's hand, snapped it in two, and threw the pieces out of the window.

Lord Harwold took this opportunity to ring the bell violently; on which summons, his own two servants entered the room.

"Now, you low-born, insolent scoundrel!" cried the disarmed Earl, stamping with his feet, and pointing to the men who stood in the door-way; "You shall be turned neck and heels out of this house. Richard, James, collar that fellow instantly."

Thaddeus only extended his arm to the men, (who were confusedly looking on each other,) and calmly said; "If either of you attempt to obey this command of your lord's, you shall have cause to repent it."

The men retreated. The Earl repeated his orders.

"Rascals! Do as I command you, or instantly prepare to be turned away. I will teach you," added he, clenching his fist at the Count, who stood resolutely and serenely before him, "I will teach you how to behave to a man of high birth!"

The footmen were again retarded from approaching, by a glance from the intimidating eyes of Thaddeus; who, turning with calm dignity to the storming Earl, "You can teach me nothing about high birth," said he, "that I do not already know. Could it be of any independent benefit to a man, then had not I received the taunts and insults which you have dared to cast upon me."

At that moment, Dr. Cavendish having heard a bustle, made his appearance. Amazed at the sight of two strangers, whom from their enraged countenances, and the proud elevation with which Thaddeus was standing between them, he rightly judged to be the Earl and his son, he advanced towards his friend; intending to support him in the attack which he saw was menaced, by the violent gestures of his visitors.

"Dr. Cavendish," said Thaddeus, speaking to him as he approached; "your name must be a passport to the confidence of any man! I there-fore shall gratify the husband of my ever-lamented friend, by quitting this house; but I delegate you to the office with which she entrusted me. I leave you in charge of her sacred remains; and of the jewels, which you will find in her ladyship's room. She desired that half of them might be given with her blessing to her daughter; and the other half, with her pardon, to her son."

"Tell me, Dr. Cavendish," cried the Earl, as Thaddeus was passing him to leave the room; "Who is that insolent fellow? By heaven, he shall smart for this!"

"Aye, that he shall," added Lord Harwold; "if I have any interest with the Duke of Portland."*

Dr. Cavendish with a flushed cheek, was preparing to speak, when Thaddeus turning round at this last threat of the viscount's, said, "If I did not feel myself as high above Lord Harwold, as heaven is from the earth, perhaps he might provoke me to treat him as he merits; but I spurn such resentment, as I despise him. For you, my lord;" added he, addressing the Earl with an agitated countenance and voice; "there is an angel above, who pleads against the insults that you have obstinately heaped on an innocent man."

Thaddeus disappeared as he uttered the last word; and, hastening from the house and park, stopped at a farmer's cottage, near the brow of the hill. The owners of this humble little place, being the parents of one of Lady Tinemouth's maids, gladly welcomed the so highly-praised Mr. Constantine; and offered him the command of their house, until he might find it convenient to quit the neighbourhood.

Any prospect of repose, promised elysium to him: with harassed and torn nerves, he took possession of an apartment, which looked down upon the road that led from the Abbey to the town. The rapidity of the late events, bewildered his senses like the illusions of a dream. He had seen his father, his brother, his sister; and most probably he had parted from them for ever! At least he hoped, that he should never again be tortured with the sight of Lord Tinemouth or his son.

"How!" thought he, whilst he walked up and down his solitary apartment, "how could the noble nature of my mother, love such a man? And how could he have held so long an empire over the pure heart of the Countess?"

Over and over again, he asked himself that question; but could return no answer: He could no where discern in the bloated features, and passionate gestures of the Earl, any of that beauty of countenance, or grace of manners, which had charmed alike Therese Sobieski, and the tender Adeliza. Like those hideous chasms which are dug deep in

---

* William Cavendish-Bentinck, Third Duke of Portland (1738–1809), served as William Pitt's Home Secretary from 1794 to 1801. Harwold intends to have Thaddeus expelled from Britain.

the land by the impetuous sweep of a torrent, the course of violent passions leaves vast and irreparable traces on the soul. So it was with Lord Tinemouth.

"Gracious Providence!" ejaculated Thaddeus; "How legibly does vice or virtue write itself on the countenance! The Earl's figure and features may be fine, but the lineaments of profligacy have degraded every part of him. Good God! Can he be my father! Can it be his blood that is now running in my veins? Can it be his blood, that rises at this moment with detestation against him?"

Before the sun set, Thaddeus was aroused from these painful soliloquies, by still more painful emotions: He saw from his window, a hearse driving at full gallop up the road, which ascended to the Abbey; and, presently return, with a more solemn pace, followed by a post-chaise and the Earl's coach.

"Unfeeling wretches!" cried Thaddeus, leaning out of the window; and pursuing with his eye, the tips of the sable plumes as the cavalcade wound round the road; "Could ye not allow this poor corse a little rest? Must her injuries be extended to the grave? Must her cold relics be insulted, be hurried to the tomb, without reverence, without decency?"

The noble heart of Thaddeus distended, beat, and writhed with horror, at this climax of the Earl's barbarity. Dr. Cavendish entered: he began to speak of the perpetrators of an act, which he deemed sacrilege against the dead; but Thaddeus could not bear it; and he interrupted him by enquiring how Lady Albina had borne such brutal treatment of her mother's remains.

"Very ill," returned the doctor; "and though I had warned the Earl, that to compel her Ladyship to follow the hearse, would be at the imminent peril of her life, yet he would not be softened. He put her into the coach in a state of insensibility with no other assistant than a woman servant, who received her into her arms; and then, loaded with the secret curses of every honest heart, I saw him set off in the post-chaise which was already occupied by his detestable son. – Heaven's malediction must follow them!"

The doctor pursued the subject. Sobieski's wearied spirits listened to him with patience; for nothing could now be said to encrease an abhorrence which had gained its height. He avowed to himself that he hated the Earl; and he hearkened in gloomy silence to the new crimes recounted by his friend.

In the midst of this depressing conversation, a courier arrived from Dr. Cavendish's Stamford patient, desiring that he would return immediately. The gentleman having sustained a relapse, Cavendish, with some reluctance to quit the Count, (whom he still knew by no other

name than Constantine,) ordered the chaise to the door. He shook
hands with Thaddeus, requested he would let him hear from him,
and bidding him many affectionate adieus, looked out of the carriage
window, till the faint light of the moon, and the fading glimmer of
the cottage candles, failed to make the little spot which contained his
friend, even discernible.

CHAP. V.

For the first time during many nights, Thaddeus slept soundly; but his dreams were disturbed; and he awoke from them at an early hour unrefreshed, and in much fever.

The simple breakfast which his cottage host and hostess set before him, was hardly touched. Their nicely dressed dinner met with the same fate. He was ill, and neither possessed appetite nor spirits to eat. The good people being too civil to intrude upon him, he sat alone in his window from eight o'clock, (at which he had arisen,) till the cawing of the rooks as they returned to the Abbey woods, reminded him that evening was coming on. He was uneasy at the absence of Somerset; not so much on his own account, as on that of Sir Robert, whose encreased danger might have occasioned this delay: However, he hoped otherwise. Longing earnestly for a temporary asylum under the roof of his friend, he trusted that the sympathy of Pembroke would heal all his wounds, and fit him, (if it were required,) yet farther to brave the buffets of adverse fortune. Nor was Miss Beaufort forgotten. If ever one idea more than another, sweetened the bitterness of his reflections, it was the remembrance of the lovely Mary. Whenever her image rose before him; whether standing with folded arms, and looking with vacant gaze on the valley beneath; or, when cast upon his watchful pillow, he opened his aching eyes to the morning light; still, as her beautiful figure presented itself to his mind, he sighed; but it was a sigh laden with balm; it did not tear his breast like those which were wrung from him by the hard hand of calamity and insult; it was the soft breath of love, which makes man dream of heaven, whilst it betrays him to the grave. Thaddeus thought it delightful to recollect how she had looked on him; it was happiness, to know that he owed his liberty to her; and the anticipation, that he should again dwell in her smiles; again draw bliss from her eyes, swelled, agitated, and intoxicated his soul.

"Sweet Mary!" murmured he, "I shall see thee once more! I shall again experience thy kindness! I will thank thee with my heart; and think myself blest, in being allowed the privilege of loving thee in silence, and for ever."

The sight of Pembroke riding through the farmer's fields towards the cottage, agreeably recalled the wandering mind of Sobieski. He went out to meet him; Mr. Somerset, putting his horse on a gallop, was at his friend's side, and had alighted, before he could cross the first meadow. Thaddeus immediately inquired after the Baronet's health. Pembroke answered the question, with an incoherency devoid of all meaning. Thaddeus looked at him with surprise. They walked towards the house, but he did not seem to recover himself; his absence of mind, and the wild rambling of his eyes whenever he was spoken to, were so striking, that the Count entertained no doubt of some dreadful accident.

As soon as they entered the little parlour, Pembroke threw himself into a chair, and, throwing off his hat, wiped the perspiration from his face, which though a cold October evening, was streaming down his forehead. Thaddeus felt suspense too painful to be endured.

"What is the matter, dear Pembroke? Is Miss Beaufort well?"

"Perfectly:" returned he, "Every body is well, excepting myself and my father, who I verily believe has lost his senses; at any rate, he will drive me mad."

The manner in which this reply was uttered, astonished Thaddeus so much, that he could only gaze on the convulsed features of his friend with wonder. Pembroke observed the amazement which sat in his eyes, and laying his hand on his arm; "My dear, dear Sobieski!" said he, "What do I not owe to you? Good Heaven, how humbled do I feel myself in your sight! But there is a Power above, who knows how intimately you are woven with every artery of this heart!"

"I believe it, my kind Pembroke;" cried Thaddeus, yet more alarmed than before; "Tell me what it is that distresses you? If my counsel, or my sympathy, can offer any thing to comfort or assist you, you know that I am your own."

Pembroke burst into tears, and covering his streaming eyes with his handkerchief, exclaimed, "I am indeed distressed! Distressed, even beyond your comfort. O! How can I speak it! You will despise my father, Thaddeus! You will spurn me!"

"Impossible:" cried he, with energy; though his flushed cheek and fainting heart, immediately declared that he had anticipated what he must hear.

"I see," cried Pembroke, regarding the altered features of his friend with a glance of agony; "I see, that you think it is possible, that my father can sink me below my own contempt."

Thaddeus felt the benumbing touch of ingratitude run through the veins; his frame was chilled, was petrified; but his just affection, and calmed countenance, proclaimed how true a judgment he had passed on the whole. He took the burning hand of Mr. Somerset in his own,

and, with a steady and consoling voice, said, "Assure yourself, dear
Pembroke, whatever be the commands of your father, I shall adhere
to them. I can understand by these generous emotions, that he objects
to receive me as your friend. Perhaps," added he, a gloom of suspicion
flashing through his mind; "perhaps Miss Beaufort may have perceived
the devotedness of my heart, and disdaining my – "

"Hush, for Heaven's sake!" cried Pembroke, starting from his chair;
"Do not implicate my poor cousin! Do not add to her disappointment,
the misery that you suspect her! No, Thaddeus," continued he in a
calmer tone, "Mary Beaufort loves you: she confessed it in an agony
of grief on my bosom, just before I came away; and only through her,
dare I ever expect to meet forgiveness from *you*. In spite of my father,
you may marry her. She has no curse to dread; she need not sacrifice all
that is most precious in her sight, to the obstinate caprice of criminal
resentment."

"A curse!" re-iterated Thaddeus, "How is this! What have I done to
deserve such hatred from your father?"

"O! nothing;" cried Pembroke, "nothing. My father never saw you.
My father thanks you for all you have done for me; but it is your
country that he hates. Some Polander, years back, injured him; and
my father took a fatal oath against the whole nation. He declares, he
cannot, he will not break it, were he by so doing, to save his own life,
or even mine; for, (Heaven forgive me!) I was this morning wrought up
to such a pitch of phrenzy, that I threatened to destroy myself, rather
than sacrifice my gratitude and honour to his cruel commands! Nay, to
convince you that his is no personal enmity to yourself, he ordered me
to give you writings which will put you in possession of five hundred a
year for ever. I have them with me."

All the pride of his princely house, rose at once in the breast of
Thaddeus. Though full of indignation at this insult of Sir Robert's,
he regarded the averted face of his friend with compassion, whilst in a
firm voice, he rejected the degrading compromise.

"Tell your father," added he, addressing Pembroke in a tone, which
even his affection could not soften from a command; "that my absence
is not to be bought with money, nor my friendship so rewarded."

Pembroke covered his burning face with his hands. This sight, at
once brought down the haughty spirit of the Count, who continued, in
gentler accents; "Whatever be the sentiments of Sir Robert Somerset,
they shall meet with due attention from me. He is your father, therefore
I respect him; but he has put it out of his power to oblige me: I cannot
accept his bounty. Though your heart, my dearest Pembroke, is above
all price, yet I will make it a sacrifice to your duty." – And by so doing,

put the last seal on my misfortunes! was the meaning of the heavy sigh which accompanied his last words.

Pembroke traversed the room in an agony. "Merciful Providence!" cried he, wringing his clasped hands; "direct me! O! Thaddeus, if you could read my tortured heart, you would pity me; you would see that this business is tearing my soul from my body. What am I to do? I cannot, I will not, part with you for ever."

The Count went up to him, and drew him to a seat; "Be satisfied," said he, "that I am convinced of your affection. Whatever may happen, this assurance will be sufficient to give *me* comfort; therefore, I entreat you, dear Pembroke, by that affection, not to bring regret to me, and reproach on yourself, by disobeying the will of your father! If we separate for life, remember my beloved friend, that the span of our existence here, is short; we shall meet again in a happier world; perhaps more blest, for having immolated our wishes to hard duty in this."

"Cease, Sobieski, cease!" cried Pembroke, "I can draw no consolation from this reasoning. It is not duty to obey a hatred little short of distraction; and, if we now separate, I know I shall never feel peace more. Good Heaven! what comfort can I find, when I know that you are exposed to all the indignities which the world levels against the unfortunate? Can I indulge in the luxuries of my father's house, when I know that you have neither a home nor subsistence? No, Thaddeus, I am not such a villain. I will not give you up, though my father should load me with curses; I trust there is a just power above, that would avert them."

Perceiving that argument at this time would not only be fruitless, but might probably incense his friend's irritated nature to the commission of some rash action, Thaddeus pretended to overlook the frantic gesture and voice which terminated this speech; and, assuming a serene air, he replied: "Let this be the subject of future conversations. At present, I must conjure you by the happiness of us both, to return to the Castle. You know my message to Sir Robert. Present my respects to your aunt; and," added he, after a pause, "assure Miss Beaufort, that whilst I have life, her goodness will be its most animating principle."

Pembroke interrupted him. "Why these messages, dear Thaddeus? Do not suppose, that if I fulfil my father's order to return to Somerset to-night, that it is our separation. Gracious Heaven! Is it so easy to part for ever?"

"Not for ever! O no:" replied Thaddeus, grasping his hand; "we shall see each other again; only meanwhile, repeat those messages to your aunt and cousin. Go, my dear Pembroke, to your father; and may the Lord of heaven bless you!"

The last words were spoken in almost a stifled voice, as he opened his arms and strained his friend to his breast.

"I shall see you to-morrow?" cried Pembroke; "on no other condition I leave you now."

Thaddeus made no farther answer to this demand, (which he determined should never be granted,) than a second embrace. Pembroke went out of the room, to order his horses; then returning again, he stood in the door-way, and holding out his hand to the Count, said, "Farewel, till to-morrow." Thaddeus shook it warmly, and he disappeared.

When the outward door closed after his friend, the Count remained on the seat into which he had thrown himself. He did not venture to move, lest he should by chance catch a second glance of Pembroke from the window. Now that he was gone, he felt the full worth of what he had relinquished. He had resigned a man who loved him; one who had known and revered his ever-lamented grandfather, and his mother; the only one with whom he could have discoursed of their virtues! He felt that he was severed from him, the link which had united his present state with his former fortunes; and throwing his arms along a table that stood near him, he leaned his aching head upon them, and in idea followed with an anguished heart, the progress and reception of his friend at the castle.

The racking misery which tortured the mind of Mr. Somerset, was not borne with equal resignation. Conscious of having inflicted fresh wounds on the breast of his noble friend, his spirits were so ill adapted for society, that he felt rather pleased than disappointed, when he found the supper-room at the castle quite vacant, and only one cover on the table awaiting his arrival.

He asked a few questions of the servants, who informed him that it was already late, past twelve o'clock; and that Sir Robert who was taken worse, had retired to bed early in the evening.

"And where are my aunt and cousin?" demanded Pembroke.

One of the men replied, that in consequence of Miss Beaufort having been suddenly indisposed, both the ladies left the supper-room before eleven. Pembroke readily guessed the cause of this disorder: he too truly adjudged it to Mary's extreme anxiety respecting the reception which the Count Sobieski would give to his disgraceful errand; and, sighing bitterly, he said no more, but went instantly to his chamber.

The restless state of his mind awoke Mr. Somerset by times. Full of solicitude for the success of an application which he intended to make to Miss Beaufort, he traversed the terrace for an hour before he was summoned to breakfast. The baronet continuing unwell, the ladies

only were in the room when he entered. Mrs. Dorothy, who had learnt
the particulars of the late events from the agitated Mary, longed to ask
Pembroke how his friend would act on her brother's command; but
every time that she moved her lips, his inflamed eye and wan countenance made her stop, and fear to venture on the subject. Mary sat in
mute dejection, watching the hurried actions of her cousin; and when,
after he had swallowed a basin of tea, he rose up, and took up his hat to
leave the room, she looked anxiously towards him. Pembroke turned
round at the same moment, and holding out his hand to her, said,
"Come, Mary; I want to say something to you. Will you walk with me
on the terrace?"

Miss Beaufort, with trepidation and a beating heart, took his arm,
and proceeded in silence till they reached the gravel walk. A mutual,
and deep drawn sigh, was the first opening of a conversation, on which
the souls of both hung with interest, hope, and dread. Pembroke was
the first who began.

"My dear, dear Mary," said he, "you are now my sole dependance.
From what I told you yesterday of my father's stubborn inflexibility,
we can have no hope of his relenting: indeed, after what has passed, I
could not flatter myself that Thaddeus Sobieski would on any account
submit to an obligation at his hands. Already he has refused, with all
the indignation I expected, Sir Robert's offer of an annuity. My dear
cousin, how can I exist, and yet witness this noble friend in distress,
and living without the succour of my friendship? Heaven knows, this
must be the case; for I would sooner perish than venture to insult the
man whom my father has treated so ill, with any pecuniary offers from
me! Therefore, dear Mary, it is on you alone that I depend. Thaddeus
adores you, and you love him. Marry him, my beloved cousin," cried
he, catching her hand to his lips, "and relieve my heart from a load
of shame and misery! Be generous, my sweet Mary," added he, supporting her now trembling frame against his breast; "Act up to your
noble nature, and offer him by me, that hand which his calamities and
disinterestedness preclude him from requesting."

Miss Beaufort, hardly able to articulate, from the emotions which
choked her utterance, replied, "I would give him all that I possess,
could it purchase him one tranquil hour; I would serve him for ever,
could I do it and be unknown; but – "

"O, do not hesitate! Do not doubt!" interrupted Pembroke, "To
serve your friends, I know that you are capable of the most extraordinary exertions; I know that there is nothing within the verge of possibility, that your generous disposition would not attempt: then, my
beloved Mary, dare to be what you are; by having the magnanimity

to act as you know you ought; by offering your hand to him, shew the noble Sobieski, that you really deserve the devotion of a hero's heart."

"Dear Pembroke," replied Mary, wiping the still gliding tears from her burning cheek, "after the confession which you drew from me yesterday, I will not deny, that to possess the esteem of your friend would render me the happiest of created beings; but I cannot believe what your sanguine affection tells me; I cannot suppose, situated as I was at Lady Dundas's, under a cloud of fashion, and surrounded by frivolous and contemptible society, that he should discover any thing in me to respect: every way embarrassed as I was, disliking my companions, afraid of my own interest in him, a veil was drawn over my mind, through which he could neither judge of my good nor bad qualities: how then can I flatter myself, or do the Count Sobieski such injury, as to imagine that he could feel any preference for such an insignificant character as I must have appeared?"

It was some time before Pembroke could shake the hold which this prepossession had taken of Miss Beaufort's mind. After having set in every possible light the terms with which his friend had spoken of her name; he at length convinced her of what her heart so earnestly wished to believe, that she was not entirely indifferent to Sobieski.

Mr. Somerset's next atchievement was to overcome her scruples against commissioning him with the message he was desirous to communicate to Thaddeus. Owing to the continual recurrence of her fears, that the warmth of her cousin might have too highly coloured the first object of debate, this task was not more easy to accomplish than the former. In vain she remonstrated, in vain she doubted, in vain demurred; Pembroke would not be denied; and as with faultering lips, she assented to the permission which he had almost extorted; she threw her arms round his neck, and implored him to be careful of her honour; to remember that she had put into his charge all that was most precious to her, the modesty of her sex, and her own delicacy.

Pembroke, delighted at this consent, notwithstanding he received it through the medium of many heavy tears, embraced his cousin with ten thousand animating promises of future happiness; and having allowed her to enter the house, mounted his horse, and set off on the full gallop, towards Harrowby-Hill.

CHAP. VI.

When Thaddeus recovered from the reverie into which he had been thrown by the departure of Mr. Somerset, he considered how he might remove out of a country wherein he had only met with, and occasioned, distress.

The horrid price which Pembroke's father had set on the continuance of their friendship, rendered it necessary that his flight should be immediate. Averse to a second interview with his friend, which could only produce them pain, he determined that not another morn should rise upon him in Lincolnshire; and taking up a pen, with all the future loneliness of his fate painted on his heart, he wrote two letters.

One he addressed to Mr. Somerset, bidding him that farewel, which he confessed he could never have taken. As he wrote, his hand trembled, his bosom swelled; and he hastily shut his eye-lids to withhold his tears from shewing themselves on the paper: his emotion, his grief, were driven back, were concealed; but the tenderness of his soul flowed over the letter. He forgave Pembroke's father, for Pembroke's sake; and, in spite of their personal disunion, he vowed that no earthly consideration should restrain his love from following the steps of his friend, even into the regions of eternity. He closed his melancholy epistle, with informing Mr. Somerset, that as he should quit England immediately, any search after him, which his generous nature might dictate, would be in vain.

Though Thaddeus Sobieski would have disdained a life of dependence on the greatest potentate of the world; though he rejected with the same sincerity a similar proposal from his friend, and despised the degrading offer of Sir Robert; yet he felt no disparagement to his dignity, no infringement on the disinterested nature of his friendship, when he accepted, and resolved to retain, the money which Pembroke had conveyed to him in prison. Thaddeus never acted but from principle. His honourable and penetrating mind knew exactly at what point to draw the tender thread of delicacy. Pride and independence, with him, were distinct terms. Receiving assistance from a friend, and leaning on him wholly for support, had different meanings: he accepted the first with gratitude; he would have thought it impossible to live and endure the last. On these premises, Pembroke was never pained by any attempt to return his bounty. Indeed, Thaddeus would have considered himself unworthy to confer a benefit, if he had not known how to receive one. This spirit left no part of Miss Beaufort's obligation on his mind, but its sweetness; and with these impressions, and a throbbing heart, he began a short address to her.

"*To Miss Beaufort.*

"My faculties seem to lose their power, when I take up my pen to address, for the first and the last time, Miss Beaufort. I hardly know what I would say – what I ought; I dare not venture to write all that I feel. But have you not been my benefactress? Did you not assert my character, and give me liberty, when I was calumniated, and in distress? Did you not ward from me the scorn of unpitying folly? Did you not console me with your own compassion? You have done all this; and surely you will not despise the gratitude of a heart which you have condescended to sooth and to comfort? At least, I cannot leave England forever, without imploring blessings on the head of Miss Beaufort; without thanking her on my knees, on which I am writing, for that gracious and benign spirit, which discovered a breaking heart under the mask of serenity; which penetrated through the garb of poverty and dependence, and saw that the contemned Constantine was not what he seemed! Your smiles, Miss Beaufort; your voice, speaking commiseration, were my sweetest consolations during those heavy months of sorrow, which I endured at Dundas House: I contemplated you as a pitying angel, sent to reconcile me to a life which had already become a burthen. These are the benefits which Miss Beaufort has bestowed on a friendless exile; these are the benefits which she has bestowed on me! And they are written on my soul. Not till I go down into the grave shall they be forgotten. Oh! not even then, for when I rise again, I shall find them still registered there!

"Farewel, most respected, most dear Miss Beaufort. May the Father of Heaven bless, with his choicest care, her, whose name shall ever be the first in the prayers of her most grateful, most devoted servant,

THADDEUS CONSTANTINE SOBIESKI."
"*Harrowby-Hill,*
11 o'clock at night."

When he had finished this epistle, with a paralyzed hand he inclosed it in the envelope which contained Somerset's; then writing a few lines to the good old farmer, he begged him to accept the note which they contained, as a small compensation for his great hospitality; and, having sealed both packets, he disposed them so on the table, that they might be the first things seen on entering the room.

It now being midnight, he thought it high time to set out on his dismal journey. Having tied some linen in a grey silk handkerchief, which had formerly been wrapped round his neck by Lady Sara, one wet evening, in Grosvenor Place; he put all his remaining money into his pocket. It did not exceed thirty pounds; the rest having been expended in his way to the Abbey, and in defraying little expences attending the illness of the Countess, to which her purse (ever kept low by the tardiness of the Earl's payments) was not prepared to answer. However, as he determined to walk to London, where he would embark for America, he hoped that it would at least hold out, until he had landed on a shore, from whence he trusted never to return.

"Ah!" cried he, as he gently closed the window by which he leaped into the little garden, "What accumulated sins, O Russia, will be heaped upon thy head! Every hasty sigh that rebels in my breast, against the almighty hand, which is again driving me out a wanderer on the wide world, calls vengeance upon thee! how many, wretched country!" added he, resting on the bar of the outward gate; "how many, hast thou driven from their homes! how many hast thou made vagabonds and murderers for that scanty pittance, of which with remorseless and wanton gripe, they were deprived by thee! – Oh, righteous Power of Justice and Mercy!" cried he, stretching his arms towards that heaven, over which the piercing winds of a bleak October night were scattering the thick and pillowy clouds; "grant me the fortitude to bear, with resignation to thy will, the miseries that I may yet have to encounter. Oh!" added he, his heart melting as the idea presented itself; "teach me to forget what I have been! Teach me to forget, that on this dreadful night, last year, I clasped the dying body of my dear grandfather in these arms!"

He could not speak farther; but leaning his pale face against the gate, remained for a few minutes dissolved in anguished recollection: then recovering himself by a sudden start, he proceeded with hasty steps through the different meadows, till they conducted him into the high road.

It was on the tenth of October 1795, that the Count Sobieski commenced this lonely and melancholy journey. It was on the tenth of October 1794, that he found the Palatine, bleeding to death, in the midst of a heap of slain. The co-incidence of his present feelings with those of a twelvemonth's past, powerfully affected Thaddeus; they recalled to him remembrances in their most vivid colours, which time, and the many intermediate events, had considerably softened.

Distressed by these painful scenes, which memory, ever true to her nature, raised before his mind's eye in rapid and long succession; he quickened his pace; he slackened it; he quickened it again; but nothing could rid him of those tormenting images, which seemed to glide around him like visible spirits of the departed.

When the dawn broke, and the sun rose, he found himself advanced several miles on the south side of Ponton Hill.* The spiry aisles of Harrowby Abbey were discernible through the mist; and the towers of Somerset Castle, from their height and situation, were as distinctly seen as if he had been at their base. Neither of these objects were calculated to raise the spirits of Thaddeus. The sorrows of the Countess, whose eyes he had so recently closed; and the treatment he afterwards received from the man to whom he owed his life, were recollections which made him turn away from the Abbey with a pang, and fix his eyes on Somerset. He looked towards its ivied head, with all the regret, and all the tenderness which can overflow a human heart: under that roof, he believed the eyes of his adored Mary were sealed in sleep; and in an instant his agitated soul addressed her as if she had been present.

"Farewell, most lovely, most beloved! The conviction, that I resign even the hope of ever again beholding thee, to the peace of my friend, shall give me comfort, when I am drawing my breath in a far, far distant world."

In this way, thus communing with his own troubled spirit, he walked on the whole day in his way to London.† Totally absorbed in meditation, he did not remark the gaze of curiosity which followed his elegant yet distressed figure, as he passed through the different towns and villages. Pondering on the past, the present, and the future, he neither felt hunger nor thirst; but, with a fixed eye and abstracted countenance, pursued his route, till night and weariness overtook him in the midst of the high road, far from any house.

Thaddeus looked around, and above: the sky was clear, and glittering with stars; the moon shining on a near branch of the Ouse, which divides Huntingdonshire from Cambridgeshire, lit the green heath which skirted its banks.‡ Thaddeus wished not for a more magnificent canopy; and, placing his wallet under his head, he lay down beneath a hillock of furze and broom, and slept till morning.

When he awoke from a sleep, which fatigue and fasting had rendered more torpid than refreshing, he found that the splendours of the night had been succeeded by a heavy rain; and that he was drenched

---

* Probably Gibbet Hill, near the village of Little Ponton and Great Ponton, about 5 kilometres south of Grantham.
† Thaddeus would have followed the Great North Road, which ran from Edinburgh to London, passing through Grantham.
‡ The setting is most likely near the town of Huntingdon, an important bridging point for the River Great Ouse, about 78 kilometres south of Grantham.

through. He rose up with a stiffness in his limbs, a pain in his head, and a dimness over his eyes, which almost disabled him from moving. He readily judged that he had caught cold; and every moment feeling himself grow worse, he thought it necessary to seek some house, where he might purchase rest and assistance.

To this end, leaning on his stick, but no longer able to incumber himself with even the light load of his bundle, he threw it amongst the brambles; believing from the symptoms which he felt, that he had not many hours to endure the ills of life, he staggered a few yards farther: no habitation appeared in sight; his limbs became more feeble, his eyes seemed totally obscured, and he sunk down on a bank. For a minute he attempted to struggle with the cold grasp of death, which he believed was fastening on his heart.

"And are my days to be so short! Are they to end thus?" thought he; "Merciful Providence, pardon my repining!"

These were the last movements of the lips of Thaddeus, whilst his blood seemed freezing to insensibility. His eyes closed, his head fell back; and pale and without animation, he lay at the foot of the tree near which he had dropt.

The Count had been a quarter of an hour in this death-like state, when a gentleman, who was passing that road in his way to a country-seat in Cambridgeshire, thought he perceived a man lying amongst the nettles and grass a little onward on the heath. The traveller immediately stopped his carriage, and ordering one of the out-riders to alight, bade him examine whether the object he saw were living or dead.

The man obeyed; and presently returning, with an affrighted countenance informed his master, that it was the body of a man, who by his dress appeared to be a gentleman, and who, being quite senseless, he supposed had been murdered by robbers. The features of the benevolent stranger immediately reflected the hue of his servant's; but ordering the chariot door to be opened, he took in his hand a bottle of drops, (which from his own invalid state, was his travelling companion,) and alighting, hastened to the side of the lifeless Thaddeus.

By this time, all the servants were collected round the spot; and the good man himself, whilst he gazed with pity on the marble features of the Count, observed with pleasure, that he saw no marks of violence. Supposing that the present accident might have been occasioned by a fit; and considering it possible by proper means to recal life; he desired that the unfortunate person's waistcoat might be unclosed; and, taking off his hat, he contrived to pour some drops into his mouth. Their warmth appeared to have renewed pulsation in the heart; for one of the servants, who was stooping, declared that it beat under his hand.

When the benevolent gentleman convinced himself that this report was true, he ordered his servants to place the poor traveller in his carriage; having only another mile to go before he reached Deerhurst, he said he hoped that his charge might be restored at the end of their destination.

Whilst the postilions drove in full gallop towards the house, the cold face of Thaddeus rested on the bosom of the stranger, who continued to chafe his temples with lavender water till the chariot stopped before the gates. Two men carried the Count to the house; and, having left him with their master, and a medical man who resided near, other restoratives were applied, which succeeded in recalling his wandered senses. When he had completely recovered his powers, and was able to look round and distinguish objects, he saw that he was supported by two gentlemen, and in a magnificent bed-chamber.

Gratitude, it may be said, was the first born feeling in the soul of Thaddeus. In the moment of his revival from that sleep, into which he believed he had fallen, till time should be lost in eternity he pressed the hands of them who held his; not doubting but that they were the good Samaritans who had preserved him from perishing.

The younger of the gentlemen, perceiving by the animated lustre which spread over his patient's eyes, that he was going to speak, put his hand on his lips, and said, "Pardon me, Sir! you must not speak. Your life at present hangs on a thread; the slightest exertion would snap it: but, as all you want is rest and resuscitation, to supply some great expence which the vital powers have sustained; I must require, that you neither speak, nor be spoken to, till I give permission. Meanwhile, be satisfied, Sir, that you are in the most honourable hands. This gentleman," added he, pointing to his friend, "saw you on the heath, and brought you to his house, where you now are."

Thaddeus bowed his head to them both in sign of gratitude and compliance; and the elder left the room.

CHAP. VII.

Next morning, when the seal was taken off the lips of Thaddeus, he expressed in the most animated terms, his deep sense of the humanity which had actuated both the gentlemen to take such generous interest in his fate.

"You owe no thanks to me," replied the one who had injoined and released him from silence, and who was now alone with him; "I am only the agent of another. Yet, I do not deny, that in obeying the benevolent orders of Sir Robert Somerset, I have frequent opportunities of gratifying my own heart."

Thaddeus was so confounded at this discovery that he could not speak, and the gentleman proceeded.

"I am apothecary to Sir Robert's household; and, as my excellent master has been long afflicted with an ill state of health, I live in a small lodge at the other end of the park. He is the best man in all the county; nay, I believe I may say, the most benevolent in the kingdom; and, should he die, (which his late melancholy fits too fearfully threaten,) both poor and rich will lose their friend. Sad and ill as he was this morning, when I told him that you were out of danger, he expressed a pleasure only known to the truly humane."

Thaddeus, not considering the wildness of the question, hastily demanded, "Does he know who I am?"

The honest apothecary stared at the look and tone of voice with which these words were delivered, and then replied, "No; is there any reason, Sir, to make you wish that he should not?"

"Certainly none:" replied Thaddeus, recollecting himself, and sighing; "and I shall be impatient till I have an opportunity of telling him how grateful I am for the goodness which he has shewn to me as a stranger."

The apothecary, surprised at these hints, (which the Count, not considering their tendency, allowed to escape,) gathered sufficient from them, united with the speaker's superior mien, to make him suppose that his patient was some emigrant of quality, whom Sir Robert would rejoice in having served. These surmises and conclusions having passed quickly through the honest gentleman's brain, he bowed his head with that respect, which the generous mind is proud to pay to nobility in ruins; and resumed:

"Whatever you may be, Sir, a peasant or a prince, you will meet with every hospitality from the noble owner of this house. His spirit is equal in magnificence with the goodness of his heart; Deerhurst will be rendered as comfortable to you, as great benevolence and great wealth can bestow; and I am certain, that Sir Robert will consider the dreadful apoplexy, that brought him from Somerset for change of air, rather fortunate than otherwise, as it has afforded him an opportunity of serving, and knowing you."

Thaddeus blushed at the strain of this speech; and, readily understanding what was passing in the mind of the apothecary, hardly knew how to reply. He paused for a moment, and then said, "All that you have declared Sir, in praise of Sir Robert Somerset, I cannot have a doubt of his deserving. I have already felt the effects of his humanity, and shall ever remember that my life was prolonged by his means; but I have no pretensions to the honour of his acquaintance. I only wish to see him, that I may thank him for what he has done; therefore, if you will permit me to rise this evening, instead of to-morrow morning, you will oblige me."

To this request, the apothecary gave a respectful, yet firm denial; and descended, to communicate his observations to his patron.

The anxiety which agitated the Count's mind, when he reflected that he was receiving all these obligations from his most implacable enemy, so occupied and disturbed him, that he passed a sleepless night. The dawn found his fever much augmented; but no corporeal sufferings could persuade him to abandon the resolution of seeing the Baronet, and immediately leaving his house: believing as he did, that all this kindness would have been withheld, had his host known on whom he was pouring such benefits, he felt as if every minute which saw him under Sir Robert's roof, inflicted a new outrage on his own dignity and honour.

To this end then, as soon as Mr. Middleton the apothecary had retired to breakfast, Thaddeus rose from his bed, and was completely dressed before he returned. The good man expostulated on the rashness of what he had done, and augured no less than a relapse from the morning symptoms of his patient. Thaddeus once in his life was obstinate, though civilly so; and, begging a servant to request Sir Robert to indulge him with an audience for a few minutes alone in his library, he soon convinced Mr. Middleton, that his purpose was not to be shaken.

The Baronet returning his compliments, that he should be happy to see his guest, the still anxious apothecary offered him his assistance down the stairs. Thaddeus needed no help, and gratefully declined it. The exertion necessary to be summoned for this interview, had imparted as much momentary strength to his frame as to his mind; and though his colour was heightened, he entered the library with a firm step.

Sir Robert met him at the door, and, shaking him by the hand, with many warm assurances of pleasure at his recovery, would have led him to a seat; but Thaddeus drawing back, only supported himself against the back of it with his hand; whilst in a steady voice, he expressed the most animated thanks for the benefits he had received; then pausing, and casting the proud lustre of his eyes to the ground, lest their language should tell all that he thought, he continued, "I have only to regret Sir Robert, that your benevolence has been lavished on a man whom you regard with abhorrence. I am that Count Sobieski, that Polander, whom you commanded your son to see no more. Respecting even the prejudices of my friend's parent, I was hastening to London, meaning to set sail for America with the first ship, when I swooned on the road. I believe I was nearly expiring; your humanity saved me: and I now owe to gratitude, as well as to my own satisfaction, the fulfilment of my declaration. I shall leave Deerhurst immediately; and England, as soon as I am able to embark."

Thaddeus, with a second bow, and not quite so firm a step, without venturing a glance at what he supposed were the shamed looks of the Baronet, was preparing to quit the room, when Sir Robert, with a pale and aghast countenance, exclaimed, "Stop!"

Thaddeus looked at him with wonder. The Baronet, incapable of saying more, pointed to a chair for him to sit down; then sinking into another himself, took out his handkerchief, and wiping away the large drops that stood on his forehead, breathlessly panted for respiration. At last, with a desperate kind of haste, he said:

"Was your mother, Therese Sobieski?"

Thaddeus, still more astonished, replied in the affirmative; and Sir Robert threw himself back on the chair with a deep groan. Hardly knowing what he did, the Count rose from his seat, and advanced towards him: Sir Robert, hearing his approach, stretched out his hand; and, with a look of agony, asked who was his father? then, without waiting for a reply, hid his convulsed features beneath his handkerchief. The Baronet's agitation, which now shook him like an earthquake, had become contagious: Thaddeus gazed at him with a palsying uncertainty working at his heart; and, laying his hand upon his bewildered brain, he answered; "I know not. I believe, the Earl of Tinemouth. But here is his picture." With a trembling hand he took the case which held it, out of his pocket; and, tearing open the clasps, gave it to Sir Robert, who had started from his position at the name of the Earl. The moment the Baronet's eyes rested on the miniature, he threw it from him, and fell senseless back on the chair.

Thaddeus, hardly more alive, sprinkled some water on his face, and with throbbing temples and a beating heart, stood in wordless expectation over him. Such excessive emotion told him, that something more than Sir Robert's hatred of the Polanders had stimulated his late conduct; and too earnest for an explanation, to ring for assistance, he rejoiced to see by the convulsion of the Baronet's features, and the heaving of his chest, that animation was returning. In a few minutes he opened his eyes, but when he met the anxious gaze of Thaddeus, he closed them as suddenly, and rising from his seat, staggered up against the chimney-piece, exclaiming, "O God, direct me!"

Thaddeus, whose conjectures were now wrought almost into wildness, followed him, and whilst his exhausted frame seemed ready to sink to the earth, implored him to speak.

"O, Sir!" cried he, "If you know any thing about my family? If you know any thing about my father, in pity answer me! Or, only tell me; am I so wretched as to be the son of Lord Tinemouth?"

The violence of the Count's emotions, during this agonizing petition, totally overcame him; before he had finished speaking, his limbs withdrew their support; and, sinking down on his knees, his head dropped breathless against the side of a chair: Though incapable of standing, his beseeching and eager eyes were yet riveted on the Baronet's averted face.

Sir Robert turned hastily round. He saw him sunk, like a beautiful flower, bruised and trampled on by the wanton foot of him who had given it root: unable to make any evasive reply to this last appeal of virtue and of nature, he threw himself with a burst of tears upon his neck, and exclaimed, "Wretch that I have been! O, Sobieski! *I* am thy father. Dear, injured son of the unhappy Therese!"

The first words which carried this avowal to the heart of Thaddeus, deprived it of motion; and, when Sir Robert expected to receive the returning embrace of his son, he found him senseless in his arms.

The cries of the Baronet brought Mr. Middleton and the servants into the room. When the former saw the state of the Count, and perceived the agonized position of his patron, (who was supporting and leaning over his son,) the honest man declared, that he expected nothing less from the gentleman's disobedience of his orders. The presence of the servants having recalled Sir Robert's wandering faculties, he desired them to remove Thaddeus to his chamber. Then following them in silence, when they had laid their charge on the bed, he watched, in extreme but concealed anxiety, till Mr. Middleton, by opening a vein, again brought back animation to his patient.

The moment the Count unclosed his eyes, they fixed themselves on the agitated father. He drew the hand which held his, to his lips. The tears of paternal love again bathed the cheeks of Sir Robert; he felt how warm at his heart was the affection of his deserted son; (and making a sign for Mr. Middleton to leave the room, who obeyed;) he bent his streaming eyes upon the other hand of Thaddeus, and said in a faultering voice, "Can you pardon me?"

Thaddeus threw himself on his father's bosom, and wept profusely; then raising Sir Robert's clasped hands in his, whilst his eloquent eyes seemed to search the heavens, he said, "My dear, dear mother loved you to her latest hour; and I have all my mother's heart: whatever may have been your faults, I feel that I love my father."

Sir Robert strained him to his breast. After a pause, whilst he shook the tears from his silver eye-lashes, he resumed, "Certain, my dear son, that you require repose, and assured that you will not find it till I have offered some apology for my unnatural conduct, I will now explain the various circumstances which impelled my actions, and drew distress upon that noble creature, your mother."

Sir Robert hesitated a moment that he might recover breath, and then went on.

"Keep your situation;" added he, putting down Thaddeus, who at this opening was raising himself up; "I shall tell my melancholy story with less pain, if your eyes be not upon me. I will begin from the first."

The Baronet proceeded to say, that very early in life he had attached himself to Miss Beaufort, the only sister of the late Admiral Beaufort, who was Mary's father; they were then wards of Sir Fulke Somerset. Mr. Beaufort had been in the navy from a boy; but his sister remaining always at the Castle, an affection as strong as it was mutual, took place between herself and her cousin Robert. When the young people applied to Sir Fulke for his consent to their marriage, he refused it on the plea of their youth. In vain the passionate Robert declared the reasonableness and ardour of his affection; his father urged his being only a younger son,* and in other ways wholly unworthy of his ward, unless he would consent to undergo the polish of a three years tour over the continent. After much altercation, this arrangement was at length complied with; and Robert and Miss Beaufort bade each other adieu at the expence of many sighs and tears. Highly indignant at the unfeeling whim of Sir Fulke; and, provoked with his brother for backing

* As a younger son, Robert will not inherit the family wealth.

his father's arguments, Robert Somerset set off for Dover, where he was joined by the present Earl of Tinemouth, (then Mr. Stanhope,) who was banished the country on the same errand: but his was to forget a mistress; Somerset's, to deserve one. Stanhope's mother, and Robert's having been sisters, the young men met as relations; mutually enraged at their fathers, (their mothers having been long dead,) they determined to change their names, and to let no one know any thing about them during their travels, except the two women, whom they best loved. To this end, as soon as they crossed the channel and had landed in France, they gave themselves out to be brothers, which their great personal resemblance corroborated, and called themselves Sackville. This business settled, they travelled pretty amicably till they reached Naples: Here Mr. Stanhope involved himself in a very dishonourable intrigue with the only daughter of an old British officer, who had retired to that climate for his health. Somerset remonstrated on the villainy of seducing an innocent girl, when he knew that his heart and hand were absolutely devoted to another; and Stanhope, enraged at finding a censor in a companion, whom he had considered as headstrong as himself, ended the argument by striking him. Somerset drew his sword; and it is likely if the servants of their hotel had not interfered, the affray would have been terminated with one of their lives. Since that hour, they never met again. Mr. Stanhope left his shame, and his wounded friend; and, fearful of consequences, fled to Palermo. Robert Somerset, when recovered from his hurts, (still retaining the name of Sackville,) took the way to Florence, in which beautiful city, determining to stay some time, he rather sought than repelled the civilities of the inhabitants. Here he became acquainted with the Palatine, and the lovely Therese, whose affections he so completely won. Soon after this intimacy commenced, Miss Beaufort ceased to answer his letters. Almost desperate with his fears, he was on the point of going to England, when he received a packet from home. On opening it, he found a letter from Miss Beaufort, wherein she informed him, that having long considered their attachment as a childish entanglement, she had tried to wean him from his former folly, by continuing an obstinate silence. Having hardly a doubt that she had succeeded, she now broke through her resolution, as it was to shew him at once, the unreasonableness of making such early engagements. Soon after his departure, a journey up to town taught her to know her own heart; and, in consequence, she had yielded her hand to Mr. Somerset, his elder brother. He had always been averse to her marriage with Robert. This shameless declaration was ended by a long homily of advice against similar fetters – and the insult, of subscribing herself his "affectionate sister," &c. On the receipt of this stab to all his hopes, he forswore his family for ever, and flying to Therese Sobieski, in a paroxysm of madness and revenge, married her. This rash act perpetrated, he in vain sought for tranquillity; he saw that she idolized him, but his thoughts were fixed on his ungrateful Mary; were always deploring her lightness, and execrating the perfidy of his brother. In this temper a second packet found him. Again he saw Miss Beaufort's hand-writing, but he dropt it with horror into the envelope, and tore open the black seal which was affixed to a letter from his father. Here, Sir Fulke confessed such a plan of deceit as petrified his son. He declared, that all which had passed, was devised by Mr. Somerset, in hopes of tempting him to revenge the affront that Mary had put on him, by a hasty marriage. The wretched old man, with many prayers for pardon, acknowledged that this bitter confession was wrung from him by the sudden death of his eldest son, who now lay a corpse in the house. The disconsolate father having related the particulars of Mr. Somerset's death, (which happened after three days illness,) added, that it was in compliance with his entreaties to preserve Miss Beaufort for him, that he had agreed to drive Robert from the kingdom. To further the scheme, of making the separation for ever, he had intercepted all their mutual letters; and, Mr. Somerset himself, had forged that one in Miss Beaufort's name, which carried the intelligence of their union. By the same means, a similar effect was wrought upon the abused Mary; believing Robert unfaithful, she fell into a melancholy, and evinced a carelessness to exterior objects, which they hoped, might in time induce her through mere weakness of mind, to give her hand to the persecuting passion of Mr. Somerset. "But," continued Sir Fulke, "death has put an end to this unnatural rivalry; and my poor girl undeceived in her opinion of you, pants to see you, and to give you that hand, which my ill-fated son, and your unhappy father, so unjustly detained."

On receipt of this packet, with a soul divided between love, humanity, and honour, Robert Somerset sacrificed all to his passions. He adored the woman on whose account he had left the country; and, though every tie of heaven and earth bound him to his deceived and injured wife, he consigned her to the full horrors of such desertion, and hastened to England.

"Shameful to relate," added Sir Robert, "immediately on my landing, I married Mary Beaufort. In her arms, I forgot for a while, Therese and her agonies. But when my dear Pembroke first saw the light, when I prest him to my heart, it seemed as if at the same instant I had stabbed it with a dagger. When I would have breathed a blessing over him, the conviction struck me, that I durst not; that I had deluded the mother who gave him birth; and that at some future period, he might have cause to curse the author of his existence. Well," continued the Baronet, wiping his forehead, "though the birth of this boy had conjured up the image of your mother, which haunted me day and night; I never could summon courage to inquire respecting her fate. When the troubles of Poland commenced, what a dreadful apprehension seized me! The success of the Russians, and the consequent distresses of the nobility, overwhelmed me with fear: I knew not, but they might be forced like the French noblesse, to fly their country; and the bare idea of meeting your grandfather or the injured Therese in England, precipitated me into such a series of apprehensions, as nearly menaced my life. I became melancholy and ill; I avoided the sight of the newspapers; and, as far as I could, (under the plea of the story which you have heard,) I withheld my family from speaking on a subject which manifestly gave me pain. But I could not prevent the tongues of our visitors discoursing on a theme which at that period interested every thinking mind. I heard of the valiant Kosciuszko, the good Stanislaus, and the Palatine Sobieski with his brave grandson, spoken of in the same breath. I durst not surmise who this grandson was; I durst not ask; I dreaded to know. At length," added he, quickening his voice, "the idol of my heart, she for whom I had perhaps sacrificed my eternal peace, died in my arms! I received the shock as became a christian: I bent beneath the blow with humility; for I embraced it as the expiation of a crime, which till then, even in the midst of my felicity, had sat on my soul like the hand of death. I bore this trial with resignation. But, when two years after, my eye fell by accident upon the name of Sobieski, in one of the public papers, I could not withdraw it again; my sight was fascinated as if by a rattlesnake; and, in one column I read, how bravely the Palatine fell; and, in the next, the dreadful fate of his daughter. She was revenged!" cried Sir Robert, eagerly grasping the hand of Thaddeus, who could not restrain the groan which burst from his breast. "I was deprived of that reason, which had abused her noble nature, for near three months afterwards. When I recovered my senses," continued he after a pause; "and found that I had so fatally suffered the time of restitution to go by, I began to torment myself, that I had not on the death of Lady Somerset, immediately hastened to Poland, and entreated Therese's pardon on my knees. This period of vivid remorse was soon terminated, by the same arguments which on the first year of my wife's loss, had deterred me from being just. I re-considered, that the Countess Sobieski having had a prior claim to my name, such restitution on my part, must in consequence have illegitimized my darling Pembroke.* It was this horrid conviction," exclaimed Sir Robert, a sudden distraction agitating his before affectionate eye, "that caused all my cruelty to you. When my dear son described the danger from which you had rescued him; when he told me, that Therese had fostered him with a mother's tenderness; I was probed to the heart: but when he added, that the young Count Sobieski was now an alien from his country, and relying on my friendship for a home, my terror was too truly manifested. Horror drove all natural remorse from my soul. I thought an avenging power had sent my deserted child to discover his father, to claim his rights, and to publish me as a villain: and when I saw my innocent son, even on his knees, petitioning for the man whom I believed was come to undo him, I became almost frantic. Under this temper," added he, putting the trembling hand of Thaddeus to his streaming eyes, "I drove out my first born, to be a guiltless wanderer on the face of the earth; not for his own crimes, but for those of his father: and heaven punished my injustice.† When I thought the evidence of my shame, divided from me by an inseparable barrier; when I believed that the ocean would soon separate me from all my fears, a righteous providence brought thee before my eyes, forlorn and expiring. It was the son of Therese Sobieski that I had exposed to such wretchedness! It was the darling of her heart, that I had consigned to the beating elements! O, Thaddeus," cried he, "can I be forgiven for this?"

Thaddeus lulled the wakeful remorse of his venerable father, with such kind arguments of excuse for his conduct, as at least imported to him, a consoling assurance in the generous affection of his son.

When this long and interesting conversation had terminated, Sir Robert, well remembering the violent effects of Mr. Somerset's grief at Sobieski's flight and declared abjuration of England, pardoned his son the outrageous reproaches which had driven him from his own house, and very joyfully dispatched a messenger to desire his immediate presence at Deerhurst.

---

* Since Sir Robert married Therese Sobieski first, and Thaddeus is his eldest son, he fears that Pembroke will be considered illegitimate and disinherited.
† Sir Robert adapts Cain's words to the Lord: 'Behold, thou hast driven me out this day from the face of the earth; and from thy face shall I be hid; and I shall be a fugitive and a vagabond in the earth' (Genesis 4: 14).

CHAP. VIII.

That sickness, which is the consequence of mental pain, usually vanishes with its cause. Long before the evening of the ensuing day, Thaddeus had quitted his chamber, and related to his father the rapid incidents of his brief but eventful career. The voice of Fame had already blazoned him abroad, as "*the plume of war, with early laurels crowned;*"* but it was left to his own eloquent tongue, to prove with all the pathos of modesty and feeling, that the most desperate conflicts are not those which we sustain in the field.

Sir Robert listened to him with affection, admiration, and delight. He was answering the interesting detail, with many grateful apostrophes to that Providence which had crowned his old age with pardon and peace, when a servant opened the door, and announced that Mr. Somerset was in the library.

Thaddeus instantly rose; but Sir Robert put him down again. "Remain here, my dear son," said he, "till I apprise your brother how nearly you are related to him. That door leads into my study; I will call you in when he is prepared."

The moment Sir Robert joined Pembroke, he read in his pale and harassed countenance how much he required the intelligence which he came to communicate. Mr. Somerset bowed coldly on his father's entrance, and begged to be honoured with his commands.

"They are what I expect will restore to you your usual looks and manner, my dear boy," answered his father, taking his passive hand, and seating him by him; "so attend to me."

Pembroke listened to the beginning of the Baronet's narrative with respectful attention; but when the name of Therese Sobieski was mentioned as the woman whom he had married and deserted; the ready apprehension of his son conceiving the rest, he had only to affirm his eager demand, that Thaddeus was indeed his brother. Pembroke looked wildly around him.

---

* James Thomson, *The Seasons: Summer*: 'Nor can the Muse the gallant Sidney pass, / The Plume of War! with early Laurels crown'd, / The Lover's Myrtle, and the Poet's Bay' (lines 1511–13). The author and courtier Sir Philip Sidney (1554–86) was a favourite of Jane Porter.

"O, my father!" cried he, "what have you done? Where is he? For what have you sacrificed him?"

"Hear me to an end," rejoined the Baronet, who, then, in as few words as possible, repeated the consequent events, with the recent meeting.

Pembroke's transports were now as high as his despair had been deep. He threw himself on his father's breast; he asked for his friend, his brother; and begged to be conducted to him wherever he was. Sir Robert did no more than open the door which divided the library from the dining-room, and in one moment the brothers were firmly locked in each other's arms.

Their father, with a speechless tongue, but an eloquent heart, stood over them with uplifted hands, invoking the spirits of their beatified mothers, to behold this heavenly scene.

The feelings of the young men for a long time denied them words, but their eyes, their tears, and their united hands, imparted to each breast a consciousness of mutual love unutterable, if not to be expressed by those looks, which are indeed the truest heralds of the soul.

Sir Robert wept like an infant whilst contemplating these two affectionate brothers; in a faultering voice, he exclaimed, "How soon may these plighted hands be separated by the harpies of the law! Alas, Pembroke, you cannot be ignorant that I buy this son at the price of your legitimacy!"

At this speech of his father's, the blood rushed over the ingenuous cheek of Pembroke; but Thaddeus turning instantly to Sir Robert, said, with a smile,

"On this head, I trust neither my father nor my brother will entertain one thought to trouble them. Had I even the inclination to act otherwise than right, my revered grandfather has put it out of my power to bear any other name than that of Sobieski. He made me swear never to change it; and, as I hope to meet him hereafter," added he, with solemnity, "I will obey him! Therefore, my beloved father, it is only in secret that I can enjoy the conviction that I am your son, and Pembroke's brother: yet, the happiness which I have received with the knowledge that I am so, will ever live here; will ever animate my heart with gratitude to Heaven and you."

"Noble son of the sainted Therese!" cried Sir Robert, "I do not deserve thee!"

"How shall I merit your care of my honour? of my dearest feelings?" exclaimed Pembroke, pressing the hands of his brother to his heart, "I can do nothing, dearest Thaddeus. I am a bankrupt in the means of evincing what is passing in my soul. My mother's chaste spirit thanks you from my lips; yet I will not abuse your generosity; though I retain the name of Somerset, it shall be only the name; the inheritance entailed on my father's eldest son belongs to you."

Whilst Thaddeus embraced his brother with affection, he calmly and firmly replied, that he would rather encounter all the probable miseries from which his father's benevolence had saved him, than rob his brother of any part of what he believed to be justly his due.

Sir Robert, with anguished delight, attempted to stop this generous contention, by saying that it should be terminated by an equal division of his estates.

"Not so, my dear father," replied Thaddeus; "I will never consent that the title of Somerset shall want wealth to support the munificence of its possessor."

After a few more arguments, of the same tendency, the controversy being settled, the remainder of the evening passed in that sweet reciprocity of confidence and peace, which the imagination can best picture.

According to the decisions of this night, Sir Robert wrote next morning to his sister, informing her, that accident had introduced Pembroke's friend, the Count Sobieski, to his presence; when, to his amazement and joy, he discovered, that this celebrated young hero, though of a nation to which he had declared an abhorrence, was the only remaining branch of a family, to which he had owed unnumbered obligations. He added, that five-and-twenty years ago, having contracted an immense debt with the Palatine of Masovia, he had, as a small compensation, signed over to the Count, (who would now resume all the honours of his rank,) the house and estates of Deerhurst, to the amount of three thousand a year. He closed his letter, with many expressions of impatience to present to his sister and niece, their interesting *emigré* under a character which reflected honour on their esteem.

This epistle was put into the hands of Mrs. Dorothy, by an outrider, as she was following Miss Beaufort and Lady Albina Stanhope into the travelling coach. Mrs. Dorothy having seated herself, read it aloud to both the young ladies; at every welcome word, the amazed and overjoyed Mary felt her throbbing heart dropping tears of bliss and gratitude. The good old lady was not backward in demonstrating astonishment. Surprised at her brother's rencontre with Thaddeus, but more at his avowal of obligations to any of that nation about whom he had always asserted directly the reverse; she was so immersed in wonder and pleasure, that her ever-cheerful tongue, clothing itself in unaccustomed volubility, entertained the attentive Lady Albina all the way to Somerset, with the public, as well as private history, of the Count Sobieski.

When the carriage arrived at Deerhurst, it was past midnight; and, to the no small disappointment of the ladies, the family had been retired to bed above an hour. Mrs. Dorothy, who would not suffer her brother to be disturbed, having ordered the girls to their rooms, was crossing one of the galleries to her own apartment, when a door opening, Pembroke, in his night-gown and slippers, looked out. He had heard a bustle, and was going to enquire the reason, just as his aunt appeared. She kissed him, bade him good night, told him to prepare for something pleasing in the morning; and, smiling, hurried on to her chamber.

Pembroke had thought so little of Mrs. Dorothy's lively promise, that he was almost the last who descended to the breakfast-parlour. Mrs. Dorothy reproached him for his undutiful laziness; but Miss Beaufort, with an anxious consciousness glowing on her cheek, embraced her cousin, who whispered, "Now, I shall see the two dearest friends I possess happy in each other."

Mary's vivid blush had not subsided, when the sudden entrance of Thaddeus, and his agitated bow, overspread her neck and bosom with crimson. A dimness seemed to obscure her faculties: she hardly heard the animated words of Sir Robert, whilst he presented him as the Count Sobieski, the darling son of one who had deserved the highest place in his heart. Whatever he was, she felt that he was lord of hers; and withdrawing her hand hastily from the timid and thrilling touch of him she would have lingered near forever; she glided back towards an open casement, where the fresh air helped to dispel the faintness which had seized her.

After Mrs. Dorothy, with all the urbanity of her nature, had declared her welcomes to the Count, she put away the coffee that was handed to her by Pembroke, and said with a smile, "Before I taste my breakfast, I must inform you, Sir Robert, that you have a guest in this house you little expect. I forbade Mary saying a word, because, as we are told that 'the first tellers of unwelcome news have but a losing office;'* vice versa, I hoped for a gaining one; therefore detained such a pleasing piece of intelligence for my own promulgation. Indeed, I doubt, whether or no it will not intoxicate some folks here," added she, glancing archly on Pembroke, who had looked suddenly round at this whimsical declaration; "suffice it to say, that yesterday morning Lady Albina Stanhope, more dead than alive, accompanied by her maid, arrived

* *Henry IV, Part 2*, I, i, 100–1.

in a post-chaise at Somerset Castle, and implored our protection as relations. Our dear Mary embraced the poor weeping young creature, who, amidst many tears, recapitulated the horrors she had suffered, since she parted with the Count Sobieski at the Abbey. The latest outrage of her cruel father, was his immediate marriage with the vile Lady Sophia Lovel; and his commands, that Lady Albina would treat her as became a daughter. Ill as her ladyship was, when she received these disgraceful orders, she determined to escape them and the degradation they would otherwise cast on the memory of her own mother, by instantly quitting home. To this end she engaged her maid to assist her flight; '*and*,' added she, '*where was I to go? Who would receive the unfortunate victim of the profligate Lady Sophia? I could think of none so likely as the father of the generous Mr. Somerset. He told me we were relations; I beseech you to be my friends!*' As I am sensible your benevolent heart, my dear brother," continued Mrs. Dorothy, "would have dictated the same, I stopped this sweet girl's petition with my caresses, and promised her a kinder father in Sir Robert Somerset."

"You did right, Dorothy," returned the Baronet, "though the Earl and I must ever be strangers, I have no enmity against his children. Where is this amiable Lady Albina?"

Mrs. Dorothy informed him, that in consequence of her recent grief and ill-treatment, her ladyship had found herself too unwell to rise with the family; but she would hope to join them at noon.

Pembroke was indeed deeply interested in this intelligence. The simple graces of the lovely Albina had, on the first interview, penetrated his heart. Her sufferings at Harrowby, and the sensibility which her ingenuous nature exhibited without affectation or disguise, had left her image in his soul, long after she disappeared. He now gave the reins to his eager imagination, and was the first in the saloon, to greet his lovely mistress.

Sir Robert Somerset welcomed her with the warmth of a parent: but his animated and enraptured son broke out into the most vehement expressions of joy, which she received with timid and grateful bows.

During this scene, Miss Beaufort, no longer able to bear the restraint of company, nor even the accidental glances of Sobieski, (whose presence, dear as it was, disconcerted and oppressed her,) walked out into the park. Though it was the month of October, the weather continued fine. A bright sun tempered the air, and gilded the yellow leaves which the fresh wind drove before her in a thousand glittering eddies. This was Mary's favourite season. She found its softness diffuse the purest melancholy over her soul. The rugged form of care seems to dissolve under the magic touch of beautiful Nature. Forgetful of the world's anxieties, the tranquillizing spirit of meditation shades the heart of sorrow with a veil, which might well be called the twilight of the mind; and the entranced soul, happy in delusion, half closes its bright eye, reluctant to perceive that such sweet repose rests in error.

Such were the reflections of Mary after her disturbed thoughts had tossed themselves in a sea of doubts, relative to the interest she might probably possess in the heart of Sobieski. Wearied out with suspense, she resolved to resign her future fate to Providence; and, turning her gaze on the lovely objects around, soon found the genius of the season absorb her wholly. Her cheek glowed, her eyes became humid, and casting their mild radiance on the fading flowers beneath, she pursued her way through a cloud of fragrance. It was the last breath of the expiring year. Love is full of imagination. Mary easily glided from the earth's departing charms, to her own waning beauty: the chord once touched, every note reviberated:* and hope and fear, joy and regret, again dispossessed her late acquired serenity.

It being near three o'clock, Lady Albina having expressed a wish to walk out in search of Miss Beaufort, the two brothers offered their attendance. Before her ladyship had passed through the first park, she complained of fatigue; Pembroke, alarmed, urged her to enter a shepherd's hut close by, whilst the Count Sobieski would proceed alone in quest of his cousin.

Thaddeus, with a beating heart undertook this commission; and bounding over the rustic bridge which crossed the Witham, hastened along the nearest dell. With the lightness of a young hunter, he mounted the heights, descended to the vallies, traversed one woody nook, and then another, but could see no trace of Miss Beaufort. Almost induced to suppose she had returned to the house, he was slackening his pace to abandon the search, when he caught a glimpse of her figure as she turned the corner of a thicket leading to the terrace above. In an instant he was at her side; with a faultering voice, his hat in his hand, his bosom panting, and cheek glowing with confusion, he repeated his errand.

Mary blushed, trembled, and was alarmed at finding herself alone with Thaddeus. Though he now stood before her in a quality which she had ever believed was his right, yet remembrance of what had passed between them, when in other circumstances, confounded and overwhelmed her. When Constantine was poor and unfriended, it was delicious to pity and to love him. When the same Constantine appeared as a man of rank, invested with a splendid fortune, and extensive fame, she

---

* revibrate, 'to vibrate again' (*OED*). Porter uses a common alternative spelling.

felt lost, annihilated. The cloud which had obscured, not extinguished his glory, was dispersed. He was that Sobieski whom she had admired unseen; he was that Constantine whom she had loved unknown; he was that Sobieski, that Constantine, who, seen and known, she now adored.

Weighed down by the weight of these reflections, she only bowed to what he said; and gathering her cloak from the winds which blew it around her, was hurrying with downward eyes to the stairs of the terrace, when her foot slipping, she must have fallen, had not Thaddeus caught her on his arm. She rose from it with a face blushing like scarlet; and that colour did not recede, when she found that he had not relinquished her hand. Her heart swelled, her head became giddy, her feet trembled; and finding that after a slight motion of her arm, he still held it fast; nearly overcome by inexplicable distress, she turned away her face to conceal its confusion.

Thaddeus saw all this; and, with a fluttering hope, instead of surrendering that hand which he had retained, he made it yet a closer prisoner, by grasping it in both his; and, pressing it earnestly to his breast, said, in a hurried voice, whilst his eloquent eyes poured all their beams upon her averted cheek, "Surely, Miss Beaufort will not deny me the dearest happiness I possess? The privilege of gratitude to her."

He paused: His soul was too full for utterance; and raising Mary's hand from his heart to his lips, he kissed it fervently. Almost fainting, Miss Beaufort struggled to withdraw it; and leaning her head, which she was now unable to support, against a tree of the thicket where they were standing, waved her released hand, in sign for him to leave her.

Such extraordinary agitation palsied all the warm and blissful emotions of the Count. Dreading that he had offended her, that she might suppose he had presumed on her kindness; he stood for a moment in silent astonishment; then dropping on his knee, (hardly conscious of doing so,) caught hold of her cloak; with an energy of action and voice, which spoke more impetuosity of feeling, than for a long time he had suffered to escape his heart; he implored her pardon, for what had passed.

"Forgive me," added he, with encreased earnestness; "forgive me, in justice to your own virtues. I meant only to thank you for your goodness to an unfortunate exile; but if my words or manner have obeyed the more fervid impulse of my soul, and declared aloud, what is its glory in secret; blame my nature, most respected Miss Beaufort, not my presumption. I have not dared to look steadily on any aim, higher than your esteem."

Mary knew not how to consider this address. The position in which he uttered it, his countenance, when she turned to answer him, were both declarative of something less equivocal than his speech. He was still grasping the drapery of her cloak; and his eyes, from which the wind blew back his fine hair, were beaming upon her, full of that piercing tenderness which at once dissolves and seizes the soul.

She passed her hand over her own eyes; with an attempt at self command, she begged him to rise, and instinctively held out her hand to assist him; he obeyed, and she continued, "You have done nothing, my Lord, to offend me. I was only fearful that my conduct – what I had done to serve you as a person my aunt esteemed, might have lessened me – might have led you to imagine, that I would not have acted the same part by any man in such circumstances."

Every emotion which faultered on the tongue of Mary, met an answering pang in the breast of Thaddeus. Fearing that he had set his heart on the possession of a treasure totally out of his reach, he knew not how high had been his hope, till he now felt the depth of his disappointment. He suffered the hand of Miss Beaufort to drop; and taking up his hat, which lay on the grass, with a countenance from which every gleam of joy had vanished, he bowed respectfully; and, in a low tone, replied, "Having the dependent situation in which I appeared at Lady Dundas's ever before my eyes, I had not the folly to suppose, that any lady could then notice my misfortunes, influenced by any other consideration than her humanity. That I excited this humanity, where alone I was proud to awaken it, was in those hours of dejection my sole comfort: It consoled me for the friends I had lost; it repaid me for the honours, which were no more. But that is past! Seeing no farther cause for compassion, you deem the delusion no longer necessary. Since you will not allow me any individual distinction in having attracted your benevolence, though I am to ascribe all to a charity as diffused as effective; yet I must ever acknowledge, with the deepest gratitude, that I owe my present home and happiness, to Miss Beaufort. Further than this, I shall never presume."

These words, shifted all the Count's anguish to Mary's breast. She perceived the offended delicacy which actuated every syllable as they fell; and, fearful of having incurred their reproof, by her cold and haughty reply, she opened her lips to say something that might better explain what she meant; but her heart failing her, she closed them again, and continued to walk in silence by his side. Having allowed the opportunity to escape, she believed all hopes of exculpation to be at an end; and, not daring to look up, she took a last despairing glance at Sobieski's graceful figure as he walked near her. His arms were folded, his hat pulled over his forehead, and his long dark eye-lashes shading his downward eyes, imparted a dejection to his whole air, which wrapped her weeping heart round and round with regretful pangs. "Ah!" thought she, "though the offspring of but one moment, they will prey on my peace for ever."

At the turning of a little wooded knoll, this silent and pensive pair heard the sound of some one on the other side, walking fastly through the heaps of dried leaves. In a minute after, Sir Robert Somerset appeared.

Whilst his father advanced smiling towards him, Thaddeus attempted to dispel the gloom of his countenance; but not succeeding, he bowed abruptly to the agitated Mary; and hastily said, "I will leave Miss Beaufort in your protection, Sir; and go myself to see whether or not Lady Albina be recovered from her fatigue."

"I thought to find you all together," returned Sir Robert; "Where is her ladyship?"

"I left her with Pembroke in a hut by the river;" said Thaddeus, and bowing again, he hurried away, whilst his father called after him to return in a few minutes and accompany him in a walk.

This immediate desertion of Sobieski, when he had come expressly to attend her to Lady Albina, nearly overwhelmed Miss Beaufort's before exhausted spirits: hardly knowing whether to remain or to retreat, she was attempting the latter, when her uncle caught her by the arm.

"Stay!" cried he, "why Mary, you surely would not leave me quite alone?"

Mary's tears had gushed over her eyes the moment her back was turned; and as Sir Robert drew her towards him, to his extreme amazement he saw that she was weeping. At a sight so unexpected, the smile of hilarity left his lips. Putting his arm tenderly round her waist, (for now that her distress had discovered itself, her agitation became so great that she could hardly stand,) he enquired in an affectionate voice, what had afflicted her?

She only answered by her sobs; till finding it impossible to break away from her uncle's arms, she hid her face in his bosom, and gave a loose to the full tide of her tears.

Sir Robert, recollecting the strange haste in which Thaddeus had hurried from them; and remembering Miss Beaufort's generosity to him in town, followed by her succeeding melancholy; at once united these circumstances with her present confusion; and conceiving an instantaneous suspicion of the reality, pressed her with redoubled affection to his bosom.

"I fear, my dearest girl," said he, "that something disagreeable has happened between you and the Count Sobieski? Perhaps he has offended you? Perhaps he has found my sweet Mary too amiable?"

Miss Beaufort, alarmed at this supposition; after a short struggle, answered, "O no Sir! It is I who have offended him. He thinks that I pride myself on the insignificant services which I rendered to him in London."

This reply convinced the Baronet, that he had not been premature in his judgment; and, with a new-born delight springing in his soul, he inquired why she thought so? Had she given him any reason to believe so?

Mary trembled at saying more. Dreading that every word she might utter, would betray how highly she prized the Count's esteem; she faultered, hesitated, stopped. Sir Robert put the question a second time in different terms.

"My loved Mary," said he, seating her by him on the trunk of a tree which had been newly felled, "I am sincerely anxious that you and this young nobleman should regard each other as friends: he is very dear to me; and you cannot doubt, my sweet girl, my affection for yourself. Tell me therefore the cause of this little misunderstanding?"

Miss Beaufort took courage at the kindness of this speech. Drying her glowing eyes, though still concealing them with a handkerchief, she replied in a firmer voice, "I believe, Sir, that the fault lies totally on my side. The Count Sobieski met me on the terrace, and thanked me for what I had done for him. I acted very weakly; I was confused. Indeed, I know not what he said; but he fell upon his knees, and I became so disconcerted, so frightened, of his having attributed my behaviour to indelicacy or forwardness, that I answered something which offended him. And I am sure, he now thinks me inhuman and proud."

Sir Robert kissed her throbbing forehead, as she ended this rapid and hardly articulate explanation.

"Tell me candidly, my dearest Mary!" said he, "Can you believe that a man of Sobieski's disposition, would kneel to a woman whom he did not both respect and love? Simple gratitude, my dear girl, is not so earnest. You have said enough to convince me, whatever be your sentiments, that you are the mistress of his fate: and, if he should mention it to me, may I tell him the scene which has now passed between us? May I tell him, that its just inference, would requite his tenderness with more than your thanks and best wishes?"

Sir Robert ended the sentence in a gay tone; but Mary, whose nice sensibility could not follow her uncle to his sanguine conclusion; looked modestly down, and with a half suppressed sigh, answered; "I will not deny that I esteem the Count Sobieski. I admired his character before I saw him: and when I saw him, although ignorant that it was he, my respect encreased. Yet, I never have aspired to any share in his heart, or even his remembrance: I could not have the presumption. Therefore, my dear uncle," added she, laying her trembling hand on his arm, and directing her fluctuating eyes to his face, "I beseech you, as you value my feelings, my peace of mind! never to breathe a syllable of my folly to him. I think," added she, clasping her hands with energy, and forgetting the force of her expression, "I would sooner suffer death than lose his esteem."

"And yet," inquired Sir Robert, "you will at some future period give your hand to another man?"

Mary, who did not consider the extent of this insidious question, answered with fervour, "Never. – I never can be happier than I am," added she, with breathless haste, seeing by the smile on Sir Robert's lips, that far more had been declared by her manner, than the words intended. Fearful of betraying herself farther, she begged permission to retire to the house.

The Baronet, now looking very serious, took her hand; and reseating her by him, said, "No, my dearest Mary; you shall not leave me, unless you honestly avow what are your sentiments of the Count Sobieski. You know, my sweet girl, that I have tried to make you regard me as a father; to induce you to receive from my love, the treble affection of your deceased parents and my lamented wife. If my Mary do not deny this, she cannot treat me with reserve?"

Miss Beaufort was unable to restrain her tears. Sir Robert continued.

"I will not overwhelm your delicacy by repeating the inquiry, whether I have mistaken the source of your recent emotion; only allow me to bestow some encouragement on the Count's attachment, should he claim my services in its behalf?"

Mary put her uncle's hand to her lips, and kissed it, whilst her dropping tears fell on it; and then replied in a timid voice; "I should be a monster of ingratitude, could I hide any thing from you, my dearest Sir, after this kindness! I confess, that I do esteem the Count Sobieski more than any being on earth. Who could see and know him, and feel it possible to regard another?"

"And you shall be his! my darling Mary!" cried the Baronet, mingling his own blissful tears with hers; "I had once hoped to have contrived an attachment between you and Pembroke, but heaven has decreed it better. When you and Thaddeus are united, I shall be happy; I may then die in peace."

Mary sighed heavily. She could not participate in her uncle's rapture. She thought that she had insulted and disgusted the Count by her late behaviour; and was opening her lips to urge it again, when the object of their conversation appeared at a little distance coming towards them. Full of renewed trepidation, she burst from the Baronet's hand; and taking to flight, left her uncle to meet Sobieski alone.

Sir Robert's anxious question received a more rapid reply from Thaddeus, than had proceeded from the reluctant Miss Beaufort. The animated gratitude of Sobieski; the ardent, yet respectful manner with which he declared her eminence above all other women, soon convinced the Baronet, that Mary's retreating delicacy had misinformed her. A complete explanation was the consequence; and Thaddeus, who had not been more sanguine in his hopes than his lovely mistress; allowed the clouds over his sunny eyes to disappear.

Sir Robert, impatient to see these two beings, so dear to his heart, repose confidently in each other's affection; the moment he returned to the house, asked his sister for Miss Beaufort. Mrs. Dorothy having replied, that she had seen her about half an hour ago retire to her own apartments, the Baronet sent a servant up stairs, to beg that she would meet him in the library.

This message found Mary in a paroxysm of distress. She reproached herself for her imprudence, her temerity, her unwomanly conduct, in having given away her heart to a man who had never seemed to require it. She remembered that her weakness, not her sincerity, had betrayed this humiliating secret to Sir Robert; and, nearly at her wit's end, with a beating heart, she was traversing the room, almost hoping that she was in a miserable dream, when her maid entered with the Baronet's commands.

Disdaining herself, and determining to regain some portion of her own respect, by steadily opposing all her uncle's deluding hopes; with an assumed serenity she arrived at the study door. She laid her hand on the lock, but the moment it yielded to her touch, all her firmness vanished; and trembling and pale as death, she appeared before him.

Sir Robert having supported her to a chair; with the tenderest and most delicate expressions of paternal love, repeated to her the sum of his conversation with the Count. Mary was almost wild at this discourse. She dreaded that the first proposal of their union had come from her uncle; and, burying her agitated face in her hands, exclaimed, "O Sir! I fear that you have for ever made me despicable in my own eyes; that you have told the Count Sobieski how weak I have been?"

Sir Robert tried to assure her, that she alarmed herself without a cause; but she would not, she could not be pacified; she believed that her tenderness and delicacy had been made a rash sacrifice; and was sitting gloomily weeping on a window-seat, when the Baronet gently added, "Well Mary, since I cannot prevail over this strange incredulity, I will call in a more powerful pleader."

He rose and opened the door which led to the dining-room. Miss Beaufort instantly got up, and flying to the opposite door, would have retreated, had not Sir Robert suddenly thrown himself in her way. He threw his arm about her waist, and turning her round, she saw the Count who had entered, standing and regarding her with an anxiety which covered her before pale features, with blushes.

His father bid him come near. Sobieski immediately obeyed, though with a step that expressed how reluctant he was, to oppress the woman whom he so deeply loved. Mary's face was now hidden in her uncle's bosom. Sir Robert put her almost lifeless hand into that of his son; who dropping on his knee, said in an agitated voice, "Dearest Miss Beaufort, do you really recal those cruel words which you directed to me this morning? May I indulge myself in the idea, that I am blessed with your esteem?"

Mary could not reply, but whispered to her uncle, "Pray, Sir, desire the Count to rise! I am already sufficiently overwhelmed."

"My sweet Mary!" returned the Baronet, pressing her in his arms; "this is no time for deception on either side. I know both your hearts. Rise Thaddeus;" said he to the Count, whilst he locked both their hands closely within his; "take him Mary: receive from your uncle his most precious gift; my matchless and injured son."

The shock which the first part of this speech occasioned Miss Beaufort, would have sunk her exhausted spirits to insensibility, had not the extraordinary assertion at its end, aroused and surprised her.

"Gracious Providence!" exclaimed she, "What do you mean, my dear uncle?"

"Thaddeus will explain all to you," returned he, "May heaven bless you both! I leave you together; and from him you will be confirmed in the truth of what I say."

Mary was too much astonished to think of following her uncle out of the room. She sunk on a seat, and turning her eyes full of amazement towards the Count, seemed to demand an explanation. Thaddeus, who still retained her passive hand, pressed it warmly to his heart; and whilst his effulgent eyes were beaming rapture and love, he imparted to her a concise but impressive narrative of his relationship with Sir Robert, and their late arrangement. He touched with short, yet ardent enthusiasm, on the virtues of his mother; he acknowledged the unbounded gratitude which belonged to that God who had so wonderfully conducted him to find a parent and a home in England; and with renewed pathos of look and manner, ratified the proffer which Sir Robert had made of his heart and hand.

Mary had listened with uncontroulable emotion to this interesting detail. Her eyes overflowed: their ingenuous language, enforced by the eloquent blood which glowed on her cheek, did not require the medium of words to declare what she felt. Thaddeus gazed on her with a certainty of bliss, which penetrated his soul till its feelings almost amounted to pain. The heart may ache with joy: neither sighs nor language, could express what passed in the Count's; he held her hand to his lips; his other arm fell unconsciously round her waist; and in a moment he found that he had pressed her to his breast. His heart beat violently. Miss Beaufort rose instantaneously from her chair; but her pure nature needed no disguise; she looked up to him, whilst her blushing* eyes were raining down tears of delight; and pronounced in a trembling voice, "Tell my dear uncle, that Mary Beaufort glories in the means by which she becomes his daughter."

She moved to the door: Thaddeus, whose full tide of transport denied him utterance, only clasped her hands again to his lips and bosom; then relinquishing them with reluctance, he suffered her to quit the room.

* That is, 'modest'.

CHAP. IX.

CONCLUSION.

The magnificent establishment which this projected union offered to Sobieski, seemed to heal the yet bleeding conscience of Sir Robert Somerset. Although he had acquiesced in the Count's generous surrender of the family honours, his heart remained ill at ease. Every dutiful expression from this long neglected son, stabbed him with an availing remorse. Conscious that his criminal marriage with Pembroke's mother, had deprived the son of Therese of his just inheritance, he could never meet Sobieski's filial attentions, without experiencing pangs of self-reproach which imbittered all his joy. Miss Beaufort's avowed and returned affection, at once removed the sting of this incessant recollection: Mistress of immense wealth, her hand would put the injured Thaddeus in possession, not only of those pure delights dependent alone on mutual sympathy of soul, but again empower his munificent spirit to exert itself in the disposal of an almost princely fortune.

Such meditations having followed the now tranquillized Baronet to his pillow, they brought him into the breakfast-parlour next day, full of that calm pleasure which promises a steady continuation. The happy family were assembled. Mrs. Dorothy saluted her brother, whose brightened eye declared that he had something pleasant to communicate; and he did not keep her a moment in suspense. With the first dish of coffee which was poured out, his grateful heart unburthened itself of its delightful tidings, that before the present month should expire, Miss Beaufort would give her hand to the Count Sobieski.

Pembroke was the only hearer who did not express surprise at this declaration: The transported Thaddeus had flown to his bed-side the preceding night, and with a bounding and enraptured heart, had related the whole of the recent scenes.

During Sir Robert's animated speech, Mary's blushing, yet triumphant eyes, sought a veil in a branch of geranium which she held in her trembling hand and affected to smell.

Mrs. Dorothy immediately rose from her chair; her heightened colour and glittering eyes spoke more than her lips, when she pressed, first her niece, and then the Count Sobieski, in her venerable arms.

"Heaven bless you both!" cried she, "This marriage will be the glory of my age."

Mary turned from the embrace of her aunt, to meet the warm congratulations of Pembroke. Whilst he kissed her burning cheek, he whispered loud enough for every one else to hear; "And why may I not participate in my good aunt's triumph? Attempt it, dear Mary! If you can persuade my father to allow me to make myself as happy with Lady Albina Stanhope, as you will render Sobieski, I shall for ever bless you!"

Lady Albina coloured like scarlet. Sir Robert took her hand with a smile of pleased surprise. "Do you, my lovely guest? Do you sanction, what this bold boy has just said?"

Lady Albina made no answer; but blushing deeper than before, cast a side-long glance at Pembroke, as if to petition his support. He was at her side in an instant; then seriously and earnestly entreating his father's consent to an union with her ladyship; (whose approbation of his passion he had obtained the preceding day in the shepherd's hut;) he awaited with hoping anxiety, the sounds which seemed faultering on Sir Robert's lips.

The Baronet, quite overcome by his darling Pembroke having like his brother, disposed of his heart so much to his own honour, found himself unable to say what he wished; and joining the hands of the two young people in silence, he hurried out of the room. He ascended immediately to the library, where kneeling down, he returned devout thanks to that all-gracious Being, who had crowned one so unworthy, with blessings so conspicuous.

Thaddeus, no less than his father, remembered the hand, which having guided him through a thorny but short path of sorrow, had in the end conducted him to an Eden of bliss: His heart did not forget, even in the midst of gaiety and smiles, the ardent gratitude which was due to the beneficent dispenser of his happiness.

Before the lapse of a week, it was discovered, that Sir Robert must hasten the marriage of Pembroke with Lady Albina, or be forced by law, to yield her to the demands of her father. After some search, Lord Tinemouth had learned that his daughter was under the protection of Sir Robert Somerset. Inflamed with rage and revenge, he sent to order her immediate return, under pain of an instantaneous appeal to the courts of judicature.

Too well aware that her non-age* made her completely obnoxious to this threat, Lady Albina fell into the most alarming fits on the first

---

* That is, nonage, 'the state of being under full legal age' (*OED*).

communication of the message. Sir Robert urged, that in her circumstances, no authority could be opposed to the Earl's, except that of a husband's; and on this consideration, she complied with his arguments and the prayers of her lover, directly to give that power into the hands of Pembroke.

Accordingly next morning by day-break, accompanied by Mrs. Dorothy and the enraptured Mr. Somerset, the terrified Lady Albina commenced her journey to Scotland; that being the only place where in her situation, the marriage could be legally solemnized.*

Whilst these young runaways, chaperoned by an old maiden aunt, were pursuing their rapid flight to Gretna Green, Sir Robert sent his steward to London to prepare two houses near his own in Grosvenor Square, for the reception of his children. During these necessary arrangements, a happy fortnight elapsed at Deerhurst. Thrice happy to Mary, because its tranquil hours imparted to her captive heart "*a sober certainty of that waking bliss,*"† which had so often animated the visions of her imagination. Morning, noon and evening, the companion of the Count Sobieski, she saw with added enthusiasm, that the sublime and princely virtues did not reign alone in his bosom. Their insufferable brightness was rendered less intense, was beautifully veiled, by the softening shades of those gentle amiabilities, which are the soothers and sweeteners of life. His breast seemed the residence of love: of a love, that not only infused a warmer existence through her soul, but diffused such a light of benevolence over every being within its influence, that all appeared happy who caught a beam of his eye; all enchanted, who shared the magic of his smile. Under what different effects had she seen this man! Yet how consistent! At the first period of their acquaintance, she beheld him like that glorious orb which her ardent fancy told her he resembled, struggling with the storm, or looking with steady grandeur through the clouds which obscured his path: But now, like the radiant sun of summer amidst a splendid sky, he seemed to stand, the source of light, and love, and joy.

Thus did the warm fancy, and warmer heart of Mary Beaufort, paint the image of her lover; and when Sir Robert received intelligence that the Gretna Green party had got to town, and were impatient for the arrival of the dear inhabitants of Deerhurst, she felt some embers of

---

* Under the Marriage Act of 1753, a person under the age of 21 could not marry in England without express parental consent. Because Scottish law held a much younger age of consent, Scottish border villages, like Gretna Green, became prime destinations for marriages and elopements.
† John Milton, *Comus* [*A Maske Presented at Ludlow Castle, 1634*] (London: Humphrey Robinson, 1637), l. 263.

human frailty sparkle in her bosom, at the anticipation of witnessing the homage which those who had despised the unfriended Constantine, would pay to the declared and illustrious Sobieski.

The news of Lady Albina's marriage, enraged the Earl of Tinemouth almost to madness. Well aware, that his withholding her ladyship's fortune, would occasion no uneasiness to a family of Sir Robert Somerset's vast possessions, he gave way to still more vehement bursts of passion; and in a fit of impotent threatening, embarked, with all his household, to spend the remainder of the season on his estates in Ireland.

This abrupt departure of the Earl's, caused Lady Albina little uneasiness. His unremitted cruelty, her brother's indifference, and the barbed insults of Lady Sophia Lovel, had wrankled too deep, to leave any filial regret behind. Considering their absence as a suspension of pain, rather than as a punishment, she did not stain the kiss which she imprinted on the venerable cheek of her new parent, with one tear to the memory of her unnatural father.

Whilst all was preparation, splendour, and happiness, in Grosvenor-square, Thaddeus did not forget the excellent Mrs. Robson. He had seen her twice, and had left her with the first payment of an annuity that would render herself and her grand-daughter independent for life. Neither did he neglect Mr. Burnett. It was not in his nature to allow any who served him to pass unrequited. He visited him one day in his rounds; and having repaid him, with a generosity that astonished the good money-lender; he took his sword, with the other relics of what were once so dear, and pressing them mournfully, yet gratefully, to his breast, re-entered Sir Robert's carriage; and was set down at his brother's house, about an hour before dinner.*

Lady Albina Somerset's arrival in London, had been greeted by the immediate calls of all the people in town, who either had been acquainted with the late Countess of Tinemouth, or were known to the Baronet's family. Amongst the earliest names whose tickets appeared at her ladyship's door, were those of Lord Berrington, Dr. Blackmore, Captain and Mrs. Montresor, and Dr. Cavendish. Lady Albina did not propose opening her gates to the gay world, till Miss Beaufort and the Count were married, and they and she had been presented at Court;

---

* In the second edition, Porter revises this paragraph and the succeeding paragraph that begins 'Thaddeus had flown to his kind friend Cavendish' to five pages (4. 228–33). In the most significant addition, Cavendish introduces Thaddeus to none other than Mr. Hopetown, the Dantzic-based English merchant to whom Thaddeus left his favourite horse Saladin. Hopetown brought Saladin with him to England, and he promises to return the horse to an overjoyed Thaddeus.

but having heard Pembroke speak of the before-mentioned persons with particular respect, (when she took the list of her numerous visitors out of her footman's hand,) she selected them as the first party which should grace her table.

Thaddeus had flown to his kind friend Cavendish, the very day on which he came to town; and telling him, with a smiling countenance, that he was that Sobieski, about whose strange fate he had so often expressed an interest; the astonished and delighted doctor embraced him with an ardour, which spoke better than language, his admiration and esteem.

When the Count alighted at Mr. Somerset's door on the day of his call on the money-lender, he was agreeably surprised by finding the invited groupe in the saloon. Lord Berrington, and the ever lively Maria Egerton, now Mrs. Montresor, ran up to him at the same instant, and expressed their sincere joy at not only seeing him again, but in a situation so consonant to his fame and quality.

Thaddeus replied to their felicitations with a frankness and grace peculiarly his own; and was not a little surprised when Dr. Blackmore, a moment afterwards, recognized him to be the stranger who had so much engaged his attention about a year ago. The Count had no recollection of this circumstance, till the good doctor brought the very hour to his remembrance, by mentioning the Hummums, and recapitulating the rudeness of the man in black, whose name he since had learnt was Loftus.

Pembroke could hardly hear the worthy clergyman to the end. He exclaimed against his vile tutor's indefatigable villainy; and, turning to Sir Robert, exclaimed, "My dear Sir, the recent hurrying events have hitherto averted justice from seizing this man; but I must beg, that his connexion with any thing belonging to us may end to-morrow. Write to him, and order him to resign his situation at Arun-house immediately."

The Baronet promised; and Sobieski trying to change a conversation which agitated his brother, addressed Mrs. Montresor on some general topic. Captain Montresor joined them, and expressed great regret at the loss he should shortly suffer in the absence of his friend Captain Roos.

"How? Where is he going?" demanded his wife.

Montresor replied, by lamenting the ill state of Lady Sara Roos's health, and the necessity which her husband found to carry her to Italy for its restoration.

"I met him this morning," continued he, "quite in despair about her."

Thaddeus too well divined, that this increased indisposition owed its
rise to his return to town; and inwardly petitioning heaven that absence
might complete her cure, he could not suppress the sigh which her fatal
devotedness to him wrung from his pity and his gratitude.

No one present, except the affectionate Mary, marked the transient melancholy which passed over his countenance. She, who had
suspected the unhappy Lady Sara's attachment, loved Thaddeus, if
possible, still dearer, for the compassion he bestowed on the victim of
a passion, which is as inscrutable as destructive.

When the party descended to dinner, Mrs. Dorothy, who sat next to
Thaddeus, rallied him upon the loss which he had sustained of one of
his most potent admirers. This strange attack, following so instantly
the information relating to Lady Sara Roos, summoned a fervid colour
into the face of the Count: he looked surprised, and rather confused,
at the good old Lady; who smiling, related, that she had been told by
her milliner this morning, that Miss Euphemia Dundas had married a
Scotch nobleman near Hamilton.

"So much the better for my dear Mary!" cried Pembroke: "Her
jealous fears are now at an end: and little Phemy was no contemptible
rival. Besides, Albina," said he, turning gaily to her ladyship, "you
may congratulate yourself on the same score. I hear that an old friend
of mine is going to take her loving sister off *my* hands. Come, Dr.
Cavendish, you must validate my report, for I learnt it of you."

The good doctor smiled, and answered in the affirmative; adding,
that his friend at Stamford had written to him as news, that "the eldest
son of Sir Halerand Shafto, was on the point of marriage with Miss
Dundas, a rich East Indian heiress, who was visiting my lady."

Sobieski wished them both happy. Lord Berrington protested, that
his lordship was more generous than just.

"I vow to heaven," cried the young viscount, "I never knew people
the end of whose lives seemed so bent on mischief. Euphemia, pretty
as she is, was better known by her spirit of tormenting, than by her
beauty: and as for the poor squire whom Diana has conjured into
matrimony, I have little doubt of his future honours."

"Ah!" cried Mrs. Montresor, "Poor Acteon! I warrant she will
allot him the punishment he merits, for stepping between her and that
delectable Endymion, Fool Lascelles!"*

"A truce, my dear Madam?" entreated Miss Beaufort.

"She does not deserve it of you," returned the laughing lady,

---

* In Greco-Roman mythology, Actaeon was punished for seeing Diana at her bath; the
  youthful Endymion was Diana's lover.

pursuing the subject, till Mrs. Dorothy and Sir Robert Somerset were both obliged to call very loudly upon charity.

Thaddeus, who knew not the nature of those sensations which constitute a rejoicing over the probable misconduct of his enemies, considered this part of the conversation, as by far the least pleasant of the day.

Pembroke's wish, with regard to Mr. Loftus, was complied with next morning. Dr. Blackmore having been prevailed upon to take charge of the young Lord Arun, reluctantly bore the mandate for his predecessor's dismission, and set out the same day for the seat of his lordship's aunt.

Whilst Sir Robert Somerset denounced the guilty, he was careful neither to plunge him into fresh temptations, nor to suffer his crimes to injure the innocent. In pity to age and helplessness, he settled two hundred pounds per annum, on the wretched man's mother and sisters in Wales. And shortly after, in consequence of Loftus confessing that all Pembroke's allegations were but too just, Sir Robert adjudged one hundred yearly, to the culprit himself, that at least he might not be seduced to obtain by deeper villainy, a subsistence. As for the living of Somerset, which had been the price of Mr. Loftus's integrity, that, Sir Robert determined to bestow on Dr. Blackmore, whenever it should fall.

The appointed day being arrived, in which Mary was to give herself and her earthly happiness, into the power of the only man, whom having once beheld, she ever could have resigned them to; she pronounced her vows at the altar, with unsteadiness of tongue, but a fixed heart: and when she alighted at Mr. Somerset's cottage in Epping Forest,* she received the congratulations of dear friends, with a tenderness, an elevation of soul, which drowned her glowing and enraptured face in tears.

The Count Sobieski was not less sensible of the favoured path which Providence had spread before him. He had passed through hosts of evils, and he now looked forward to a long Sabbath of peace and gratitude. He found it at the cottage.† He enjoyed its full possession, when he returned to town he saw his beautiful wife at the head of fashion, not only adorning his house, but filling his home with all the ineffable comforts of domestic life, and domestic virtues.

---

* Epping Forest is an ancient woodland some 20 kilometres north of central London. The location is changed to 'her own paternal mansion, in Kent' in the third edition.
† Changed to 'He found it at Beaufort-hall' (that is, Mary's 'paternal mansion') in the third edition.

One fine evening in which they were out together, she ordered the carriage to stop in Covent Garden; when it drew up, she expressed a wish to walk through the church-yard. Thaddeus immediately complied; and before he had time to express his surprise at the strangeness of her request, she led him towards the grave of his revered friend Butzou, who had been buried there. It was no longer the same; a white marble tablet occupied the place of grass and yarrow. The Count bent forward, and read with swimming eyes, the following inscription:

> *Stop, traveller, thou treadest upon a hero!*
> *Here*
> *rests the body*
> *of*
> *Lieutenant* GENERAL BUTZOU.

Sobieski's soul was pierced. Incapable of speaking, he led his wife back to her carriage; and, placing her in it, clasped her suddenly and fondly to his breast. His tears gushed out in spite of himself, and mingling with hers, poured those thanks, those assurances of animated approbation through her heart, as made it even ache with excess of happiness.

Thus mutually endeared, we leave the family of Sir Robert Somerset. We leave Thaddeus Sobieski, blessed in the fruition of every earthly good. Whilst he, each morning, opens his eye to fresh prospects of joy, his pure and manly heart, derives its best felicity from gratitude to heaven; and owns, that the retrospection of past misfortunes, like shade to a picture, gives to our present bliss greater force and brightness.

THE END.

APPENDICES

APPENDIX F

Appendix A: Third Edition Ending

Following his December 1796 release from prison, Tadeusz Kościuszko travelled to the United States of America, stopping in Sweden and England on his way. In May 1797, Kościuszko arrived in London, and there he met with numerous admirers, including the artist Benjamin West and Jane Porter's brother, Robert Ker Porter. For the third edition of *Thaddeus of Warsaw* (1805), Porter imagined Kościuszko's visitors to include Thaddeus Sobieski, and she extended the novel's conclusion to portray the reunion of her heroes.

> Thus mutually endeared, we leave the family of Sir Robert Somerset. We leave Thaddeus Sobieski, blessed in the fruition of every earthly good. The Virtues, the Muses, and the Charities, were the guests at his table. Misfortune could not veil Genius from his eyes; nor Calamity obscure the brightness of the Just. Though banished from his native country, where his birth gave him dominion over rich territories, now in ruins; and a once numerous and happy people, now no more; – he had not yet relinquished the love of empire: – But it was not over principalities, and embattled hosts, that he wished to extend the sceptre of command: – He wished to reign in the soul: – His throne was in the hearts of the Good, the Amiable, and the Unfortunate. The Unhappy of every rank and Nation, found refuge, consolation, and repose, amongst the shades of Beaufort.[1] No eye looked wistfully on him, to turn away and weep; no voice addressed him with the petition of distress, to close it with the sigh of disappointment: His smiles cheered the disconsolate; and his protecting arms, warded off the approach of new sorrows. *Peace was within his walls, and plenteousness within his palaces.*[2] And when a few eventful months distinguished their course with the death of the implacable Destroyer of Poland,[3] and General Kosciuszko (who

---

[1] Beaufort Hall, Mary's inherited property. See footnotes to page 395.

[2] From Psalm 122: 7; see also the anthem *Laetatus sum* ('I was glad'), traditionally sung at coronations of the British monarchy since that of Charles I.

[3] Catherine the Great died in November 1796. Her son and successor, Paul I, released Kościuszko and his imprisoned colleagues on the understanding that they would not return to Poland.

was set at liberty by her successor) arrived in England, he was received with the warmest welcome, by his now happy friend. – "Ah, my dear General" said he, as he clasped the veteran to his breast; "I am indeed, favoured above mortals – I see thee again, on whom I believed the gates of a Russian prison had closed for ever! – I have all that remains of my country pressing upon my heart – all its valour, virtue, and heroism, is now within the circle of my arms! – Kosciuszko, my friend, my father, bless your son!"

Kosciusko did bless him; and embalmed the benediction, with a shower of tears, more precious than the richest unction that ever flowed on a royal head; – they were drawn from the heart of a Hero. – Sobieski presented his lovely wife to his illustrious friend; and while he gratefully acknowledged the rare felicity of his fate, he owned that the retrospection of past misfortunes, like shade to a picture, gives to our present bliss, greater force and brightness.

Appendix B: Critical Reviews of *Thaddeus of Warsaw*

Critics warmly received *Thaddeus of Warsaw* when it first appeared in 1803, praising its balance of historical particularities with sentimental romance. In 1831, Porter produced an extensively revised edition, which included a new introduction and footnotes, for Henry Colburn and Richard Bentley's Standard Novels series. Poland was again at war against the Russian empire in 1830–1, and the timely new edition of *Thaddeus* led to a renewed interest in Porter's hero and the novel's historical contexts.

Critical Review 39 (September 1803), p. 120

Miss Porter has availed herself of a very interesting period in history for the foundation of her tale. Often have we felt our heart rent by indignation and pity, at the dismemberment of Poland, and the cruel fate of Stanislaus. Truth and fiction are blended with much propriety in these volumes; and we have turned with sincere pleasure the pages that praise the valour of Kosciusko; and recount, though but as a novel, the adventures of a Sobieski.

Imperial Review 1 (February 1804), pp. 309–14

… Miss Porter has given us, in Thaddeus Sobieski, not merely a model of magnanimity, but a true hero – a man never above the feelings of humanity – a noble of nature, formed to enjoy and to dispense felicity, fitted to endure and to surmount adversity … . Thaddeus is a work of genius. It is not invariably correct, nor universally excellent: some little inaccuracies and redundancies are discernible, which the mere mannerist in literature is not liable to commit, and at which the hypercritical inquisitor of literature will not fail to declaim: but these we predict, with confidence, will be by few perceived – by fewer still regarded. Thaddeus has nothing to fear at the candid bar of taste: he has to receive the precious meed[1] of sympathy from every reader of unsophisticated sentiment and genuine feeling.

Monthly Review 43 (February 1804), pp. 214–15

Many of the incidents in this novel partake much of the nature of romance: but it is founded on real events, and the scene of the first volume is laid almost entirely in Poland, at the time when that country and its unfortunate inhabitants became the prey of the ambition of the surrounding monarchs. This part is perhaps too deeply involved in bustle, and, in order to be understood, requires a larger portion of attention than the generality of novel readers are accustomed to bestow. The business of the other volumes is more connected, and our own country is chosen for the scene of action. Thaddeus Sobieski, after the fall of his devoted country and the ruin of all his hopes, flies to England for refuge; and the story, which the author has thus interwoven with historical fact, exhibits some situations of considerable interest. The meeting of two friends, between whom a misunderstanding had been created by the unworthy practices of an interested agent, is described with peculiar propriety; and dignity of character is well preserved in the immediate and unreserved credit with which the mutual explanations are received.

Altogether, the work has more merit than can be ascribed to the crowd of productions of this class, and inculcates virtuous and magnanimous sentiments. It is inscribed to Sir Sydney Smith in a very neat and well managed address.[2]

Edinburgh Literary Journal 135 (June 1831), pp. 370–1

... 'Thaddeus of Warsaw' is indeed one of the shortest – it is the first – and we are much inclined to add – the best of Miss J. Porter's performances. We need not, however, talk of its merits now; for the verdict of public judgment has long ago pronounced in its favour by a very considerable majority. The present edition, according to the reigning fashion, has undergone the careful revision of the author, of which the fruits are occasional notes of

---

[1] meed, 'a person's deserved share' (*OED*).
[2] Ralph Griffiths, editor of the *Monthly Review*, identifies the author of this review as 'Capt. B....y': that is, Captain James Burney (1750–1821), brother of novelist Frances Burney. Nangle, Benjamin Christie, *The Monthly Review, Second Series, 1790-1815* (Oxford: Clarendon Press, 1955), p. 97.

explanation – none of any importance – respecting the principal incidents and characters of the story. …

… Some having evinced surprise at the very vivid, yet accurate, delineations of the principal actors and real scenes in which they were engaged, she explains her means of obtaining such information, from the frequent conversations she was enabled to hold with those who had dwelt in these very homes, and struggled on these battle-fields. 'The features of the country also,' we are told, 'were learned from persons who had trodden the steps she describes.' Now this is the only point where we are forced to quarrel with Miss Porter, for want of honest candour. For a very superficial comparison of the first volume of Coxe's Travels in Russia, with this romance, must convince every one who will 'believe the truth avouch of his own eyes,' that the passages alluded to in the latter, are, if not a copy *verbatim*, at least a very continuous transcription from the other work. And though Coxe *has* 'trodden the steps she describes,' it is scarcely enough, while she is so lavish of gratitude to others, to make such an equivocal acknowledgment of her obligations in this quarter. Nor is there any need of being ashamed to do this; since Mrs Radcliffe[3] has always readily allowed that her finest descriptions of the scenery of the Alps and Apennines are borrowed from this very source.

Independently of these considerations, the appearance of this volume at this moment is most opportune. It is a highly-coloured chronicle of events and characters, whose memory is now inciting thousands to enforce their repetition with all the prospect of a happier issue. And to the not altogether indifferent, but more distantly interested spectator, it presents a picture of the local scenery and manners of Poland, in a period of excitement very similar to the present, which is not always to be found drawn so pleasantly, and at the same time with such observance of truth.

Athenaeum 189 (11 June 1831), p. 377

This edition has been revised and corrected by the author, who, after the usage of Sir Walter, has written an explanatory introduction, in which she gossips pleasantly enough of herself, the original of the tale, and the historical persons and circumstances referred to in it. These trifles certainly give additional value to a volume that in itself must be a welcome addition to every library.

---

[3] Ann Radcliffe (1764–1823), prominent Gothic novelist.

These very cheap republications we have from the first cordially
recommended, and we are glad to hear that the speculation has
been as successful as it deserved to be.4

Gentleman's Magazine 101 (June 1831), p. 622

The influence of Novels in effecting the formation of character,
upon such abstract principles of morality, wisdom, and heroism
as overpower the sordid and mean motives of interest or fear, is
a subject far too refined for common apprehension, and too pure
for designing worldliness ... . An exemplar how to form a noble-
minded young man, is delineated in this novel, which has been
too generally read for years to need any extract.

Monthly Magazine 12.67 (July 1831), p. 96

It is now thirty years since Miss Jane Porter published her
Thaddeus of Warsaw – the first of the class of biographical
romances which Sir Walter Scott has since brought into such
fashion and repute, and in which, she observes, he had done her
the honour to adopt her precedent. In her turn she is delighted to
follow his example, in communicating to the world all it is desirous to know of a writer's views, when first framing these particular fictions. Her interest in favour of the Poles was first raised by
seeing numbers of the refugees, after the last partition of Poland,
roaming forlornly in St. James's Park. Some years after, when
Kosciusko was released by Paul of Russia, and came to London
in his way to America, Miss Porter's brother was introduced to
him, and thus he became the topic of family talk; and finally,
when she took to writing, the hero of the young lady's romance.
Mrs. Radcliffe ate raw steaks to stir her imagination, and Schiller
hung his room with black drapery, and wrote by the glimmer
of a farthing rush-light;5 – while Miss Porter worked away in

4   Colburn and Bentley's Standard Novels series aimed to distribute novels at low cost for
    a wide readership with volumes priced at six shillings (6s) instead of the average price
    of a guinea and a half (31s 6d). Wallins, Roger P., 'Richard Bentley, Henry Colburn
    and Richard Bentley, Henry Colburn, Henry Colburn and Company, Richard Bentley
    and Son', in *British Literary Publishing Houses, 1820–1880*, eds Patricia Anderson and
    Jonathan Rose (Detroit: Gale Research, 1991), pp. 39–52 (42–3).
5   Rumours circulated that Ann Radcliffe ate raw or undercooked meat before bed to
    induce nightmares as inspiration for her novels. Norton, Richard, *Mistress of Udolpho:
    The Life of Ann Radcliffe* (London: Bloomsbury, 1999), pp. 215–16. German poet
    Friedrich Schiller (1759–1805) reportedly wrote at night in dim and sombre conditions

her brother's study or painting room, in which was suspended Abercrombie's 'war-dyed coat,'[6] and the waistcoat, bullet-torn, of some other commander, to give intensity to the strokes with which she dashed off the campaigns of Thaddeus Sobieski.

to inspire his art. Carlyle, Thomas, *The Life of Friedrich Schiller* (London: Taylor and Hessey, 1825), p. 149.

[6] Porter, Jane, 'The Author to her Friendly Readers', in *Thaddeus of Warsaw* (London: Colburn and Bentley, 1831), p. xi. Lieutenant-General Sir Ralph Abercromby (1734–1801; often written Abercrombie) died from wounds sustained during the Battle of Alexandria. Robert Ker Porter's third panorama, *The Battle of Alexandria* (1802), celebrated Abercromby's heroism.

Appendix C: Poland in the Nineteenth-Century British Literary Imagination

In Kościuszko and his stalwart attempts to defend Poland's independence, many Britons saw an exemplar of national heroism. Although the events recounted in *Thaddeus of Warsaw* had faded into the past, Kościuszko retained a strong presence in the imagination of numerous British writers. These writers – including Samuel Taylor Coleridge, John Keats and Lord Byron – reflected on Polish–Russian relationships and the Polish partitions in the context of contemporary political philosophies and celebrated the heroism of Kościuszko in a variety of verse forms.

Samuel Taylor Coleridge, 'To Kosciusko', in *Poems on Various Subjects* (London: G. G. and J. Robinson, 1796), p. 52

Like many of his contemporaries, Samuel Taylor Coleridge (1772–1834) viewed Kościuszko as a model of patriotism. Coleridge first published this sonnet on 16 December 1794 in the *Morning Chronicle*; it was the fifth in his series of 'Sonnets on Eminent Characters'. A revised version appeared in his 1796 collection.

> O what a loud and fearful shriek[1] was there,
> As tho' a thousand souls one death-groan pour'd!
> Ah me! they view'd beneath an hireling's sword
> Fall'n KOSKIUSKO! Thro' the burthen'd air
> (As pauses the tir'd Cossac's barb'rous yell
> Of Triumph) on the chill and midnight gale
> Rises with frantic burst or sadder swell
> The dirge of murder'd Hope! while Freedom pale
> Bends in *such* anguish o'er her destin'd bier,
> As if from eldest time some Spirit meek
> Had gather'd in a mystic urn each tear

---

[1] 'When *Kosciusko* was observed to fall, the Polish ranks set up a shriek' [Coleridge's note].

That ever furrow'd a sad Patriot's cheek;
And she had drain'd the sorrows of the bowl
Ev'n till she reel'd, intoxicate of soul!

Peter Courtier, from *Revolutions: A Poem* (London: C. Whittingham, 1796), Book 1, lines 457–67

English clergyman-turned-poet Peter Courtier (1776–1847) situated his poetic reflections on war and despotism in the context of three political events that had captured the British literary imagination of the 1790s: the American Revolution, the French Revolution and the Polish partitions. The passage offered here evinces a contemporary literary trend of presenting Kościuszko as an emblem of patriotism, heroism and anti-imperialism.

And thou too, hapless Poland! thou shalt rise
Above the storms of war; yes, thou shalt quit
The wiles of Russia, and her harpy fangs:
Then, KOSCIUSKO! yet awhile bear up
Beneath the tedious yoke; remember still
Thy suffering Country, and exist for her.
For she remembers thee; and waits the day
(Soon it will dawn,) of Retributive right.
Then, with the laurels of eternal Fame,
She'll bind thy patriot brow; and with her own,
Avenge the injuries which thou hast felt.

Thomas Campbell, from *The Pleasures of Hope* (Edinburgh: Mundell and Son, 1799), Part 1, lines 349–82

Scottish poet Thomas Campbell (1777–1844) became a friend of Jane Porter's in the months before the publication of *Thaddeus of Warsaw* in 1803. Campbell's enormously popular poem draws inspiration from Samuel Rogers's *The Pleasures of Memory* (1792), which Pembroke Somerset reads to Countess Sobieski and Princess Sapieha. *The Pleasures of Hope* was first published six months after William Wordsworth's and Samuel Taylor Coleridge's *Lyrical Ballads* appeared and explores contemporary political topics, including slavery, the French Revolution and the partition of Poland. The first part of the poem, from which the following lines are excerpted, presents a descriptive catalogue of the triumph of hope over various miseries, particularly warfare and political injustice.

Oh! sacred Truth! thy triumph ceas'd awhile,
And Hope, thy sister, ceas'd with thee to smile,   350
When leagu'd Oppression pour'd to Northern wars
Her whisker'd pandoors and her fierce hussars,
Wav'd her dread standard to the breeze of morn,
Peal'd her loud drum, and twang'd her trumpet horn;
Tumultuous horror brooded o'er her van,   355
Presaging wrath to Poland – and to man![2]
   Warsaw's last champion from her height survey'd,
Wide o'er the fields, a waste of ruin laid, –
Oh! Heav'n! he cried, my bleeding country save! –
Is there no hand on high to shield the brave? –   360
Yet, though destruction sweep these lovely plains,
Rise, fellow men! our country yet remains!
By that dread name we wave the sword on high,
And swear for her to live! – with her to die!
   He said, and, on the rampart-heights, array'd   365
His trusty warriors, few, but undismay'd;
Firm-pac'd and slow, a horrid front they form,
Still as the breeze, but dreadful as the storm;
Low murm'ring sounds along their banners fly,
Revenge, or death, – the watchword and reply;   370
Then peal'd the notes, omnipotent to charm,
And the loud tocsin toll'd their last alarm! –
   In vain, alas! in vain, ye gallant few!
From rank to rank your volley'd thunder flew: –
Oh! bloodiest picture in the book of Time,   375
Sarmatia fell, unwept, without a crime;
Found not a generous friend, a pitying foe,
Strength in her arms, nor mercy in her woe!
Dropt from her nerveless grasp the shatter'd spear,
Clos'd her bright eye, and curb'd her high career; –   380
Hope, for a season, bade the world farewell,
And Freedom shriek'd – as KOSCIUSKO fell!

---

[2] Campbell adds an endnote here quoting the *New Annual Register*'s description of the 10
October 1794 Battle of Maciejowice. Porter's own description of this key battle appears
in Volume I, Chapter VI of *Thaddeus of Warsaw*.

Leigh Hunt, 'To Kosciusko', in *The Examiner* (19 November 1815), p. 746

Leigh Hunt (1784–1859), like Coleridge, greatly admired Kościuszko. As Keats reports in the poem 'Sleep and Poetry', Hunt had a bust of the Polish general in his Hampstead cottage. In the sonnet's subtitle, Hunt praises Kościuszko as one '[w]ho took part neither with Bonaparte in the height of his power, nor with the allies in the height of theirs'.

'Tis like thy patient valour thus to keep,
  Great Kosciusko, to the rural shade,
  While freedom's ill-found amulet still is made
Pretence for old aggression, and a heap
Of selfish mockeries. There, as in the sweep
  Of stormier fields, thou earnest with thy blade,
  Transform'd, not inly alter'd, to the spade,
Thy never-yielding right to a calm sleep.
Nature, 'twould seem, would leave to man's worse with
  The small and noisier parts of this world's frame,
And keep the calm, green amplitudes of it
  Sacred from fopperies and inconstant blame.
Cities may change, and sovereigns; but 'tis fit,
  Thou, and the country old, be still the same.

John Keats, 'To Kosciusko', in *The Examiner* (16 February 1817), p. 107

John Keats (1795–1821) followed in the footsteps of his contemporaries in penning a sonnet in praise of Kościuszko. The content of Keats's poem and his choice of publication venue espouse his political liberalism and his friendship with Leigh Hunt.

GOOD KOSCIUSKO! thy great name alone
  Is a full harvest whence to reap high feeling:
  It comes upon us like the glorious pealing
Of the wide spheres – an everlasting tone:
And now it tells me that in worlds unknown
  The names of Heroes, burst from clouds concealing,
  Are changed to harmonies, for ever stealing
Through cloudless blue, around each silver throne.
  It tells me, too, that on a happy day,
When some good spirit walks upon the earth,
  Thy name, with ALFRED'S, and the great of yore,

Gently commingling, gives tremendous birth
    To a loud hymn, that sounds far, far away,
To where the great GOD lives for evermore.

George Gordon, Lord Byron, from *The Age of Bronze* (London: John Hunt, 1823), lines 158–67

Lord Byron (1788–1824) wrote elegantly on his anti-colonialist stances, particularly in regard to the Turkish presence in Greece and the Russian presence in Poland. His poem, *The Age of Bronze*, offers a critique of European and English colonial politics. In addition to his admiration of Kościuszko, Byron also discusses key figures of the American Revolution, George Washington and Benjamin Franklin (245–50, 383–9), and implores readers to forget the conquests of Francisco Pizarro and instead to embrace liberators like Simón Bolívar (251–66).

                                                  ye who dwell
Where Kosciusko dwelt, remembering yet
The unpaid amount of Catherine's bloody debt!
Poland! o'er which the avenging angel past,
But left thee as he found thee, still a waste;
Forgetting all thy still enduring claim,
Thy lotted people and extinguished name;
Thy sigh for freedom, thy long-flowing tear,
That sound that crashes in the tyrant's ear;
Kosciusko!

Appendix D: Porter Family Correspondence

Jane Porter worked closely with her sister, novelist Anna Maria Porter, while composing her works. These selections, written while Anna Maria was at the Porters' Gerrard Street residence in London and Jane was visiting Bath, concern preparations for the second edition of *Thaddeus of Warsaw*. They give insight into the sisters' collaborative practices, their family concerns and their ideas on heroism.

Anna Maria Porter to Jane Porter, 31 March 1804

MS: Huntington Library Jane Porter Papers POR 442

My dearest Jane,

You know not with what Joy, I hasten to tell you, that a second edition of your Thaddeus is required <u>immediately</u>. – pray procure a set from the Circulating Library at Bath, and make notes of the alterations you wish to appear; you must then forward them, volume, by volume to me; and I will insert them properly in the printed copy, from which the 2d Edition will be taken. – be careful to say in what page of each vol. these corrections are to come, and that will be sufficient. – Longman[1] has settled the remaining account, (very handsomely) and has given you a bill of 24 pounds: My mother without scruple has appropriated this, to her present necessities; for indeed my dear Jane – the difficulties of Robert, and the amazing disappointments of John,[2] render us at this period, almost insanely happy at the sight of 24 pounds! – such is our <u>real</u> situation, while the world, considers us rolling in riches. – by a Frank[3] next week, we will send you a two pound note, or more if you require it. –

---

[1] Thomas Norton Longman III (1771–1842), printer and bookseller, proprietor of the Longman publishing business and publisher of *Thaddeus*.

[2] Robert Ker Porter (1777–1842) and John Porter (1772–1810), two of Jane Porter's brothers.

[3] Letters could be sent for free with the stamp or 'frank' of a peer or a member of Parliament. See *New Guide for Foreigners* (London: S. W. Fores, [?1789]), p. 23.

pray do not forget the alteration of the burying place of old Butzou – and do not neglect restoring Saladin to his master.[4] Mrs Crespigny[5] annoyed me again about Prague – and talked of your novel being <u>pretty</u>, while I told her, what Mr Rees[6] said of it: – Good God, if she had not been humanely listening to my intercessions about Miss Mortimer,[7] five minutes before, I think I could have torn her limb from limb! –

Bob bids me tell you, that <u>4 sheets</u> of MS, will make the Alexandria Book, a proper size.[8] – you are to remember that Buonaparte is a favorite in America, and therefore though you cannot <u>praise</u>, you must not <u>censure</u> his actions: – all the poisoning business is to be omitted.[9] – We got your letter for Henry,[10] which I forwarded by the Post. – Bray,[11] tells me, that you look wonderfully well – I fear <u>my</u> looks have declined of late; though I am otherwise perfectly well. – the Cottage Bonnet was unluckily sent to Mrs W Porter,[12] many months ago; my mother recommends you to buy some C muslin,[13] and have one made. –

adieu. – all are well – and all unite in warmest love – the Post is going I can only say, that I am ever, ever your most affte[14]

A. M. Porter

---

4   In the second edition, Porter corrected the location of General Butzou's grave and restored the horse Saladin to Thaddeus.

5   Mary, Lady Champion de Crespigny (?1748–1812), author and literary mentor to the Porter sisters.

6   Owen Rees, printing and bookselling partner with Longman, publishers of *Thaddeus*.

7   Little is known of the actress Miss Mortimer, a Porter family friend who played Ophelia in her Covent Garden debut in September 1803. Wewitzer, R., *A Brief Dramatic Chronology of Actors* (London: John Miller, 1817), p. 16.

8   Robert Ker Porter's 1802 panorama *The Battle of Alexandria* had been shown throughout Britain and Ireland, and in 1804 it was heading for North America. Robert apparently asked Jane to create an accompanying pamphlet for American audiences. The result was *A Correct Account of the Battle of Alexandria* (New York: Southwick and Hardcastle, 1804).

9   At the siege of Jaffa, Napoleon ordered the poisoning of French soldiers who were suffering from the plague. See Wilson, Robert Thomas, *History of the British Expedition in Egypt* (London: T. Egerton, 1802), pp. 74–6. A print of the episode, after a drawing by Robert Ker Porter, was published in 1803.

10   Captain Henry Edwin Allen Caulfeild (1779–1808), actor and close friend of Jane Porter.

11   Bray is likely a female attendant with the Porter family (Huntington POR 1494).

12   Lydia, first wife of Jane and Anna Maria's brother, William Ogilvie Porter (Huntington POR 1422).

13   Calico muslin, a simple, inexpensive, cotton fabric.

14   An abbreviation for 'affectionate', often used in epistolary valedictions in the eighteenth and nineteenth centuries.

Jane Porter to Anna Maria Porter, 3 April 1804

MS: Huntington Library Jane Porter Papers POR 1504

My dear Maria!

I hope the enclosed remainder of the MSS: will please Robert. I assure you the want of a guide has been a great plague to me – Had I had an Alexandria-Book, I could have compiled it better to my mind. – [15]

I shall daily expect Thaddeus – the moment it arrives, I will commence alterations with all diligence. – I have been advised to add a second Title – for stupid people forget the first – which in enquiring for the book, is a great injury. – suppose I call it, "Thaddeus of Warsaw – or – The Hero." – The addition is simple, and easy enough to be remembered. – To please that illiberal woman Mrs Crespigny, I will change the word Prague, to Praga. – But I will say something about it – so I wish you would look into Campbells book for me, or any other – just to give me authorities for spelling it in my own way[16] ... .

Anna Maria Porter to Jane Porter, [?6 April] 1804

MS: Huntington Library Jane Porter Papers POR 443

My dearest Jane,

... apropos of Heroes – I am no friend to any alteration in the title of your Book; whoever advised you to put "Thaddeus or the Hero" – advised you, to do that which would have damned you. – all the world says, (truly) that you have drawn the portrait of a Hero, but you should not say it. – the moment Thaddeus sets up for a perfect Hero, (like the woman that sets up, for a perfect beauty) he will cease to appear so; (in five mens eyes, out of ten.) – you know well, that no one more sincerely assents to the unexampled excellence and yet possibility of Sobieski's character, than I do; but I honestly confess, that such a title would arm me against it, if I did not know the writer. – suffer your

---

[15] Jane wishes she had a copy of *An Historical Sketch of the Battle of Alexandria, and of the Campaign in Egypt* (1802), the explanatory pamphlet that accompanied *The Battle of Alexandria* on its first exhibition in London.

[16] In an 'Advertisement', dated May 1804 and added to the second edition, Porter quotes from Thomas Campbell's *The Pleasures of Hope* to defend her spelling of the Warsaw suburb.

Book to remain with its first name; – it is unassuming, modest, like your own character, and the reader is therefore more deliciously surprized when he discovers the grandeur of the work it is to designate. – but my opinion is not <u>Law</u>. – ...